Tom Clancy
Commander in Chief

This Large Print Book carries the
Seal of Approval of N.A.V.H.

TOM CLANCY
COMMANDER IN CHIEF

MARK GREANEY

LARGE PRINT PRESS
A part of Gale, Cengage Learning

GALE
CENGAGE Learning®

Farmington Hills, Mich • San Francisco • New York • Waterville, Maine
Meriden, Conn • Mason, Ohio • Chicago

GALE
CENGAGE Learning®

LIBRARY OF CONGRESS CATALOGING-IN-PUBLICATION DATA

Names: Greaney, Mark, author.
Title: Tom Clancy : commander-in-chief / Mark Greaney.
Description: Large print edition. | Waterville, Maine : Thorndike Press Large Print,
    2015. | Series: A Jack Ryan novel | Series: Thorndike Press large print basic
Identifiers: LCCN 2015041346 | ISBN 9781410484727 (hardback) | ISBN 1410484726
    (hardcover)
Subjects: LCSH: Ryan, Jack, Jr. (Fictitious character)—Fiction. | BISAC: FICTION /
    Thrillers. | GSAFD: Suspense fiction.
Classification: LCC PS3607.R4285 T655 2014 | DDC 813/.6—dc23
LC record available at http://lccn.loc.gov/2015041346

ISBN 13: 978-1-59413-901-7 (pbk.)
ISBN 10: 1-59413-901-6 (pbk.)

Published in 2016 by arrangement with G. P. Putnam Son's, an imprint
of Penguin Publishing Group, a division of Penguin Random House LLC

Printed in the United States of America
1 2 3 4 5 6 7 20 19 18 17 16

PRINCIPAL CHARACTERS

United States Government
Jack Ryan: President of the United States
Scott Adler: secretary of state
Mary Pat Foley: director of national intelligence
Robert "Bob" Burgess: secretary of defense
Jay Canfield: director of the Central Intelligence Agency
Dan Murray: attorney general
Arnold Van Damm: President Ryan's chief of staff
Peter Branyon: CIA chief of station, Vilnius, Lithuania
Greg Donlin: CIA security officer

United States Military
Roland Hazelton: admiral, chief of naval operations, United States Navy
Scott Hagen: commander, captain of USS *James Greer* (DDG-102), United States Navy
Phil Kincaid: lieutenant commander, execu-

tive officer of USS *James Greer* (DDG-102), United States Navy

Damon Hart: lieutenant, weapons officer on USS *James Greer* (DDG-102), United States Navy

Richard "Rich" Belanger: lieutenant colonel, 3rd Battalion, 5th Marine Regiment, 1st Marine Division, United States Marine Corps; battalion commander of the Black Sea Rotational Force

The Campus

Gerry Hendley: director, The Campus / Hendley Associates

John Clark: director of operations

Domingo "Ding" Chavez: senior operations officer

Dominic "Dom" Caruso: operations officer

Jack Ryan, Jr.: operations officer/analyst

Gavin Biery: director of information technology

Adara Sherman: director of transportation

The Russians

Valeri Volodin: president of the Russian Federation

Mikhail "Misha" Grankin: director of the Kremlin Security Council (Russian intelligence)

Arkady Diburov: chairman of the board of directors of Gazprom, Russian natural gas company

Andrei Limonov (Mr. Ivanov): Russian private equity manager

Vlad Kozlov (Mr. Popov): intelligence operative in the Kremlin Security Council

Yegor Morozov: intelligence operative in the Kremlin Security Council

Tatiana Molchanova: television newscaster, Novorossiya (Channel Seven)

Other Characters

Martina Jaeger: Dutch contract killer

Braam Jaeger: Dutch contract killer

Terry Walker: president and CEO of Black-Hole Bitcoin Exchange, cryptocurrency trader

Kate Walker: wife of Terry Walker

Noah Walker: son of Terry and Kate Walker

Eglė Banytė: president of Lithuania

Marion Schöngarth: president of the Federal Republic of Germany

Salvatore: Italian paparazzo

Christine von Langer: former CIA case officer

Herkus Zarkus: Lithuanian fiber-optic network technician; Land Force soldier

Linus Sabonis: director, Lithuanian State Security Department

Common Acronyms and Abbreviations

ARAS: Lithuanian police antiterrorist operations unit

ASROC: Antisubmarine rocket

ASW: Antisubmarine warfare
CIA: Central Intelligence Agency
CIWS: Phalanx close-in weapons system
CNO: Chief of Naval Operations
DIA: Defense Intelligence Agency
FSB: Federal'naya Sluzhba Bezopasnosti, Russian State Security
JSOC: Joint Special Operations Command
NATO: North Atlantic Treaty Organization
NGA: National Geospatial-Intelligence Agency
NSA: National Security Agency
ODNI: Office of the Director of National Intelligence
ONI: Office of Naval Intelligence
RAT: Remote Administration Tool
SAU: Search and Attack Unit
SIPRNet: Secret Internet Protocol Router Network — Classified network for U.S. Intelligence community
SOF: Special Operations Forces
TAC: Tactical Air Controller
TAO: Tactical Action Officer
USWE: Undersea Warfare Evaluator
VHRJTF: Very High Readiness Joint Task Force — NATO

NORTHERN EUROPE

PROLOGUE

The Norwegians sold their secret submarine base to the Russians, and they did it on eBay.
Really.

In truth, the transaction was conducted on Finn.no, the regional equivalent of the online trading site, and the purchaser was not the Kremlin but a private buyer who immediately rented out the facility to a Russian state-owned concern. Still, the base was the *only* non-Russian permanent military installation on the strategically important Barents Sea, and the very fact that NATO condoned the sale in the first place spoke volumes about the organization's readiness for war.

And it also said something about Russia's intentions. When the purchaser clicked buy, Norway gave up Olavsvern Royal Norwegian Navy Base for five million U.S. dollars, a third of what Norway was asking and a pitiful one percent of what NATO spent building it in the first place.

With this purchase Russia won two important victories: It gave them the strategically located installation to use as they saw fit, and took it out of the hands of the West.

Olavsvern is an impressive facility, something out of a Bond film. Carved into the side of a mountain near the city of Tromsø north of the Arctic Circle, it has direct access to the sea and contains underground tunnels, massive submarine bays with blast-proof doors, a dry dock capable of receiving large warships, a 3,000-square-meter deep-water quay, infantry barracks with emergency power, and more than 160,000 square feet of space that is virtually impervious to a direct nuclear attack because it is hewn deep into the rock.

At the time of the sale, those in favor — including the Norwegian prime minister — rolled their eyes at anyone who said such a deal was ill-advised; the buyer promised that the Russians would use the facility to service their oil rigs — the Russians drilled all over the Barents Sea, after all, so there was nothing nefarious about that. But once the ink was dry, the oil-industry ruse was quickly forgotten, and the massive mountainside submarine lair was promptly employed to house a fleet of Russian scientific research vessels for a state-owned concern run by Kremlin insiders.

And those who knew about Russia's Navy and intelligence infrastructure in the Arctic knew research vessels often worked hand in hand with both parties, conducting surveillance and even moving combat mini-submarines around in international waters.

The Norwegian prime minister who sanctioned the deal with the Russians soon left office, only to become the new secretary general of NATO. Shortly thereafter, Russia moved its Northern Fleet to full combat readiness, and it increased activity out of the Barents Sea fivefold as compared to the last of the days when Olavsvern maintained a watchful eye over them.

Russian president Valeri Volodin stood in the Arctic cold with a pleased expression on his face, because he was thinking of Olavsvern now, even though he was some 250 miles to the east.

This was an auspicious morning here at Yagelnaya Bay, Sayda Inlet, the home of the 31st Submarine Division, and Volodin had the massive base in Norway on his mind because he knew without a shadow of a doubt that if NATO still operated Olavsvern there was no way today's operation would have had a chance for success.

The Russian president stood on the bow of the *Pyotr Velikiy,* a Kirov-class nuclear-powered heavy missile cruiser and the flagship of the Northern Fleet, his Burberry coat buttoned tightly across his chest and his wool hat keeping most of his body heat where it belonged — in his body. The commander of the 31st Submarine Division hovered just behind him on the deck, and he motioned to the fog ahead. Volodin saw nothing at first, but as he peered deeper into the mist, a huge shadow appeared on the cold water, pushing out through the veil of morning vapor.

Something big, slow, and silent was coming this way.

Volodin remembered a moment from the time of the Olavsvern sale. Members of the Norwegian media had pressed the ministers responsible for approving the deal about the danger posed by their neighbor Russia. One of the more frank of these ministers replied with a shrug. "We are a NATO member state, but we are also a small and peaceful nation. America, on the other hand, is large and war-like. Jack Ryan will see to Norway's security if the day comes. Why shouldn't we use our money for the important causes and let America do the fighting for us, because they love it so much?"

Volodin smiled now as he looked into the fog hanging over the gray water. Jack Ryan would have no time for Norway. True, the American President loved war, and the excuse of a Scandinavia in peril would be a good one for him, but Valeri Volodin knew something that few on earth knew, least of all Jack Ryan.

America was about to have much to deal

with. Not here in the Arctic, but damn near everywhere else.

The silent shadow began to take shape, and soon it was visible to all on the deck of the *Pyotr Velikiy.* It was the pride of the new Russian Navy. A massive new Borei-class nuclear ballistic submarine.

Volodin knew if NATO was still operating a base here in the Arctic, the vessel before him could have been detected and it would have been tracked by Western craft, both surface and submersible, well before it made it into the safety of deeper waters. And that would have been a shame, as far as the Russian president was concerned, so it was a damn fine thing that the Norwegians sold their strategic base off for pocket change.

Volodin glowed with satisfaction. Five million U.S. was a small price to pay for Russian naval supremacy of the Arctic.

The vessel before him had a name, of course; it was called the *Knyaz Oleg.* But Volodin still liked to think of this one, as well as the four others already in his fleet, by their original code number. "Project 955A" had a nice ring to it; it felt like a fitting title for Russia's most powerful and most secret weapon.

The Borei was the fourth generation of what the Americans called SSBN (Ship, Submersible, Ballistic, Nuclear). At 170 meters long and 13 meters wide, it was huge, although it wasn't the biggest sub Volodin had ever seen. That would be the Typhoon class, one of the Borei's predecessors. But while the Borei might not have been as big as the Typhoon, it *was* far more advanced. It could dive to 1,500 feet and make 30 knots while submersed, and its pump jet propulsion gave it something submariners called "silent speed," meaning it could travel quickly with very little noise, and it was damn difficult to detect.

There were ninety crew members on board, and most all of them, including Captain Anatoli Kudinov, stood on the deck and saluted their president as they passed the *Pyotr Velikiy.*

Project 955A was no secret to the Americans, but they did not understand the full scope and operational capabilities of these vessels, nor did they realize the *Knyaz Oleg* was already in service. Soon enough, likely just north of here in the icy waters of Kola Bay, Volodin was certain an American satellite would take note of a Borei leaving Sayda Inlet, sailing away from the protection of its hangar and out into the Barents Sea.

It was no matter. It might take the Americans a few hours to be sure they were looking at the *Knyaz Oleg,* but then they would lose interest, as they had no idea it had already been assigned to fleet ops. For a few days the Americans would think the newest Borei was undergoing more sea trials, but that would not last for long, because Valeri Volodin had no plans to make this mission a secret one.

No . . . Volodin was sending this submarine out on a mission of terror, and the mission hinged on everyone in the world knowing both *what* it was and, in a general sense, *where* it was.

Also standing on the deck of the heavy missile cruiser behind Volodin, ringed by his deputies, was the admiral in command of the 12th Main Directorate of the Ministry of Defense of the Russian Federation. He was the overall commander of all naval nuclear ordnance, and he'd come along today to wish bon voyage not to the *Knyaz Oleg,* but to the twelve devices of his that had been loaded into the sub's weapons stores.

On board the floating titan passing now just one hundred meters in front of President Volodin were a dozen Bulava ballistic missiles, each one carrying ten warheads. This gave the *Knyaz Oleg* the ability to prosecute 120 nuclear detonations, meaning this one vessel could, with only slight exaggeration, replace the United States of America with a smoking hole the size of a continent.

But *only* if it was close enough to the East Coast of the American shoreline to render America's missile defense systems irrelevant.

Volodin spoke softly in the morning cold, his words turning to vapor. "Amerika. Washington, D.C."

The men standing behind him at the bow looked at one another. If this was an order, it was an unnecessary one; everyone knew the *Knyaz Oleg* was heading exactly there — to within forty-five miles of the capital city of their adversary.

But even though Volodin was sending 120 nuclear warheads into the territorial exclusion zone of the United States, he had no plans to lay waste to the United States. He did, however, have every intention of scaring the living shit out of every man, woman, and child over there, and in so doing, to persuade the American populace that Russia's territorial integrity 8,000 miles from home was none of their goddamned business.

Volodin's scheme to be played out in the weeks ahead was wide-ranging, but the *Knyaz Oleg* was the opening move on the chessboard, and for this reason he had flown all the way up here to the Arctic, to pay his respects to Captain Kudinov, and to bestow on the mission and the men the weight and force of his presence.

The vessel Volodin liked to call "Project 955A" disappeared in the distance now, fading silently into the mist just after leaving Sayda Inlet and moving toward Kola Bay. Valeri Volodin continued to stare at the wisps of vapor left hanging in its wake, his military leaders looking on.

The emotions he wore on his face — pride and excitement — were both real, but there was another emotion welling inside, and this sentiment he would not allow himself to express.

Apprehension. Apprehension bordering on dread.

Today represented one facet, a single moving part of an intricate mechanism, a multifaceted operation that would span the globe.

And while Valeri Volodin was proud and hopeful and defiant . . . he also knew this *had* to work.

This had to work or he was a dead man.

1

The *Independence* was a ship, but its job was not to sail from here to there. Instead, it remained stationary at anchor in the port of Klaipėda, on Lithuania's Baltic coast, and it just sat there, connected to a long jetty with mounting and mooring devices, steel connecting bridges, and a massive pipeline link.

The supertanker had sailed into port to much fanfare a year earlier because everyone knew it was going to be a game changer for the Lithuanians. And although now it was, essentially, a fixed object bobbing in the water and no longer much of a ship, it had achieved its mission.

Independence was its name, but this was also its objective. It was a floating liquefied natural gas (LNG) storage and regasification unit, the first of its kind.

Lithuania had been dependent on Russia for its gas and electricity needs for decades. On a whim determined by the political winds of the region, Russia could either raise the price of gas or reduce the flow. They had done this multiple times over the past few years, and as tensions between the Baltic nations and Russia grew, Lithuania's dependence on its neighbor's goodwill became a clear and present danger to its national security.

An LNG import facility stood to change this. With the *Independence* and the pipeline from the port, LNG shipments from Norway now could be delivered by tanker, offloaded onto the regasification facility, and turned into the natural gas necessary for the nation.

This way, if the Russians once again turned off their gas pipelines, or once again raised the prices to extortionist rates, Lithuania and its allied neighbors needed only to exercise their option to turn on the safety valve provided by the *Independence.*

The process for regasification is highly technical and precise, but surprisingly simple to understand. In order to transport a large volume of gas, it needs to be converted into liquid, thus condensing it by a factor of six hundred. This is accomplished by dropping the temperature of the gas to −160 degrees. The liquefied form of the commodity is transported at this temperature in specially designed tankers, in this case from Norway to Lithuania. Here the LNG is pumped into the storage tanks of the *Independence,* where the regasification system superheats the liquid with propane and seawater, returning it to its gas form. The gas is then pumped into tubes that offload it through the port of Klaipėda and then along an eighteen-kilometer pipeline to the metering facility. From there it goes directly to Lithuanian homes, where it provides much-needed heat for the long Baltic winters.

The $330 million project was already serving its purpose from an economic standpoint. Russia dropped the price of its gas the day the *Independence* went online so they could compete with the Norwegian gas.

But to say that the Russians weren't happy about this was a great understatement. Moscow did not take kindly to energy-export competition in Europe. It was accustomed to its monopoly and it had used it to threaten Russia's neighbors, to enrich the nation, and, perhaps most important, to mask Russia's myriad other economic problems. Russian president Valeri Volodin, in typical hyperbolic fashion, had even gone so far as to claim that Lithuania's new natural gas facility was nothing short of an act of war.

Lithuania, like many of the other former Russian satellites, was used to incendiary rhetoric from Moscow, so the government in Vilnius just ignored Volodin's threats and imported large quantities of natural gas via Russian pipelines and small quantities of LNG from Norway via the Baltic Sea, and the *Independence* served as a model for other Baltic nations to work to develop their own secondary option for energy.

The rest of Europe had a hand in the building and delivery of the *Independence* to Lithuania. Stability in the region was in everyone's interests, after all, and NATO nations who could be pressured or controlled outright by Russia's energy exports were a weak link in the chain.

It was therefore said that while Lithuania relied on the *Independence* for its energy, Europe as a whole relied on the *Independence* for its security.

A middle-aged German electrical contractor walking along the jetty noticed the body floating in the water, and this saved his life.

He'd come to work early this morning to check some misbehaving circuits in the offloading pumping station, only to find his truck stuck behind a locked gate. Deciding it would be faster to walk to the pumping station than to wait for someone to bring a key, he'd started off along the 1,400-foot-long jetty at a pace spurred on by his annoyance that his morning hadn't started out well at all. He was only a quarter of the way along when he looked to his left and noticed something bobbing down below in the water, at the far reaches of the jetty lights.

At first he thought it was just a large piece

of trash, but he stopped to make sure. Stepping up to the railing and looking over, he pulled an industrial-grade headlamp out of his backpack and flipped it on, holding it in his hands and shining it out on the water.

A diver in a wetsuit, a silver tank on his back, floated facedown, arms and legs out.

The German electrician spoke little Lithuanian, but he called out anyway. *"Labas!"* Hi! *"Labas?"*

There was no reaction from the diver twenty meters from the jetty. As he looked closer he could see long blond hair floating around the body's head, the small, thin form, and he realized it was a woman, perhaps quite young.

The contractor struggled to get his walkie-talkie out, but by the time he did so it occurred to him that there would be no one else on his channel till his coworkers got in to work in another hour. He couldn't remember the security channel, so he just began running back along the jetty in the direction of the Port Security office.

And this decision, born out of panic, made the German electrician Lithuania's luckiest man of the year.

Several hundred yards from the frantic electrician, the *Independence* sat quietly on still, black waters on a cold October morning, bathed in the lights on the deck and

25

positioned on the attached jetty and pumping station.

The ship and the jetty were not attached to the Lithuanian mainland; instead they were connected to Kiaulės Nugara Island in the Curonian Lagoon, at the mouth of the port of Klaipėda. The waters all around were busy with port traffic during the day, but now, at eight minutes after four in the morning, the water was nearly empty from the LNG facility to the sea gate at the mouth of the lagoon, other than a pair of small rigid-hulled inflatable boats crisscrossing the water slowly and nearly silently. The security men on the boats had no clue the electrician was racing along the jetty, because the enormous supertanker was positioned between the patrol boats and the running man.

The boats passed within twenty yards of each other on their patrol. The men on the decks of the boats glanced across the water at one another, but they passed close too many times a shift to call out greetings or wave hands every time.

Security here at the port was relatively tight, and there were all sorts of impediments to a terrorist attack by land or by water. But even though the guards at the pumping station, on the island, on the *Independence,* and in the patrol boats were reasonably vigilant, nobody thought anything serious could ever happen here.

Yes, a month earlier protesters had shown up in small wooden boats and charged the facility through the sea gate. They brought along colorful signs demanding an end to globalization and they had a bullhorn through which one of the protesters shouted expletives at port workers, and they had milk jugs full of oil they planned to sling at the supertanker to demonstrate something of desperate importance.

They hadn't been altogether clear on just what that was.

It was lost on the protesters that this was a natural gas operation, not oil, and their jugs of oil would inevitably end up in the water.

Fortunately for the ocean around, the two patrol boats had converged on the wooden boats and detained the protesters before they could get close enough to the supertanker to be any sort of a danger.

This was the main type of threat the security guards had in mind, because the *Independence* was built incredibly tough. It had a double hull of milled steel, and inside that, the hyper-chilled LNG was protected by thermally insulated membrane tanks. An RPG from the coast or Molotov cocktails or IEDs would have little effect on the big structure.

Fully loaded with six million cubic feet of liquefied natural gas, the *Independence* possessed the energy of fifty-five nuclear bombs, but there was only an eighth of its maximum capacity in its storage tanks, and again, it would take one hell of a massive bomb to breach the side of the ship and ignite the gas.

The patrol boats passed near the LNG tanker, just two hundred yards to the east or so, but it was exceptionally dark here. The two men on the decks would have required superhuman vision and focus to see the anomaly right in front of them. Instead, both boats motored on. One to the north, one to the south.

In their wake several small trails of bubbles rose to the black surface, then quickly dissipated. The security vessels had noticed nothing, and they just continued their patrols.

The electrician flagged down a security officer in a pickup at the end of the jetty and in broken English explained that he'd spotted a dead female in the lagoon. The security officer was dubious but deferential. He told the German to climb into his vehicle so he could direct him to the spot on the jetty.

Just as the electrician closed the door, a flash of light caused both men to look out the windshield, straight ahead at the giant ship. A glow emanated from the far side of the vessel and silhouetted it, then a thin flame skyrocketed up, ripping open the darkness, and the fireball that came next turned the night to day.

The security officer behind the wheel of the pickup had been well briefed on the fact that the *Independence* was toughly built but nevertheless essentially a huge bomb. He jacked the pickup into reverse, stomped on the gas, and raced backward over an eighth of a mile, literally chased by a series of roaring explosions that rocked the jetty and sent debris and shock waves in all directions.

The pickup finally bounced back into a ditch along the side of the access road into the facility. Here the guard and the electrician bailed out of the vehicle and dove into the mud.

They felt the heat over them, they heard shrapnel sprinkle the ground all around, and they heard the sirens from the jetty, but above all they heard the thundering death of Lithuania's game changer.

The communiqué from the perpetrators arrived the way these things do nowadays: A Twitter account was registered, and a single tweet was posted. This linked to a nine-minute video that began with a nighttime shot of a group of four masked men and one woman standing together, apparently somewhere along a dark highway.

A low-quality night-vision lens on the camera gave an eerie feel to the footage as they crept through a forest, but to military experts the five subjects of the video moved less like trained special operators and more like children playing a game. A man used bolt cutters on a barbed-wire fence, then he and the others passed through, right next to a sign that read:

ZONE PROTÉGÉ

More creeping around paved roads and concrete buildings, a shaky zoom-in on a guard sitting in a tower in the distance. Then a chain on a cargo container was defeated with the same bolt cutters, and soon all five individuals were hauling crates out of the facility, back through the barbed-wire fence.

Inside a room with plenty of light now, the five crates were shown lined up on the floor, their lids open. Inside were bread loaf–sized boxes, a half-dozen in each crate. The only writing visible on the boxes read *Composition Four.*

Again, those in the military would easily recognize C-4, a military plastic explosive.

A lot of it.

A woman with a French accent spoke English; she held up what she said was a detonator, claimed all the equipment was from the American military and it had been liberated from a NATO storage facility in France.

The scene moved and the camera was back outside in the dark again, filming in grainy green night vision. Five people knelt at the water's edge wearing wetsuits, swim masks, and snorkels. Tanks and vests were stacked next to them. Through a telephoto lens the camera recorded jerking images of the *Independence* LNG facility and the port beyond.

A close-up shot of the shoreline showed a coffee table–sized item completely enshrouded in black plastic next to the divers. Strapped to the plastic-covered box were several scuba vests, and one scuba tank was strapped to the top. A different woman spoke now, her voiceover narrating the scene; her accent was later determined by authorities to be from Barcelona.

"The bomb was made buoyant by the attached scuba equipment. The revolutionaries took the device into the water and sunk it to where it descended below the surface. Then they delivered it to their target, over a kilometer away."

The five disappeared in the darkness off the water's edge, pushing the large floating plastic item attached to the scuba equipment between them.

The camera stayed on the shoreline, then the scene cut again. Now the gargantuan *Independence* was in the center of the frame, illuminated by bright lights. After only a few seconds of calm, the explosion bloomed on the near side of the ship, the rolling flame ascended, and secondary and tertiary detona-

31

tions erupted, some causing the camera operator, who must have been a very long distance from the blast, to flinch noticeably.

For the denouement of the video, the long-distance shot of the destruction of Lithuania's liquefied natural gas facility switched abruptly to a person in a ski mask sitting in front of a small table. Despite the concealment of her face, the exposed skin around her mouth and her slight build revealed her as a Caucasian female, likely a young woman.

Behind her, a white flag had been pinned to the wall. In the center of it was a circle, clearly representing planet earth, covered by a maze of pipelines. An oil well jutted out of the top of the circle, and a red drop — presumably representing blood — hung below it.

Across the bottom of the flag were the words *Le Mouvement pour la Terre.*

The Earth Movement.

She spoke in English; investigators would later determine her to be the same woman with the Barcelona accent who narrated a portion of the video.

"You have just borne witness to the opening salvos of a war. For too long, violent and destructive acts perpetrated against our planet at the hands of the energy industry have gone without counterattack.

"Those days are over now. We will fight back on behalf of Mother Earth.

"There will be no peace until our demands are met. The Earth Movement will retaliate against any and all examples of greed and materialism at the expense of Mother Earth that we can find. We invite others to join us in battle as we return the planet to its natural position of harmony.

"We honor our sister Avril, who was tragically lost in the battle in Lithuania. Let the oil and gas industry know that her spirit burns bright in the fight we continue in her name."

In the last few seconds of the video the camera panned to the other side of the room. Here four men and women, all in black and all masked, raised their fists in salute. Some held automatic weapons.

Eight hours after the explosion, the body of twenty-four-year-old Avril Auclair, a French citizen and former university student, was pulled out of a thick marsh in the lagoon. She was identified quickly, almost immediately, really, because the YouTube video had mentioned "sister Avril," and a woman with this name had been well known to authorities keeping an eye on the sometimes-violent eco-terror movement in Europe.

Auclair had made a name for herself by being kicked out of Greenpeace two years earlier for hurling a fusillade of punches at the deputy director of the Paris branch of the organization. The police report said it was an argument over tactics. Auclair had been too radical for Greenpeace, so they'd sent her packing, and she then beat up the sixty-year-old woman in charge of the Paris branch.

The director ultimately did not press charges, and Auclair disappeared from view, completely dropping off the map for the past six months.

An autopsy later determined Avril Auclair's scuba tank had a faulty pressure gauge, and although it read that she had a full tank, her tank had run out of air. It was determined that she must have passed out underwater during the mission and then drowned, although she had been found so far away from the explosion, in the exact opposite direction from the point of entry of the divers as shown in the video, nobody understood how she could have floated to the jetty unless she had been on a completely different mission from those who attached the explosives to the hull of the ship.

It was a small mystery, however, as she had been identified in the video by her mother as the first woman speaking, and she'd led a life that made her death during an ecoterror incident no great surprise to anyone.

And video of the theft of the explosives was authenticated soon after the *Independence* explosion, when French authorities revealed a previously unreported theft of hundreds of pounds of C-4 and detonators from a military depot west of Montpellier.

European police and intelligence officials immediately began the hunt for an ecoterror group no one had ever heard of.

2

The good-looking Dutch couple stood out here in Caracas. They were tall, the man every inch of six-five and the woman nearly six feet herself. Both of them wore identical shades of auburn hair, his styled professionally short, while her shoulder-length curls blew in a warm fall breeze.

Even here in the upscale and exclusive neighborhood of Los Palos Grandes, where tourists and well-heeled foreign business-people were common, the couple turned a few heads because they were particularly attractive and stylish. They were dressed in chic business attire that bordered on extravagant: She wielded a large orange Hermès bag that cost more than the average annual income of a Venezuelan laborer, and he wore a white gold Piaget watch that sold for twice what she paid for her bag.

They might have been in their thirties, or perhaps their early forties. He appeared the elder of the two, but this was often the case with husbands and wives, and from the band on his ring finger and the massive rock on hers, they were clearly married.

They walked arm in arm along the Parque del Este on the Avenida Francisco de Miranda, and she giggled from time to time in response to a story he was telling. Then they turned to take the steps in front of the Parque Cristal, an eighteen-story cube-shaped building that looked south over Francisco de Miranda to the park, and they continued to the lobby entrance, looking up to marvel at the remarkable architecture.

Just behind them a Lincoln Navigator pulled to the curb and two men climbed out. One of them opened the door for a backseat passenger, a balding fifty-year-old in an expensive suit. He pushed his briefcase out the door in front of him and followed behind, and as the Navigator returned to follow the traffic to the west, the three men ascended the steps to the Parque Cristal, walking just feet behind the striking couple from Holland.

In the middle of this trio of Latin men was Lucio Vilar de Allende; to anyone who noticed him, he appeared to be just any other businessman with dealings here in the large office building, with the one exception being that he was shadowed closely by a pair of serious men in suits with open coats and flitting eyes.

And then they would recognize that the

man in the middle wasn't just anyone, because most people in Caracas knew bodyguards when they saw them; it's that kind of town.

Lucio Vilar had a protection detail because he was one of Venezuela's top federal prosecutors. He was moving light today — just the pair of bodyguards, the armored SUV, and the driver with an Uzi in his center console — because Vilar wasn't on official business. He'd taken the afternoon off to visit his son at his school, and now he was meeting the mother of his child to discuss his boy's grades. His ex-wife worked in a real estate office here in the Parque Cristal, and she had agreed to her ex-husband's request that he meet her in the coffee shop on the top floor for a talk.

Vilar checked his watch and picked up his pace, and his bodyguards stayed with him, step for step.

Though Vilar had family matters on his mind as he entered the lobby, that didn't stop him from noticing the attractive woman just in front of him. She was a head taller than he was in her heels, so she was hard to miss. He stepped to the elevator bank just behind the Caucasian couple, who, he could plainly hear, were speaking to each other in Dutch. When the elevator car arrived and opened and the tall couple stepped in, Vilar's principal protection agent put a gentle hand on his protectee's arm. It was a suggestion that they wait for an empty car, but Lucio Vilar ignored the hand and followed the Dutch couple inside, so his bodyguards dutifully followed.

Vilar nodded to the Dutch couple as they turned around.

"Good afternoon," the woman said in English.

"Good afternoon," Vilar replied. His English was not as strong as hers, but it was serviceable. "You are from Holland, I hear. I have visited Amsterdam. Very beautiful."

"As is your country, *señor,*" the woman said, with a pleasant smile.

One of the two bodyguards pressed the button for the eighteenth floor, and the Dutchman pressed the button for the seventeenth. As the elevator ascended, the woman stepped into the front corner of the elevator, and her mate stood on her right, directly in front of the doors, facing forward.

"It is always wonderful to see foreigners here," Vilar added. "Are you here on vacation?"

The woman shook her head. "Sadly, no. We are working."

"I understand," Lucio Vilar said, and he checked his watch again.

But Lucio Vilar did not understand at all.

Martina Jaeger glanced up to the digital floor-number readout over the door and saw they had passed the fourth-floor restaurant without stopping to pick up more passengers. This told her the odds were good they would likely go all the way to floor seventeen without stopping.

Lucio Vilar smiled up to her, and he seemed to want to use the short ride to practice his English. "May I ask what business brings you to Caracas?"

But Martina ignored him. In Dutch she said, "On eight."

Braam Jaeger, still facing the door, replied calmly in Dutch. "Agreed."

Lucio Vilar furrowed his brow at being ignored by the woman, but he said nothing more.

When the elevator reached the eighth floor, Martina Jaeger slipped her Hermès handbag off her shoulder and then she lifted it, raising it into the upper corner of the car.

It took the two bodyguards less than a second to realize what she was doing. The tall Dutch woman was covering the security camera.

Braam Jaeger continued to face the elevator door and did not turn around, but just as the two younger men at Vilar's side started to react to the woman's action, two pistol silencers appeared around the sides of his suit coat, both pointing backward toward the guards. He'd cross-drawn them from his waist inside his coat and now his left hand pointed one gun around the right side of his body, and his right hand aimed the other gun around his left. He glanced up at the reflection in the polished metal doors.

Both weapons fired as one. Even suppressed, the bark of two automatic pistols rang loudly in the small space.

The two bodyguards slammed back against the wall, then dropped to their knees, perfect holes in their foreheads. They'd both drawn their guns, so two weapons tumbled from their hands. The man on the left collapsed a second slower than the man on the right, but they both fell facedown onto the floor of the elevator car.

Lucio Vilar de Allende stood still, his briefcase in his right hand, the bodies of his protection agents crumpled on either side of him.

Braam Jaeger turned around now, reholstered the weapon in his right hand inside his coat like an expert, and raised the weapon in his left.

Vilar spoke in a hoarse whisper. "I . . . I do not understand."

The statement was directed toward the man with the gun, understandably, but Martina Jaeger answered. Her handbag still covered the camera. "No? I think it should be obvious. Somebody out there doesn't like you very much."

And with that Braam shot Venezuela's top

federal prosecutor in the right eye. His head slammed back against the rear wall of the car and he crashed to the floor, settling perfectly between his bodyguards.

Braam fired twice more into the already still form. Control shots, just to make certain the target was dead.

With the second bark of the silenced pistol, a few drops of blood splattered up and onto Martina's lavender Louboutin pumps.

"Verdomme!" she shouted.

"Het spijt me" — Sorry — Braam replied, then knelt and took the pulse of the prosecutor, who was clearly dead.

He scooped up spent shell casings — all of them still hot — while Martina Jaeger began unbuttoning her blouse with her free hand. She unfastened only two buttons below her breasts, then peeled up a black square of fabric held to her skin with electrical tape. She raised it up under her handbag, and she pressed it over the camera's lens.

Once done, she lowered her purse and glanced up at the floor-number readout. *"Vijftien,"* she said. Fifteen. She turned, watching Braam as he stood up from collecting the casings.

She said, "One in each guard, three in the target."

Martina said nothing else. Quickly Braam realized what she meant. He'd collected only four shell casings. He knelt again and found

42

a fifth. It had rolled under the right forearm of the principal target. He pocketed it while Martina stepped in front of him to shield him from view of anyone waiting for the elevator when it reached their floor.

It opened at seventeen, which was undergoing renovations and therefore empty. Braam pulled a small wedge-shaped doorstopper from his coat pocket and propped the door open, then they exited and moved quickly to the stairwell, with Martina slipping off her pumps as she did so.

They hurried down the stairs and made it to the underground parking garage in less than six minutes. Martina put her shoes back on and they walked naturally through the lot, until Braam folded himself behind the wheel of their parked Audi A8, and Martina climbed in next to him.

They left the Parque Cristal one minute and four seconds before the first alarm bells rang.

They drove north along the Caracas–La Guaira highway in the direction of the airport, and most of the trip was conducted in silence. The pair had done this sort of thing before, so even though the fight-or-flight chemicals coursing through their central nervous system increased their heartbeat and blood pressure, they remained outwardly cool and calm.

The Audi pulled into the parking lot of the

Playa Grande Caribe Hotel and Marina, on the shoreline of the Caribbean Sea. Braam parked and each of them grabbed a rolling duffel from the trunk, and with the luggage trailing behind them they walked through the hotel's entrance. Passing the reception counter, they strolled through the large facility, until finally they exited the back and continued down a winding sidewalk that led them to the marina itself.

Here they climbed into a small gray dinghy, Braam started the engine, and they motored out to a forty-two-foot sailboat moored in the marina.

Braam started the engine while Martina unhooked the line from the mooring ball, and in moments they were churning out of the marina and into open water.

Braam kept one eye on the sea in front of him and the other on his laptop. Open in his browser was a weather forecast for the southern Caribbean. The conditions looked fair for the next twenty-four hours, which was crucial if they were going to make it to Curaçao by three a.m. There was a six-forty a.m. direct flight to Amsterdam the next morning, and the Jaegers had tickets and every intention of being home by tomorrow night.

Twenty minutes after setting sail, Martina stepped up to the bridge with two glasses of champagne in her hands. She passed one to Braam, seated at the helm, and with it she gave him a high five.

No one was around to see this, they were miles out to sea, and if anyone had been, they would have adjusted their show of affection to tie in better with their cover for status: that they were husband and wife.

Braam and Martina Jaeger were not, in fact, married. They were brother and sister, and they were contract killers working for Russian intelligence.

3

Three days after the explosion of the liquefied natural gas facility in Lithuania, two well-dressed businessmen sat together at a café table in a little restaurant attached to the main hall of Warsaw's Centralna station. The older of the two was nearing fifty, short but powerfully built, with curly dark hair flecked with a significant amount of gray. The younger was in his thirties and of average height, with short brown hair and a trimmed beard and mustache.

The men drank coffee and checked their watches from time to time; the older of the two perused an English-language newspaper and the younger kept his phone in his hand, but he mostly just sat with his legs crossed, his bored eyes drifting around the station. The appearance of the two was indistinguishable from twenty-five other pairs of businessmen in the central hall, and not markedly different from any of the three hundred or so standing or sitting here at the station.

When the men spoke, they did so in English, but even that wasn't unusual at all in a cosmopolitan city such as Warsaw.

An announcement of the impending departure of the 9:55 Warszawa–Berlin express came over the PA in Polish, German, then English, and the men stood, hoisted shoulder bags and briefcases, and headed for the stairs down to the platforms.

As they walked through the middle of the crowded hall the younger man spoke softly. His business associate would not have been able to hear him if not for the earpiece transmitter the size of a hearing aid hidden in each man's ear.

"If he's a no-show, do we still board the train?"

The older man responded: "No sense sitting around Warsaw if we don't have intel on his location. This is all we've got. We'll take the train and check it out, maybe he boarded and we just missed him in the station."

Dominic Caruso nodded without speaking, but the truth was he would have preferred to stick around Poland a little longer. They'd only just arrived the evening before, but already he could tell this was his kind of town; the history of the city was fascinating, the beer and the food were good and cheap, and the few people he'd encountered seemed laid-back and nice. He'd also noticed that the women were stunning, though this was nothing to keep him here. He was in a relationship at the moment, so he told himself it was probably just as well that he was about to climb on the next train out of town.

On the platform the two men took a moment to look around before boarding. A large crowd of travelers were moving in all directions, too many for either of the Americans to positively identify their target in the sea of faces. Still, they took their time, keeping an eye out for any countersurveillance operatives watching the platform to check the scene for the target.

Neither Domingo Chavez nor Dominic Caruso saw anything that concerned them, so they found their first-class carriage at the back of the EuroCity express train to Berlin. Here they sat in a cabin with six seats and a sliding glass door to the narrow hallway, and they both positioned themselves near the window so they could continue to monitor the platform.

Chavez said, "Lots more cops than I'd expect to see."

Caruso nodded as he scanned all the way to the stairs at the far side of the platform. "It's that thing up north in Lithuania. A new terror actor over here with the skills to pull that off has all the European governments on edge."

"Yeah, but for how long?"

"It's hard to keep an edge," Caruso acknowledged, and he also wondered if the increased police presence here in Europe, due to a completely unrelated situation, would have the unintended consequence of screwing with his surveillance mission.

He pushed away the doubt and kept scanning.

Their target here in Poland was named Yegor Morozov. He was thought to be a senior officer in the Federal'naya Sluzhba Bezopasnosti, Russian intelligence. He was in his late forties, and to make the two Americans' job over here more difficult, he was just about as plain-looking as most of the men in his chosen profession.

Chavez and Caruso worked for an American private intelligence outfit that called itself The Campus; through the research and analysis shops of their organization they had managed to uncover a Cyprus-based shell corporation associated with the Kremlin and Russian intelligence. The CIA had already ID'd Morozov as a spook, but The Campus tracked him here in Warsaw after he'd used a credit card linked to the Cyprus shell that was under one of his known aliases. By the time the two Americans made it to Poland, Morozov had checked out of his hotel, but his card had been used to book a pair of first-class tickets on this morning's Warszawa–Berlin express.

The men had a picture of their target from

his Polish visa application, but they didn't know who he'd be traveling with, why he was going to Berlin, or any intel at all about what he was doing here in the West.

Still, they were here; their focus for the past few months had been on Russian money networks, after all, and Morozov was a name with a face tied to one company in one of the networks. He wasn't much of a lead, but he was all they had, so they'd been sent to tail him.

And now it looked like he was going to be a no-show.

Dom Caruso said, "This could turn out to be a boring day."

"Yeah, well, this whole investigation is more analysis than footwork. Jack Junior and the other analysts are the brains; you and I are just the feet and the eyeballs, so we pulled this thrilling gig."

Caruso nodded while he scanned, then he blinked hard in surprise, as if doubting the image in front of him. "I'll be damned. I got him."

He saw the target on the other side of the window, walking along the platform in a leather bomber jacket and jeans, and holding a large leather duffel bag in his hand. There was a female pulling a rolling duffel a few feet away from him, and they walked in step with each other. She was much younger than he was, with dark hair and fair skin. To Dom she didn't look Polish, nor did she look Russian, but he told himself he had not been checking out the females over here all that much, so he wouldn't admit to being an expert.

But Chavez was thinking the same thing. "I'd say the unsub is North African. Morocco. Algeria. Maybe Spanish, possibly Portuguese."

Caruso nodded. Ding Chavez had been at this a lot longer than he had, and the older man was usually right with his first assumptions.

Caruso added, "She could do a lot better than a guy like Morozov."

"Frankenstein's bride could do a lot better than a guy like Morozov."

The Russian and his fellow traveler climbed into the same car as Chavez and Caruso, which was not pure luck. Of the six carriages in the train, only one was first class.

Dom climbed out of his seat and moved to the sliding glass door to the hall, glanced down and saw the woman following Morozov into a compartment two down from the American operatives.

Moments later the conductor stepped onto the platform just ahead of where Caruso and Chavez were sitting and blew his whistle, then he climbed back aboard and the massive Siemens electric locomotive began pulling the six carriages out of the station.

Once they had been on the way for a few minutes, Chavez and Caruso decided they'd recon the entire train to look for any countersurveillance before they decided how to get a closer look at their target and the young woman with him. They left their compartment and passed Morozov's compartment without glancing in, then they moved through the vestibule to the dining car. On the other side of the dining car, the vestibule was open to the first second-class carriage. Here a group of a dozen or so men, all in black tracksuits with red piping, sat together. Chavez and Caruso had seen them in the station a short while before boarding, and they assumed the men to be members of a soccer team. Most of them wore earbuds, but a few of them chatted. A couple of their number looked like they could be the team's coaches, but the rest were the right general age and build of athletes.

Chavez and Caruso continued on to the next car, where they saw no one but tourists, a couple of men and women in business attire, and several senior citizens.

In the second-to-last car, both Americans took note of a trio of men in their thirties. Two were white and one was black; they sat together, wearing jeans and North Face jackets. In the lap of one of the white men was a high-end backpack with military-style webbing on the outside. The black man wore a tactical diving watch, and the other white male had a Panasonic Toughbook, a rugged-case laptop computer used commonly in the world of military and security contractors.

The final car was full of tourists, families with small children, and senior citizens.

Back in their compartment, the men talked about what they'd seen on their recon. Dom said, "The three dudes in car five were definitely in the biz."

"Yeah," said Chavez. "But our target is FSB. No way a follow team for Morozov would outfit themselves like that. Way too conspicuous."

Caruso thought it over and agreed with a nod. "What about the soccer team? I can't read Cyrillic like you can."

"Yeah," Chavez said. "Their logo said they were FC Luzhany. Not sure who or what that is."

Dom looked them up on his phone. After a minute he said, "Here they are. A competitive amateur soccer team from Ukraine. Down south, near Odessa."

"Can you find out what they're doing here?"

A little work on his phone gave Dom more information. "There is an amateur tournament in Leipzig next week."

"Okay," Chavez said. He wasn't really thinking there were a dozen bad guys on his train dressed as a soccer team, but he wanted to check them out anyway. He said, "Ruling out the team and the three G.I. Joes, I didn't see anyone else on the train worth a second glance. Other than Morozov and his lady friend, that is."

"Right," Caruso said. "You want to get closer?"

Chavez nodded. "We can sit at a table in the dining car and have lunch. From there we can get eyes on their compartment through the windows in the vestibule doors. The angle isn't perfect, but at least if anyone comes or goes we'll get a look. If the girl makes a trip to the john, I'll try to get a picture of her. That's about all two of us can do."

"I could plant a bug on her or Morozov."

Chavez shook his head. "We can't expose ourselves like that. Back when there were more of us, maybe that would have been an option, but with just two of us, we need to play this soft and smart."

Caruso knew Chavez was right. The team was smaller now than it used to be, and every day in the field something reminded them of this fact.

4

John Clark felt the enormous impact of Arlington National Cemetery — he appreciated the majesty of the 624 acres, and the sacrifice of the 400,000 buried there. But the truth of the matter was . . . John Clark wasn't much on visiting graves.

It was no sign of disrespect to the departed; on the contrary, he saw those who worshipped tombstones to be the ones who failed to remember the fallen as they wanted to be remembered. He'd lost many friends over the years, and it was important to him that he remembered them all, but he told himself he did not need to go to their final resting place in order to do it.

But despite his reservations, he was here today at Arlington, in the cold rain, his umbrella forgotten in his car, and he stood over the grave of a friend.

The headstone said very little, and much of what it said was untrue.

SAMUEL REID DRISCOLL
1SG
U.S. ARMY
JUNE 26, 1976–MAY 5, 2016
PURPLE HEART
AFGHANISTAN

The name was right, though he went by Sam. The rank and service were correct as well, but Sam had left the Army Rangers years before he died. The birth date was accurate, though his actual date of death was a few weeks off from the one hewn into the white marble. Clark was absolutely certain of this, because Clark had been just fifty feet away from Sam when he died.

And unless Afghanistan had been somehow picked up and moved south of the U.S. border, the location of his death was incorrect as well.

Sam Driscoll had been shot dead by a North Korean intelligence agent in a dark hallway of a luxury villa an hour outside Mexico City.

No, the marker didn't mention any of that.

And while it was true that all the misinformation and errors of omission on Sam Driscoll's tombstone bothered Clark a little, he knew they were for the best. The marker could not have said Sam was an operations officer for an off-the-books intelligence shop called The Campus, and it sure as hell couldn't have stated the fact that Sam had been down in Mexico hunting the people behind the nearly successful assassination attempt on the President of the United States.

Sam had been good, no doubt he was a hell of a lot better than the North Korean who killed him — a man who, in the same instant, died at Sam's hand. But Sam had been dealing with multiple attackers, and while he got them, *both* of them . . . one of them got lucky in his last breath.

There are no promises in combat. When men are in fierce battle for their lives, fighting hand to hand and slinging hot lead at one another with a muzzle velocity of a thousand feet a second, bad shit is bound to happen, and to Sam, bad shit did.

John Clark stood there in the rain and thought about that night in Cuernavaca for another moment, but then he thought about his own life, his own mortality. It was hard not to do, standing here in a massive garden of stone, each white slab of rock representing another man or another woman, each with his or her own story about how the end came.

A hundred thousand ways to die; the only constant to these markers was that virtually everyone buried beneath them had, in some way, served the United States of America, and many of them, a great many, had lost their lives while in that service.

Just like Sam.

It wasn't fair.

John Clark was sixty-seven years old. Sam Driscoll had been twenty-seven years younger than Clark, and many of the other men and women buried here at Arlington had been half Sam's age when they'd met their maker.

Nope, not fair at all.

If he could, Clark would have taken the bullet to the heart that dropped Sam Driscoll, but Clark had been in harm's way the vast majority of his lifetime, and if there was one thing he had learned, it was that there wasn't one damn bit of sense involved in any of this, and even with all the skill in the world, there is a pervasive randomness to a gunfight.

John looked around at thousands of white tombstones.

Anything can happen; the good guys can die, too.

Slowly, *very* slowly, he remembered the flowers in his hand.

If Clark wasn't one to stand at gravesites, he *really* wasn't the sort to walk around carrying flowers. But this wasn't his idea. No, it was the fulfillment of a promise.

At Sam's funeral he met Edna Driscoll, the mother of the deceased. She knew nothing about how her son died; in fact, she knew only that her son had left the Army and had taken a job for a private contractor involved with homeland security. She understood his work was top-secret and he could not discuss it, but she did not know it would prove to be even more dangerous than his time in the 75th Ranger Regiment.

At the funeral, Clark expressed his condolences seriously and solemnly to the gaunt and drawn woman, but when she'd asked for details of her son's death, all Clark could tell her was that he'd died for his country.

It was the God's honest truth, and he hoped it would be enough, but he'd been through this before, and he knew.

It was *never* enough.

Clark's wife, Sandy, had come to his rescue, as she had done at so many funerals in the past. She stepped into the conversation, introduced herself, and then directed Edna Driscoll away. She commiserated with her, and after the service, Sandy asked the woman if the two could stay in touch.

It was an act of kindness, a chance for a widow from Nebraska who lost her son to have some small connection to those he served with, although she did not understand who or what they were.

Sandy contacted Edna a few days later and told her an account representing her fallen son's pension had been established as part of his compensation package with the private security contractor, and it was all hers, and when Sandy told her the amount in the account, Edna Driscoll was even more confused about her son's employer.

She found $3 million to be a shockingly large sum, but still, it was no replacement for her loss.

And then, a few weeks after Sam was buried and the account was settled, his mother e-mailed Sandy Clark with a request. She said she was overcome with sadness by the fact she was sure the flowers she'd left at her son's grave had by now withered and died, and she wondered if Sandy wouldn't mind placing a fresh bouquet on the headstone from time to time.

Sandy and John lived in Emmitsburg, Maryland, which wasn't exactly next door to Arlington National Cemetery, but this was lost on the woman from a little town outside Omaha, so Sandy agreed, promising Edna she'd take care of it.

John Clark would have loved for his wife to do just that, to take care of it — cemeteries were not his thing, after all — but Arlington was on the way to his office in Alexandria, so it made no sense for Sandy to make the drive when he could do it so much more easily.

And now he was back again for a third delivery of flowers. John placed them on Sam's headstone, feeling the weight of the deaths of Sam and all the others around him, but soon he shook out of it. He wasn't too sentimental about all this. He missed Sam and felt the same amount of responsibility for the man's death as he had for others who had died under his leadership, but Sam wasn't here, lying under this headstone, under this dirt.

This was just an earthly memorial.

And it occurred to Clark that Edna Driscoll's realization of this just might help her heal in some small way.

His phone rang in his jacket, and he welcomed the distraction, even though it was a struggle to answer in the rain.

"Clark."

"Hey, John. It's Jack."

Jack Ryan, Jr., was in Italy, this Clark knew because he'd sent him there two weeks earlier. Clark looked at his watch and saw it was afternoon there.

"How's the girl, kid?"

There was a slight pause. "You mean Ysabel?"

"How many girls do you have over there?"

Jack laughed uncomfortably. "She's fine, thanks. You *do* know I'm working, don't you?"

"Of course I do. Just giving you a little grief." He looked down at Sam's grave. "Nobody wants to deprive you of your personal life. There's little enough of that as it is."

Jack paused before speaking again. Then, "You okay, John?"

"Absolutely." The connection was silent until Clark said, "You called *me*, remember?"

"Yeah. Wanted to see if you could get the guys in the conference room for a ten-minute talk. Nothing earthshaking, just wanted to give everyone a progress report on what I've found over here."

"You learn anything interesting?"

"Yeah. I learned Russian financial shenanigans are complicated."

Clark turned from Sam's headstone and began to walk back to his car. "We paid for a first-class seat on Alitalia and a month lease on a furnished apartment in Rome for you to figure that out? Hell, I knew that sitting on my back porch."

Jack laughed again, more naturally this time. "Well, yeah, I've managed to piece together a bit more than that. You guys have time for a briefing?"

Clark said, "Not at present. I sent Dom and Ding on a quick trip to Poland yesterday."

"Lucky guys."

Clark snorted. "Says the lucky guy shacking up with his girlfriend in Rome."

Ryan chuckled awkwardly again, then said, "Okay, how about I just brief you and Gerry?"

Clark replied, "Actually, I'm out of the office at the moment."

"Really? It's nine-fifteen in Virginia. Not like you to sleep in."

"Do you *really* think I slept in?"

"No, I was just trying to get you to tell me

where you are."

Silence on both ends of the line, until Jack Ryan, Jr., said, "And, apparently, I failed." Still nothing. "Okay, we can do the call tomorrow."

"Let's, but give me the five-second version," Clark said.

"I've identified a lawyer in Luxembourg who is definitely involved in this scheme. When I'm done here, I'd like to go to Luxembourg City to look into him a little more closely."

"Do you need me to send you some help?"

The answer came quickly. "No, I'm good. This is straight analytical work, nothing dicey. Ysabel and I have it covered here in Rome, and I don't think I'll need any more resources in Luxembourg than I do here. I will need another week or so here to finish the job before moving on."

"Right," Clark said. John Clark was no fool, he knew what was going on. Jack's girlfriend was an Iranian national named Ysabel Kashani. She was assisting him there in Rome, and Rome was closer to Tehran than Luxembourg City.

It was also several orders of magnitude more romantic.

Clark almost admonished his young operative. He considered telling him to get his head in the game, but he stopped himself. He'd go easy on Ryan, for a day or two. This operation was important, but this wasn't a matter of life or death.

The kid could enjoy himself a little bit more. It wouldn't hurt anybody.

"Okay, kid. I'll get a conference call set up for this time tomorrow and you can fill us in on what you know." His voice turned louder and more commanding. "And don't get complacent over there. I want you practicing your proper OPSEC twenty-four/seven. No excuses, no compromises. Got it?"

"Roger that. Hey, you sure you're okay, John?"

"I'm outstanding, kid. Talk to you tomorrow."

Clark hung up the phone, gave one last look to the hillside full of identical white stones, then he bent his head into the rain and climbed into his car.

Jack was right; Clark was late for work.

5

Jack Ryan, Jr., slipped his phone back into his blazer and downed the last few drops of his double espresso. He checked his watch, then picked up the newspaper folded in front of him and glanced at it absentmindedly.

Jack was in his early thirties, just over six feet tall, with short dark hair and a trimmed beard. He wore sensible eyeglasses that, along with his tailored blue blazer, made him look older than his years, but his jeans and easy smile lessened any sense of stuffiness about him. He weighed two hundred five pounds, much of it muscle, but his clothing choices went a long way toward hiding his athletic physique.

He dropped the paper down on the table and looked across the nearly empty café, his eyes searching intently.

He just realized his date had been in the bathroom for a long time. He felt stress growing inside, a sudden feeling of foreboding.

Ysabel reappeared from the women's restroom as if on cue, looking boyish but beautiful in jeans and a fitted leather jacket, her black hair up in a tight bun.

Jack stifled a sigh of relief, chastised himself for freaking out because a girl just spent a few minutes in the little girls' room, and reminded himself they weren't in the middle of a damn war zone.

Not anymore.

Jack stood from the table and pulled her chair out for her, and he called for the check as they both sat back down.

Ysabel said, "Sorry. I know you think I was just preening at the mirror for the last ten minutes."

"Were you gone long? I hadn't noticed."

She smiled. A look that said she didn't believe him. Shaking her head, she said, "I was touching up my makeup and another woman at the mirror knocked my purse on the floor. Everything fell out." She giggled. "A girl keeps a lot in her purse, you know."

"I've lifted your purse. Did she at least help you pick everything up?"

"Yes. She was very apologetic and helpful. Just a klutz. What about you? Is everything all right? I thought you said you'd be on the phone awhile."

"Everything is fine. My boss is out of the office, so I'll have to make my report tomorrow."

In a hopeful tone, Ysabel asked, "You're going to ask for more time here in Rome before you have to go?"

Jack nodded. "Told him we'll need another week. We're not quite finished here; plus, I have a lot of analytical prep work to do before I need to be on the ground in Luxembourg. Might as well do it here, since the apartment is paid up until the end of the month." He affected an air of nonchalance, picking up the folded newspaper again and looking it over as he crossed his legs.

Ysabel frowned, but for only an instant, because Jack slowly looked up at her and grinned. "Kidding. All that's true, but I'm going to stay another week so you and I can spend some more time together. This working-vacation thing has been awesome. You think we could license it?"

She stood up and came around to his side of the table, sat in his lap and kissed him, but only after punching him on the arm first. He'd gotten used to her playful attitude, to the point he was slowly starting to adopt his own version of it.

Ysabel's eyes widened suddenly. "I've got an idea! To celebrate, I am going to make you a fantastic dinner tonight."

Ryan did not adopt her same sense of excitement. With an air of suspicion, he asked, "What's on the menu?"

"A dish my grandmother taught me. *Kookoo sabzi.*"

"I really hope that's not Farsi for 'Grandma's vegetarian mush.'"

She punched him playfully on the arm again. "Of course not! It's an herb-and-vegetable quiche."

"Oh, boy."

Ysabel sighed and climbed off Jack's lap. "It's delicious, you're gonna love it. I'll go by the Persian market on the way home and get everything I need."

Jack looked up at her without speaking, but he faked a look of enthusiasm.

Clearly, she saw right through it. "Why don't you pick up some steaks at the butcher? Get a cut you would eat at home. You can grill while I make stew. We will have the *kookoo sabzi* as a side dish. An Iranian-and-American meal."

Jack almost leapt up from his chair, his enthusiasm real this time. "The world in harmony, right there on our plates. I like it. I'll meet you back at the apartment in a half-hour."

They kissed again and Ysabel left the café, turning south. Jack headed east, a spring in his step because he was already thinking about dining on juicy steaks and drinking great wine on the balcony of his apartment, all with such a beautiful and amazing woman.

As he walked through central Rome's late-afternoon swarm of pedestrians, cars, trucks, and scooters, he thought about his situation,

68

and some of the spring left his step because he was reminded how temporary this all was. He and Iranian national Ysabel Kashani had spent the past two weeks here in one of the most romantic cities in the world, and he'd loved every minute of it, but it wasn't going to last much longer.

He didn't know what kind of a future he had with Ysabel, it was too early to say, because they had known each other for just over a month. They met on an operation in Asia and a relationship had developed quickly, and despite his reticence about getting into anything serious at this stage of his life, Jack had to admit he found himself falling for this girl.

And he knew this could be problematic for a few reasons, not the least of which was that they lived in different hemispheres.

Jack quickly scanned his six o'clock as he reached the left bank of the Tiber River and began walking south toward the nearest bridge to the east. He didn't see anyone tailing him. Even though he wasn't expecting anyone to be following him on this op, he didn't need Clark reminding him to keep his personal and operational security at the forefront of his thoughts; OPSEC and PERSEC came naturally to him now. His countersurveillance tactics had become ingrained in his past several years working with The Campus. Everywhere he went, even back in the States, he used varying routes to and from his apartment; he didn't go to the same coffee shops, restaurants, or markets every day; and he made subtle checks of the people around him, both in front and behind, at irregular intervals.

He completed his scan, and then he allowed his fertile brain to go back to work. His thoughts drifted off Ysabel — for the time being, anyway — and he started thinking about finances.

Not *his* finances — he was making good money, and he came from a well-to-do family. Hell, his dad was President of the United States and his mom was chief of ophthalmology at Johns Hopkins.

But the finances on his mind at present were those of the upper echelon in the Kremlin.

He'd come here to Italy on a mission that was one part operational fieldwork and two parts analysis, and Jack considered himself perfectly suited to the job, as he was both an operations officer and an analyst, specializing of late in the financial analytics helpful in tracking money laundering.

The U.S. intelligence community knew that the key to dealing with the criminal regime at the Kremlin was to understand both where their money came from and, perhaps more important, where it was going. Russia was a kleptocracy, all the power in the hands of a corrupt few. The term thrown around these days was "elite capture"; the privileged of the nation had taken over the democratic process, wresting the power from the masses through bribery, election rigging, and other underhanded tactics.

Around the time Russia's foreign and domestic intelligence agencies merged with each other, the CIA began tasking a lot of analytical manpower to identifying the personal assets of the small cabal of Kremlin and FSB policy makers at the center of influence, many of whom were themselves ex–intelligence officials. Jack's father, the President, had managed to convince several other nations to join him in imposing sanctions on many in this group of Russian elite as a way to press back against that nation's aggression against its neighbors. This wasn't a perfect foil to the Kremlin's actions by any means, but it hit several of Russia's top power players where it hurt, and it had increased pressure on President Valeri Volodin from within.

But while some of the oligarchs' accounts were seized and their travel privileges in the West curtailed, The Campus had begun focusing not on the oligarchs aligned with the Kremlin themselves, but on the economists, mathematicians, bankers, money managers, offshore business experts, and accountants who worked under them. Jack knew Volodin's top men weren't themselves hunched over computers setting up foreign trusts and buying and selling holdings, property, and other assets. No, it was the men and possibly women — though so far The Campus had identified only men — below these powerful Kremlin players who possessed both the financial talent and the political reliability.

These Russian money movers had been a project of the analysts at The Campus for some time, though Ryan himself had been away, involved in operations around the world, so he had only recently gotten involved.

Together Jack and the other analysts had identified roughly three dozen men who seemed to be in the trenches controlling the two-way spigot of money that propelled the Russian government kleptocracy. There were undoubtedly many more than those they knew of, but the deeper Jack got into the weeds while looking into the known players, a question in Ryan's mind grew and grew: Which of these men, if any, did Valeri Volodin *himself* entrust to handle his own finances?

It was rumored Volodin had untold wealth — before the recent huge drop in oil prices it had been suggested he had north of $40 billion. Presumably, it was held in a combination of stakes in state-owned businesses, offshore banks, and other property. Most in the U.S. government suspected Volodin's own money traveled through the same secret financial-haven networks as that of the other members of Russia's powerful elite, so it was just a matter of peeling apart the layers of the network and looking for the masterminds who build it, and then perhaps The Campus would find the men in control of Volodin's hidden riches.

The U.S. government, of which Jack's father was the chief executive, had expressly precluded the Department of Justice from targeting Volodin's personal wealth. There were international treaties and accords set up to prevent one nation from dredging up world leaders' personal finances, set in place to keep bickering countries from simply filing charges against one another's heads of state as a means of diplomatic pressure.

But The Campus had no such restrictions.

The director of The Campus, Gerry Hendley, had given his analytical shop the green light to seek out the players involved with Volodin's personal amassed billions. That had led them to a lot of sleepless nights of work, but finally it had led one of them — Jack Ryan, Jr., to be exact — here to Europe.

Mikhail "Misha" Grankin was a key player in Volodin's inner circle, and currently under sanction by the West. As the new director of the Kremlin's Security Council, Grankin had in the past year become Volodin's principal go-to adviser on all matters diplomatic, military, and intelligence. But in addition to his duties for the government, like a lot of Volodin's cronies, he was also part owner of several large private companies with government contracts. By tracing funds paid by the government for these contracts tied to Grankin, The Campus identified a shell company in Rome as a money-laundering vehicle for several works of art at galleries across the Italian capital. The company had used Russian government money to purchase several dozen paintings, and the art was still physically here in Rome, still displayed in the galleries from which it was purchased. If and when the artwork sold, the gallery would get a hefty commission, and then payments would go to a private trust to be deposited into some offshore bank somewhere.

The entire scheme seemed plain enough to Jack and his fellow analysts at The Campus: Mikhail Grankin's people had purchased the paintings with the sole intention of expatriating millions of dollars of his nation's wealth by laundering the money through the sale.

The opacity of the art world meant a person could walk into a gallery or an auction house, purchase a painting for a million dollars in cash, and walk out with it without even giving a name. It was an excellent way to launder money, and a terrific way to hide the portfolio of a man who was on America's list of sanctioned members of the Kremlin.

Jack had come to Rome to dig into the transactions and to try to identify the facilitators of the purchase. Whoever offered up the money for the paintings, Jack knew, would be deeply involved in the scheme, and Jack didn't think for a second this would be a one-off crime. His working theory was that whoever was involved in the operation was part of the intricate network the Kremlin used, and it stood to reason that Valeri Volodin himself might use such a conduit to hide his money.

His goal had been to identify the next link in the chain, and then to pass his intelligence about Grankin's money on to the U.S. Justice Department, so they could lock down these funds, same as they had all the other accounts of Mikhail Grankin that they had found outside Russia.

There was another reason Jack had come to Rome, though he tried to deny it, even to himself. Rome was pretty damn romantic, and Ysabel had been helping him in his investigation.

They had planned on taking a vacation to Tahiti together after their last operation, but the Mikhail Grankin information had cropped up suddenly, and Jack realized he instead needed to go to Rome. He'd talked to his higher-ups, explained the situation, and reminded them what Ysabel had just pulled off in Dagestan. John Clark and Gerry Hendley allowed her to support Jack on his operation, and she had jumped at the chance to meet Jack in the Eternal City and help.

Ysabel's part of the op was straightforward enough. She simply served as the face of Jack's investigation; she went from one gallery in the city to another, places where Grankin's front company was selling the art on commission. She posed as a representative for a buyer, and she used a hidden camera and a mike to look at the goods, to see what had sold already, and to try to get a feel for whether the prices asked and the prices paid indicated the whole scheme was indeed some sort of a payoff.

And Ysabel had one more role. It was her job to film enough of the computer systems in the establishments to work out what sort of technology the galleries used to store their account data.

Jack then did what he could to identify the buyer of the art. The director of information technology at The Campus was an MIT grad and a hacker of the first order; at most galleries, he had been able to simply break into their files to glean sales information. But at some of the galleries Ysabel herself had needed to plant RATs — Remote Administration Tools — on the systems, so that connections could be created between the network at the gallery and Gavin Biery's own system.

Ysabel had been up for the work from the

76

start. In fact, Jack realized, she loved this sort of thing. At first he worried she could be in some danger, but all the research he had done into the specific art galleries they were targeting indicated no relationship with organized crime or any real nefarious elements. These were just retail establishments that were unwittingly laundering money for the top goons in the Kremlin.

Ysabel's only danger was being seen by a security guard poking around behind a counter while a gallery manager stepped into the kitchen to make her a cup of tea.

For these awkward moments Jack had always remained close by, outside the gallery in a vehicle, with eyes on Ysabel's real-time camera feed — ready to swoop in and get her out of any jam, though she'd been so slick with her tradecraft he'd not once been called to sort out a problem.

As Campus operations went, this one had been a breeze.

And it had recently borne fruit. All three galleries Campus IT director Gavin Biery had hacked the sales info of showed the same thing. Pieces of art being sold on commission by the Russian front company were bought by a single entity. A trust based in Luxembourg.

Ryan's digging into the trust had taken some time, but he'd successfully identified an attorney in Luxembourg who managed the trust's finances. Although Jack didn't know where the money came from that went into the trust to buy the paintings, he assumed this was nothing more than a way to take the Russian money that went into the art and launder it with the clean Luxembourg money. If the money purchasing the art at inflated prices was simply payoffs, then there would be other people and business entities involved. Many more. Ryan knew he had a long way to go to untie this Gordian knot, but he was happy he'd managed to swim downstream this far at least, from Grankin, to the art galleries, to the Luxembourg trust, to the individual lawyer.

His next step, he knew, was to dig into this lawyer in Luxembourg himself, identify what other companies he worked with, and identify who was helping Grankin in this deal.

If he was lucky he would be able to trace this scheme right back around to Grankin himself, but that was a long shot. He knew from his experience as a financial investigator that a well-resourced and well-backstopped money-laundering structure would involve dozens of companies, blind trusts, registering agents, banks, and even nations. By the time Grankin profited personally from the money expatriated from Russia, it would have moved around the world like a shell in a fifty-cup shell game.

But that didn't matter to Jack. Even if

Rome, Luxembourg, or the next five places Grankin's money went didn't give up the evidence he needed to disrupt the network, little by little he was removing layers of the onion, and someday he'd have the man at the top of the illegal enterprise.

Jack wanted to invite Ysabel to Luxembourg, but he'd need the approval of Hendley and Clark for that. He'd ask them tomorrow, and he was pretty sure they would say yes.

She'd done a great job so far; she and Jack had worked hard every day and into the evenings, but they did not miss this opportunity altogether. The young couple was getting to know the restaurants and amorous corners of the city as they got to know each other better in the process.

Jack smiled a little as he checked his six again. John Clark's commanding voice was always there in his mind, telling him to watch his back.

He was clean.

Luxembourg, even with Ysabel, would not be as much fun as Rome. Jack would need to move on from the beautiful art galleries and into static surveillance operations on office buildings and conference rooms to identify the associates of the lawyer.

Not quite the same thing he'd done in the past couple weeks, but at least he and Ysabel would be together.

With that pleasant thought on his mind, Jack Ryan stepped off a curb, looking in all directions as he did so.

Suddenly his face morphed into a mask of terror.

A small blue Citroën ran a stop sign and barreled down on him as he walked in the middle of the street.

6

Jack launched forward in a broad jump, avoiding the front bumper of the speeding car by less than two feet. He spun around to look at the vehicle, which was now in the process of making a screeching left turn at the intersection.

The blue Citroën almost slammed into a middle-aged couple walking on the crosswalk on the other street. The woman gestured and screamed at the driver, a heavyset man in his fifties, who seemed oblivious to the fact that his bad driving had nearly caused a bloodbath.

If this had been anywhere else Jack would have thought someone had just tried to kill him, but this was Rome, the most dangerous city in Europe for pedestrians. This wasn't an assassination attempt; it was just some asshole who didn't know how to drive.

And this town was full of them.

"Son of a bitch," Jack muttered under his breath, but he didn't yell. OPSEC demanded he not reveal himself as American in the field unless it was necessary to do so.

He started walking again, and he thought about something he read when he was doing research for his work trip. A writer talking about the poor drivers in the Italian capital had remarked that Romans park their cars the way he would park his car if he had just spilled a beaker of hydrochloric acid on his lap.

Jack thought that line was as true as anything he'd ever read, and he wondered if Gerry would give him hazardous-duty pay for living here in central Rome for the month.

He smiled at his own joke — working for The Campus meant *every* day involved hazardous duty, and nobody got a bonus for danger.

He crossed over the Ponte Regina Margherita and ducked into a butcher shop he had noticed earlier in the week. He used his pidgin Italian to pick up a pair of fat rib eyes, cut to order by the owner himself. His mouth watered while the steaks were wrapped in paper, and after leaving the little shop he began to pick up the pace so he could hurry home, careful to keep a close eye on the motorists around him. It was nearly four p.m. and he imagined they wouldn't eat for another three hours or so, but like all good things, he knew these steaks would be worth the wait.

Jack's eyes roamed constantly while he thought. It was on probably the fiftieth such quick scan of the day, just before reaching the corner of Ferdinando di Savoia and Maria Adelaide, when he glanced at the reflection in a passing bus and noticed a man behind him in a leather jacket with his long brown hair pulled back in a ponytail. The man wasn't looking right at Jack, but something seemed familiar about him. Jack wasn't certain he'd seen this person before — central Rome was full of men, many had long hair, and this guy didn't look or act different from the norm — but something inside Jack triggered when he noticed the man.

Jack had long ago learned that the moment you think there is any chance whatsoever that someone might be following you, suddenly *everyone* looks suspicious. He had been living with this phenomenon for years, and over time he had trained himself to keep a cool head and a dispassionate, analytic eye scanning the world around him. He saw no one else in the area who piqued his senses, so he simply filed the man's appearance in his mental database and kept walking.

But by the time he reached the large, open Piazza del Popolo, he was convinced something was wrong. He'd slowed down significantly a block before so he could window-shop. This wasn't a countersurveillance ruse — a magnificent Breitling watch really did catch his eye in a shop window, and although he wouldn't let himself go in and inquire as to the price, neither could he tear his eyes away from the big chronograph for nearly a minute.

When he made his way into the piazza a few moments later he glanced into the glass of another passing car and realized Mr. Ponytail was still behind him, at the exact same distance he was before.

Either this guy had managed to stumble across a distraction that lasted exactly as long as Jack had been looking at the watch, or else the man slowed down or stopped so that he did not overtake Ryan on the sidewalk.

Suddenly Jack knew he was being tailed. He had noticed during his last reflection check that the man had a small backpack over one shoulder, and he wondered what was inside.

Jack crossed the street and entered the piazza. A stage was being erected in the center — he assumed there would be some sort of open-air concert here this evening — but for now it was easy to walk across the cobblestones among the small crowd milling about.

Now everyone *did* look suspicious. A man sweeping the piazza, a young woman sitting on a scooter and talking on her cell phone, an ice cream vendor standing behind his cart and gazing Jack's way.

Jack picked up the pace for a moment, then turned suddenly at another vendor's cart and purchased a bottle of water. While he fished a few euro coins out of his pocket he glanced back to his left and saw Ponytail tying his shoe, his foot propped up on an iron bench.

Yep, he was most definitely a follower, and not much of one at that. It looked to Ryan as if this guy had trained in surveillance by watching shitty made-for-television movies.

Ryan thought if this guy was part of a crew, he was either the weakest link or else they would all be as obvious as he was. As he began to walk away from the vendor cart, sipping his bottled water, Jack scanned the crowd more intently, all the way south across the Piazza del Popolo.

It was a three-minute walk, his wrapped steaks in hand, and through it all Jack ID'd no one else who appeared to be interested in him.

He chanced a quick look behind him as he tossed the empty water bottle into the trash. Ponytail was still there, seventy-five feet or so back, and he looked away as Jack turned in his direction.

Jack's body tensed, and his mind began working on the situation. He'd been compromised, and that was bad, but he was too in-the-moment to think of the ramifications this surveillance had on his operation at this point. Now it was just about slipping this character and getting back to the apartment.

He'd work out his next move after that.

It occurred to Jack that the best way to shake this incompetent flunky, if he was in fact alone, was to simply climb into a cab. Ponytail probably didn't have wheels close by, he would have no way of knowing that Jack would be heading to the Popolo, so the likelihood that he'd staged a vehicle right here was next to none.

Ryan walked to the curb of the street ringing the piazza, watched the cavalcade of small Italian cars whip around, each driver seeming to have his own idea about both the speed limit and the location of the lane markers, and he picked out a taxi approaching in the closest lane. He waited until it was a reasonable distance away at the speed it was traveling, then he held out his hand.

The cab driver whipped his little Fiat over to the curb and came to a stop. Behind him scooters and cars slammed on their brakes.

Jack jumped into the back and the cab lurched forward again.

Chavez and Caruso had finished a meal of schnitzel, sauerkraut, and mashed potatoes, washing it all down with a couple of beers. There was no rule about drinking on the job at The Campus; the operatives were supposed to maintain their cover for status and cover for action at all times, and sometimes that meant downing a drink or two while working surveillance. It was part of adapting to the surroundings, and while the men knew better than to overindulge, they also knew better than to draw attention to themselves.

While they sat, Dom kept an eye out through the doors to the compartment containing Morozov and the young brunette female he seemed to be chaperoning into Germany. She'd made one run to the bathroom and Caruso had taken a picture of her. He'd sent it to The Campus so the analysts could run it through facial recognition, but she didn't turn up in any of the criminal databases.

Caruso and Chavez were talking over their surveillance options for when they arrived in Berlin when the train passed out of Poland and into Germany at the town of Frankfurt an der Oder. There was no scheduled stop here at the border; both Germany and Poland were in Europe's Schengen Area, a collection of twenty-six nations with common visa requirements and no passport controls between the nations.

So the two Americans looked out the window in surprise when the train began to slow.

Ding went to the counter to order a coffee while a voice over the train's PA system, broadcast in several languages, announced that German customs police would be making a quick pass through the train with dogs.

When he sat back down with his coffee, Dom said, "Must be because of the Lithuania thing."

"Right," agreed Chavez. "They don't know how much C-4 those ecoterrorists used to blow up that ship. Might be enough left over to take down the Reichstag or something."

Here in the dining car, Caruso was seated facing the first-class area, and back over Chavez's left shoulder he had a clear view of the door to Morozov's compartment, plus their own compartment farther on. He saw no activity from Morozov or the girl. Over Dom's right shoulder Ding could see into the open second-class cabin. There, many members of the Ukrainian soccer team had gotten up to look out the window, and once the train came to a full stop, six officers in the Bundespolizei, the German Federal Police, entered with two Belgian Malinois on leashes. One of the dog handlers and two officers made a right, deeper into the train, and the other three turned toward the forward three cars. Quickly Chavez realized these were not customs officers, as the train conductor said; nor were they just making a simple pass down the length of the train. Instead, they were taking their time, asking to see everyone's passport.

Chavez said, "They are doing a full immigration check."

The train began to roll again.

Caruso chuckled. "I hope Morozov has his papers in order. It would be a shame to see him frog-marched out of here."

Chavez smiled, too, but not for long. "Hey, are these Ukrainians starting to look a little squirrelly to you?"

Caruso turned to look back over his shoulder, and he saw what Chavez noticed. Several members of the soccer team, including one of the coaches, were constantly looking back over their shoulders at the three approaching officers. "Yeah," he said. "These guys have something to hide."

But when the police arrived at them, one of the coaches pulled a stack of passports out of a vinyl messenger bag and handed them over to the officers. One man looked them over quickly while the dogs sniffed around the young men. Both Dom and Ding saw continued evidence of nervousness in the players, but after matching each passport with a face, the Bundespolizei officer handed the documents back to the coach of the team, and the three moved on toward the dining car.

Caruso said, "Wonder if they have performance enhancers in their luggage in the racks above them. They were scared they'd get searched."

Chavez said, "They are amateurs. It's probably weed."

The two Campus operatives produced their

documents when the trio of armed officers arrived at their table. Dom noticed one of the men carried an HK MP5 submachine gun on his chest, and all three, including the female dog handler, wore big Glock 17 pistols on their belts in retention holsters.

"Gibt es ein Problem?" Chavez asked the officers. Is there a problem?

"Not at all," the female officer replied in English, after their documents were returned to them.

Chavez had hoped for a little more information, but he wasn't surprised the German police weren't terribly forthcoming with an explanation about what was going on.

The three cops and their dog moved through the vestibule and into first class, and now Caruso focused on Morozov's compartment, visible through the glass window in the vestibule doors. When the police arrived they opened the door and stood in the hall outside the compartment. The dog sniffed around inside for a moment, then returned; he seemed utterly uninterested in his work and ready to move on. Caruso could see the passports the two inside the compartment handed over to the police. They were both burgundy in color, which meant they could have been Russian, but there were also lots of other countries, even here in Europe, that used the same color.

One of the passports was returned quickly,

but the other was checked for a long time. Caruso slowly got the impression that something wasn't right. Dom could tell one of the three officers was asking a series of questions to one of the people in the compartment, presumably the Russian spy.

Chavez was facing the opposite direction, so Caruso kept him informed. "Looks like Morozov is getting the third degree."

Chavez did not look back. "That's weird. You'd think the FSB could at least send their man out into the field with clean papers."

"Dumbasses," Dom muttered with a little grin.

"Don't get too excited, 'mano. If they take him off the train, we just wasted a trip."

"We can follow the girl."

Chavez shrugged. For all he knew this was Morozov's daughter and they were on their way for a vacation in the art galleries of Berlin.

A minute later the other three police and their dog passed through the dining car, went through the vestibule to first class, and joined the others, all standing in the hall.

"Damn," Caruso said now. "They *are* taking him off." He could see the police motion for someone to come out of the compartment, and he assumed it was the Russian spy. But to his surprise he saw the brunette female escorted out of the little room.

For a moment Caruso caught a glimpse of

91

Morozov as he leaned out of the compartment, trying to talk to the police, but they weren't listening to him. Instead, they began walking the girl toward the exit of the first-class cabin. One of the cops pulled out his radio, presumably to order the conductor to stop at the next station.

Morozov turned and walked toward Dom and Ding, passing them in the dining car without a glance. Dom could see an intensity on the man's face that worried him.

"Where's he going?" Chavez asked.

He got his answer quickly. The Russian FSB man rushed into the second-class cabin, walked right up to the coach of the soccer team, and leaned in close to his ear.

Chavez said, "Oh shit. What does *this* mean?"

Caruso turned and his eyes went wide. "I guess it means the amateur soccer team is a professional security team, and Morozov has himself a dozen goons."

The soccer team stood as one and began to reach for their luggage, which was all positioned on the racks high above their heads. Morozov moved back through the dining car, passed Dom and Ding again without looking at them, and continued into his compartment, where he closed the door. The six police farther down the car, standing around the woman by the exit, didn't even notice he'd left his compartment.

Dom saw all this, but Ding wasn't looking. Instead, he had his eyes on the Ukrainians. They'd all slung bags over their shoulders, placed their hands inside the unzipped bags, and they were flooding toward the dining car.

Chavez said, "These dudes are packing. They are going to try to get the girl back."

Caruso said, "And we're unarmed."

Chavez lifted a dirty steak knife off the table and hid it under the cuff of his suit coat.

Caruso gave Chavez a look. "You're going to engage a dozen armed dudes with a steak knife?"

"No. I'm going to engage *one* armed dude with a steak knife, and then I'm going to engage eleven armed dudes with a gun."

Dom grabbed his own knife, wiped some sauce from it with his napkin, and hid it in the cuff of his jacket.

7

Domingo Chavez knew he wasn't breaching his cover by staring at the men in black storming up through the dining car toward the police. It would have looked completely inauthentic to continue drinking his coffee with his eyes on his empty lunch plate while a dozen men with intense faces marched by in single file, every one of them holding something hidden inside a gym bag. So he stared, tried to ID who they were and how far they were willing to go with this. Quick eye contact with Dom, then an almost imperceptible nod, passed on the message that these men were the real deal; they looked willing to kill some police to keep this mystery woman out of the hands of German authorities, and Dom and Ding had to keep this from happening.

After the first ten men passed the table, then went through the vestibule door, the last two turned around in the dining car by the door, drew black automatic pistols from their bags, and covered the dining car and second-class car beyond. This put their eyes right on Dom and Ding, a dozen feet ahead of them on their right. They held their guns low in front of their bodies.

Chavez instantly realized these men were well trained, otherwise all dozen would have just attacked the known threat, and they wouldn't have set up a rear guard for any other potential threats.

Still, both Caruso and Chavez saw that they were within a dozen feet of the pair of armed men, close enough to engage. They just needed to act with speed, surprise, and violence of action, and they could even the odds of this one-sided contest.

As the door to the vestibule between the dining car and the first-class car closed, Dom raised his hands and began to stand in the aisle, drawing the attention of both men.

"Don't shoot! Just tell us what is going — "

Ding Chavez spun low out of the chair with his coffee cup in his hand and flicked the steaming liquid out and up toward the faces of the men. He took one step to square his body with the gunmen standing shoulder to shoulder in front of the door, and he launched himself forward. Both pistols rose toward the motion, but the hot coffee in their eyes caused them to flinch and recoil before they could aim. Chavez slammed into the midsections of both men, sending them back hard onto the floor. One man banged his head against the door and dropped his pistol, and the other man's gun hand was pushed high to his right by Chavez's left shoulder. A shot rang out in his first-class cabin just as Caruso arrived, leaping through the air over Chavez's prostrate form, then landing, his knees slamming onto the chests of both men. One man drew a folding knife from the pocket of his tracksuit and clicked it open, but Ding stabbed him through the heart with his steak knife, ending him instantly. The second man still had his pistol in his hand, but a hailstorm of punches from Dom onto the man's nose and jaw rendered him senseless quickly.

By then, sustained gunfire from first class shattered the glass window of the vestibule door just over both Americans' heads.

Chavez and Caruso both scooped up the weapons of the two gunmen. They were GSh-18s, Russian military-issue nine-millimeter pistols. They entered the vestibule, crawling low, listening to the booming gunfire just past the next door. The gunfire grew heavier by the second, but Chavez chanced a look through the broken window. He saw the female dog handler lying still in the hallway of first class, the big Belgian Malinois tearing into the arm of a flailing man in a black tracksuit, and more police taking cover in the first compartment and down at the end of the hall near the exits to the train. More men in black leaned out of Morozov's compartment and two more closer to the dining car, all firing pistols.

Chavez aimed quickly at the back of a gunman's head and fired, dropping the man to the hallway floor, but immediately the German police began firing at Chavez, thinking him to be just one more attacker shooting at them. He hit the floor, turned to Dom, and said, "The shooters are in the nearest three compartments in first class."

Dom said, "I'll go outside, engage through the windows."

Chavez said, "The hell you will. This isn't *Mission Impossible*. They don't put handrails on the outside of trains."

Just then, the train began to slow again. Its brakes wailed and squealed. Dom and Ding were thrown to the ground in the vestibule.

Dom looked outside. "Shit, we're in a forest."

The conductor was just stopping the train so people could get off, but Caruso and Chavez knew this would help Morozov and his team escape.

Even before the locomotive came to a complete stop, the Americans could hear glass shattering in the first-class compartments. Dom opened the door to the outside, leapt to the ground, and saw men dropping to the tracks, weapons in hand. He started to aim at the closest gunman, but the cracks of a pistol from one of the windows sent him back inside the train.

He found Chavez involved in a firefight through the vestibule window. "They are escaping out the windows!" Dom shouted over the gunfire.

"Good! Let them go, just don't let them flank us!"

Dom aimed back through the door just as a gunman spun around, trying to get a shot off on the unknown shooters behind the gunmen in first class. Dom fired twice, hitting the man in the left clavicle and spinning him to the train tracks.

A second shooter had made it to a row of trees beyond the train tracks, and with his pistol he took careful aim at the men in gray suits in the vestibule between the dining car and first class. His first shot went high over Ding's head, but his second grazed Dom in the back, sending him diving into the bathroom.

The door to first class slid open without warning, and Chavez spun his gun toward the movement. A man dressed in black slammed into him, knocking him to the floor.

The German police continued firing up the length of their carriage, and bullet holes tore through the metal door as it closed again, the rounds going just a few feet over Chavez's head.

Dom aimed at the man on top of Chavez

from his position on the floor of the bathroom, and he pressed his trigger, but the attacker lowered his head quickly and the round went high. The slide of Dom's GSh-18 locked open, letting him know he was out of ammo.

The man on top of Chavez delivered a powerful right cross into the American's face.

Dom leapt from the bathroom and onto the man, ripping him off Chavez and throwing him against the wall of the vestibule. The man launched himself back toward Dom, eyes red with fury.

The attacker in the black tracksuit landed on top of Caruso now, but not before Dom got his steak knife out and up. It buried into the man's throat, sent him rolling off, grabbing at his mortal wound.

More gunfire from the outside of the train forced the Americans to crawl out of the vestibule and back into the dining car, where they took cover with a terrified porter behind the counter. They weren't sure what had happened to the German police, Morozov, or the woman, but they'd done what they could to minimize the slaughter, and now it was all about survival.

The entire gunfight, from when Chavez and Caruso took down the two rear sentries to the last sound of men running off into the trees, lasted only three minutes.

Chavez's mouth was bleeding and his lip

swollen from the punch to the face, but he was most concerned about the wound to Dom's back. Dom pulled his jacket off, and when he did so Chavez saw blood on his white shirt.

"How bad?" Dom asked. It was in the small of his back on his left side, but too far behind for Dom to be able to see the wound.

Chavez looked at it quickly. "You're fine. Wrap it with a tablecloth and put your coat back on. I'm going to go check on the cops."

Ding Chavez found three police officers and one dog still alive in the first-class carriage, though one of the men had been shot twice in the legs. Chavez stabilized him while he talked to the other police. He denied knowing anything about any other shooters on the train other than the cops, and asked the three police what happened to the woman they were trying to detain.

"She got away," one said, his voice cracking with emotion as he looked at his dead comrades. Chavez thought the man might go into shock within minutes.

More civilians appeared in first class now, as well as the train conductor and a cashier from the dining car. Ding used the influx of new faces to slip back to the dining car, where he found Caruso going through the pockets of the unconscious men. He looked up at Chavez and shook his head. "More ammo. Their bags have clothes, a few toiletries, small wads of cash."

"Where are their passports?"

"Remember, the guy dressed up as a coach had them. I guess he's in the forest somewhere."

Chavez sighed. "It's time for us to do the same. How do you feel?"

"My back stings like I just got a tattoo. My pride is hurt that I took a bullet. Do the cops suspect us of anything?"

"I doubt it, but it will just take one witness to put us with a gun in our hands to get us stuck here at the German border till things get straightened out. I think we need to get off this train."

Dom nodded. "I'll get our bags."

Chavez said, "These guys were good. *Very* good."

Caruso nodded. "Could be a Spetsnaz unit of some sort. If that's the case, if Russian special operations boys *are* running around in the West carrying guns and shooting cops, you can bet none of those bodies will have any IDs."

Chavez said, "We get out of here and call it in. That's all we can do."

"Roger that."

8

Jack Ryan, Jr., was sure he'd lost the man who had been following him, so he climbed out of the taxi two blocks from his apartment on Via Frattina, in the center of Rome. Glancing at his watch, he realized he'd been in the cab for a quarter-hour. He could have walked home from the Piazza del Popolo faster than the vehicle had gotten him here, since the tiny one- and two-lane streets in this part of town made footpower and scooters more efficient than four-wheeled transport. Still, he was sure he'd lost the man in the pandemonium of Roman traffic, especially with all the twists and turns the taxi driver took to get around the worst part of the chaos.

He approached his apartment on foot, a little warily, because he had not been able to rule out the fact that one follower he'd identified could have confederates. But he checked the four or five places he figured someone might position himself if he wanted to watch the front door of his place, and he saw no one who did not belong.

He opened the door to the building and entered a long echoing hallway of black-and-white-checkered tile. His place was four stories above, on the third floor, and the slow, rickety, coffinlike elevator gave him the creeps, so he headed for the enclosed stairwell on his right.

Thirty seconds after Jack entered the stairwell and started heading up, a brown-haired man with a ponytail, wearing a brown leather jacket and carrying a backpack on his right shoulder, entered the front door of the apartment building, carefully shutting the door behind him so it would not echo in the large entry hall. He then stepped to the stairwell, cautious to ascend softly so the noise of his footfalls would not carry upstairs.

He climbed the stairs almost silently, taking his time doing so, and stopped at the first floor. Here he slowly leaned his head out into the hall. He looked left, then right. Seconds later he was back on the stairs and ascending again, making the turn on the landing between the floors. At the second floor he poked his head out into the hall and looked left, then right.

Once again he returned to the stairwell, climbed up to the third floor, and moved to the doorway to the hall. He slowly craned his head out and looked to the left.

The tall bearded man stood there facing him, just two feet away.

Jack reached out and grabbed the man by his jacket, spun him around 180 degrees in the hall, and slammed him hard against the wall. The man with the ponytail was stunned by the blow, but he was still aware enough to reach down to the backpack hanging off his shoulder. His right hand shot inside through a partially opened zipper, and he clutched something there.

Ryan fired a right jab straight out, connecting with the man's nose, snapping his head back.

"Che cazzo . . . ?" the man shouted. What the fuck . . . ?

Ryan grabbed the forearm connected to the hand in the bag in order to prevent the man from pulling out a weapon, and he smashed the man against the wall again by slamming into him with his left shoulder.

"Che cazzo . . . !" the man screamed again, his words echoing down the tiled hallway of the old building. The man started to reach into his front pocket with his left hand now, so Jack headbutted him in the face.

The man with the ponytail dropped down on his knees, completely dazed, his bloody face wrapped in his hands, and Jack ripped the backpack off him. In doing so the pack slammed hard into the wall.

"What were you going for, asshole?" Ryan shouted at the man. His own words echoed down the hall, but they were partially drowned out by the groans of pain from the lungs of the man with the ponytail.

Jack pulled out a large thirty-five-millimeter digital camera, cracked from the impact, a couple of high-end lenses, both shattered, and a see-through plastic neck pouch. In it was a media identification card containing a passport-sized photo of the man kneeling on the floor in front of him. The writing on the card was in Italian, but Jack recognized the word PRESSE stamped in large letters across it. Jack then knelt down and found the man's wallet in his front-left pocket. This had an ID card that said the same thing.

Ryan dug through the man's bag some more, found a few small Baggies of off-white powder, a metal spoon, a cigarette lighter, and a cluster of syringes, all rubber-banded together. There was also a cell phone, but Jack had apparently smashed it, as well, when he banged the pack against the wall. He dropped everything back into the bag, put it on his own shoulder, yanked the man back to his feet, and pushed him up the hall.

"If you're press, then I'm the Pope," Ryan said.

Ysabel rushed to the door when she heard Ryan and another man shouting in the hallway. She looked out the peephole, then opened the door just as Jack came through, his hand pulling the bleeding man by the collar behind him.

Ysabel said nothing, although her eyes revealed her surprise.

Jack all but dragged the man through the living room and into the kitchen, their footfalls on the hardwood floors echoing off the high ceilings of the luxury apartment. He shoved the man onto a chair at the kitchen table and the man crumpled there, still stunned by the vicious head butt.

Ysabel walked up behind Jack now. Sarcastically, she asked, "Will our guest be staying for dinner?"

Jack didn't answer. He took a moment to let his adrenaline dissipate, and while he did this he watched Ysabel take ice from the freezer and put it in a wet cloth. She cracked the cubes inside the cloth with a metal ladle.

He looked down at his hand now. It was scuffed, and he knew from past experience the knuckles would probably bruise to a yellowish gray, but his hand wasn't bleeding.

"I'm fine," he said.

She did not look up from her work. "It's not for you. It's for him."

"The hell with him."

"I'm not going to let him bleed all over the place."

Jack would have done just that. He was furious that his feeling of safety and anonymity had been destroyed in the blink of an eye. His time here in Rome, his utterly perfect two weeks, was over, just like that, and he was having a hard time accepting this fact.

Ysabel asked, "Who is he?"

"He's been following me."

"Then why on earth did you lead him here?"

"I didn't. I shook him at the Piazza del Popolo, I'm *sure* I did. I spent fifteen minutes in a cab checking behind me the entire time, then I came back here and he followed me in. Somehow he knows where we live."

"What's in the bag?"

"Camera equipment, mostly. And some fake creds that say he's a journalist."

"No weapon, then."

Jack shrugged. "No. No weapon."

"What are you going to do with him?"

"I'm going to find out who sent him."

"Before you do that, I'm going to clean him up and stop the bleeding."

Ysabel knelt in front of the man at the kitchen table, and Jack took the man's backpack into the living room and sat down, careful to position himself so he could keep an eye on him in the kitchen.

He watched Ysabel kneeling in front of the man. He still seemed to be dazed, and she worked expertly on cleaning his bloody face, applying ice to the lacerations to slow the bleeding.

The man wasn't badly hurt. Jack himself had taken blows much harder and kept his wits about him.

For just a quick flash it occurred to him that he should be appreciating the kindness of his girlfriend. Ysabel was in the same boat as he was; the appearance of this son of a bitch was a death knell to the perfect little world they had created. A temporary respite after the time of great danger and stress they'd shared on their last mission, and before Jack inevitably returned to real field-work with The Campus.

But Ysabel's compassion for this man just annoyed him. He didn't have the humanity she did, he supposed. He was just pissed.

Jack stood back up and stormed into the kitchen now. Playtime was over. It was time for answers.

He asked, "Do you speak English?"

The man had clearly come out of his stupor, because he shouted, "Eat my shit, Jack Ryan Junior!"

Jack scooped the backpack up again and began to recheck it, looking for a false partition or hidden compartment. As he did this he said, "So . . . you know who I am. You are going to tell me who you are and who you work for."

"You going to hell, man!"

This guy was pissed. Not scared. That

seemed odd to Jack. He pulled out the camera. "This is a nice rig. Where did you get it?"

"From your mother."

Jack sighed. "Right. Well, I found your fake media credentials in your bag and a fake ID in your wallet. I am going to do some digging into these and see if I can figure out who you really are."

"Fake? What shit are you saying?"

"I'm saying your name isn't" — Jack looked at the ID card again — "Salvatore." He cocked his head in confusion. "What, you couldn't be bothered to make up a fake last name?"

The man touched his face. "You broke my nose!"

Jack knelt down directly in front of the man now. He had four inches and twenty-five pounds of muscle on the seated man. "It's not broken, but I'll break your neck if you don't talk."

"I'm Salvatore."

Jack just looked at him.

"Salvatore!"

"Right! I got it! You're Salvatore. But who the fuck are you?"

"You see the ID, man. It say who I am. I am photographer. You know . . . celebrity photographer."

Ryan looked down at the credentials again. "Wait . . . you are saying you are a paparazzi?

Bullshit."

"Paparazzo, sì," Salvatore said, and he fingered his swollen lip.

Ysabel had been listening in. She walked over to her laptop on a desk next to the doorway to the kitchen and began to type the man's name into a search engine.

Jack asked, "Why were you following me?"

"You're a celebrity, you son of a bitch."

Ysabel called across the room. "Jack? Can I speak with you in here for a moment?"

Jack stepped up to Ysabel's desk, a sudden pang of worry filling the pit of his stomach. When Ysabel looked up from the desk to face him, he said, "Don't tell me."

"He is exactly who he says he is. He's just a photographer. A paparazzo." She turned her laptop so he could see the website of Salvatore — just the first name, along with several celebrity photographs. Ysabel added, "And you just beat him up."

Jack's jaw muscles flexed under his beard. *Oops.* He turned and headed back into the kitchen. "Who sent you?"

"Nobody send me nowhere."

"Bullshit," Jack said again.

Salvatore said, "You had coffee at Café Mirabelle. The hostess . . . she send me tips when somebody famous comes in. She recognize you, and she send me a text."

Jack remembered the hostess now. A beautiful college-age girl with eyes that stayed on his an uncomfortably long time. He'd mistaken the look as one of attraction.

It was a mistake that had nothing to do with vanity, just experience. More women looked at Jack because he was good-looking than due to the fact he came from a famous family, because he'd done everything within his power to change his appearance. His beard, his powerful physical bearing, the eyeglasses with the uncorrected lenses — he was night and day a different person from the much younger man who had been on TV some when his dad was in the White House for his first term.

But every now and then, somehow someone still realized who he was.

"How did you find my apartment?"

"I followed you."

"No, you didn't."

"You didn't see me," Salvatore said with a smile. Jack could see blood captured between the man's teeth. "I am good."

"If you're a photographer and you saw me, why didn't you take any pictures?" Jack had checked the man's cracked camera and found nothing but a few pictures of a fountain.

Salvatore said, "The girl at restaurant told me who you were, but I no sure. I want follow you, wait you are sitting so I can get good pictures."

That made sense to Ryan, and he caught himself actually wishing this guy had been some sort of an assassin, because he'd roughed him up so bad.

Ysabel stepped up behind Jack now. She whispered, "You need to let him go."

Jack nodded. Of course he did.

He looked down at the man on the chair. Blood dripped from his chin again, and his shoulders hung slumped.

This was going to be awkward.

Jack knelt down and, with a tone much more conciliatory than before, said, "Look . . . Mr. Salvatore. Here's the situation. I don't have security protection, I don't really need it . . . but the Secret Service insisted I go through some . . . *specialized* training so I could protect myself if something bad happened."

Salvatore said nothing.

"I've had a couple of crazy people come after me in the past. I guess I just overreacted a little this time." Jack held out a hand. "I hope you will accept my apology."

The Italian just stared at him, but after a moment he shook the extended hand.

Jack said, "I think you'll be fine, but I'd be more than happy to take you to a doctor."

Salvatore shook his head. He said, "You got anything to drink?"

"Sure, of course." Jack stood quickly, headed to the refrigerator, and pulled out a bottle of still water. As he turned toward the paparazzo sitting at the kitchen table, the man shook his head. "Wasn't talking about water. You have grappa?"

Jack didn't have any grappa, an Italian brandy, but he did have a six-pack of Moretti beer in his fridge. He wanted more than anything to get this guy out of his apartment, but he felt obliged to drink a beer with him.

Salvatore drank in silence — mostly, he seemed like he wanted the alcohol, not the fellowship of sharing a beverage.

Jack muttered a few words here and there about wanting to protect his privacy for the benefit of the people around him, but Salvatore did little more than nod and drink.

When he finished he stood. Jack said, "Your camera equipment and your phone. What's that worth?"

"Ten thousand euros."

Jack shook his head. "Try again. That camera is fifteen hundred, and it's repairable. The lenses might be five hundred each. Another five hundred for the phone. That's less than three thousand euros." Jack sighed. "I'll give you five."

Salvatore shrugged, then nodded.

Jack always carried a lot of cash when he worked an operation. Less this time than usual, because this was only half a mission, as much analysis as anything else. Still, he had exactly five thousand euros hidden under a shelf in the bathroom. He pulled an envelope containing one hundred fifty-euro notes out of a hiding spot in the back bathroom, then handed them over to the Italian.

Salvatore took the bills and tucked them into his pocket. Ysabel held out the backpack, and he took that and left the apartment without another word.

Ysabel locked the door behind him, then turned to look at Jack. He could see what she was thinking by the look on her face. She was also worried about what this meant for their time in Rome.

She asked, "Are you okay?"

"I don't know. Something about that guy . . . I don't know."

"What do you want to do?"

"I have to leave. Get out of town. It's the only way to protect the operation."

She said, "Why? I'm sure you aren't the first person to punch a paparazzo in the nose. It's a known job hazard for guys like Salvatore."

"He'll talk about this, you can bet on it."

"Do you think he'll call the police?"

Jack shook his head. "He had enough dope in his backpack to get himself thrown in prison. He knows that I know, so the last thing he's going to do is go to the cops. They'll give him a drug test, and that guy is an addict. He won't be clean, and he knows it."

Ysabel shrugged, as if the matter were settled. "So . . . he tells some friends. Some

114

other paparazzi. Maybe somebody camps out with a camera outside. We'll just deal with that when it happens."

Jack shook his head. He'd been playing the double game of espionage a lot longer than Ysabel Kashani had. "I wish we could do that, I really do. But I need to get out of here. You, too, just to avoid any hassle if more media show up. We can sanitize this place and get a hotel room tonight, and I'll head up to Luxembourg tomorrow." He wanted to invite her with him, but he had not yet cleared that with his bosses at The Campus.

Ysabel said, "I thought we had more galleries to check out."

"We do. There is another week's worth of work here. But I can't compromise the mission by sticking around. If Salvatore really did have a confidante at that café, he might have others all over town. Who's to say someone in the hotel won't tip him off, too?"

Ysabel thought for a moment. "I can stay here, Jack. I'll just stay in a hotel and visit the remaining galleries. I'll be finished in less than a week. Done by Saturday."

Jack hesitated.

Ysabel smiled at him. "You said I was a natural."

Now Jack chuckled. "Okay. But only to look for pieces that have already been purchased. If you find one of the paintings that has sold, you call me, and I'll call Gavin to have him hack the gallery. If he can't, we just move on. I don't want you sneaking around, trying to plant bugs on their computers. Without me ready to help you out of there, it's too dangerous."

"No problem." She looked around and sighed now. "I'm going to miss this place."

"Me too. I'm sorry. This is my fault. I just thought he was going for a weapon when he reached in his bag."

She nodded. "That's good to know. I won't make any sudden moves in front of you."

"I guess I'm a little jumpy. We saw a lot of action in Dagestan. When this guy started following me, then showed up again, it felt like the real deal."

She stepped over and kissed him slowly, running her fingers up the back of his neck and into his hair.

Jack smiled a little. He was in a shitty mood, but Ysabel was helping. He put his arms around her.

Ysabel said, "I can hear it in your voice. You feel like you've done something wrong. You haven't. You are very good at what you do, Jack, but you will always have to deal with the fact that your father is a public figure."

He shook his head. "Nobody has recognized me in months. Doesn't happen more than a handful of times a year, and almost never when I'm outside of D.C."

She shrugged. "Obviously the guy was telling the truth. You were recognized."

Jack nodded, then he changed the subject. "Listen. I was going to ask you after I got it approved, but I'm sure it will be okay. I'd like you to come up to Luxembourg when you're done here. You can fly up next week. You can help me on my surveillance there."

Ysabel broke into a wide smile. "I was hoping you'd ask."

"We work well together, don't you think?"

She kissed him again. "I think so. We also play well together, wouldn't you agree?"

He nodded. "I would." In minutes they began sanitizing the apartment together. Regardless of the fact that today's compromise didn't put him or Ysabel in danger, Ryan knew he needed to get moving, because just the possibility another paparazzo might show up would destroy the operation he was working on, and he could not let that happen.

There was something else Jack knew he should do now, but he decided to wait. Standard operating procedure was to report this contact to John Clark. Clark was director of operations for The Campus, and he'd want to know that one of his ops guys was compromised in the field, even if it wasn't by any foreign intelligence agency or enemy actor.

Clark would be pissed, not at Jack but at the situation. Jack had busted his ass to transition from straight analytics into field-work, and he'd acquitted himself well during many operations, but there was always the possibility that his cover would be blown. Not by any errors in his operational security, but simply by virtue of the fact that he still looked just a tiny little bit like the son of one of the most well-known people on planet earth.

Jack decided he could wait till tomorrow to let Clark know. For now he grabbed the two beautiful rib eyes wrapped in butcher paper, and he tossed them in the garbage. He had to get moving. For operational security reasons, he and Ysabel had no time for a cookout tonight.

A half-hour after he left Jack Ryan's rented apartment, Salvatore pulled his scooter into the little driveway next to his apartment on Via Arpino in Municipio V, east of the city center. He locked it to a rack in front of his building, then took the outside stairs quickly to his first-floor flat.

Inside his apartment, he threw his backpack on a chair, then opened his freezer. He pulled out a frosty bottle of grappa and poured himself a double shot in a water glass, and he drank it down while he walked back to his bedroom.

Here he grabbed his cordless phone off his bedside table and headed straight to the bathroom, dialing a number from memory as he walked. He looked in the mirror while he waited for the connection to be made.

A man answered in Italian, with a thick foreign accent. *"Prego?"*

Salvatore touched his broken lip with the tip of a finger. He replied in English, "It's him. You were right."

"You're sure?"

"I just drank a beer with him."

"You *what*?"

"It's fine. He does not suspect anything. The identity is confirmed."

There was a long pause. Then, "You will find the money in your mail slot in the morning. We have more work for you."

Salvatore was surprised by this. "For the same fee?"

A pause. "The fee is acceptable to us. But the work will be outside of Rome. In Brussels."

"No problem."

"Good. One week from now, maybe two. We'll let you know."

"Tutto bene." Then, "Wait . . . there is something else."

"Yes?"

"He is suspicious. He thinks someone is after him. And he's ready. For trouble, I mean."

Salvatore heard the man chuckle, then the line went dead.

9

Kaliningrad Oblast is a strange artifact of the Second World War: a Russian province that is not connected to the rest of Russia. It was created out of the redrawing of German borders, when Stalin demanded for himself the German Baltic seaport of Königsberg and the territory around it.

For nearly fifty years the sequestration of the province from the rest of the Soviet Union served as a strategic benefit for Moscow. Bordered by Poland to the south and east, and Lithuania to the north and east, Kaliningrad Oblast was nestled between Soviet client states, so there was minimal threat of losing it to the West, and it gave the Navy of the USSR easy access to the Baltic. Their Baltic fleet became their most strategically important, as it patrolled waters bordering several NATO nations.

Kaliningrad was called the most militarized place on earth during the Cold War, because the Soviets staged so many armaments and troops throughout the oblast, ready to defend the Iron Curtain or attack south through Poland and into Germany.

But after the fall of the Union, the fact that tiny Kaliningrad hung out alone, surrounded by nations no longer obligated to the whims of Moscow, made it extremely vulnerable. And then, when Poland joined NATO in 1999, the segregation of the half-million Russians living hundreds of miles from the Russian mainland became a significant issue indeed. And when Lithuania joined NATO in 2004 along with Estonia and Latvia, the Kremlin went apoplectic, as this meant a Russian province and home to their Baltic Fleet was now surrounded by NATO member states.

These days the oblast was, essentially, a forward operating base for the Russian military, because Valeri Volodin had spent the last three years pouring troops and matériel into the province en masse as his relationship with the West became more adversarial. The Baltic Fleet had been beefed up with new ships, new missiles, and new naval infantry battalions, all of which threatened both land and sea around the Baltic. The naval air base at Chkalovsk, just a few miles north of Kaliningrad City, housed the Baltic Fleet Air Force, a naval aviation detachment of Su-27 Flanker fighters as well as helicopters, anti-submarine platforms, and transport aircraft.

The most robust airfield in the oblast, however, was fifty miles east of Kaliningrad City, at Chernyakhovsk. Here Su-24 Fencers and MiG-31 Foxhounds lived in hardened bunkers and patrolled the skies over the oblast and west over the Baltic Sea.

Getting all this equipment and personnel into Kaliningrad was no easy feat, but the Russians had it figured out. Supplies were brought in by air transport, of course, but that was only a small fraction of the military needs of the oblast. Since the Russian mainland did not border its most western province, Moscow hashed out an agreement with both Belarus and Lithuania, stipulating that Russia be allowed unrestricted access to Kaliningrad. Russia and Belarus were close allies, but Moscow's deteriorating relations with all the Baltic nations caused the rail and highway transit routes through Lithuania to become a potential flashpoint for another European war.

The situation had worsened to the point that many said it was only a matter of time before Volodin threatened Lithuania directly, and after Russia's one-day attack of Estonia and their armed annexation of the Crimea, many Kremlin watchers determined it would take nothing more than a railroad strike in Lithuania or well-attended protests in Poland for Russia to send troops into their neighbors to establish a permanent corridor to Kaliningrad with the stated purpose of ensuring transit to their western province.

And if they did this, it didn't take an expert to know that the reverberations would reach far beyond the Baltics.

Lithuania was a NATO member state, and one of the major founding principles of NATO's charter was the concept of "collective self-defense." This was embodied in the charter's Article Five. "The Parties agree that an armed attack against one or more of them in Europe or North America shall be considered an attack against them all and consequently they agree that, if such an attack occurs, each of them, in exercise of the right of individual or collective self-defense . . . will assist the Party or Parties so attacked by taking forthwith . . . such action as it deems necessary, including the use of armed force, to restore and maintain the security of the North Atlantic area."

During the Cold War it was presumed that any attack of any NATO country would be part of an all-out Soviet invasion of the West, so the prospects of NATO's being drawn into a regional war it didn't want by Article Five were slim. But now, as small NATO nations in Central Europe found themselves in the crosshairs of Valeri Volodin, NATO leaders across Europe had become shaky, to put it mildly.

France, for example, wasn't crazy about the

idea of fighting a nation with 310 nuclear-tipped ballistic missiles to defend the honor of tiny Lithuania.

It was clear that Volodin wanted more territory, and it was somewhat less clear, but still reasonable to assume, that Volodin did not want war with NATO. His Kremlin had become incredibly adept at taking the political temperature of the NATO countries and then waging a kind of "hybrid war" in the Baltic, careful to keep their actions just below the threshold of an Article Five violation — or, more precisely, below the threshold of what the NATO nations could plausibly deny was an Article Five violation.

But across the Atlantic, President of the United States Jack Ryan was pushing for tougher reactions against Russia. He had suggested, both publicly and privately to NATO leadership, that the organization's indecisive moves and nonconfrontational stance to virtually all provocations by Russia was only encouraging a full-on attack. There was nothing stopping Russia from coming over the Lithuanian border, save the prospect of NATO countermeasures, so Ryan quite reasonably felt Europe's feeble responses to Volodin's threat and low-intensity action only encouraged him to do more.

It also kept Lithuania in a constant state of frustration and uncertainty. Recent polls in the small Baltic nation showed most citizens believed their country would be invaded by Russia within the next year.

All it would take would be that one spark, and the low-intensity hybrid action Volodin had been waging could morph into a full-on military invasion.

The troop train rumbled west over Belarus's border with Lithuania, passing by the immigration-control buildings and the lines of fences shortly before midnight. It continued on without slowing, and the border guards from both nations barely gave it a glance.

On board were nearly four hundred soldiers, most from the 7th Guards Motorized Rifle Regiment, but among them were a few dozen members of the 25th Coastal Missile brigade and a mishmash of men and women from other Kaliningrad-based forces returning from leave.

Two dozen Kaliningrad Oblast government workers returning from vacation in Russia rounded out the personnel on the train, riding exclusively in the first-class cars in the rear.

The train also carried several military trucks, mostly Army GAZ light cargo vehicles and heavier Ural Typhoon mine-resistant vehicles, along with more than twenty tons of ordnance ranging from handgun rounds for the Army to 130-millimeter high explosive shells for the Navy's AK-130, a massive auto-fire cannon used by the destroyers in the Baltic Fleet.

To the average Lithuanian there was no outward clue this twenty-car train passing in the middle of the night through their nation was carrying Russian military forces and their equipment; it looked much like any other train coming from the east and heading to the west. But anyone around here who followed the news was well aware that Russia had the right to transit Lithuania on the way to Kaliningrad.

There had been a mutual agreement that said in exchange for Lithuania being allowed to board and inspect the trains whenever they wanted, the Russians were allowed to inspect Lithuanian border security facilities, but the agreement fell by the wayside when Valeri Volodin came to power.

The Russians would pass through, they would show the Lithuanians nothing, and the Lithuanians would just have to get used to it.

The Lithuanian government had not gotten used to it. Not at all. But they had learned to pick their battles with the regional power-house to the east, and they let the trains pass. They were never allowed to stop inside Lithuania; stations along the route were lined with guards, and the trains were always followed a few minutes behind by three high-rail inspection trucks to check for anything or anyone left behind.

A minute before the Russian military train passed through Vilnius Central Station, a pair of nearly identical gray Ford Transit vans drove along the Švitrigailos rail overpass due west of the station. The vehicle in front pulled to the curb slowly, then stopped, and then the van in back, fifty meters behind its twin, did the same. Simultaneously, men climbed out of the front passenger seats of the two vans, then they jogged out into the middle of the street with flashlights in their hands.

The man in the rear turned to the south; the man in front looked north.

There was no one else on the overpass at this time of night, but had there been, they would have reported that the men who leapt from the vans wore identical black armbands with two lances crossing each other. It would mean nothing to any potential witnesses, because few people in Lithuania would recognize the insignia of the Polish People's Lancers, a small civilian paramilitary outfit based in Łódź, Poland.

While the first pair stood ready to block the overpass from any traffic, the side doors of the two vans opened simultaneously and two more men jumped out of each vehicle. These men, also wearing the Polish Lancers insignia, immediately turned back around into their vehicles and hefted large, long metal devices.

These they carried over to the sidewalk near the overpass railing.

Again, no one outside of the men from the vans saw any of this, but if they had, they would need to know their military weapons and perhaps a bit of history to recognize the Soviet-era B-10 smooth-bore recoilless rifles, first put into service in the 1950s and taken out of service by most modern armies by the early nineties.

The two big metal cannons had wheels, but they were not placed on the ground until they were almost in position by the overpass railing overlooking the rail line below. Then they were rolled left and right, oriented generally on a fixed point on the train tracks between the overpass and the station in the distance.

Each B-10 possessed a simple optical sight fixed to the left of the long 82-millimeter barrels, and one man on each gun used the sight to refine the weapon's positioning a bit more. They were not precise, but they didn't have to be. They were aiming at a point just two hundred meters away.

The big diesel engine of the twenty-car Russian military train on its way to Kaliningrad rumbled through Vilnius Central Station after the two guns had stopped moving. The men on the overpass watched it approach, pulling the long train behind it. They waited a few seconds more, then they heard a call on the radios they wore hooked to their belts.

"Atak!" The command was in Polish.

The two recoilless rifles fired almost simultaneously.

The diesel engine at the front of the train took two direct hits of high-explosive shells, and although it did not disintegrate or flip off the tracks, it was knocked out of commission instantly, its two-man crew was killed, and several of its rail wheels were damaged. The derailment came, but it did not come until the engine was almost directly under the overpass. Though the damage had been less than any of the attackers expected, they reloaded and aimed again quickly; the gun on the left fired down onto the ninth railcar, and the gun on the right sent an HE shell into the eleventh.

Two more direct hits tore into both cars.

The B-10s were reloaded a second time, this time aimed farther back along the long train. The recoilless rifle on the north side of the overpass managed to miss its target by a dozen feet, but the high-explosive round sent thousands of bits of shrapnel into the fourteenth car, killing and maiming almost as many as if the shell had hit the roof of the train.

While the attack was under way, a taxi with a passenger in the back on its way to the train station turned onto the Švitrigailos Street overpass. The driver slammed on his brakes as a man in the road waved a flashlight, and an instant later, a pair of flashes near the railing ahead on the right illuminated the entire area. Both the driver and the passenger saw the men and the small artillery pieces, and they heard the detonations down below on the train tracks.

The sixth and final shell fired by the men wearing the Polish civilian paramilitary insignia did the most damage. This 82-millimeter projectile impacted on the sixteenth car, and just by luck this car housed, among other items, a dozen 100-millimeter naval gun rounds. They did not all detonate, surprisingly, but the four that did created a colossal secondary detonation that affected seven other cars on the tracks.

The attackers didn't know it, but they had the time to fire at least two more salvos, because the police at the station checkpoint had taken cover, thinking somehow the passing Russian train was attacking *them,* so they were only just orienting themselves to the situation when the assault ended.

The two Ford Transit vans raced off to the south one minute, twenty-seven seconds after the first round was fired, leaving both B-10 recoilless rifles there on the overpass, still smoking from the attack.

The two witnesses in the cab mentioned the black armband worn by the man wielding the flashlight in the road, and its distinctive crossed-lance crest. Within half an hour of the attack, officials of the Lithuanian State Security Department were huddled over computers, running searches of known insignias, all the while fighting the panic that locals had just started a war with the biggest and baddest actor in the region.

But when they found a match for the symbol worn on the arms of the attackers, the men and women of the Lithuanian SSD blew out sighs of muted relief, and they scratched their heads in confusion, unsure how this news would play out.

They had the identity of their culprits, or they *thought* they had anyway, but they found themselves more than surprised that a few farmers from Poland would do something of this magnitude against the *fucking* Russians.

10

President of the United States Jack Ryan wasn't sleeping much these days. The pressures of the job and the physical requirement that the chief executive be present for an ungodly amount of meetings, photo opportunities, official functions, state dinners, diplomatic trips, and the like meant getting eight consecutive hours a night was a rarity, if not a pipe dream for the leader of the free world.

And that was in times without any particular crisis or calamity affecting the nation. In the past year Jack Ryan had endured an enormous succession of emergencies, from hurricanes on the eastern seaboard, to Russian invasions of its neighbors, to terror attacks on Middle Eastern consulates, to coups in South America.

And then there was the big one — the event that defined the past twelve months for the President: North Korea's assassination attempt of Ryan himself.

The heavy burdens of serving as the nation's President made catching a reasonable number of hours of sleep all but impossible, but it was this nearly successful attempt on his life several months back, and the continued pain resulting from it, that made his nighttime hours difficult now.

He'd broken his collarbone and suffered some soft-tissue damage in his shoulder during the attack, along with a concussion. The effects of the concussion dissipated in a few days, but even after surgery and a daily physical-therapy regimen, often overseen by his loving but incredibly persistent wife, he found himself waking throughout the night with stiffness and soreness, if not jolting pain.

Cathy Ryan had explained it this way to her husband on more than one occasion: "Face it, Jack. Getting blown up can be tough on the human body."

Ryan's physical therapy had been a part of his daily routine in the months since surgery; today he was just finishing up his monotonous afternoon ritual of spinning an arm-pedal exerciser in the gym in the White House living quarters. Although this machine wasn't particularly difficult or challenging, his surgeon had told him he needed to spend twenty minutes a day on it to prevent a frozen shoulder after the surgery. His shoulder was getting better, slowly but surely, so Ryan followed his doctor's orders and added the arm-pedal machine to the end of his regular daily routine.

Ryan had worked up a sweat on the treadmill before sitting down at the arm machine this afternoon, and this is what Cathy noticed when she peeked in.

"You okay, Jack?"

"Not really."

She came in and stood behind him, began rubbing his shoulders through his sweat-covered AIR FORCE ONE T-shirt. "The pain is flaring up?"

Ryan kept pedaling away with his arms, but he shook his head. "No, I'm suffering from acute boredom. I figure in the past month on this damn thing I've completed the Tour de France with my hands, and I didn't even get to enjoy the French Alps."

Cathy laughed, ended the shoulder rub with a tousling of her husband's salt-and-pepper hair, checked her watch, then looked to Joe O'Hearn, Jack's principal Secret Service agent. O'Hearn often worked out with his protectee in the residence, and right now he was doing barbell military presses in the corner. She said, "Joe, I have to go down to the formal dining room to check on the arrangements for tonight's state dinner. He's got seven minutes to go. Don't let him slide."

"Yes, ma'am."

As if Jack weren't in the room, Cathy said, "You know how he is. He'll try to charm you

135

with conversation so he can take it easy the last few minutes. You need to watch out for that."

O'Hearn smiled and did one more rep of the heavy bar. "I'm utterly uncharmable, ma'am."

"Good. I watched Jack flirt with Andrea for many years. Always trying to get her to go easy on him when he wanted to do something he wasn't supposed to do." Andrea Price O'Day had been Jack's lead agent, but she was badly injured in the assassination attempt. She'd be okay, eventually, but her career on the presidential detail, or any detail, for that matter, was over, and now O'Hearn was in the role Andrea had filled for so long.

O'Hearn regarded the First Lady's comment. He deadpanned, "If your husband tries to flirt with me, ma'am, I'll inform you immediately."

Cathy laughed again, gave her husband's shoulders one more squeeze, and headed back into the hall for the stairs. She was just out of earshot when the President said, "Joe, what happens in the White House gym stays in the White House gym."

O'Hearn put the barbell down and toweled off. "Yes, sir." And then, "But I think you should shoot for the full twenty minutes. It's for your own good."

Ryan grumbled and kept spinning the arm pedals.

But for only a minute more. Then the phone on the wall rang and O'Hearn snatched it up. "Gym." After a moment he looked up to the President. "It's DNI Foley for you, sir."

"More like my reprieve from the governor," Ryan said. He stopped pedaling, grabbed a towel off a rack, and began to rub his stiff shoulder while he took the phone from the Secret Service agent.

"It's six p.m. on Saturday, Mary Pat. Something wrong?"

"I'm afraid so, Mr. President. There has been an attack on a Russian troop transport train. Word is just coming in. Looks like there are multiple fatalities. Perhaps dozens."

"Ukraine?" Ryan asked quickly. The assumption was reasonable; Russia and Ukraine had been fighting a protracted positional war for more than a year. But if this had happened in Ukraine, he wasn't sure why the director of national intelligence was calling to let him know.

"No, sir." A pause. "Vilnius."

Ryan sat slowly in a chair by the phone. "Oh, boy." Now it made sense why Foley was calling. He thought it over. "This is the sort of thing we've been worried about. Culprits?"

"Unknown, but it's very early still. Of course, with the attack on the Baltic coast, one has to look at this Earth Movement organization, but this is a very different type of target."

"Right. Bad guys have been coming out of the woodwork lately. Let's get everyone in the Situation Room." He looked at a clock on the wall. "Forty-five minutes."

"I know you have the state dinner tonight with the Japanese prime minister at seven-thirty."

"That's right. I can't duck out of that completely, but I'm going to need to multi-task. Pop back and forth if I have to. Can you call Arnie for me and get the ball rolling on this while I get changed?"

"Of course. See you in forty-five."

Ryan shrugged at O'Hearn after hanging up the phone. His right shoulder ached unnaturally as he did so. "Sorry, Joe. Gotta run."

"You're the President, Mr. President."

Ryan wore his tuxedo as he hurried through the White House Situation Room, a five-thousand-square-foot collection of rooms on the ground floor of the West Wing. He'd just left the gym fifty minutes earlier, his shoulder hurt from the exercise and the injuries he'd received in Mexico, and his bow tie still hung untied on his shirt.

As he entered the conference room he was pleased to see he had a full house. Twelve seated in chairs around the table, and nearly that many others in chairs that ran along the wall on both sides. Four or five of the impromptu meeting's attendees were also dressed formally. The state dinner was always a big deal, but other than the UK and Canada, no nation was closer to the United States than Japan, so the White House always kicked it up a few notches when the prime minister and his wife came for dinner.

Sitting just to the left of the head of the table was Secretary of State Scott Adler. He wore his tux and looked ready for the party, but he was hunched down, reading a cable to himself from his embassy in Vilnius. And the national security adviser, Joleen Robillio, sat next to him in an attractive gown, but she was huddled over her iPad, reading the latest from her staff on the incident.

Everyone rose when they saw the President enter, and he waved them back down and slid into his chair, which was at the head of the table, nearest the door.

"Those of us going to the state dinner *will* be there. On time. Let's do this quick, set up things so we can get out of the way of those we're leaving behind to do the heavy lifting tonight."

He looked around the room at all the men and women of the military and Department of Defense, the National Security Council, the Department of State, and the various intelligence services, all of whom would be tasked with staying either in the West Wing or at the Eisenhower Building next door, and no doubt working through this Saturday night.

Ryan said, "Damn inconvenient of whoever it was that hit that train at dinnertime in D.C. I'll have the dining stewards bring everybody something from the state dinner." He shrugged. "Beats pizza."

He looked to Mary Pat Foley, who sat near the opposite end of the conference table. "Have we learned anything more about the incident?"

"Yes, and it's not good. Two witnesses to the attack both report the terrorists wore armbands of the Polish People's Lancers."

Jack looked around the room to see if anyone else recognized the name, because he sure didn't. "What the *hell* is that?"

Foley said, "A small paramilitary outfit. Civilians. They are a nationalist, anti-Russian group, so that falls in line, generally speaking, with the possibility of being responsible for an attack on the Russian military, but so far we know of exactly zero violent attacks against the Russians committed by the Polish People's Lancers. The attackers employed two" — she looked down at her notes — "B-10 recoilless rifles to fire on the train from an overpass near the Central Station. The weapons were then left at the scene. I suppose they decided it would take too long to get them out of there after the assault."

"Have these Lancers released a statement?

Either claiming responsibility or distancing themselves from it?"

"Neither. Not yet."

Ryan cocked his head. "You'd think if they *weren't* involved they'd not wait around to make that known."

Secretary of Defense Robert Burgess was also in a tux. He shook his head. "Mr. President. It takes training and coordination to move a pair of small artillery pieces through the middle of a foreign city and then assault a particular moving train. From the little I know about the Lancers, they aren't much more than weekend war-gamers. It's basically a gun club. They do some camping in the woods and marching around. As Mary Pat said, they've never orchestrated any violent attacks *anywhere* against *anybody*. We found a few references in the newspaper in Łódź, Poland, where one of their more outspoken leaders made some threats against Russian speakers living in his neck of the woods, but other than some arrests for graffiti and demonstrating without a permit, they haven't run afoul of the law. I find it hard to believe for one second they pulled this off."

"So . . . who did it?"

CIA director Jay Canfield said, "Wouldn't rule out the Russians themselves."

Ryan said, "Are you suggesting this was a false-flag attack? That Russia attacked their own train?"

"I know it's too early to make any informed guesses, but we've seen it in the past, haven't we?"

It had been determined by the CIA that Russia had staged an attack in eastern Ukraine that killed pro-secessionist protesters, Russia's supporters in the troubled region. The Kremlin used the event to justify an invasion, and their tanks rolled over the border shortly thereafter to signal the beginning of the Ukrainian war.

Ryan said, "Yes, we've certainly seen it before. What was the train carrying?"

Mary Pat looked down at her notes. "Our Lithuanian partners say it was a scheduled Russian troop and matériel transport. The Lithuanians had beefed up their security at the station like they always do when these trains come through, but they weren't watching this overpass, because it was a half-mile away or so."

"Casualties?"

Canfield said, "This is subject to change, because you can be sure there is a lot of stuff on that train that can still explode and cause damage, but right now we are told twenty-two Russian soldiers were killed in the attack, and another sixty-one injured. The train and its cargo are a near complete loss, and five Lithuanian firefighters were killed fighting the blaze. Again, follow-on detonations are going to be a problem."

"Christ," muttered Ryan. "Reaction from Moscow?"

"They've already gone up to their highest state of military readiness. Here we are, two hours after the attack, and they have made statements on social media blaming NATO, the CIA, Lithuania, Poland, Ukraine."

"The usual suspects."

Secretary of State Adler said, "You can't say they aren't consistent."

Ryan drummed his fingers on the table. "If the Russians did it, we'd have to proceed on the assumption that this is an opening move to grab a corridor to give them direct access to their military installations along the Baltic Sea. I've worried for a long time that Kaliningrad could well be the next Crimea."

Adler added to his President's comments. "Actually, sir, Kaliningrad is more Crimea than Crimea. Where Crimea was a Ukrainian province with a Russian majority and a Russian Navy base, Kaliningrad actually *is* Russian territory, with a Navy base and two air bases, not to mention missile batteries all up and down the coast and multiple Army bases. It's a legit strategic interest like Crimea and, in this case, Russia has a rightful claim to it."

Ryan said, "But they don't have a claim to southern Lithuania, and that's what they'll have to take to get to it."

Adler agreed with this point with a nod, but said, "The question isn't legitimacy, the question is: Does Valeri Volodin think NATO will actually fight him over a swath of Lithuania?"

Mary Pat said, "Volodin is looking for some sort of diplomatic or military victory. He needs a win badly. Fossil fuel prices are way down, and this has been a disaster in the Russian economy, because over half their exports are oil or gas. The sanctions we pushed through a few months back are already squeezing the nation even more.

"When we armed the Ukrainians we made his easy rout of that nation turn into something more costly than he was prepared to pay for. He lost in Estonia, even though he framed it to his people as a win with a negotiated withdrawal."

Canfield added, "In the past thirteen months his domestic approval rating has gone from eighty-one percent to fifty-nine percent. That's not a nosedive, but it's bad. Considering the fact he virtually outlaws negative media coverage of him and his policies, a twenty-two-point drop is remarkable."

Ryan said, "A year ago the booming economy made him invincible. The economy is not booming anymore, and there's nothing he can do about it. So he's totally changed hats. Now he frames himself as a nationalist, he whips up national symbols, portrays himself as the savior of the Slavic people, who are being oppressed by the West. Blames us,

NATO, whoever, for all Russia's problems."

Scott Adler said, "The one thing that will bring his poll numbers back up, barring a major jump in energy prices, is a real military triumph. But he's not winning anywhere. Ukraine is a stalemate."

Ryan added, "Ukraine is a stalemate because Volodin keeps it there. He could push harder toward Kiev if he wanted to, and he might do that still. But we have to keep our attention on the new flashpoint. These two different attacks in Lithuania could be used as a catalyst, whether or not Volodin was directly involved in them."

Adler said, "We essentially blackmailed Volodin last year. Told him we'd reveal what we knew about his ties to organized crime and how that brought him to power in Russia. He backed off in the Ukraine, turned his tanks around, and locked his territorial gains at the Crimea and Donetsk."

Ryan said, "Our blackmail didn't solve our problem with Volodin, but it did help things. When he stopped his push to the Dnieper River it gave the Ukrainians time to regroup and improve their defenses. We armed them with the best defensive missiles and armor we had, and we increased our military advisers."

National Security Adviser Joleen Robillio said, "Mr. President, we did the right thing in Ukraine, and we handed Volodin a stalemate, which, considering how fast his troops were moving, is just as bad as a defeat to him. But I worry that if we back this man into a corner, at some point he will realize the only way out for him is to employ nuclear weapons."

Ryan replied, "You're right, and he knows that we are factoring that into the equation. He expects us to harass him at every turn, but ultimately he does not expect us to call his bluff. If this Lithuania attack was his doing, perhaps he is considering a new front. Ukraine didn't work, so he's probing another location."

Scott Adler said, "You're speaking of this as if it is already a war."

Ryan thought that over for a moment. Then he turned to his secretary of defense. "Bob, what are our options as far as responding to the attack in Lithuania?"

SecDef was ready for this question. "We'll have to go through NATO to move any of our NATO forces, of course. There is the NATO Response Force based in six Central European nations — Lithuania included, of course — but we're talking six thousand troops in total. Not more than four hundred in Vilnius. There is a bigger contingent in eastern Poland, but still, not anything close to being enough to thwart a Russian invasion. We'd need a major mobilization."

"How fast can the NRF deploy in an emergency?"

"The NRF can deploy within a week. Of course, NATO now has another unit that can deploy even faster, within forty-eight hours. That's the Very High Readiness Joint Task Force, and they are good troops, even though there aren't enough of them to stop the Russians."

Mary Pat said, "Let's not get ahead of ourselves. Russia isn't coming over the border in the next week in any numbers, Mr. President. They don't have forces in predeployment positions."

Ryan was not terribly comforted. "But these timelines don't take into account the decision-making time of the Europeans. None of our partners has the political will to snap their fingers and send troops off to meet the Russians without needing a lot of hand-holding. We've got the NATO summit coming up soon in Copenhagen. Why don't we use this as an opportunity to appeal to the other heads of state to develop some ways to streamline the process of moving forces into defensive positions? With the LNG facility explosion and now the attack in Vilnius, hopefully enough of the member states will recognize how quickly this could develop into war."

Robillio said, "I really hope you are met with a receptive audience, but you know how these summits go. A lot of talk, not a lot of action."

Ryan nodded, turned back to his SecDef. "What if NATO sticks its head in the sand? What about U.S. assets not tied to NATO?"

Burgess said, "We have a battalion of Marines, twelve hundred men, assigned to the Black Sea Rotational Force. They are set up as a rapid response, and they aren't tied to NATO forces."

"Where are they now?"

"They are in Romania, but they are twenty-four hours away from wherever we need them in theater. This is just the sort of thing they train for."

Ryan raised an eyebrow. "Twelve hundred Marines train to fight off a Russian invasion?"

"Absolutely. They know they are a stopgap. Something to put into place, coordinating with other U.S. forces if possible, certainly along with local friendlies."

"Okay. Any other options?"

Burgess gave a little shrug. "One destroyer is in the Baltic on a presence mission. But no carriers, and no real combat capability in comparison to a Russian invasion force. We do have a Marine Expeditionary Unit along with several ships practicing with the Brits on the west coast of the UK."

Ryan said, "That's a long way from the Baltic."

Burgess held his hands up. "That's true,

but it's two thousand Marines. A couple thousand well-equipped, well-positioned, and well-supported Marines could, in theory, seriously degrade a Russian invasion, if we gave them enough air, but we'd lose a hell of a lot of them in the process." Burgess's shoulders sagged. "The good old days of hundreds of thousands of U.S. Army and hundreds of tanks ready and waiting in Europe are behind us."

Nobody in the room thought those days were particularly good, but his point was understood by all.

Ryan addressed Mary Pat Foley now. "It goes without saying, but we need to be watching military movements in Belarus. Russia will have to go through Minsk to get to Lithuania, unless of course they attack from the Kaliningrad side."

Mary Pat said, "We'll add to our eyeballs in Belarus and along the Lithuanian border."

One of Jay Canfield's aides entered the room and leaned over the CIA director, conferring with him for a moment. Canfield looked up at the President.

"What is it, Jay?"

"Good news. The fire on the train is out and Lithuanian Land Force personnel have been through the wreckage. The ordnance on the train was all conventional artillery shells, small-arms ammunition, that sort of thing."

Ryan knew what Canfield was saying. There

were no ballistic missiles on board the train. According to rumor and intelligence reports, the Russian Federation had moved dozens, even hundreds, of Iskander-M short-range ballistic missiles into Kaliningrad province in the past year. These missiles had the capability to be armed with nuclear warheads. The fact no Iskander-Ms were present during the train attack was a relief to everyone.

Burgess said, "Interesting there were no missiles on that train."

"Interesting why?" Ryan asked.

"That train just had vanilla troops, and vanilla ordnance. No Spetsnaz, no sophisticated weaponry."

Ryan had been at this for a long time, so he understood what Burgess was getting at. "From that you infer it was targeted by Russia, because an attack on it wouldn't destroy anything too valuable?"

"If there had been Iskanders on that train I would have had a hard time believing Russia would be involved in any attack. With the attack comes an inspection of the wreckage, after all, and that would mean that ordnance is going to get examined, possibly seized. The fact there was nothing controversial on board does make me a bit more suspicious of who the actual culprit was."

Ryan said, "We can speculate all we want, but we do so at our peril. We need hard and fast answers. Volodin is playing a game, ladies and gentlemen. He knows the rules. He has the plan. He is not as masterful as many people make him out to be, and I no longer believe he has the power to do whatever he wants, but make no mistake about this: Volodin is at the controls."

"The controls of what?" Adler asked.

Ryan stood and motioned for all those heading to the state dinner to follow him. As he walked through the door and began tying his bow tie, he looked back to Scott Adler. "I don't know, Scott. I hope we figure that out before it becomes apparent to everyone on earth."

11

Six months earlier

The café on Krivokolenny Lane was legendary, but to only a select few here in Moscow. To most it was just one of thousands of simple eateries in the city. It certainly wasn't much to look at: just three rooms that didn't get sufficient light from the street, walls with worn wood paneling, and simple wooden tables upon which dim votive candles burned in cheap glass holders. The building that housed it was old, dating back to before the Second World War.

The restaurant had changed hands many times over the years, but now it was called Café F, and it was a high-dollar gastro-pub, attracting hipsters and tourists. Most of the hipsters didn't know it, because even Russian hipsters didn't think about such things, but Café F was only two blocks from Lubyanka Square — the headquarters of FSB, Russian State Security, and before that the HQ of the KGB. The café had been the location of a popular watering hole for KGB, FSB, and military intelligence types. To a man, the personalities who now ran Russian State Security and controlled the nation had once sat at the bar in the front room by the door, downed shots of vodka, and complained about their bosses and the direction their nation was heading.

The venerable dive two blocks from the back door of the FSB building had turned into a posh local eatery and was even shilled to tourists on TripAdvisor.com. To the old guard still around it was a goddamned shame that somehow the edgy insider joint from the old days had morphed from a smoke-filled spy haunt into a swanky date-night destination.

But not tonight. Tonight the new-money clientele of Café F had been shuffled away at six p.m., a sign had been put up out front explaining that a private party was being thrown, and soon after that cars and trucks full of armed men began pulling up out front. These were security officers and advance-detail men, most of them driven over from Lubyanka, but by nine p.m. bodyguards had arrived from the Kremlin, just a kilometer to the southwest.

By ten p.m. there were three dozen armed men blocking Krivokolenny Lane and manning the rooftops and filling the sidewalk out in front of the closed restaurant. The building had been swept with dogs and bomb-detection equipment, and it had been swept again for listening devices and pinhole cameras, and only when the advance men and the security shift leaders pronounced the location clear did the arrival of the principals begin.

Most came in armored SUVs and armored limos, but Pyotr Shelmenko was head of the GRU, Russian military intelligence, and he landed in a helicopter in Revolution Square, which was three blocks to the northwest. From here he walked with an entourage of twelve armed men. When he got to the restaurant he left most of his security unit out on Krivokolenny, and he went through the door of Café F with just a pair of close protection officers. Inside, Shelmenko grabbed a vodka at the bar and greeted several men around him with bear hugs.

These were the top men of the *siloviki,* the former intelligence and military officers who were now the billionaires in charge of the Russian government, both behind the scenes and in the public eye.

The nation's foreign minister, Levshin, was there, as was Pyshkin, minister of the interior. Both men had served in the KGB in the 1980s. Arkady Diburov, the head of Gazprom, the state-owned natural gas concern, showed up in the middle of a phalanx of silver Cadillac SUVs, and he didn't make it through the alcove in front of the restaurant before finding himself in deep conversation with Mikhail Grankin, the director of the Kremlin's Security Council, who happened to be entering at the same time.

Security men were not allowed inside the bar itself; it was a long-standing rule of the get-together that had the effect of making the street outside look like the front lines of a war zone throughout the evening. Dozens of men with rifles stood outside cars and scanned the area. Inside, chiefs of staff and aides-de-camp filled the front room and bar area of the café, while the back room was completely reserved for the *siloviki*. Diburov and Grankin followed the other principals inside, and soon sixteen men were in the back, drinking vodka and sitting at simple tables, chatting quietly.

The oldest was the eighty-one-year-old interior minister, and the youngest was Grankin at only forty-five.

This was the twenty-third consecutive year of this event, although there had been quite a few additions to and subtractions from the guest list along the way. The first meeting, in '94, was well before the *siloviki* wrestled power away from the more democratic government types and installed the first in a series of presidents in the Kremlin. Back in the beginning of the annual meetings they all just came to lament their fall from grace, or to use the get-together to help one another bolster their new fledgling companies, concerns, and holdings, in order to use their networks in the military and intelligence communities to navigate the difficult days of Russia's return to a market economy via brash and brazen criminality.

But by 1999 every single one of the attendees was a millionaire, some many times over, and they had taken control of the Kremlin, and since that year the annual meeting on Krivokolenny Lane had taken on even more importance as vital matters of state were discussed and decided on. Most of the last seventeen years had been good times for these men, and often this event at the café two blocks from the Lubyanka was a raucous affair, with much back slapping, tears of laughter, jokes about one another's mistresses, and invitations to parties, palaces, and private islands tossed around between them.

But not this night. Tonight the men were somber, quiet. Worried.

Angry.

The Russia of just a few months ago seemed like a distant memory now. Oil prices and gas prices had nose-dived, and the American government had placed economic sanctions on nine of the sixteen men in the room, blocking their movements out of Russia and freezing foreign assets that could be identified. These men weren't broken, but they were damaged, to be sure, and every one of the others wondered if he might be the next man in the crosshairs of the West.

The Russian economy had dipped significantly due to these two events, and these problems had revealed just how weak an economic system Russia had. Prices had risen, employment was down, potholes in the street weren't getting fixed in Moscow, and garbage wasn't getting picked up with regularity in Saint Petersburg.

The public was furious, the nation was unstable, the *siloviki* were feeling the pressure.

The sixteen men drinking and smoking in this small room needed a scapegoat, and their scapegoat arrived at eleven p.m.

Six armored vehicles from the Kremlin pulled up to the barricade blocking off Krivokolenny Lane from the main streets. The motorcade barely slowed before the wooden lane blockers were moved and the vehicles were allowed through. In front of Café F, all six stopped as one.

Valeri Volodin looked out through the bulletproof glass of his limousine as his security team formed around the vehicle, and he waited for his door to be opened. He wasn't looking forward to tonight. Back before he was in charge of things he enjoyed the annual visit to the old bar, the get-together with the powerful men of the intelligence and military. This used to be a place of great plots, alliances, and allegiances, of multimillion- and even billion-dollar deals and decisions that would change the course of men's lives.

Or end them.

But now, as president, he loathed these evenings. Even when things were going well, which they had been until just months before, the others in the *siloviki* sat stoically while he held court and gave them a rundown on events at the Kremlin that would interest them, as if he were some sort of PR man, a talking head on the television. At the end he took questions from men who should have been more than satisfied to just enjoy the billions of dollars he'd helped them make, and they should have been climbing over one another to be the one to get to shine his shoes.

Volodin distanced himself from organized crime and wrapped himself tighter in the flag of Russian nationalism.

His approval rating had dipped, but despite the fact he was the leader of an ostensible democracy with many enemies, Volodin wasn't going anywhere. He retained control over the media, the defense ministry, the intelligence services, and, more important, he retained the support, if not the love, of the oligarchs he had made rich and powerful in exchange for their support and compliance,

and the *siloviki,* the former intelligence officers who now held power over the nation.

Volodin was not in a good place politically,
but he was essentially a dictator, so it didn't
really matter.

Now things weren't going as smoothly as
far as the national picture went, and he knew
the sixteen other members of the *siloviki* who
would be here this evening would be a
particularly surly bunch. His talk would be
met with more skepticism and fewer toasts
than usual.

Volodin told himself he didn't need this
bullshit. He owed these men nothing. It was
they who owed him everything for his careful
management of their lives and careers.

But he did not tell his driver to leave. This
yearly summit was set in stone; if he missed
it he would be perceived by these weaklings
as intimidated, and he could not let that happen.

And in truth, he *did* need them.

Volodin had been owned by a Russian
organized-crime syndicate as far back as the
late 1980s, even if he never actually admitted
this to himself. They'd propped up his career
in KGB, and then FSB, and then they'd
advanced his business interests in the 1990s.
The *siloviki* meetings had been more important for the other men than they had for him,
because he had the protection of the Seven
Strong Men.

Now that protection was gone, the Mafia group to which he had been tied wanted him dead, so his *siloviki* brotherhood was more important now: a necessary evil.

A gentle rapping on the window of his limousine brought him back to the moment, and he opened the door and climbed out into the cold night.

Volodin entered the café and looked around at the familiar confines; Café F had the same floor plan and tables and wall paneling as had all the other iterations of the venerable locale — it looked much the same as it did forty years earlier, the first time Volodin set foot inside the door.

In his twenties he shoveled hot borscht into his mouth at the bar on quick lunch or dinner breaks, before rushing back two blocks south and returning to his office. He'd spent entire evenings at a table in the corner here, designing plans and operations, and he'd met with coworkers from KGB or colleagues at GRU here, and he'd made plans of a tactical nature here long before he was entrusted to make plans of a strategic nature at the Kremlin.

He entered the back room now, shook hands that weren't as firm as usual, exchanged bear hugs that were not as long, strong, or demonstrative as they had been in years past.

He shook hands with Derevin, the president

160

of the massive oil concern Rosneft, and he drank a vodka with Bogdanov and Kovalev, former KGB rezidents and now directors of the state-run mining and timber concerns.

Though these men still addressed Volodin using his patronymic, Valeri Valerievich, he felt the malevolence in the room, and although he couldn't say he did not expect it, this was a new feeling for him.

A year earlier the group was cautious. Estonia had not gone well, but this was before his annexation of the Crimea, when the Ukrainians put up surprising resistance, and a phone call from the President of the United States to Volodin revealed that the Americans knew about Volodin's ties to organized crime.

Volodin had then pulled his troops back to the eastern and southeastern oblasts of Ukraine, and he'd kept them there, giving in to the blackmail of the Americans. To the men in this room this looked like Volodin had suffered a defeat, but Volodin knew they simply did not understand the full dynamics of the events.

Estonia had not gone well, Ukraine was still in question, Volodin could concede these facts, but he knew the men were angry about the economic problems that most affected them. And these, Volodin was adamant, were not his fucking fault.

He addressed the men in the back room of the café for a half-hour, most of it extolling the good things that had happened in Russia during the past year. Virtually all of his examples involved his successes in reining in his opposition, quashing media and Internet outlets that spoke ill of the Kremlin, the *siloviki,* and the governmental decrees and decisions that Volodin claimed perpetuated the success of the sixteen men in the room — seventeen including Volodin himself, who was essentially the crown prince of the *siloviki.*

At the end of his planned speech he tacked on a few minutes more of extemporaneous talk, mostly because he was putting off starting the Q&A portion of the event.

As he neared the end, a round of vodka shots was passed around. Every year there was a toast to him before the beginning of the questions.

But he was still speaking, wrapping up by talking about the new breeze of nationalism blowing across the nation and how this benefited the status quo, when he noticed that Levshin had begun drinking his vodka, not waiting for the toast.

Diburov noticed this, too, and he downed his own.

Around the room, others began reaching for the glasses on the table in front of them.

This was an insult.

As Valeri Volodin offered a high, reedy *spasiba,* thank you, at the end, he saw that almost all the glasses were empty, facedown on the table.

These men had been his peers, his equals, for most of his adult life, but in the past few years Valeri Volodin had become a reverential figure among them. He was not their equal, this he knew.

But now he saw they were treating him as if he was their lesser. Beneath them. *Who the fuck do they think they are?*

A combination of fury and paranoia began to well up in the pit of his stomach.

Slowly, he nodded his head. In a measured tone he said, "I see the malice. You express it clearly. So . . . which of you would like to begin? Who among you wants to start off by telling me how you would have steered the national economy in a manner that would have brought the past year to a different conclusion? Who here would have been a better steward for Mother Russia? You, Levshin? Are you the one to say your face should be on every newspaper and not mine?"

Levshin looked back at Volodin with a placid smile. "Of course not, Valeri Valerievich. You were chosen to lead because of your skills, your abilities. No one is denying this."

It was a smooth backhanded compliment, Volodin knew. "Chosen to lead" indicated to Volodin that the foreign minister was pointing out that he didn't think Russia's president could have made it into that role without the help of the other men in the room.

Volodin said, "You are my foreign minister. This precludes you from complaining too much about international events, because you are our conduit to the rest of the world."

Levshin simply said, "I follow your instructions, Valeri Valerievich." Again, he was smooth, but there was ice in his words.

Bogdanov sat at a table right in front of Volodin. He spoke up now. "We are concerned about the oil prices, but no one blames you for this. But the sanctions . . . these are a direct result of the attack in the Ukraine. This was your decision, and you are in day-to-day control. I speak for those of us caught up in the sanctions. We are angry, Valeri. We could have weathered the storm caused by the drop in oil prices. But our international relations have been a disaster."

Volodin shook his head vigorously. "Events in Ukraine have not gone according to plan, but we hold several oblasts along our border and we now control Crimea. The Black Sea Fleet is secure in a way it has not been in a generation."

He saw that he wasn't going to be getting a round of applause for the stalemate he'd entered into in Ukraine, so he spoke of other foreign initiatives.

"We have reached out in positive ways to the Chinese."

Diburov parried this away. "Reaching out isn't very specific, is it? Our pipeline talks with China stalled the day oil dropped below eighty U.S. dollars a barrel. It's trading below sixty now, so China can buy from anywhere. They don't want or need a pipeline now —"

Volodin did not wait for Diburov to finish speaking. He said, "And Saudi Arabia, long an adversary, is reaching out to us on many fronts."

Now Levshin spoke up. "They are doing this because they have cash we need, and they think we are desperate enough to chance our policies on Iran and Syria to get it. Those are your policies, Valeri Valerievich, and it is through your mishandling of the economy that we are in such desperate need of their cash."

Volodin's eyes scanned the room, saw men sitting up straighter, looking to one another. Something was coming. A threat, a demand. He felt the hair on the back of his neck stand up, his palms begin to sweat.

He knew he needed to head this off.

For the first time this evening, Valeri Volodin looked to Mikhail Grankin, the head of his Kremlin Security Council. From what he had seen, Grankin had been the only man in the room to save his vodka for a toast to Volodin.

Grankin was young, only forty-five, a full twenty years below the average age in the room. He had been FSB, a bold and success-

165

ful foreign intelligence officer, then he left intelligence work to serve under Volodin in Saint Petersburg. When Volodin came to the Kremlin a few years earlier, Grankin came with him, rising through the ranks from junior consultant to senior adviser on security matters. Volodin had been Grankin's *krisha,* his roof, his benefactor.

And then, some months earlier, the head of the FSB had been killed by his own security force. Of course Volodin had been responsible for the death of Roman Talanov, and it was up to him to replace him. He sent Mikhail Grankin to Lubyanka to take the reins, not because he was smart and crafty, although he was. He was not necessarily the best man to lead one of the largest intelligence agencies in the world, but he was a Volodin confidant in the ways the fifteen other men in this room were not.

Grankin was *siloviki,* like the others, even though he was younger. His time in FSB had led him to riches and influence, but Volodin determined that Grankin was also young enough to be spared the hubris felt by every other man in this room.

Valeri Volodin no longer trusted the *siloviki,* nor did he trust the FSB, but he did trust Mikhail Grankin to comply with his wishes.

After a few months in power at Lubyanka to right the ship Grankin had left the FSB at Volodin's request, and he came to lead the

166

Kremlin's Security Council, a small, tight group of men who advised Volodin on all matters of intelligence, diplomacy, and military. The hyper-compartmentalized and secretive president of Russia listened to Grankin and his small team, and he gave them directives, plotting the course for the nation.

Grankin, next to Volodin, was the most powerful Russian when it came to international affairs.

With a nod from the young Kremlin Security Council chief, Valeri Volodin turned his eyes back to the room and said, "Gentlemen. I can see you have all put your heads together and come up with a solution. But I am the president. So why not listen to *my* solution first?"

Shelmenko said, "You brought a solution to our problem with you tonight?" The skepticism was obvious in his voice. "Well, then, the boys and I can't wait to hear it."

After Grankin nodded to his president, urging him on, Volodin said, "You all want a change. I see this. A return to prosperity. I understand. Who wouldn't? What if I told you there is an initiative I have been working on with Misha Grankin that will cause a transformation in the order of things? I wanted more time to perfect every note in this concerto, but I see from your faces that you men are not the type to wait. You've been sharpening your knives since last year's meeting, and tonight your knives are out."

Diburov sighed, blowing out smoke from his cigarette as he did so. "Details, Valeri Valerievich. Give us details. Without specifics this is just talk."

"This is an operation of wide scope and immeasurable depth. I can't give you details, but I can tell you that once it begins, you will know, and when it ends, that is to say when we all come back here in one year's time, Russia will be a very different and much improved place."

Pushkin called out from the back. "You are going to throw *another* lady punk band in prison for dancing in the Christ the Savior Cathedral?"

This line got the biggest, and perhaps only, real laugh of the evening.

Volodin even smiled at this, but his sharp, angular face showed the malice he felt.

He said, "I smile, Pushkin, not because you are funny, but because I am already picturing the reception you will get here next year when I remind the room of your comment. No. Something big is on the horizon. It involves our military, our intelligence organizations, and the diplomatic offices at the Foreign Ministry."

Heads turned to the foreign minister. Levshin shrugged. "First I am hearing about this."

Volodin snapped back, "Because you have

168

no orders yet. You'll get them soon enough."

"This sounds like the fantasy of a man trying to stave off the ignoble end of his tenure."

Volodin bit his lower lip, the shaking of his hands nearly visible now.

Mikhail Grankin stood suddenly, surprising everyone in the room, even Volodin. "With your permission, Valeri Valerievich, I would like to address the group for just one moment. I know you are too wise and careful to provide specifics, but I am willing to stick my neck out."

Volodin made a dozen calculations in his head, then slowly he nodded. "Be as sparing as possible, Misha."

Grankin turned to the room. "We will bring the West by the nose to the negotiating table."

The men looked at one another. Confused. Unconvinced.

"Negotiating for what?"

"The Baltic."

There was laughter, jeers, and hisses, but from only half of the group. The others sat silently, curious to know more.

Grankin talked for ten minutes only, but this was more than Volodin had been willing to do. He was short on the details of the operations, but he went to some length about the results he expected to attain. When it was over, a show of hands indicated the *siloviki* were at least willing to let the opening volleys of the plan play out, to see where it went.

169

Diburov muttered that things couldn't get much worse, so he'd watch Volodin's scheme for a while.

The meeting broke up at three a.m. The mood, while certainly not ebullient, at least was decidedly more upbeat than it had been an hour earlier.

Grankin shook Volodin's hand in the little lobby in front of the bar. Volodin said, "Are you heading back to the office or to your home?"

"I am going home."

"Good. Come with me, I will take you. We can discuss matters in the car."

"Thank you, Valeri Valerievich."

On the drive through the darkened streets of Moscow, Grankin addressed his president. "They were even bigger old pigs than I expected them to be. They showed you no respect, and you handled them expertly."

"But?"

"But we are not ready. Our plan is more aspirational in nature."

"We have one year."

"Yes, Mr. President. I was there. I heard you assure everyone that the world would be quite different in twelve months. But what if it's not?"

Volodin chuckled. "Then we'll both be sacked, of course."

Grankin was not laughing. "Me they can

sack. They can put pressure on you to have me replaced. But you? They can't just remove the president!"

Volodin smiled. "You're right." With a shrug he said, "I'll most likely be assassinated." He held a finger up. "That reminds me, Misha. I want a list of the best offshore banking specialists known to the FSB. Your staff can compile it quite easily, I should think."

Grankin cocked his head. "This is part of the operation? Something you haven't told me about?"

"This is just one piece of my puzzle. I will work the diplomatic front, the military front, the cultural front, domestic avenues. Financial resources. There are many moving parts."

"And you need to move some money, I take it."

"Exactly so. But just give me the names of the people the FSB trusts the most. Men whose discretion is beyond reproach. Check with their leadership, and make sure you have a consensus from them."

"I'll have it for you in a week's time, Valeri Valerievich."

The motorcade pulled into Shvedskiy Tupik, a blind alley a kilometer from the Kremlin, and the limo pulled over to the curb in front of house number 3.

After shaking his president's hand once more, Grankin climbed out of the limousine and entered his apartment, his security force converging on him around the pavement as he climbed the steps to his building.

Volodin looked out the window at the dead city as his motorcade headed back to the Kremlin. His mind was not as quiet as the roads here at half past three in the morning. The city looked dead as he thought over all he had learned this evening. His mistrust for the men he had been with his entire career was complete now. Any one of these sons of bitches would do him in if it benefited them to do so. Grankin was better than the others, but that was only because his debt to Volodin was more obvious. He'd follow along with the plan as long as it moved in his favor, but he'd go running off after a new *krisha* if the storms became too heavy.

Hell, Volodin thought to himself. Grankin didn't need a *krisha* anymore.

Volodin looked forward to getting the list of the FSB's most trusted minds in the world of offshore banking. There would be dozens of names; the FSB was always moving money and managing holdings for the *siloviki,* so there were quite a few men in the upper echelon of the industry they called on. But Volodin wasn't interested in the names that would be on the list. He was looking for a name *not* on the list. One of the great financial minds of Russia who, quite simply, the FSB did *not* trust to move their money.

That was the person Volodin needed to find,

because if the FSB trusted a man, that meant the FSB could control the man, and Volodin needed to find someone with a unique level of discretion to help him prepare his escape in case this whole thing went to hell.

12

Present day
Thirty-eight-year-old American Peter Branyon considered himself to be the luckiest man in the intelligence business. Not because he'd uncovered any particular nugget of information that would change the world. No, that hadn't happened yet. But simply because of his current position. He was station chief in Vilnius, Lithuania, and it seemed like fate had given him one hell of a good opportunity to shine.

He'd come a long way in a short time, and he was smart enough to realize he hadn't completely made it on his merits. A year earlier, one of the top men in the Ukrainian Intelligence Service was caught spying for the Russians, but not before he had passed on the names of many of the top CIA officers working in Ukraine.

As a result of this outing of CIA officers, dozens of men and women, all of them experts in the region and most of them Russian speakers, were recalled to the United States. Consequently, their roles had to be filled by CIA officers whose identities had not been revealed to the Russians. A massive reshuffling happened at the CIA's Near East desk. The former chief of Lithuania Station was promoted to the more important Ukraine Station, and a case officer in Vilnius was promoted to run the CIA operation in Lithuania.

This man's tenure at the top of Lithuania Station did not work out. He was a field man, fair to good in his role as a case officer but completely unable to manage an office full of case officers from the top, delegate with authority, and administrate effectively. He was brash and direct to the point of being rude, and consequently lousy at building liaison relationships with the Lithuanians. Within a few months of his taking over, the new CoS had alienated longtime partners and delivered no real guidance or discipline over the men and women in his station who were out in the field, running agents and operations in the nation.

Langley belatedly recognized they had the wrong man for the job, so they demoted the CoS back to case officer, moved him to Jakarta, and then they went looking for his replacement.

And they found Peter Branyon in Buenos Aires.

Branyon had been CoS in Argentina only a few months, but before that he made a name for himself in Chile and Brazil. He was a hard-charging case officer, able to recruit and manage many agents, and his work running a network of Chilean embassy staff at the Chinese embassy in Santiago had won him the appreciation of Langley. An operation he managed in São Paulo involved bugging business-class hotels and recruiting tipsters at an executive airport, and it led to solid intelligence material on many visiting government employees of several nations, including breaking up a Russian SVR operation to plant listening devices in the U.S. embassy and an Al-Qaeda terrorist plot against a synagogue in the city.

Pete Branyon earned his way to the top of the Argentina Station, no doubt about that, but the Lithuania posting had fallen in his lap only due to the misfortune of others. Any Central European nation was a huge posting for a young CIA station chief, but the Baltic was the center of the action these days, and for a number of reasons, Lithuania was the star of them all.

And that was even before somebody killed a bunch of Russian soldiers in the heart of the nation's capital and blew up a natural gas facility on the coast.

Branyon told himself that although he might have lucked his way into his present predicament, he was going to make the most of it and prove that he merited the post.

To that end, in only seven weeks in the position Branyon had taught himself an impressive amount of Lithuanian, he'd taken a tiny and inefficient network of informants in the eastern part of the small nation and whipped them into shape personally. He acted not just as a station chief, but also as a case officer, unafraid to roll up his sleeves and get his hands dirty, and unwilling to sit at his desk in the embassy all day. But unlike the last station chief, Branyon led from the front, had no problem delegating a dozen different jobs to a dozen case officers under him, and had no compunction about demanding hard work and discipline from all his staff.

Branyon wasn't really supposed to be as hands-on as he was, but he was getting things done, sending back nightly cables to Langley about his quick progress in the station.

The only ding on his time here was a worry by others about his personal security. He was CoS, and he was sitting in cars in gas stations a mile from the Kaliningrad border, or walking down blind dark alleys in the capital, looking to meet with petty criminals who might have information to sell about shady foreign elements in the city.

After some prodding from the CIA security office, Branyon accepted a bodyguard, but only under the condition his was to be a low-profile version of personal security. Greg Donlin was a forty-seven-year-old ex-SEAL, and a longtime CIA security officer, with stints all over Southeast Asia and the Middle East. He could work low-pro, just an MP5K hanging under his arm and hidden by his jacket and a subcompact Glock pistol under his shirt, a hidden radio earpiece that linked 24/7 to both the CIA security office and the Marine guard force at the embassy.

It wasn't much protection for a chief of station who enjoyed hanging out in bandit country. Donlin would have preferred three or four guys with him, but Branyon said he didn't want to wander the streets with a half-dozen other dudes like a goddamned boy band about to take the stage.

So Donlin worked alone keeping Branyon alive.

It was just dawn now, below freezing here in Vilnius, and Peter Branyon made a mental note to buy a thicker coat as soon as he could. His jacket was barely keeping his body heat in, and it was just October. By December he figured he'd be dead up here in Lithuania, found frozen stiff on the sidewalk after trying to walk to work.

He looked next to him to his security man, and he saw Greg was feeling it, too.

Donlin was from California, and Branyon

from New Mexico. This was the first autumn in the Baltic for either man, and their first winter was just around the corner. Neither man was accustomed to the cold, and they both hated it with a passion.

Branyon looked his security officer over for another second and said, "I guess the reason I'm station chief and you're not is because I'm smart enough to button my coat."

Donlin sniffed, rubbed his red nose. "I'd *love* to button my coat, but I can't. Got to have quick access to my piece, because my station chief insists on standing on a train platform out in the open."

Branyon chuckled. "Okay, how about we go down to the train and warm our hands on a smoldering artillery shell?" He headed off down the platform, closer to the derailed Russian train.

"You're just full of great ideas today, aren't you, Chief?"

Branyon approached the massive crime scene; the cold air was full of the scent of burnt fuel and plastic, the sound of construction equipment and men hard at work cutting the dead out of the wreckage. He saw a small cluster of men in trench coats right next to a car torn open as if by a giant can opener, and he recognized the man in the middle. Branyon made his way through the group and up next to his local counterpart, the Vilnius director of the Valstybės Saugumo Departamentas, the State Security Department. The man held a cigarette in one hand and a telephone in the other, and he stood talking into his phone alongside the tracks as a dead Russian soldier was carried out in a blue body bag.

Branyon didn't wait for the man to stop speaking into the phone before greeting him. "Morning, Linus. You've had a busy week."

Linus Sabonis, head of the SSD, hung up the phone and shook Branyon's hand. "Peter, nice to see you down here, but I hope you've just come as a friend of Lithuania. I hope Washington did not send you to investigate this. Everyone knows already who is responsible. All the people with one half brain know Russia did this to themselves."

Branyon looked into the twisted mass of barely distinguishable items in the center of a train car. He saw some smoldering wreckage, but it gave off no warmth. "I'm just here to poke around. I had to see this for myself."

Donlin kept his head moving in all directions, even up on the overpass nearby.

Branyon also looked above. The weapons there had been roped off, and there were guards standing around them, even though morning traffic was allowed to traverse the overpass. "Those are B-10s, right?"

"That's right," Linus said. "But don't get any bad ideas. The Lithuanian Land Force

180

can vouch for every one of those old things in our inventory."

"What about Poland?"

Linus sighed. "No, Peter. Don't be fooled by Russia. Even if those weapons turn out to be from Poland, it is still just a Russian ruse."

Branyon shrugged. "I know I'm the new guy around these parts, but you'll forgive me if I go where the facts lead. Everybody is saying Russia did this to foment the conflict, and you may be right. We just don't know for sure yet."

Linus said, "I know your government is looking for answers, but just look at who benefits from this. There are Russian troops to our east in Belarus, and west in Kaliningrad. The Russians have spent the past years putting a lot of troops and equipment very close to our western border. With this attack here, they have all the excuse they need to come over and say hello."

Peter Branyon said, "We're with you, Linus."

"Is NATO with us?"

"You know I don't speak for NATO."

The director of the SSD nodded slowly and took a drag on his cigarette. "I know you don't. I only hope you guys know that we do not trust NATO to come to our aid. Maybe America will help like they did in Estonia, like you guys are doing in Ukraine. But France, Spain, Italy? Forget about it. They are sorry they let us join their little group, and they will bow to Russia, let it do whatever it wants, even if they fill our skies with para-troopers."

Branyon shrugged. "That sounds like an Article Five violation. They'll have to come if that happens."

Linus shook his head. "No. NATO will just say the Russians are only coming in for a visit."

Branyon knew Linus was probably right, and he also knew he never had to worry about this sort of thing in Buenos Aires. The idea that Brazil would invade his host nation was laughable.

But here nobody was laughing about the prospect of the skies filling with Russian troops under parachute canopies.

Branyon said, "Tell you what, Linus. Let's you and me work our asses off to keep our governments aware of the situation around here. That's all we can control, so let's stick to that."

Linus nodded and puffed on his cigarette, then motioned to the train. Another body bag was being removed, and the sun glowed in the east over low buildings and factories. "You and I are standing on ground zero, my friend. This piece of train track. Believe me, people will look back and say this was the beginning of it all."

Linus and his entourage turned and headed

back up the tracks toward the station.

Branyon looked at his security officer. "What do you say we take a drive to the eastern border today? I want to see what our agents there say about the news coming out of Belarus."

Donlin sighed a little. "What do you say you let one of your case officers handle your network on the Belarusan border?"

"It will be fine, Greg. We'll be back before lunch."

In a resigned voice the security officer said, "Not worried about lunch. Worried about Little Green Men."

Branyon give Donlin a wink. "We see some Little Green Men, I'll be the first guy in the country to turn around and run."

"And I'll be the second."

13

Oud-Zuid is the most desirable quarter in Amsterdam. It's centrally located, expensive, cosmopolitan, and beautiful.

Sibling assassins Braam and Martina Jaeger lived here in the neighborhood, residing together in a comfortable and ultramodern condo that took up the top two floors of a brownstone on leafy Frans van Mierisstraat.

They'd been home from Venezuela for just days; they'd spent them relaxing mostly, enjoying the neighborhood cafés along with late nights in clubs. Last night brother and sister had gone to a trendy nightclub and while Braam had sat on a VIP sofa lording over the scene, his sister had danced in the hot, thick space till four in the morning.

It was just ten a.m. now, and Braam had made breakfast for them both. Martina had just finished picking through her omelet, and now she took her coffee to the table in the middle of the living room and she opened her laptop. She logged on to Tor, software that enabled "onion routing." Tor was an acronym for The Onion Router — and it offered the user anonymous communication by directing Internet traffic through some six thousand relays around the world, hiding both the sender and the receiver of a message.

She opened an e-mail sent late the night before, and reading through it saw she and her brother had been given their next assignment. The uniqueness of the situation was not lost on her, that here, sitting in a bathrobe and holding a mug of steaming coffee, her mind heavy from the booze and the noise and the pills she'd taken the night before, she could receive and accept a contract to kill a human being somewhere in the world, on the other side of the planet, even.

Braam sat across the room, himself in a robe, with a copy of *De Telegraaf* open on his lap.

She called out to him. "Braam. *Kom hier.*"

He climbed from the sofa and stepped behind her at a desk in the middle of the large open living area, nestled his chin on her shoulder, and they read their instructions together silently.

When he finished, Braam said, *"Amerika. Mooi."* Nice.

She smiled herself. "Beverly Hills." And then, in a fake American accent, she added, "Darling, this will be so much fun."

They both stood up and went to start packing, because the timeline on this operation was short.

The conversion of the Jaegers from normal middle-class kids from Utrecht to international contract killers employed by Russian intelligence began quite innocently when their father, a colonel in the Royal Netherlands Army, convinced his video game–loving ten-year-old son to come with him on a hunting trip. Braam took to the shooting and the stalking naturally and with ease, but it would have been no great love of his had he not seen the pride in his father's eyes.

When he did see it, he realized, quite simply, that his father's love was conditional on his ability to hunt game.

Soon enough Braam began to enjoy the competition of shooting, so much so that he became a well-known teenage biathlete. After school he joined the Dutch military instead of going to college, for the simple reason that the military had a program that would allow soldiers to compete in national and international sporting competitions. He soon became an infantry sergeant, with plans to leave the military after four years to go on the professional biathlon circuit.

Then came Holland's entrance into the Afghanistan war.

Braam found himself engaging in, and

riveted by, the combat. By the end of his first day in a "real" war he had no further interest in wearing Lycra with a number on his back and shooting paper targets. No, the only *real* competition in a man's life, as he saw it, was the two-way gunfire of battle.

He left the Dutch military after four years to take a job as a civilian military security contractor in Iraq. He found himself under fire with regularity, and life was good.

Martina was beautiful and intelligent, and she worshipped her brother and had followed in his footsteps since she was old enough to walk. She hunted and shot with her father, and she competed in the biathlon and other shooting sports. At eighteen she became world ranked in the ten-meter air rifle and ten-meter air pistol categories, and she missed out going to the Olympics at age twenty only because of a neck injury she picked up while training for a European championship judo competition.

In her early twenties she took up mountain climbing with all the gusto she put into everything she enjoyed, and by age twenty-six she had summited seven of the fourteen 8,000-plus-meter mountains of the world.

Her try for an eighth ended in disaster, however, when an avalanche on K2 killed four in her party and left her with broken bones.

While Braam was engaging insurgents in

Iraq, Martina convalesced at home, bitter that all her competitive endeavors had ended in failure.

Eight years earlier, when they were still in their late twenties, Martina was working in a sporting-goods store in Amsterdam when Braam called and asked her to drop everything and meet him in Mali, Africa. She was surprised to learn he was no longer in the Middle East, but he explained he'd taken a job doing security investigations in the Third World.

As soon as she arrived she realized her brother had not asked her to Africa for a family reunion. Instead, he was working on a low-profile assignment and he needed a cover story — more specifically, he needed someone to play the role of his wife.

The cover worked, the operation was a success, and Martina Jaeger knew she would never work in some mundane profession again.

Braam began to use his sister on several more jobs, he found himself working deeper in the shadowy world of private security, and much of his work involved deep-cover operations.

It was Martina Jaeger who first suggested they offer their services as contract killers. They found work immediately, and they killed their first target together in Namibia. He was a white South African reporter who'd run afoul of local organized crime. Their white skin and their cover as urbane tourists allowed them to slip into bars and restaurants where black gangsters would have brought security officers running, and their skill and calm under fire helped them see the difficult assignment through.

After a few more hits in Africa, Martina decided they would branch out, so she contacted a Saint Petersburg *bratva*, a Mafia-like criminal organization.

Neither Martina nor Braam cared for politics. They worked for money and the thrill of it all, and the Saint Petersburg syndicate gave them two years' worth of work around Europe. After this, they found themselves coopted into FSB operations, because of the close nexus between Russian business and Russian government interests.

They didn't care. They were paid well and on schedule, and the FSB had all the work Braam and Martina could handle.

The Jaegers absolutely loved their work.

Killing, they agreed, was the best adventure sport on earth.

14

John Clark woke early on Sunday morning, long before his wife, and he dressed for warmth. He slipped a weathered gun belt through the loops of his jeans, holstered his large SIG Sauer P227 .45-caliber pistol, and pulled on a thick flannel lumberjack shirt.

After a pit stop in the bathroom and a drop into the kitchen to fill a thermos with coffee from the automatic pot, Clark headed out the back door of his Emmitsburg, Maryland, farmhouse. He pulled on a pair of muddy and weathered boots and made a beeline to his garage. Here, in a locked storeroom, he filled an old canvas pack with several hundred rounds of .45-caliber ammunition, several extra magazines, hearing and eye protection, and a gun-cleaning kit. A small medic pouch and his thermos also went into the pack; then he slung it over his shoulder and headed back outside.

Clark walked nearly ten minutes to his own private shooting range, down deep in a dry gully that ran to the creek on his farm. Here, several steel plates of different shapes were set up in front of a hay-bale backstop, and behind that the wall of the gully kept any examples of poor marksmanship from straying too far, although Clark was certain he'd never once placed a single bullet in the mud.

An old wooden workbench on wagon wheels sat in the middle of the gravel-covered ground, and here John Clark took his time disassembling and cleaning his handgun, and sipping his coffee, while the sun rose.

Even this early, John heard the occasional crackle of gunfire in the distance. There were hunters on land nearby, and instead of being annoyed by the noise, Clark welcomed it, because as far as he was concerned it gave him carte blanche to conduct target practice on his own property whenever the hell he pleased.

Sandy had made John promise to never open fire before seven a.m. unless he was using a weapon with a silencer. John, who was a loving and dutiful husband, always added a half-hour to his wife's moratorium, so he never started before seven-thirty.

As his watch beeped the half-hour, Clark loaded his gun. His everyday sidearm was the New Hampshire–manufactured SIG Sauer P227 .45-caliber Enhanced Elite model. It carried ten rounds in the magazine, along with an additional round in the chamber.

Clark was the only member of The Campus who carried a .45 and the only one who carried a SIG. All the others carried Glocks or Smith & Wessons in nine-millimeter, but Clark had been a fan of the big and fat .45-caliber round since Vietnam.

Ryan and Caruso teased him a bit for being old-school with his pistol, and even Chavez liked to joke that Clark could run a little faster and jump a little higher if he didn't wear a howitzer on his belt, but Clark didn't find the eleven-round SIG to be as heavy as the eight-round Colt 1911 he'd carried for decades, so he felt secure in his choice of weapon.

He let the others chide him; it was his opinion that reasonable people could disagree on caliber, but the most reasonable people agreed with him that the .45 was the way to go.

Clark brought this and other weapons out to his homemade gun range regularly, but today he'd decided he would make a major shift in his daily training.

Clark's eyesight was fair for a normal sixty-seven-year-old man, but Clark was not a normal sixty-seven-year-old. Few men his age ever found themselves needing to shoot at anyone shooting back at them. And Clark was fast for his age, but few men his age ever called on their speed to engage a threat with a firearm.

In both cases, John Clark was one of those few.

He knew he was getting slower and less sure with his weapon; it was a fact of life that his skills would deteriorate with age. Sure, he was still a hell of a lot better, at all handgun distances, than the vast majority of those who carried a weapon for a living, but to Clark that wasn't good enough.

It was about carrying out his missions, but it was more than that.

Clark thought about the death of Sam Driscoll, and he knew objectively that Sam's death had had absolutely nothing to do with any mistake Clark made. But with the news that Chavez and Caruso had found themselves outgunned in Germany two days earlier, Clark realized he could possibly find himself back out in the field, and his ability to handle his share of the duty and protect his team from harm was paramount to him.

And he wanted to be ready, despite the negative effects of his age on his skill sets, so he told himself he needed to work his ass off to maintain and even increase his own abilities in the field.

Point shooting was a technique that involved focusing on the target, not the weapon's sights, in order to quickly and accurately engage a threat. Clark had been trained in point shooting; all operators who spend time in close quarters battle training need the ability to bring a rifle or a pistol up for a snap shot when there was no time to engage through the sights. But Clark knew his advancing years meant it would be greatly beneficial for him to adapt point shooting to engaging targets farther out than the very close distances he'd been accustomed to. If he could teach himself to draw his pistol and hit chest-sized targets at twenty, thirty, even forty feet, he could greatly decrease his engagement times with a firearm.

So much of point shooting involved orienting the body and using the body to aim the weapon. Without the benefit of the sights, proper body alignment to the target helped get the barrel of the gun pointed in the right direction. From there it was just a matter of refining fundamentals. Proper grip on the gun, perfect trigger control, a good understanding of how to manage recoil and get the gun back on target.

Clark exhaled a long, full breath that turned into vapor in the cold, and he reached over to the table and tapped a button on the top of his automatic shot timer. Once the button was pressed, it would wait a random amount of time — somewhere between three and ten seconds — and then it would beep loudly. This served as his starting gun, his indication that the steel target forty feet away was a threat.

Clark lowered his hands to his sides, and

he eyed the target, waiting to explode with action. He always started his training rounds cold, meaning he did not warm up at all. He knew if he ever needed to employ his weapon in the field, he wouldn't have a chance to tell all the bad guys to take a smoke break while he shot some paper targets off to the side, just to make sure his synapses were firing and he was ready to go.

The shot timer beeped. Clark dropped his hand to the pistol and drew it from his belt. As he did so he turned his body toward the target, so when the gun cleared leather and he began to raise it, he was already oriented in the right direction.

Clark fired one round in nearly half the time it would have taken him to bring the weapon up to his sightline and focus on it.

He saw a massive splatter of mud in the wall of the gully, behind and a foot to the left of the steel target.

Clark sighed and reholstered his weapon.

He didn't let it get to him. This was why he trained. If he had succeeded his first time out, he would have known he wasn't making the training challenging enough.

Clark ran the drill again, and again he got the same results. On the fourth try he was slower, but at least he dinged the edge of the steel target, just where the "right elbow" of the "man" jutted out from his body.

He spent an hour dumping more than two

hundred rounds at the steel man-sized target forty feet away. One draw at a time. It was hard to keep himself from bringing the weapon up to eye level for each shot, but it got easier as he retrained his muscles to respond to the new technique.

At the end of his training, he was speckled with mud from splatter that came back at him, and his clothing and hair smelled like gun smoke. On top of this, he wasn't where he wanted to be with this skill, not even close. But he was a hell of a lot better than he'd been when he woke up.

He cleaned his gun at the table, then reloaded it, and he was just slipping his hot pistol back into his holster for the last time of the morning when his cell phone rang in his pocket. He didn't even look at the caller ID on the screen, so sure he was it was Sandy letting him know that she had breakfast almost ready and the table set on the back porch. She'd dutifully listened to an hour of gunfire on a Sunday morning, and as he brought the phone to his ear he decided he was going to make it up to her. "I'm on the way back, honey. How about we go to that antiques place up in Gettysburg after breakfast?"

There was a delay, then Clark heard the Kentucky drawl of Gerry Hendley, director of The Campus. "Uh . . . John?"

"Oops. Sorry about that, Gerry. Thought

you were Sandy."

"I'm not, but that doesn't mean I don't like antiques."

Clark laughed. "What's up?"

"I hate to do this to you, but Mary Pat asked if she could come to the office today for a meeting."

Clark said, "Does this involve the shootout in Germany?"

Gerry said, "Not sure. Dom and Domingo just got back in town last night, but she asked that everyone come, so I'll call them next."

Clark did not hesitate in his response. Mary Pat rarely came to the office. After all, she was the head of all U.S. intelligence, a cabinet-level official. "Just tell me when and I'll be there." He looked down at himself. "I'll be honest, though. I could stand a shower first."

15

The office of The Campus was on Fairfax Street in Alexandria, Virginia, with views over the Potomac River. Autumn had come to Virginia weeks before; now the red and yellow leaves blew down the narrow streets of Old Town as John Clark's Chevy Suburban rolled into the neighborhood and then descended into the underground parking garage below the Hendley Associates Building. He noticed the four-car convoy of vehicles the director of national intelligence always traveled in had not yet arrived.

He'd changed into fresh jeans and a button-down shirt back at home, but as soon as he entered the building he went to his office to grab a blue blazer out of his closet. He was just heading back out on his way to the conference room when Domingo Chavez and Dominic Caruso stepped into the hallway from the elevator.

All three men entered the fourth-floor conference room and poured coffee for themselves out of an urn. A tray of danishes and bagels sat on the middle of the table, and Dom and Ding both dug in.

Gerry entered a few minutes later with Mary Pat Foley. She shook the men's hands and sat down at the head of the table.

She started by asking, "Where's Jack Junior?"

Gerry said, "Forgot to tell you. We have him in the field. In Rome, actually. He's got a line on a network of shell companies being used to launder money out of Russia. Not sure how wide or deep the network is yet, but he feels strongly that he has them linked to Mikhail Grankin, Volodin's confidant. The hope is we can pass this on to DOJ to get more of Grankin's assets in the West seized."

Mary Pat nodded appreciatively. "The son has become the father."

Dom said, "In all ways other than politics. Jack's got no use for it."

Mary Pat looked at Clark with a smile. "John and I remember a time when Jack Senior said the same thing."

"Sure do," Clark agreed. "Wonder how much he likes it now, even."

Ding said, "Mary Pat, we haven't seen you since Sam's funeral. I guess, in some ways, it's good news if DNI doesn't drop by that often, from a world-crisis perspective."

"Yes. But as you see . . . here I am." She turned to Caruso and Chavez. "I understand you were both injured in the firefight in Germany."

Chavez still wore a gray bruise on the right side of his face and a cut on his lip. "Dom caught the worst of it."

Dom said, "It was nothing, really. A little graze to my back. Adara gave me a couple of stitches on the plane ride home. I would like to know more about what happened over there."

Mary Pat said, "I can help you there. The Germans were on the lookout for a woman named Nuria Méndez. She is Spanish, sort of an ecowarrior who had been wanted for questioning after attacking a pipeline in Hanover last year. They didn't know she was traveling with the Russian FSB agent, and they certainly didn't know there were a dozen other men on the train who were willing to kill to keep her out of the hands of the authorities."

Dom said, "Do they think she was part of this Earth Movement group that did the attack in Lithuania?"

"They had no intelligence that led them to that conclusion. There was an arrest warrant for Hanover. That's all."

Clark said, "Which is why they were totally unprepared to take her in. This certainly makes it look like she was part of something big going on, and something that involved Russian intelligence."

Mary Pat nodded. "Nothing conclusive here, but we sure would like to get our hands on Ms. Méndez and find out."

Gerry asked, "What did the Germans learn about the dead guys in the tracksuits?"

"Nothing at all. No documents, no tattoos, no survivors. The six who were killed, either by the police or by you two, are lying in a morgue in Berlin now, so I'd call the entire attack a dead end."

Clark said, "And Morozov? Up in smoke?"

"Afraid so." Mary Pat folded her hands in her lap. "But this is not why I am here. I'm not going to shock anyone here by telling you the location of the newest danger zone for the United States."

Ding said, "I keep thinking the situation with Valeri Volodin can't possibly get any worse. Time and time again I'm proved wrong. This issue with the Baltics and Kaliningrad seems like it's coming to a head."

Mary Pat nodded. "Yes. And this is a particular problem for the U.S. intelligence community."

Clark finished the thought. "Because the leak from Ukrainian intelligence a year or so ago compromised a lot of CIA assets in the Near East section. I assume you've had to move a lot of operations personnel out of the region and replace them."

She said, "In many cases with younger, less experienced case officers."

"Ouch," said Dom.

"The chief of station in Vilnius, Lithuania, is one such example. Peter Branyon. Solid officer, he was in Brazil and Chile for the early part of his career, then did a stint as CoS in Buenos Aires. But after we reshuffled in Central Europe, Jay Canfield sent Branyon to Vilnius. Long-term, he's got the potential to go to the top of the heap in the Agency, but it's a tough post right now."

"And he's screwing up?" asked Chavez.

"Not at all. He's really good, in fact. In any normal scenario he'd be able to mature in time. But events on the ground in Lithuania . . . He's just . . . in a little over his head."

Hendley asked, "Why can't you replace him with someone more experienced?"

"Anyone we bring in there is going to be more junior, with less understanding of the lay of the land. Like it or not, for the time being, Pete Branyon is all we've got."

Ding Chavez said, "We could go over there and watch his back."

Mary Pat did not respond to Chavez directly. Instead, she turned and looked at Hendley. "I had something else in mind, actually. Branyon is cultivating a fair-sized network of agents in the east of Lithuania. These people are absolutely crucial to our understanding of what the Russians or Belarusans are doing along the border. And in case of an invasion, we'll need good intel behind the lines."

Gerry raised his eyebrows. "Behind the lines? We are just giving up any pretense that we can hold the Russians back?"

Mary Pat said, "I am not a battlefield commander, but I am told that unless NATO agrees to move forces into Lithuania before an invasion begins, the Russians can take Vilnius at will."

"That bad, huh?" Dom asked.

Mary Pat nodded somberly. "That's why a good intelligence picture on the ground is critical. Branyon has a good team, but there are only a dozen case officers, many of whom are new to the region, or even new to the Agency. We simply don't have the experienced manpower available to assist him. The people who could be helpful are already in Ukraine, in Moscow, in Estonia, in Moldova, in Georgia. Other places just as hot, or nearly as hot, as Lithuania."

Ding asked, "What is it you need us to do?"

She said, "If you agree to go, I'm going to send you a file. I'll send a duplicate to Dominic. It's a list of GPS coordinates, all near the Belarusan border. A big list."

"What's at the coordinates?"

"Now, nothing. They are street corners, building rooftops, ditches, fields. Parking lots. To be honest, I don't know what all you'll find at the coordinates. But I need you to go to each of these locations and take pictures using a device we will provide you."

"Pictures of what?"

Mary Pat said, "Of whatever is there."

Ding cocked his head. "What on earth for?"

"You'll have to forgive me for this, but I'm not at liberty to say."

Gerry was taken aback. "You can't tell me what I'm sending our men to do?"

"It's for their own good. As you all know, the Russians' modus operandi before an invasion is to send troops over the border with no markings. *Little Green Men* is what they call them in the media. They intimidate the populace, hold roads and fortified positions for the follow-on troops. But even before they do that, they send over plainclothed operatives. Our guess is there are already foreign infiltrators in Lithuania. If that is the case, and they should, God forbid, take you by force, I don't want you knowing about the operation you are undertaking."

That sunk in for a moment, until Mary Pat said, "Obviously, the best situation would be if you didn't get caught."

Dom said, "Okay. How many locations are we talking about?"

"There are over four hundred."

"Wow," Ding said. "That's a lot of photography."

"It is," Mary Pat agreed. "But you'll just have to trust me. It is important."

John Clark said, "We're not actual members of the intelligence community. How do we do this without raising red flags with CIA station?"

Mary Pat said, "We have an established cover for you. You go in as private intelligence gatherers. You are a private enterprise working with the CIA under contract, which means you can collect atmospherics and data. You can't run agents, you can't take part in any sort of direct-action work, officially speaking, of course, but there is no reason you can't go over there and take some pictures under contract for the ODNI."

Clark asked, "How are we going to be able to take four hundred photographs out in the open without drawing attention to ourselves?"

Mary Pat said, "I think I can help in that department as well. From time to time we work with an American company that does business in Central Europe. They are electronic technicians, laying fiber-optic Internet cable all over Lithuania, both underground and aboveground on poles. It's a real company, so the work is real, and twenty-five percent of the workers are from the U.S. Ninety-five percent of the techs working over there have no affiliation with the U.S. intelligence community, but we have a good relationship with the owner of the company, so we can fold you into his operation and you can travel all over the country with no one batting an eyelash. It will get you into buildings, on the streets, wherever you need to go."

Chavez said, "Excellent. We'll study the requirements for the job and be ready to hit the ground running when we get there."

Off a look from Caruso, Mary Pat said, "Dom, is something wrong?"

Caruso gave a half-smile. "That sounds like real work."

Chavez slapped him on the back, well above his wound. "Don't worry, kid. As my apprentice, I'll take good care of you as you enter the exciting world of the fiber-optic field service technician. Of course, you will have to do most of the heavy lifting, dirt digging, and pole climbing. I have to supervise you."

"Why the hell can't I be the supervisor and you be the apprentice?"

Chavez said, "I'm older. Seniority has its privileges. Not very many, that's for sure. But enough to keep me off a pole and out of a ditch."

Clark had been entertaining the idea that he could go to Lithuania as well, but he realized there was no way he could pass himself off as a cable technician. Sure, he could dig a ditch and drive a truck, but there would be aspects to this physical work that would make it too hard for him to fit in.

Gerry Hendley looked to John Clark. "You're the director of operations. What do you think?"

Clark didn't hesitate. "I think the DNI is asking us for help. Ryan is in the field on an analytics job, so Dom and Ding can go. I'll stay here, help in any way I can from HQ."

Chavez said, "You sure about that, John? You're a Russian speaker. We could use you over there."

"You're a Russian speaker, too. They speak Lithuanian in Lithuania. If you find yourself needing your Russian very much, that probably means you are in a whole lot of trouble." There were chuckles around the table, except for Chavez, who only smiled. He looked at John for another moment, clearly surprised he wasn't sending himself along for this trip. Finally, Ding extended a hand to Mary Pat Foley. "Sounds good to us. Dom and I will get everything together here and get going as soon as possible."

Mary Pat shook Ding's hand and looked to Gerry again. "Obviously, Gerry, if you agree to send your men to Lithuania, you need to be prepared to get them out of there. If an invasion happens, I don't want Dom and Ding caught behind the lines."

"That makes three of us," Dom quipped.

Gerry said, "I'll have our plane ready to go over there at a moment's notice. If things look really bad I'll keep the aircraft at the airport in Vilnius twenty-four/seven so we can exfiltrate them in an hour if necessary."

"When do we go?" Dom asked.

Mary Pat smiled as she stood. "I'll leave you boys to work out the details, but as soon as possible would be my choice. I'll notify Pete Branyon's station that you're coming. I want you to know I appreciate your help, and my secure phone is always on me. I'm available whenever you need me."

Gerry drummed his fingers on the table. "Mary Pat, I'm going to go ahead and address the elephant in the room here. This seems important, maybe more important than we are able to understand at this point, but this doesn't seem like the kind of crisis that would bring the head of all the U.S. intelligence agencies out on a weekend to make a personal appeal for two operatives to go into a theater to collect data. Are we missing part of the puzzle here?"

Mary Pat shook her head. "I'm not hiding part of the mission or anything like that. I could have done this over the phone with you, Gerry, and left you to task your men. But I wanted to come in person, as a sign of respect for all The Campus did for us in Mexico . . . and what you lost in the process."

The men of The Campus nodded at this.

Gerry said, "We're a small outfit. Losing one of our own hits us in the gut, that's for sure."

Mary Pat looked to Dom Caruso now. "The Campus has paid a terrible price in the

past several years, and yet you all keep showing up in the most dangerous situations. This
country can't know what you are doing, but I
know, and I want to convey my thanks."

The men thanked her, then Chavez and
Caruso each immediately began a well-
practiced routine of prepping and packing to
leave town.

16

A deckhand hard at work clearing fishing nets of their mackerel just happened to look up and off the starboard bow of his fifty-foot trawler. It was sunrise, thirty-eight miles northwest of Scotland's Shetland Islands, and there were no other fishing boats or cargo ships in sight. This meant this boat should have had the sea to itself, because no pleasure craft ever came up here, since there was not one thing pleasurable about bobbing and rolling and freezing to death on this stretch of the North Atlantic.

The deckhand glanced away from the bow and back down to his work, but then his head lifted back up quickly and his eyes focused on a point less than a mile distant. It took a second to pick out the anomaly in the waves that caught his attention, but once he found it again, he knew what it was. The fisherman was still a young man, and his eyesight was excellent. The low form was gray like the water around it, but a few shades darker, and its edges were unmistakable. Man-made. It was also massive, easily the length of a train car and three times the height.

He looked out across the water by himself for a moment, ignoring the fish falling out of the net and onto the deck behind him, but soon he grabbed the man next to him and pointed.

This deckhand was much older, his eyes weren't so sharp, and he agreed only that he saw "something."

The younger man said, "It's a bleedin' submarine."

"You're bleedin' daft. That out there is not as big as a submarine. Haven't you seen one?"

"It's the . . . It's that hat thing on the top of the cigar thing. I don't fuckin' know what they call them."

The young fisherman waved his arms up toward the bridge of the trawler, where the captain sat on the other side of a pane of glass. When the captain noticed the movement, the deckhand pointed toward the squat form off the starboard bow.

Quickly the captain stopped the nets, grabbed his binoculars, and looked out into the early-morning waters.

But not for long. After just a few seconds he flipped a switch on the console in front of him and his voice came high and flat over the speaker over the deck. "It's a fuckin' sub, Danny. Big bloody deal. The Brits have submarines. Back to work!"

Danny dropped his shoulders, the excitement robbed from him, and he bent down to scoop up the mackerel flopping around on his deck, but the captain lifted his binoculars back to the big conning tower moving through the water off his bow, now just crossing over to the port side. The captain assumed the sub was British, but he saw no markings on the black form, so it was only a guess. It ran like a knife's blade through the rough water on a southwesterly course, and he knew in minutes he'd lose sight of it.

As he told the young man below, military vessels here were normally nothing to get excited about, but a year earlier, a fishing boat off the Orkneys had reported a sighting of a periscope, and the British Navy had reacted with alarm. They claimed to have no boats in the area and, even though an exhaustive search had turned up nothing, the final conclusion by the Royal Navy had been that it was a Russian submarine patrolling off the Scottish coast.

Of course, the captain of the mackerel boat could not imagine why a Russian submarine would sail with its conning tower proudly on display to a Scottish trawler if it wished to skulk around the United Kingdom, but, the captain thought, it wouldn't hurt to reach out to officials in the area, just to let them know he'd seen an unidentifiable sub.

Before he radioed in his sighting, however, the captain grabbed a point-and-shoot digital camera with an eight-power optical zoom. He stepped out of the bridge and into the cold, fought the roiling sea for balance, and took a few pictures with the camera zoomed in as tight as it would go.

After taking the snapshots he returned to his helm on the bridge and reached for the radio.

Within ninety minutes of the deckhand on the trawler seeing a queer sight off the starboard bow of his boat, Her Majesty's Naval Base Clyde, known more commonly in the area as Faslane, had the images of the sighting in its possession. And in less than another half-hour, the base went on full alert. Faslane was on the Scottish mainland in Argyll and Bute, a good 450 miles from the incident, but they notified their ships in the area, as well as those along the Atlantic coast, of the general heading of the sub sighting.

The HMS *Bangor* was a mine hunter, but it was closest, just west of the Orkney Islands and directly on the path of the conning tower. The *Bangor* headed northeast in search of the mysterious vessel.

The HMS *Astute,* a nuclear-powered attack submarine, was just leaving Faslane on an eighty-day patrol mission of the North Atlantic, so it was ordered to make best possible speed to a position ahead of the submarine.

It would take two and a half days for the *Astute* to arrive on station, so no one was optimistic about its chances.

A more immediate chance for identifying the sub came from the Royal Air Force. RAF stations in the Scottish Highlands scrambled helicopters with antisubmarine capabilities, but it was known from the outset that the distances required would mean the helicopter missions would be less about search patrols and more about hoping for another sighting from a fishing trawler that could vector the helos in to exactly the right coordinates.

But one after another the helicopter missions returned to base without locating their quarry.

The British used to have the perfect tool for this job, but no longer. The Nimrod maritime patrol aircraft had been recently retired from service, a victim of British defense budget cuts. This left few options for the British short of calling up the United States to ask for help.

So they did.

A pair of U.S. Air Force P-3 Orion aircraft were flown from their home station at RAF Mildenhall, up to RAF Lossiemouth in the Scottish Highlands, and from here they began launching on patrols. The Orion could fly racetrack patterns over the sea for many hours and use its high-tech cameras and sen-

214

sors, built expressly for antisubmarine warfare.

While the Orions flew off the west coast of Scotland and the British naval vessels hunted from the surface, the British submarine *Astute* closed on its quarry.

By now it was certain the sub had gone deep, since the hunt itself turned up nothing, but the identity of the sub was determined thousands of miles away in an office just southeast of Washington, D.C. The Office of Naval Intelligence Farragut Technical Analysis Center spent days with the photographs taken by the captain of the fishing trawler, looking over each pixel.

Finally, their analysts came to a consensus about just what it was they were looking at.

At the same time, the HMS *Astute* picked up faint acoustic readings of a large submarine passing to the northwest, but they were unable to catch up to it, and within moments of the dim signals, they lost it. The only thing they were able to determine with near certainty was that it was heading westerly, into the Atlantic Ocean.

From this, inferences could be drawn. The sub seen on the northern tip of Scotland was sailing, almost certainly, to America.

17

President Jack Ryan sat on a sofa in the Oval Office, a stack of photos in his hands. He examined them carefully, took in every bit of the meager intelligence he could derive from them, then laid them down on the coffee table.

Admiral Roland Hazelton, the chief of naval operations, sat on the couch across from him, and next to him was SecDef Burgess. Scott Adler, Mary Pat Foley, and Jay Canfield also were present, as well as Arnie Van Damm, Ryan's chief of staff.

The President looked up from the photos. "I used to know subs inside and out. I could still give you specs on Kilos and Ladas and Typhoons, or at least the specs that haven't changed since I was in that world, but to tell you the truth, all I can see here is a distant conning tower on rough seas. It's big, but not shockingly so. I'm guessing it's one of the new Boreis or Severodvinsks, otherwise you two wouldn't be sitting here looking at me like that."

CNO Hazelton said, "It took us a couple of days to ID it, but the Office of Naval Intelligence is convinced it is the *Knyaz Oleg*. It's a boomer, a brand-new Borei. It's so new we had no idea it was taking part in fleet ops. From the track of the sightings, it's definitely heading out into the Atlantic. There's not much for it to do there in the middle of the ocean, so it is a reasonable assumption that it's making a crossing."

Ryan flexed his jaw. "It's coming here, then."

With a nod Hazelton said, "*That's* why SecDef and I are here looking at you like this."

"What are we doing to find it?"

"The Atlantic Fleet is on notice. We are moving surface ships and subs out of Norfolk to augment what is already out on routine patrol. We have P-3s and P-8s either en route or prepping on both coasts, and ONI is working to plot possible courses."

Ryan detected something in Hazelton's voice. "But?"

"But the Borei will be difficult to detect. Damn near impossible. Frankly, all the advantages in this hunt are in favor of the *Knyaz Oleg*."

"Why didn't we pick it up sooner?"

"Olavsvern, Mr. President. When the Norwegians sold off their Arctic naval base, it hurt our efforts to find, fix, and track subs coming out of Kola Bay."

Ryan rubbed his eyes under his glasses. "Kill me now. Just put me out of my misery." After a moment he said, "How many Borei are in the Russian fleet?"

"We thought they had three operational Borei-class subs. Now it appears they have five. The two that were under trials are apparently further along than we thought."

"Where are the five?"

"One in the Pacific Fleet, two in the Northern Fleet, one in the Black Sea near Sevastopol, and one, from what the intel tells us, is heading over here."

"They can launch Bulavas, right?"

Hazelton nodded. "The Borei has the capability to carry Bulava missiles, yes."

Ryan said, "Talk to me about the specs of the Bulava."

Burgess took this one. "It's a new and relatively unproven system, but our intelligence on it makes it look impressive. It's hypersonic, faster than anything else out there; it has the ability to conduct evasive post-launch maneuvers and deploy decoys to shake off anti-missile ordnance."

Ryan said, "We have no idea if the *Knyaz,* or if any of them, for that matter, are actually carrying Bulava missiles, do we?"

"None whatsoever. My guess is some are, some aren't."

Ryan said, "Still, we operate under the assumption that the *Knyaz Oleg* has a full complement of nuclear weapons in its stores."

"Of course, Mr. President."

"Assuming this submarine does park along our coastline, what are the chances our antiballistic missiles can defeat a Bulava launch?"

Hazelton shook his head gravely as he spoke. "Next to none. It's too close, it's too fast, and it's too smart. We can put several Aegis platforms near D.C. Destroyers with missile defense, but they've never successfully brought down anything with a Bulava's capabilities. Frankly, Mr. President, our only real hope is launch failure."

Ryan had heard this before, but he wanted to be certain.

"What else do you suggest we do?"

"Sir," Burgess said gravely, "I would never tell my President what he has to do . . . but you asked me directly."

"I did."

"You have to make sure that sub doesn't launch. I'm sure that's easier said than done, but I can assure you that once those missiles fly . . . we aren't stopping *any* of them. As a military man, it might seem strange to say it, but our best defense is diplomacy on this one. A world where Valeri Volodin doesn't order that sub commander to fire is the world we need at the moment."

Scott Adler said, "Mr. President, if we've indeed identified this as a Russian nuclear ballistic missile sub, and if we are confident it is heading across the Atlantic, I suggest we go public with it. It might embarrass the Russians on the world stage enough for them to recall it."

Burgess said, "I agree we go public. Don't know if they'll be embarrassed, but this is a case where I think revealing our capabilities at detection will be good for our national defense. Make the Russkies aware that we're tracking closely. They won't know that we've lost them, only that, at one point, we had them fixed."

Ryan nodded. "We let Russia know that we know, although it doesn't look like they were going to great lengths to hide the fact. I wonder if that was their point from the outset. Create a panic."

Burgess said, "It's possible. The Borei is a terror weapon, just like its predecessor, the Typhoon." He shrugged. "At least until we got our hands on *Red October* and unlocked its secrets."

Jack Ryan gazed out the window for a moment, through glass thick enough to stop a sniper's bullet. He thought about his own short stint as an impromptu crew member on a Russian SSBN. "For a long time we had an incredible advantage on Russia in the antisubmarine-warfare realm. We essentially deconstructed the Typhoon we captured, and learned a lot in the process.

"But the Borei is using all new technology. It's a game changer. The advantages go with the subs, not with the ships hunting the subs." He sighed. In an annoyed tone he said, "Olavsvern. At the NATO summit, can we add a line to my speech politely requesting that no more strategic NATO bases be given to the Russians?"

Eyes turned to Adler, who said, "Diplomatically speaking, that will come off as an insult to Norway."

Ryan said, "Well, they have it coming. I'm not going to this summit to ruffle feathers, but the fact I have to go hat in hand to make my case to increase the readiness state means our NATO partners" — he held a finger up to correct himself — "*some* of our NATO partners, are shockingly out of touch."

Burgess said, "Remember, Mr. President. This isn't the first time Russia has sent a ballistic missile sub across the Atlantic. They sent a Typhoon over two years ago, took a few pictures off North Carolina, and went home. We only found out about it after the fact when Russia reported it as a major success."

Ryan said, "At the time it looked like they did it for the prestige, their way of saying the Russian Navy was coming back strong. Looking at that now, I wonder if it wasn't some sort of proof of concept."

He then asked, "Will the *Knyaz Oleg* go back to North Carolina?"

Hazelton shook his head. "Doubtful. They figure we'll look there, and there is a lot of coastline to choose from instead."

Adler said, "What I don't get is why. Why is Volodin doing this, and why now?"

Ryan said, "My guess is that Volodin ordered this sub to come over here because he wants to remind the U.S. we have our own problems close to home so that we're not too focused on events in Europe. He wants to threaten us directly, to use his submarine as a terror weapon, so we won't be emboldened in advance of the summit."

Adler said, "Mr. President, your performance in Europe next week is becoming more important by the day. You have to convince twenty-seven nations, in the face of all the increasing danger coming out of Russia, to do something that many will call provocative. They will say you are poking at a wasps' nest with a sharp stick."

Ryan said, "Well, then, I'll have to convince them that I just want to position a few cans of bug spray around the yard in case the wasps begin to swarm."

18

Two months earlier

Valeri Volodin sat at his desk in the Kremlin, his eyes running over a single sheet of paper lying on his blotter. It was the list of the FSB's most trusted financial minds in the nation. He read every name on the list — thirty-eight in all. He knew of all the men, of course — these were well-known technocrats involved in government finance and, more important, the personal finance of the government elite.

He was looking for one name in particular, and when he came to the end of the list, he smiled with satisfaction, because Kremlin Security Council Director Mikhail Grankin's list confirmed to Volodin exactly what he expected.

There was no mention of a local private equity manager named Andrei Limonov, and this meant, to Volodin, that Andrei Limonov would do just fine.

He'd researched Limonov through the

Interior Ministry officials as well, just to make certain the man was trustworthy politically, and found the man had a refreshing lack of ambition in politics. Volodin appreciated this greatly, because if one thing could corrupt a man faster than money, it was the power that the Kremlin offered.

Volodin recognized Limonov as a bean counter, a damn good one, but nothing more than that.

He snatched up the phone on his desk, and his assistant answered immediately. "Yes, sir?"

"I am playing hockey tonight?"

"Yes, sir. The match is at ten p.m. Shall I cancel it?"

"The match will continue. I want to add a player to our team."

"Of course."

"Who is our left-winger this evening? Is it Kuklin?"

There was a pause as Volodin's secretary scrambled to pull up the right file on her computer. Finally, she said, "That's correct, sir."

"Remove him. Contact Andrei Limonov, director of Blackmore Capital Partners, and tell him he will be playing on my left tonight. He suited up against us once, a year ago. He was terrible, couldn't skate the wings if his life depended on it, but no matter. I'll see him through."

"Yes, sir." A pause. "Shall I tell him he will

be meeting with you here in the Kremlin after the game?"

Volodin's secretary knew the president liked to invite men to play sports with him before a meeting. It was a good way to take the measure of the man, and to also show who was in charge. Volodin replied, "No. Tell him nothing. I'll decide if I want to speak with him after the game."

Andrei Limonov pulled up to the VIP entrance to Luzhniki Olympic Complex at nine p.m., rolling his sleek Mercedes S65 coupe through the gates after giving his name to a guard with a clipboard.

The coupe rumbled, restrained by Limonov's foot on the brake pedal. The 621 twin-turbo V12 wanted to blast through the complex, but the driver controlled it expertly, negotiating a second security check and two more open gates before coming to a stop in front of the Luzhniki Small Sports Arena, the only major building in the area with its lights on on this August evening.

Limonov climbed out wearing a black suit with a burgundy tie, his blond hair combed into a part that partially covered a small bald spot that bothered him in a way he could never let on to others. In his line of work it helped to be young and vibrant and vigorous, and although he was only thirty-five, he was already considering a hair transplant that would help him hold on to his youth for a few years more.

Limonov was met at the player entrance to the stadium and checked in, and then an attractive young female employee from the Kremlin introduced herself and led him to the locker room.

Limonov had been only fair at hockey, and that was back when he was fifteen years old, so he was surprised to be here. He hadn't played hockey in several months, though he retained a great passion for the game.

He'd been told the president himself had invited him to join the weekly match, which was stunning, but Limonov had heard that Volodin extended invitations to important people in the city, mostly when he wanted something from them.

Limonov had met Valeri Volodin only a couple times, most recently a year earlier, when Limonov's amateur hockey team, made up of friends from university, had been invited to play against Volodin's team.

Volodin's side won that night, as they did every night they played, for two important reasons. One, Volodin's team was partially made up of current and former players from Dynamo Moscow, Volodin's favorite professional squad.

And two, nobody wanted to body-check the man who controlled the military police and the Army.

Valeri Volodin, consequently, scored a lot of goals.

While he kitted up for the game, Limonov looked around at the other men on the team. He recognized all of them, as most had been famous national hockey stars just a few years ago, and those that weren't former pros were well-known Volodin confidants in the government who, thanks to their boss's passion for the sport, spent a lot of time playing hockey. The private equity man knew he was out of his league, to put it mildly. This was an uncomfortable feeling for him, because he was normally the most confident man in the room.

Andrei Limonov was smart, and he was successful. He also was supremely self-assured. He knew without a doubt that if he'd been more than a small child back in the nineties he would be one of the main power players in the nation now. Back then the assets of the Soviet state were carved up and handed out to a select few in Russia, then snatched up by the most ruthless of them, making a hundred billionaires in a nation with a quarter-billion in abject poverty. Limonov was certain he would have been one of the toughest, smartest, and shrewdest, had he only been around to enjoy that brief moment in time when all the fortunes were made.

Still, he was making good money now. He

was a millionaire, and his private equity firm could not have been on stronger footing.

One could not work with banks or in trading here in Moscow without having ties to the Kremlin and the FSB, as the *siloviki* ran both institutions as well as the Russian economy. Business and government were one and the same here, so many of Limonov's top clients were also the powerful elite who ran the government and government-controlled ventures. That said, Limonov was no inside man in the Russian government. He'd worked for senior officials at Gazprom and Rosneft and other state-controlled companies, and he'd done work for senior officials at FSB for a time, building up shell networks to launder funds into Western banks, but recently he turned down an FSB offer to handle a large portfolio for them. He looked at the proposition carefully, but in the end he didn't need the headache, so he rejected the offer. From this decision he'd lost a couple of *siloviki* clients, but in the long run he was sure it would work to his advantage. He'd shown several top men in the government that he wasn't going to be their bitch, and he kept his nose cleaner than many of the other men in his profession here in Russia's capital.

At ten-fifteen p.m. the door to the locker room opened and several men in suits entered. They were clearly security, and they quickly walked the room. A pair of bomb-sniffing dogs on leashes did the same, sniffing every locker, gym bag, and even a jock strap that had been cast aside by one of the ex–Dynamo Moscow players.

A few minutes later when the team was stretching and chatting in the middle of the room, Valeri Volodin entered, wearing a suit and tie. He nodded to the group perfunctorily and began to change clothes at his own private locker.

Limonov had wanted to speak with the president as soon as possible to thank him for the invitation, but soon it became clear that unless he thanked the man through his mouth guard on the ice, he wouldn't get the opportunity till after the match.

The game started after eleven p.m., with only a minute or two on the ice for Limonov to warm up. He'd been told the opposing team was made up of bodyguards of the Russian prime minister, and although they would not touch Valeri Volodin, they could be extremely aggressive toward the other players on Volodin's team. One of the Dynamo guys patted Limonov on the helmet right before the start of the match and told him the other team couldn't catch the pro players on Volodin's team, so they took out all their frustrations by body-checking the hell out of any amateurs invited as the president's guest.

And tonight there was only one man in that category.

And the prediction had been correct. Within the first minute of play Limonov had been knocked on his back twice, and in the first period he'd been slammed violently against the boards so many times he'd lost count.

In the second period he thought he'd broken a rib after a pass to the president that Volodin converted for an easy, uncontested goal. Limonov climbed slowly off the ice to his knees and asked for a substitution, but Volodin just skated up past him and said, "Be tough, Limonov. That was nothing."

Andrei Limonov used his stick to hoist himself back up to his feet, and then he went back to his position.

The fact the opposing side battled as hard as they could against most of Volodin's team — even taking their frustration out for having to play the role of whipping boys by body-checking some of the big-name players — made the game look legitimate in some respects, but it also drew a stark contrast with the play reserved for Valeri Volodin. When the Russian president was on the puck, he was only lightly grazed by a shoulder here and there.

Consequently, Valeri Volodin scored four goals, and no one else scored more than one.

Limonov had not managed to get into position to take a single shot.

When the match was over, Limonov was literally doubled over in pain. He had to ask one of the other players what the final score was, because it was too much effort to look up at the scoreboard.

He staggered back to the locker room, well behind the other players, and just as he sat down on a bench at his locker and began removing his gear, Volodin appeared in front of him and punched a fist into Limonov's shoulder. It hurt like hell, but Limonov thought this was a good sign. The president was treating him like a childhood chum.

"You played better than I thought you would, Andrei Ivanovich."

"Thank you, sir."

"Of course, I had expected you to be horrible, so you didn't have to do much to exceed my expectations."

Limonov nodded. "You were excellent, Mr. President. Your third goal was a thing of majesty."

Volodin's half-smile disappeared. "And what of the others?"

Limonov hesitated, but then said, "Number two was very good, also. Number one should have been called back after the illegal check Pavel Yurievich placed on their defender to take the puck in the first place. I hope you don't mind my saying that, or the fact that your fourth goal was handed to you. Dmitry Petrovich sent you a back pass that rightfully should have been his shot. He had an open goal, yet he passed to you."

Other than a hint of nervous laughter, there was no sound in the locker room for several seconds. Finally, Volodin said, "A detailed accounting of tonight's ledger. Spoken like a true accountant."

Only when Volodin smiled at his joke did the other men in the room recognize it as a joke, at which point they themselves broke into uproarious laughter.

Volodin put his hand on Andrei Limonov's shoulder again. "I want you to come and see me. Tonight."

He turned and walked off without waiting for a response.

Limonov wanted an ice bath more than a visit to the Kremlin, since the pain in his side and in his legs and in his lungs was at the forefront of his mind now, but he knew there was no way out of such an invitation. He had no idea what the president wanted from him, but Volodin was already out the door to the locker room, and he would not have dared ask, anyway.

"Don't worry, Andrei Ivanovich," a forty-year-old ex–Dynamo right back named Pavel said. "If Volodin wanted something bad to happen to you, it wouldn't happen at the Kremlin." He smiled. "It would just happen."

The other men chuckled, but Limonov could see on their faces that they were all worried for him.

Limonov pulled himself up into a standing

position by using the door of the locker, and then he headed for the showers.

19

It took an hour for Limonov to move from a bench in a locker room at Luzhniki Small Sports Arena to a red velvet gold-framed baroque chair in a sitting room overlooking the Kremlin's Tainitsky Gardens. He was washed and his blond hair combed in a part and he wore his suit and tie, but his rib cage was seized with pain and he was covered with black-and-gray bruises. He sat here drinking a glass of tea, but he wished he were home with something stronger and a few painkillers. The pair of beautiful and impossibly tall attendants who had given him the tea probably could have found him something for his pain, and they stood just feet away now, on either side of the door to the main hallway, but Limonov sat there with his mouth shut and pretended he was fine.

Volodin had orchestrated tonight's meeting to show his virility and physical prowess. It wouldn't do for Limonov, more than a quarter-century younger than his president, to show any weakness at all.

Outside a window on his right he could see Volodin's Mi-8 helicopter, its rotors slowly spooling up, and this gave Limonov the impression that, just after their meeting, the president would be heading home to his private residence in Novo-Ogaryovo just west of the city.

It was well after two a.m., so Limonov thought it was a safe bet his was the last meeting of the day, but he'd read stories about how the president would sometimes work straight through the night and then work a full twelve hours the next day.

Volodin charged into the room without even looking up at the women on either side of the door. He sat down, then finally raised his eyes in Limonov's direction. "Why doesn't the FSB like you?"

Limonov almost pissed himself. The pain in his ribs disappeared as the muscles in his back cinched even tighter. "I . . . well, I don't know. I didn't know there was a problem. I certainly have done nothing that would —"

He stopped talking when Volodin raised his hand.

"No, no, nothing like that. You just aren't on their list of most trusted financiers."

Limonov's bladder was safe, for now. He let out a little sigh of relief, but he realized Volodin had intentionally rattled him. He recovered and said, "Oh. Yes. As I am sure you know, I worked for Gazprom, Rosneft, and several other state-controlled companies. Many of my colleagues also did work setting up FSB and SVR shells around the world. My colleagues, from what I understand, floated my name to the FSB, mentioning I had created a robust international business network that could have been useful to them. FSB asked me to arrange the international finances for some of their corporate entities and move it through my existing system. I looked over the terms and didn't think they were in my best interests. Nothing dramatic, just no money in it."

Volodin took tea from one of the tall young ladies. "Many would say that gaining favor from the State Security services would be all the reward one would need."

Limonov just replied, "No one told me these matters were important to Mother Russia. It just looked like bad business for my firm. I stay busy enough." He shrugged. "I am happy to serve this nation if I am called to do so, Mr. President."

"I heard about your financial network." Volodin nodded. "It's very clever."

"Thank you."

"Small potatoes. But clever nonetheless."

Limonov said nothing.

Volodin smiled now. Held eye contact with Limonov for several seconds. The younger man fought the desire to speak, sensing

Volodin was testing his patience. Finally, the president said, "I need you to do something for me. Large potatoes. It will be good for Russia, but it will also be good business, I assure you."

"Of course."

"This matter is of utmost secrecy."

Limonov almost said "Of course" again, but he caught himself, said, *"Konechno,"* which was more like "Sure," and a little familiar under the circumstances.

"I have a number of personal assets throughout the world, as well as a few accounts."

A few accounts? Limonov thought. It had been rumored that Volodin had been one of the richest men in the world before the worldwide plummet of energy prices. Limonov had heard enough gossip around Moscow's financial circles for him to assume the president still possessed assets somewhere in the neighborhood of twenty billion U.S. dollars. Most of that, Limonov knew, was in shares of state-owned companies, but a fair chunk of it would be in offshore accounts.

With a poker face Limonov said, "Yes, sir. I am friendly with men here at the Kremlin. Your financial advisers. Obviously, they haven't told me details, they are good men, but these are men who do not trifle with small change."

"I am told my portfolio is valued at twenty-one billion euros, or thereabouts. Is that a number that shocks you?"

Limonov was not shocked, except for the fact that the gossip had proven so close to the accurate number. Still, he said, "You have worked hard building your fortune, and you have worked hard strengthening our nation. You have excelled in both endeavors."

Volodin went silent again, his eyes locked on Limonov's. His thin smile was so tight his lips had lost some of their color. "Eight billion U.S. dollars, give or take, is held in banks abroad. My problem, Andrei Ivanovich, is that too many people know exactly where these foreign accounts are."

Limonov knew the total number of people involved in establishing and maintaining Volodin's riches was five, which didn't seem to him to be a large number, especially considering the sums these men were dealing with and the number of accounts involved.

Still, he said, "Yes. The five bankers here at the Kremlin were necessary, however, because of all the financial intelligence required in order to ensure your assets were well hidden from outsiders."

Volodin looked down at his fingernails. "So that nobody knows where my money is, many people have to know where my money is. Is that it, Limonov?"

Volodin seemed to be pointing out an irony,

but Limonov wasn't certain. He just nodded a little.

"The locations of my foreign holdings, these are banks also used by other members of my government, other individuals, other people in my circle who require offshore accounts."

"Yes, sir. That is often the case. As it is with the network I have created, several investors here in Russia benefit from single entities that we have created as shells to —"

"The problem, Andrei Ivanovich, is that the more people who know where my money is, the more people who can either get to it or stop me from getting to it."

"I assure you, no one knows where your holdings are. I'm sure your investment team went to unprecedented lengths to ensure this."

"But you just told me five people knew. Not including me."

"Well . . . yes, but I mean no one outside of the inner circle of accountants who you entrusted with your money."

Volodin said, "Don't you think the West is looking at people like those five technocrats? Don't you think they will use them to get to me? All five of these men are tight with FSB, with other known groups that outsiders know of. Don't you think it is just a matter of time before someone in the FSB will accept a bribe or a political rival will promise the moon and the stars to one of the men involved with my portfolio?"

Limonov had no answer, because he saw no solution to the problem. If Volodin wanted to stick his $8 billion in his mattress, he was welcome to do this, but Limonov felt certain that would be even more dangerous than having a deep network of bank accounts hidden under the names of dozens, if not hundreds, of trusts and shell companies.

He only said, "I feel certain your accounts are safe."

Volodin shook his head. "Well, I feel less certain. I need to move money. I want you to help me. Only you. No one else must know. The fact that you turned down government work, you aren't in the confidence of the FSB, and you are not a known Kremlin cashier will help obfuscate the fact you are involved."

Limonov understood why he was here now. "I see. What percentage of your total offshore holdings would you like to move?"

"All of it."

Limonov did not mask his shock. It would have been impossible to do so. "But *why*? I understand the sanctions have made many in the Kremlin nervous, but they won't touch your money. They can't. Plus, there is no indication the Americans are aware of specific holdings, and by moving money around, securing different locations, you will only draw attention from the Americans —"

"This is not about America. This is about home."

Limonov thought for a moment, worked it out for himself. "Your assets were put in their present locations by men trusted by the FSB. Is there someone at FSB you do not trust?"

Volodin nodded. "Of course there is."

"Well . . . Mr. President. I am no chief executive. But can't you simply remove this person from his position? Replace him with someone you do trust?"

"No. Replacing my potential enemies with other potential enemies is more problematic than simply moving my holdings. You are not known at FSB as being one of my financial planners, so they aren't going to be expecting me to give you this access.

"As it stands now, my personal assets are tied up in vehicles that are known to the FSB. In many cases they are controlled by the FSB. It is only via the goodwill of the Russian government that I have any money at all."

Limonov understood what Volodin was really saying. The Russian president had created a nation where he, the chief executive, made all the rules. It worked to his advantage now, but where would this arrangement leave him when he was no longer the chief executive? Basing his future on the hopes that his nation's intelligence service carried benevolent feelings for him wasn't much to bank on.

Volodin wanted his money away from the gravitational pull of the next Kremlin leader.

Limonov couldn't imagine Valeri Volodin lying on a beach in Tahiti with a fruity drink in his hand, living out his days. But that wasn't up to him. Volodin wanted a golden parachute, and he was willing to pay Andrei Limonov to set it up for him.

Limonov said, "This . . . what you are asking, it will be very difficult. I have never dealt with the numbers you are speaking of."

Volodin continued to speak as if he had not heard Andrei Limonov. "And we need to do this quickly. Speed is our friend in this endeavor."

Limonov persisted. "The sums in discussion, even if I could mask the movement of the money, the arrival of the money somewhere else would cause certain suspicion. If I do this, I need to do this very slowly and carefully."

Volodin just shook his head. "This must begin within the next month or two. I will need to see your plan before that."

"This is an incredibly short time frame. May I ask what is the reason for the rush?"

"You may not. I understand your current assets under management are three billion dollars. You have also moved tens of billions of dollars offshore in the past several years. I need you to do that which you already do, but in a larger scale, and faster. Much faster."

Limonov wondered if Volodin had any clue just how difficult this would be. In an instant he told himself, *Of course he knows*. He's just putting the screws to an underling to do his bidding.

Volodin put his hand on Limonov's shoulder, which did not convey the fraternity that he might have been intending. "Look, friend. You do this, your commission will be substantial. What do you think of one and a half points?"

Andrei Limonov was an accountant, a moneyman, so he could not help making a quick calculation in his head.

If he pulled off this impossible task for his president as directed, he stood to make $120 million.

In a matter of months.

A small gasp came from his already open mouth.

Volodin squeezed his shoulder. "Yes, I see you are interested in this partnership. I will leave you to get to work. Come up with a plan, and then we will discuss implementation. I will instruct my staff to give you access to me twenty-four hours a day. You do nothing without my knowledge." He leaned in a little and offered a thin smile. "This scenario doesn't give you power of attorney over my finances or anything ridiculous like that. I have to trust you more than anyone else to offer you this job . . . but that's not saying much."

Andrei Limonov just nodded a little. "All my actions will, of course, be utterly transparent to you."

Volodin stood. "Good." He leaned over Limonov, and his thin smile came back. "Because there are two ways this ends for you, Limonov. Only two. Either you become rich beyond your wildest imagination and you have a job for life managing my assets . . . or I gut you like a fucking fish."

The threat was completely out of phase with the rest of the conversation. It stunned Andrei Limonov, and as Volodin turned and walked out of the beautiful sitting room in his customary quick gait, Limonov realized that had been the man's intention. He found himself frozen with fear, unwilling to even let himself consider for an instant any outcome other than success in the contract he had just agreed to.

After Limonov had sat there for a few minutes, one of Volodin's beautiful assistants returned to the room. It was nearly three a.m., but she looked perfectly made up and wide awake. She said, "Can I walk you back to your car, sir?"

Limonov stood on shaky knees.

The job was impossible, but he'd done the impossible before. He wasn't sure where to start. He knew it would take some time to create a new and impenetrable network of companies, banks, accounts, trusts, agents, and cutouts. He'd get started tonight, and he would work straight on through for weeks before giving the president his proposal.

Valeri Volodin wasn't a man to be kept waiting.

20

Present day

Jack Ryan, Jr., was on his second day here in Luxembourg City, sitting in a tiny and dark sixth-floor office on Avenue Émile Reuter and peering up the street through a spotting scope set up to a video camera pointed at a fifth-floor window in a building on Boulevard Royal. There a man in his shirtsleeves sat hunched over his desk while his frumpy secretary sat at her own desk across the room and talked on her telephone.

Jack felt like he was looking through a soda straw at the world's most boring zoo exhibit, watching the nearly still-life experience of a European attorney at work.

The tiny nation known officially as the Grand Duchy of Luxembourg kept itself out of the world headlines, but in some respects it was the heart of Europe. For starters, it was the third-wealthiest nation on the planet. Even though this was the case, most of the money that passed through Luxembourg, certainly the vast majority of it, did not belong to the Luxembourgers themselves. It was instead owned by offshore corporations, companies who used Luxembourg only for their banking and registration, so they could avoid revealing information to the actual home country of the companies' owners.

Luxembourg had been at this game a long time. It became a purveyor of offshore corporations in 1929 and today it is one of the largest tax havens in the world.

Ten percent of all wealth on earth is held offshore, somewhere in the neighborhood of $7 trillion, and there were dozens of offshore financial havens; experts had pegged sixty that fit into the category of secrecy jurisdictions. There were differences in how the jurisdictions operated, but their mission was all the same. These nations were able to make money by doing things for citizens of other nations who wished to get around the laws in their home countries. The secrecy jurisdiction was happy to oblige in this endeavor . . . for a cut of the winnings.

Of course these financial haven nations did not afford the same rights and privileges to their own citizens. No, they were taxed and tracked and held completely accountable for their finances. The foreigners were treated with deference, and the locals were "ring-fenced," kept away from the financial goodies.

The process was done through offshore banks. In nations with little regulation, any physical address could be registered as a bank. A guy sitting in a windowless cube with his feet on a cardboard box and a mobile phone in his hand could be a bank.

You could go on the Internet and buy a bank. A service would set you up in a tax haven with two employees — a director and an assistant director — a filing cabinet, and a physical address. Money could be moved through accounts from one place to the other, and the two bank employees would never even see the amounts, the sending bank, or the receiving banks. They served only as ways for the owner of the money to check off a box on a regulatory document in the nation where the money was coming from, and another box on a regulatory document where the money was going.

Not all offshore companies were involved with laundered money, not by any stretch, but those that were usually set up a complicated network, or ladder, using secrecy jurisdictions to get around revealing the details that would make experts like Jack Ryan, Jr., suspicious.

The point of the ladder was very simple: It took money, made it disappear, and then made it reappear somewhere respectable and clean. A hundred million dollars from a heroin deal in Afghanistan between Chinese and Pakistanis, for example, could turn up in a Chicago bank, totally separate from the crime, the criminals, and, most important, those looking for the culprits.

The criminals could access their money, and in doing so, they would not look like criminals. They would look like businessmen.

And then there was something in the financial world called a "flee clause." A flee clause in a trust agreement states that if the assets of a trust come under inquiry — if a financial examiner in Grand Cayman poses an inquiry about the trust's ownership, for example — then the trust would automatically transfer out of the Caymans and into Panama.

Jack understood why business in this field was booming. The business of money, not surprisingly, came down to money. Simply stated, the people hiding the money were paid a lot more than the people looking for the money.

Jack was one of the lookers, and he felt the title particularly apt today while he stared through his scope and wondered how he was going to get closer to the answers bouncing around in the head of the man in the office down the street.

Jack enjoyed the puzzle, even if several times a day he wanted to pull his hair out trying to piece together the murky parts of the relationships among all the players.

He did know one thing above all. Next to

the actual holder of the assets — the individual attempting to launder money — no one in the ladder was more important than the attorney. Rarely did they know the entire picture — only the person who set up the network did — but attorneys usually knew more than anyone else along the ladder.

Lawyers were integral to financial shenanigans for one reason above all. With an attorney, Jack knew, a person attempting to hide assets from regulators had one more tool in the toolbox. A lawyer could represent a shell company as a nominee in lieu of the actual owner of the assets and keep things organized, all with the get-out-of-jail-free card of attorney-client privilege.

Guy Frieden was just such an attorney. He was involved, at what level Jack still didn't know, in a complicated scheme to launder money for Mikhail Grankin, a powerful government intelligence official in Russia. And Jack told himself he wasn't leaving Luxembourg until he knew where to find the next rung in the ladder.

When Jack was just fifteen minutes into his surveillance of Guy Frieden's office, he realized something that had held true for the past forty-eight hours.

Surveillance, even surveillance of one man, was no one-man job.

Although Jack's target didn't move around the city during the workday other than his daily eleven a.m. foray for coffee with his secretary and his afternoon lunches with clients, it was damn difficult to keep eyes on someone all day long in hopes of identifying his associates.

After two weeks of sitting outside art galleries in Rome while Ysabel hobnobbed with those inside, and now two more days' worth of nine-hour stretches peering into cameras, binos, and night-observation devices, he was bored stiff.

Jack told himself the next time Frieden went to the bathroom, he would do five minutes of yoga on the floor to loosen up his aching muscles.

But for now, while he watched and waited, he thought about Ysabel down in Rome. He missed his romantic evenings with her, and each night as he walked the fifteen minutes from his rented space across the street from Frieden's office to his rented apartment, he made mental note of the nicer restaurants he passed, hoping he'd have an opportunity to take Ysabel out to dinner a few times when she finally made it up here.

Jack's apartment here wasn't as spectacular as the place they'd shared in Rome, but it was in a great neighborhood, in the Old Town, overlooking the small and serene Place de Clairefontaine. It met all his requirements, which were not necessarily the things he would personally look for in an apartment.

The Campus maintained a long list of security criteria that needed to be satisfied any time one of their people rented a safe house, so Jack had to make sure from his first arrival there that he'd be as protected as possible. He'd been relatively impressed with the building he'd found, the apartment inside, and the options for dining and exploring in the quarter around it. But still, his place wasn't anything like his place in Rome.

Jack thought about Ysabel now while he looked through his spotting scope at the back of Guy Frieden's bald head. He worried about her, hoped she was keeping an eye out for anything out of the ordinary that might spell danger. They'd spoken on the phone each of the last three evenings and they exchanged texts throughout the day. While half their correspondence was just the idle chat of two people who missed each other and enjoyed each other's company, the other half was work-related; she'd managed to track even more sales back to the trust maintained by Guy Frieden, putting the total amount of the sales well above ten million U.S. dollars.

More than satisfied Frieden was a willing participant in the Russian/Roman art world money-laundering scheme, Jack had e-mailed Gavin Biery the night before, asking him to research the man's office computer network to see if The Campus could get a look at his files. Jack had learned from digging into the art galleries' systems that it was a hit-or-miss proposition, and often Biery would come back to him and tell him he'd have to physically plant a remote access tool to give The Campus the on-ramp into the network they needed to begin the encryption process.

Jack hoped that wasn't going to be the case here, since he was alone, and while Frieden's office didn't look that terribly secure, Frieden's building did have standard security measures that would take time to defeat.

Jack sat up, taking a break from looking through his scope at the office across the street. He checked his watch and realized it was two p.m. here, which meant it was eight a.m. in Virginia. Gavin Biery would just be arriving in the office.

Jack pulled his phone out of his pocket and dialed the number.

As he expected, the portly IT director answered his phone just slightly out of breath.

"Biery."

"Morning, Gavin. Sorry for hitting you right as you come through the door. Do you at least have your coffee and your doughnut in front of you?"

"It's a bear claw, but yes." Jack heard the squeak of Gavin's chair as he sat at his desk. "I got your e-mail last night and spent some time looking into the network of this Guy Frieden character."

"How did you do that?"

"I just used a secure Linux system at home and pinged Frieden's network, took a look at his firewall, tried to find some open ports, all the basic stuff. Bad news, Ryan, he's locked down tight."

"Damn," Ryan said.

Biery said, "Yeah. I'm a genius, but I'm not a freaking magician. Whoever set his computer network up knows enough to keep it safe from outside vectors. You are going to have to gain physical access to his system and plant a RAT on it for me to hack into it. Even then, that will just get me into his network. I can't promise he won't have good encryption on his actual files, so you'll need to allow me some time to get into them."

Ryan deflated. "How do I get a RAT onto his system?"

"You are the secret agent man. I'm the computer guy. Remember?"

"Right." He thought a moment. "Has Clark made it in yet?"

"Saw him in the elevator."

"Good. Can you transfer me?"

"Now I'm the freakin' switchboard?"

"Gavin!"

"Just kidding."

Clark came on the line seconds later. "John Clark."

"Hey, John, it's Jack. I'd like permission to take Gavin off your hands for a day or two."

"Okay. Tell me why."

Ryan briefly explained what he needed.

When he finished, Clark said, "You keep telling me that what you're doing over there in Europe is mostly analysis. But what you are talking about sounds suspiciously like espionage."

"Yeah, I know. This is going to take a bit more subterfuge than what we've been up to recently, but this will be a lot less than normal Campus fieldwork. Guy Frieden works with one secretary in a busy office building; security to get into that building is controlled by RFID badges. I just need to get Frieden out of his office and in a situation where I can steal the electronic data on the badge, then have Gavin make me a quick working copy of it. This can be done in a day. At that point Gavin can go back home, and I can slip into Frieden's office while he and his secretary run out. They go out for coffee together each morning, and their office is totally empty for at least twenty minutes."

"You can see their entire office from your vantage point?"

"Not exactly. I can't see the door to the hall, and he has a little conference room to the left of his secretary's desk that I can't see into. But when Frieden and his secretary step out of the building, they shut off all the lights. I'm sure they aren't leaving anyone in his office behind."

Clark asked, "How are you going to manipulate Frieden so you can be in a position to clone the badge?"

"I haven't worked that out yet. I'll have to get him someplace where I can be within a couple of feet from him, but I can't let myself get compromised, because who knows how close I'll have to get at other times? Maybe you could send Ding or Dom over with Gavin, they can help me out."

Clark said, "No can do. They are on a business trip."

Jack knew that meant his mates were operational, and he suddenly felt an immediate twinge of regret bordering on jealousy. He preferred working on the team with the other ops officers of The Campus, and all three hadn't operated together since Sam's death. Still, he'd gone to Iran on his own volition, then Dagestan, and then Rome. He'd put himself here, and he believed in his work.

He didn't regret anything other than the fact that he wasn't there, in an obviously dangerous theater, to help his friends. "Everything okay?" he asked.

Clark said, "Sure. Just some technical support work for one of our clients. Still, it's a crazy world. You know how even on a business trip you've got to keep your head on straight."

"I do indeed." Jack's mind drifted off his own mission for a moment. The work over here was child's play compared with most everything he'd done in the field in the past few years. He knew he should appreciate it, and he certainly had when he'd been with Ysabel, but at the moment his mind was with Chavez and Caruso, somewhere out in the field without him there to help them out.

Clark brought Jack back to Luxembourg when he said, "I think I know someone who might be able to help you over there. At the Agency I worked with a woman named Christine Hutton. Hell of a case officer. She got out of the biz a long time ago, she's got to be fifty-five or sixty now. Anyway, I think she's a German noblewoman."

Jack thought he misheard. "Sorry, she's a what?"

"She left the Agency when she married a German diplomat. He came from nobility, which used to be a big deal in Germany, but now it isn't terribly useful. Poor guy died of cancer several years back, left everything to his wife. They have a couple of grown kids, but last I heard she was living in the family estate in Bitburg, just over the border from Luxembourg. She is completely out of intel work, has been for a long time, but she might be up for an afternoon of excitement."

"How do you think she can help?"

"Simple. She's filthy rich, and it's old European money."

Jack understood. "She won't have any problem getting a meeting with a financial lawyer in Luxembourg City."

"Right. She's a down-to-earth girl who married into money but didn't let it ruin her, so she doesn't flaunt what she has. Still, I am sure if I called and explained the situation to her, I could get her to show up at your lawyer's office putting on all the airs of Catherine the Great."

"I like it."

"Obviously, she'll be going in without any cover at all. You'll have to pull it off cleanly."

"That won't be a problem. We'll come up with a legit reason for the meet."

"I'll get Gavin packed up for the trip over, and then I'll reach out to Christine."

21

There was no fanfare to the scene this day at Zapadnaya Litsa Naval Base, only a persistent sleet under overcast skies. Valeri Volodin was not present for the passage of *this* submarine out of Sayda Inlet and into the deeper waters of Kola Bay, although the Severodvinsk-class sub was, like the Borei that left a week earlier, departing on its maiden mission in the service of the Russian Federation.

The *Kazan* was also similar to the *Knyaz Oleg* in that it was the best, most modern vessel of its class, and the Americans and other Western powers thought this *Kazan,* like the big Borei on its way across the Atlantic, was still undergoing sea trials. They had no idea it was operational.

At 111 meters long and 12 meters wide, the *Kazan* wasn't as impressive as the Borei ballistic missile sub in sheer size, but it had a different role, and this role required it to be smaller and sleeker. The *Kazan* was a nuclear attack submarine, SSGN in the parlance of the U.S. Navy. To call it the most advanced submarine in the world was no stretch. Like the Borei to its U.S. counterpart Ohio, the Severodvinsk class was more sophisticated and cutting-edge than the comparable U.S. version, the Seawolf.

Powered by a pressurized water reactor, its steam turbine could generate thirty-five knots below the waves and twenty on the surface. It also had a silent speed of twenty knots, and though it wasn't quite as quiet as the Seawolf, it was far quieter than any nuclear attack sub any Western power had ever come up against.

And far more powerful.

The most potent weapon on the *Kazan* was the P-800 Oniks, a long-range antiship missile that could do Mach 3 — a mile every two seconds — and deliver a conventional or nuclear payload out to a range of 327 miles, using an awesome assortment of computerized offensive and defensive measures to do so. There were thirty-two Oniks missiles on board at present, along with two dozen Type 53-65 torpedoes.

With a hull made from low-magnetic steel, the 13,800-ton warship itself was incredibly difficult to detect, but with a bow array, flank arrays, and towed arrays, its own spherical sonar could "see" the water in all directions. This made the vessel a lethal hunter as well as a particularly difficult quarry.

It was a big muscular fighter, a great white shark in the water, and the water it was heading to was rich with prey.

Today marked the beginning of what was expected to be a long patrol for the *Kazan.* Most of its eighty-eight crew members knew little about their mission other than the fact it could last up to three months.

But the captain had his orders. The *Kazan* would sail submerged into the Barents Sea, and from there through the Norwegian Sea and into the North Sea. After that things would get interesting. The Øresund Strait separating Denmark from Sweden is only two and a half miles wide at its narrowest. The Russian nuclear attack sub would need to negotiate these heavily trafficked and more heavily monitored waters without being detected, using intelligence and supreme stealth to do so.

After the stress of the Øresund Strait, the Baltic Sea would seem as vast as the Atlantic to the sailors of the *Kazan,* but the captain and a select few of the boat's thirty-two officers knew what they would be doing when they got there. They also knew that, unlike the *Knyaz Oleg* on its way into the two-hundred-mile exclusion zone around America, the *Kazan*'s mission was not merely about the threat of action.

No, the captain of the sub fully expected to engage his enemy in battle.

Russia's Baltic Fleet, based in Kaliningrad, currently had only two operational attack submarines, older but capable Varshavyankas, called "Kilo class" by NATO forces. But with the arrival of the *Kazan* to the Baltic, the Varshavyankas would have a capable ally.

As soon as the *Kazan* made it to its patrolling zone north of Poland, the Varshavyankas would begin seeking targets and destroying them with torpedoes, following a checklist that came from the Kremlin itself. The *Kazan* would join them with cruise missiles and torpedoes, and together they would intimidate all ships traveling in the waters around Kaliningrad.

After standing for a while in the conning tower, enjoying the stinging impacts of sharp sleet on his face, the captain finally gave the order for his warship to submerge as soon as it was safe for it to do so. Western satellites might have identified the boat in the thirty-five minutes it was out of its hangar this morning, and they might even have been able to deduce it was putting out to sea. But the experts would only think it was off on sea trials, like the *Knyaz Oleg* before it.

They would learn the truth soon enough, and if the captain did his job correctly, they would know the *Kazan* was in play only when wolf packs of Oniks missiles began screaming toward their targets.

22

After a nine-hour flight from Baltimore, Ding Chavez and Dominic Caruso arrived in Vilnius, Lithuania, during a mid-morning rain shower. There to meet them at the airport's fixed-base operator was Herkus Zarkus, a thirty-one-year-old American of Lithuanian descent. Herkus was a technician for the CIA-linked company with a contract to install high-speed Internet service throughout the southern half of Lithuania.

Though Herkus wasn't a spy himself, he held a security clearance and he had been read in on Ding and Dom's mission, at least as far as his responsibility in it. He knew it was his job to take the two American contractors wherever they needed to go, both in Vilnius and in the countryside, and make sure their cover as fiber-optic linemen remained sound.

The two Campus operators loaded their bags into a van with the name DATAPLANET on the side, and all three men climbed in for the ride into town from the airport. While Herkus drove he explained that he had served in the U.S. Army with an electronic system maintenance military operational specialty. After working a few years in a support unit for 10th Special Forces Group, he left the service to go back to school for an advanced degree in electrical engineering.

After he graduated he was heavily recruited for the job with DataPlanet, a Maryland-based fiber-optics technology company that worked government contracts around Central Europe installing and upgrading fiber-optic networks. He was surprised that the company pulled out all the stops to get him on board, but as soon as he accepted the position he was let in on the fact DataPlanet actually had an affiliation with the Central Intelligence Agency. Herkus found out he had been head-hunted not only because of his job-related education and work experience, but also because of the security clearances he'd held in the Army.

DataPlanet would have been a nearly perfect CIA front, but it had, in fact, started organically and only later become involved with U.S. intelligence. A CIA officer noticed an opportunity in the company and, over time, developed an informal "relationship" with the owners, themselves former defense contractors with high security clearances. Most of the work the firm did overseas was unrelated to the mission of the U.S. intelligence community, but from time to time CIA and NSA electronic intelligence specialists accompanied men like Herkus Zarkus into the field, using the lineman-technician cover to move virtually anywhere in Central European nations where Russian intelligence had many eyes and ears. And while the company techs and the intelligence operatives actually did install the high-tech networks in houses, towns, and buildings, they also sometimes added a few optional extras to the nets, allowing electronic surveillance in parts of the world where Agency techs working out of embassies would not have been able to avoid scrutiny by opposition intelligence services.

In this case, it had been explained to the technician that his two "tag-alongs" would not be doing any technical work of an electronic intelligence nature on this op. They would, instead, simply need to go to a number of different locations and take pictures with a special camera.

On the flight over, Dom and Ding had watched an hourlong video that served as a crash course on working as fiber-optic technicians. After this they sat through three more hours of Lithuanian language study, which was effectively nil, but they did learn a couple dozen phrases that might prove useful in a pinch.

Chavez spoke Russian, but here in Lithuania only seven percent of the population spoke Russian daily. That said, Russian was understood by many here, and Ding's Lithuanian was only what he had on his iPhone translator and what little he'd picked up on the flight over.

Herkus brought the men to his office in the center of town, and here they had coffee and chatted for a while, then he got down to business, showing the men a PowerPoint presentation on the legitimate work they'd be doing here in the region. It was straightforward, and not too terribly technical, because Herkus himself would be with them every step of the way.

They needed to know only the basics so they could act naturally in their covers and get on with the real reason they were over here in the first place.

In the late afternoon they piled back into the DataPlanet van and drove through the city, ending up on the third floor of an old building in the Old Town. This was a CIA safe house. Herkus had been instructed to drop the men off here and then pick them up for work early the next morning.

Dom and Ding had just gotten their luggage into their rooms when there was a knock at the door. Dom looked through the peephole to see two men wearing blue jeans and insulated jackets.

"Yeah?" he asked through the door.

One of the men answered, "Mary Pat sent me over. You should be getting a text to that effect just about any second."

Dom checked his phone and saw nothing, but Chavez entered the foyer of the apartment, looking at his phone. "It's okay. Just got a text from Clark. It's the CoS."

Caruso opened the door and let the men in.

"You must be Dom," one of the men said. He extended a hand. "Pete Branyon. Good to meet you, and welcome to Lithuania or, as we like to call it, tomorrow's ground zero."

The CIA chief of station Vilnius, Peter Branyon, entered the room with his security officer, Greg Donlin. After shaking Dom's hand, he walked toward Chavez. "I'm Pete. Domingo, it's an honor to meet you."

"Likewise."

Branyon said, "When I got the cable that you'd be coming over to help, I was surprised, to say the least. But since you come on the recommendation from the DNI, that's good enough for me. Mary Pat Foley's office is all the bona fides I need."

Branyon and the two newcomers sat down in the small living room, while Donlin stood near the window, keeping one eye on the street outside.

Branyon said, "We swept this apartment for

267

bugs just before you arrived. We'll do it every day, just to be sure, but we don't expect you'll garner too much attention from the opposition."

Ding said, "Can you fill us in on the situation?"

"Sure," Branyon replied. "As I'm sure you know from the news, Valeri Volodin has convinced a sizable portion of his nation that Ukraine is inhabited by Nazis, all Russia's neighbors want to destroy them, and American spies are running amok here in Lithuania." He chuckled. "I'm pretty sure none of that is true, but I can promise that third assertion is absolute bullshit. We aren't running amok, we are barely treading water. We spend all our time trying to keep tabs on Russia's spies on the ground here, and working to discern Russia's intentions."

Ding said, "I'm sure you've been told, but we've been given an assignment by the DNI. But when we're not doing that, we're available to help your station any way we can. Our cover is fiber-optic linemen, so we should have pretty good freedom of movement."

"Yeah, DataPlanet can get you guys anywhere you need to go. They are one hell of an asset. Me and the rest of my covered case officers can't go anywhere without doing a lengthy SDR, but DataPlanet is so ubiquitous around here the Russians don't bother with them."

Chavez said, "Mary Pat told us your station was a little short-staffed."

Branyon said, "We were barely able to keep up with our work as it was, then the LNG regasification facility on the coast was blown up. A few days later, the Russian train transport was attacked here in Vilnius. Now we're up to our eyeballs in problems and marching orders from Langley. Half the world thinks Lithuania is looking like it is going to be the epicenter of the next war."

"Anything we can do to help out your station?" Dom asked.

"I know you guys have plenty of work to do, but it sure wouldn't hurt for us to have a couple more sets of eyes looking out for Little Green Men near the border."

"Which border?" Dom asked.

"A damn good question. Russia could send sappers in from either the east or the west, since Belarus is to the east and Kaliningrad is to the west. But my main concern is the east. Belarus is friendly with Russia, as I'm sure you guys know, so even though Kaliningrad has a lot of Russian troops on our western border, if there is an invasion Russia would be idiots not to hit from both directions. If you guys are laying cable to the east it will put you in the little villages and on the highways close to the Belarusan border. Just keep an eye out. We have a network of agents in the towns there by the border, but the rules

269

say you guys can't have any involvement with agents, so I'll keep working that myself."

Ding said, "Sorry, Pete, it's not my place to say, but you are the CoS. Is it really a good idea for you to be traveling near the border?"

Branyon shrugged. "I'm a hell of a good case officer. Just because I'm station chief doesn't mean I can't still get out into the populace. I do my SDRs, I move light and low-profile, so I don't have much to worry about." He nodded toward Donlin. "Greg here keeps me safe."

Greg Donlin had barely spoken, but he said, "I keep warning him about the dangers. He keeps overruling."

Chavez said, "Well, okay, but if you need any help from us involving your PERSEC, just shout."

Branyon raised an eyebrow. "You guys aren't carrying weapons, are you?"

"No," Dom said quickly. "I think my partner is talking about help getting you *away* from a fight."

Ding nodded. "Yeah, Dom and I aren't here to go up against Russia's Army. I guess we'll just have to leave that to Greg."

Greg Donlin sighed. "I've got a pistol, but I'm an armored division or two short if I have to fight the Russians."

The men laughed, a moment of gallows humor, nothing more, because if Russia decided it wanted to move into Lithuania, there wasn't a damn thing anybody sitting in this little living room could do to stop it.

23

Jack Ryan, Jr., met Christine von Langer, née Hutton, at a café on the Rue Notre Dame. When she first walked in the room, he was happy to see she absolutely looked the part of a woman of means. Mature, stately, and attractive, she wore chic clothes that looked expensive, and she held a fur coat over her arm that must have cost a fortune.

As she shook Jack's hand and sat down, placing her Hermès bag on the chair next to her, she gave him a wide smile like she'd known him his whole life.

"Sorry, Mrs. von Langer, but can I ask why you are looking at me like that?"

"Oh, I'm sorry. You just remind me so much of your father."

"I guess it makes sense that you would know my dad, but John didn't mention it."

"Can't say I knew him well, but I had occasion to work with him from time to time." She lowered the wattage of her beaming smile a little. "I don't do politics, it's never been my bag. Working in the government, under administrations of all different persuasions, I just found it better that way. But I knew your dad to be a hardworking man of impeccable character. That's good enough for me."

"Thanks. I hear that a lot, but I can't help but just think of him as Dad."

With a serious eye she said, "They beat him up in the press over here, you probably already know that."

Jack gave a half-shrug. "They beat him up at home, Mrs. von Langer. I'm pretty sure it bothers my brother and sisters and I more than it bothers him."

"Please. Call me Christine. Okay. Down to business. John says you are private sector, this is financial forensic accounting, but this might lead to something that traces back toward Moscow."

Jack said, "It most definitely traces back to Russia, probably to Moscow, perhaps even to a specific building in Moscow."

She raised her eyebrows. "Kremlin or Lubyanka?"

"Either/or."

With a smile she said, "I love it already, Jack. I'm in."

He told her exactly what he needed her to do; she asked a few questions about her target. He could tell she was a little disappointed she didn't have more to her role, but she was certainly game, and he had no doubts she'd do one hell of a good job.

When he was finished she said, "This lawyer . . . do we think he's corrupt?"

Jack thought about that a moment. "He definitely knows the kind of money he's working with, and I doubt he's into the art for the sake of art. He is an adviser for this offshore trust, so he's funneling money into the art, paying inflated prices, obviously either as a kickback to a Russian or as a way to replace dirty money for clean money. So, in that respect, he's corrupt but . . ." Jack's voice trailed off.

Christine von Langer said, "But we're talking about a lawyer here in Luxembourg, where ethics are . . . murky."

"Right," Jack said.

The fifty-six-year-old woman said, "I will have to be honest with you, though, I left the company twenty years ago. I'm not exactly up on the newest tech." She started to ask about the technology she'd be using for the operation, but before she got very far, Gavin Biery entered the café. Ryan motioned him over and made the introductions.

He immediately opened his backpack and revealed a black box the size of a hardcover book, with a digital screen and a few buttons.

Gavin said, "This is an RFID emulator."

Von Langer's eyes flitted around the room nervously while Ryan reached over and put his hand on the backpack, closing it. "That's okay, Gavin, we can do that later."

"Oh . . . okay. Sorry."

It was an uncomfortable moment, more for Christine than for Jack, because he was used to Gavin doing awkward things when out in the field. Jack dispelled the awkwardness by saying, "I want you to know how much we appreciate your help, Christine."

"I am happy to be involved. I hope if your . . . *organization* needs me in the future they won't hesitate to ask. My husband is gone and my kids are doing their own thing. I've got hobbies and diversions, but . . . nothing as cool as this."

They all went back to Jack's rented apartment on Place de Clairefontaine. Here Gavin set up his equipment and gave Christine a primer on how the scanner worked. After a few minutes of this — Gavin would have spent all day on the details if Jack didn't hurry him along — Jack walked Christine through the best way to use the skimmer to steal the information off Frieden's building access badge. She'd merely have to get it within three feet of Frieden's access card, and keep it in the same position for at least three seconds while the antenna of the little device passively stole the coded information on the card.

With the technical and physical aspects of the job behind them, Jack and Christine worked together on a backstory that would have Frieden excited to meet with her. She would tell the attorney that she needed to set up an offshore, and was looking for an attorney to serve as the director. Frieden regularly represented such clients, Jack knew from his investigation into the man, so they both agreed that, despite the fact he was already making money working with a Russian oligarch, the prospect of taking on a client like Christine von Langer would be very appealing to him.

The next morning a call to the office of Guy Frieden earned Christine an invitation to get together for coffee that afternoon. They met and sat across from each other in an outdoor café. Christine kept her purse on the table with the skimmer on while she told an impressive story about a scheme by a half sister to use the courts in the United States to grab a share of Christine's European riches. A property deal between the two women went bad, according to Christine, and her sister was sending lawyers to the courts in Germany in an attempt to settle her claim.

The Luxembourger nodded throughout the story with the necessary gravity to express concern, and then he assured the wealthy American that protecting estates from unmanageable relatives was one of the reasons he went into this line of work and one of his most fulfilling duties as an attorney. He talked about the way he would set up a trust to sequester money Christine's husband had bequeathed to her and keep the German courts from having any access to it.

While Christine sipped her coffee and listened to the attorney, the real work was being done inside her Hermès handbag. The reader pulled the information off the card as if Frieden were swiping it at a security kiosk in his building, but Christine's reader did it secretly and from farther away.

After coffee Christine said she'd be in touch, and she left on foot. She did a forty-five-minute SDR, passing once through the Gare de Luxembourg, the main train station, where Jack sat drinking espresso at a stand-up table next to a bakery, his eyes out for anyone trailing behind or interested in Christine. He saw nothing that aroused suspicion, and this gave him and Christine one more layer of certainty that she was not being followed.

They met back at the apartment and Christine passed the reader to Gavin, who had his equipment set up in the kitchen. With a kiss good-bye to Christine and more effusive thanks for her help, Jack sat at the kitchen table and watched the Campus IT director work.

He extracted the info from the reader via a digital SD card and he programmed it into an RFID tag machine. Gavin had brought a photo of Jack from a file on the Campus network, and he affixed this on the card, along with the name of the building and other information represented on the cards held by building employees.

Last, he attached a black neck lanyard that perfectly matched the one worn by the employees of Frieden's building.

All totaled, Gavin finished the job in under thirty minutes. He held it up for Jack to look at.

Jack asked, "How sure are you it will be accepted by the scanner?"

"One hundred percent."

Jack looked at Gavin with incredulity.

"I'm serious, Ryan, find some other part of this op to stress about. That was a breeze." Gavin then handed over an electronic device to unlock Frieden's office door and asked Jack if he remembered how to operate it.

Jack said, "You're kidding, right? You put me and the guys through two days' worth of training on that gadget."

"And now that training will pay off," Gavin said, with a hint of satisfaction in his voice. He also handed Jack a completely nondescript thumb drive. "Here's your RAT. It's just like the one Ysabel used down in Rome. Get it into a port on any networked device in his office, wait nineteen and a half seconds for the program to upload, and then pull it out. After that, you're done, I'll take care of the rest remotely."

Jack and Ysabel had joked in Rome about Gavin's precise instructions to wait nineteen and a half seconds. They both agreed the first nineteen seconds went by quickly, but that last half second felt like an eternity.

Gavin returned to D.C. that afternoon on a commercial flight, and Jack spent the evening in a local gym, trying to undo some of the damage he had done over the past weeks wining and dining Ysabel and sitting on his ass all day.

The next morning at eleven a.m. Jack stood in a doorway six floors below his rented office and watched Guy Frieden and his secretary leave their building, the same as they had the previous four days. He knew they were headed to a café around the corner from Frieden's office on the pedestrian shopping street. As soon as they disappeared up Grand Rue, Jack crossed the street, a purposefulness to his walk that gave an air that he did this every day.

He wore a gray suit under a brown Fendi wool overcoat and he carried a black leather Tumi bag. His beard was trim and neat and he wore Tom Ford clear-lensed eyeglasses with no correction to give him even more of a professional presence.

He entered the building and marched up to the counter, waved the badge Gavin made for him over the reader, careful to glance away from the camera that recorded his entrance while he did so. He was rewarded with a green light and a rotating turnstile. He pushed through and headed for the elevators, continuing the appearance of utter relaxation.

On the fifth floor Jack passed a dozen individual offices, most of them private bankers or attorneys, before he made it to a door with a gold nameplate that read *Guy Frieden, Avocat*. He continued on down to the end of the hall, then he turned and started back toward the door. When he was certain no one was coming, he reached into his pocket and pulled out a white box the size of a deck of cards. This he placed over the card reader lock next to Frieden's door. Automatically the device began pulling in data from the reader and then decoding it.

It was another one of the Campus team's inventions, and Jack knew it didn't always work, but Gavin and company had researched the locking protocols used by this office building, and Gavin assured him he'd get in.

As usual, it took a little longer than Gavin said it would, but, also as usual, it worked as advertised. The door opened thirteen seconds after Jack pushed the lock decoder against the card reader.

Frieden's office was dark and quiet. Jack looked out the window to his vantage point across the street, then hurried to the computer on the desk, pulling out the RAT as he moved. He plugged the device in, initiated it with the simple movement of the mouse on the desk, and left it there while it worked its magic.

He had a few seconds to snoop around, so he looked through the drawers on Frieden's desk. He didn't see anything that looked very interesting, so he headed back into the lobby to check the secretary's desk.

Jack saw Guy Frieden's secretary had a calendar blotter on her desk, so he pulled out his phone and began taking pictures of the handwritten notes on the pages. Each and every day of the exposed month had some sort of notation, but they were all in German.

He carefully checked the following month, but this page, and the two calendar pages representing the rest of the year, were completely blank.

Jack assumed at the beginning of each month Frieden's secretary took all the appointments off whatever computer program she kept them on for scheduling, and she then hand wrote them on the calendar for quicker reference. It left him with a very incomplete picture, but enough notes were written on the blotter that Jack knew he didn't want to pass it up.

He gave the RAT a full minute to do its thing, more than three times as long as Gavin said the device needed to install itself, but

Jack figured it couldn't hurt.

Jack was out of the building seven minutes after he entered — he doubted Frieden had managed to finish his biscotti yet — and he was on the phone with Gavin as soon as he was back in his tiny sixth-floor office. Gavin promised to get to work on hacking into the system immediately.

Next Jack called Clark, following the orders of the director of operations to notify him the moment he was clear. Jack felt a little silly checking in, like he was calling his mom to let her know he made it home safely, but Clark had requested the contact. Jack knew Clark didn't like his men operating in the field, even if it was a low-risk mission in such a serene place as Luxembourg.

24

One month earlier

Russian private equity investor Andrei Limonov assumed he would have his next meeting
with Valeri Volodin at the Kremlin, so he'd
been surprised when the car that picked him
up at his apartment at the prearranged time
took him not east to the president's offices,
but west, to Volodin's private home, the
palatial estate of Novo-Ogaryovo.

Volodin was famous for his late-night meetings, often conducted in his offices in Building One of the Kremlin complex, or even in
sitting rooms in the Grand Kremlin Palace,
normally reserved for ceremonial functions.
But meetings in his private residence were
exceedingly rare. Limonov had heard a few
rumors from his friends working high in the
Economic Ministry that the president had
changed many of his habits in the past several
months, giving them the impression he was
becoming more paranoid about those around
him. Limonov didn't know any of this first-

hand, of course, but he could well imagine that the Kremlin had become a difficult place to work since the recent economic downturn and Russia's military forays of the past year.

The private equity manager was no fool. He had no doubt in his mind that his task of moving Volodin's secret wealth was directly related to the president's concerns about those around him.

Limonov was X-rayed and passed through a biometric scanner and his briefcase was searched, then he was led through the entrance to the property, and a few minutes later he sat alone in an ornate sitting room, looking out a window at a massive lawn. His eyes tracked a pair of guards and their dog walking at the edge of the property, and saw the sweep of a spotlight running across a wood line on a hill beyond the property's outer fence.

Limonov thought once more about his plan, running over details in his mind knowing fully well this would be the last opportunity before he presented it to the president. He committed himself to its implementation, telling himself it was as close to foolproof as he could possibly make it.

Valeri Volodin entered the room, his gait fast and focused as he approached, his eyes locked on Limonov as if he might attack. He made no apology for his late entrance, but Limonov had expected none.

Volodin got right down to it. "When we last met you agreed to a plan to move my holdings to someplace out of the established network and into new secure accounts that will be invisible to not only those in the West hunting for them, but also those at home who might not have my best interests in mind."

"Yes, Mr. President. I believe I have come up with an infallible strategy to remove your money from existing accounts where they might be monitored by FSB auditors and those who might report to FSB, then move it via a network of companies, banks, trusts, and special purpose entities to initiate the obfuscation of its disbursal, and then . . . suddenly, to make it altogether disappear."

Volodin said, "You've lost the plot, Limonov. I don't want my money to disappear."

"Right, well it will reappear, only to you, and not tied to the chain of previous movements. It will not be money that was shuffled around. It will be money that existed, then ceased to exist. And then, as if by magic, new money will appear in different accounts, known only to you, all over the world."

"You have my attention, Andrei Ivanovich."

"The plan revolves around cryptocurrency. Bitcoin. Are you familiar with this?"

"I am familiar with it, but not familiar enough to give you eight billion dollars. Keep talking."

"Removing your assets from their existing

accounts, I will channel them through a network of shells to slow down anyone trying to track the transactions. Then I will use the money to purchase digital currency, which is untraceable. Once we have the digital currency we will use this to purchase fiat currency, that is to say government-backed money, and this money, completely distanced from your original assets, will be deposited in a collection of banks around the world. The beauty of it all, Mr. President, is that no one will know where your money is other than you."

"This is your *objective.* That is not the same thing as a plan. Tell me how this will happen."

Andrei Limonov spoke for the next ten minutes, taking small charts out of his stack of papers in his briefcase to use as illustrations. When Limonov was finished with his presentation, Volodin tapped his fingers together several times. It was an affectation that, in others, would likely appear thoughtful, but Volodin was so full of nervous energy it looked utterly manic.

Volodin said, "This man you mentioned. The man you will need the assistance of to ensure our little project's success, do you think he will work with you?"

"For what we will pay him, he would be a fool not to."

Volodin sniffed. "The world is full of such fools."

Limonov was taken aback. He expected to have to defend some of the technical aspects of the plan, but not whether he could employ the services of someone by giving them an incredible sum of money to do the very job they were already doing.

Limonov said, "I will need this man to work with me for two weeks, no more. I will oversee him while he makes the trades, in increments of a few million at a time, so we do not draw more attention than we need. He is a businessman, and this is his business. The only change to his normal business is that I will require being present while he works, and the amount of money will be more than he has ever dealt with. He will be compensated for this alteration in the normal working relationship he uses with his clients."

Volodin said, "Andrei Ivanovich, I foresee this as being more difficult than you expect. People might want information who don't need it. People might try to find out about you and your client. I can't allow that to happen." Before Limonov could respond, the Russian president asked, "Do you know a man named Vlad Kozlov?"

Limonov's stomach suddenly began to churn. His voice cracked when he answered. "I am aware of the name."

Volodin touched a button on his desk.

"Send him in."

Limonov turned to look toward the door of Volodin's private office. His heart pounded against his ribs.

The real reason Limonov had refused to work with the FSB was because of people just like Vladimir Ivanovich Kozlov. He'd never met the man, had no idea what he looked like, but the name *Vlad Kozlov* had been breathed by some of his banker friends who worked for the government. As the man entered and approached across the floor now, Limonov stood, suddenly feeling meek and small. The new arrival was forty-nine and athletic. He had gray hair so short it was spiked, and a surprisingly good sense of style. His suit and tie made him look like a Kremlin pol, but Andrei Limonov knew what the man crossing the room was.

He was an ex–operations officer in the FSB. Well known as ruthless and cunning, and also regarded as extraordinarily cold.

He wasn't the man to pull the trigger himself, not anymore, but Vlad Kozlov was the type of man who got a lot of people killed on both sides.

He had been internal security previous to Volodin's rise to power, but once the man on the other side of the desk from Limonov took over in the Kremlin, Kozlov had left the intelligence services and gone to work for Volodin personally. People around Moscow whispered that he had orchestrated the assassination of a couple of prominent journalists here in the city in the past few years, and his name had come up in a recent ruthless and effective hit of a popular Volodin opponent on a bridge right outside the Kremlin.

Limonov knew all this through rumors and inside gossip, but looking at the man in the flesh now, he had no reason to doubt any of it. He looked like a cross between a gorilla and a snake.

Limonov stood to shake hands with Kozlov, and when both men sat down, Limonov looked back to Volodin. "I do not understand."

Volodin nodded. "Which is why Vlad will be your guide through all this. He works for Grankin at the Security Council, but I've had him tasked to me personally. You are the private equity manager. He is the facilitator. When you need something, he will get it for you. When you need some*one,* he will get *them* for you. When you run into trouble, he will spin you around and run you right out of trouble."

"With due respect, what sort of trouble do you think I will get into? I will be setting up a business network, I will be acquiring digital currency, and I will be establishing offshore accounts. I have been doing this sort of thing for a dozen years without anyone there to guide me."

"There will be people in Russia who do not want you to liquidate assets, people overseas who will require information you are not allowed to provide. It is the nature of the world that sometimes certain pressures must be applied to influence outcomes."

Limonov glanced at the man seated next to him. Kozlov looked straight ahead, at his president. "May I ask if Mr. Kozlov is also responsible for keeping watch over me? Exerting this pressure you speak of on me to ensure I do what I am supposed to do?"

Volodin replied matter-of-factly, "I find it is better to trust two men partially than one man wholly."

He said nothing else. Limonov did not know whether he should follow up that comment with a protest about the arrangement — sitting here with Volodin and Kozlov, he quickly determined the better course of action was to hold his tongue.

But despite himself, words flew out of his mouth.

"What if something should happen to me?"

"Like what?" Volodin asked.

Like you have your man slit my throat as soon as I set up your new accounts, Limonov thought. But he said, "I fulfill my end of the bargain, and then an accident befalls me."

"You see monsters in every dark corner, don't you, Limonov?"

The young financier did not reply.

Volodin said, "If you do not trust our arrangement, I can't depend on you to fulfill our agreements, can I? You will be paid what I told you I would pay you, and you will have a job for life."

Limonov knew what Volodin meant. Limonov would know all about Volodin's money. He would always know, as long as he lived.

"I know you could have me killed."

"And I know you could have me destroyed in the event of your untimely death. You must already be thinking about your dossier."

"My *what*?"

"A secret file, hidden, but with an automatic launch mechanism. You die, you are threatened, and my account numbers are handed over to my enemies."

A clock ticked somewhere outside the room.

"I wouldn't do that."

"*I* would," Volodin said.

Limonov didn't feel much better about the arrangement, but he let it go. He said, "I need to relocate to London. I will require an office outside of Moscow to be certain I am not monitored by FSB."

Volodin said, "You don't think I can reach you in London?"

Limonov said, "Of course you can. But it would be an annoyance for you to do so. I plan on making you incredibly satisfied with my work, and I plan on you putting your trust in me for years to come. I only ask that you assure me of my protection."

It was a shrewd demand, especially considering the fact that Andrei Limonov was scared shitless at the moment, but once Volodin thought it over for a long time, silently, letting the tension build in the room almost to the point where the equity manager told his president to forget the whole thing, Volodin smiled. "I only hope you treat my money as cleverly as you considered this arrangement."

"Your money will be safer the moment we shake hands to begin the deal, Mr. President."

A minute later Limonov found himself out in the hall, with Vlad Kozlov in front of him.

Kozlov said, "Mr. Limonov, the president has conveyed to me the importance of your task. You can expect to find me at your side throughout the entire process."

Limonov could not hide his discomfort. "Very well. But . . ." He searched for the right words.

Kozlov helped. "You are in charge. I am here as a problem solver. Nothing more. Will we be traveling soon?"

We? Limonov's concern increased even more. "I will need to set up the London office. I will then begin the preliminary work of setting up the network. This will take some weeks, and not a single ruble will move until the entire structure is in place. There are bankers and lawyers and registration officials in several places throughout the world I will need to speak with. There is a man in Luxembourg I know who can make the introductions I need to the Bitcoin expert. I really don't think it's necessary for you —"

"I am coming with you. These men you speak of. Do you know them already?"

"Some of them, yes."

"Find other men. Volodin wants no existing network used."

"But —"

"He was clear on that, but I can tell him you have doubts about his plan. See what he says."

"No . . . let's not do that. I'll need some time to find suitable replacements, but I will go to London immediately."

"Of course," said Kozlov. "I will pack my bags. Then I will meet you at your office in the morning. We will go over the logistics of your plan, and then I will wait until you are ready to go."

Limonov cocked his head. He was going to ask why Kozlov needed to sit in his office day in and day out, but he didn't bother. He realized the ex–FSB operative was part of the deal, and he needed to just accept it and move on.

He told himself he should not be at all

surprised that $120 million came with a few strings attached.

25

Present day

Jack Ryan, Jr., woke from a dead sleep, and he realized his mobile phone on the bedside table in his Luxembourg apartment was chirping. He could tell by the cobwebs in his brain it was early in the morning, and that gave him a pretty clear idea about who was calling. As he lay down the night before, he fully expected to be yanked out of a deep sleep — the IT director for The Campus was sure to hack into Guy Frieden's network, and Jack had no doubt Gavin would do so at a speed that ensured he'd call Luxembourg at an inappropriate time.

Jack answered the phone with a tired voice. "Morning, Gavin. Ten p.m. there, I see."

"Ten-oh-five. I didn't want to call before four a.m. your time."

"Thanks for the five-minute snooze," Jack said sarcastically. "You got into Frieden's network?"

Biery said, "Well, the decryption of the files

themselves is going to take a little more time. But I did manage to crack into his contact list and his calendar. These applications weren't locked down like the files, which he keeps under special protocols to take into account attorney-client privilege. Thought I'd share what I had, since it might give you something to go on in the short term."

Jack rolled out of bed. His body was sore from last night's workout. "That's great. I'd be interested in anyone he has been in contact with, either by phone, e-mail, or instant messaging in the last six months."

"Done. It's a lot of people. You ready for the number?"

"Hit me."

"Twelve hundred eighty-eight."

Jack rubbed his eyes. "You're joking!"

"This guy gets around."

Ryan said, "How about people with Slavic names. Can you sort those out?"

"Done."

"How many?"

"One hundred fourteen."

"Damn." Ryan sighed. "Well, that's better, anyway. Can you send everything to me? I can run pattern analysis, see if anything jumps out."

"It's already waiting for you in your inbox. Going to take some days to get deeper into Frieden's network."

Jack said, "Honestly, his contact list is the

most important piece of this puzzle. The files themselves will be a maze of shells, offshores, and other ways to obfuscate his clients and their relationships between each other. I am certain that decrypting the files will just lead us to another layer to break through. I'll get started on his contacts, and I'll take whatever else you get, whenever you get it."

"Okay. Enjoy your beauty sleep." Gavin hung up.

Ryan rolled out of bed and into the shower, knowing he wouldn't be able to fall back to sleep. Twenty minutes later he was sitting at his desk in his apartment, hot coffee in his hand, scrolling up and down a list of the 1,288 names. After a quick check, he looked at Gavin's tab on the spreadsheet of the Slavic names. He recognized some of them, they were the usual suspects — Kremlin-affiliated cashiers, investment bankers, economists, and the like — but eighty percent of the names meant nothing to him.

He poured them all into a computer program that ran data and link analysis, checking them for relationships to one another, as well as against other sources The Campus kept in a database for Russian money laundering.

From the results of the analysis it looked like Guy Frieden was a busy guy, well connected to a lot of the players in the known realm of offshore banking, but almost instantly Ryan felt a sense of disappointment. It was clear by his associations that he had only mid-level access. There wasn't a single big fish in his contact list, not even the secretary or the attorney of a CFO or the assistant to a CFO at any one of Russia's state-owned companies. No. Frieden's Russian contacts were secondary moneymen — worker bees.

And certainly not Kremlin big shots.

Frustrated, Jack began to scan down through Slavic names he did not recognize in the hopes there would be someone who, somehow, had been missed by the link analysis. He checked through the graphs that showed the relationships among the different names, and when he did this, he immediately noticed something curious. Almost every single person had at least four or five affiliations to someone else in the group, but one name stood to the side of the others. No lines went to it or emanated from it.

The name *Andrei Limonov* looked like a little island off to the side of the graph.

Ryan knew nothing about Limonov, and that was curious. Clearly, whoever he was, he'd managed to keep his name out of any list of Russia's most notorious offshore finance experts, and Jack wondered if that in itself was notable.

Ryan looked him up on SPARK by Interfax, a database of information on tens of thousands of Russian companies, hundreds of thousands of businessmen. There were quite a few hits on Andrei Limonov, but it wasn't a particularly uncommon name in Russia, so he had to keep digging. After a while, he decided the man who showed up in Guy Frieden's appointment book was the same Andrei Limonov who directed Blackmore Capital Partners, a Moscow-based private equity enterprise with a decidedly British name, no doubt to give it an air of panache.

Ryan dug around in a database of Russian newspapers and magazines for more information on Limonov, using automatic translation software that, although nowhere near as good as a real translator, at least would tell him basic information if any existed.

But he found nothing. The man did not exist in Russian social or media circles.

Another database Ryan had access to proved more helpful. It held information of attendees of business schools around the world. From here he saw Limonov graduated with honors from Lomonosov Moscow State University Business School, and then he received a degree from Saint Petersburg University Graduate School of Management. The dates on the degrees told Ryan the man was probably still in his mid-thirties, and from SPARK he saw that Blackmore Capital

Partners had come into existence ten years prior.

Impressive, thought Jack. It looked like this guy walked out of business school and into the world of international finance as the head of a private equity firm.

And there was one more matter of note regarding Limonov. According to Frieden's appointment calendar, the man was here in Luxembourg, right this very moment. He had held a meeting at four p.m. yesterday afternoon with Frieden, and he was due to lunch with him today at two p.m. at a place called La Lorraine, in the Place Guillaume II.

Jack realized he must have photographed Limonov entering the office the day before. He'd taken dozens of pictures during the day, but unless this guy had missed his meeting and Frieden's secretary had failed to strike it through on her blotter, he should have an image of the man.

Jack went back through his notes. Yes, at four p.m. exactly the day before, Frieden had entered his conference room for a meeting.

He'd found not a single photograph of the Russian online, so he had no idea who he was looking for. Nevertheless, he began to scan the men who entered the bank building between three-thirty and four p.m. There were nearly five dozen images to go through, and he did this one at a time, ruling out any men or groups of men where at least one of the men was not in his thirties, possibly Slavic, and male. A few men had entered in blue-collar work clothes, and one duo had paint cans and a ladder, and all these men were omitted as well.

When he was finished going through the images a second time, he had it narrowed down to only four pairs of men. These he sent to Gavin for processing through a Department of Justice classified database of known faces, culled from Interpol and individual "Five Eyes" national crime information, as well as open-source media files.

It was a couple hours too early to reach Gavin at the office in Virginia, and Jack did not want to just sit around and wait in his office, so he decided to head out to La Lorraine to see if he could get eyes on Frieden's mystery man, Andrei Limonov. Normally he would need to clear an operational move like this with John Clark, but Jack justified his lapse of OPSEC; he knew there was a McDonald's on the Place Guillaume II, and he hadn't had a greasy American hamburger for months. There was no Campus protocol that said Ryan had to call in to HQ to request permission to go to lunch.

At five minutes till one Jack sat outside the McDonald's on the other side of the Place Guillaume II, Luxembourg's central square, eating a Big Mac and drinking a Diet Coke.

It was a frigid afternoon, but he wasn't alone. A dozen or more locals and tourists sat around the McDonald's, and this gave Jack the comfort that his surveillance position would remain undetected.

At just after one in the afternoon, Guy Frieden entered the restaurant alone, looking dapper in a gray suit and carrying a briefcase. Jack glanced up and down the square on the offhand chance there was some countersurveillance around the meeting location, but he saw nothing.

Ten minutes later a black Jaguar XF sedan pulled to the curb next to the restaurant. Two men climbed out and headed directly to the door of La Lorraine. They both wore dark suits; the shorter one had thinning blond hair and appeared to be younger than the other, who was tall and broad and had spiked gray hair. The Jaguar turned right, leaving the square, and Jack was unable to get a look at the driver.

He lifted his burger and took a bite, but his eyes remained up on the men until they disappeared into the restaurant. He gazed again around the area before pretending to check his phone for messages, making a show of being just one more working stiff on his lunch break.

Just as he put his phone back into his coat it started buzzing. He pulled it out and saw it was John Clark calling. "Hey, John."

302

"Actually, it's John and Gerry. We've got you on speaker in the conference room."

"Oh . . . okay. Good morning, Gerry. Hey, this isn't about that Bugatti I put on the company card, is it? I can explain that."

Gerry Hendley ignored Ryan's joke. "What are you up to over there, kid?"

Jack walked away from the others sitting outside the McDonald's and found a quiet bench on the Place Guillaume II, fifty feet from anyone else. "I thought you knew. I've got eyes on an attorney here in Luxembourg City who is part of the Grankin money-laundering ladder."

"Tell me about the photos you sent Gavin."

"I sent Gavin some faces to push through the DOJ facial-recog system. That's it. You can ask him."

Clark said, "Don't have to. Gavin brought them to us a few minutes ago."

"Is something wrong?" Jack asked, confused by the interrogation.

Gerry said, "You are looking for a private equity guy named Andrei Limonov. No known criminal ties."

"Right."

"One of the pictures was interesting. One guy came up with nothing, but that might be Limonov, because there are no other images of him anywhere."

"Okay. What about the other guy? Any idea who he is?"

Clark responded to this. "We know exactly who he is. He's Vladimir Kozlov."

The name didn't mean anything to Jack. He was a little embarrassed by this, because he was supposed to know names in the Russian banking and investment world, and he'd drawn a blank on both men. He said, "He's some kind of a banker or something?"

"Nope," Clark said. "He's a spook. He's Kremlin now, but he's ex-FSB. Active-measures operations."

Suddenly, Ryan knew he was on the trail of something big, he was certain of it. He looked out across the square at the restaurant, his heart rate increasing. "Well, hot damn!"

"No, Ryan," Gerry said, "this *isn't* good. Look, I'm glad you seem to be on the right track over there, but in every conversation we've had about the analytical work you'd be doing in the field in Europe, you've gone out of your way to stress that there were no indications of physical involvement by organized crime or FSB in your investigation."

Jack said, "That was true, up until now. Look, guys, this man Limonov had nothing to do with the work I was doing in Rome."

"But he's tied to the same lawyer who set up the company who purchased the artwork."

"Yes, that's true. But I think it's just a coincidence. I know the players in Rome — they were Russians, sure, but I didn't get one ping down there on this guy Limonov. I am somewhere between highly confident and absolutely positive that Limonov is a guy who just happens to be meeting with the same lawyer as the Russians operating in Rome. I have no idea what he's doing here, but I sure am curious because he's so opaque."

Clark said, "Well, I'm curious, too, but Kozlov is no one to mess with. He's trouble, pure and simple. He was originally identified as Russian intelligence about three years ago on an operation here in D.C. Then he showed up in Kiev last year. According to our links into CIA SIPRNet there are suspicions he was the brains behind that assassination on the bridge in front of the Kremlin a few months ago."

Jack slowly scanned the square again. For an urban area, this space couldn't possibly have been any more tranquil. There was nothing to worry about here, he felt sure. "Well, that's interesting," Jack said. "Wonder what he's doing with Limonov. Moving Kremlin money?"

Clark said, "I have no idea."

Jack thought about it. "He wasn't mentioned on Frieden's appointment book, only Limonov was. Looks like he's traveling as Limonov's hanger-on. I wonder if Limonov could be moving money, and this ex-FSB thug is here protecting Limonov."

Gerry said, "I'm liking your involvement in this less and less."

"Look, we are a small team. Smaller now since Sam died. But this is important, and I'm being careful." Jack thought of the incident in Rome with the photographer Salvatore. He'd never gotten around to mentioning it to Clark, and now sure as hell didn't seem to be the time to bring it up.

Jack said, "If there is a chance we can get at some of Volodin's money, then we can —"

Gerry said, "Wait. *Volodin's* money? You're taking a hell of a leap. What makes you think Limonov is working for Valeri Volodin?"

Jack demurred, chastised that he'd gone too far in justifying his operation. "I don't know that he is. But whoever he is working for, apparently it is some Kremlin fat cat, somebody who can send this Vladimir Kozlov to babysit him."

Gerry said nothing.

"Think about it. It's someone high at the Kremlin. We've dug up a lot of bit players involved in Kremlin finances, but not this guy. He has to be working with someone whose assets we haven't uncovered yet. Someone like Volodin."

"Someone like any one of fifty other guys with Kremlin ties."

"Fair enough, but I've got a strong feeling about this one. Limonov only shows up in business-related searches. He doesn't have any criminal background, and he obviously isn't any sort of a politician, or we'd know him. If he is what my analysis says he is, and if I was the kleptocrat leading a nation who needed someone to control my money, he's exactly the guy I'd want doing it. Some finance manager who isn't looking to make a name for himself. Who keeps out of trouble and out of the news, and who quietly makes a lot of money."

Clark said, "If he's such a big-shot manager, how come we don't know about him?"

"I asked myself the same question. But then I thought about it. You don't get famous by getting rich. You get famous by getting rich and using your riches to acquire power. The wealthy guys who've parlayed their wealth into a seat at the table in the Kremlin are the guys on our radar."

"Very true."

"And this Limonov just sits at his desk and sets up shell companies, moves money out of Russia and into offshore vehicles."

Gerry said, "Okay, with Clark's permission, we'll let you keep soft surveillance on Frieden for a little while longer. You can dig into Limonov all you want via analysis, but I don't want you walking the streets behind him, tailing him in your car, or anything idiotic like that."

Jack was poised on the bench, watching the restaurant, and ready to do just that. Instead, he stood up, tossed the rest of his lunch in a garbage can, and started back to his office. "I wouldn't even consider it, Gerry." He said it behind a sly grin.

26

The prince sat in his Mercedes limousine, idly looking out the window at the tourists and the shoppers strolling by on Rodeo Drive, many of whom were staring back at his vehicle and the smoked-glass windows. He imagined they were wondering if some sort of a movie star was sitting inside, and this made him chuckle.

He was no actor, but there wasn't an actor on this planet with a portfolio a tenth the size of his. The prince was Saudi Arabia's deputy minister of petroleum and mineral resources, which meant he was second in line to one of the highest positions in the nation. He was also from the House of Saud, the royal family, which meant his personal wealth was all but incalculable.

The prince enjoyed his visits to the West, but not quite so much as his wife did. She loved to shop and he loved to make her happy, or at least he understood the benefit to him if she remained happy, so he placated her with a little time in which to shop, and a lot of money to spend while she did it.

Every time they left the kingdom he gave her at least a full day of roaming the stores, and she had become an expert at taking advantage of these days. In Milan, in Paris, in Monaco, in Singapore, luxury boutiques had been raided by the prince's wife, and usually the prince felt like the getaway driver, because he preferred to wait outside in the car.

His security detail preferred it as well.

He'd met his wife at a Formula One race in Abu Dhabi eight years ago; she was a Czech national and a model. Since the day they met she'd done her best to spend his money. He didn't care, she treated him well in the process, and she couldn't possibly put a dent in his riches, no matter how many bags, necklaces, shoes, and designer pedigree dogs she purchased.

And as much as she loved to shop, she loved to get out of the kingdom even more. This trip to California had a business component to it, of course. The prince was being courted by the American government. It was known to all that the current minister of petroleum and mineral resources, the prince's uncle, was suffering from inoperable bowel cancer. He did not have long, and the Americans hoped relations on the energy-trading front would remain the same or even improve when the younger man took over. To that end, they brought him over as often as they could and did their best to show him and his wife that America was a friend to the Saudis — especially the Saudi oil industry.

But the prince wasn't thinking about work now, he was thinking about his wife. He sat in the backseat of a Mercedes-Benz S-Guard, one of the most expensive armored cars on earth, and he looked out the window onto Rodeo Drive. His wife was in the Bulgari store with one of their bodyguards, and he was outside with two more, plus his driver and a personal assistant.

He considered asking his PA to text her and demand she hurry it up — it was nearly lunchtime, after all. But just as he turned to give the command, his phone chirped and he answered it.

"Can you come in?"

"Why?"

A pause. "I need you to see something."

The prince sighed to the others in the Mercedes. "I'll be right back."

His close protection agent called back from the front seat, "I'll go with you."

"No need."

But the guard insisted and climbed out and opened the door for the prince, and the two men crossed the sidewalk.

The prince pressed the button for the door to be unlocked, and he entered the exclusive shop when he heard the click of the lock disengaging. With no attempt to hide his impatience, he climbed the steps up to the sales floor, his bodyguard at his side, and looked around for his wife.

Quickly he realized the little store was empty other than his wife, a single doorman in a dark suit, and a tall, attractive salesclerk standing on the other side of a glass counter from his wife.

The two Saudis passed the security guard standing along the wall.

The prince said, "I told you to get whatever you wanted. Why do I have to see it?"

She stood over a case of necklaces, so his eyes scanned down the merchandise.

Next to him, his guard spoke to his wife as well. "Where is Faisal?"

When she did not immediately answer either man, the prince looked up at her for the first time, and he noticed the terror in her eyes.

"What is it?"

Braam Jaeger drew his silenced .22-caliber pistol and shot the prince's bodyguard in the back of the head, just behind the ear, at a distance of three feet. The big man pitched forward along with the snap of the round, and he dropped to his knees. Braam stepped closer behind him and shot him execution-style where he knelt, and by the time he lifted his weapon to train it on the prince, he saw the prince was already beginning to run in his direction, back toward the door.

The prince lurched forward, stumbling as he passed by Braam, and slid across the cold marble floor.

Martina Jaeger stood behind the counter, and she held out her own silenced .22. She had shot the man between the shoulder blades from behind.

Braam fired his weapon twice more at the man writhing on the ground at his feet, then he turned and left the showroom, heading down to cover the entrance in case more of the prince's guards tried to enter. As he walked he holstered his pistol, and from a shoulder holster he drew a Brügger & Thomet machine pistol. It was not a suppressed weapon like the .22, but was fully automatic, fired a larger, heavier nine-millimeter round, and was much more suitable for a real gunfight with multiple attackers than the little .22.

The prince's wife had dropped to the floor the moment the shooting began, and now she cowered there. "Please! No!"

Martina walked around the showcase slowly, taking her time, her high heels rhythmic on the marble. She stood over the trembling ex-model from the Czech Republic for several seconds, enjoying her fear.

"If you are a smart woman, then you know

that I must kill you."

"No!"

"Yes. We just spent ten minutes talking about platinum bracelets. I have a striking face, perhaps not as beautiful as your own, but certainly you will be able to provide a detailed description of me if I let you walk out of here."

"I swear to you. I will say nothing!"

"And I saw the way you looked at my brother when you came in. You wanted him for yourself. Pity that won't happen." She smiled. "It would be something to see."

"I won't tell anyone."

Martina pushed the muzzle of the .22 into the woman's blond hair. "Stop lying! Stop sniveling! Can't you die with dignity?"

The Czech woman began to sob loudly.

Martina said, "When I die, I will make my death as graceful as my life. I have self-respect. Honor."

Just then, Braam Jaeger called out in Dutch from the stairs. "They are coming!"

Martina cleared her head quickly, and she took two steps back from the woman on her knees in front of her.

She was thinking about the inevitable splatter and her ivory blouse.

Just as the prince's wife looked up at the movement, Martina Jaeger fired four times into her heart. The Czech woman cried out, grabbed at the wounds for an instant, then slumped over dead.

Martina knelt and picked up her tiny hot brass, giving no more thought to the dead bodies lying around her.

Braam walked up to the counter next to Martina and shattered the glass with the butt of his pistol. He and Martina pulled out several trays of rings and necklaces, taking no real time to distinguish specific pieces.

The pair left via the rear of the boutique seconds later, stowing their weapons out of sight and stepping over the two employees of the store and the wife's bodyguard, all of whom were piled on the floor behind the counter. Even before the Saudi guards were able to break down the front door and rush onto the small sales floor, Braam was behind the wheel of an Aston Martin, and he and his sister were pulling out of the loading area, heading toward Wilshire Boulevard.

Within an hour they would be in the air, leaving Van Nuys Airport, and within fifteen hours they would be back in Holland, waiting for their next operation. They doubted they had long to wait, because it sure seemed like the Russians were really picking up the intensity of their operations.

27

It was Saturday afternoon, and President Jack Ryan was supposed to be with his wife and two youngest kids enjoying the beautiful fall day at their home in Peregrine Cliff. He'd been looking forward to the getaway all week, anticipating looking out over the waters of the Chesapeake Bay surrounded by autumn colors, the leaves floating down all around him.

Instead he looked at a stack of white papers on the table in front of him. A National Intelligence Estimate was a poor substitute for blowing fall leaves. He was stuck here at work, sitting at the conference table in the Situation Room in the basement of the West Wing.

This meeting could have been held in the Oval Office; there were just a half-dozen in attendance, and this wasn't an imminent national security situation, but the White House staff had chosen today to clean the carpets in the West Wing, the President's secretary's office, and the Cabinet Room. Jack had been told this in advance, but it was only a young uniformed Secret Service guard with an awkward expression on his face standing in the West Colonnade who called out to the President as he opened the door, one step away from entering and trampling all over wet carpet.

That would have made his dark mood even darker, but the moment was saved, and now he was here facing the secretary of energy, the attorney general, and the secretary of state, along with a couple staff members for each of them.

The President sat at the end of the conference table, his head in his hands and his glasses on the papers in front of him. Slowly he rubbed his eyes. The director of the CIA and the director of the Office of National Intelligence were supposed to be here as well, but they hadn't made it in yet, so his questions about the international intelligence ramifications of the current situation went unanswered, and Ryan wasn't pleased about this at all.

Ryan slipped his eyeglasses back on and sighed.

"The heir apparent to be the next Saudi minister of petroleum and mineral resources. A prince of the nation, a friend of our government. Where does this assassination take place? Riyadh? Jeddah? London? Istanbul?

Nope. Beverly *fucking* Hills!"

No one spoke.

Ryan shook away a measure of his anger and said, "Dan . . . who did it?"

Attorney General Dan Murray shrugged his broad shoulders. "LAPD says it looks like a very professional, but very ruthless contract hit dressed up to look like a smash-and-grab robbery. Obviously the perpetrators had intelligence on the security setup, that's how they knew how to swipe the video footage, as well as get in and get out without being picked up on any cameras in neighboring shops."

"Where did they get the intel?"

"It's a chain store. Chain stores use the same equipment, same security protocols. They might have cased one of these shops anywhere in the world, then when they walked into the one on Rodeo Drive they knew what to do."

"Go on."

"Lots of stuff was taken, a couple million in missing jewels, but it doesn't smell like robbery to LAPD. Our agents just arrived on scene this afternoon, so maybe we'll get a better picture later today."

Ryan said, "I'll state the obvious. This will hurt our relations with the Saudis and the prince's loss will affect the world energy markets, at least in the short term." He turned to the secretary of energy, Lester Birnbaum. "Any idea how much, Les?"

"I hate to be crass, Mr. President, by converting the prince's death to a dollar figure."

Ryan nodded. "I feel bad for the guy, and for his wife, same as I would for anyone who is murdered. But we're not here to grieve for them, Les. We have another job."

Birnbaum nodded. "I'd say a dollar a barrel, at least for the next ninety days." After he said this, he added, "And what about the assassination of the federal prosecutor in Venezuela last week?"

Ryan cocked his head. "What about it?"

"I'm just pointing out another event that took place recently that is having an effect on the oil markets. Not as big a deal as the Beverly Hills assassination, but if that Venezuelan prosecutor had managed to pass down some indictments it would have negatively affected world markets. He died before he revealed his information, and the price stayed flat."

Ryan turned back to AG Murray now. "Dan? What do you know about the Caracas murder?"

Murray said, "We're on the outside looking in. Our liaison relationship with Venezuelan federal law enforcement is effectively nil, but that killing appeared to be very professionally done. Everyone down there we've talked to asserts this couldn't have been a local hit, not even something arranged by the government.

It was too slick."

Ryan said, "Vilar was working on indictments against the Venezuelan government, right?"

"That's right. He claimed to have evidence of bribes given by the Russian state-owned gas industry to Venezuelan oil and gas officials, paying them off to release low Venezuelan production numbers to keep prices higher."

Ryan was intrigued. "So if the Venezuelan government didn't have him killed, that leaves the Russian government, although it doesn't seem to me like it would be that easy for a group of Spetsnaz gunmen to roll into Caracas and kill a top federal prosecutor. Any ID of the killers at all?"

Dan Murray said, "Caracas is tight-lipped about the investigation. We wondered if they were putting a lid on it because the killer came from within. But considering their good relationship with Moscow . . . it could just be the case that they suspect the Russians, too. Both governments would benefit if the assassin or assassins got away scot-free."

Mary Pat Foley and Jay Canfield entered the conference room together, their pace indicating they knew they were running late. Jack looked up at them long enough for them to know he was annoyed. "We've been spitballing theories around here without you two. Take a seat and help us out."

320

Mary Pat said, "I'm sorry, Mr. President, but there is a situation under way in Nigeria that required our attention."

"Nigeria?"

Canfield said, "It looks like a well-armed force of over one hundred, presumably Boko Haram fighters, attacked and took over an oil rig near Lagos. Unknown number of dead, you can bet many will be foreign contractors. The Nigerian Army is prepping an op to retake the oil rig. I asked my counterpart over there to allow us to consult with them, at least on the intel side. Burgess is talking to them about allowing American military advisers from JSOC to come down and give advice."

Scott Adler asked, "Have any Americans been taken hostage?"

"None, surprisingly. Ocean Oil Services out of Houston owns the rig, but it's run by the French and staffed mostly by Nigerians. Still, it's a U.S.-owned company, so we're asking for a seat at the table."

"Christ," Ryan said, and the glasses came off again.

Lester Birnbaum muttered under his breath. "There's another buck right there."

Ryan started to ask more questions of his intelligence advisers, but instead he turned to the secretary of energy. "What did you say?"

"Nothing, Mr. President. Sorry." Ryan kept his eyes on him until Lester Birnbaum realized he had to explain himself. "It's just that . . . the assassination in Caracas of the prosecutor investigating government price rigging of Venezuelan oil, the explosion of the LNG plant in Lithuania, the assassination of the Saudis' number-two fossil fuels man in Beverly Hills, and an attack on a rig in Nigeria. All happening within a week and a half. Each one of these separate events will have an effect on energy prices. Add that to the general conflagration in the Baltic . . . and I can't even predict where prices will rise to. Honestly, Mr. President, my ability to foretell oil and gas futures becomes a lot shakier every time you throw another crisis into the equation."

Ryan stared at his reflection in the polished table. "Jay, when has Boko Haram attacked an offshore oil rig?"

"Well," Jay Canfield said, "they've attacked the fields and the processing facilities. But out at sea? No, they haven't. First time for everything, I guess."

Ryan next asked, "Why would they do something that's exponentially more difficult than hitting a refinery on land? I mean, what's in it for Boko Haram?"

Mary Pat said, "They are showing their power and reach."

"Right, but can't they do that by hitting other targets? They could even hit oil targets. Why put a hundred guys in boats and conduct a completely different type of mission, for no more obvious gain?"

Birnbaum chanced another comment, although he was not directly in the intelligence loop. "Well . . . Mr. President, if they wanted to really affect the markets, they would do just this very thing. It conveys the fragility in Nigerian energy. The foreign energy companies' facilities were already at slight risk for a refinery attack every couple of years, so that risk is already priced into the market, more or less. But *this?* This is a new level of danger to the supply out of Nigeria. It will have a market effect equal to or more than the death of the Saudi prince, I should think."

Ryan looked to Jay Canfield. "Is Boko Haram sophisticated enough to take this into consideration?"

Canfield shook his head. "*Hell,* no. Not in a million years." Mary Pat shook her head in agreement with Canfield's dismissal of the strategic thinking of the Nigerian rebel force.

Ryan said, "Then maybe someone is doing their thinking for them."

"What do you mean?"

Ryan said, "Think about it. Every percentage point oil or natural gas goes up means billions in the coffers of the Russians, and millions in the personal accounts of Valeri Volodin."

Scott Adler said, "Wait. I know you suggested Russia was possibly responsible for the *Independence* explosion, and the train attack in Vilnius. But now you are suggesting they murdered a Saudi prince in California?"

Jay Canfield was equally skeptical. "And a prosecutor in Venezuela? And they encouraged Boko Haram to go big against the local energy sector? Sorry, Mr. President, but that's one heck of a conspiracy theory."

Ryan held his hands up. "It's not a theory, Jay. It's a hunch. I can't back it up enough to raise it up to theory status. But what if Russia is using its reach through the FSB to orchestrate all these events?"

Adler cocked his head. "To make money?"

Ryan shook his head. "No, to increase their power. Look how bad the energy sector has fallen. If Russia recoups ten to twenty percent of that, it makes them ten to twenty percent stronger. And if they reach out into Lithuania, or into Poland . . . it's only going to cost Europe that much more to confront them."

Adler wasn't buying it. "They are sending FSB out around the world to boost oil prices, so when they attack Lithuania NATO won't respond, because that would be too expensive? I don't know, Mr. President."

Ryan just shrugged now. "I don't know, either. Maybe I'm reaching. But the shooting in Germany showed us an FSB officer and a group of armed unknown operators in cahoots with a Spanish ecoterrorist. We know Russia has done false-flag ops in the past."

His conclusions were met by stares around the room.

He looked to Mary Pat Foley.

Mary Pat knew this look well. "Yes, Mr. President. As details from these events come out, we'll look into your hunch." She didn't sound any more convinced than Canfield or Adler had.

Jack said, "I know you will. Now, if you'll excuse me, I have to call an angry and grief-stricken sultan in Saudi Arabia and then run off six hours late to see an angry and disappointed wife in Maryland." He stood. With a slight bow he said, "Thanks for coming in on your Saturday. I sincerely wish you all a better weekend than I have in store for myself."

28

The DataPlanet truck sat on the loose shoulder of a winding gravel road to the east of the town of Pabradė, Lithuania. Within fifty feet of the road both to the north and south, tall, ramrod-straight pine trees shot up seventy-five feet into the air. While Herkus Zarkus pulled rolls of fiber-optic cable out of the back of his vehicle and set them up in neat stacks, Ding Chavez attached a toaster-sized optical laser surveying station to an already positioned tripod, turned it on, and pointed it along the road to the east.

Twelve miles beyond the next bend was the nation of Belarus, and just beyond that was Russia. There, Russia's Western Military District, numbering thousands of tanks and tens of thousands of men, could be in position to attack Lithuania within days. There was no notice from the CIA that the Russians were on their way here, but the two Campus operators not so far from the border of Russia's closest ally were taking the events there seriously, to say the least. They knew at any point they might be relying on that little DataPlanet van on the side of the road to outrun tanks and Mi-24 attack helicopters.

Caruso, Chavez, and Zarkus all wore identical uniforms, blue cold-weather coveralls, reflective vests, and orange helmets. Their vest had the name of their company written across the back, and they each wore a utility belt adorned with radios, tools, phones, and other gear.

While Chavez stood next to Caruso, he consulted a tablet computer with the geo-coordinates sent by Mary Pat Foley's office. Next to the GPS location, a small icon of an arrow directed him to move the tablet computer to the right two meters. He stepped the corresponding distance on the wet grass, and this put him just inside the tree line. The GPS coordinates on his tablet turned green.

"Right here," Dom said.

Ding moved the tripod to exactly where Dom stood, and he turned the laser surveying device slowly, from left to right. The display on the device gave him a 360-degree reading of the direction of the lens, and Dom told him to turn to heading 098. Ding complied, and the heading marker turned green the moment he pointed his camera in the correct direction.

"On it," he said.

"Mark it," Dom instructed, still looking at

his tablet.

Chavez pressed a button on a remote device in his hand, the camera inside the laser surveying station took a series of high definition images, and Dom's tablet signaled the data had been received with a green checkmark.

"Got it," Dom said.

Ding called out to Herkus, who was just fifty feet away by the truck. "That's it. Load it up."

While the Lithuanian American threw his rolls of cable back into the van, the two Campus men began breaking down their equipment, a process that they'd perfected in the past two days of long shifts. While Ding lifted the legs of the tripod out of the soft earth he said, "What was that, forty-nine?"

Dom corrected him. "No. That's an even fifty. We'll hit sixty by the end of the day."

"Which means, at this speed, we'll be done in ten days."

Dom helped Ding carry the big device back up a little rise toward the truck. "I hope Lithuania has ten days. I wonder if it would make us work faster if we knew what the hell we were doing."

Ding said, "I've been thinking it over."

"Any conclusions?"

"Obviously, this is some sort of survey of the battle space. Not sure why they are just doing it now, or what's different about this that makes it so classified. Normally, with an area like this they'd just have local forces send back images for the military planners. I don't get all the subterfuge, but that's not the thing that really confuses me."

"What's that?"

"Well, if the Russians come, we assume they will take the Kaliningrad Corridor from Lithuania."

"Right. So?"

"So we're about thirty miles north of the corridor. That stretch of Belarus over there isn't the quickest route to Lithuania's capital, and it isn't the closest point to link up with the Kaliningrad side."

"So your question is . . . why are we here?"

Ding loaded the tripod, turned around in the road to remove his helmet, and started back for the front passenger seat. He looked up and said, "I have a feeling that is *their* question, too."

A four-door Toyota drove up the gravel road from the distant bend. Herkus started for the driver's seat, but Ding said, "No, let's take our time. Talk to these people and feel them out."

The car pulled up and three men and one woman climbed out. They were of varying ages, but they all looked confident.

And suspicious.

"Labas rytas," Herkus called out to the group. Good morning.

One of the group, a short, fat man in his fifties, waved back idly. Speaking Lithuanian, he asked, "What are you boys doing here?"

Dom and Ding were both looking for the telltale signs of weapons printing under their jackets. Neither man saw anything, but with the thick coats the locals were wearing, it was difficult to be sure.

Herkus said, "Fiber-optic maintenance and survey. We're putting in super-high-speed Internet cables."

The man in charge of the little group nodded distractedly, still looking at the men and the equipment.

"Is this your property?" Herkus asked.

To that the man responded, "Do you have some identification?"

The woman and two other men stood in the road, and their body language showed the Campus operators that they were most definitely on guard.

Herkus pulled out his employee badge. "Some kind of a problem?"

The man didn't even look at the badge. "Where are you from?"

"USA, but my parents are from here. Used to spend my summers near here when I was a kid."

The man nodded. "And them?"

"We're all Americans. Look, friend, what's the —"

"Tell them to say something in English."

Herkus cocked his head. "What?"

One of the men in the road let his right hand slip inside his open coat. Dom saw this and moved close to the man, ready to drop him with a punch to the jaw if he saw a gun. "Don't try it, asshole."

The hand stopped moving, slipped out of the coat. Shaking.

The woman spoke in Lithuanian now. "Tell them to speak English."

Herkus looked to Dom and Ding. "Say something in English."

Dom said, "What do they want us to say?"

The bald man turned to the woman. "You don't think Spetsnaz can learn English?"

Herkus tipped his head, then relaxed noticeably. Turning back to the Campus men, he said, "I get it. They are locals. They think we are Russians."

Ding slowly pulled his passport out of his coat. It said his name was Thomas Kendall, but it was as good a U.S. passport as any of these four rural Lithuanians had ever seen. Dom pulled his own identification out, giving his name as Andrew Martin. The four Lithuanians looked them over in the road, and collectively they breathed an audible sigh that was almost comical to the two Americans by the van.

The relief was so complete the woman began to laugh. She spoke in halting English.

"Sorry. We thought you are Little Green Men."

Dom looked down at his coveralls. "No, ma'am. We're medium-sized blue men. We're just here to work on the Internet."

The bald-headed man wasn't smiling. "We don't need Internet from America. We need tanks from America."

Chavez nodded. "Trust me, if I had a tank, I'd give it to you."

Dom said, "Why did you think you would find Little Green Men up here? Russia is threatening the south."

The woman replied, "That's what we think, too. But the Green Men are already here."

"Wait. You've seen Russians? Are you sure?"

"We are here our entire lives. We know when someone not belong here."

Dom and Ding looked at each other. They both knew they had to be careful to not give their cover away. Even though these locals weren't the enemy, if rumor got out that a group of Americans wearing linemen's uniforms were asking questions about the Russians, it wouldn't take a spymaster to put together what was going on. And in rural communities such as here, rumors had a habit of spreading like wildfire. Ding said, "We don't get paid enough to deal with Russians. Where did you see them?"

"They were in Zalavas yesterday, near the

border. Ten men, maybe more. Taking pictures."

Kind of like us, Dom thought but did not say.

The woman continued. "We told police, but the Russians left before police came."

The three men in the DataPlanet uniforms broke away from the Lithuanian locals soon after and headed off to the next GPS coordinate on their list. They had planned on breaking off for lunch at noon, but the three men agreed it would be better for everyone if they just kept working as long as there was light to do so.

They were more convinced than ever that Lithuania didn't have ten days.

29

On Jack Ryan, Jr.'s fifth day of surveillance of
the Luxembourg attorney Guy Frieden, he
realized he had managed to reach a level of
symbiosis with his target that he had never
wanted to achieve. All week Jack had been
taking bathroom breaks at the same time
Frieden did. This was by necessity, of course;
he had learned through uncomfortable mis-
steps in the field that he needed to take
advantage of every available opportunity to
go when there was a lull in the action.

But now as Jack zipped up his fly and
washed his hands he realized his last few calls
of nature had corresponded naturally with
Frieden's. His bladder had fallen into a
rhythm with the man's down the street.

Jack found it both depressing and funny
that his biology had melded sympathetically
with his target's, but he shook the feeling
away and headed back into his dark little office.

Not to watch Frieden so much — although

that remained his main duty — but to get back to his computer.

So far, the only interesting person who had come into contact with Frieden — physically, anyway — was Andrei Limonov. Jack had gotten no closer to the money-laundering network used by Mikhail Grankin, and it didn't look like he would do so unless and until Gavin Biery cracked the man's files.

But while the objective that sent Jack to Luxembourg in the first place seemed — temporarily, at least — out of reach, he had been able to dig into Limonov and uncover a few things about the man's patterns. He had no information at all about Blackmore Capital's clientele, so he didn't know if Limonov invested one thousand rubles for one million clients, or one billion rubles for a single client. But through his research he had succeeded in discovering that Blackmore Capital Partners of Moscow had just very recently opened an office on Callcott Street in the Kensington district of London.

The computer techs at The Campus had successfully managed to tap into London's municipal camera feeds on an operation there a year and a half earlier, so Jack logged on to a Campus portal that served as his way in. It was estimated there was a camera for every eleven citizens of the United Kingdom, and through the portal Jack had access to every cam in the nation.

He tapped the address of Blackmore Capital into the program, and instantly he was shown the seven cameras within a one-block radius. One of these cameras even pointed right at the street and pavement in front of the little house with the gold BCP sign on the front door.

He saw no activity on the street or obvious movement through the half-open blinds of the house.

Between glances up to his monitor showing him the activity in Frieden's office, Jack closed the program displaying the London CCTV feeds, and he began to research how Limonov and Kozlov had gotten to Luxembourg.

He knew they'd first visited Frieden on Monday, so he looked at direct flights from both Moscow and London that arrived on that day. Through a Department of Homeland Security database, he checked passenger manifests on the airlines, but found nothing. If the men were traveling under their real names, they hadn't flown commercial on that day. He widened the search, but still came up with nothing.

The next step, he knew, was to check private aircraft. Luxembourg Airport was really the only potential location for a private flight to deposit someone into the city, so Jack pulled up a list of fixed-base operators working there. Within minutes he had a list of all the registered flights that came in on Sunday or Monday. There were seventy-three, which sounded like a lot to Jack until he considered the amount of money in play here in the city, at which point he realized it should come as no surprise that a bunch of people with private planes would come here to bank or to shop.

Of these seventy-three, eight had come directly from Moscow and nine directly from London.

Jack started with the London aircraft first, thinking it relevant that Limonov had opened an office there just a month earlier. He researched each plane to try to determine the owners and their passengers.

This took a half-hour, and when he was finished there was only one plane, a Bombardier Global model 6000, that he could not identify. It had arrived in Luxembourg just ninety minutes before Limonov and Kozlov met with Frieden in his office and, according to civil aviation information, it was still at the FBO at Luxembourg Airport.

Jack jotted the tail number down, not positive this was Limonov's aircraft, but certain he had no other leads.

He expected it to just return to London soon, so he wasn't over the moon with his potential discovery. Perhaps the two Russians were meeting with other bankers here in Luxembourg, setting up some new network for a big player in the Kremlin. Jack knew short of switching his surveillance from Guy Frieden to Andrei Limonov, finding out which hotel he was staying at, and trying to get photos of the man with any other associates here in town, he had pretty much exhausted investigative potential.

With a sigh of frustration he looked up at his monitor and saw that Frieden was putting on his coat. Jack checked his watch and saw it was after five p.m. He'd been working on Limonov all afternoon.

It was time to call it a day.

Five minutes later Jack walked among the heavy pedestrian traffic on the Grand Rue, his mobile phone against his ear.

"Gavin Biery" answered the voice on the other end.

"Gavin, I just wanted to let you know that everyone here in Luxembourg is still talking about that dashing American who blew through town the other day."

"Ha. I'll bet the natives have erected statues in my honor."

"There was already a Burger King here, so they'll have to think of something else."

"Somebody's in a joking mood. You must have found a new lead. What's up?"

"There's a plane parked at the airport here. Privately owned. I drilled down into the ownership as deep as I could, but couldn't find out too much. Still, I have a tail number. Will you be able to tell me when it leaves and where it goes?"

"If it publicizes its route, you can watch it yourself. But if they BARR the flight, then I'll have to roll up my sleeves and do some real work."

Jack knew what Gavin was telling him. While most private aircraft registered their flight numbers and destinations with air traffic authorities, certain private planes used the Block Aircraft Registration Request system to hide this information. Celebrities, corporations hoping to keep their competitors in the dark about their actions, and the über-wealthy who didn't want anyone to know where they were simply requested their aircraft and destination information not be placed in the system.

The Hendley Gulfstream used this service every time it went on missions for The Campus.

"Yeah," Jack agreed, "they might BARR it. But on the flight into Luxembourg they flew in the open."

Gavin said, "No worries either way, Ryan. Even if they try to hide it, I can probably find it. What kind of aircraft?"

"A Bombardier Global Six-K."

"Shouldn't be an issue. I can find your Bombardier if it takes off and tries to go ghost."

Jack said, "While I should probably just leave well enough alone and not ask you for details, I'm curious. How will you do it?"

"The FAA uses ASDI, Aircraft Situation Display to Industry, which is just a big public database so everyone can see what plane is where. When you use an app like Flight-Aware, it gives you information on where a flight is, although that is class-two info, which means the data is five minutes old. ASDI class one is real-time . . . It's what the people in the aircraft industry see.

"BARR flights mean the aircraft disappears from the list, so we look for planes in the air that are not showing on ASDI, then employ advance machine learning and data analytics to suck info from other public sources. If I'm searching for a single plane I can find it by using times, refueling info, catering info, private car hire info at the FBOs. Much of it is done automatically through the system. I can put in a flight number and then, within a certain time period, it will tell me exactly where to look for it. From there, all I have to do is download audio from the suspected airport and use a speech-to-text app, then do a rundown of aircraft landing there. I'll check every one that doesn't match ASDI and figure out who's who." Gavin chuckled. "The bad guys can't hide from me."

"You're awesome, Gav," Jack said.

"Tell me something I don't know."

"Pretty sure that's impossible."

Gavin gave a satisfied snort. "What's your tail number?"

"November, two, six, Lima, Charlie."

"Got it. I'll keep an eye on activity at Lux Airport. When it takes off we'll track it, whether they try to go ghost or not."

Just then, Jack's phone buzzed in his hand. He looked down and saw it was Ysabel calling. "Sorry, Gavin, I'd better take this. Keep me posted on the plane."

"Sure, Ryan. Tell her we all said hi." Gavin hung up.

Ryan shook his head and laughed, embarrassed that Gavin had seen through him so easily, but appreciative of the man's powers of deduction all the same. Quickly he switched to the incoming call. "Hey, there. How are you?"

"I'm great. Better than great, actually."

"Really? Why's that?"

"I finished early. Got the info from the last art gallery this morning."

"That *is* great. Did you run into any problems?"

"Everything went fine. You should hire me, I'm pretty good at this."

Jack laughed. "You are *very* good. Hey, since you're done a day early, why don't you try to get on a flight tonight? I just finished for the day. I can meet you at the airport and then we can —"

"I'm way ahead of you, Jack."

Jack cocked his head and slowed. A grin grew on his face. "You're already here, aren't you?"

Ysabel laughed. "Guilty. Hope that's okay."

"Okay? It's the best news I've had since I left Rome."

"I wanted to call you and not just barge into your apartment. No offense, but I know how jumpy you were last week."

Jack smiled wider, started walking along the Grand Rue again; he felt his feet pick up the pace automatically; he couldn't wait to see her.

"I'll be home in ten minutes." There was a long pause, and this surprised him. "Ysabel? Did we get cut off?"

"You're not at your apartment right now?"

"Not yet. Won't be long." After another pause on the other end he asked, "What's wrong?"

"Nothing. It's just . . . your doorman said you were home and I should go right on up. I'm standing outside your place now. I guess he was mistaken."

Jack slowed a little. "You must have the wrong building. What's the address?"

"It's the address you gave me. Five Place de Clairefontaine. Apartment Four E."

Jack Ryan, Jr., broke into a sprint. He tore down the middle of the pedestrian street as fast as his legs would take him. As he darted around the afternoon foot traffic, a sense of dread grew in the pit of his stomach.

Ysabel *was* in his building, but his building did not have a doorman.

30

As Jack ran he kept the phone to his ear and forced himself to keep his voice calm. "Listen carefully. I want you to step away from my apartment, but do *not* go back into the stairwell or the elevator. Just stand there, hang up, and call 112. That's local emergency services. Stay on the phone with them till I get there."

"What is it? What's wrong, Jack?"

"Tell them you are being mugged."

"Why would I do that? There is no one up here in the hall but me. What's going —"

Before Jack could respond he heard a scream from Ysabel, and the phone clanged to the ground.

"Shit!" He ran as fast as he could, pushed aside pedestrians in his way, leapt over a bum lying on the corner of Grand Rue and Rue des Capucins. As he sprinted he dialed 112, the phone rang three times, and then it was answered in German. He told the operator he needed the police at his address, and he recited it slowly. He described the situation, a woman had just been attacked, but when they asked for more information, he just hung up. He wanted to free up his hands to sprint — he needed two free hands more than they needed any more information from him.

From his first day here in Luxembourg Jack had noticed how few police he saw around on the streets. Other than the occasional squad cars driving by at speed on the main streets and a few bored patrolmen at the train station, he had not encountered much law enforcement at all. That had been a benefit to his operation, of course — no one doing surveillance work likes to worry about roaming law enforcement bumping up against their operation — but now he wished like hell this little burg were crawling with cops.

Instead he sprinted through the middle of the town square, the Place Guillaume II, then made a hard right onto the Rue du Fossé. The occasional tourist glanced at the well-dressed businessman running as if his life depended on it, but his actions didn't cause any alarm.

He slowed quickly right before he entered the pedestrian square in front of his apartment building, then he walked at a normal pace toward the front door. As he did so his eyes scanned the square, looking for any signs of trouble.

It didn't take him long to see an unmarked

panel truck parked in a fire lane on the far side of the little square. A man stood next to the driver's-side door smoking a cigarette, and when Jack focused on him he turned away.

Jack stepped up to his building and reached for the door, but to his surprise a man in a suit and tie stepped out through the door and held it open for him. He was young, in his twenties, with a dark complexion and broad shoulders. He smiled at Ryan, but Jack saw the recognition on the man's face.

Jack smiled back as he passed by. *"Merci beaucoup."*

"Avec plaisir, monsieur," the man said. He had an accent, but it didn't sound French to Jack.

Just as he passed through the door, with the fake doorman right on his heels, Jack quickly scanned the tiny lobby, looking for anyone else. As he suspected, this man was serving as a lookout and there was no one else down here, but Jack was certain there were men in and around his place.

He barely broke stride as he headed toward the elevator. Taking three steps into the lobby, he felt the continued presence of the "doorman" close on his heels.

Jack spun and reached out with his left hand, grabbed the man's necktie, and yanked him along with his spin. The man had his right hand on the grip of a pistol tucked in

346

his belt under his jacket. Ryan grabbed the man's wrist and then pivoted on his feet to his left. As he did so he brought his right elbow up, using the spin and all the muscles in his back and shoulder for added velocity.

His elbow connected with the man's face, snapping his head back and dazing him, and Jack shook the man's wrist as he fell, freeing the pistol from his grasp. It fell to the floor with a thud and bounced on the carpet.

Ryan had disarmed the man, but he didn't have control of the situation yet. He threw another punch, following his right elbow with a powerful left jab, again into the man's face. The man started to fall onto his back, but Jack leapt at him, spun his weak and dazed body around, and put him in a vicious choke-hold.

The fake doorman couldn't get his hands behind him, so tight was the hold, and the man's knees gave out fully. Jack went down with the man, slamming him onto the ground.

Into his ear, Jack said, "How many? How many men?"

The man did not answer, so Jack released the hold, leapt off the man, and launched toward the pistol on the floor. It was a CZ Omega nine-millimeter. Jack wasn't that familiar with it, but it operated like most other pistols. He found the external safety and flipped it off, then racked the slide just to make certain there was a bullet in the chamber. A cartridge arced high and dropped to the carpet, leaving fifteen more in the weapon, assuming the fake doorman had his gun fully loaded.

He pointed it at the man. "Last chance. How many?"

The man slowly raised his hands, rolled up to his knees, and then cleared his throat.

He pinched his thumb and forefinger together. Jack noticed this, but he didn't understand what it meant, until the man shouted, *"On imeyet svoy pistolet!"*

Jack realized the man had a tiny push-to-talk button in his hand, probably wired through the arm of his suit coat, and although he couldn't understand what he was saying, he assumed the man just transmitted to his confederate or confederates upstairs that Jack had his gun. Jack rushed up to him quickly, whipped the heavy pistol across his body, and struck the man across the side of his head, steel against skin and bone. Blood spilled onto the carpet as a massive wound opened on the man's temple, and he dropped down into the blood, wholly unconscious.

Jack was running to the elevator before the man hit the ground, and he saw the car was open at the lobby. He reached into the car and pressed the button for the fourth floor, but he did not enter.

As the car headed up, Jack ran for the stairs.

Time was his enemy now; every second worked against him, and against Ysabel.

Andrei Limonov stepped into the shower in his seventh-floor suite at the Meliá Luxembourg. He'd spent the day working in his room, although mostly he just sat around and waited.

He had come to Luxembourg to meet with Guy Frieden because Limonov knew Frieden had worked on a deal with a man in the Caribbean who was extremely choosy about who he worked with. Normally, in the world of international finance a man in charge of the amount of money Limonov now controlled would have no problem arranging meetings on his own, but this was a special situation, and Limonov had been unable to get a response from the man in the Caribbean on his own.

Frieden seemed agreeable enough about helping Limonov make contact. He promised three days earlier he would call the man immediately and set up the introduction, but in those three days he'd come back only with apologies. Apparently, his contact had been reticent about taking on new clients.

Limonov was annoyed, but he knew business relationships sometimes took time. Kozlov, on the other hand, was livid about the delay. He'd begun to do his own research on the man Limonov sought, and made his own arrangements to force the meeting. Limonov wasn't happy about this, of course, but Vlad Kozlov had been ordered by Valeri Volodin to keep the wheels of this operation turning, and there was nothing Andrei Limonov could do to put him off his mission.

Limonov had wanted to return to London to wait for the go-ahead to fly to the Caribbean, but Kozlov had insisted they wait in Luxembourg until the meeting was arranged, because if the meeting could *not* be arranged, Kozlov insisted he could simply go back to Frieden's office and encourage the attorney to be more persuasive.

Fortunately for all parties involved, Guy Frieden had called this afternoon with the news that the mysterious man in the Caribbean had agreed to meet the two Russians in twenty-four hours' time. Limonov and Kozlov would fly out this evening, so Limonov wanted a long shower before the all-night flight across the Atlantic.

As he showered he thought about his trip. This was the big moment, the step in the process where money would actually begin leaving Volodin's accounts and then disappearing, where it would exist in the ether before solidifying again in new accounts already set up by Limonov.

Limonov shuddered, thinking about the weeks to come. And then he smiled. They might be fraught with stress, but at least they would be spent in paradise.

He turned off the water and had just stepped out of his shower when he heard the door to his room open. He grabbed a towel and wrapped it around himself quickly, stuck his head out of the bathroom, and found Vlad Kozlov rushing across the suite toward him.

"What the *fuck,* Kozlov? Who gives you the right to barge into my room?"

Limonov could see the worry on the older Russian's face.

Kozlov said, "We have a problem."

"What problem?"

"Jack Ryan."

Limonov just stared at the other Russian. "President Ryan is everyone's problem."

"Not the President. His son."

"He has a son? What about him?"

"Jack Ryan, Jr., works for a private equity company in the USA, Hendley Associates. He and a colleague, a woman, were running around Rome last week, looking into a sale of art Guy Frieden was handling for Misha Grankin."

"Okay."

"Grankin's men sent local contract hires to get better photos of the woman, and through her they found Ryan, but then Ryan disappeared after confronting the surveillance on him."

Limonov said, "He doesn't sound like any private equity manager I know."

"Me either. They kept a tail on the girl, nothing happened for several days, but at noon today she went to the airport in Rome and boarded a flight here. They had a man in a cab when she came through arrivals. He picked her up and she gave him an address. They were waiting for her when the cab arrived. It was *Ryan's* apartment. He's been here in Luxembourg."

"Here?" Limonov did not understand the significance, and Kozlov could read it on his face.

"Grankin's office knows I'm here. They don't know what I'm doing, but they contacted me to warn me to get out of town. The men are waiting for Ryan to get back. I don't know what they will do to him, but we don't want to be anywhere around when it happens."

Limonov still missed the point Kozlov was trying to make. He said, "Grankin can't know we are meeting with Frieden."

"They *don't* know, damn it! But what if Ryan *does*? If he was looking into Frieden in Rome, and now he's here . . ."

Limonov got it now. "He could have surveillance on Frieden here."

"Which would mean he has seen us. Twice." Kozlov grabbed Limonov's underwear and pants off the bed and threw them to him. "You and I need to get to the aircraft. We are leaving tonight. Grankin's people are going

352

after Ryan as we speak. Move, man!"

Jack Ryan, Jr., stood on the fourth-floor landing, listening to the sounds in the hallway. He had beaten the elevator car up, this he knew when he heard the chime announcing its arrival. The elevator was only five feet from the stairwell door, so he waited to hear the doors open, then he swung out, the CZ pistol aimed forward, but close to his body so no one standing there could get a hand on it.

The hallway was dark; someone had removed the bulbs from the sconces along the wall. In the dim he saw two men wearing blue jeans and warm-up jackets in the hallway; both had weapons pointed toward the elevator. One man was crouched, facing away from Ryan, and the other was just stepping inside the car to look around.

Ryan took the first man from behind, striking straight down on the back of his neck with the grip of the heavy pistol. The man crashed, dazed, to the carpeted flooring without so much as a grunt, but there was no hiding what had just happened from the other man, because the sound of the impact of steel on bone had been loud enough to echo throughout the hall.

The man in the elevator reached out with his pistol, pointed it into the hallway without looking. Jack found himself staring down the barrel of a gun.

He dove flat for the floor just as the pistol cracked and the flash from the barrel illuminated the scene.

Jack fired back, through the wall of the hallway and into the elevator. He knew his rounds would be inaccurate and less potent after going through the wall of the hallway and the wall of the elevator car, but he also felt confident the nine-millimeter rounds from the CZ would penetrate. He fired over and over, desperate to suppress the threat there so he could get to Ysabel, who he assumed now was in his apartment, being held by others.

After seven shots through the wall, Jack heard a voice cry out inside the elevator. He stayed low, crawled with one hand and both knees along the hallway, keeping the weapon pointed at the elevator as he closed on the danger. Unsure whether the man in the elevator was trying to trick him with his continued moans.

Inside the car he found a middle-aged bearded man in coveralls, an earpiece in his ear. Blood poured from his groin area, pooled around him. He'd dropped his gun — it lay in the dark red — and he pressed hard against the wound.

He looked up at Ryan with resigned, fatalistic eyes.

Ryan climbed to his feet now, stuck his foot in the elevator to keep the doors from closing, switched his gun to his left hand, and aimed it at the door to his apartment, just ten feet away. Looking at the wounded man on the floor of the elevator car, he asked, "*Combien?* How many?"

The man replied in English with a heavy accent. "Eat shit and die, Ryan."

Jack reached a foot out and dragged the pistol back out of the car, through the blood. He kicked it behind him in the hallway. He reached down and pulled the man's earpiece and radio set out of his coveralls. Then he pressed the button for the ground floor.

The car closed and descended.

Ryan looked back at the other man on the floor. He was coming to, but slowly.

Jack stepped forward, sent a massive front kick into the man's face, and dropped him back down and out. On top of this, Jack knew he'd broken the man's nose and given him whiplash that would render him immobile for days, if not weeks.

Jack turned for the door to his apartment, and he fought every urge to forget his trade-craft and barrel through at top speed. He knew Ysabel was in there, and he seriously doubted she was alone.

He felt the latch and realized the door was unlocked, so he went flat on the floor, lying on his left shoulder. He switched his pistol to his left hand, used his right to unlatch the door above him, then quickly switched the gun back again to his dominant hand. With a quick breath to ready himself, he shoved the door open with his left hand, holding it in place so it didn't bounce back on him.

His living room was in front of him. He saw no one there, but a floor lamp lay across the ground and the glass coffee table was shattered as if someone had fallen through it.

Jack rolled up to his knees but stayed as low as possible. He crept into the room, keeping his gun arm pivoting back and forth between the two exits in front of him. The kitchen was on the right, and the hall to the bedroom and bathroom was on his left.

He cleared the kitchen first, and what he saw here made him recoil in horror. Blood on the floor, smeared on the wall at knee height. Ysabel's luggage lay open and strewn about the room. The room was empty, so he turned back out and headed for his bedroom.

His ears were tuned to hear any sound in the apartment, but it was deathly quiet. In the distance he detected some movement in the hallway, but quickly he heard the sounds of neighbors talking to one another, screaming at the sight of the unconscious man and the guns lying about. He knew he'd have civilians on him in moments, and police here shortly after that, but his only focus now was on getting Ysabel away from any danger.

Jack cleared the bathroom with his pistol, then lowered his body and pivoted into the bedroom.

He saw her hair first, down on the floor and matted on the far side of the king-sized bed. Behind it, a bloody handprint streaked the wall next to an open window.

"Oh, *God,* no," he whispered.

31

"Ysabel?" He retained the presence of mind to keep his gun on the blind corner, and he moved carefully over toward the large walk-in closet, training his weapon inside to make sure it was empty.

He passed over Ysabel's body without allowing himself to focus on it yet as he moved to the window. He looked outside at a fire escape, trained the CZ pistol up toward the roof and then down to the street.

Three men ran across the little cobblestoned square in front of his apartment building and jumped into the back of the panel truck he saw earlier, just as a pair of police cars rolled onto Place de Clairefontaine.

Ryan tossed the gun under the bed and then ran to Ysabel's lifeless body, sliding across the polished hardwood floor on his knees for the last several feet. Cradling her limp head in his hands, he felt wetness in her hair. He knew it was blood; he didn't have to look.

"Ysabel?"

He started to lean down to listen for a heartbeat, fearing the worst, but just as his ear rested on her chest she coughed, weakly.

Her eyes remained shut and her breathing remained shallow.

Jack shouted loud enough to be heard all over the floor of the building in both French and German. *"Aidez-moi! Hilf mir! Ambulance! Krankenwagen!"*

Ryan shoved his hand into the side pocket of his blazer and breathed a prayer of thanks that he found what he was looking for.

John Clark had demanded of his team that they never went anywhere without their personal trauma kit, a tiny package of items designed by Clark and Chavez. Jack and Dom hated the things; while Clark touted them as being tiny, as far as the two rather fashionable men in their early thirties were concerned, they weren't nearly small enough. Dom derisively referred to the PTK as his "diaper bag," and Jack called it "Clark's boo-boo pouch."

After listening to the two younger members of his team bitch long enough, Chavez came up with the idea to have the kit items taken out of their pouch and put in plastic bags, which could then be vacuum-sealed, and this made them just larger than two decks of cards stacked on top of each other. They would just fit in the front pocket of a pair of pants now, and Jack and Dom stopped their complaining. It was still a hassle to carry a med kit twenty-four hours a day, even when they weren't in the middle of a mission, but both men knew when to pick their battles, so they kept the packets on them at all times.

Now Ryan thanked God that he'd been forced into carrying the damn thing, and he tore the PTK open with his teeth and dumped the contents onto the floor next to Ysabel. He tossed the tourniquet to the side; she wasn't hemorrhaging from an appendage, although she was bleeding badly from several head and neck wounds.

He used one of the pressure bandages on her forehead and another on a gash on her neck that looked like a deep puncture wound. While covering the bloody cut, he realized she'd come a half-inch from having her carotid artery severed by a knife's blade.

He used gauze and electrical tape from the kit to stanch the bleeding on her upper-left arm and the bridge of her nose.

He knew the paramedics would likely just remove the majority of his bandaging and apply their own dressings, because they would want to evaluate the wounds. But Jack didn't care. He had no idea how much blood Ysabel could lose between now and when they'd get here, so stopping the bleeding and keeping her stable were paramount.

With cuts and bruises as bad as he could

see, he feared she might have many broken bones and even damage to her organs. He had no idea if she was bleeding internally. He'd done good work on the injuries he could see, but he had no idea if he'd done enough to save her life.

Her face was pale under the smeared blood and the gray and purple contusions.

After stabilizing her head, he moved her arms onto her lap. While doing so he noticed all the defensive wounds on her hands. There were cuts on her palms and fingers. In addition to this, her knuckles looked like she'd punched one of her attackers, and hard.

"Good girl," he whispered, his voice cracking with emotion as he did so.

From behind he heard a man's voice, speaking English. "Who are you?"

Jack spun around quickly, his right hand moving closer to the gun hidden under the bed.

A heavyset man in his early twenties stood in the doorway to the hall, shock on his face. His hands were empty.

Jack slipped his hand away from the pistol. "I live here. Who are *you*?"

"I am a neighbor."

"Call an ambulance."

"Four C has already called. The ambulance is coming."

Jack had no idea who this guy was, but he needed the help right now. "Did you see who did this?"

"No. I only just arrived."

Jack felt the man staring at him.

"You are husband? Her husband?"

"No." He thought while he worked on her arm. "I am her friend. I just got here myself."

The young man relaxed a little; he'd been scared by the possibility he'd stumbled onto some sort of a domestic fight, and the man who now treated the woman had just minutes ago beaten the woman. This made Jack confident the man had not been involved in the attack himself, although this guy was too portly to fit in with the three other members of the crew Jack had already encountered.

The neighbor asked, "Who did this?"

Jack shook his head while he frantically treated her. He had the presence of mind to answer the man carefully. He knew the police would be here soon, and they would take statements. What he said to this neighbor could mean the difference between the cops letting him leave Luxembourg or throwing him behind bars. "I don't know. She comes from a political family back home. There had been some threats."

The young man nodded again, and he asked no more questions.

Other neighbors entered soon after, and the police made it up to the fourth floor not long after that. They assured Jack the ambulance was on its way.

Ryan knew he needed to call Clark or Gerry and let them know what had happened, but he had no idea if Ysabel was going to survive the next few minutes. There was no way he was going to make a phone call until she was stabilized. Instead, he just huddled over her, rubbed her hand and her forehead with a wet compress one of the neighbors brought, and kept talking to her, telling her she would be fine.

The police let him stay with her, only because they didn't have a clue he'd just shot a man and severely injured two others in the building. As they tried to figure out what was going on, Jack hoped they didn't look under the bed and find the pistol he'd slid there. To reduce the chance of this even more, as he knelt behind the police, he pushed his left foot back, slid it under the bed, and shoved the gun further out of sight of anyone who wasn't specifically checking for something hidden there. They might find it eventually, but Jack was hoping he'd be long gone by then.

Ysabel's eyes opened a little, and they focused on his face. He soothed her with his words, again told her she would be okay, although he had no idea what sort of internal injuries she might have suffered.

She said, "I'm sorry, Jack. There were too many."

"Don't be sorry. You did great. You're going

to be fine, just rest."

But she wanted to talk. "The men . . ."

"The men? Yes? Do you know who they were? I couldn't identify the accents."

She just shook her head. "The one . . . the one in charge. The one who did this to me."

"Yes?"

Ysabel's voice cracked, and tears drained down the side of her face.

"Russian."

Jack felt the life drain out of him. *Russian.* He felt certain this had happened to her because of him. Because of his safe little operation in Western Europe, the one with the opportunity to roam art galleries during the day and enjoy nice restaurants at night.

"God damn," Ryan muttered under his breath. Looking at Ysabel's impossibly swollen face, the blood seeping through her bandages, her lip split and her eyes blackened, he knew this was all his fault.

Two paramedics pushed through the growing crowd in the apartment, then they all but knocked Ryan out of the way. He stood back against the wall by the bedside table.

They concentrated on stabilizing her neck, then they rolled her onto a backboard for transport.

Within three minutes of arriving in the apartment, the paramedics were yelling for the police to make a pathway through the dozen or so people standing around so they could get by and back down to their unit.

Jack stood to the side for most of this, but he helped clear out some space in the living room for Ysabel's stretcher to pass.

Jack started to walk out the door behind the paramedics and the stretcher, but one of the policemen stopped him. He said, "We'll take you to the hospital, but we have questions."

"Ask me on the way." Jack wanted to rush to be by Ysabel's side, but he also wanted a few minutes to think about his story.

"One moment first. Do you have identification?"

Ryan handed over his actual passport, because he was not traveling undercover here. The police officer looked it over quickly, showing no recognition of the name. "What is the woman's name?"

"Ysabel. Ysabel Kashani."

"American, as well?"

"No, Iranian."

The cop looked up at Ryan. After a moment he said, "This is your apartment?"

"I am renting it, just for a week or two. Did you find the men outside of the apartment?"

"The *men*? There was just one man. In the elevator."

Shit, thought Jack. The two less wounded goons managed to get out of the building before the police arrived. Still, at least they had picked up one of the men.

"How is he?"

"He's dead. Did you shoot him?"

"*Me?* No, of course not. I was on the phone with Ysabel when she was attacked. I raced over here and found the men outside. Then I found her." Jack could not have admitted shooting someone without getting detained for a long time. Even if he could convince them he'd taken a weapon from one of the attackers, he knew it would take longer to sort out than he wanted to spend as a guest of the Luxembourg police.

The police officer didn't seem to buy his story. "There are cameras down in the lobby and in the elevators. One on each floor. We'll see what happened."

Jack nodded, then said, "I think I'm going to be sick."

Two cops stood outside the bathroom while Jack stumbled in. They were obviously suspicious of him still, though not enough to search him.

In the bathroom he turned the water on, faked a few hacks, then he pulled out his phone and dialed a mobile number in Alexandria, Virginia. Jack held his breath, hoping the man who owned the phone would answer quickly.

To his relief, he heard a voice. "Gavin Biery."

Ryan hacked loudly again, then whispered, "It's Ryan. Listen carefully. Five Place de

Clairefontaine, I need the security cam footage of the last hour removed from the drive. You have five minutes, tops."

"How many things can I do for you at one time, Ryan? Hack this art gallery, hack this lawyer, tail this aircraft, erase these cameras. You don't think I have anything else going on?"

"I just killed a man. The police have me and they are about to watch the footage."

The pause was short. "Holy shit! I'm on it, Ryan." He hung up the phone.

Jack hung up as well, flushed the toilet, and left the bathroom.

There was a moment of confusion in the apartment while the police worked out who was going where and with whom, and men started to lock down the crime scene. Violent crime in Luxembourg was rare, rare enough that Jack saw the police weren't defaulting to any real standard procedure. There was a lot of talking and even a little arguing, all of it in German. Jack took advantage of the moment to go into the kitchen and get a glass of water, and while he did so he saw Ysabel's purse lying on the counter, its contents strewn all around it.

He ignored the contents and concentrated on the bag itself, began feeling around in the material quickly.

In ten seconds he found it, feeling a small, hard shape in the leather in a place where he could find no button or zipper. He pinched at the material for a moment more, then pulled out a one-inch-long pin with a small black head.

He knew what this was, and he knew how it got there.

32

By the time Jack's police minders got him to the hospital it had been worked out by the authorities that the man in their control was the son of the U.S. President. Jack explained he was in town working for his company, Hendley Associates, doing some forensic accounting on some potential acquisitions for the private equity firm. Ysabel was a friend who had just arrived for a visit, and she'd obviously stumbled onto a robbery in progress.

The police weren't sure about anything other than the fact that this crime made their tiny nation look bad, especially because of the high-profile friend of the victim.

The police immediately became deferential to him, but Jack imagined they would change their tune quickly if the handgun at the crime scene was found and dusted for prints, and he refused to give his up.

He wanted to be long gone by then.

Ysabel had been given an MRI to check

her head, neck, and torso for any internal injuries. Jack had only just arrived when a doctor came out of an exam room, introduced himself to Jack as a neurosurgeon, and told him that Ysabel was a lucky woman, considering all she'd been through, but she wasn't out of the woods just yet. A small fracture in a cervical vertebra meant she would need immediate surgery.

Jack went pale. "You are telling me she has a broken neck."

The doctor gave a sympathetic shrug. "It is something we can repair. There is no damage to her spinal cord." He patted Jack on the arm. "A one-level cervical fusion is an extremely common procedure. Trust us, Mr. Ryan, we will take good care of her."

Jack wasn't next of kin, and the doctors knew this. They were going ahead with the surgery despite any reservations he had. Jack just nodded distantly and sat back down, staring off into space.

He thought about everything he and Ysabel had experienced together over the past month. He felt sick with the thought that after the events in Dagestan that nearly killed them both, he had led her headlong into even more danger.

Ryan's mobile buzzed in his pocket, bringing him back to the present. He pulled it out distractedly, looked down, and saw the call coming in was from Clark. He launched out of the chair and began to walk away from Ysabel's room. "Please tell me Gavin got the camera feeds."

"He did. I just watched the entire event, including you taking out three hostiles. Obviously, I don't have the context I need to understand what the hell is happening over there."

"Neither do I, to tell you the truth."

"Are you secure now?"

"Yeah. I mean, I think so. Might have to slip the police at some point, but they don't seem too interested in me, considering. I don't think they have much of a plan to deal with a big gun battle around here. I get the feeling it never happens."

"How is Ysabel? I saw her removed on a stretcher."

"They say she'll live, but she's being taken in for surgery on her neck."

"Christ. I'm sorry, Jack."

"Yeah."

"Look, you need to take it from the top, tell me everything you know." He paused for a beat, then said, "And I need you to do it *right now.*"

Jack told him what had happened, and although he had no idea who was responsible, he let Clark know this looked like it could have been related to the work they were doing in Rome. He said, "It's obvious by the fact they were asking her about me that she wasn't the real target. I was."

Clark said, "Any idea how they found your place?"

Ryan said, "Yeah. They used Ysabel to find the location. I found a GPS tracker in her purse. It's the size of a pushpin. Top-flight tech."

"That doesn't sound Russian."

"No. It looks commercial, but top of the line."

"Do you know how it was planted?"

"Last week she told me a woman knocked over her purse in the bathroom, then helped her pick up all the contents. About a half-hour after that a man who was following me showed up in my apartment building."

As soon as Ryan said this, he winced, anticipating the admonitions to come.

Clark's voice rose and his tone lowered. "What man?"

"I should have called this in, John. I screwed up. It's just that he didn't —"

"*What man,* Ryan?"

"An Italian paparazzo tailed me in Rome. I thought I shook him, but he showed up back at the condo. I roughed him up a bit, thought he was a bad actor of some sort, but when he proved he was just a stupid photographer, and convinced me he'd been tipped off to me by a girl in a café who recognized me, I didn't think it was anything related to the op I was on. Just the occasional negative aspect of being Jack Ryan's son.

"Still, though, just to be safe, Ysabel and I left the condo immediately. She got a hotel down there to finish up our work in Rome, and I came up here to Lux City. I thought that was the end of it."

"Damn it, Jack! It is your job to call in contacts and compromises. Do you have any idea the danger that exposure put you in?"

"Yes . . . I mean, no, I didn't. It's pretty fucking clear now," Jack said darkly. His eyes shot back up the hall toward Ysabel's room. A pair of orderlies were rolling her unconscious body down the hall to surgery.

Clark asked, "Who was the photographer?"

"Salvatore."

"Salvatore *what*?"

"He just goes by one name."

Clark mumbled softly, "I hate him already."

"Tell me about it. I didn't trust the bastard, but we checked him out online, and he is a legit paparazzo . . . if such a thing exists. Anyway, I was satisfied he wasn't working with the Russians."

"But if it was the same GPS tracker that got him to your Rome condo that the attackers in Luxembourg used to track Ysabel, then obviously they are related."

"Yeah," Jack said. "As soon as she gets out of surgery and into a room here, I'm going back to Rome to get my hands on this Salvatore."

373

"No, Jack. You are not. You aren't going to be operating alone anymore. You need to get out of there."

"I need to protect Ysabel."

Clark ignored the comment. "I'll get Christine there now. I have associates from my days in Rainbow right over the border in France. I can put two tier-one shooters outside Ysabel's door when she comes out of recovery, and keep them there twenty-four/seven. That's more than you could do."

"I'm not leaving her side!"

"Look, Jack. She was attacked because she was *by* your side. You aren't going to help her with your proximity to her. You said it yourself: You were the target, not Ysabel. I know it feels wrong to leave her, but that's just exactly what you have to do."

The realization hit Ryan like an ax handle to the head. Yes, he knew she was attacked because of him, that was obvious. But now he recognized that not only could he not protect her, but the longer he stayed around her, attempting to do just that, the longer she was going to remain in mortal peril.

It took him half a minute to respond to Clark. "You're right."

"Good. You are coming home. Now. It will take the Gulfstream ten to twelve hours to get to you, and I want you gone before then, so get yourself on the first train out of Luxembourg, and then the first transatlantic back to the States. Don't use the main station. Too dangerous. Take a taxi to the burbs and board there."

Jack wanted to argue some more, but he knew Clark was exactly right about everything. He just said, "When I get home, I'm going to see what I can find on Salvatore. We might have other avenues of attack beyond just threats. He's a drug abuser. Heroin. Normally, that might be incriminating, although in his line of work I don't suppose anyone gives a damn what he does in his free time."

Clark said, "We'll also run this video through facial recog, see if we get some pings on the faces of these men who attacked you and Ysabel. The quality is shit, but we might get lucky."

Ryan got off the phone a minute later. He had a direction now, a plan to find the men responsible for what happened to Ysabel. He wouldn't leave the hospital till Christine arrived, but he knew that was just to make himself feel better.

Clark was right, Ysabel was in more danger when he was around.

33

Kaliningrad's Chernyakhovsk air base was blanketed by fog at five thirty a.m., but this was of no great concern to Captain Chipurin, the pilot of the Ilyushin Il-20M on the taxiway. He flew through the clouds all day long, after all, so taking off into thick, obscuring vapor was hardly an issue. Landing, on the other hand, required more skill, but Chipurin and his crew would not be landing for another eight hours, and that would be 800 kilometers away at Saint Petersburg, where the weather was predicted to be cold but clear.

The one thing that was a potential concern for Chipurin today, however, was the weather out over the Baltic Sea. Massive thunderstorms had developed overnight and moved northeast from Germany, and at sea level now there were reports of forty-mile-per-hour winds and twelve-foot waves. It was a typical Baltic autumn storm, lots of cells popping up then petering out, and other pilots in the area had reported that the tops of many of the cells rose above 40,000 feet. Chipurin knew this meant he'd have to be on the lookout for weather, even at his cruising altitude of 38,000 feet.

Upon gaining clearance from the control tower, the captain goosed his power levers forward slightly, turned the nose of the big, dull gray aircraft to face the length of runway 6, and then he pushed the levers all the way forward, sending full power to his four turboprop engines.

This aircraft wasn't based here in Kaliningrad — rather, its home was Chkalovskaya, near Moscow — but it had left for its reconnaissance flight of Sweden two days earlier, and halfway to its destination it had developed a problem with its electrical system. Chernyakhovsk had been the nearest friendly place to land, and as this was a spy plane, Chipurin very much preferred landing at friendly airports, lest he be stripped of his rank and thrown out of the military.

The electrical problem was fixed after a day, so this morning the Il-20M was again taking to the skies.

At five thirty-four a.m. it did just that. The controllers in the tower watched the plane lift off, fading quickly into the mist above their runway. Only the small red star on the vertical stabilizer was visible at fifty meters off the ground, and this too disappeared within a few seconds as the gray airship melded with the saturated air.

Of course the aircraft's flight path had been altered by the fact that it was beginning its day at a different airport than planned, but once Chipurin left Kaliningrad and got up to his cruising altitude he would merge with his original flight path and carry out his orders. This would take him northwest over the Baltic to Sweden's Gotland Island, which he would circle, just outside Swedish airspace, at an altitude of 20,000 feet. After this he would turn due north, flying along the Swedish coast, passing Stockholm out his portside window before performing a series of racetrack patterns in the Gulf of Bothnia between Sweden and Finland. Here the sensor operators in their seats behind Chipurin and his copilot would conduct tests on Swedish radar capabilities and listen in on military communications. After two hours of this, the big Ilyushin would leave the skies over the gulf and return to the Baltic Sea proper, heading east past Helsinki before descending over the Gulf of Finland to land finally in Levashovo air base, north of Saint Petersburg.

It was a routine electronic intelligence flight for Chipurin and his ten-person crew in most respects, other than the fact they were taking off in Kaliningrad and would have to change their route to avoid the storm cells.

Just after takeoff Chipurin turned off his

aircraft's transponder, the electronic signaling device that emits information to air traffic control and other nearby aircraft giving its location and identity. This meant the military turbo prop was essentially invisible to other aircraft, as its radar signature would be all but lost in the clutter from the storms around. Nor would Chipurin make or respond to radio communications with civilian air traffic control or non-Russian military aircraft.

This was a military reconnaissance flight, after all; Captain Chipurin did not take to the skies to make friends.

There was no international law that said military aircraft needed to use transponders, follow standard routes used for civilian traffic, or communicate with air traffic control. But despite the lack of a mandate to do so, flying without a transponder was inherently dangerous.

Civilian aircraft do have onboard radar, but contrary to much public perception, these are not designed to identify other aircraft in the sky. They are instead used for weather and, at low altitude, terrain, but an aircraft in the sky on an onboard radar would appear as a tiny speck, if at all. Tiny specks could also represent rain, birds, or false echoes of nothing that the radar displayed in error.

Commercial aircraft do carry onboard traffic avoidance systems, but these simply collect the transponder codes from aircraft in the area that choose to broadcast them, and show the location and heading of these flights to the pilot.

If a plane does not use its transponder and if the aircraft controller looking at his radar just sees a vague, intermittent, primary signal on his screen, there is a chance, a good chance, that another pilot in the area would never know there was another big, fast-moving, and heavy mass racing along nearby unless he looked out his window and saw it.

And pilots, as a rule, hated such surprises.

But Chipurin thought nothing of this. He was just following his standard procedure for an electronic intelligence reconnaissance flight. Russian ELINT planes virtually always operated in international airspace without using their transponders. Chipurin and his copilot had been doing this sort of thing in steady rotation for several months, and they had been flying for several years, so they had become masters at both getting near and staying clear of other planes in the skies.

In today's weather there was no way the aircraft controller watching over this section of the Baltic could relay every primary signal to every pilot he was responsible for. Chipurin knew this, but he just told himself he'd stay out of known aviation lanes, he'd avoid the most congested airspace around Stockholm and Helsinki, and he'd keep his eyes sharp.

The first hour of the flight went by quickly. While the captain and his copilot negotiated the weather, altering their path to proceed directly toward Gotland Island as opposed to their original planned-on northwesterly course near Lithuania, the men and women in back calibrated equipment and began listening in on civilian maritime traffic to check audio levels.

Around Gotland, Chipurin ignored the radio calls from the Swedes like he always did when flying near his target's airspace. He normally didn't like being noticed up here, but on a day like today, when the weather on so much of their flight path was shit, he was secretly pleased to see that some Swedish ATC had his eyes in his scope.

Just after eight-thirty a.m., they finished what they assumed would be the most difficult part of their day. The area around Stockholm was thick with both heavy thunderstorms and air traffic, but the Il-20M had avoided the commercial jet routes, giving them an even wider berth than normal in case other pilots had decided to deviate from the lanes due to the weather.

This had gone well. Both the pilot and the copilot knew they now had a few easy hours of racetrack patterns before things got tight again as they passed Helsinki on the way to Saint Petersburg, but the weather there would not be as much of a factor, so as far as Chipurin was concerned the rest of the day would be a breeze.

He did, however, have to get around the last of the multicell cluster thunderstorm in the middle of the Baltic, so he changed course to a heading of 353 degrees, turning slightly back toward Sweden.

Doing this helped him avoid the heavy cell, but he did not avoid moving through an updraft that seemed to develop around him on the radar. Storms like this propagated new cells with regularity, so he wasn't concerned, and it wasn't particularly strong yet. The Il-20M encountered moderate turbulence, but Chipurin knew it would not be an issue for either the passengers or the equipment, so he decided to just climb a few thousand feet to see if he could find his way out of the clouds.

During a surprisingly heavy buffet the copilot dropped his clipboard, sending dozens of pages onto the floor of the cockpit. The first officer left his seat to pick up several of the pages, but both the pilot and copilot simultaneously turned to help, because pages had spilled all around them. It took only a few seconds before the pilot was back up and gazing at the gray covering his windshield.

Chipurin said, "Where is the top of this shit?"

The copilot said, "Could be sixty thousand. You want to try a new heading?"

Chipurin looked at his radar and saw returns all around him.

"No. We'll go over it or through it." Chipurin kept scanning out his windscreen, looking for blue sky. Suddenly they broke out of the storm and began racing over the clouds, giving visual reference to the plane's speed. When this happened it always felt to the captain like he was flying over a massive snowy field at low level, and he enjoyed the sensation. He rode along here for just a moment, then reached forward to change to a steeper climb that would take them up to 34,000 feet.

Out of his left eye Chipurin detected movement, something outside his windscreen in the clouds. He turned his head toward the motion at his ten-o'clock position, focused on the spot less than a half-mile away, and he saw a puff of white emerge from the top of one of the gray storm clouds like a flower's bloom. Suddenly, in the middle of the puff, a large white aircraft with a blue vertical stabilizer appeared, just ahead and below the Il-20M, rising out of the clouds in a shallow climb.

"Tchyo za ga lima?" What the fuck?

It was an Airbus A330, a Swedish Airlines commercial flight. Chipurin recognized the aircraft and its distinctive markings. It did not belong right in front of the Ilyushin, there was no reason for it to be where it was, at this altitude, but Chipurin knew he needed to initiate evasive maneuvers because the Airbus was climbing on a heading that would take it up and through his starboard wing if he did not act immediately.

He turned the yoke hard to his left and pulled it back, raising his nose and banking hard to port.

This would have worked, sending the A330 just below his starboard wing, had the pilot of the Swedish airliner not also pulled up his own nose and executed a turn to starboard in response to the impending collision.

Chipurin realized both planes were converging, so he jammed the yoke to the right now and shoved it forward, trying to somehow push himself below the ascending Airbus.

But there was not enough time. His countermovement merely had the effect of correcting the climb and the bank to port, and this ensured his Ilyushin was flying straight and level when the massive A330 drove belly-first into the rear section of the Russian electronic intelligence flight at a converging speed of more than seven hundred knots.

Mercifully for those on board the Swedish Airlines Airbus, the deaths of all came nearly instantaneously as the full center tank exploded just two seconds after slamming into the fuselage of the gray Russian spy plane.

But many of those on the Russian spy plane were not as lucky. Captain Chipurin was, at first, unaware he'd lost the tail of his aircraft. He frantically put on his emergency air supply and fought the unresponsive plane all the way down with his copilot, a futile three-minute-and-twenty-second attempt to fly the unflyable through the middle of the heavy storm.

The men and women in the main cabin had parachutes, but they were not wearing them, and the dying spiraling plane meant not one of them had a chance to do anything to save themselves. Instead, all they could do was whip around in their harnesses, strapped into their chairs, arms, legs, and heads flailing, screaming helplessly into a roaring wind. Most passed out within a minute, but a few managed to get their masks on, which did nothing for them but ensure that they suffered their terror longer than their more fortunate colleagues did.

Finally, Chipurin's broken craft slammed into the water at latitude 59.0404 and longitude 19.7576, near the middle of the Baltic Sea, well before the first bits of debris from the Swedish airliner began raining down on the water around.

None of them would ever know that Swedish Airlines flight 44, just twenty-five minutes after takeoff from Stockholm, had been given permission to deviate from its course by twenty degrees to avoid the new storm cell growing in front of it, but its request to climb out of the weather was delayed because of a Latvian cargo plane that had just been vectored into that altitude. When the final approval for flight 44's altitude change was approved by ATC, the Airbus pilot and his copilot had missed the transmission, delaying their ascent by more than two minutes before ATC noticed the error and repeated the transmission.

The deviation and the delay put the Airbus eleven miles south of its normal route and four thousand feet lower than its normal altitude, which would not have been an issue, if not for the Russian spy plane transiting the area without squawking its transponder.

Twenty-two minutes later, at three a.m. in Washington, D.C., a man residing at 1600 Pennsylvania Avenue was awakened and given the news. He did not go back to bed. Instead, he headed for his bathroom to shower, his closet to dress, and then began the familiar walk to his office.

34

The USS *James Greer* (DDG-102) was an Arleigh Burke–class guided missile destroyer assigned to the Sixth Fleet and based in Naples, but at the moment she sailed west through the Gulf of Finland in moderate seas.

She was two months into a four-month cruise, having already been to Gibraltar, Portugal, England, Germany, and Gdańsk, Poland, before sailing here, the northernmost point of her voyage. She left Helsinki first thing this morning after a three-day port visit, and just prior to that she had been participating in passing exercises with the Finnish Navy's fast attack craft *Tornio* and a pair of ships from the Finnish Coast Guard. PAS-SEX were joint drills between the ships from the two nations involving simulated air attacks, tactical maneuvering, and bridge-to-bridge communications set up around increasing coordination between the U.S. and allied ships that might find themselves working with the U.S. in a real fight.

The drills had gone well, and when they were finished the sailors and officers on the *Greer* enjoyed a performance of the Finnish Naval Marching Band, which was nice, plus thirty-six hours of liberty in the bars and restaurants of Helsinki, which was better. Not all the sailors and officers were granted shore leave, of course, but enough did to where the executive officer of the ship, Lieutenant Commander Phil Kincaid, had wandered the passageways for several minutes late the previous evening before encountering another living soul.

The Baltic PASSEX with Finland had been exciting, to a degree, but the 383 officers and crew on board the *James Greer* hadn't joined the Navy to drill and listen to a Finnish marching band. They had joined to serve the United States, to project its interests and values around the world and to keep the peace, even if keeping the peace meant going to war.

Guided missile destroyers were known as the most versatile warships in the Navy. Larger than frigates but smaller than cruisers, they were capable of antiair, antisurface, and antisubmarine warfare, and they used the latest technology in the furtherance of each task. The *Arleigh Burke* was the first ship in the newest class of destroyers, designed around the Aegis Combat System. Commissioned in 1991, the class had gone through several flights of modernization over the past twenty-five years, and the *James Greer* was one of the most modern in the Navy's sixty-four-ship inventory.

Destroyers are so named because they are descendants of a class of ships known as torpedo-boat destroyers. Torpedo boats are a thing of the past, but torpedoes themselves are still a threat to surface warfare. They are now normally fired from submarines, of course, which is why destroyers are equipped with the most advanced antisubmarine warfare capabilities known to man.

The *James Greer* was capable of antiair and antisurface missions as well, but there were no real surface threats to speak of in the area. Russia's Baltic Fleet had several small corvettes and old frigates in port in Kaliningrad, but no surface ship captain would steam out to do battle with an Aegis-equipped guided missile destroyer unless either he was part of a large armada or he was insane.

There were air threats around here; the Russians had been throwing a lot of aircraft in the theater to spy on, intimidate, and essentially piss off all the other nations that sailed on or flew over the Baltic, but the real menace to the *James Greer* in these waters would come from below the waves. There were a pair of upgraded Kilos in the Baltic Fleet, and while the vessels were not the newest Russian technology, they were quiet diesel subs, they were deadly, and, most important of all, their commanders and crew knew these waters better than anyone.

It was for these reasons that the men and women on board the *Greer* took their jobs exceptionally seriously. For the last few weeks of their cruise they had been here in the Baltic Sea, so they were in the middle of Russia's turf, and they had even been buzzed by two Russian Su-27 interceptors two weeks earlier while north of Poland.

The captain of the *James Greer* was not a captain in rank, he was a commander. Commander Scott Hagen had been in the Navy since the Academy, he was forty-three now, and his wife told her friends he was going to stay in until the Navy sent armed men to drag him off base for sticking around past retirement age.

He was a lifer.

Hagen sat behind his desk in his wardroom at 1100 hours, scanning through some reports from his acoustical intelligence officer. He heard movement outside in the passageway, and then his XO rapped gently on his door before leaning in. "Message for you from the N3."

Hagen sighed in frustration. He'd been hoping this message wouldn't come. "Bring it in, although I have a feeling I know what it says."

Kincaid entered the wardroom and handed

the single page over to his captain without comment. Both men had seen the news about the missing plane over the Baltic late this morning. They had discussed the chance that they would be contacted by the Sixth Fleet's director of operations (N3) and ordered into service. Hagen had bet they wouldn't get that order. They were half a day away from the location of the crash, so they wouldn't be involved in any real rescue, and due to the increased tension in the Baltic region, he felt the Navy would want to keep one of its most powerful weapons in the area, ready to employ quickly if shots were fired.

But the XO took the other side of the bet. He couldn't imagine the U.S. Navy missing out on the PR boon of taking part in such a high-profile public interest mission.

Hagen nodded as he read, then summarized the order for Lieutenant Commander Kincaid. "You called it, XO."

A minute later, Commander Hagen wore a headset and patched himself into 1-MC, the shipboard PA system. He punched the transmit button, sending his voice throughout virtually every space on the ship. "This is the captain speaking. All hands give me your attention for a minute.

"Some of you might not be aware that at around oh-eight-thirty Zulu time today, approximately two and a half hours ago, a Swedish passenger jet traveling from Stockholm en route to Dubai collided with a Russian military surveillance aircraft over the Baltic Sea, roughly one hundred ten nautical miles from our position. We have been ordered to make best possible speed toward the crash of Swedish Air 44 and assist with search-and-recovery operations.

"This is going to be a grim job for all of us, to put it mildly, but it's damn important. We owe those victims our best work, whether we rescue anyone alive or only recover remains."

He stopped transmitting for a moment while he ordered his thoughts, then pushed the button again. "While we are in the process of this recovery, we cannot and we *will* not allow ourselves to lose focus of our larger mission here in the Baltic. The tension between the Russian Federation and other national actors in the area was plenty high before this incident. It will only get higher. We might find ourselves called upon at any moment to . . . to respond to threats. The *James Greer* will suffer no loss of mission readiness while we are assisting in the recovery mission. None at all."

After he finished his address he put his comm set back in its cradle on the desk in his stateroom, then looked up at Phil Kincaid. "You know, XO, there's one thing about this mission that I really don't care for."

"That we're heading due west when Russia is due east?"

Hagen shook his head. "It's not that. No, I guess our politicians haven't noticed it just yet, but we are smack dab in the middle of a potential war zone, and we are operating in an AO that also contains naval combat forces of our adversary."

The XO nodded. He finished the thought. "And we're about to go to a fixed spot on the water and let everybody in the world, including the opposition in the area, know where we are."

"That's it. By the time we get on scene there will be zero chance for survivors, even if someone managed to live through a midair collision and impact with that cold water. So we'll be there to pick up wreckage and bodies. Yeah, it's important, but I sure as hell wish surface ships that *aren't going to be* called to fight the Russians in a shooting war would spend their time on victim recovery, while the *James Greer* stays a hell of a lot more low-profile. Once the bad guys know where we are, it's going to be hard to slip them if the time comes."

The XO just nodded.

Hagen shrugged and stood up, heading for the passageway. "Nobody is asking us, so let's head up to the bridge and get this ship hauling ass toward that well-publicized point in the middle of the ocean."

35

The most-watched news channel in Russia was Channel Seven, Novorossiya, or New Russia, and the most-watched program was *Evening News with Tatiana Molchanova.* The striking raven-haired broadcaster was not only the favorite television news personality in the nation, it was clear she was also the favorite of Russia's president. Volodin spoke to any journalist who managed to get a mike in front of him when he was out and about, but when he had either information or spin he wanted to deliver to the nation, he almost always went to the *Evening News* to sit live with Molchanova.

It had become such a routine that Tatiana had taken for granted that Valeri Volodin would come to her, but in the past six months things had changed. Yes, she still got exclusives with the president, but he no longer appeared in her studio — now she, and her production team, had to go to him.

Before the change in the arrangement

between interviewer and interviewee, there had been difficulties of a logistical nature every time the Kremlin called the *Evening News* and said Volodin was on his way for an on-camera interview, because rarely did the TV station have more than an hour or two to prepare for his arrival. But the producers, the technicians, and Molchanova herself looked back to those days fondly now, because these days, the arrangement was significantly more difficult for them.

Now a call would come to a senior producer from one of Volodin's trusted inner circle, and notification would be given that the president was requesting Molchanova and her crew to arrive either at his offices in the Kremlin or, and this had been the case exclusively in the past three months, at his personal residence in the suburbs.

Tonight was the fourth time the entire crew packed into a pair of helicopters and made the twenty-minute flight, landing on the lawn of a neighbor's property and then rolling equipment to the gate in the wall of Volodin's presidential residence. From here everyone was frisked and X-rayed before being loaded back into a van kept on the property for transporting deliveries up the hill to the main house. From the driveway they were led into a living room. Furniture was carefully moved, light stands were erected, audio and video equipment was plugged in and tested.

The satellite truck would pull up outside an hour after the helicopter arrived, and usually with only a half-hour or so to spare.

While the techs and producers worked together to assemble the set, Molchanova was led by one of Volodin's female attendants into a bathroom off the kitchen, and here she took care of her own makeup. While doing this she listened to one of her producers through her earpiece while he read her intro and the few questions they had prepared. Tonight, as was often the case, she demanded some changes.

The questions were softballs by design. The crew of the *Evening News* had no specific knowledge of why they had been summoned by the president, so they needed to have only a few general setup questions ready to get the ball rolling. But even in the simple prepared opening, Tatiana Molchanova thought the tone wasn't right.

She changed her opening because she had noticed a change in her president in the past three months or so. He seemed more defensive, more nervy and testy with her questions. Gone were the days of the easy sly smile and the subtle sexual tension she felt during the interviews. Now he was on guard, ready to take issue with the smallest point.

She knew her role — people joked that Channel Seven was "Volodin's Megaphone," after all — so she had never hit him particularly hard in her interviews, but now she wore kid gloves during their time together. And tonight, after the plane crash, she expected her president would be especially touchy.

At six-thirty Volodin entered the living room and strode past nearly two dozen attendants, inner-circle confidants, and Channel Seven employees on his way to the lighted set. He greeted Tatiana with a friendly kiss and a smile; outwardly, this looked much the same as it had for his entire presidency, but Tatiana could see a change in the look, feel a difference in his touch.

This used to be both business and pleasure for Volodin. Now it was all business.

He looked older to the reporter than he had the last time they saw each other, just a month earlier, at the opening of a new restaurant in central Moscow.

Volodin spoke first, because Volodin always spoke first. While she was still close in his grasp he said, "Miss Molchanova, you are looking more beautiful than ever." Her blush had been painted on, but she flitted her long eyelashes and looked down with a wide smile. She felt his attraction to her, though there used to be some actual urges behind the sixty-two-year-old man's words, and those seemed to have disappeared.

It was the stress of the job, she assumed.

"You are too kind, Mr. President."

She started to escort him to his chair, but he held her tight for a moment more. "You will ask me how I can ensure the safety of our sons and daughters serving in the military when traveling into Kaliningrad Oblast. Let's not get distracted by attention-grabbing headlines and salacious events. The main issue is Lithuania."

He had given her hints in the past, directions for the interview, so she was not surprised.

"Of course."

Nor was she surprised when he went further with his stage-managing of the interview.

"But not directly. We will come to it slowly. We'll deal with the accident in the Baltic first, then the attack on the train."

"Medlenno, da. Ya ponimayu." Slowly, yes. I understand.

"Khorosho," he replied with a thin smile. Good.

A producer wired the president with a microphone as he sat down, and then everyone sat awkwardly for a few moments, waiting to go live. Molchanova noticed Volodin fidgeting more than normal, but she averted her eyes, pretending to look down at the cards that held the same remarks and questions that would be broadcast on the teleprompter under the camera in seconds.

Mercifully, as far as she was concerned, they went live quickly. She sensed Volodin's fidgeting stop suddenly on her left as she began to read the opening that she'd demanded be softened to spare her any icy response from the president.

"Mr. President, thank you so much for agreeing to speak with us today, as I know this must be a busy time for you."

Volodin smiled. "It is my pleasure, but frankly, I have been busy since I first entered government service forty years ago. These days are consistent with what I have experienced for a long time."

"Let me begin by asking you your thoughts of this morning's apparent midair collision between a Russian aircraft and a Swedish aircraft."

Volodin nodded; he was ready with his spin. "Of course it goes without saying, I regret all loss of life in this incident. In this regard I am unlike President Jack Ryan of the United States, who quickly ran to the first lectern he could find with a microphone on it and passionately decried the deaths of two hundred ninety-eight people, omitting the eleven on the Russian military transport aircraft. I find it telling that the American President can be so flippant by conveniently forgetting about the deaths of Russians, whose lives clearly hold no value to him.

"I will also add that the Russian aircraft was flying a legal flight in international airspace over the Baltic Sea. It had every right to be where it was and do what it was doing. It was the Swedish flight that had gone astray, though the Western media will make no mention of this.

"As our great military has taken to international waters and international skies, the West has reacted with fear and anger, and they have resorted to reprisals. This has been coming for a long time, and I have predicted something just like this would occur.

"The unfortunate souls on the Swedish airliner were pawns in the West's game to pressure the Russian Federation to stay crouched and compliant within its own borders. The aircraft was sent off course by Swedish air traffic control under orders from the Swedish government, who in turn was taking its cues from the United States of America and Great Britain. It was their plan to create a provocative situation, a near miss, so they could use this as propaganda against Russia's legal military maneuvers around the world.

"I truly hope nothing like this ever happens again, but to ensure this, I call on the governments of the West to stop their aggressive behavior in peaceful international skies." He looked into the camera. "Russia rejects your detestable premise that we are not allowed to engage with the rest of planet earth. We have as much authority to go places and do things as the West does, and we will never surrender our right of self-determination to those who would keep all Russians boarded behind fences and walls."

And that was that. Molchanova saw a restlessness in Volodin's eyes and mannerisms that told her he was ready to move away from this subject.

She thumbed through her cards deftly, omitting some follow-up questions about the crash. Then she said, "Even before the accident of the two aircraft, Mr. President, there were other recent events, all in the Baltic region, that seem to have the world on edge."

Volodin held a finger up and quickly leaned forward, a blast of energy. Molchanova was used to his mannerisms, so she did not flinch the way many foreign journalists did when interviewing the Russian president. "You put it magnificently, Tatiana Sergeyevna. You said they 'seem' to be on edge. And I am sure the simple population of many of these countries are genuinely horrified by the quickening of events there, but I ask them all to take care and say to themselves . . . Does this seem natural? A plane crash in the Baltic Sea, an attack in Lithuania on a train, on a natural gas facility? All in the same month? No, of course there is nothing natural to this all. This is well orchestrated."

"By whom, Mr. President?"

"By the West. It is known by our intelligence services that the West feels their power waning over the nations that border the Russian Federation. A region we refer to as the 'near abroad.' Jack Ryan, the EU, NATO: They all want to surround Russia with their client states. Subservient governments who do the bidding of the cabal of countries who don't share Russia's strategic, economic, and national interests.

"The attack on the natural gas facility. Done by environmentalists? I am suspicious of this. The attack on the Russian military transportation train. Perpetrated by a little-known Polish paramilitary unit? I think this highly unlikely."

"If you reject the official findings, Mr. President, who do you think was involved?"

"We Russians can point fingers at specific groups, actors, and states, but we would do well to get away from this, because we have one adversary. The West. Whether these were the actions of the CIA, the British MI6, Central European groups working on the behalf of America, or anyone else hardly matters any longer. Russia is under threat from a broad coalition of aggressive, hostile nations. Our safety and security threaten them for some reason, our love for our country and our customs and our desire for prosperity only enrage them. I find it sad to say this, but the evidence is clear. They are, simply put, enemies of the Russian Federation."

Molchanova nodded thoughtfully and turned her head away from the president and back to the viewers at home, if only to read the next question on the teleprompter.

She said, "The United States has reacted with anger after claiming a Russian Borei-class ballistic missile submarine is now crossing the Atlantic Ocean toward its shores. Is there anything you would like to say to respond to the allegations?"

Volodin shrugged with an easy smile. "If you like, I'd be happy to respond." Molchanova marveled at how completely he'd been able to morph himself from the man beset with nervous energy he'd been moments before the camera turned on to the calm, clever, and supremely self-assured chief executive he appeared to be now.

When he did not, in fact, respond, Molchanova cleared her throat. "And what is your response, Mr. President?"

A wider smile. "Perhaps it is out there. Perhaps it is not."

"Do you mean a submarine in general or, like the Americans allege, the *Knyaz Oleg*?"

"The Americans should pat themselves on the back. They are correct in their determination that the *Knyaz Oleg* is fully operational and now part of Russia's Northern Fleet. Whether it is in the Atlantic, in the Pacific, or patrolling the waters on Jack Ryan's bathtub . . . this is something I will not reveal."

"Of course," Tatiana said, and she looked down at her next card.

"Unless you twist my arm," Volodin added.

Molchanova glanced back up. She was a little confused about what she should say next, but Volodin's testiness in some of their recent encounters was nowhere to be seen now, so she relaxed a little.

"Our viewers always appreciate your candor, when you are able to be candid, that is."

"I will be very candid. It is very possible that one of our newest, greatest, and technologically superior submarines is, at this moment, in international waters, operating peacefully and within all maritime and international norms and limits . . . in the backyard of the United States of America."

Volodin grinned.

Molchanova was stunned, and she struggled for both elucidation and closure of this topic. "If the Americans are correct that it is out there, on its way across the Atlantic, can you say what the purpose of such a mission would be?"

Volodin shrugged, leaned forward. *"Pokazuka."* Just for show. He reached out and touched Tatiana Molchanova's exposed knee, taking the hem of her skirt and pulling it down a little to cover it. It was an odd gesture, almost fatherly in a way that made it even creepier. Despite her years of experience, Molchanova was utterly taken aback. She struggled for something to say, but Volodin did not need her to say anything. He barely needed her in the room.

The audience was watching him, not her.

Molchanova remembered his direction to her and recovered quickly. "I wonder if you can tell the viewers, both here in Russia, as well as our large Russian-speaking audience all over the near abroad, how we can ensure the safety of our young service people who are stationed in the enclave of Kaliningrad Oblast, in light of the attack on the troop transport train passing through Vilnius last week?"

She saw from his look at her that she had pleased him by asking this question at this time, and she felt a wash of relief come over her.

He said, "I like you very much, Miss Molchanova, so I will use the opportunity of your news program tonight to make an announcement that I would normally make from my desk at the Kremlin. It is *that* important."

She just nodded, urging him on.

"Our prosecutor general's office has been loyally going through old cases for a number of years now, at my direction. Cases of theft, I am speaking of. I have long been concerned about things that may have been stolen from the Russian people — from your viewers, in fact."

Molchanova was good, but she wasn't used to working without a net. She had no idea what the hell the president was talking about now. Criminal matters in Russia?

405

"What . . . what things?"

"In the latter days of the Soviet Union, decrees and decisions were made without respect to the Russian people. One must distinguish Russia, the nation, from the Soviet Union, the amalgamation of nations."

"*Da,*" Molchanova replied, only because Volodin looked at her in a way that told her a reply was demanded of her.

He continued. "The Baltic is an interesting case, I have always thought. This was land the Soviet Union won from the Nazis, on the backs of the Russian people. Russia bore the brunt of that war. *Russia.* Despite the fact the Soviet Union was the organizing body during the war, Russians fought, died, and earned the land of the Baltic through blood.

"The Soviet Union was acting illegally when it recognized Baltic independence in 1991, as at this time, the Soviet Union was an unconstitutional body. This land won by Russia, through a decree by an illegal body, was permitted to leave Russia's area of influence. Everyone knows contracts signed by someone unauthorized to sign said contract are deemed immediately null and void."

"But . . . what does —"

"The prosecutor has not been directed by me at all, although I have long felt the Baltic States should never have been granted release from our influence. Of course, he will do his work and look into all the details, the documents, the signatures, but in light of what has happened in Vilnius last week with the death of so many young, brave Russians, I encourage him to work diligently and quickly. There is no time to waste.

"Assuming he does, in fact, determine the recognition of independence was an illegal act, this will open the doors for Russia to revive the corridor between our friends and neighbors Belarus and Russia's enclave of Kaliningrad. Lithuania is situated in the way of the safety of Russia's commerce with itself, and if we need to ensure the corridor is protected from danger, we will do just that."

Molchanova's eyebrows were almost touching, so confused was she by what she was hearing.

But Volodin beamed as he spoke. "I have just today spoken with our wonderful friend and partner President Semyonov of Belarus, and explained to him the situation. He has promised his full cooperation with the results of the prosecutor's office. If we need to reopen the corridor through Lithuania, Belarus will support us in that endeavor."

Molchanova sat in awe now, staring at her president. He smiled at her, a cocked smile, almost a smirk of self-satisfaction. Like a chess champion who just declared checkmate.

She broke out of her stupor quickly, shrugged a little, almost apologizing for stating the obvious. "Yes. But . . . the Lithuanian government, it can be assumed, will not just let Russians enter their country and take the territory between Belarus and Kaliningrad."

Valeri Volodin's smile did not waver. "Tanks don't need visas, Miss Molchanova."

36

It was just before noon in Washington, D.C., and in the conference room off the Oval Office, a dozen men and women watched the live transmission of the Russian president's interview on a large monitor. The volume was turned down, and a running translation came from a pair of interpreters sitting with their headphones on at the far end of the table. Helpfully for all, the female translator gave a running commentary for the female reporter, and the male translated the words of Valeri Volodin.

Jack Ryan was there in the room, along with several of his national security staff. They listened to every word in silence.

When it was over, all eyes turned to the President of the United States.

" 'Tanks don't need visas,' " he said, a tone of resignation in his voice. "The president of Russia just declared the nations of the Baltic illegal states, and he all but promised to invade and take the corridor to Kaliningrad, at the very least."

Mary Pat said, "Which, by the way, goes right through Vilnius, the capital city and the largest city in Lithuania, and Kaunas, the second-largest city in the nation."

Arnie Van Damm wasn't part of the President's National Security team, but he almost always sat in on these meetings for the very simple fact that he ruled the roost of the President's schedule, and national security issues required adjustments to this schedule. But although he was usually in the room when this group had their discussions, he rarely ever spoke unless Ryan's schedule was in question.

Which meant every head in the room turned when he spoke now.

"You know . . . it's remarkable. It's brilliant, really."

Jack Ryan said, "What's brilliant, Arnie?"

"At the beginning of the interview, when he blamed the Swedish commercial flight for murdering eleven poor innocent Russian airmen who were just minding their own business. Then he switched gears and cast doubt on the official stories about the explosion in Klaipėda and the attack in Vilnius. But what if Russia was behind these two things? Obviously, he'd be involved with it, or at least know about it, and he would know the cover story set up by his minions."

"Right," Ryan said.

"And then he goes on national TV and says he doesn't believe the official stories, which are actually *his* cover stories."

Ryan nodded thoughtfully. "There is a depth to his scheme, isn't there? Again, assuming these things to be the case."

Secretary of State Scott Adler slowly leaned back in his chair. "How do we even respond to his comment about Lithuania?"

Before anyone could answer, Bob Burgess entered the conference room and looked to President Ryan. He offered no deference to any of the cabinet members, however, because he had something he needed to say. "Pardon me, Mr. President. While Volodin was speaking, a Twitter account belonging to Russia's Western Military District announced a snap drill in Belarus in three days, involving Russia's Sixth Army. Not a lot of specifics, but if it is like other drills in that area, they will move some land and air units to staging facilities west of Minsk, work with the Belarusan military for a few days, and then pull out. They say it's to test emergency operational readiness for both forces in the case of an attack from a Central European nation."

"Right," said Scott Adler. "In case Lithuania or Latvia begin a push toward Moscow." The sarcasm in his comment was obvious.

Burgess said, "They'll put a useful mix of front-line forces close enough to Poland and

Lithuania to represent an immediate threat to both nations. Of course, they already have troops in Kaliningrad, too, but they'll move them out of garrison and put them in predeployment points, exactly as they would do if they were coming over the border. All totaled, their snap drills involve somewhere around fifty thousand troops."

"And Lithuania has how many troops in total?"

"Including their ready reserve . . . twelve thousand."

"Christ." Ryan turned to Mary Pat. "What's your take on this?"

"They've done snap drills a half-dozen times in the past decade, so it's not terribly threatening in itself. Still, the timing is . . . provocative, and that's a word that I've all but stopped using when speaking of Volodin's actions, because it has lost all its meaning and context."

Burgess said, "Mr. President, this might well be a drill and not the precursor to an invasion, but if it *is* an invasion, if we don't move NATO forces into Lithuania, right now, there will be no way whatsoever that we can stop an invasion."

Ryan said, "NATO's Very High Readiness Joint Task Force needs to move before the invasion starts?"

"Yes, sir. Without a doubt. Otherwise, Russia will own Vilnius before the first NATO troops get into Lithuanian airspace."

Ryan thought it over, then he addressed Scott Adler. "Scott, how do we get NATO to move on this?"

The secretary of state said, "Since there has been no Article Five violation yet, it will take a consensus of the member states. And since the summit is already kicking off the day after tomorrow anyway, the Lithuanian president, as the threatened NATO member, can call an emergency session at the beginning of the summit. She can make her case to move NATO High Readiness units into her country, and then the other member states will have to agree."

Ryan nodded. "Okay. I'll call President Banytė as soon as we're finished here and encourage her to request an emergency session for the day after tomorrow."

Burgess said, "If the NATO forces can get there in time, it will provide a helpful tripwire. Hopefully that will encourage Volodin to keep his forces on the Belarusan and Kaliningrad sides of the border. But realistically, Mr. President, the VHRJTF is not strong enough to repel fifty thousand Russian troops."

Ryan knew this already. "We need to be ready to help them out. You mentioned the battalion of Marines we have in Romania."

"The Black Sea Rotational Force. Right now it's the 3rd Battalion, 5th Marine Regiment, of the 1st Marine Infantry Division."

Ryan, a former Marine, leaned back in his chair. "Darkhorse."

"Correct, sir. The Darkhorse Battalion. One thousand two hundred of the best Marines in the Corps, and they can be ready to move in days."

Ryan said, "Give the Black Sea Rotational Force a heads-up now, but quietly. *Very* quietly. If the other NATO member states find out we're ready to do an end run around and throw non-NATO forces into the gap, that might complicate things before the emergency meeting."

"I understand," said Burgess. "I'll talk directly to the Marine Corps commandant, as well as Lieutenant General Blanchard, the commander of MARFOREUR. That's Marine Forces Europe. He is based in Germany, and he's the commander of all Marine forces in theater. Lithuania is his battle space, and he will be the one who is tasked with deploying them effectively."

"Good," Ryan said, then looked back to the others in the room. "Now, we're not done yet. I think there is still a chance, a good chance, that Valeri Volodin is just escalating things here as a bluff. He wants to see NATO back down so he can move into Lithuania without firing a shot. So we need to be able to identify the difference between a legit drill and the precursors to an invasion."

Mary Pat Foley said, "We have methods,

Mr. President. One thing we'll do on our end is have the DIA and CIA take a look at specific military personalities in Russia, to see if we can figure out where they are."

Ryan cocked his head. "Explain."

Mary Pat looked to SecDef Burgess. "Bob?"

Burgess said, "I know off the top of my head of three Russian Army generals who I guarantee will be involved in any invasion of any former satellite. These are their go-to guys. They were in Georgia, in Estonia, and they were in Ukraine. The oldest was also a company commander in Chechnya, and a battalion commander in Dagestan. These generals' physical proximity to a border region can spell trouble. Of course, the Russians are smart, so they move these gents around, just to keep us guessing. But if we can get intel on their location, and we find out they are not in Belarus or Kaliningrad, then my concern about an invasion will go down precipitously."

Ryan summarized this. "So if they show up in Minsk, that doesn't necessarily mean there will be an invasion, but if they are back in Moscow or in three different parts of the country to the east, an invasion probably won't be coming anytime soon."

Mary Pat said, "That's the way we see it. We'll work hard to fix their positions in the next few days."

The meeting broke up and Ryan returned

through his secretary's office into his own. Arnie Van Damm followed in behind him, looking down at his mobile phone as he walked.

Ryan turned around inside the Oval. "You need something, Arnie?"

The chief of staff chuckled aloud. "You'll love this. The Russian embassy here just relayed a request from New Russia Television. That's Channel Seven over there. They are asking for fifteen minutes for a sit-down interview with you while you are in Copenhagen."

Ryan was surprised. "Really?"

"They pledge to not edit your comments." He sniffed. "You know it will be a total hit job."

Ryan raised an eyebrow. "Mexico City was a hit job, Arnie. This is a TV interview." He was referring to the assassination attempt against him, a bit of a gallows-humor joke.

If it had been anyone other than Van Damm, Ryan's comment would have mortified them, turned them white with embarrassment, thinking they had offended the President. But Arnie just rolled his eyes and clarified. "Cute, Jack. You know what I mean. They will come at you hard, try to misrepresent what you say."

Ryan said, "Hell, all those presidential debates I had to endure during the campaigns should have taught me how to take on a tough interviewer."

Van Damm kept reading the e-mail, then he said, "One perk to it, though. Tatiana Molchanova will be the one conducting the interview."

Ryan replied sarcastically, "Sorry, Arnie, but I've been slacking. I haven't been watching as much Channel Seven as I should. I don't know their on-air personalities."

Arnie said, "You just watched her interview Volodin. An eleven on a scale of ten in beauty, brains, and the amount of Kremlin Kool-Aid she's drinking."

"Oh . . . *her.*"

Van Damm said, "I'll tell them no."

"Tell them yes."

Arnie was taken aback. "You're kidding, right? There is nothing to gain by following their format for a sit-down interview."

"I want to communicate directly with the Russian people. I'll give her fifteen minutes, and I'll be on my best behavior." After an incredulous look from his chief of staff, Ryan said, "Think about it, Arnie. Volodin has been on every American network multiple times. You can't get that guy to shut up. And what Volodin just said to his people was absolute insanity; he's driving them headlong toward war and pinning it on the West. I know I can't get my message to them unless I offer their state-backed TV exactly what they want." He shrugged. "I owe it to the process to give this a shot, Arnie."

Van Damm said, "I don't like this, boss."

Ryan smiled a little. "Put me in, coach. Give me a chance."

Van Damm chuckled. He stood to leave the Oval and, while doing so, began to type a message on his phone. "I'm about to surprise the hell out of some producer in Moscow, because nobody over there seriously thought you'd accept this invitation."

Ryan headed for his desk. He called out to Arnie as he left the room. "The big surprise in Copenhagen will be if I manage to convince twenty-six member states to predeploy forces in Lithuania before Russia invades."

37

Ding Chavez and Dominic Caruso had been working twelve-hour days for the past week, scrambling all over the central eastern portion of Lithuania, photographing streets, fields, villages, creeks, even brick walls.

They had no idea why they were doing what they were doing, but they'd both spent the majority of their careers working for the U.S. government, so they had some background in following curious orders that didn't seem to make a hell of a lot of sense.

Today they worked along the banks of the Neris River, beginning in the northern suburbs of Vilnius, and then heading north and east, going to nearly two dozen locations designated by the Office of the Director of National Intelligence. Following the river through the villages of Skirgiškės and Bratoniškės, and ending on the second of two bridges at Nemenčinė. The photographs today were much the same as all the others they had taken this week, although the two men were noticing some trends they hadn't picked up on before. Several of the photos, maybe twenty-five percent of the total, seemed to be different positions of high ground looking north and east. They were even tasked with photographing from building rooftops and upper-level balconies in the towns.

And Herkus Zarkus was with them every step of the way. At each stop he contributed to their cover, usually just unpacking and prepping equipment, but occasionally actually digging trenches and climbing poles when the Campus men ran into unexpected delays.

He'd gotten them into private apartments, behind locked gates, and once even came up with a ruse to have them set up their "survey" equipment in a drainage culvert while curious traffic passed, claiming to the most inquisitive onlookers that a plan was in place to dredge below the culvert to expand the super-high-speed network.

While they worked, Ding and Dom had kept their eyes out for anything out of the ordinary, and this was tough for a couple guys who weren't familiar with the area, but the pair had both been in Ukraine the year before, just prior to the invasion there, so they had some recent experience operating in similar territory.

An hour before nightfall they ran into

another group of suspicious locals when they were parked on Highway 108. Just like last time, after convincing the locals they were fiber-optic linemen from America and not Little Green Men from Russia, Dom, Ding, and Herkus were told about suspicious vehicles in the area. It was anecdotal evidence that something was going on, nothing more, but the Campus men had no reason to doubt what they were hearing.

Tonight, once it got too dark for any more high-res photographs, the men headed south, taking a roundabout route back to the capital just to get a look at the area. The military presence they encountered to the east of Vilnius was impressive from a quantity standpoint. Lots of troop trucks, sandbagged positions, and young men carrying HK G36 battle rifles filled parking lots, roadsides, and other congregation points, but there were no roadblocks or any armor positions in sight.

As they drove along the E28, the main highway that went west from Kaliningrad, passed through Vilnius, and continued on to the Belarusan border, a pair of MI-17 helicopters churned the air above the DataPlanet truck.

Herkus looked up through the truck's windshield as he drove. "You won't believe it, but you guys are looking at about fifteen percent of Lithuania's entire air force."

Caruso said, "You've got to be kidding."

"Nope. They only have one fighter, an old Czech trainer from the seventies. That and a few transport planes and helicopters. A few years ago we didn't have any money, so we couldn't spend it on defense. Now we are more prosperous, but we joined NATO, so our leaders told us we didn't *need* to spend money on defense."

Caruso said, "Figures."

Chavez said, "No offense, but the military equipment we've passed on the road doesn't make your army look a hell of a lot better than your air force."

Herkus agreed. "Not a single tank in the Lithuanian Land Force. We've got some antitank weapons, a few artillery pieces, and a bunch of mortars. If the Russians come, and nobody shows up to help us . . ." Herkus surprised the Americans with a smile. "Well, at least everyone will get the news quickly with our superfast Internet."

Jack Ryan, Jr., sat at Amsterdam's Schiphol Airport, waiting for his seven a.m. flight to Dulles. He'd positioned himself in a corner of the waiting area at the gate, his back to a wall and his eyes scanning those around him.

He'd arrived from Luxembourg City less than a half-hour earlier, which meant he was probably out of danger, but failures in his OPSEC had led to the situation he now found himself in, so even though he was in an airport terminal where no one should have a gun or a knife, and even though he was hundreds of miles from where he'd been attacked the afternoon before, he wasn't going to let his guard down for one second.

Not again.

As soon as his flight from Luxembourg landed he called Christine von Langer at the hospital to check on Ysabel. Christine told him his injured friend had made it through surgery with flying colors. Ysabel was still in a medically induced coma because of the dangers of swelling of her brain, but all her vital signs were stable and the doctors felt she would make a slow but full recovery.

Christine also mentioned that a pair of very polite but very tough-looking Frenchmen who were friends of John Clark's had arrived at the hospital and presented themselves as friends of Ysabel's family. Out of earshot of the doctors and nurses, they assured Christine that they would take good care of her, but Christine insisted on staying around, at least for the first few days, to make sure the doctors knew Ysabel had a lot of people watching out for her.

Relieved that the situation back in Luxembourg had stabilized, Jack next thought about calling his mother at the White House, asking for her take on Ysabel's medical situation. He knew his mom would know a lot more about the care Ysabel would need than Jack would, but Jack ultimately decided against it. There was really no way he'd be able to explain to his mother that a woman he was involved with had just been beaten and stabbed to within an inch of her life without Jack's mom needing a lot more information.

He told himself when he got back home he'd run over to 1600 Pennsylvania Avenue and drop in on his parents. Maybe when they saw he was safe Jack could ask for a little bit of medical advice "for a friend."

He wasn't looking forward to that conversation at all, but he felt like he owed it to Ysabel to help in any way he possibly could.

He'd just completed a scan of a group of men near the gate when his phone rang. He looked down and saw it was Gavin calling. There was no one close to him at the gate, but he was careful to keep his voice low nonetheless. "Wow, Gavin. It's early there. Must be midnight."

"Yeah, I've been working through the evening." He paused a moment. "Heard about what happened to your girl. I'm sorry, man."

"Thanks." Jack wasn't used to tender moments with Gavin Biery. It made him uncomfortable. "Uh . . . You have something for me?"

"I've got info on that plane out of Lux City you asked me to track."

Jack had all but forgotten about Gavin's

promise to find out where Limonov and Ko-zlov went next. "What about Salvatore? Clark said he'd get you to look into him."

"We're on him. Nothing yet. It will take a little time."

Jack didn't try to mask the annoyance in his voice. "What's the holdup?"

"He doesn't have anything to latch on to. No network to crack. He's not employed officially, just a freelancer. He has a mobile phone — who doesn't? But so far we haven't gotten into the network to check his contacts or movements. We're working on getting into the police systems there, checking him against Interpol, that sort of thing, but it is going to take a little time."

"Okay," Jack said. "I understand." Distractedly, he asked, "What about Limonov's plane? Did it go back to London?"

"Nope. That tail number took off from Lux City just after eight p.m. last night. They blocked his flight plan, which I thought you might find interesting, because you said they didn't block the flight into Luxembourg. So I lost them for a couple of hours, but I found a flight heading out over the Atlantic on a southerly route that reported a tail number that didn't correspond to any departures anywhere in Europe. Not the one you gave me, but some aircraft will actually file under a different identity to hide the movement. Anyway, there were other ghost flights up and around Europe at the time, but nothing else that fit perfectly, time- and distance-wise, from Luxembourg, considering the cruising speed of a Bombardier 6000."

Jack wanted to just tell Gavin to get to the point, but he was too sapped of energy at the moment to resist the computer geek's intense desire to ramble. "Okay."

"So this one looked good, but I had to rule out another that was heading out over the Med with a similar profile. Took a half-hour to determine the other flight was a Citation owned by a shipping concern in Sardinia, so I went back to the plane over the Atlantic. For a couple more hours I thought it was flying down to South America, but eventually it checked in with ATC over Bermuda, and by then I determined it was heading to the Caribbean."

Jack felt his excitement rising. He wasn't sure why Limonov would need to go in person to the Caribbean if he was planning on moving accounts offshore there, but Jack knew he could keep an eye on the man there better than he would have been able to watch over him if he returned to Moscow.

"Where in the Caribbean? Antigua? Grand Cayman?"

"Nope. They flew twelve hours straight, landed in the British Virgin Islands."

"British Virgin Islands?" It was a known offshore location, although not one commonly used by Kremlin-associated Russians. Again, he didn't have a clue why the Russians needed to personally visit the location, but he wasn't going to look a gift horse in the mouth. "Any more info?"

"Just that the jet landed at Terrance B. Lettsome International six minutes ago, taxied to Beef Island Air Services, a fixed-base operator at the airport. Don't know where they will head from there. Just looking online, there aren't a ton of hotels in the BVIs, but there are hundreds of private apartments and villas to rent."

"Okay, thanks for the info."

"Anything you need, Jack, you just shout."

There was unmistakable empathy in Biery's voice.

Jack thanked him, hung up, then he boarded his own transatlantic flight, the whole time wondering why two Russians working for the Kremlin would go to the British Virgin Islands, especially right after meeting with a lawyer in Luxembourg.

Most of the *siloviki* money he and the other analysts at The Campus had been following had gone through Cyprus or Switzerland or Gibraltar or Singapore. Cyprus had gone through severe financial hardships but there were still tens of thousands of offshore companies there owned by Russian entities, completely free of regulation. Cyprus's money problems had nothing to do with Russia's money, other than the fact that the newly flush-with-cash Cypriot banks had invested heavily in Greek bonds, which were rendered worthless due to Greek financial mismanagement.

The BVIs, on the other hand, were a place where many Chinese billionaires parked their accounts on the way to moving them back into China as investment capital.

Jack thought about it while he sat down in his first-class seat. Softly he said to himself, "If I was a big-shot Russian billionaire, I'd keep my money away from shell banks in the same neighborhood as the Chinese."

Even if the money was in numbered accounts, some shell corporation or bank in the BVIs could make deductions about where it was coming from, and while they were sworn to secrecy, the power of the tens of billions coming out of China could encourage someone to say something about this other client.

China and Russia had come to blows in the past decade, and even when they were allies, their partnerships were fragile.

Jack muttered, "No way would I move my Kremlin money into China's offshore turf."

Jack wondered if there was some other reason Limonov and Kozlov had gone to the British Virgin Islands.

He doubted it had anything to do with their suntans.

■ ■ ■ ■

After takeoff he pulled out his laptop and opened his IBM i2 Analyst's Notebook analytics software. He looked again through his data sets on Frieden, trying to find something in the British Virgin Islands that looked like it might warrant a trip down.

But he found nothing. None of Frieden's known associations seemed to have anything going on in the BVIs, nor did any of his contacts. Sure, some of his clients had gone there, for what reason he did not know, but they didn't seem to have any connection to banks down there.

Jack knew there had to be something. Limonov didn't seem to be connected to Rome, and he didn't show up in anything he had on Mikhail Grankin's network.

Jack widened his search, pulled in data on known financial networks used by other members of the *siloviki* from Justice Department and Campus investigations going back years.

There were little bank accounts, shell companies, and trusts registered there, no doubt every last one of them money-laundering vehicles, but Jack didn't see any obvious connection to Limonov, nor did he see why a Russian private equity manager and the ex-FSB goon shadowing him would have any reason to go down physically to move money there.

On a whim he ran the rest of Frieden's contacts, looking to see if, perhaps, Limonov had met with Frieden to find information that led him to the Caribbean. This wasn't an easy endeavor, because only a portion of Frieden's contact list had physical addresses for the contacts listed. Jack threw these known addresses into a spreadsheet and searched for BVI references, and then, after finding none, he looked up the phone code for the British Virgin Islands.

Seconds later, he ran a search of the number 284 in the database.

He got two hits. The first was a business registration firm on the island of Tortola. The second, Jack saw, was a man named Terry Walker.

Jack didn't recognize the name, so he ran it through his database of people involved in the world of international finance. He found no hits on a Terry Walker of the British Virgin Islands, so, assuming there were probably fifty thousand references in Google for both men and women named Terry Walker, he simply typed in the phone number.

Nothing.

With nothing else coming to mind, Jack typed the name into Google, ready to refine it by adding "British Virgin Islands" after his initial search, but he didn't have to.

The first reference to the name in Google was the man Limonov had gone down to the BVIs to see, Jack knew this beyond a shadow of a doubt.

The flight attendant leaned over him, distracting him from his computer. "Can I get you anything?"

Jack looked up. "Yeah. Scotch. Neat." And then, "Better make it a double."

38

Jack sipped his scotch, reading about Terry Walker on the Internet. The Australian was the inventor and owner of BlackHole, the world's largest and most notorious Bitcoin exchange. Jack found a recent article about the man, and learned his company was registered in the British Virgin Islands, and Walker was a resident of Tarpon Island, an exclusive beachside resort popular with millionaires and billionaires.

Jack knew about Tarpon Island because it was a famous retreat for famous people, and he knew about BlackHole because it was, without exaggeration, a nightmare for those in the world of anti–money laundering. It was something referred to as a hopper, or a tumbler, where all virtual currency transactions could be jumbled together to completely disguise both the buyer and the seller of the currency.

Bitcoin was difficult to trace on its own, Jack knew, but if someone used BlackHole, the best forensic accountants in the world couldn't trace the transactions back to their origin.

Jack wasn't certain why Limonov would physically need to meet with Terry Walker to use BlackHole, but he'd obviously gotten the name from Frieden, and he'd obviously made the BVIs his next stop, so Walker *had* to be the reason for Limonov's trip.

Jack Ryan suddenly felt his entire operation slipping away from him.

Jack thought for a moment, then pulled out his mobile phone. He was on a European airline, so there was no prohibition against making a call in the air. It was two a.m. in Maryland, and Clark had clearly been asleep, but he answered quickly; a lifetime of never being far away from a crisis meant he knew how to flip his "on switch" at a moment's notice. It took a second for him to say anything, but Jack knew that was just because John was stepping out of his bedroom so he didn't wake up Sandy.

"You okay, Jack?" Clark finally asked.

"Yeah. I'm over the Atlantic, inbound to Dulles. Sorry for the late call, but I think I've got some actionable intel."

"Not a problem," he said, and then, "We'll get to your intel in a second, but first . . . I'm glad to hear you got on that aircraft."

"You ordered me to. It's not often I don't

follow orders."

"I just know how you feel right now. Trust me, I do. As soon as you get home you can start looking for the men who attacked Ysabel."

"Actually, I'm calling about something else. Gavin has tracked Limonov and Kozlov to the British Virgin Islands."

Clark took a minute to change gears. Jack figured Clark was surprised he was working on something other than finding Salvatore and Ysabel's attackers. But finally Clark asked, "What are they doing there?"

"I think they are going to meet with an Australian national named Terry Walker. He is the world's leading trader of cryptocurrency. Bitcoin and others like it."

There was a pause. "Jack, I'm old. I understand the financial markets, more or less, but I haven't been keeping up in this computer-currency stuff. Sounds like a bunch of nonsense."

"I can explain it to you in a couple of minutes."

There was a slight pause. Then, "Clock is ticking, kid."

Jack said, "The first way to buy things was trade, right? I have a cow, I want your wheat, so I give you milk for the wheat."

Clark chuckled. "For the record, I'm not old enough to remember that part firsthand, but yeah, I'm with you."

"Somebody had to come up with a way strangers could trust each other to give them something else of value. Otherwise everybody would be lugging their yak or whatever to the market."

"Right."

"Money came along. Coins at first, but there was no known, specific intrinsic value in the metal. Intermediaries had to insure it. Middlemen — banks, who were like referees. They said, 'This guy you've never met is going to hand you a little chunk of metal for something of value, but you can use that chunk later to buy something of value. It's okay, it's legit, we'll cover it.' Of course, the banks took their cut for this service, and of course the banks had to have a little information about you if they held on to your chunks of metal for you or loaned you other chunks of metal so you could exchange them for goods or services that you wanted to pay back over time. Borrowers and savers."

"I'm still with you," Clark said.

"And it's been like this for a thousand years. Works pretty well, unless you don't feel like paying someone in the middle, and unless you don't want anyone to know who you are."

"And I guess there are a lot of people who fall into that category."

"Damn right there are," Jack said. "World economic output is ninety trillion a year.

435

Think about how much of that goes to middlemen. Banks are necessary and extremely powerful. So along comes cryptocurrency. It cuts away the middlemen. It removes centralized financial institutions and replaces them with self-directed computer networks, decentralizing the process. Once someone figured out how to ensure transactions without recording any identity data about the payer or payee, the system began to grow quickly."

"How does that work?"

"It's an independent network-based ledger. It's called a blockchain. It automatically tells one party that the other party in the transaction is legitimately paying for a good or service. It's completely computerized, completely peer-to-peer. No third party involved."

Clark said, "And no real regulation."

Jack said, "It's complicated, but yet it's awesome in its simplicity, and its potential. It reduces fees in doing business, and it completely eliminates the corruption in intermediating institutions, because there is no one in the middle who can misuse information or steal money."

"So how do you get the little coin into the computer?" Clark asked.

Jack assumed he was being sarcastic, but he explained anyway. "Bitcoin is not a physical coin. It's digital cash — a long number that you enter. It's not tangible, not issued by a government, it's not a semiprecious metal with a dead person's face on it. It resides nowhere, but it can be accessed anywhere."

"But who controls the system?"

"The system is set up, and then it is monitored by everyone. Each person who takes part in cryptocurrency commerce has the same ability to oversee the operation. There is this blockchain, this ledger, which is updated in real time, and everyone can see. It won't show me that John Clark just bought a pizza, but it will show me that the holder of this Bitcoin just bought something from someone who received this Bitcoin. Once that person buys something it will show the movement of the Bitcoin itself, not the product."

Clark whistled. "A money launderer's dream."

"Yeah. I love the brilliance of this system, but as a guy who chases corrupt money around the world, I've got to say . . . it sucks for me."

Clark said, "You are telling me all this at two a.m. because you want me to understand that once this money is converted into Bitcoin, it will be even harder to track."

"No. Not harder. Impossible. We have to stop this from happening."

"How do you know Limonov is going to see Walker?"

Jack explained how he had come to his conclusion.

Clark asked, "You think Limonov is working with him?"

"I think it's a strong possibility. I don't see any other reason for him to go down there to set up accounts for the money. There will be dozens of locations of these accounts around the world, no way he'd visit them all."

Clark was confused. "So he's going down to buy Bitcoin from Walker? To do what with it?"

"The Bitcoin isn't a destination. It's just a vehicle to get the money out of Russia without it being tracked by other finance people in the FSB. Once he has the digital currency, he can just sit at a computer and exchange it for government-backed currency. He'll just buy dollars or euros or something, and he'll plop that into accounts. The new money won't be tied to Russia. He can put it in Chicago if he wants. I guess he won't own the Bitcoins for any time at all."

"What can you do to track it, then?"

"There's only one thing. I have to get to Terry Walker before he agrees to work for Limonov, and I have to turn him, to get him to work for us."

Clark said, "I see why this is important. Your whole case looks like it's racing headlong into a dead end."

"I'm not going to let that happen, John. I want to go down there. I assume Limonov is going to approach Walker at his office, but I

438

found out he is staying with his family on Tarpon Island."

Clark had heard of the place. "Fancy."

"Yeah, I was thinking we could slip ashore as soon as possible and then we can talk to him at his house. If we can convince him to work with us, maybe we can unwrap Limonov's network and figure out where he's getting his money from."

"You keep saying 'we.' "

"John, to get to that island quietly, I'm going to need a boat. I don't know a thing about boats, but that's not a problem, because I know somebody who does."

"Me?"

"Yep."

"Jack. There is no way in hell Gerry is going to let you out of the country again before we know what happened in Luxembourg, and why."

Jack said, "Let's get Gerry in on this conversation."

A moment later Clark conferenced Gerry Hendley onto the call. He had been sleeping as well, and he wasn't as easy to wake up as Clark had been, but finally he understood the situation. He also understood that Jack Ryan, Jr., was asking to take John Clark and the Gulfstream to the BVIs.

Hendley said, "The problem I have with all this, Jack, is that you don't have any way of knowing who Limonov is working for, do you?"

"No. I wish I could say he was definitely Volodin's cashier, but I can't. Suffice it to say this money that's about to be moved belongs to someone high up at the Kremlin, and time is critical if we are going to have a chance to intercede. Limonov is hiding the money, and I think that is interesting."

Gerry was confused. "Of course he's hiding money. That's what laundering is all about."

Jack said, "No, I mean he is hiding it from the others in the *siloviki*. He's avoiding traditional routes for Russian money. Instead of using a financial network, he goes way out of his way to use Bitcoin to steer clear of other Russian transit means."

"Who is he hiding from?"

"The only people who have the power to see into the Russian offshore transit networks."

Gerry Hendley said, "The FSB."

"Bingo. Whoever Limonov is moving money for, it is someone who doesn't trust the FSB. Someone who is getting his money the hell out of Russia. Someone with enough time to set up his golden parachute with care, but someone with concerns about the FSB learning what he is doing."

"Who does that sound like?" Gerry asked, knowing the answer to his question.

"It's very possible this could be Volodin's

money. Limonov could be the personal cashier for the president of the Russian Federation."

Now Clark asked, "Do you think Limonov and Kozlov were involved in the attack at your apartment last night?"

Jack didn't answer for a moment. When he did, he was equivocal. "I wish I knew. It's clear to me there were two different groups we ran across. One in Rome and one in Luxembourg. It looks to me like the people from Rome tracked Ysabel to me, and they might not have any connection to Limonov. But I don't know. The fact his plane took off right after the attack . . . and it blocked its flight number . . . It looks suspicious.

"I am going to find the sons of bitches who hurt her, and I'm going to hurt them. But right now I know we don't have a minute to lose in stopping Limonov."

Gerry thought about it for a long time. Finally he said, "Jack, your plane doesn't land in Dulles until eleven a.m. If you turned right around and jumped on the Gulfstream, you still wouldn't make it to the BVIs before evening. It seems to me the faster someone gets down there, the better the chance we get to Walker before Limonov does."

"What do you suggest?"

Gerry said, "I'm approving the G550 to travel to the BVIs, but John will go down alone. He can be there and set up before nightfall, and waiting for you will only slow that down. Jack, I want you here, in Alexandria. You can brief John on what to say to Walker over the phone while he's en route."

This wasn't Jack's first choice, but he recognized that Gerry was right. If Clark could get to Walker before Walker even came into contact with the Russians, then maybe he could avoid whatever the Russians had planned from coming to pass.

Jack said, "That's fine, Gerry."

Gerry said, "Of course, John, this is up to you. I know you have stayed out of operations for the past few months. This does look important, though."

Clark said, "Agreed. I'll call Adara and get myself packed."

39

Air Force One left Andrews Field on Joint Base Andrews at ten p.m., lifting off into a clear October sky and turning north over the Atlantic Ocean to skirt the eastern seaboard on its way toward Europe. On climb-out President Ryan looked out the portal next to his desk, down at the black water below, and he wondered if somewhere down there, lurking below the waves, was a 113-meter-long metal tube filled with Russians, nuclear weapons, and bad intentions.

He'd been getting daily updates about the hunt for the *Knyaz Oleg*. Five of the Navy's newest antisubmarine warfare aircraft, the P-8A Poseidon, flown out of Naval Air Station Jacksonville, had been patrolling the length of the coast in rotation twenty-four hours a day since the evening before the best estimates put the *Knyaz Oleg* in the area. U.S. Navy destroyers, cruisers, and littoral combat ships were off the coast now, too, using their sonars as well as their helicopter-based sonar systems, trying to find a needle in a haystack.

The U.S. Coast Guard was also out in force, although they had lost their principal antisubmarine warfare role in 1992 with the fall of the Soviet Union. Much of their mission now involved searching for periscopes and conning towers, sending cutters out from the Mid-Atlantic state ports and investigating potential sightings from civilian surface ships, of which there had been hundreds.

There was an immense area for the Navy and Coast Guard to search, obviously. The Office of Naval Intelligence had determined that the Russian vessel was heading toward the United States from the North Atlantic, which meant the entire East Coast of the United States was its possible destination. There were assumptions made after that, of course; ONI assumed the Russians would want to stay in international waters, which meant it would remain at least twelve nautical miles from any U.S. land. By looking at the oceanic geography of the East Coast — areas of shallows, areas of high current or other poor conditions — and taking into consideration busy shipping lanes that would hamper the submarine's task of remaining invisible while having a perfect understanding of all threats in the water around them, the Navy and Coast Guard could eliminate more area from the search.

Of further consideration to the analysts was

the United States' missile defense system. The Navy knew that the Russians knew that if they could enter to within seventy nautical miles of the U.S. coastline, it would dramatically increase their chances of evading America's ability to knock their weapons out of the sky.

So the ONI had worked for days, and they had "pinpointed" the possible location of the *Knyaz Oleg* to something like a million square miles. Twelve miles from shore to seventy miles out, in international waters, for most of the way up and down the East Coast.

Chief of Naval Operations Admiral Roland Hazelton had been frank with his President — he'd said it was his feeling from discussions with Navy and Coast Guard brass that they would only pinpoint the Russian Borei when it launched a Bulava ballistic missile out of the water and the bloom showed up on MASINT — Measurement and Signature Intelligence data.

Hazelton had been so frank in his portrayal of the *Knyaz Oleg*'s advantages in the present scenario that he'd immediately offered to turn in his resignation. An offer Ryan declined angrily, telling Hazelton he wasn't getting out of the present crisis so easily. He'd sent the CNO out his door with orders to work harder, twist more arms, motivate his people and lead them.

To find a way out of this mess.

After the waters off the U.S. coastline disappeared before Ryan, he began focusing on the other, not unrelated situation, the reason for his trip. He spent the first couple of hours of the flight in his office, then he had a working dinner with Bob Burgess and Scott Adler in the dining room just aft of the senior staff meeting room.

He'd received some rare and welcome good news during dinner. Burgess had just come from a conference call, and he informed Ryan that French Special Forces had finally retaken the Nigerian oil rig from Boko Haram fighters with no losses to themselves or the hostages.

After dinner Ryan made a quick call to the French president to congratulate him on his good work and to tell him he looked forward to seeing him in Copenhagen. It was true that Ryan was impressed and happy about the French president's decision to hit the rig, but it was not true, not true at all, that Ryan was looking forward to seeing the president at the emergency meeting the next afternoon. France would be one of the least inclined to send NATO troops to Lithuania, and the French president was a hell of a good debater.

Now Ryan was in the nose of the plane, lying on his bed in the executive suite, just below the cockpit of the massive 747. He told himself he'd shoot for five hours of sleep, which would get him up just prior to landing in Copenhagen.

But he'd settle for four. Hell, he'd be thrilled with four.

He'd be lucky if he got three.

And when he closed his eyes his fears were realized. Sleep would *not* come. Instead, his brain refused to shut off; it wanted to keep working, to compute, to analyze, to mind-map the Russian problem and plot a solution to it.

As a historian, and then as an analyst with the CIA, Jack Ryan always had a feeling the answers were out there. Information was attainable; he didn't discount the difficulties encountered by those in the operations end of things who had to go out and attain it, but once they did, people on the analytic side of things had all the more responsibility to divine the correct answers from the data. And the answers were there, passing by in the wind, and he just had to snatch them out as they passed by.

Those days were a long time ago, but he still felt the same way. As President of the United States, he had access to all the information, and that to him meant he had access to all the answers.

The answer to the question of what Volodin was doing now was attainable. He just had to take all the information, data about economics and military firepower and logistics and geography, and his adversary's impressions of the world around him and even the psychology of the man. This and dozens of other factors needed to be calculated and evaluated, and from this he should be able to conclude what Volodin's game was.

The answer was attainable, Ryan still believed this, but as he lay there on his bed, he realized the answer remained out of his grasp.

Something Burgess had said tonight was bothering him, though. During dinner the talk had turned to Russia's actions down in Ukraine over the past month. After nearly a year of stalemate the Russian Army had ticked up the fighting, surprising the Ukrainians and knocking them off-balance, although the Russians had failed to capitalize on this tactical advantage.

Burgess had said, "They are increasing attacks, artillery and rocket fire. Some fronts are seeing forty percent more volume in the past month. But it's harassing actions only. That's expensive, Russia is blowing through a lot of ordnance, but for what gain? They aren't taking territory. They aren't even amassing troops for any sort of a push."

Ryan had asked, "You're sure?"

Burgess replied, "We saw some reserve battalions move into border positions, almost like they were thinking about doing something, but it looks like it was just show for our satellites."

"Why do you say that?"

"Fuel reserves for the battalions are minimal, they aren't stockpiling equipment. They just took a few thousand men out of Volgograd, Russia, and moved them west to Duby, Russia. It's just over the border from Luhansk."

Ryan had been confused. "But Russia already has Luhansk."

"Exactly. Why stage combat troops in Russia when you can just move them into Ukraine, closer to the front lines?"

Ryan thought over the conversation with his SecDef now, trying to figure out what that information meant.

His eyes opened quickly. Alone in the dark, he said, "Son of a bitch."

President Ryan sat in his darkened office in Air Force One with his desk phone to his ear. He looked down at his watch and realized the person he was calling was likely in bed, because it was one a.m. in Washington, D.C.

"Hello?"

"Hold the line for the President of the United States. Mr. President, I have Director Foley."

"Thanks, Lieutenant." Getting the communications desk upstairs in the 747 to make his calls for him made him feel a little useless, but the truth was, he couldn't remember Mary Pat and Ed's home phone number to save his life. On top of that, Ryan admitted to himself, he didn't even have a clue how to dial an outside line on Air Force One.

He guessed it was probably 9.

"I'm sorry, Mary Pat. You know I don't do this often."

"Is something wrong, Mr. President?"

"No. Well . . . I don't know." He took a second to compose his thoughts. "You know my hunch, right? That Volodin has been behind the spate of attacks on the worldwide energy sector."

"Yes, sir."

"And my working theory is that he is doing this to affect energy prices, specifically natural gas and oil, to bolster his economy?"

"Right."

"Well . . . if he was planning on invading Lithuania, wouldn't that have the same effect?"

She thought it over. "That's a question for Les Birnbaum, I guess, but as DNI I feel pretty confident in fielding it. Yes, tanks crossing into a NATO member state will have more effect on energy prices than everything Volodin's done to date. That is, assuming he has done the things you suspect. In fact, I can't imagine anything that would have a greater effect than a Russian war with a NATO power."

"Exactly. And wouldn't Volodin know none of this other stuff was important if ultimately he planned to invade?"

Mary Pat said, "Yes, of course he would. So, you don't think he actually plans on invading?"

"Maybe not. The Borei coming to the East Coast, the troops on the border, the chaos in the energy sector. The uptick of attacks in Ukraine. What if he's not trying to foment war? What if he's trying to foment fear? Instability."

"Interesting theory," Mary Pat said, but Ryan could tell from her voice she wasn't on board. "You think he's bluffing on his attack?"

Ryan had been thinking about this. He said, "He might be. He can't win a protracted war and he knows it. The only game he can win is a game of chicken. He keeps upping the stakes incrementally, and at some point we'll either confront him or stand down. He's putting all his money on us backing down."

She said, "Escalation dominance."

Ryan nodded. "Escalation dominance. Yes. He looks like he is the one in control of events, simply by virtue of the fact he is the one making moves. Right or wrong, whether they work out for him or not. It's been his modus operandi for years."

Mary Pat said, "I see it in the media when they talk about Volodin as the chess master. Sometimes, unfortunately, I see it in my own staff. They make a list of everything Volodin has done, and they point to it and say it's

451

proof of his plan, regardless of the fact that nothing he has done has ultimately worked for him."

Ryan nodded in the dark office. "Five snap decisions in a row looks like a plan if you write them down." He rubbed his eyes. "Maybe if we can push enough NATO into Lithuania he'll come up with some other measure to declare victory. I don't know what, but I do know one thing."

"What's that, Mr. President?"

"I know if we don't get troops into Lithuania, his tanks will roll right over that border in the next week. If that happens, Volodin will be unstoppable. Lithuania will be just the first domino to fall."

40

Tatiana Molchanova checked her appearance in a handheld makeup mirror and realized the interior lights of the SUV didn't give her enough illumination to see if she needed to pluck her eyebrows. She sat in the back of the Suburban while the rest of her team climbed out and pulled bags from the back, and she took her time touching up her makeup. Tatiana never went out in public without looking perfect, because she was a celebrity, and airports were nothing if not crowded public spaces.

This was not to say Tatiana was a complete diva, really; she knew she'd be lugging something on this trip sooner or later, even if it was just her roll-aboard and her purse.

Finally she slipped out of the vehicle and stood with the others in her crew outside Terminal 1 at Moscow's Vnukovo International Airport. It was four p.m. and there was a lot of activity around her, but even passengers rushing to catch flights turned to look her way. Many pulled out cameras and took pictures of one of the most famous women in the country.

Tatiana smiled at the attention without slowing to make eye contact with anyone. Instead, she put her mirror back in her purse and waited for the audio technician to finish stacking up the gear so they could go.

Her mobile rang and she answered it without looking. *"Allo?"*

"Tatiana? It is Lidiya Maksimova, from the office of the president."

Tatiana's eyebrows furrowed with concentration. "Yes, Lidiya. How are you?" Molchanova knew Lidiya well; she was one of Volodin's top appointment secretaries.

"I am fine. I am in the vehicle directly behind you. We are to bring you directly to the president for a meeting. Here at the airport. Shan't take any time at all."

Tatiana looked to the street, to the four-door Jaguar directly behind where the Channel Seven car was parked. "The black Jaguar? Well . . . okay, but I do have a plane to catch."

"Your plane will go nowhere without you, Tatiana. I can assure you of that."

Valeri Volodin's aircraft always flew out of Terminal 2 at Vnukovo. Tatiana knew he had been up in Saint Petersburg today and would just be returning about now, but she'd had no plans to meet with him.

As surprised as she was by this, she told the others in her party she'd meet them on board the plane, and she climbed into the Jaguar with only her purse.

Fifteen minutes later she was brought on board the president's plane and escorted into Volodin's office. He had just landed, and much of the staff was already out on the tarmac or in the hangar, but Volodin seemed to be in no rush to leave.

He stood and crossed the small office, his hands outstretched. He appeared calmer and more at ease now than he was during his interview a few nights earlier.

"Miss Molchanova, thank you for coming today."

"Yes, of course." Together they sat close on a love seat across from his desk. She could smell his cologne. "I want to thank you for allowing me this opportunity to visit you on your aircraft. This is very thrilling."

He smiled like a Cheshire cat, still holding on to her hand. "My duties are so numerous and stressful, I have forgotten the thrill of entering my own aircraft." He softened his grip, but only a little. "I miss the days when I was just a simple, obedient, hardworking agent of the KGB."

Tatiana beamed at him.

"Any idea why I asked you here?"

"I am at a complete loss, Mr. President."

"You are flying out tonight to Copenhagen.

Tomorrow you will interview the President of the United States."

"Yes. My producers communicated this with the Kremlin as soon as our request was approved by the embassy. We solicited a list of questions to your office, and I have been given my notes from Lidiya. I believe everything is in order."

Volodin smiled a little. Molchanova thought he seemed pleased by her discomfort. "You are not on the firing line, my dear. No reason to be so defensive. On the contrary, I have a favor to ask."

She let her relief show. "Of course."

"I want you to do something for me. A bit of statecraft."

"Statecraft?"

"Yes. Would it excite you to know that you will be engaging in high-level communications between the Russian Federation and the United States of America?"

Tatiana Molchanova brought her shoulders back and lifted her chin. "That would excite me greatly, Mr. President. But . . . why me?"

"Because you have the intelligence and qualities to see this through." He held up a finger. "And you have proven yourself a reliable conveyer of Russia's interests."

No journalist likes to be called a shill for her government, not even a journalist who is a shill for her government. But she only nodded a little, and made no remark.

He said, "I am certain you will do a good job, but one thing is important to remember above all. No one can know about this but Jack Ryan. No one."

"I understand."

Volodin's smile disappeared. His eyes narrowed. "I really hope you do. I would hate for anything to threaten our good relationship."

"I will reveal nothing of my mission," she said meekly.

Volodin nodded, smiled again. "You will ask for a private audience with Ryan as soon as your interview is over tomorrow night. I am going to tell you what to say to him. You will repeat my words verbatim to Ryan, that is crucial."

"Of course."

"He will, no doubt, have a message for me. Perhaps not immediately. He will want to confer with his brain trust. He doesn't think on his feet like I do."

"No. Not at all."

"You will stay in Copenhagen until you have his message for me, and then you will return immediately. Once you get back to Vnukovo I will send a helicopter for you, and it will deliver you to me. Either at my home or at the Kremlin, depending on where I am at the time of your return. You will give me his message, exactly in content and tone, as he gave it to you."

"I understand everything and will do as you ask. I am proud to serve you . . . serve Russia."

Volodin spent the next several minutes telling Molchanova what to say to the American President. When he finished she repeated it back to him several times, as he commanded. He was not happy with her delivery at first, so they went over it for a while. A taciturn schoolmaster and an approval-seeking student. It was not a difficult task, but Tatiana Molchanova had difficulty because it was so incredibly hard for her to fathom that this was, by far, the coolest thing that had ever happened to her, and yet she could never tell anyone about this at all.

John Clark climbed the stairs up into the G550 Gulfstream executive jet. As he reached the top he was greeted by Adara Sherman.

"Good morning, Mr. Clark," she said, taking his small pack from his hand and ushering him through the door.

"Ms. Sherman."

Adara served, officially at least, as the Hendley Associates logistics coordinator and flight attendant. In reality, almost all her work revolved around The Campus, where she was not only a coordinator of logistics and a flight attendant, but also a security officer for the aircraft, and something of a fixer for the team to help them get out of the jams they often found themselves in overseas.

She helped stow Clark's duffel while he poked his head through the cockpit door to greet the pilot and copilot, and then he took one of the big leather cabin chairs for himself. Adara set him up with a bottle of water, and she quickly discussed the flight plan for the day, along with the menu for lunch.

When she was finished with this, Adara said, "We'll be taking off immediately. Can I get you anything else, Mr. Clark?"

"Yes, actually. I need a sailboat."

She nodded, headed up to the galley, and grabbed a book full of cocktail recipes. "I don't know that one, offhand. It's probably here in *Mr. Boston's.*"

Clark laughed. "No, Ms. Sherman. I need a *real* sailboat. And I need it ready for me by the time we get down to Tortola."

"Oh." She moved across the cabin to her laptop and sat down behind it. "I can do that, too."

"Nothing too fancy or complicated. I will be staying within the BVIs, but I'll need to slip quietly right up to an island resort with restricted access."

"And make your own access," Adara said with a little grin.

"You got it. I'll need a short list of equipment as well."

"I'll arrange as much as I can while we're in flight, and if I need to I'll go out and scrounge up the rest when we land."

"Excellent," Clark said. Sherman had impressed him every time he had worked with her, and he knew she had also proven herself in the field once, when she and Dominic Caruso had found themselves in an in extremis situation in Panama.

He regarded her for a moment more and thought about how lucky the men were to have her on the team, especially now since Sam was gone. They were a thin operational outfit, so having a force multiplier like Adara Sherman was all the more important.

Clark went to work going over maps of the area of operations he was going to be working in when he got to the British Virgin Islands. He saw his ingress to the target to be the easy part of this operation. The difficult part would be convincing this virtual currency trader to work with him. He imagined the man wouldn't be doing what he did, and working in a place like the place he was working in, because he had a great love of authority. Clark assumed Walker was a typical money-laundering crook, so as soon as Jack Junior landed in D.C. and got into the office, the two men would work on Clark's game plan to encourage, cajole, or even threaten Walker to work against some very powerful and probably very dangerous Russians, and instead work for some very motivated, but not terribly forthcoming, American.

41

Terry Walker missed his home country the way many of his fellow countrymen do when they become expatriates, because Australia is a beautiful place, but he had to admit that his temporary digs weren't half bad. As he looked around his massive bedroom, his eyes slowly adjusting to the early-morning light, he knew he was in the midst of pure luxury, and he wondered why this didn't make him happier.

As he lay there in bed, the dawn approaching through the curtains to the balcony, he thought about his life for a moment. It wasn't lost on him that he had most everything he ever wanted; those who knew him thought he was living a dream. But it also wasn't lost on him that the dream he'd assembled for himself had come at a great cost.

He did his best to push all his worries from his mind, and he climbed out of bed quietly. He dressed in workout gear in the dressing room adjacent to his bedroom, then he kissed the mop of chestnut hair sticking out from between a clump of overstuffed pillows. The hair belonged to his wife, Kate, who would sleep for another hour, and when he tiptoed down the hall and looked in on his seven-year-old son, he saw that Noah was sound asleep as well, with a stack of comic books next to him in the bed.

A minute later Terry was out in the early-morning air, walking through the lush tropical property toward the five-thousand-square-foot gymnasium down at the bottom of a hill lined with jacaranda and coconut palms.

Tarpon Island was no regular resort hotel; it was an exclusive resort on an even more exclusive private island, owned by a British billionaire and a celebrated bon vivant. The man had purchased the island in the 1980s to use as his own private refuge, but he'd taken to inviting so many of his well-heeled guests to the place in the past three decades his entrepreneurial spirit told him he could simply open a corner of the island up as a resort for the rich and famous.

Perhaps rich *or* famous was a better way to frame it.

Rock stars, movie stars, and fashion icons all stayed here, but these were just the famous guests. More common were men and women like the Walkers, fabulously wealthy but unknown to anyone but a very few within their industry.

The Walkers were unique in one respect, however. Where most other guests at the Tarpon Island resort stayed a week or two at most, the Walkers had been living here for the past six months, and they planned on being here for six months more.

Terry worked out in the gym for nearly an hour, his mind appreciating the focus exercise gave him, and then he headed home, past the smallest units on the island, cottages that could sleep six, and back up the hill to his place, the four-bedroom mansion with floor-to-ceiling views of the Caribbean Sea from almost every single room.

At eight a.m. a showered, shaved, and fed Terry Walker walked around the breakfast table, kissing his wife and child as he went. He waved good-bye to the cook, then headed down the steep hillside pathway to the beach, just fifty yards from his back door. He wore a suit and tie today because he had a meeting, but on most days he just wore board shorts and a polo. Even with the suit, Terry carried a backpack over his shoulder, a particular affectation of his because his large collection of electronic gadgetry wouldn't fit into a regular briefcase or messenger bag.

A candy-apple-red Robinson helicopter landed on a beachside road promptly at 8:05, as it did every day, and Walker climbed aboard as the aircraft's only passenger. He chartered the helo every day to cut his commute time down from what it would have been if he had taken a launch, and this gave him a little more precious time in the mornings and evenings with his family.

As he did virtually every morning, Walker sat in the back of the helo and looked out at the villa as he lifted into the air. Then, when he could see it no longer he regarded the resort below, and the rest of the hilly island. And then, when the island twisted out of view, he gazed across the blue-green water that shot below him.

Terry was blowing nearly ten grand a day on the house, the office, the helo, the food, and the rest of this operation, so it was a good thing he was averaging about $75,000 a day in profit from his work. He was making too much money to shut this temporary gig down yet, but, he told himself, the day was coming.

This bit of paradise would not be theirs forever. He'd promised Kate they'd spend no more than one year here in the BVIs. After that they would return to Sydney and then they would do . . . well, Terry wasn't sure yet.

He was only certain of one thing: They wouldn't do *this* anymore.

Kate didn't understand exactly why Terry had to work here, and he'd done his best not to burden her with the details. It wasn't that she wasn't smart enough to understand her husband's work. No, Terry Walker did not want his wife to know the ins and outs of it all, the reason he really had to stay here in the BVIs to do his job, because the truth was that in virtually any other place, what he was doing would get him thrown in prison.

Twenty minutes after lifting off, the Robinson dropped him at a helipad just a block from his office in Road Town, on the island of Tortola, and he walked the rest of the way to work. Unlike his rented home, his rented office was utterly nondescript. It was a suite of rooms on the second floor of a two-story glass box building on Lower Estate Road. It might have been the nicest and most modern non-hotel structure in Road Town, but that wasn't saying a hell of a lot.

Terry's operation only used a couple local assistants to serve as file clerks and, when clients came in, something of a fake secretary to sit at the desk in the lobby and pretend to do real work. It wasn't that Terry didn't have work that needed doing. It was just that Terry didn't trust anyone else to do it, so he did it all himself.

Walker found it necessary to work here in the BVIs to get around money-laundering laws that he didn't feel rightfully applied to him. BlackHole was a Bitcoin exchange, and in most every other country his company was considered a financial institution. With this designation came all sorts of regulations, the most important of which was that if he had doubts about the source of income of a client, he had to report it to local financial regulators.

In the BVIs, however, he was able to skirt this restriction, as well as a number of others. He merely had to establish his business here, pay his taxes — plus a few bribes — and then he and his young business were left in peace.

It wasn't that Terry *wanted* to dodge the laws of other lands, he simply did not agree with them. He felt the British Virgin Islands was one of the few countries that understood his business, understood that he wasn't trading, he was merely purchasing something on the Internet for a client, and then selling that something on the Internet to another person.

Of course he was trading, *of course* Black-Hole was a financial institution, and *of course* Terry Walker knew this, but his moral compass had been knocked out of alignment by the fact he was making half a million dollars a week managing his company, and handling trades for large investors.

He was in a different boat from most people who had to concern themselves with the financial reportings of their clients, because Walker's clients were temporary. He'd work with a person who wanted to buy a few hundred thousand, or a few million — in some cases tens of millions had been traded — and he'd manage the transaction for them, putting their purchase in his computerized hopper, where it was rendered invisible to anyone who might have the ability to track Bitcoin transactions.

And for a premium, Terry offered another service, one that was not advertised on the BlackHole website or promotional material. For a few well-heeled clients he had arranged their travel here to Road Town, and then he'd structured their transaction in a way that made the movement one hundred ten percent invisible. Even Terry had no way of knowing where the proceeds of these special sales went after the trade was made, since BlackHole automatically wired the money received for the sale of the hopper-hidden Bitcoin into an account entered on the physical computer at Terry Walker's office. He simply executed the buy of Bitcoin, threw it into the hopper, sold it, then left his office for a moment. His client sat at his desk and entered routing information for the new money, sending it anywhere in the world he wanted it to go with a few keystrokes. The record immediately erased itself from the hard drive.

The perfect move for a money launderer.

This necessitated face-to-face meetings, of course, but normally the person showing up at his office was a cutout a dozen times removed from the beneficiary of the money, so Terry never knew who was profiting from his services.

Obviously Terry Walker was no fool, he

understood these special transactions were likely being conducted by criminals, corrupt government officials, or other ne'er-do-wells, but again, Terry Walker was making seventy-five grand a day.

Walker was not concerned about the occupations, habits, or predilections of his clients, but he was obsessed with not getting hacked. It was the terror of everyone in the cryptocurrency market, but for a man like Walker, who dealt with powerful clients with regularity, he knew that losing either money or information that belonged to someone else just might mean a death sentence.

To keep his data ultra-secure, he had something called a cold wallet, a completely offline file kept on a computer in a room with no Internet access of any kind, and he moved his Bitcoin information to it with handwritten sheets of paper from another room in his office, this with computer access. Once he received a new wallet of valuable coins on his computer, he would register the information on his pad, check it three times, then rip out the page from the pad and walk it into his "cold room." Here he would input it in the file, then immediately slip the paper in a crosscut shredder next to the desk.

When he needed to transfer the Bitcoin from the cold wallet to the network to make a transaction — depositing funds into an account owned by a private trust set up on

Mauritius or Dubai, for example — he would merely reverse the process, taking the information off the cold wallet and walking it into his room with Internet access. Here, again, he had a fingerprint scanner, a retinal scanner, and a voice scanner, all of which had to be satisfied that he was, in fact, Terry Walker. He then entered his twenty-digit alphanumeric code, which he had memorized, combined with double-factor authentication.

To Walker it seemed he had the perfect system, with one obvious flaw. It wasn't scalable. Walker himself had to work, day in and day out. He had to input the "special trades" into his system, and he had to be here on those occasions when his "special clients" came to input their account information into the system.

It was this lack of scalability that was burning him out. He told himself that in a year's time he would sell BlackHole to some other wealthy tech-minded cryptocurrency maverick. He'd make tens of millions more for the sale on top of what he was banking now, and he would then explain to the new owner about the special transactions he had been conducting in person. While the new owner weighed this information, Terry Walker would take his family home, and when he got home he would park his money in offshores and work in something else; he didn't know what just yet, but one thing he told himself he would not do was deal with any more dangerous people. He had a wife and a son, and while he was providing for them in a way most people could never dream of, he was very aware they were, ultimately, in as much danger as he was.

This job was great for making money in the short term, but it was terrible as a long-term plan.

Terry told himself he'd keep at it for a while, but he'd pick and choose his clients now. He wanted no more dealings with dangerous individuals, so he planned to keep an eye out for business opportunities that seemed too good to be true.

Today Terry worked away the morning, and then into the afternoon, pausing for only a few minutes to exchange texts with his wife and a few minutes more to eat a rice-and-sausage dish brought in by one of his local employees.

At three p.m. his secretary came over the intercom in his office, even though she was sitting just a dozen feet away in the front room. "Mr. Walker? Mr. Ivanov and . . . and a colleague are here for you."

Terry had forgotten about this afternoon's meeting, but with the call he immediately brushed the last of the rice off his face and took a long swig of bottled water to do what he could to hide the garlic from his breath. He tightened his tie and headed for the little lobby of the office.

Most offices in this building belonged to local attorneys, and Terry doubted many of them had ever had a client visit them in person. That wasn't what the BVIs and several other Caribbean offshore financial havens were all about. But Terry found himself face-to-face with one of his special clients or potential clients every week or so.

Walker shook hands with the two men and introduced himself.

One of the men spoke in a heavy Russian accent. "My name is Ivanov, and this is my associate, Mr. Popov."

Walker knew that Popov and Ivanov were two of the most common surnames in Russia. Virtually a third of the mysterious Russians he'd ever had dealings with had called themselves Ivanov, and probably one in six had gone by Popov. Walker assumed they were not the men's real names; the Ivanovs and Popovs he'd met in the past had not really been named that either, any more than a couple Americans introducing themselves as Mr. Smith and Mr. Jones would really be named that.

Walker found himself completely unfazed to learn he was probably being lied to. It went with the job.

When they sat down, Ivanov said, "I appreciate your time."

"It's my pleasure. Either of you care for a

471

cup of tea?"

Ivanov shook his head, as did Popov, and they both sat down in simple chairs across from Walker. Ivanov said, "I represent a client who wants to convert a large amount of his assets, an extremely large amount, into cryptocurrency. He then would like the currency traded on BlackHole for U.S. dollars and he would like me to enter his new account numbers for disbursal of the funds."

Walker stifled a yawn and told himself he should have had a second Red Bull after lunch. He said, "Mr. Frieden contacted me yesterday and said you'd be coming right over. I don't normally work this quickly, but he assured me this would be something I wouldn't want to pass up."

"I should think not," Ivanov said.

Walker just nodded. He reached for a pen. "How much?" He knew better than to ask who the client was.

"There will be future transactions. But for now, let's say eight billion."

With wide eyes Walker reached for his calculator. "Good Lord. That is . . . that *is* a lot of money, indeed. I'll just need to check the exchange rate and convert that from rubles to U.S. to get an idea of —"

Ivanov said, "Eight billion U.S. dollars."

Walker stared at Ivanov, then put his pen down with a little sigh. "Eight billion dollars. Is this a fucking joke, mate? Because I've no time for jokes."

"No joke."

"Mr. Ivanov, the entire market capitalization of Bitcoin is barely six billion dollars."

"I understand that. That's why this must be done piecemeal, but it still must be done quickly. You could transfer two hundred sixty-six million dollars a day into the market, in which case you would have the transfers completed in thirty days. This is five percent of the market capitalization."

"That's ridiculous! All the activity on BlackHole combined is less than five hundred million a day."

"So our transactions would be less than three-fifths your normal daily trades." Ivanov added, "People watching the cryptomarkets will immediately recognize there are new big players involved, it will push the value of the currency up, and it will increase the total market value, and the total trading volume. That happens, and we will increase our daily transactions. Our thirty-day plan will become a twenty-day plan, or even a fifteen-day plan. It all depends on how others in the markets react."

Walker sighed again. "You aren't thinking this through, mate. As this money is introduced into the markets so quickly, so dramatically, the increase of the price of one Bitcoin will be dramatic. Others in the market will react by freaking out."

Andrei Limonov had taken his cover identity from his father's name, Ivan — he went by Ivanov. He had no idea why Kozlov called himself Popov, but he hadn't asked.

He had expected Walker to say exactly what he had said. Limonov replied, "My client requires the conversion. He is willing to pay you a premium in addition to your normal rate. He is offering an additional ten million dollars U.S. to you when this is completed."

Walker hesitated for nearly a minute. Finally, he said, "Often it benefits me to beat around the bush a little. To avoid being too direct. It's good business. And it's good for my relationships. But right now I feel the need to be quite direct."

Limonov said, "I welcome that, Mr. Walker."

"Good." He leaned closer. "You are out of your *fucking* mind, mate. Whoever your client is, it is obvious he is doing this for the sole purpose of laundering money. And that amount of money, it's safe to say, is bad news." Walker pointed an accusatory finger out. "That's bad bloody business for me. If eight B U.S. enters into the market and then disappears out of the market in a bloody month, Bitcoin will be known as nothing more than a money-laundering transfer vehicle. It will bring in more regulators, it will push away nervous clients, and it will attract more nefarious blokes like you who cause trouble. We don't fuckin' need any of that, mate, and we will be better off without your eight billion than we would be with your eight billion popping in and out of the market."

Andrei Limonov was surprised by the words of the man in front of him, and the ethics they implied. *Of course* cryptocurrency was a money-laundering tool.

He said, "This client of mine is not laundering money. He is using this vehicle to liquidate assets abroad so that the Russian government cannot confiscate them. The money was legally acquired, but it cannot be protected where it is."

There was irony in the fact that Limonov was fingering the Russian government as the villains, but he wasn't thinking about that now.

Walker said, "Look. I understand. I really do. If you would like, I can, perhaps, take a portion of these assets and buy Bitcoin with them. Maybe three, four hundred million U.S. I'm just not ready to draw the attention to myself by dealing with the amount of money you're talking about."

"You won't be drawing attention, Mr. Walker. BlackHole's daily trades are averaging more than we need to trade. If you simply do not make the purchases for your other large clients for the next few weeks, you can take this money and not draw the attention to yourself that you fear. You will purchase our Bitcoin, in lieu of making purchases for your other clients. Only for a short time. I doubt your clients would know, or even much care, if you waited a week or two to make their trades."

"Are you mad? I can assure you they will both know and care."

Limonov leaned closer. "A year ago you had a two-week-long break in trading. A technical glitch, you called it in the media. What was that?"

Walker looked blankly back at the man. Finally, he said, "It was a technical glitch."

"I think not. I think you were making trades for Vadim Rochenkov, a Ukrainian billionaire. I think the amount he had you trading made you worry you would remove liquidity from the Bitcoin market and reveal what you were doing, so you faked a technical issue. Your other clients were annoyed, but you were the only game in town, as it were, so you continued on. I merely ask you to repeat the system that you yourself invented and utilized."

Walker stood up from his desk. "I don't know how else to tell you this. No. Not interested. You need to find some other avenue, Mr. Ivanov. Surely the world is full of schemes that will work for you."

He stepped toward the door. "Now, if you will excuse me."

The Russians climbed back into their SUV outside. Around them sat four other men, all called up by Vlad Kozlov as protection after the incident with Jack Ryan, Jr., in Luxembourg the day before. They were private contractors from Steel Securitas LLC. They were as tight with the Russian government as any Spetsnaz unit, although their allegiance was financial, not ideological or patriotic.

Steel Securitas was one of the largest private security contractors in the world. Based in Dubai, it was big in executive protection, site security, tactical training, and even direct-action operations, and it was used by small governments and large corporations all over the planet.

Its vetting process was robust, but with 40,000 employees around the world, a few bad apples were to be expected.

The Kremlin Security Council, run by Mikhail Grankin, had actively sought out these bad apples and their managers, paid them dearly for no-questions-asked work, and ensured their trust with the not-so-veiled threats that these men were now working for the FSB, and the FSB could fucking ruin them if they didn't take their money and keep their mouths shut about the work and their clients.

Another Land Cruiser with four more Steel Securitas men idled in the street behind them.

As they rolled off down the street, Kozlov pulled out his phone and held it up toward Limonov. He said, "I see no alternative."

Limonov looked like he was going to be sick. He said, "Perhaps if we wait a day and call on Walker again. Maybe I can —"

Kozlov shook his head, turned away from Andrei Limonov, and dialed a number on the mobile. After a moment he heard someone answer. A male voice spoke English. "Yes?"

Kozlov spoke English as well. "Pick them up. Carefully. We need them alive."

Limonov thought he heard a sniff, like that of laughter, on the other end.

"Of course," said the man, and the phone went dead.

42

The Hendley Associates jet touched down on Beef Island in the mid-afternoon, and after the jet cleared customs, John Clark and Adara Sherman climbed into a jeep left for them on the tarmac. Together they drove to a marina in East End Bay in the adjoining island of Tortola. They were met at the dock by a man standing next to a floating dinghy, and after handshakes he handed over a set of keys to Adara.

"Everything you asked for is already stocked and on board. You're moored at number fifty-three. It's the 1978 fifty-two-foot Irwin ketch you picked from the rental photos."

"Excellent," Adara said, and she tipped the man $200 for his quick work.

The man looked Adara and John over for a second. She was in her mid-thirties and he in his mid-sixties, and John caught the inference by the look — he clearly thought John and Adara were a couple. Clark felt a twinge of anger that this stranger took him for a geezer with a trophy wife or — because Adara wasn't wearing a ring and Clark was — perhaps the marina employee assumed Clark was taking his girlfriend down to the islands for some frivolity away from his wife back home.

Clark didn't like it, but he did nothing to dissuade the man's assumptions. He figured he wasn't the first rich old philandering bastard renting a sailboat in the marina here.

It was a good cover story.

As John sat at the helm of the dinghy and pulled out into the marina with Adara next to him, he leaned closer to her. "I hope you didn't have him stock this boat with too many things. With a little luck we'll only need it for one night."

"Not too much. There's enough for a few days, because I thought it might look fishy if we went to all this trouble just for a twenty-four-hour cruise."

"Good thinking."

Adara added, "I think that guy back there was rendering judgment on us both."

Clark nodded. "Yeah, but he sure took our money, didn't he?"

Adara laughed. "Yes, he did. Maybe I should have dressed differently, played into my cover story a little." Sherman wore khakis and a white polo. Her short blond hair was pulled back in a small ponytail. She was young and attractive, but hardly the image of a gold digger on a Caribbean vacation with her sugar daddy.

"And maybe I should wear more rings on my fingers and a fat chain around my neck," Clark said. "I could get some Botox, too."

Adara laughed at the thought.

They piloted out into a field of mooring balls, most of which had sailboats or catamarans attached to them. Quickly they found mooring ball number 53, and they motored slowly around the white monohull sailboat attached to it.

Clark liked what he saw. It was big enough to be comfortable, but not too big to be difficult to captain. It wasn't new and flashy. Adara had told him on the plane it was nearly forty years old, but it looked like it had been lovingly maintained.

They tied the dinghy off on a cleat on the Irwin's gunwale and climbed up onto the deck. Another dinghy, this one a little smaller, was tied off on the back of the boat.

Together they walked around the deck, then went through the cockpit and stood at the helm. Adara said, "She'll do twelve knots on her engines. More under sail, depending on the conditions." She raised a finger as she thought of something else. "These Irwins heel over pretty dramatically in the wind, though, so don't forget to hold on."

Clark just smiled. He told himself no thirty-five-year-old was going to teach him anything about boating, but he caught himself. She wasn't patronizing him, she was looking out for him, and he knew he should appreciate it.

After a walk around belowdecks and a quick survey of the navigation area, the radios, engines, and emergency pumps, Clark rendered his judgment on the boat. "You've done well, Ms. Sherman."

"Good. Ready to head out?"

Clark looked at his watch. It was just after five p.m. He figured the cruise from East End Bay in Tortola to Tarpon Island would take four hours under engine power. Once there, he'd wait a few hours more to head to shore, timing his arrival to avoid anyone else on the water in the bay or walking along the sand.

"Let's do it."

It was a beautiful afternoon on Tarpon Island, but that was no surprise to anyone. This was paradise; even when it rained it was beautiful here.

Today there was no rain; the weather was characteristically perfect, the sky a deeper blue than usual, the ocean clear as glass in the foreground and perfectly aquamarine in the distance.

Seven-year-old Noah Walker splashed as he swam in the shallow surf. His mother, Kate, watched him from her beach chair, looking over the top of her book at him from time to time, just to assure herself he hadn't wandered too far out in the deep. His snorkel, his tuft of jet-black hair, and the backside of his red swim trunks were the only things sticking out of the water anywhere in the bay.

Kate knew she was in heaven here, and she hoped Noah was able to appreciate it. She'd come from a lower-middle-class family; she'd worked for everything she'd ever had in life. It was hard for her to get her head around her son's utterly different childhood experience, but she did her best to keep him as grounded as possible.

That was hard here in paradise, of course, with the maids and cooks and other attendants. With the seaplanes and fine dining, and daily celebrity sightings at the dining pavilion.

Noah knew nothing different from this life; even in London and Sydney they'd had it extremely good since he was three or so, but Kate still had a hard time accepting it all as part of her own existence.

She was no trophy wife, and nothing on earth infuriated her more than when she felt someone treated her as such. She'd worked as a waitress in Sydney while she went through school, then she'd met Terry when they were both programmers at a small software company.

When they were first married, neither of them owned their own car, and within a year they were parents, which made their financial situation even more precarious. Kate left work to take care of Noah, and soon after that Terry, much to Kate's consternation, quit his job to spend his time developing new software products for the new virtual-currency exchanges cropping up on the Internet. They moved to London, where prices were even higher than in Sydney.

It had taken him years to bring his first piece of software to market, and he'd made a lot of money off it, and five years after that his masterpiece was finished and live — BlackHole.

For the first years of BlackHole they'd been rich beyond her wildest imagination, but then Terry explained to her that he needed to relocate from London, move to the Caribbean, and there he could *truly* realize the dream of making BlackHole the biggest and best virtual-currency exchange on earth. She agreed, provided he put a time limit on their relocation, and the next thing she knew, they were here and her husband was making $2 million a month.

The Walkers' lives had changed dramatically, to put it mildly, but Kate often caught herself feeling wistful about those days in London when they were scrounging coins in the sofa cushions to pay for Noah's diapers. At least they were together. These days, in order to keep Terry's system up and running he had to work seven days a week; he had a never-ending array of clients to meet and trades to execute, and there was nothing but promises from him of when he would take a break, when they would get to enjoy their lives, when they would finally get a vacation from paradise.

Six more months was his promise, and it was a promise she planned on holding him to.

The beach here was nearly empty this afternoon, but that was usually the case. She came out here with Noah most every day around this time, after the worst of the sun's rays, and she read while her son swam around, hunting shells in the shallow water of the bay.

She was just thinking about how boring paradise could be when a woman's voice startled her. "Oh, hello there. Mind if I join you?"

She turned to find an attractive smiling woman sitting down in the next beach chair, a piña colada in her hand. She wore a conservative bikini with a wrap around her waist, and a wide-brimmed hat on her head. The woman's European accent was noticeable, but Kate couldn't place it.

"Hi," Kate said. "Of course not. You must be new."

"Just in today. We're on the other side, in the little cottages. I hope it's okay for me to be here."

Usually this stretch of beach was reserved for the three villas up on the hill above them, and the cottages on the far end of the bay had their own, less exclusive stretch of sand. But it was not Kate's job to enforce the rules of the resort, so she wasn't about to send this lady packing. Plus, she realized she was happy for the adult company. She extended a hand. "Of course you can be here. Kate Walker."

"I'm Julia."

Kate thought the woman was beautiful, and she assumed she was someone famous. Most of the vacationers here on Tarpon Island were not rock stars or actors, but a significant portion were, and this lady sure had the looks, bearing, and confidence of a celebrity. The fact she'd given only her first name also contributed to Kate's suspicion that Julia fully expected to be recognized.

Not wanting to appear to be a typical star-struck civilian, Kate didn't ask her anything else. There was an unspoken rule here on the island: You didn't question anyone about what they did for a living. At a place where many people went in order to get away from attention, it was seen as improper to peer into private lives.

Julia looked out to the water at Noah. "He's got so much energy. All I want to do is lie around and sun."

Kate smiled. "Same here." She raised her own glass. "With a drink in hand."

Julia tapped her glass to Kate's. "You're here on vacation?"

Kate could have answered simply "Yes" and shut down further inquiry, but she didn't have many opportunities to talk about her life. "Not really. My husband is in the BVIs on business, and I homeschool Noah, so we are living here, for the time being." She realized the tone she'd affected, and quickly added, "Not that I'm complaining. We're living in a villa. This place is wonderful."

Julia said, "It's wonderful enough in the cottages." She looked over her shoulder. "But I suspect that villa is exquisite."

Kate nodded. "Sure is. We've been here quite a while, though, so I am looking forward to returning to Sydney." She motioned to Noah. "He could stay right here forever."

The two ladies were the same age, give or take a couple years, and it was bothering Kate that she couldn't place Julia. She tried to picture her on a stage with a microphone in her hand, or in an ad in a glossy magazine, or even in a movie.

Nothing. She didn't look familiar at all.

She decided she'd break Tarpon Island protocol. "How about you, Julia? What brings you here?"

"I'm here for work as well."

"I see," Kate said, but she didn't. That Julia added nothing, just sipped her piña colada and looked out at the water, kept Kate from making any further inquiries.

It was quiet for several seconds, only the breeze and the squawks of a few grackles in the distance.

Finally, Julia broke the stillness. "My boyfriend and I are thinking about getting a tour of one of the villas before we leave. He has a big family, he's Italian, Catholic, you know what I mean."

"Sure," Kate said. Now she was trying to picture the woman's boyfriend. Maybe *he* was the famous one.

"Anyway, we thought on our next visit to the BVIs we might try to bring everyone down for a family reunion."

Kate knew all three villas were occupied at the moment. A well-known film producer was in one; from the rumors Terry had picked up at the pavilion cigar bar, he was spending his days with a constant rotation of starlets.. And a French winemaker was with his family in the other. The management here at Tarpon wouldn't dream of giving a tour through the occupied villas, not even for other guests staying on the island.

Kate held her tongue for a minute, but as she weighed the situation, she decided she could just take Julia up the hill herself and give her a quick tour. Hell, she was bored, and it would be fun to show her around.

"Would you like to come up and take a look at our place? Noah and I were just about to leave. My husband usually gets home by seven, and the cook will be here to make dinner by six-thirty. I have to run up anyway."

Julia's eyes widened dramatically. "That would be wonderful, but I don't mean to intrude."

"Not at all. I'll show you around and we can have a glass of wine. You'll love the view of the bay from up there."

Julia stood with her drink in her hand. "Well, then, lead the way."

Twenty minutes later, the tour of the villa complete, Kate poured two glasses of Chardonnay in the kitchen and took them out to Julia, who sat in the living room on a sofa by the window overlooking the bay. Noah lay on the floor in front of the television, playing Xbox on the large-screen TV on the wall.

Julia took a glass from Kate with a smile and then took a sip.

"Very nice."

Kate sat down next to her, looked out into the bay, and noticed a large slate-gray sailing catamaran at anchor a few hundred yards from shore. She couldn't see anyone topside.

She motioned with her wineglass to the boat and said, "That's interesting. You don't usually see anyone anchored over here. The staff at Tarpon Island doesn't like boats mooring in the bay. When the island security boat comes back by here they will run them off."

Julia looked out at the boat herself now and took another sip of wine. "The island security boat only makes one pass an hour. The last one was twenty minutes ago. Otherwise it's perfectly secluded over here."

Kate was surprised Julia knew anything about the security here, since she said she'd just arrived that day.

Julia continued, "For an island with so many wealthy and influential people staying on it, I have to say I am rather surprised there isn't more in the way of protection."

Kate chuckled at this. "This is the most peaceful place I've ever been, to tell you the truth. I do worry about Terry, a little. He is in international finance and offshore banking, which brings in its share of shady characters. But nothing has ever happened to him."

Julia took another sip of her Chardonnay, then placed her glass on the end table next to her. She leaned closer to Kate.

The Australian woman cocked her head, confused by her proximity.

Julia whispered, "I am a little concerned."

"About what?"

"About Noah."

Now Kate was really confused. An unease grew in the pit of her stomach. "What about Noah?"

"Children can be a problem. I will ask your help to keep him calm throughout all this."

Kate felt the foreboding growing from

within. "I don't understand, Julia. What on earth are you talking about?"

Julia smiled a little, pointed toward the entrance to the villa. Kate looked around and saw a tall, broad man with auburn hair. He wore a linen shirt, cargo shorts, and boat shoes, along with sunglasses and a baseball cap. His hands were empty, but he moved with purpose.

Kate launched off the sofa, dropping her glass of wine to the floor. It shattered on the tile. "What's going on?"

Julia stood with her and took her by the arm roughly. A knife appeared in her hand, and she touched it to Kate's ribs. Kate stared down at the knife while Julia spoke softly in her ear. "Listen carefully, bitch. We are going outside, and then down to the water. We will take a skiff out to that boat. You will not cry out, and you will keep that little brat of yours quiet. You understand?"

Just then, Kate heard Noah call out, "Hey!"

She turned and saw that the big man had taken the Xbox controller out of her son's hand and tossed it to the side. Now he grabbed Noah by the shoulder and lifted him to his feet like he was a rag doll. He turned him around and pushed him toward the door.

"Get your hands off of him!" Kate screamed out, and she tried to move to the aid of her son.

Julia yanked her back around to face her,

and the knife moved up to her left cheek. The two stood with their faces inches apart. Kate saw nothing but cold in the other woman's brown eyes. Julia said, "They don't want me to kill you, but I *will* cut your pretty face. Make Noah afraid to look at his mother. Make Terry disgusted to be in your presence."

Kate's voice went hoarse. "Who the *fuck* are you?"

Julia just said, "To the boat. Quietly, or I will drain your blood across the sand."

Kate Walker was crying now, but she nodded, turned to her son. "It's okay, Noah. Do what they say." She turned back to Julia. "We will go with you. Just, please, don't hurt us."

Julia said, "I thought you might come around."

Ten minutes later Kate and Noah Walker were helped out of the dinghy and onto the deck of the big gray catamaran. Julia followed them up onto the deck. The huge man in the linen shirt had been at the wheel of the dinghy. He tied it off and climbed on board the catamaran as well.

On the deck Kate saw four big men standing around, all wearing T-shirts and shorts, muscles rippling on their arms, tattoos of different colors and shapes on every one of them. They said nothing, just kept their eyes on the newcomers.

Kate turned to the woman who called herself Julia and asked, "Who are these men?"

"These are your babysitters, darling."

"Why are you doing this to us?"

"Your husband has something my employer wants. When my employer gets it, you will go home. If my employer doesn't get it . . ." Julia smiled. "You know? Why don't we just stay optimistic?"

The Walkers were led down the stairs from the cockpit and into the saloon, and then from there into a large master cabin. Julia was close on their heels. She said, "You have a bed and a bathroom. Food will be brought to you three times a day. They will not tie you, unless you give them a reason to." She looked at Noah. "My advice, Kate, is to watch this kid of yours. He's just about reaching the age where he thinks he is invincible. Don't make the men on board prove to him he is not."

Noah just stared at the strange woman with wide eyes.

Kate said, "You aren't staying here?"

"No, my dear. I am not a babysitter. You will remain in the care of these men." She turned and left the room, but as the door shut Kate heard a bolt being slid into place. She checked the door and saw the lock had been removed, obviously so it could be attached to the other side.

■ ■ ■ ■

Martina Jaeger climbed the stairs out of the saloon, pulling a mobile phone out of her bag on the way. She walked forward on the catamaran's main deck, just next to the anchor chain, which drooped down into the water from the center of the bow.

A local number was answered moments later by a man with a Russian accent. She didn't know the real identity of the man called Popov, but she assumed he was FSB.

"Yes?"

"We have them."

"Any problems?"

"Of course not. They are on the boat with the contractors. My husband and I will be returning to Europe immediately."

"Very well. Leave Kate Walker's phone with the men on the boat. I will be there within the hour." The line went dead.

Martina turned to find Braam standing close to her. They high-fived on the bow with a grin and went back downstairs to grab their backpacks, then they tossed them onto the dinghy and motored off. The four men on the boat had said nothing to them, nor they to the men.

As Braam opened the throttle on the dinghy's engine, he leaned over to Martina. "It's nice here. I'd like to come back."

Martina said, "This job was beneath us. I'll only come back if they have something for us to do."

Braam shrugged a little. "The pay was the same."

Martina looked at her brother for a moment. "You do this for the money still? Braam, darling, you really worry me sometimes."

43

Terry Walker looked up from his computer and checked the clock on his wall. It was almost seven p.m., which meant he had only a few minutes before the Robinson landed at the helipad to fly him back home for the evening.

He rubbed soreness from his eyes and started to close down his computers for the night, but his mobile phone rang. Looking down, he saw that it was Kate's number. "Hello, darling. I'm on schedule. I'll be home in half an hour."

To his surprise, a man replied. He immediately recognized the Russian accent of Mr. Popov. "We are very sorry to have to take these measures, Mr. Walker, but you forced our hand."

"What?" He looked down at his phone, double-checking to make sure it was, in fact, Kate's line calling. "Where . . . where is my wife?"

"She is perfectly safe. I promise you that.

She will remain so, as long as you comply with our requests."

Terry Walker was overcome with a feeling of disbelief. That some joke, some trick, was being played on him. He even coughed out a little laugh. "You've got me, Popov. Bloody good joke, mate. I don't know how or why —"

He heard a shuffling on the line, then a new voice. Soft, distant, unsure.

"Dad?"

Walker's blood ran cold. "Noah?"

"They say you have to do a job for them, it will only take you a couple of weeks. You'll do it, right? Mom and I need you to do it. They wanted me to tell you that."

Tears poured down Walker's face and his voice cracked. "Where's your mother, Noah? What have they done?"

"Her mouth is all covered with tape. Dad, I think they are pirates. Tell me you'll do what they want you to."

"Yes, of course. Don't worry, buddy."

There was a knock at the door to Walker's office. He leapt to his feet, unsure.

Popov said, "You can answer the door." He hung up the phone.

Walker ran to the door, thinking Kate would be on the other side. He flung it open, only to find the man called Ivanov standing there. Two big, tough-looking men stood

497

behind him, their hands held behind their backs.

The Russian called Ivanov said, "I'm sorry, Mr. Walker. But I need to come in and talk."

A few minutes later Ivanov and Walker sat in the office, staring at each other across Terry Walker's desk. The Australian's eyes were rimmed red, and he'd made no attempt to wipe his tears off his cheeks.

The two big men remained in the lobby. They hadn't said a word.

Ivanov said, "So, Mr. Walker, it is very simple. We know your security setup. You have retinal scanners and fingerprint scanners here that you have to use to log in. You can only make trades and purchases from your office computer so that no one can steal your credentials and operate under your identity. For this reason we cannot take you somewhere else to do this, we must remain here. This makes things difficult, but we have a plan. You and I will live at a private residence here on Tortola. We will simply go to work every day, but you will not work with any other clients. Only our account. You will purchase two hundred sixty-six million dollars a day in Bitcoin in automatic small increments, then you will sell it for dollars in other small automatic increments through your tumbler system. The dollars will be deposited in accounts that I have already established throughout the world. I will enter the information at the end of each transaction to disburse the money."

Walker said nothing.

Ivanov added, "Obviously, the more quickly we conduct this operation, the better it will be for everyone. I am hoping the addition of the money into the marketplace will bring up the market, and we can increase our trading volume." He smiled. "And shorten the amount of time you are inconvenienced by all this."

Still, Walker did not reply.

"You will also let the staff at Tarpon Island Resort know that your wife and son have been called away to tend to a family illness. They will be well taken care of, but we will hold them until you fulfill your end of the bargain."

Slowly Walker rubbed the wetness from his face, and he sat up. "I won't be staying with my family?"

"No. They will be held somewhere else."

"I will work with you. I will do whatever you want. But I want my family to remain here in the area. I don't want you shipping them off to Siberia."

"Certainly. No one is going to Siberia."

"Return them to Tarpon Island."

"Out of the question."

Walker held firm. "Look. You need my compliance. You made that obvious by the

499

steps you have taken. You will get what you need, but you have to give me something in return."

"I'll give you your family back. Not enough for you?"

"No, it's not. I want to see them while I work. You deliver me to them, every single night. I don't care what you have to do to do it, I don't care what I have to do."

Ivanov said, "My colleague, Mr. Popov, said you would ask for this. Here is what we are prepared to do. I will give you a walkie-talkie. Its range is fifteen miles. You can communicate with your family once a day. If they can transmit to you, then you know they are in the area."

Ivanov pulled the device out of his coat and turned it on. He held it out and Walker took it.

Immediately, he pressed the talk button. "Kate? Kate, are you there?"

His wife's voice came through the speaker after a few seconds. She sounded impossibly far away, but Terry wondered if what he was hearing was just her fear. "I'm here, Terry."

"How are you? Have they laid a finger on you?"

He could tell she had been crying. "We are okay. They taped my mouth for a bit, but I'm fine."

Terry started crying himself again. "Good. It's going to be just fine. These men just need me for a couple of weeks."

"They told me. Please do what they say."

"I promise I will. Where are you?"

"I can't tell you. They told me not to."

"Are you sure you are all right?"

"I'm . . . I'm feeling better than I was, actually. No more of that damn nausea, which is a surprise, considering."

Suddenly Walker knew his wife was trying to tell him something. He wasn't sure what it was. He thought a moment, but then Ivanov motioned for him to wrap up the conversation.

"I have to go, darling, but we'll talk tomorrow. They told me I could talk to you every night."

To this she just said, "Okay."

"I love you, Kate. I'm sorry, but this will be over soon."

Instead of his wife, Popov came over the radio now. "You start work in the morning."

Terry Walker looked up to Ivanov. The Russian looked upset by having to listen to the conversation between Walker and his kidnapped wife. His face was pale, his eyes narrow, almost as if he was taking it all in for the first time.

Walker said, "I'll fulfill my end of the deal, mate. You just see that you fulfill yours."

Ivanov's eyes cleared and he nodded forcefully. "Mr. Walker. I want you to understand that, despite this uncomfortable arrangement we have established, we are still paying you, and paying you an incredible amount of money. When this is all over, when you are reunited with your family, I hope you will take that money and remain quiet about all this. What I know about your operation could ruin you. What you know about us, on the other hand, could realistically only get you killed. You go to the police, and men like Mr. Popov will find *you* long before the police find *us*."

Walker decided to make one last play to end the kidnapping. "I understand, and I agree totally to your terms. So just let my family out of this."

Ivanov's obvious insecurity about the arrangement disappeared in an instant. Walker saw this man was not going to call the whole thing off. Ivanov said, "Mr. Walker, you are a businessman, after a fashion. You understand the fundamentals of indemnification. Your family, sadly, is insurance for us. Nothing more."

Walker saw there was no reason to protest. He told himself he would do everything they wanted him to do. What alternative did he have?

Walker and Ivanov left the office together a moment later, the two big men following them down to a waiting car.

Terry Walker was taken to a luxury villa on

the top of Saint Bernard's Hill, far on the west side of Tortola Island. He was marched along with three guards through a tiled entryway, past a formal dining room with views out to the sea, and down a hallway to the first-floor master bedroom. Along the way he saw no fewer than six men, all dressed casually. Some were white, some were black, others appeared Hispanic. He was certain few of them, if any of them at all, were Russian other than Popov and Ivanov. He had no idea who they were, but he knew without reservation they were armed, and they wouldn't hesitate to do the bidding of their Russian masters.

Walker was frisked thoroughly by a guard, then locked in the master bedroom. He walked around the space and saw all the windows were secured and he heard the rhythmic footsteps of a sentry on the colonnade that wrapped around the outside of his room. He had no doubt another guard was posted outside his door.

Walker lay down on the bed, facing the rotating ceiling fan above.

He thought about his conversation with Kate. What had she said? Something about her stomach feeling better, and that this surprised her, considering the situation. She hadn't said a thing about her stomach since they'd rented a sailboat a few months back. The plan had been for Terry to take a few days off from his work to sail up to Anegada Island, but the trip turned into a disaster. Kate had been so violently ill that they'd had to return the boat after just one day.

Why would it surprise her she was not feeling the same effects now? Clearly, Terry deduced, because she was not on land.

And what had Noah said? Something about pirates?

Yes, Terry realized. His wife and child were clearly being held under guard on a boat.

He rolled over and put his face in his pillow, curled up into the fetal position. It didn't matter where they were, Terry told himself, because no one was going to come and help them. The only way he could save his family was by making Ivanov and Popov satisfied that he had fulfilled his end of the bargain.

Andrei Limonov stepped out on the patio off the living room with a bottle of vodka and a glass. He sat next to the infinity pool, looking down the side of the hill, to the lights of West End Bay below. The water in the bay on the far side of the lights was blacker than the sky above.

He drank two shots of warm vodka in close succession to calm his nerves. He'd just poured his third glass when he saw the headlights of a big SUV approach up the long and winding driveway. The lights disappeared on the other side of the house, and soon Vlad

Kozlov joined him by the pool, sitting in a chair on the other side of the little table. The gray-haired Russian poured himself a shot from a glass he'd brought with him from the bar. He drank it down quickly before turning to Limonov. "How did it go with Walker?"

Limonov said, "He is here. He will comply. We won't need to use him for very long. I think all the transfers will be complete within three weeks at most. We can then release the family and let them get on with their lives."

Kozlov said, "I understand."

Limonov added, "This man knows what he's dealing with here. If he speaks about this with anyone, even years down the road, he understands you'll kill him."

Kozlov did not reply to this.

Limonov decided he would say no more. Instead, he poured another shot of vodka. While he drank it he wondered if, despite any arrangements already made or understood by all the parties, the Australian locked in the master bedroom of this villa was nothing more than a dead man.

44

John Clark climbed into the dinghy tied off on his sailboat just after midnight, leaving Adara Sherman behind on the fifty-two-foot Irwin. He cut engine power when he was still a half-mile off Tarpon Island, which meant he had to paddle for nearly fifteen minutes, but the water in this bay was nearly as placid as a swimming pool, and he had the added benefit of being able to point himself directly at all the lights coming from the big villas on the hillside to guide him to just the right spot for his landing.

It had been a long while since the ex-SEAL had hit a beach in a small watercraft, but he was certain he'd never conducted a midnight raid on a five-star resort. He had a feeling he could have had Adara call ahead to arrange a piña colada and a grilled lobster under glass waiting for him once he landed on the shore, except for the obvious wrinkle that he was not a guest at the exclusive island retreat.

He pulled his boat up off the white sand

and dragged it under some meticulously maintained foliage, alongside a pair of high-end wooden recliners. Then he passed a little copper bucket where he could dip his feet in water to wash off the beach sand, which he declined to do. Quietly he headed up the pathway on the hill toward his target location.

When he was halfway up the path he heard a noise ahead of him. He stepped into the sandy area below the mangroves just to his left and ducked down behind a jacaranda. Other than the loud pops in both of his knees as he knelt, he didn't make a sound.

Fifteen seconds later two young men passed, both holding rakes. One had a mesh bag over his shoulder, and Clark got the idea they were on their way down to the beach to comb it for any tiny bits of seaweed that might have washed ashore.

The guests of Tarpon Island didn't want to wake up to a pristine paradise marred by nature.

Clark shook his head. As a member of Navy special warfare, he'd swum through swamps so green and gooey he could have written his name on the surface with his fingertip. He was cut from a very different cloth from the average patron of this swanky place.

When the two men were out of sight he pulled a night-vision monocular out of his pocket and used it to lead him the rest of the way up the winding stone path that led directly to the sliding back door of the immense villa.

There were lights shining on the second floor, he'd seen this from the bay, but the ground floor appeared to be completely dark. John looked for the telltale tiny red lights of a security system or motion detector anywhere on the ground floor, but he saw nothing.

He tried the glass door and, to his surprise, found it unlocked. He pulled it open a foot, then retreated back to a thick copse of bushes off the patio.

A few minutes later, when no one came to investigate the breach, he felt certain there had been no security system activated at the villa, so he returned to the back door and entered slowly.

It took him nearly five minutes of slow, steady movement to make it from one end of the ground floor to the other. The space looked neat but well lived in, but there was no one here at present.

Eventually he doubled back to the stairs out of the living room, and he took these up, still moving at a near glacial pace. He had his night-vision device in his hands, but he'd taken the time to let his eyes adjust to the low light, so he didn't use the monocular.

On the second floor he found a child's room. Again, it looked like someone was living there now, but they weren't in the bed or the adjoining bathroom. He'd been told Walker had a young son, and he found himself surprised the kid was out of his bed well past midnight.

He made his way into the master bedroom next, crept in complete silence, and moved to the bed. Here he did use his monocular to confirm it was empty.

Another minute to check the second floor more carefully and he was done.

It was on his second pass around the property that he noticed the shattered wine-glass by the couch. That someone had just left it there along with the wine on the tile floor made no sense, unless they had to leave in a hurry.

Unless it was something bad.

As he headed back down the stairs, Clark spotted a security camera high on the wall. For a moment he was worried this camera linked with the resort's security office, but that didn't make much sense to Clark. He couldn't imagine some millionaire checking into this chic place with the full understanding he or she would be watched like a research specimen.

He looked closer at the camera. It was attached to a small radio system. A tiny antenna stuck up a few inches.

Clark had seen these units before. They could broadcast only one hundred feet or so.

He realized this was a private system. Used

for a guest's own security detail that might travel with them to the resort.

Clark walked through the entire villa looking for the security station, finally finding it outside the building in a small one-room cottage on the far side of the driveway. The door to the cottage was locked, but he picked the lock quickly, then moved inside, careful to keep the lights off and his head below the level of the windows, just in case anyone was around.

He saw there were five cameras set up to run on the monitors, but the three inside the building had been shut off, obviously for the privacy of the guests. The other two feeds, one on the front drive and one at the rear of the property, including the path that led down to the beach, were up and running, and now they broadcast black-and-white images taken from the infrared low-light-capable camera.

Clark looked down at the security board. It didn't look like anyone was using this room at all, so he didn't know if the video recorders would be working, but to his surprise he found the attached computer made a digital recording in a loop that recorded over the file every eight hours.

Quickly he pulled up the front-of-the-house camera, backed it up to the beginning, and began to look through the video on the monitor. The timestamp said it was four-thirty that afternoon, and the image of the driveway and lush vegetation alongside it was in color and very clear. He began racing through it at sixteen-times speed, looking for any clues.

At six-thirty he brought it back to normal speed. A golf cart had pulled up in front of the house and a heavyset black woman was climbing out with several pots and pans and trays. She seemed to be a hired cook. She disappeared into the house, making a couple of trips to move all her equipment.

Clark raced through some more time, stopping again when the woman came back out at seven-thirty, talking on her cell phone. He watched her for a moment, then sped it up again.

At eight p.m. the woman packed up her kitchenware and left in the golf cart.

Clark went to sixteen speed again and watched the recording until the point where he saw himself lurking around the driveway and the security shack. He fumbled with the controls for a moment to erase the video, then he started with the back of the house.

On this feed he watched for a moment, then sped it up to eight-times speed. Nothing was happening, so he reached down to increase the speed again, but just as he did so he saw movement on the path. He rewound the recording, then hit play, watching it in regular time.

A young boy with black hair, Clark put him

at about seven or eight years old, appeared on the path from the beach, then shot below the camera, heading toward the house. Behind him, two women, one with chestnut hair, the other with auburn hair and wearing a wide-brimmed hat and large sunglasses, came up from the beach, towels and drinks in hand.

Clark waited for a minute to see if Terry Walker would be following them, but there was no one else. He gave it another minute, then increased the speed, his finger idling above the key that would return the video to normal speed. He tapped it when a large auburn-haired man with sunglasses and a baseball cap walked purposefully up the path.

After less than a minute, the man appeared again. He held the shoulder of the boy. Behind them, the two women walked closely together.

This, Clark realized in an instant, was probably the strangest-looking kidnapping he'd ever witnessed, but he was sure that's what it was. The two tall Caucasians had taken Terry Walker's wife and child, and rushed them down to the beach.

John Clark spent the next five precious minutes cussing under his breath as he tried to figure out how to save the video recording onto a DVR disc he found on a shelf. He finally gave up with more bitching about the technology, then used the camera of his own mobile phone to record the film. He could already hear Gavin Biery chastising him for his low-tech method to a high-tech problem, but Clark knew he couldn't spend the entire night here.

He then erased the remaining video and left the cottage.

His exfiltration of the property and the island took more than twenty minutes. As soon as he was back on his sailboat he called Jack Junior, who was in Virginia.

Ryan had been ready for the late-night call, so Clark didn't have to wait for him to wake up.

"Bad news, Jack. Walker's family has been kidnapped."

After a pause over the line, Jack blew out a sigh. "Well, *that* complicates things. I presume it was Limonov and Kozlov."

"I have no doubt they are behind it, but they did it through proxies. I have video of the kidnappers, one male, one female. Their faces are obscured by hats and glasses."

"Any idea where they went?"

"I suppose they used a boat to get them out of here, but the kidnapping took place around five-thirty, so they have a seven-hour head start."

Jack said, "So they could be halfway to Moscow now if they wanted to be."

Clark said, "If they left the country, they

didn't do it in Limonov's aircraft. Adara has a man at the airport here who's watching Limonov's plane for us, and it's sitting right there. No way they would take the Walkers out of here on a commercial flight. Either they went across the open water to Puerto Rico and flew out on an exec jet there or else they are still here in the area. If that's the case, they will be in a rented house or they'll be on a boat."

Jack thought about this. "I've been doing some research on Walker. If they are going to use BlackHole to launder money, they might need to keep Walker there at his office or close by. Depending on his security setup, it's possible he has to make large clandestine trades from his own server. If that's the case, they'll probably do it tomorrow." Jack added, "Maybe he refused to comply, so they just snatched his wife and kid to help convince him."

Clark said, "Yeah, and when they don't need Walker's help anymore . . ."

Jack said, "Right. Do you have any ideas?"

"Yeah," Clark said. "I'm going to take a look at his office setup. If Adara and I head back to Tortola now, I can be in position by early morning. Maybe I can get eyes on Walker and find a way to get him away from Limonov."

"I can be on the first flight down."

"No, Jack. You stay up there. Run the video

I sent you, keep looking into Salvatore, and keep trying to find out what Limonov and Walker are up to."

Jack said, "Okay, I'll do that, but if you gain access to Walker, I have a funny feeling you'll learn a lot more than I will up here."

Clark and Sherman motored west through the night from Tarpon Island toward Tortola, pushing the sailboat's motors to full power. Clark sat at the helm at first, but after an hour or so Sherman asked if she could relieve him.

Clark said, "It wouldn't hurt for me to get a couple hours' sleep before I get there. Tomorrow might be a long day."

Adara said, "You should go below. The bed in the master stateroom is made up. We'll be in port by five a.m. It's only a five-minute drive from the marina to Walker's office building."

"Thanks, Ms. Sherman," Clark said.

Adara hesitated for a moment, then said, "Mr. Clark, I know you want me to return to D.C. in the morning, but I'm a little concerned that it might be dangerous down here for just one operative."

John said, "Are you offering to stick around?"

She said, "This is a big boat, you could use the help."

"I am sure you are right, but I don't want

to take you away from your other duties. Ding and Dom might need an extraction at any time. Even in D.C. you are five hours closer to them than you are here. Plus the Gulfstream can fly there direct. If you had to haul ass to Lithuania from here, you would need to stop for fuel, tacking on another ninety minutes, minimum."

He could tell from her look that she was concerned. He said, "I need you to support them, not me. My work here won't be nearly as taxing as what the others are doing."

Adara said, "I hope you're right about that."

"Me, too." Clark went below deck, and Adara Sherman took the wheel and looked out over the black water.

45

The tires of Air Force One touched the runway of Copenhagen Airport–Kastrup just after six p.m. A steady rain shower ensured the crowd around the airport was light, and the reception was minimal, but Ryan was met on the tarmac by the U.S. ambassador to Denmark, a few senior NATO staff, and a representative of the Danish prime minister.

The pleasantrics out of the way, he folded into his motorcade and headed into the city.

The NATO summit would open at the Eigtveds Pakhus conference venue, in central Copenhagen, next door to the Ministry of Foreign Affairs of Denmark. Ryan and his entourage would spend the night at his hotel. Tomorrow morning he would go to the Amalienborg Palace for a friendly breakfast with the Danish royal family, and then he'd be on his way to Eigtveds Pakhus, where the real work would kick off at noon.

The afternoon meeting would involve a short speech by the Lithuanian president,

Eglė Banytė, requesting help from NATO in both the Baltic Sea and its border regions, to counter the threat of invasion. After this, President Banytė had agreed to yield part of her time to Jack Ryan, so he could back her request for the NATO deployment.

The Lithuanian president would then immediately return to her threatened country; she insisted she had to be in Vilnius if the Russians came; it wouldn't do for her to be any more safe than her citizens.

The real battle in Copenhagen would begin the next day. Ryan would reconvene with all the other leaders and discuss the emergency proposal. This would be conducted in a roundtable format, and Ryan fully expected a lot of pushback from a large number of the European member states.

There was, officially speaking, anyway, no voting in NATO. The organization bragged about its principle of consensus decision-making, meaning, essentially, that all members had to come to an agreement for anything to happen, except in the case of responding to actions that had been codified into the NATO charter. In theory, this meant that an Article Five violation such as an actual attack on Lithuania would be met with an automatic response from all twenty-eight member states, but the reality was a lot murkier.

Ryan wanted to move troops now, before

hostilities began, but the truth of the matter was he wasn't even convinced NATO would agree to move troops *after* an Article Five violation.

A final meeting would be held the following afternoon, and there a poll would be taken to see if all members agreed on the proposal. Usually, if a member state or two knew they were seriously outnumbered in their dissent, they would abstain for the good of the institution and allow the action to proceed, but the consensus decision-making principle had the effect of giving veto power over any proposal to twenty-eight out of the twenty-eight nations.

It might have been a great way to avoid war, Ryan acknowledged, but it was no way to fight one.

As soon as Ryan was secure in his suite at the Radisson Blu hotel, he began going over his speech with his staff, troubleshooting any rough spots. When he finished with this he tasked both his NATO ambassador, referred to officially as the United States' permanent representative to NATO, and the deputy chief of mission, the number-two member of the U.S. embassy here in Denmark, to play the part of NATO members ready to shoot down every one of his proposals.

The three sat around a table in the dining room of the suite. Both the NATO ambassador and the DCM had folders and notebooks full of reference material, but President Ryan had only an empty pad and a pen in front of him.

After the first round of the mock discussion Ryan called a time-out, and lectured the two diplomats about their performance. "Ladies, we're going to have to take this from the top. You are talking to me like I am the President and you are a couple of people I could fire at will."

The deputy chief of mission cast a confused look at the NATO ambassador, and then one at Ryan. "Well, Mr. President. That *is* the case."

Ryan said, "Nobody's getting fired for being too tough on me. Take off the kid gloves and tell me what I'm going to hear tomorrow."

The NATO ambassador said, "Yes, sir, but don't say we didn't warn you."

They then spent another hour on the drill, and when they were finished Ryan felt like he'd been put through the wringer. His two faux-European leaders had brought up every possible protest Ryan could think of, and many he never would have considered.

Secretary of State Scott Adler had watched the entire affair in silence while sitting on a nearby couch, ready to render judgment at the end.

Ryan turned to Adler and took a bottle of water off the table to wet his dry throat. He felt like he'd been talking nonstop. "How did I do, Scott?"

"You did well, Mr. President. You will make a good case for our cause."

Ryan picked up a negative implication in the comment. "But you don't think we'll get the votes, do you?"

Adler said, "If I was a betting man, I'd bet on the Europeans moving with caution, not action, and telling you they would need to see an Article Five violation before deploying into Lithuania."

Ryan said, "And if there *is* an Art Five violation? Will they move even then?"

Adler sighed a little. "I hope I'm wrong, but I wonder if they would excuse one event, write it off to hotheads in the military over-stepping their bounds, and then demand evidence of a second Article Five."

Ryan said, "Which will come when Russian Spetsnaz officers high-five each other over beers in the dining room of the Presidential Palace in Vilnius."

Adler said, "Again, I hope I'm wrong, and I hope there is consensus."

Ryan asked, "Anything I can do to up my chances?"

"Just give it your best shot, don't make it personal between you and them, and be ready to roll with the punches."

Ryan knew Adler was worried about his President losing his sense of decorum and becoming argumentative. Ryan found himself sharing his secretary of state's concerns. He said, "And you be ready to deal with the diplomatic fallout if I screw up."

Adler chuckled. "Trust me, Mr. President, I'm ready. Frankly, sir, if you didn't have a mouth, I wouldn't have a job."

The meeting kicked off more or less on time, although the arrival of twenty-eight world leaders to a single place resulted in what Ryan considered to be a maddening amount of protocol, mostly unofficial, in the form of who had to shake whose hand first or which prime minister stepped up to greet which president in which order. There were cameras present as the principals entered the conference room and posed for a group photo, and Ryan knew media in each nation here would talk themselves silly if their leader was shown less deference by the behavior of other leaders.

The photographers in attendance were given fifteen minutes to chronicle the absurdity of it all, and then the cameras were shuffled out of the room and the twenty-eight men and women and their senior advisers got down to work.

The secretary general of NATO was the former prime minister of Norway, and well liked by everyone in the room. Ryan wasn't a fan of the man's policies, but got along well enough with the guy. After his short speech to kick off the emergency meeting, he recognized Lithuania's president, and she read a prepared statement to the room.

Eglė Banytė was an eloquent speaker, her words were impassioned, and the English interpreter kept the running translation up in Ryan's ear with incredible skill.

After ten minutes she ceded to Ryan, and the secretary general turned the floor over to the American President. He stood at the lectern and cleared his throat while the eyes of twenty-seven national leaders turned in his direction.

"Ladies and gentlemen, I appreciate the opportunity to speak before you today. My staff has placed a briefing booklet in front of you that covers what I am going to say here in more detail. I'd just like to ask for a few minutes of your time so I can make my case directly to you.

"When Russia's president Valeri Volodin was the beneficiary of a strong energy sector, he was a dangerous man. He increased military spending by twenty percent, he adopted or restarted provocative and threatening initiatives involving his intelligence, military, and even his nuclear weapons programs. He brought his Navy to full combat readiness; he began overflying NATO nations from the border of his country all the way to the United States with strategic bombers. He threatened maritime commerce with his Navy, commercial airline routes with his air force. He harassed dissenters, he assassinated enemies, and he imprisoned those with whom he had business disagreements. He used his police, his spies, and his soldiers as blunt instruments to increase his power, both domestically and internationally.

"Again, he did all this at the height of his success. During the good times.

"Now Valeri Volodin is failing on all fronts, and for this reason, I submit to you, he has only become *more* dangerous.

"Back when things were good for him it appeared nothing could touch him. Certainly he felt he was invincible, and one of the consequences of this was the Ukrainian invasion.

"Ukraine looked toward the West to increase its economic and cultural ties, and Volodin panicked. Other former nations of the Soviet Union who have chosen freedom have found prosperity, and the Kremlin sees these nations as an existential threat to its backward and autocratic ways. The Kremlin cannot allow its subjects to witness the success of its neighbors, because then they would demand change for themselves.

"Volodin calculated that we would do nothing when he attacked Ukraine, so he attacked Ukraine. We did not do nothing, so he doesn't own all of Ukraine. But we did not do enough, so today a large swath of that country is nothing more than a Russian puppet state.

"We've lost eastern Ukraine, but its loss illustrates something important. In the eyes of Valeri Volodin, Russia's security depends on the insecurity of its neighbors.

"Now he sees a new threat: a Baltic region allied with NATO, increasing their ability to meet their energy needs without dependence on Russia. He sees Lithuania specifically as a successful and independent nation that serves both as demonstration of the failures of his policy and a potential corridor to his province on the Baltic Sea. He needs a victory. It will help Russia's economy, bolster the Kremlin's power, and take the pressure off him after his string of losses.

"Russia's hybrid warfare against Lithuania is purposefully ambiguous. As long as Russia's aggression stays below a certain threshold, there will be enough pundits and pacifists in the West assuring everyone that the real threats are not in Russia, but in the West. They will continue saying this until the facts on the ground are so utterly different from what they assert that the world will have no choice but to come to the conclusion that the pacifists were wrong, but by then it will be too late to do anything about it.

"People speak of hybrid warfare like it is a new phenomenon. But there is nothing new about it. Valeri Volodin's Kremlin is executing the time-tested battle plan of using the full spectrum of power. In the United States, we refer to this under the acronym DIME. Diplomacy, information, military, and economics.

"DIME starts with diplomacy. Volodin's Russia is pulling away from all international norms, violating treaties, making pacts with our enemies to increase Russia's power at the expense of democracies, world bodies, agreed-upon standards of behavior. They've left the European Court of Human Rights, and they have breached every agreement and security assurance they have given in the past twenty years.

"He is diplomatically isolated because of the hostility of his regime, but his diplomats continue to aggressively pursue Russia's policy in whatever venues remain open to them.

"On the intelligence front, he is swinging for the fences. For one, I believe FSB has a worldwide operation to bolster energy prices. If he can get oil and gas prices to rise, this will augment his power, both at home and abroad. The assassination of the prosecutor in Venezuela going after corrupt oil officials, the killing of the Saudi deputy minister of petroleum and mineral resources, the oil rig attack in Nigeria. Plus the attack on the LNG facility in Lithuania. It is no coincidence that all these events have happened in the past few weeks, and it is also no coincidence that they all have the effect of benefiting Volodin. We've seen gas prices shoot up fourteen percent in the past month, and crude prices a shade over nine percent.

"On the military front . . . well, we all saw what happened yesterday with the crash of SA44. Volodin is blatantly positioning an invasion force near his neighbors, threatening ships in the Baltic and filling the skies with military aircraft, with catastrophic results. He's doing all this because he is gambling that the West isn't committed to the fight against him, that we will allow him to absorb the Baltic back into his sphere of influence.

"It is on the last letter of DIME — economics — where we have seen his greatest failure. He began with this, and it was all he needed for a time. When oil and gas prices were high, Volodin used his energy companies, Gazprom and Gazprom Neft, as a weapon. But oil and gas prices have plummeted from last year's highs, and Europe is an unfriendly market because Volodin has used Gazprom against you for so long that you found other sources of energy.

"The notion that energy only flows from East to West is outdated. Right now Western nations are supplying Ukraine, via Poland and Slovakia. The Nord Stream pipeline is up and running, and the Central Europeans are better off, because LNG going directly into Germany could be sent from Germany into Central Europe if Russia cuts them off again.

"At the height of the market Gazprom was worth three hundred sixty billion U.S. dollars. Now it is worth fifty billion. I will put it very simply. Gazprom's business model is dead.

"Russia's business model: using energy revenue to build the military, and using Europe's need of energy as a way to threaten it . . . *this* model is also dead."

Ryan took a sip of water before continuing. "So what is Volodin doing to reclaim his power? He has decided that if he can't stay big, then he must make his adversary small. He is trying to drive a wedge between the United States and Europe, and to emasculate NATO by ripping away Lithuania, showing the weakness in the organization. He wants to turn NATO into nothing more than a piece of paper. If he accomplishes this he will give himself the strongest military power in Europe, and he will do it without a protracted war.

"Russia can't win a protracted war, but it can harass, it can block, and it can terrorize. I ask you all to look around at the state of the world today. This is exactly what Russia is doing.

"President Volodin knows that many Western European nations take the stance that dialogue is preferable to confrontation. They talk in circles while they look at the chessboard, but they do not move any pieces. But the Baltic States are allies of America and NATO partners. If they are attacked and we do nothing, our friends will know the NATO they once respected has become an empty promise.

"Deterrence only works if Volodin believes the West will act. Right now he doesn't believe that, so there is really no limit to what he might try to achieve. We, as an alliance, need to show the Russians our collective resolve."

Ryan looked around the room slowly, taking his time. "How do we do that? What's the solution to the crisis? Step one, recognize and come to terms with the fact Russia's actions of the past year have changed European security forever, and we will not return to where we were before. The realization that a new normal is upon us is crucial if we are to take the bold steps necessary.

"Step two, more economic sanctions against the Russian elite. Thousands of Russia's most prominent do their shopping in the West, their banking in the West, they send their children to school in the West. Increasing sanctions on the privileged and powerful would be easy for us and relatively harmless *to* us, but devastating for the decision makers in Russia.

"Step three . . . We call on NATO to immediately deploy the Rapid Deployable Corps into Poland. A decision in the next days could put substantial forces into the area within a week, and within a month the risk of an invasion from Russia would be greatly reduced.

"Step four, ladies and gentlemen, is the most urgent and most important of all. We call on NATO to *immediately* deploy the Very High Readiness Joint Task Force to Lithuania, positioning them on both the Kaliningrad and Belarusan borders. The VHRJTF could be moving within twenty-four hours, and they could be in position in seventy-two. While this force is no match for any real Russian attack, it could serve as a tripwire, and may cause President Valeri Volodin to pause, to reflect on the consequences of an attack. It would show him NATO was willing to fight for Lithuania.

"I am talking about a temporary NATO presence in Lithuania and Poland, not a permanent NATO base. As soon as the current crisis comes to an end, we will move to withdraw the rapid response units from Poland and Lithuania.

"I am under no illusions here. I fully expect Russia to react negatively to these proposals. They *will* respond to this move by us, and we will *not* like their response. But it is my fervent belief that the actions they are making now are a result of our inaction in the past, and we cannot let this continue."

Ryan paused again and looked around the room. "Volodin does not have a better military, a better economy, or better ideas than the West. To date, Volodin has had an advantage over the free nations of the West in one valuable commodity." Ryan held up his finger. "Just one." After a pause for effect, he said, "Simply put, he has will. President Volodin has the will that we do not. And he has this in excess."

Ryan said, "There is an impression in the West, even now after all that has taken place, that the existing security order in Europe is stable. There are rules by which nations live, and those rules ensure peace. And since peace is in everyone's best interests, why would this ever change?

"Ladies and gentlemen, Russia is rewriting the rulebook right in front of us. They are not waiting for tomorrow. We should not, either."

Jack Ryan sat down. The room was quiet after his speech, but these were never raucous affairs, so he hadn't expected anyone to throw confetti.

After the meeting was adjourned, Ryan spoke privately for a few minutes with President Eglė Banytė and assured her he'd do everything in his power to support Lithuania. She thanked him, expressed her belief that the motion would be approved, and headed for the airport.

Ryan appreciated her positivity and her staunchly brave face.

But he wasn't nearly so sure.

46

Terry Walker had sent his staff home today as soon as they arrived for work at eight a.m. He told them his new clients required a higher level of discretion, so he would attend to them alone. He paid his two locals in advance for three weeks, wished them a pleasant vacation, and watched them gleefully collect their things and shoot out the door. One woman actually cried with joy.

After Walker's staff left, Kozlov and two of his men from Steel Securitas arrived and set up shop in the tiny lobby of the office. They carried pistols and they allowed the grips of their guns to show under their suit coats as they moved around near Walker, upping the intimidation factor and reducing the chance the young Australian might think about some sort of a double cross.

Walker spent the first hour of the morning looking over notes Limonov had prepared about how he wanted the exchange to be made. The transactions would be done in $8 million increments. As they needed to convert a daily total of $266 million from cash in various worldwide accounts into Bitcoin via the BlackHole hopper, and then sell the Bitcoin for U.S. dollars which Limonov would deposit into a new set of accounts, the two men had to make thirty-three separate transactions throughout the day.

At ten a.m., Limonov and Walker sat down next to each other in front of the terminal on the desk in Walker's office, and they conducted their first trade of the morning. Walker did this sort of thing all day, every day; even the individual amounts of the trades weren't out of the ordinary to him. The only major differences between today and any other day were the sheer number of trades he'd have to make for the same client, the armed men looming over him, and the fact that Kate and Noah were somewhere themselves under guard.

His hands shook through the entire first transaction. When he stepped away from the desk so Limonov could put in his account information to deposit the new, fully washed U.S. dollars, Walker put his hands against the wall to steady his legs, and he had to fight a wave of nausea.

Soon enough, Limonov called up from the desk with a big smile. "That's it, Walker. One down. Nine hundred ninety-nine to go." The Russian seemed positively beside himself with satisfaction.

Walker said, "Yeah, but only thirty-two more today."

The process had been initiated, and soon fell into a repetitive rhythm. By initiating a new transaction every twelve minutes, the two men could transfer the planned $266 million worth of trades in a day. Each complete transaction took only three to five minutes from start to finish, so Walker spent the rest of the time staring at the wall while Limonov spoke with Kozlov in the other room.

After they finished the seventh trade of the day, Walker looked up and saw it was just after eleven. He stood to stretch his legs and announced, "I'm going to the toilet."

Kozlov heard him from where he sat on the sofa in the lobby of the little office. As Walker passed him by, heading for the door, the Kremlin operative looked to the security man from Canada. In English he said, "You go with him. Search it."

"Yes, sir."

Walker and his armed guard walked down a short hallway and nodded to a local attorney who passed them on his way out of his office for the stairs, and then they came to the second-floor restroom. The Canadian opened the door and saw it was just a simple space with two urinals and two stalls along with a sink and a garbage can. There were no windows, but he quickly opened the stalls, found them empty, and then looked to Walker.

"You going to be long?"

"Heaps longer if you stand there looking at me, mate."

The big man gave Walker an annoyed look, turned around, and stepped out the door. "I'm in the hall."

Walker did his business and returned to the office with his guard following behind him.

At one p.m. a Steel Securitas man with a German accent entered the office and brought paper plates of rice and sausage for Limonov and Walker, bought from a corner restaurant, along with bottles of soda from the machine in the lobby of the office building. The two men continued to make the trades, even while they ate. Walker wasn't in the mood to eat, but Limonov finished quickly and asked the armed security man to go out and grab coffee.

By now Walker had relaxed enough to stop shaking, and he found himself spending much of the time between the trades dispassionately answering Limonov's constant questions about the technological aspects of BlackHole and the Bitcoin markets in general. The Russian seemed fascinated by it all, and genuinely impressed by the incredible intelligence of Terry Walker.

Walker, on the other hand, just wanted this Russian in his office to shut up and get on with it.

At four p.m. Walker again announced that he needed to use the toilet. The same Canadian security man escorted him down, opened the bathroom door, and looked inside. This time, both stalls were wide open and visible from the doorway, so the man just waved Walker in while he remained in the hall.

Walker entered the restroom, and as the door closed behind him he heard a click. He turned to find a man with gray hair locking the door.

The older man turned back to Walker. Softly he said, "Don't make a sound, Terry. I'm here to help."

John Clark looked carefully at Walker, gauging the man's reaction. If he was going to call out to his guard he would likely do it in the first few seconds, so Clark knew he had to be ready to launch forward the five feet that separated them to stifle the man's shouts. But Walker just stood there, a look of confusion on his face, along with incredibly bloodshot eyes, obviously from the fatigue and stress of the past day.

To Clark's relief, Walker replied in a whisper. "Who are you?"

Clark said, "We know the Russians have

537

your family."

Walker's whisper was delivered now almost as a shout. "Yeah, and they will kill them if they think I am talking to Americans! Get the fuck out of here before Popov finds you!"

"He won't know I'm here. You need to trust me."

"You are FBI?"

"No."

"CIA?"

"Look, Mr. Walker," Clark said. "We are experts at doing this sort of thing, all while remaining in the shadows. We know you are converting assets into Bitcoin for someone in the Kremlin. We also know you are doing it to protect your family."

Walker cocked his head. "The Kremlin?"

"Yes."

"You mean, like Volodin? The fucking psycho who runs Russia?"

"I was hoping you could tell us."

Walker rubbed his eyes. "I knew it was a rich Russian, obviously. I just figured it was some sort of Mafia boss."

"After a fashion," Clark said.

"Popov, the tough one, acts like a gangster."

"That would be Kozlov. He works for the Kremlin. Ex-FSB. A very bad man."

Walker sat down on the toilet slowly. "And the other one? The finance guy?"

"Andrei Limonov. He's moving money for a high-ranking Kremlin suit. We don't know who, but it could be Volodin himself. How much money is involved?"

Walker put his head in his hands. "Eight billion. Dollars."

Clark just said, "Wow."

Walker said, "Popov will kill them. Noah and Kate. He will really do it, won't he? If I don't give him what he wants he'll kill my wife and kid."

Clark moved into the other stall and closed the door. Sat down on the next toilet, ready to lift his legs if the guard returned. He said, "I'm not going to lie to you, Terry. Even if you do exactly what they say, these aren't the type to just say thanks at the end. They are not going to let you or your family go. You just know too much."

Clark could hear Walker sobbing softly. "What the fuck am I gonna do?"

"You are going to let us find Kate and Noah and get them away from the Russians, and then you are going to help us."

After an audible sob Walker asked, "Can you really do it?"

"We can and we will. You keep doing what you are doing. Raise no alarm. But we also need you to help us find your family. Have you gotten any information about where they are being kept?"

"Somewhere here in the islands, within fifteen miles or so. On a boat. That's all I know."

"How do you know they are on a boat?"

Walker explained the clues Kate and Noah had given him.

Clark said, "She normally gets seasick?"

"Yeah. Violently ill. Don't know what's different about this boat." Walker said, "I've got to get back out there. Look, you can't tell anyone else. The CIA, the FBI. They'll just come down here and make noise."

Clark said, "I agree with you there. How much longer till you are finished moving the money?"

"I don't know. Depends on what the markets do. If trading volume goes up, we'll increase daily transactions."

"What's your best estimate?"

"We'll probably be finished in two weeks."

Clark regarded this information. "Can you stall them while we look for your family?"

"That's impossible. Ivanov . . . you called him Limonov . . . he doesn't know Bitcoin that well, but he is a bloody expert on finance. He really knows his shit. He's watching me all the time, he sees everything I do. Asks me about anything he doesn't understand. There is nothing I can do to change this process that he won't see."

Clark said, "Okay. Don't try anything. We'll get your family back, and then you can help us catch these guys."

Instead of gratitude, Terry Walker said, "You guys better be fucking *certain* of your plan.

You get my family killed and I'll give the Russians whatever the fuck they want. You understand me?"

Clark just said, "Go."

Walker flushed his toilet, then stepped out to the sink and turned on the water. While looking at himself in the mirror he said, "I can't fucking handle this."

Clark opened the door to the stall he had been in. "You can, Terry. You *have* to. Kate and Noah are depending on you." And then, "You've got to get back out there."

Walker nodded distractedly. "I really did need to go to the toilet." And he stepped out through the door.

Terry Walker returned to his office suite moments later, followed by the Canadian security man. Limonov barely looked up as he entered the office, but Kozlov followed him from the reception area.

Standing in the doorway, Kozlov barked, "What took you so long?"

"I was in the loo. You figure it out."

The Russian stepped forward quickly and grabbed the small Australian by the back of his neck. He squeezed tightly. "What were you doing?"

"Do I have to fucking spell it out for you?"

Kozlov turned to the Canadian. "Were you with him in the toilet?"

"No, but I searched it, and I stayed just

541

outside."

Kozlov pointed to their prisoner. "Search him. Search every inch of his body." He turned away, stormed out into the hall toward the bathroom. As he moved he drew his gun and held it down by his leg.

The security men pushed Terry Walker against the wall roughly, unsure what the problem was, but unquestioning in their compliance to their client. As men lifted Walker's shirt and yanked down his pants, he looked toward the door to the hallway, terrified Kozlov would find the American in the bathroom. His stomach clenched and he wondered if he would pass out from the terror.

Walker turned to Limonov. The Russian was typing an e-mail on his notebook computer, barely paying attention. The Australian said, "Your friend is completely mental, you must know that."

Limonov did not look up from his work. "He's not my friend, but otherwise you are correct."

Kozlov opened the door to the office again, looked to the two men who were finishing stripping Walker down. He had holstered his weapon. "Anything?"

"He's clean, boss."

As Walker put his clothes back on, Kozlov pointed to the security officer who'd escorted Walker to the bathroom. "From now on you stand with him in the bathroom at all times. Is that clear?"

The Canadian contractor said, "Whatever you say, sir."

Kozlov went back into the little lobby of the office and sat down on the sofa.

Limonov called out to Walker, "Time for another trade, Terry."

It had taken Clark almost an hour to defeat security cameras and pick locks in the building early this morning, and he wouldn't have been able to manage it without Gavin Biery's help from Alexandria. And now that he was finished with his meeting, he would have to wait hours more, till the end of the business day, before he could get out of here.

He knelt in the back of a janitor's closet, just twenty-five feet from the bathroom and deeper in the building. He'd brought with him two bottles of water and a Snickers bar, not really expecting to spend the entire day inside the building, but wanting to be lightly equipped if he had to. But Gavin had texted him not long after he arrived, letting him know that two security guards had shown up in the front lobby, and he could find no escape route visible on the hacked CCTV that looked clear.

Even this wouldn't have been a problem if this office building received clients like most every other office building in the world. But

Gavin had been reporting throughout the day that this was the deadest commercial space he'd ever watched during its hours of operation. Other than the people who worked there, virtually no one had come or gone.

Clark settled in for the long wait, and then he sent a text to Gavin and another to Jack, telling them both what he had just learned. He might have to sit here for another three hours before he could return to his boat, but that didn't mean his two colleagues couldn't work remotely to start looking into the kidnapping.

He didn't really know what they would be able to accomplish up there, but Clark liked his chances, whenever he did get out of here. If the Walkers were on a boat and the boat was still here in the BVIs, Clark knew exactly where he needed to start his hunt to find them.

47

Chavez, Caruso, and Herkus Zarkus stood on the roof of a high school assembly hall in the town of Pabradė, looking out to the east at the Belarusan border in the distance. They took pictures of the farmland between their position and the border from three different points of the roof, pleasing the men greatly because they got to check three more objectives off their list without having to load up the vehicle and drive to a new location each time.

The two Americans were now more convinced than ever that the work they were doing was in support of a military defense of Lithuania. It seemed odd to them that the director of national intelligence would be the one sending them here, or that they would go at all, as the Defense Department had its own intelligence service that normally did these sorts of things.

Still, Dom Caruso and Ding Chavez weren't complaining about the technical collection work. It gave them the opportunity to get a feel for the area.

Dom had joked dryly earlier, when he was certain Herkus was out of earshot, that the work they did now might help CIA operations behind the "New Iron Curtain" in the future. Both men knew the ground they walked on could easily be Russian territory in a matter of days, just as the ground they walked on in the Crimea a year earlier was now as much a part of Russia as was Red Square.

They finished their precision imagery, climbed down off the roof of the high school, and waved thanks to a really confused but compliant building supervisor.

As they were packing up the van to go to the next location, the phone in Chavez's pocket chirped.

"Chavez."

"This is Greg Donlin, Branyon's PPA."

Chavez remembered meeting CoS Pete Branyon's personal protection agent the week before when the chief of station dropped in on their safe house. "Hey, Greg. You doing okay?"

"I remember you guys offered to help us out in your downtime. I'm hoping that offer still stands."

"Of course it does. We don't normally knock off till the light gets too bad to work, usually around seven or so. But if you're in a jam we can make an exception."

"This would be at five p.m. Branyon needs to go east this evening, to meet with an agent in a village called Tabariškės. It's about a half-mile, tops, from the Belarusan border."

"Oh, shit."

"Yeah. I have tried to dissuade him from his decision, but he says it's vital. His network in that area is reporting more Little Green Men sightings. He wants to meet with them in person to see what we're dealing with here."

"Sounds dangerous."

"Might be, but we had a NOC in Tabariškės last night, and he reported it was all clear. We're not too worried about the town, but the drive down has us a little concerned. Lithuanian police and military presence is light on the road there, it's just too far off the main highway, and the cops and soldiers around here are stretched thin enough as it is."

Chavez said, "We'd be happy to escort you guys down, but, as you know, we don't have any weapons."

"I'll fix that. If you come along I'll hook you up with some bang sticks. One thing, though. Branyon doesn't want you in Tabariškės village. He is worried about compromising people in his network with strangers showing up. He asks that you guys just follow us down, find a place to park to

547

the west of town, and then wait for us to call and let you know we're en route back toward Vilnius."

Chavez asked, "Do you feel safe being Branyon's only security man while he walks around in this town by the border?"

"Hell, no, I don't. I'd roll in with an Abrams tank if I was calling the shots, but I'm not."

"I hear you," said Chavez. "We'll watch over you guys on the road down and back. Stay in comms with us in case you need us in the village."

"Sounds like a plan. Let's meet up at seventeen hundred hours so I can give you guys some weapons and we can discuss the movement."

Branyon and Donlin pulled into the parking lot of an IKI chain grocery store in Nemėžis, a southeastern suburb of Vilnius. It was five p.m., there was still a lot of light out, but storm clouds were rolling over the area, with heavy rains predicted by sunset. As they came to a stop in a space well to the side of the entrance, a black Toyota Land Cruiser pulled into the spot next to them. Chavez and Caruso climbed out of the Toyota, and then got into the back of the CIA men's vehicle.

Branyon was in the passenger seat. Everyone shook hands quickly, then the station chief said, "Appreciate the company, guys."

Dom replied, "Our pleasure. You guys are cutting it close on the light, though. Not sure how long you plan on being at your meet, but it looks like we'll be coming home in a pitch-black storm."

Donlin said nothing. Both Campus men had the impression he didn't like this scenario at all, which meant they weren't too crazy about this movement, either.

Branyon saw the expressions on the men's faces. "Look, I'm not doing this because I want to. There are a lot of people down there by the border that are relying on the U.S. to protect them. They work for me, and they are skittish as hell, but I still need them to do their jobs. I can't just call them from the safety of the U.S. embassy and tell them I've got their backs. I need to go down and convince them I'm still looking out for them, so they'll continue providing intel to me." He shrugged. "For whatever that's worth. Fucking Volodin going on TV and saying he basically owns their homes is creating more anxiety than I can dispel with my handsome face."

Chavez and Caruso smiled.

Greg Donlin said, "At your feet you'll each find an AK and a pistol, along with some extra mags. The guns are a little old, but they function, and they'll put holes in people if it comes down to it. Stay on our ass on the way down, but peel off before we get to the village. I'll let you know when we're about to leave the meet."

"Roger that," said Chavez. The two men in the backseat collected their new weapons. Each was folded into a blue gym bag so they didn't have to climb out in the grocery store parking lot waving guns around. Instead, they just hefted the bags and returned to their vehicle.

Back in the Land Cruiser they took a moment to check the rifles and the pistols. The AKs had folding wire stocks and simple iron sights. The pistols, big Glock 17s, looked just like the AKs: well used but also well maintained. They shoved the pistols in their waistbands under their jackets, then placed the rifles on the floorboard of the backseat, where each man also had a Maxpedition sling bag filled with surveillance equipment, medical supplies, and other odds and ends they knew they might need on an escort mission like this.

As they began following the CIA men's white Mercedes SUV, Dom began looking at a map of the area near the border on his phone, trying to find a place for them to wait for Branyon and Donlin while they conducted their meeting in Tabariškės. As he looked over the map, he said, "Ding, does any of this feel right to you?"

"From a personal-security perspective?"

"Yeah."

"Not at all," said Chavez. "I respect Branyon for not riding a desk, but like he said, I don't know that there is much he can do by coming down here. If the Russians start shelling the area, those mortar rounds aren't going to know or care the CIA is in that village."

Dom said, "From the map it looks like there are some low hills on a farm about five hundred yards to the southwest of the village. How would you feel about us finding a layup position that gives us a little overwatch on Branyon's poz?"

Chavez said, "I like it. Not much we can do to affect things from five hundred yards, but I guess we can call in to Donlin if we see anything in the area we don't like."

"Like Russian T-90 tanks or incoming rockets?"

Chavez laughed. "Yeah, for example. In the meantime, let's keep our eyes peeled on this road. We've been driving five minutes and we've already passed a half-dozen perfect places to get bushwhacked."

Light rain began to fall on the SUV as they headed for the border.

48

Pete Branyon and Greg Donlin rolled into the village of Tabariškės, just a half-mile from the Belarusan border. Branyon was behind the wheel, and he drove his white 1998 Mercedes M-Class SUV through the rain, along the narrow, flat streets, passing only a few other vehicles on the road. After a few minutes he turned off the road, and crunched up the gravel driveway in front of a mustard-colored wooden church. A small, bleak cemetery sat in front of the building, with tombstones on both sides of a path from the entry of the church to the parking lot out front.

Branyon put the vehicle in park, then just sat there, peering out through the rain in all directions.

There was only one other car in the church driveway, and Branyon did not recognize it.

He'd come out to the church this evening to meet the agent who ran his cell here along the border. Albertas Varnas was a parish priest living in the village, and he had been reporting to Branyon about the situation in the area, as well as organizing others in his parish. Branyon had recruited him just a month earlier, and the only thing Varnas and his people had been used for so far was setting up a few remote Internet-based cameras that beamed images of the road to the border back to the CIA shop at the U.S. embassy, and calling in tips about border activity.

Branyon decided to come out here this evening because he wanted to ask Varnas personally about his claims that villagers were reporting sightings of foreigners in the area.

Branyon had been advised by Langley to get Varnas on the phone and question him a little deeper, but Branyon felt he'd be better able to gauge the veracity of the reports in person. Plus, if there were any Little Green Men out here in Tabariškės, he wanted to see them firsthand. He knew if the chief of station told Langley the Russians had breached the border, it would carry more weight with Langley than if some untrained parish priest just called in the sighting secondhand.

Greg Donlin sat in the passenger seat with his eyes fixed on the east. The border was beyond a wood line that began on the other side of a field, right outside the village, and it also jutted out to the west just south of the village, meaning it was also a mile and a half behind them. He said, "Closer than we need to be, boss. We've got Belarus on two compass points of this poz."

"I know, Greg," Branyon said, still looking at the unfamiliar car in the lot. He checked his phone for any missed messages, then he dialed Varnas. After twenty seconds with his phone to his ear he said, "No signal. Perfect."

Donlin checked his own phone. "Same here. Wonder if the Russians are jamming this area from over the border."

Branyon chuckled a little. "Now you are getting paranoid. I talked to Varnas an hour ago, phones were fine then. I've had this happen before. No sweat."

He grabbed his umbrella, opened his car door, and climbed out.

Donlin climbed out as well. "That's a Honda Civic. Varnas has an old Škoda. He isn't here, Pete. Why don't we wait a bit?"

Branyon answered back, "Why don't we go light a candle and make an offering? Can't fuckin' hurt."

"I don't like it. Whose car is that?"

Branyon was already moving, but he turned back to his personal protection agent. "Let me ask you this, Greg. If the Sixth Army *does* invade Lithuania, do you imagine they'll all pile into the back of a Honda Civic to do it?"

As usual, Greg Donlin did not share his superior's cavalier attitude. He caught up with his boss on the pathway up to the church. Both men stood in the rain. "Pete, I'll go in first, see if he's here. You get behind the wheel and wait, just in case."

Branyon sighed. "Really, Greg? Are you going to ride my ass on this?"

Donlin said, "Just make me feel better. Okay, boss?"

Branyon turned and headed back to the Mercedes, but he didn't get behind the wheel. Instead, he leaned against the hood, pulled a pack of Marlboros out of his jacket with his free hand, and poured a cigarette into his mouth. He dropped the pack back in his jacket and pulled a lighter from his pants pocket.

Donlin gave him a slightly annoyed look, then turned and headed up to the church.

Branyon took a long drag on his cigarette and fumbled with his umbrella to check his watch. It was almost seven, the clouds made it look like dusk, and he knew it would be pitch-black by the time they left, even if Varnas was here now.

He had put on an air of nonchalance with both his bodyguard and the two contractors shadowing him this evening, but the fact was he wasn't taking this lightly at all. He knew he was pushing his luck being here now, and the last thing he wanted to do was hang out here after dark. But his cell of agents here near the border was more important than ever. Not just because they could send him information in advance of an invasion, but if NATO did not rush up and save the day, if the Russians poked holes in the eight-foot-tall wire fence that was the only thing separating a hundred villages like this from the Sixth Army, then this cell would be absolutely crucial working behind the lines in Russian-held Lithuania.

He *had* to be here, he *had* to do this, and if he got his ass shot off in the process — well, he told himself, he'd ignored his dad's advice to go to dental school, so it would be his own damn fault.

Dom Caruso and Ding Chavez sat in their black Toyota Land Cruiser, parked on a hill 550 yards to the west of the mustard-colored church. Chavez had pulled off the main road and up a hill into an abandoned junkyard, then continued out into an open field, finally stopping in a copse of trees. He turned off the engine and listened to the sound of the rain on the roof of the vehicle.

Through the enhancement of the 500-millimeter lens of his camera propped in the partially open window, Dom could easily make out the scene to the northeast of their position: Branyon leaning on the hood of the white Mercedes SUV with an umbrella in one hand and a cigarette in the other, and his close protection officer disappearing alone into the church.

Dom said, "Can you freakin' believe it? The CIA station chief heading all the way out here in the boonies like this?"

Chavez agreed. "I know why he's doing it, but it's the wrong call."

"I guess he thinks he's invincible."

"All we can do is hope he is. If there are Little Green Men out here, or any of the local pro-Russian civilians, knowing that the Agency chief for the entire country is wandering around this remote area with a target on his head is almost too good to pass up."

Dom asked, "Do we want to think about moving closer? Just in case?"

Chavez held his own camera up now, focused in on the church in the distance. "No. Branyon was right about us not entering the village. If there are bad guys around, we'd be made in two seconds flat. Plus, I like our view here. If we break off to get closer we'll lose sight of him for two or three minutes. Let's just keep watch."

Within a few seconds, however, Dom noticed a pair of big covered flatbed trucks pulling out of a tree line due south of the village. They began moving over fallow farmland, three hundred yards east of the church. They seemed to be heading directly toward Branyon and Donlin in the middle of the village, and they were increasing speed over the mud and tilled earth.

"What the hell is this?" he asked. Chavez had been looking up the road to the west, but he oriented his camera on the trucks. Quickly he said, "Call Donlin."

Caruso lowered his camera and yanked his phone from his jacket. Quickly he dialed Greg Donlin's number. He held the phone to his ear for several seconds, then checked it.

"Can't get a signal."

"Use the sat phone."

Dom spun around, grabbed his Maxpedition bag, and yanked it into the front seat with him. His Thuraya phone was in its waterproof case in an inner pocket. "It's going to take me a minute to get through."

Ding just watched the trucks get closer through the rain. "Do it, anyway. We don't know for sure what's happening."

Branyon stood up from the hood of the SUV, turned around and looked back over his shoulder. He saw a row of homes with white fences in front of them, and a line of big oak trees behind them. He thought he heard the noise of a vehicle somewhere back there, which was strange, because he'd been here before, he'd studied the map, and he knew it was nothing but farmland on the south side of the trees.

Just then, a single gunshot cracked inside the church, spinning Branyon's head in the direction of the noise. The cigarette flew from his mouth and he threw the umbrella to the side. His hand went inside his jacket and formed around the butt of his compact Glock 26 pistol, but before he could draw it the front door of the church flew open and Greg Donlin appeared in the doorway at a run. He shouted, "Get out of here!"

Branyon ran around to the driver's side, jumped behind the wheel, and fired up the engine. Directly in front of him Donlin ran through the cemetery in front of the church, his own pistol pointed back behind him at the door.

From the darkened doorway came a flash, then the pounding beat of a single rifle shot. Donlin stumbled in his run, then he fell onto the gravel of the drive. His body stilled.

"Fuck!" Branyon screamed, then he threw the Mercedes into gear and spun the tires, racing forward, trying to get to Donlin. He had no plan for pulling the big man into the vehicle while under fire from less than one hundred feet away, but he was operating on impulse now.

Another burst of gunfire came out of the church. Branyon assumed whoever was there was shooting at him, as the Mercedes was only twenty-five yards from the front door. But looking at Donlin's still form lying facedown in the drive, illuminated by the headlights of the Mercedes, Branyon saw mud and rock kicked up around him.

Someone was firing an automatic rifle, not at Branyon or his SUV, but at Donlin's body.

Pete Branyon saw his bodyguard's lifeless form kick up with the impact of the bullets.

Blood splattered the brown gravel around him.

The CIA station chief screamed again in fury, then stomped down hard on the brake pedal, skidding on the loose gravel and puddles of water. He threw the SUV into reverse and punched the gas, backed down the drive and into the street, then executed a three-point turn and shoved the gear shift into first. Stomping the gas to the floor now, he took off to the west.

He made it less than seventy-five yards. At the first intersection a large truck with a canvas bed top appeared around a building on his left, and it slammed into the left front of the Mercedes SUV, spinning it around on the street. Branyon's head smacked the door pillar by his head so hard he saw stars in front of his eyes.

The Mercedes stalled out in the middle of the intersection. Branyon was dazed, but he was still able to draw his Glock 26. He raised it at the movement in the headlights in front of him, but just as he did so, the passenger-side window exploded on his right. He turned to point his weapon at the noise, expecting to see an armed man there taking aim, but instead he saw something else.

In the front passenger seat, just a foot or so from where Branyon sat behind the wheel, was a flash-bang grenade. The pull ring was missing.

The device exploded in the confined space, blinding Branyon with light and disorienting his ears with a shrieking ring.

Chavez and Caruso watched helplessly as the action unfolded 550 yards away. It was tough to see the entire scene in the poor light and heavy rain, but when the CIA station chief was dragged from his vehicle by several men in civilian dress and carried in front of the headlights of the Mercedes, both Chavez and Caruso saw movement in Branyon's arms and legs.

Chavez said, "He's alive!"

Caruso spoke through a jaw tight with frustration. "A fucking kidnapping."

Chavez said, "And those aren't local yokels. That was slick as bird shit."

"Spetsnaz," Dom said.

"Or something like them," Chavez agreed. "We can't lose visibility till we see which direction they're heading."

"*Then* what do we do?"

Chavez fired up the engine of the Land Cruiser. "Donlin's dead. We go after Branyon."

"Roger that."

The two canvas-covered trucks headed east down the main road out of the village, directly toward the tree line, which was no longer visible to the Americans in the low light. But they didn't need to see the trees to know the fence line separating Lithuania from Belarus was just beyond, and they didn't have to jump to any great conclusions to figure out what was happening.

Pete Branyon was being taken back over the border.

Chavez threw the Land Cruiser into gear and launched forward, heading down the hill through the center of the farmland that ran along south of the village. "If we don't run into any natural obstacles we can beat them to the border."

Dom asked, "Are we going to shoot it out with Spetsnaz?"

Chavez said, "If the Russians get the CoS they will know the name of every U.S. asset in this country. When they take Lithuania they can scour the nation to remove all our eyes and ears."

Dom nodded as they bounced along the uneven ground, splashing through low mud puddles and up over small levees dividing the fields. He struggled to grab one of the rifles in the backseat. Once he had it in his hand he said, "We're not going to let that happen."

49

Chavez and Caruso had spent the last five minutes slamming around the inside of their Land Cruiser as it hurtled along through a rain-soaked pasture just a quarter-mile from Lithuania's border with Belarus. Even though they wore their seat belts, their upper torsos and appendages had been battered by the impacts of the relentless crashing as the big off-road-capable vehicle dipped and lurched and splashed and skidded along.

They drove without their lights, which had not been such a problem just five minutes earlier, but the last of the light was leaving the sky now, and as Chavez looked from behind the wheel toward the scene in front of him, he realized he was about one minute away from leaving the open field and plunging into a dense forest, and at that point he had to either flip on his headlights or slow down considerably.

He didn't want to slow, but he sure as hell did not want to turn on his lights, because the two big trucks were dead ahead, following a road that led due south to the border, and there was no one else out here. Turning on the Land Cruiser's headlights would reveal the presence of the Americans to Branyon's kidnappers.

Ding saw where they were going, and he wished he could have just veered to his right, to continue along the field to a convergence point with the trucks. But he realized that this wasn't possible. A small creek, not more than fifteen feet wide, twisted through the farmland just this side of the road Branyon was being taken along, and the only way to reach the road from where Ding now drove was to cross a small bridge right in front of him.

This meant he'd have to pull onto the road a couple hundred yards behind the Russians and then just chase them. It looked from here like it was a gravel surface, but even on gravel Chavez felt confident he could overtake the trucks, if given enough time.

His problem, however, was that the road entered the forest soon after the bridge, and neither he nor Dom had any idea what they would find in the forest between them and the border fence.

And their troubles didn't end there. As soon as they took off in pursuit of Branyon, Dom had tried to call the U.S. embassy in Vilnius. He wanted them to send help in the form of local police, national military, or even U.S. embassy Marines or CIA security officers.

But his phone still would not get a signal. After trying twice while he bounced along as a passenger in the vehicle, he stowed his mobile and pulled out his sat phone. He fired it up and dialed the embassy, but to his astonishment, this signal would not go through, either.

"You've got to be kidding me! No sat signal, either! Are we on the fucking moon?"

Chavez kept driving, his eyes wide to catch as much light as possible in case he needed to avoid anything in the pasture in front of him. "They jammed it."

"*Jammed* it?"

"Yeah. Somebody has to have a big piece of equipment to jam a sat phone, or else they have to be close."

Dom said, "Maybe that's what all those foreigners people reported seeing have been up to. They could have planted remote jammers in the towns along the border. Ready to switch them on the moment the shit hits the fan." He slipped his sat phone back into his coat now. "It's just us, then."

"Yep," Chavez confirmed.

"How many did you count in that group?"

Ding thought it over for a second. "Including drivers . . . eight to ten."

"That's what I came up with." He blew out a long sigh. "Jesus."

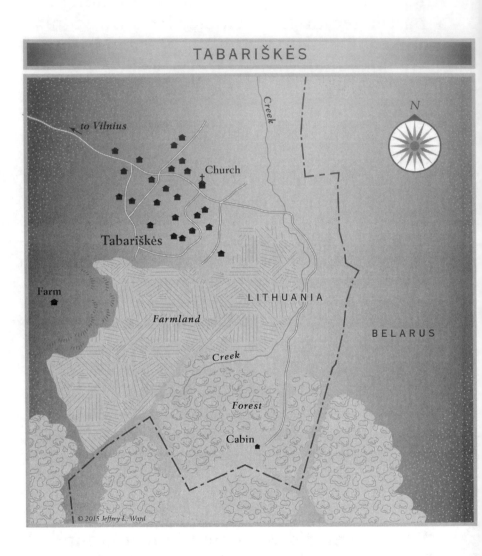

Chavez had to slow during the last thirty seconds before he arrived at the little bridge over the creek because visibility was so bad, but once he got over the bridge and onto the gravel north-south road, he was able to pick up the pace. The taillights of the rear truck were close to three hundred yards ahead now, so Chavez increased the speed of the Land Cruiser. Through the rain he could barely see his way ahead, but he just concentrated on holding the wheel steady and making sure those lights in the distance did not stop abruptly.

As Chavez drove, Dom said, "If they have a way through the border fence already prepared, then they are just going to drive on through. Are we going over the border after them?"

"No," Chavez said. "That would be suicide. You know they'll have people there ready to reseal the border, and we'd be driving right into them." After saying this Chavez stepped down even harder on the pedal, speeding his Land Cruiser up, desperate to reach Branyon and his captors before it was too late.

Dom had been looking at the map of the area, and he spoke up when they were just a few hundred yards from entering the forest. "The border is two hundred yards beyond the trees. You think these kidnappers will set security?"

Chavez thought about it for a moment, then

began to slow down. "Yeah, good call. Those guys are well trained. If they have to park and get over that fence somehow, they'll know to have someone watching their six."

Instead of pulling over to the side of the road, Ding just came to a complete stop in the middle of the lane, the grille of the big SUV just inside the start of the trees. They sat there for a moment, rolling down their windows to listen for any noise.

They heard nothing but the steady rain.

Caruso disabled the interior light before they quietly opened their doors; then each man climbed out with a rifle in his hand and a Glock 17 pistol jammed in his waistband. They both reached into their gym bags and pulled out two extra magazines for the rifle and one more for the pistol, and stowed the added gear in various pockets.

Each of the two Campus operators now had ninety rounds of rifle ammo and fifty-two rounds of pistol ammunition. This would be a lot of ammo for most any imaginable scenario, but neither Caruso nor Chavez felt confident in their ability to defeat eight to ten well-trained operators with their weapons in hand.

Still, they both knew they needed to get moving. They pushed their way into the trees going just west of the north-south road, planning to skirt anyone left on the gravel road as a sentry to watch for approaching traffic.

As they moved through the woods the rain picked up dramatically. It obscured their vision ahead, but they also knew the rain made it tougher for the opposition to see or hear, so they welcomed the bad weather.

After just three minutes of quiet movement, Caruso grabbed Chavez by his forearm and both men dropped to their knees. He said, "Lights ahead."

Ding squinted into the darkness; he saw nothing, but he trusted Caruso's eyes over his own, since Caruso was fifteen years younger.

Both men slung their rifles on their backs, reached into their packs, and pulled out monoculars. Ding's was a fat rubber device that looked like half of a set of waterproof binoculars, with a battery pack on the bottom. It was a FLIR scope, capable of picking up heat sources in darkness or behind thin concealment.

Dom's device was a three-power fourth-generation night-vision monocular. It rendered the blacked-out area in front of him in soft green hues. The image was essentially two-dimensional, but it provided excellent illumination in the darkness.

At first all either man saw was more trees, but after another two minutes to get into position, they arrived fifty yards away from the two trucks, finding them parked in front of a small cabin in the trees. Next to the cabin, a tiny barn was open on both sides.

And just beyond the two trucks and the two structures, Dom saw the eight-foot-high metal fence that separated Belarus from Lithuania.

The Campus men crawled forward a little more, just until they each had a good position on the floor of the forest — Ding behind a large pine tree, and Dom down behind a fat root system sticking out of the mud at the base of a partially felled maple.

The men were a dozen feet from each other, but close enough to see hand signals or converge quickly if they needed to speak.

Chavez held his FLIR monocular up to his eye. As soon as he directed it in the right area, he saw several men running along next to the cabin. The motion had drawn his attention, but when the men disappeared around the other side, he lost them, so he scanned back toward the location of the two trucks. The first vehicle seemed to be empty except for a driver sitting behind the wheel. The second vehicle also had a driver, but in the back, through the canvas wall of the vehicle, Ding could make out a large luminescent blob in his optic. He knew this would be several men, at least three or four, sitting close together on the bench in the back of the vehicle.

He assumed Branyon would be in the middle of the pack, surrounded by kidnappers.

Chavez estimated there were ten men at this location other than Branyon, which was the high end of their earlier estimate, but at least it meant the kidnappers had not picked up any more gunmen who'd been back here waiting for the trucks to return.

While Chavez had been scanning the driveway and the house and barn with his FLIR, Caruso had been using his night-vision monocular to look at the fence line in the distance. It was only sixty or seventy yards away from where he now lay, so he had a decent view of all of it except the portion he could not see on the other side of the house.

As near as Dom could tell, there was no breach in the fence at all.

He crawled over to Chavez. "You can't see the fence through that, can you?"

"Not at all. I see people, and I see warm truck engines. That's it."

Caruso nodded. "Well, I don't think these fuckers have cut a hole in the fence. You think they are going to climb it?"

Just as he asked this, both men could hear the noise from an engine, its low rumble growing out of the sound of the heavy rain.

The men put their optics back up to their eyes and trained them on the scene. Three men removed Branyon from the rear vehicle. His arms were bound behind his back and he wore a bag over his head.

And beyond the fence, a large truck pulling a trailer came into view. On the trailer was a crane with a basket: a medium-sized cherry picker. The truck began a slow process of backing through the mud in the heavy rain, positioning the trailer right up to the metal fence.

Chavez said, "There's your answer."

Caruso cussed. "Shit. They're about to take him over. We're going to have to engage them right now."

"Yeah," replied Chavez. Quickly, he reached into his Maxpedition bag and retrieved a roll of duct tape. He laid his rifle on the wet ground, quietly removed a long strip of the tape, and began to wrap his infrared monocular onto the left side of the weapon.

Caruso watched this for a moment. "What the hell are you doing?"

"Poor man's nightscope, I guess. Better than nothing."

Caruso said, "If you are trying to make it a scope, why aren't you putting it on top of the weapon?"

"I still need to use the iron sights, for distance. This will be helpful for close in. I'll aim left when I shoot."

Caruso shrugged, took tape from Ding's roll, and attached his night-vision monocular to his simple Kalashnikov rifle in the same fashion.

As he did this, Chavez said, "We need to

separate. It might make them think there are more of us."

Caruso nodded. "Okay. You're a better shot than me. I'll move off to the west, try to flank them and get a little closer."

Chavez whispered, "I'll move closer to the road, I'll have a more complete sightline on their poz there. I'll engage from seventy-five yards or so, any further out in these conditions and I might hit the CoS. I'll wait till I see as many of them together and as close to the light as possible, and then I'm going to open fire, left to right. You follow my lead, shooting right to left.

"Watch out for Branyon, okay?"

Caruso looked to Chavez. "We can't let him fall into the Russians' hands."

Chavez shook his head. "Don't even think about it. I'm not shooting a CIA officer, and neither are you. You do have a green light on any combatant you see. Do what you have to do."

Dom nodded slowly. "Roger that, Ding." And then he held out a hand to Ding. "Let's do it."

The two men slapped hands and pounded fists. Chavez said, "Sixty seconds. On my 'Go.' Don't fuck it up."

Dom rolled off to the right and began to crawl away quickly with his rifle on his back.

50

Pete Branyon knew his ribs were broken, several, in fact, all on his right side. He could feel an awkward and painful catch every time he took even a shallow breath. He had a broken tooth, at least one, and as bad as this was, it was even worse because he had a gag in his mouth and had been working for five minutes to dispel the tooth through the fabric before he swallowed it. This, and a blow to his nose that left it swollen and bloody, had made Branyon concentrate on little besides breathing for the past few minutes.

He finally managed to use his tongue to push the broken tooth fragment out through the gag in his mouth. It made its way out onto his lower lip and became stuck there on the thick blood that had been pouring out of his nose.

He'd taken a rifle butt to the side of his head ten minutes earlier for trying to escape out the back of the moving truck. The broken ribs came in the initial assault, when he'd been dragged out of his Mercedes disoriented and he'd had the side of his body slammed on the running board of the SUV.

He didn't remember how he hurt his nose, which meant it might have been when the flash-bang rendered him stupid for a good ten seconds. Hell, for all he knew he'd caught a fist or a rifle butt right to the snout the moment the men reached in for him.

And now, through the pain and the continued disorientation, he understood the kidnappers' plan. They were going to lower a cherry picker over the metal fence between Belarus and Lithuania, toss him in it, and pull him back over.

God damn it, Branyon thought. His concern about his own situation was secondary; in fact, he wasn't thinking about it at all at the moment. Instead, running through his mind now were the names of all the agents in his network, the CIA NOC officers under him, the Lithuanian SSD intelligence operatives he'd worked with in the nation, and dozens of other agents and assets, and codes, safe houses, and other compromising information.

He knew he couldn't let them take him over the border. At least not while he was still alive.

As they pushed him toward the cherry picker, his shoulders still wrenched halfway out of their sockets with his arms tight behind his back, he decided he'd try to break away again, to make another run for it, this time through these dark woods. He knew he wouldn't get fifty feet, but he thought he just might get lucky and coax one of these amped-up armed men to raise his rifle and fire at the escaping prisoner.

Dead men told no tales, and Branyon knew he had a lot of tales in his head.

Twenty feet from the border fence, one of the two men with a hand on his shoulder loosened his grip for a moment. Branyon had been submissive since they'd beat him during his escape attempt in the truck, and his compliance had led the one man into relaxing his guard now that at least half a dozen other men were standing around.

Branyon took two more steps through the mud, then ducked his head and slammed his left shoulder hard into the man who was holding his arm tight, simultaneously breaking away from the first man. He knocked the man on his left to the wet ground with the hard blow, then turned away from the fence and the armed men standing around, and he began to run down the gravel road, back in the direction the trucks had come from.

Ding had pulled the key fob for the Toyota Land Cruiser out of his pocket. He used his other hand to line his weapon up on the cluster of four men next to the border fence, some twenty-five feet away from the cherry picker, and he pressed the remote engine start on the fob.

A second later the lights of the Land Cruiser, two hundred yards back through the trees, illuminated the scene, casting distant ghostly shadows through the trees. Instantly some of the men by the fence turned and looked in the direction of the light.

Others were running after a man who himself was running in Chavez's direction on the gravel road.

Ding realized it was Branyon, and he realized the men behind him would have him in seconds.

There wasn't much illumination, but there was enough to help Chavez line the front blade sight of his AK-47 up on the group of men. He flipped the fire selector switch down to semiautomatic, and he opened fire.

Dom Caruso knew the light from the Land Cruiser was Chavez's "Go," his cue to engage. Dom had moved himself much farther to the west than he had planned to, but the noise of the heavy rain and the relatively clean forest floor made it easier for him to move than he'd expected.

As the gunfire started from Chavez's side, Caruso was about to engage the man closest to him. But just then both trucks began moving. They lurched forward, toward the men by the cherry picker, either so they could climb in or else to provide cover for them.

Quickly, Caruso got an idea. He centered his front blade on the driver of the first vehicle, then he squeezed off a single round. At fifty-five yards he hit the man in the right temple, toppling him dead against his driver's-side window and spilling him to the floor of his cab.

His truck continued to roll toward the other men. Caruso knew this would be an added distraction for the nine gunmen, a distraction he, Chavez, and Branyon could use right about now.

He slipped his right thumb on his weapon's fire selector lever, and he flipped it up to the fully automatic setting. Just as intense gunfire began, all in the direction of Ding Chavez, Dom Caruso leveled the rifle on a group of men lying prone in front of the fence, and he pressed the trigger.

Chavez found himself flat on his face behind a tree. He was impressed as hell with the quality of the shooting of the men some seventy yards away. They'd seen his muzzle flashes through the trees and pinned him down in mere seconds.

Realizing he didn't have any choice but to withdraw, he launched to his feet and began to run through the woods, zigzagging as he retreated. He heard the chatter of gunfire back behind him, and the hot *zing*s of bullets whizzing past, but he continued his run for five full steps before diving forward and sliding between two more trees. Here he went flat, spun around, and used his FLIR taped to the side of his rifle.

He saw men prone in the distance, and he saw others on their knees, most firing off toward the west in Dom Caruso's direction. The muzzle flashes were huge in Chavez's optic.

He also saw one other form, lying on the east side of the gravel road, crouched down in a small gulley. The man had both hands behind his back. Chavez knew it had to be Pete Branyon.

After seeing this, Chavez rolled out on the other side of the pine he hid behind and he finished off his magazine in fully automatic fire, spraying the area by the fence with the other gunmen. When his weapon went dry, he tucked tight behind the tree and began reloading from his last magazine.

When he only had a few rounds left in his second mag, Caruso peered quickly through the night-vision monocular and saw a man climb out of the cabin of the cherry picker and raise his head above the metal fence. He pointed a pistol in the direction Branyon had run, back near the gravel road. Caruso moved his eye to his sight, lined it up on the flash of the man's handgun, and moved his weapon a fraction of an inch to the right. He squeezed off three rounds just as fast as he could control his AK's recoil.

Checking his scope again, Caruso didn't see anyone peering over the fence there. He knew he couldn't be sure if he'd hit the operator of the cherry picker, or if there was anyone else who knew how to work the machine, but he had a feeling he'd bought Branyon some time.

Dom clicked his last magazine into place as he ran through the woods, back toward Chavez, Branyon, and the Land Cruiser.

Pete Branyon lay facedown in the mud as crashing gunfire rocked all around. Right in front of him one of his kidnappers lay on his side, desperately holding a wound on his neck with his hand as blood spurted between his fingers.

Branyon had never been in a gun battle; he'd never seen a man die. He couldn't believe the ungodly noise of everything going off around him, and he saw no way out of this for himself. He wasn't sure who was shooting back at his attackers, but he thought briefly about standing up in the middle of the fire, hoping he might get shot in the head so he wouldn't be dragged over the border.

But he stopped himself. Somebody in the trees was fighting like hell on his behalf; he realized the least he could do in return was not commit *fucking* suicide in the middle of the battle.

Chavez had been leapfrogging through the trees, moving to his right now, away from Branyon, trying to draw attention and fire from the restrained man lying in the little gulley. Chavez would move only three or four steps at a time, then drop flat, roll behind some sort of cover, and pop out to aim. The forest was thick enough that he could not just reach his weapon back around toward the shack and the trucks and spray — the bullets would just hit other trees. Instead, he picked his targets, using muzzle flashes to guide him, then he'd squeeze off three or four rounds in the direction of the flashes. He knew he was expelling ammunition too fast for the number of attackers, but by creating consistent muzzle flashes in a number of different locations in these woods, he felt he could give the men the impression they were facing more opposition, and this might help encourage them to keep their heads down and slow their return fire.

He made one more bound to the right, slid on the ground, and aimed toward the muzzle flashes in the distance. He squeezed the trigger of the AK-47, and the weapon did not fire.

He was out of ammo.

Just then Chavez heard a noise in the trees on his right. He reached down to the Glock

17 jammed in his jeans and drew it, but before he could level it at the approaching sound he heard someone call out to him.

"Hold fire, brother! It's me."

Caruso slid up next to him in the thick mud and wet, matted leaves. He was holding his pistol in his hand as well. "You hit?"

"I'm good, but these bastards sure can shoot."

Just then a massive chunk of pine bark blew off the trunk three feet above Caruso's head. Both men ducked lower.

"No shit," Caruso said. "We've thinned the herd. I think there are four or five left. Have you seen the CoS?"

"Yeah. Down in a gulley just off the road. Alive, the last time I saw him."

"What do you want to do?" Dom asked.

Chavez didn't hesitate. He pulled the key fob out of his pocket and put it in Caruso's hand. "You're faster, I shoot better."

"So?"

"I'm going for Branyon, you're going for the truck. Turn the lights off and roll up to fifty yards from the cabin. I'll be there with Branyon . . . or neither of us are coming. If you don't see us when you get there, take off and don't look back."

Dom just said, "Sure I will," and he began to run through the trees back in the direction of the Land Cruiser.

Chavez had no confidence Caruso would

just leave if Chavez and Branyon didn't show up at the rally point. No, Caruso would fight until his last breath to save his teammate and the CoS.

Chavez reloaded the Glock, leapt to his feet, and began leapfrogging through the trees back in the direction of Pete Branyon.

Branyon struggled out of the ditch with his arms secured behind his back during a lull in the shooting, then rolled into the trees on his right. He was fifty feet away from where he'd heard the last gunfire behind him at the fence, which wasn't far at all, but at least he felt like the way forward was clear of gunmen.

Just as he stood to run, constrained by the bindings on his wrists behind his back, he heard a new volley of fire, coming from multiple rifles, all behind him.

He decided to drop in his run, but he had to do this with care with his hands behind his back. Just as he began to lower down, he heard the banging and ripping sounds of bullets tearing into the trees around him.

He fell to his knees and pitched himself forward. Then he felt an incredible blow to his right shoulder — so hard it spun him around and he landed on his back on the wet ground.

It took a moment to realize he'd been shot, but when he did he found himself surprisingly calm about it. He just lay there, staring into the black above, feeling the rain on his face, and waiting for the pain to grow right where he'd felt the dull blow.

But there was no pain.

He heard new gunfire now, closer, on the other side. Seconds later he saw the flashes of light as someone stood over him, shooting. He couldn't make out the image, the light had blinded him, but he felt spent cartridges bouncing off his chest, and he wondered why it was he couldn't feel the bullets tearing into his body.

What he did feel now, however, was a hand, grabbing him by his injured shoulder. Suddenly an electric pain came from nowhere, blinding him, as he was lifted off the ground by someone grabbing him at his wound.

He found himself on his feet now. Someone was pulling him backward for a moment, coaxing him on, and all the while the gunfire continued from the pistol in the hand of the man directing him.

Branyon ran as fast as he could, using the other man for balance as he tried to stay upright on the unsteady footing.

He and the other man must have run for thirty seconds before the man yanked Branyon to a stop alongside the gravel road.

Sporadic gunfire back by the cabin continued, but the CoS realized the man with him was no longer returning fire.

"Shoot!" Branyon shouted.

"I'm out of ammo. Our ride should be here any sec. Hey, are you hit? There's blood all over my hand."

Branyon recognized the voice of Domingo Chavez.

In the darkness a black vehicle slid to a stop right next to them. As soon as it did, Branyon heard a car door open, and then he heard the sound of a bullet shattering the windshield.

Chavez pushed him into the backseat, then leapt in on top of him, slamming right into Branyon's torn shoulder.

The CIA chief of station screamed in agony.

Chavez said, "Go!"

And then the black vehicle revved, spun mud and water, and began racing to the north in reverse.

Branyon tried to climb up to a sitting position, but Chavez covered him with his body and held him down. "Stay put, Branyon! We're not out of this yet!"

The Land Cruiser took five rounds to the grille, the engine, and the windshield before Caruso backed out of the forest and spun around, then turned on the headlights and stomped on the gas. They raced north on the gravel road that would take them back to Tabariškės, and from there they could hit the two-lane blacktop road that led all the way back to Vilnius.

Chavez used his med kit on Branyon's shoulder. A massive flap of bloody tissue, easily the size of a peach, hung open off the man's rear deltoid.

"Fuck! That hurts!" Branyon shouted.

Chavez said, "I bet it does. But you're okay. Might have a broken clavicle, but it won't kill you."

"Fuck!" Branyon said again, the pain of Chavez's manipulation of his open wound almost too much to bear. Then he said, "Donlin's dead."

"Yeah," Ding confirmed. "We saw it all go down. Tried to call you, but they jammed both the cell and the sat."

Branyon looked up to Chavez in surprise. "You're kidding."

"No. Why? They were trying to kidnap you and take you, a CIA chief, over the border. Why does it surprise you the Russians would also jam the comms in the area?"

Branyon winced with pain again as Chavez pressed QuickClot, a blood-clotting agent, into the open portion of the wound. Once he recovered, he said, "Because they weren't Russian."

Both Ding, sitting next to Branyon, and Dom, behind the wheel, said, "What are you talking about?"

Branyon just shook his head. "They weren't Russian. They weren't Belarusan, either."

Ding said, "You've lost some blood, man.

You aren't talking straight."

Branyon tried to shrug his shoulder but the pain almost made him vomit. After a few seconds he said, "I don't know what language they were speaking, but it wasn't Russian. Could have been Czech, Bulgarian, Hungarian, Croatian, something like that. But definitely not Russian."

"Did they say anything to you?"

"Not a damn thing. They got their point across with the butt of their rifles."

The men drove on through the rain, heading back away from the border. In light of Branyon's information, Dom and Ding realized they had no idea what the hell had just happened.

51

John Clark motored his dinghy up to the wooden dock alongside a black ninety-eight-foot schooner with the name *Willie T* painted in white alongside.

The *William Thornton 2* was an old cargo hauler that had been turned into a bar just offshore of Norman Island. Among yachties here in the BVIs it was an institution, a dump of a place that served booze and fried food to anyone who could make it to its dock.

Its namesake had sunk right here when it wasn't too much older than the current version, and it was only a matter of time before this one found its way to the bottom of Davy Jones's locker, but tonight it was raucous and alive, so alive Clark had heard the music all the way from where he was moored on the other side of the bay.

Right now it looked like the majority of the people here on the crowded boat were young; girls in bikinis leapt off the upper deck at the stern and into the water, a drop of no more than a dozen feet that was met by riotous applause, as if the girls had just dove from a cliff in Acapulco.

Clark climbed out of his dinghy, passed by a large group of kids dancing on a dock that didn't seem to Clark like it was built to be a dance floor, and he made his way through the rowdy main deck of the bar. There were easily one hundred people in an incredibly small area, and Clark wished he'd come earlier in the day so he wouldn't have to push through all of them. But he made his way through easily enough, simply because most of the people here were drunk and happy, and therefore particularly pliable, especially to a man trained in using his body and his gaze to encourage compliance in others.

At the bar he ordered a Cruzan rum and ginger ale, then he pushed his way back out through the crowd trying to get the lone bartender's attention so they could get another round.

He sipped his drink for a moment, taking in the scene that could not have been any less appealing to him, then he climbed a circular staircase to the upper deck of the *Willie T.*

It was crowded here as well, but less so, and after a minute he found a stretch of real estate along the rusted railing of the boat. He leaned against it and looked out at the lights of the ships in the mooring field near the bar.

He counted twenty-four boats in total, nine of them catamarans, and he wondered if one of them might be his target.

He'd arrived at his conclusion that he was looking for a larger-sized catamaran by process of elimination. Walker had mentioned that he was being watched over by a group of four heavies, as well as the two Russians. Even though Clark had watched Kate and Noah kidnapped by just two people, he couldn't imagine an operation that put a half-dozen bodies against a compliant man going to work, and left a pair of unwilling kidnap victims with only one or two guards. There would be at least as much security on Kate and Noah to keep them restrained as there was on Terry, Clark felt certain of this.

Four to six bad actors, plus the two victims, meant the vessel he was looking for had to accommodate eight people, for possibly as long as a month.

That would necessitate a decent-sized boat.

Terry had said Kate expressed surprise she'd not gotten sick on the boat, and that had Clark wondering if she was on a catamaran. If her previous experiences had been on a monohull sailboat, she would find the cat much less unsteady, and therefore there was less chance she'd feel the effects of nausea.

There was one more thing. The kidnappers had arrived in a private aircraft, they were here forcing a deal worth $8 billion, and there were, if Clark's assumptions were correct, at least ten of them.

It stood to reason that they would have no problems spending money on their boat. They would buy something, not rent it, and it would be well outfitted and likely fast.

Clark checked the mooring field taking all this into consideration.

There were two catamarans out there that were more than fifty feet long, which as far as Clark was concerned made them big, but both of them had the name of the rental company they'd come from on the side. Neither of them looked any faster than any other boat in the water around them, so he thought it was less than likely either of these boats was involved.

His problem, Clark knew, was that there were easily twenty-five mooring fields this big or larger in the British Virgin Islands, as well as dozens more that were smaller. On top of this, there was no law that said the kidnappers had to park their boat in a mooring field at all. No, Clark thought it was possible, if not probable, that they just found a dark, quiet cove around one of the seventy islands and dropped anchor.

Clark would never find them just sailing around and looking for them. Not in a year of searching.

So he needed to enlist some assistance.

Through the gaggle of young people sitting

591

and standing around on the upper deck, Clark noticed a group of men who didn't look like tourists. They were older than average, which was a bit harder for Clark to judge, because not one of them was over forty-five, but they had a look to their dress and a stature that made him lock on to their conversation from across the deck. He tried to pick up bits of their voices from where he stood, but he failed miserably. He did have a clandestine listening device he could pop in his ear to pick up normal speaking voices from as far away as one hundred feet, but if he used it right now all the rap music and revelry would blow his eardrum, an eardrum that had somehow survived countless gun battles.

Although he couldn't hear the men talk, Clark watched the men's gesticulations and tried to discern what they were talking *about*.

For the first minute or two the topic of conversation was most definitely women: namely, women who were shapely — bordering on the cartoonish. But after this their gestures told Clark what he wanted to know.

These guys were boat captains.

Confident he had found what he had come to the *Willie T* looking for, he made his way over to the five men and leaned into their conversation. "Good evening, gentlemen. I wonder if I could buy you a round."

The men looked up in confusion, but not

suspicion or any animosity. This was the Caribbean; these were boat captains, so their answer to him was predetermined. Some nodded, others said yes. Clark stepped away, and in minutes he sat back down with six rum drinks. He was in with these guys now, at least as long as the booze held out.

The captains were nice enough, but while they included Clark in their conversation, they weren't terribly interested in him. He asked them about their vessels, and he immediately suspected at least one of them would indeed be able to provide him with some intel. Two of the five were down here on vacation but kept their own vessels here and sailed regularly. The other three were all captains for hire: one from the U.S., one from Uruguay, and the other from Jamaica. They all lived here year-round, made money off tourists who employed them to captain their chartered boats to sail them to all their favorite locales. All three of them were currently on a charter, but their clients were tucked away in their cabins somewhere out in the mooring fields, and these men were meeting up for drinks and girl-watching.

Clark had to almost yell over the sound of the god-awful music; some woman yammering something about milk shakes, if Clark could at least understand the monotonous chorus. He told the five men he was down here renting a monohull Irwin, trying to find his way around the islands.

The captain closest to him, an American from Florida, nodded almost like he gave a damn, then said, "Know anything about captaining?"

Clark shrugged. "Just a bit. Used to have a forty-foot diesel cruiser back in Chesapeake Bay. Did a little sailing on leave in the Navy."

The men looked at one another knowingly. He knew he'd not impressed them.

Another man, this one with a British accent, said, "You had yourself a rust bucket, did you?"

Clark laughed good-naturedly. He knew all these men identified him as a "renter," a man who comes down to the islands once or twice a year to rent a boat and, as far as they were concerned, not a real captain. In fact, these guys probably thought him something of a menace.

"How about another round?" he asked, and their looks softened.

"How 'bout yes?" said the tall, thin Jamaican captain.

After he returned with six more rums Clark leaned closer to the American sitting next to him. The others had started chatting with one another, blocking Clark out of the conversation. He asked the man about where he had been recently, and the captain explained he'd been going to at least two or three different islands and marinas a day all week.

Clark nodded, then said, "Big catamaran. Fast and expensive. Half-dozen men on board, maybe more. Seen anything like that?"

The man turned to Clark. "Uh . . . Why?"

"Let's just say I'm looking for a guy." Clark wiggled his right hand on the table. There was a fifty-dollar bill in it.

The captain looked down at it, then up at Clark. "What kind of cat?"

"I don't have a clue. Would have just started showing up this week. The boat itself might not be new to the area, but I'm sure the crew is. My guess is they don't all look like the sailing type."

The man slowly reached out for the money, but Clark flipped it away. "Give me something, I give you something."

"Who are you?"

"I'm the dumbass offering you a hundred bucks to answer an easy question."

Another fifty appeared in Clark's hand.

The American captain nodded slowly. "I know a guy who mentioned to me he ran into exactly who you are looking for. Seriously. Exactly."

"I need to talk to that man."

The captain said, "A hundred-dollar finder's fee and I'll take you to him. He'll want a hundred as well."

Clark said, "If the info pans out, I'll give him another hundred."

The captain snatched the hundred dollars,

gave a wide smile, then looked across the table. "Diego?"

A tan man in dreadlocks who'd said he was from Uruguay looked up.

The American captain said, "That sixty-eight-foot gunboat you passed the other day. Where did you say you saw her?"

The man on the end said, "Last night I was at the south tip of Guana. It was in a little cove just west of Monkey Point."

Clark cocked his head. "A *gunboat*?"

The American captain laughed and said, "It didn't have a cannon or anything. It's a type of racing boat. Fucking beautiful. It looks like a cross between a catamaran and a spaceship."

Clark's eyebrows rose. He sure as hell hadn't seen anything like *that* sailing around here in the BVIs.

Clark asked Diego, "What color was it?"

"Cobalt gray. It's called *Spinnaker II.*"

Clark hadn't even considered asking for the name of the boat. He had no idea he'd be getting this much information. He pressed his luck. "Did you see who was on board?"

"Bunch of guys. White guys, black guys. Didn't look like racers. They are renters, that's for sure."

Clark was confused. "How do you know they were renting?"

"The dumbass had the thing moored in the wrong place. Boat like that, you want people to see it. It was anchored like they were trying to hide out or something."

Clark nodded, then asked, "A catamaran like that? How fast could it go?"

"Thirty-five knots, easy. Fast as hell." Diego returned to his conversation with the other men.

Clark nodded again, making a show of his interest in the boat as a sailing vessel, not as a potential target.

The American whispered to Clark, "I'll take Diego's hundred. Make sure he gets it."

Clark felt like telling the man to go screw himself, but he didn't need animosity from the locals. For all he knew he'd see this guy again. He fanned him the money. "You be sure to pass that on, okay?"

"I'll do that. Hey, does that sound like the boat you are looking for?"

Clark had a feeling it was indeed the right boat. But he shook his head. "Don't think so. Still, I'd love to pass it someday. Sounds nice."

52

Jack Ryan, Jr., sat at his desk facing three large monitors full of information. His eyes scanned back and forth, and then he lowered his head into his hands and rubbed his eyes.

It had been a long and completely fruitless day, yet it had begun with so much promise. He'd been given good-looking intelligence from many different sources, but so far nothing had panned out.

The video feed of the cameras on Tarpon Island had led him nowhere. These two obviously white, obviously tall people who'd kidnapped the Walkers knew how to simply and effectively obscure their faces. They both wore hats and sunglasses, probably because they knew some asshole was going to sit at his desk, pore over every frame searching for clues, and push images through the best facial-recognition suites in the world.

Jack was that asshole and he'd come up with nothing.

As Jack watched them conduct their brazen

act, he was struck by just how calm and nonchalant they appeared to be. The woman followed her would-be victims into the home with a big smile. Then the man, her co-conspirator, appeared up the walkway from the beach, strolling into the big villa like he owned the place.

This couple weren't newcomers to this sort of work. They appeared to be in their element during the kidnapping.

This gave Jack the idea to investigate other unsolved kidnappings around the world using intel from Interpol and SIPRNet. He watched surveillance videos of sixty crimes, read the reports on a hundred more, but he saw no other kidnappings that matched the MO of this one.

He'd skipped lunch to keep searching for information about the Walkers' kidnappers, but he attained nothing other than a lot of doubt. His supposition that this couple were experienced kidnappers was contradicted by the fact no kidnappings he could find anywhere involved suspects matching their description.

Still, Jack knew, they were experienced in *something* that gave them a hell of a lot of confidence while snatching a kid and his mom out of their home.

After spending the morning working on the kidnappers, he spent the afternoon working on Andrei Limonov, spending hours trying to track the man's aircraft before it arrived in Luxembourg, to see where else he might have gone and who else he might have spoken with. This too had been a fruitless hunt. The Bombardier owned by Limonov's shell had spent most of the previous month, from what Ryan could tell, sitting in a fixed-base operator at Biggin Hill, an executive airport twenty minutes southeast of London.

The plane flew nowhere, which probably meant Limonov was in London during that time, but that didn't tell Ryan anything of value.

Another failure.

He'd also made several calls to Christine von Langer throughout the day. Ysabel had been taken out of her medically induced coma and upgraded to good condition, and this was obviously great news, but she would remain in the hospital for at least another two weeks.

Christine had remained by Ysabel's side, even though the two did not know each other. The American millionaire widow had slept on a tiny vinyl couch and eaten hospital food, which admittedly was better in Luxembourg than it was in the United States, but still was a far cry from what she was accustomed to.

Jack thanked her profusely, and she said she only wished she could do more.

Jack thought she was doing plenty; in fact, he was certain Christine had accomplished a hell of a lot more today than he had.

It was exactly the moment when he felt like giving up for the day, as he sat there with his elbows on his desk, rubbing his eyes, when Gavin Biery leaned his head into his cubicle.

"How is she?"

Jack looked up to find Gavin looming over him. "Oh, hey. Ysabel? She's going to be fine. Eventually. I can't figure out if she's really lucky or really unlucky."

Gavin sat down in the one other chair by Jack's desk. "Lucky to be alive. Guess that's all that matters now. The rest is over and done."

"Yeah." Jack noticed Gavin had a folder in his hand. "*Please* tell me there's something in that folder I want to see."

"Okay. There is something in this folder you want to see."

"What is it?"

"The phone records of one Luigi Vignali."

"Who the hell is" — Jack stopped himself and sat up straight — "Salvatore?"

"That's right. Salvatore isn't his real name. Big shocker there."

"What did you learn about him?"

Gavin chuckled. "This guy is a piece of work."

"You found something incriminating on him?"

"Yeah, but I don't really know where to

601

start. Maybe with the drug charges, or the petit larceny stuff." Gavin glanced down at the file. "Lots of arrests for disturbing-the-peace kind of things, all over Europe. Most involving his paparazzi harassment of celebrities, but he also has been heavily involved in the environmental and antiglobalization movements. He's been arrested in Paris for protesting nuclear power, in Frankfurt for a sit-in at the European Central Bank, and he had an attempted-arson charge in Davos, Switzerland, at the World Economic Forum."

"*Attempted* arson? What does that mean?"

"He threw a Molotov cocktail at a bus full of rich conference attendees, but didn't douse the rag with gasoline, so the thing burned out in the air."

"Genius," Jack said. It didn't sound relevant to his investigation into the man, but it still showed him something of both the Italian's character and his aptitude. Jack was disappointed. He wanted to see collusion between this man and Russian intelligence. "That's it?"

Gavin looked back down. "Pretty much. He punched out his mom once, put her in the hospital, and did a couple of days in the slammer for that, but Mommy dropped the charges."

"Jeez," muttered Ryan.

"Aren't moms the best?" quipped Gavin. "There is also some interesting logistical stuff. I geolocated his phone and found out he's not in Rome."

"Where is he?"

"He flew to Brussels today, went to a hotel in the European Quarter and spent the night. I pulled up the hotel's guest info, and he's staying there under the name Salvatore. Reservation for a week at the Stanhope Hotel."

"What's going on in Brussels?" Jack asked.

"What do you mean?"

"He takes pictures of celebrities for a living. Is there something happening in Brussels that would be of interest to a paparazzo?"

Gavin just shrugged. "I wouldn't really know, Ryan."

Jack thought about it. "Yeah, me either."

The computer geek and the intelligence analyst both sat in silence for a moment. Neither of them was exactly dialed in to the pulse of celebrity goings-on these days, if ever.

Gavin said, "I could do some research."

"How?" Jack asked.

"Dunno. Turn on a TV or something."

Jack broke into a smile, his first one since Luxembourg. "Wonder if Gerry would let us expense a *People* magazine for research purposes."

Gavin said, "He let Clark expense a freakin' sailboat, so I bet he'd be okay with it."

Jack spun around in his desk and started looking at goings-on in Brussels in the next few days. There were concerts and plays and political conferences and corporate conventions, but with no idea what he was looking for, it was hard to know how to narrow down his search.

He shrugged. "The only way to find out what he's up to is to go over there and watch him. Or else go over there, grab him by the throat, and throttle the information out of him."

Gavin said, "I know which method you'd prefer."

"Yeah. He was involved with the people who hurt Ysabel. I don't know if he knew what was going on or if he was just a patsy." Jack shrugged. "I'm not sure I give a damn. I've got to use him to find them."

Gavin leaned forward a little. "There is no way in hell Gerry is going to let you go back to Europe alone."

Jack knew this was true.

Gavin surprised him by saying, "Tell you what. I'll talk to him, maybe he'll let me go along with you to watch your back."

Jack smiled affectionately at Gavin. If Gerry wouldn't let Jack go alone, he sure as hell wouldn't let Jack go supported by an overweight IT director pushing sixty whose experience in the field in the past few years had been extremely hit-and-miss. He patted Gavin on the shoulder. "I appreciate it. But I need to handle this on my own for now. I'm going to walk into Gerry's office and tell him how important it is."

"Good luck."

Ten minutes later Jack walked out of Gerry's office, his face a mask of utter frustration. Gerry had said just exactly what Jack feared he would: His request to return to Europe to conduct physical surveillance of Salvatore had been denied. He returned to his desk, opened up the security feeds at the Stanhope Hotel in Brussels, and began to scroll through the different cameras.

He told himself he'd sit here all night if he had to, but he was going to learn something.

53

John Clark sailed his fifty-two-foot sailboat around Monkey Point, at the southern tip of Guana Island, just after noon. He wasn't sure of the exact location of the cove mentioned by the captain in the bar, but it wasn't a large island at all, so Clark knew he could circle the entire landmass in under an hour.

But he didn't have to. Within five minutes he found exactly what he was looking for. A massive but sleek catamaran, bigger and more impressive than anything in the waters of the BVIs that he'd seen to date, bobbed at anchor in a little cove on the south side of the island. It was tucked away, but not that hard to see from the main sailing route.

Clark was a quarter-mile from the other vessel as he passed by, but he didn't use his binoculars to look it over. Instead, he just sailed on, standing by the helm with the wheel in his hand, doing his best to keep his eyes on the water in front of him. He knew if this was the boat the kidnap victims were be-

ing kept on, there was a good chance someone on that catamaran — on the deck, in the
cockpit, or up on the flying bridge — was
watching him right now with optics that
could easily see every move he made. As long
as he appeared nonchalant and concentrated
more on sailing than on searching the coves
for hidden boats, he'd arouse no suspicions.

An hour later Clark's boat lay at anchor
itself, three coves over from where he had
noticed the *Spinnaker II,* and Clark was in his
dinghy, motoring toward a remote secluded
beach on the southwestern side of Guana
Island.

When he came ashore he pulled in his
outboard and heaved the ten-foot-long craft
onto the sand, then he threw a small backpack
over a shoulder and began to walk.

The island was all but deserted other than
a single resort hotel, and it was covered in
high and sometimes steep hills, but there was
a decent network of rustic hiking trails. Clark
followed one such trail across the southern
end of the island, taking almost an hour to
bisect the little landmass sticking out of the
perfect water before finally coming close to
the crest of a steep hill. Here he checked his
GPS carefully, then left the sandy trail and
pushed into the mangroves alongside.

After ten minutes of slow-going progress
through the bushes, seeing somewhere along
the lines of a hundred lizards along the way

and poking his hands and legs so many times with cactus needles that he'd stopped responding to the pain, he lowered his body down into the sand and crawled the rest of the way to the crest.

At the top he looked out over a small cove. Tortola was due south in the distance, and on his left a twin-engine Pilatus was lining up on final at the same airport he and Sherman had arrived in three days earlier.

But he wasn't here to look at Tortola. No, much closer, in the little cove below him, the *Spinnaker II* sat right where Clark had seen it two hours earlier. Putting his binoculars up to his eyes, he first scanned along the beach in front of him. The last thing he needed was to be discovered by someone from the *Spinnaker II* sitting on the shore.

There. Two men sat under a tree in small beach chairs. They each had a pair of binoculars in their laps and bottles of beer in their hands. They looked relaxed enough, but Clark wondered if that was just because there were no other signs of life in sight other than lizards and birds.

Confident there was no way the two men could see him, he began looking over the *Spinnaker II.* The deck was empty, but he saw two men in the cockpit and another man up on the flying bridge. They all had their shirts off, and they were big, muscular, and relatively young. The man on the bridge was obviously another lookout; he used his binos to glass the waterway to the south twice in the five minutes Clark watched him.

Clark tallied five men: two on shore and three on the boat. They appeared relaxed, but they all looked like they could switch on quick enough and become formidable. They didn't appear Russian to him at all. One man was black, and another was darker-complexioned than any Spetsnaz guy he'd ever seen.

He had nothing but circumstantial evidence that these men were holding the Walkers, not even enough to go on. He decided he needed more information about what was happening inside that boat.

At three p.m. he turned around and headed back down the hill, planning on coming back at night to set up surveillance.

Clark returned to his Irwin and got a few hours' sleep. When he woke he cooked a steak on the gas grill on the deck and made a salad in the galley. He sat in the cockpit in front of the helm and ate his dinner, knowing he was in for a long night.

At around ten p.m. he started getting his gear together to move to his hide overlooking the *Spinnaker II.* He packed water, food, optics, night-vision goggles, bug spray, and a knife.

He also knew there was a chance he might

see something on the boat that would necessitate him hitting it immediately in an in
extremis one-man raid. While he didn't like
his chances against five men, he recognized
the fact that he wouldn't be able to just watch
if one of the hostages was in jeopardy. He
packed his swim fins, his mask and snorkel,
and his pistol, on the chance he'd have to use
them.

At ten-thirty he was ready to go. He was
standing in the cockpit, just finishing a bottle
of Gatorade before loading the dinghy with
his backpack, when he heard the faint sound
of a small engine purring across the water.
He stepped out onto his deck, walked around
for a moment, then realized it was coming
not from land but from outside his little bay.
Since there were no more boats moored in
the bay, and no rational person would take
his dinghy all the way across the water from
Tortola, he immediately decided he was hearing the dinghy of the *Spinnaker II,* and it was
approaching his boat.

With his mast lights on he couldn't see well
more than fifty feet in any direction, so he
pulled a flashlight off a table in the cockpit
and stood out on the deck.

His SIG Sauer pistol hung in his shorts on
his right side under his T-shirt, a folding knife
in the cargo pocket on his left. Extra magazines for both were tucked in his back pocket.
He was ready for a fight, but he knew if he

stood on the deck in the lights, he'd be exposed to any armed person in the dinghy.

On the other hand, if he ran onto the deck and crouched behind cover, he would quite obviously blow any pretense that he was just some sailboat renter out for a little peace and quiet here in this cove.

When the dinghy came into view he saw two men on board, and he recognized them both as the men he'd seen on the gray catamaran. One waved a hand in his direction as they neared, and he belted out an accented "Evening, Captain!"

They threw their line up to Clark, who took it, then tied it off on a cleat on the deck.

"Good evening," he said, doing his best to sound chipper and unsuspicious.

As they climbed aboard, Clark saw they were both in their thirties and they were physically fit. One had short brown hair and an impressive beard; the other was completely bald and his arms were inked from his wrists to his shoulders. The bearded man climbed aboard with the confidence and dexterity of someone very accustomed to his actions, but the bald-headed man didn't seem particularly comfortable with boats; he took a moment to heave himself up onto the deck from the bobbing dinghy, an action that came naturally to a real sailor.

Clark scanned the tattoos on both men, but he couldn't derive any intel from them.

"How's it goin'?" the bearded man asked. He was obviously South African, which surprised Clark some. They all shook hands, and the South African introduced himself as Kip, the bald-headed man as Joe.

"Doing fine," Clark said, still affecting the genial nature of a vacationer. "Welcome aboard. Care for a beer?"

"Always," said Joe.

Clark went down to the saloon, grabbed three cold Caribe beers, and came back up. As he passed them around to his two visitors, Kip said, "Nice ketch you've got here. Out here by yourself, are you?"

"Sure am," Clark replied. "Just about to shut down for the night, actually."

The other man looked the boat over slowly. He spoke with an American accent. "You're renting?"

"Yeah. Just down for a couple of weeks."

Clark could tell the men were suspicious of him, but only to a small degree. He thought this was odd, because he was certain he'd not been seen earlier on the hill, and he could think of no other way he could have possibly given any indication he was interested in them.

Kip said, "This is a bit of a lonely vacation, wouldn't you say?"

Clark nodded. "You're telling me. My girlfriend was supposed to come along, but she couldn't make it at the last minute."

Clark was wearing his wedding ring, but a married man with a boat down here talking about his girlfriend wasn't going to raise suspicions.

The pair just stood there on the deck, facing down Clark without speaking. He realized the men were trying to be intimidating, and to the average man in his mid-sixties, Clark imagined they might have been able to pull it off.

Clark, on the other hand, had a plan to kill them both if necessary. He wasn't intimidated, just annoyed.

That said, his cover persona, a semi-sleazeball retiree down here for a few weeks of recreational boating, would be easily intimidated by a pair of men looming over him like this, so Clark swallowed hard and let his mouth twitch a little, as if from nerves.

"You know," said the man called Kip, "there's a pretty nice marina and yacht club over there at Scrub Island. Only about twenty minutes from here. Seems like a guy down here by himself would do well to pick up a mooring ball over there, wander up to the bar, and meet himself a nice, mature lady."

Clark said nothing.

The other man spoke now. "Instead of hiding out over here in this little nothing bay."

Clark shook his head. "I'm not hiding from anything."

The South African shrugged, took another

sip of his Caribe.

Clark knew he needed to ask them about themselves. He said, "You guys come from shore?"

"Us? No. We've got a little cat in the next cove."

They didn't have a little cat and they weren't in the next cove, but Clark just nodded and sipped his beer.

The discomfort of the situation was palpable, and Clark played it up, even wiping his forehead a few times, as if to remove the sheen of sweat there. Finally he said, "Look, guys. Like I said, I was just about to call it a night."

The men finished their beers in silence.

On the main deck the bald-headed man said, "This bay isn't really that safe in case of a storm. The marina is much safer."

Kip added, "This sure is a nice boat. I'd hate for anything to happen to it."

Clark cocked his head, still playing the role of a nervous senior citizen. "What might happen to it?"

"Some weather's coming in is what I heard," Joe said, the malevolence strong in his voice.

Clark nodded. He'd checked the weather, of course. There was nothing but clear skies and moderate winds predicted.

Clark said, "Okay. Maybe first thing in the morning I'll pull anchor and find another place. Something more suitable."

Kip winked at Clark. "Sounds like a solid plan, old-timer. You have yourself a good one." He put the bottle down and headed over the side.

Joe followed Kip back into the dinghy and the pair motored off. They disappeared as soon as they were out of the glow of the Irwin's mast lights, but Clark heard their motor for another minute as he stood there on the deck.

He then went back to the cockpit and sat down, thinking about the exchange. He felt convinced the men had no real reason to be suspicious of him. Likely they were just assholes given instructions to keep all threats away from their operation, and they were being proactive.

These guys weren't decision makers in this crime. Just muscle given enough responsibility to fuck it up. Of course, Clark knew, that didn't mean they weren't able to do their job when it came to using their guns or their fists, or following their boss's orders.

Clark waited till midnight to go to shore. The original plan had him taking the dinghy in, of course, but he didn't know if the two goons from the *Spinnaker II* would come back and look over the boat while he was gone. If they saw the dinghy ashore in the middle of the night, their suspicion would switch to outright certainty that Clark wasn't what he appeared to be. So instead he stripped to his shorts, jumped in the water with his bag, and donned his fins. In seconds he was kicking in the black water, heading to the beach.

He was out of breath when he arrived, but he'd made good time, and in just minutes he recovered enough to begin the long hike.

An hour after this Clark climbed the rise, dropped down to his knees, and covered the last few feet in a crouch. When he peered over the top of the hill, he took a moment to orient himself. He looked down at the little cove below him, then pulled his night observation device from his pack.

After scanning back and forth through his NODs, he dropped his shoulders in resignation.

The big catamaran was gone.

54

President Jack Ryan sat back down at the round table in the conference room in Copenhagen, surrounded by twenty-six other national leaders, everyone minus the president of Lithuania, who had returned to her country to deal with the crisis at home.

His biggest ally in all this was gone, he told himself.

Before the discussion began he took stock of his base of support. He felt secure that he had the backing of Poland, Latvia, and Estonia, as well as other NATO member nations in Central Europe. As for the Western Europeans, he was counting on the United Kingdom and Germany, although the latter had not given him any direct indication they were on board with his plan.

Most all of the other nations were question marks, and he knew he was about to find out just where they all stood.

While Ryan hadn't exactly expected a coronation after his ten-minute speech, he quickly realized he'd also been unprepared for the daggers to come out quite so quickly. As soon as the meeting reconvened, the president of France was recognized by the NATO secretary general. He was a swarthy sixty-year-old with a sparkle in his eye from a quick wit. He was a socialist, of course; five hundred times more liberal than Ryan, yet always respectful in his dealings with the American President. He addressed the room in French, but his words were deftly translated through the FM wireless earpiece in Ryan's left ear.

"We've all read the briefing book you delivered to us, President Ryan, but, quite frankly, so much of what you assert is based upon conjecture. You are alleging the FSB has been involved in nearly every bad thing that has happened in the last few weeks."

Ryan kept a measured tone. "I've cited five events I feel have been influenced or orchestrated by Russia. I am sorry to say it, but much more bad has happened in the world in addition to these five. I haven't blamed Valeri Volodin for the bomb in the mosque in Tunisia on Tuesday, for example, or the drug cartel crisis in Mexico, just to mention a couple of things in the news."

The French president waved his hand. "Be that as it may, your accusations feel like a stretch. And even putting aside the inflammatory proposal of moving armor from the alliance into Lithuania, your request for further sanctions troubles me as well. All this talk about the wealthy wrenching power from the masses. You are essentially accusing the Russians of operating a criminal state. A rogue regime."

"In a manner of speaking, yes, I am."

The president of France said, "What you are talking about is corruption. Shall we outlaw any nation with corruption in their system?"

"Corruption isn't in Russia's system, Mr. President. It *is* their system."

"Be that as it may, we are not an enforcement body over the domestic policies of anyone, much less a non-NATO power. We have to leave Russia to fight their own organized crime."

"Forgive me," Ryan said, careful to keep his tone lighter than his darkening mood. "But when the state is a criminal organization, the state won't do a good job combatting criminal organizations."

The prime minister of the Netherlands spoke up now. He was a good-looking man in his late forties who spoke English as well as Ryan did. "Mr. President, you talked as if Russia had something to show for their invasion of Ukraine. I disagree with this assessment. They have been effectively held in place for a year. They are not winning."

Ryan nodded. "Compared to their original

goal? No, they have not been successful, you are correct. But look at a map of two years ago, and then tell us Russia is not in a better position now. Compared to a two-year-old map, they are winning."

The Dutch leader said, "A fair point, Mr. President. But you are asking us to risk war with Russia over Lithuania."

Ryan said, "Mr. Prime Minister, I am merely asking you to live up to the NATO charter, of which your nation is a signatory."

The young Dutchman shrugged a little, a dismissive gesture. "Over a Russian land bridge through Lithuania to its own province. Look, I'd love to help in this endeavor. Russia's involvement in the plane crash was horrific, and both their actions and their rhetoric have been deplorable. Further, I recognize NATO will appear weak if we do nothing. But there has been no Article Five violation yet, so we aren't *obligated* to do anything."

Ryan said, "But when the violation comes, there will be no *chance* to do anything. Russia can take Lithuania at will."

The Dutch prime minister said, "And my nation can't prevent that. Look . . . let's talk facts. Russia has seven hundred fifty thousand ground troops. The Netherlands has *seventeen* thousand. They have seven hundred sixty attack and interceptor aircraft. We have sixty-nine. They have three hundred fifty-two warships. We have twenty-three."

He paused for a moment, cleared his throat, then said, "They have fifteen thousand tanks. We have zero." He smiled, as if he had just checkmated Ryan, then repeated more forcefully, "*Zero, Mr. President.*"

And whose fucking fault is that? Ryan didn't say it, but he thought it so hard he wondered if the interpreters might pick up his feelings and translate them to the room. Europe as a whole had made a high-stakes gamble on permanent world peace, or at least on permanent European peace, and their bet had not paid off. Now Ryan had to convince them to agree to put a few thousand of their troops into action to prevent a European war, while America would carry the water for them all.

He said, "I recognize your nation and many nations here are hopelessly outgunned by Russia. That is all the more reason to accept this proposal. If Volodin walks into Lithuania without a response from us, he will walk, or he will fight, his way into Poland. The rest of the Baltic will look good to him then. At that point, we will be at war, I feel sure, but the question is, how many tanks will you have then? Zero still? Or will you go on an all-out defense buildup and buy twenty-five?"

The Dutch prime minster glared at Ryan.

Ryan said, "You can prevent a larger conflagration by standing firm now."

The prime minister of the United Kingdom was ceded the floor for a moment, just long enough to assure President Ryan that the UK was behind him and in support of his proposals, and then to implore the rest of the room to carefully consider the blow NATO would take for losing a member state to Russia's tanks. As soon as he was finished, the young president of Poland echoed the UK's statement, and assured Ryan the Poles were with him in this fight all the way.

But after this, the French president spoke again. "My intelligence agency does not see an attack on Lithuania as imminent. Yes, it is provocative that Russia is conducting such a large-scale training exercise at this time, but it seems they do this every couple of years."

Ryan wanted to say, "Yeah, and it seems like they invade a neighbor every couple of years." But he fought himself, and he held his tongue.

The French president continued. "So we do not feel there is a crisis like the one you describe. Further, at the moment France carries a large percentage of the forces and armor in NATO's VHRJTF, larger than anyone other than the United States. We feel our burden would be disproportionate, should the Russian invasion come."

Ryan thought about being diplomatic for a moment.

But not for long.

He said, "Mr. President, you are saying Russia will not attack, so it is not necessary to move the VHRJTF into Lithuania, and then, with the next breath, you say you don't want to move the VHRJTF because if Russia attacks, your forces would be most affected."

Ryan looked at the president of France, and he looked at the president of Germany, his close friend Marion Schöngarth. From the expressions on both leaders' faces, he quickly registered that with his last comment he had lost France and won Germany.

A push.

The prime minister of Denmark had never been a fan of Ryan, he knew this from his dealings with her, and he *really* knew it from everything she said about him in the press. In the entire room, she probably came the closest to outright hatred of the U.S. President. She pulled her microphone closer to her mouth to speak, and Ryan reached for his glass of water, knowing he was going to need to be ready for a vigorous response to whatever she said.

The Danish prime minister said, "If we move troops to Lithuania, we are asking Volodin to invade. We are giving him the excuse he needs. Is that what you really want? Are you *trying* to draw us into a fight?"

Ryan shook his head. "By not putting a blocking force in Lithuania we are asking Volodin to invade, because he sees this as nothing but weakness, and the success of his intimidation tactics. You think we would be doing nothing, but we would be doing something. We would be quite actively backing down. The sooner we realize how Valeri Volodin sees the world, the sooner we will understand how we need to counter him."

The Danish prime minister said, "Apologies for articulating what many people in this room are thinking, Mr. President, but I think this is how *you* see the world. *You,* President Ryan, *you* are the reactionary zealot. Valeri Volodin is no one to fear. He is a tin-pot dictator with an old and inefficient military."

Ryan wondered how long Denmark could hold out against Russia's "old and inefficient" military. He presumed their fifty-seven tanks would put up a good fight, but if they survived half a week against Russia, their tankers' heroics would be spoken of for hundreds of years.

Ryan said, "I respectfully disagree. Yes, he has a poor hand of cards, but he is playing them like the best poker player on the planet."

The Danish leader said, "Volodin has done nothing against the people of Denmark, and nothing he has done in Lithuania, not even his threats, have risen to the level of an Article Five violation. I will support increasing sanctions — we can fold in the midair collision as part of the reason why. But I don't want to antagonize a man like Volodin."

Now the German president, Marion Schöngarth, spoke up. "Our intelligence agencies are quite good, Mr. President. Maybe they aren't as good at spying on allies as your CIA, but they know Russia."

Ryan ignored the dig. A whistle-blower had revealed a CIA eavesdropping operation in Germany, and Ryan knew he'd hear about it here. He made no reply, he'd already apologized over the kerfuffle, and he was content to leave it there.

Schöngarth continued, "And my intelligence service says Volodin is looking for a sign from us. He will do all these things you speak of up until an attack, hoping to see clear evidence we will not fight back. When we reveal ourselves as not willing to put up a fight for Lithuania, only then will he move in."

The Spanish prime minister all but shouted into his microphone: "So he's bluffing. You just said it. All we have to do is insist we will retaliate, and he will back down. We shouldn't move forces, because that will be too provocative. That will invite a response when none would come if we kept our cool heads."

Ryan fought his exasperation now. "When we allowed the former Eastern Bloc nations into NATO, we knew this could happen. NATO isn't an economic partnership. It's not a cultural exchange. It's a military alliance. We didn't all agree to this union so that we could trade cheese between our nations. No, it is to protect one another." He paused.

"And one of us is in danger of being erased from the map."

The French prime minister said, "The alliance is to prevent a European war. The former Eastern Bloc nations want revenge on Russia." He sipped his water. "NATO is not in the revenge business."

Ryan said, "This is not about revenge for the crimes of a quarter-century ago. This is about protecting people, livelihoods, and futures from a current, imminent, and existential threat."

Patiently, Ryan added, "I firmly believe moving the troops to Lithuania will reduce any chance there is for war dramatically. That is why I am here today."

The prime minister of Denmark spoke up now. It was becoming something of a gang attack in here, with Ryan as the victim. She said, "If what you say is correct, that he is trying to draw us into war, then there is nothing to worry about. Other than you, no one in this room wants to go to war. We can't be drawn in."

The predictability of the comment left Ryan at a loss. He'd expected better arguments for non-involvement than what he'd heard, almost a preemptive declaration of surrender.

Ryan leaned in to his microphone. "It might be inconvenient for you all that we accepted nations into NATO that might now actually call on NATO to help, but where will we be if we do not respond forcefully to an Article Five violation?"

The Danish prime minister barked angrily, "Where will we be if we do?"

The Italian prime minister spoke up now. "You said he will invade without war if he sees he can get away with it. Well, he invades and we are drawn in, or he invades and we stay out of it. Well . . . I fall firmly on the side of staying out of it. Of course we will intervene diplomatically, perhaps economically. We will express that this is not how one behaves in this day and age, and we will demonstrate our moral superiority."

Ryan said, "A show of our moral superiority will not help the Lithuanians nearly as much as a show of our air superiority will."

An hour later President Ryan, Scott Adler, and his NATO ambassador emerged with the others from the meeting, and after some handshakes he entered his armored car. On the way back to his hotel, Ryan rubbed his eyes under his glasses while his assistant chief of staff got his SecDef on the phone. Ryan took the phone from him as he looked out the window. "Bob? Well, we've got Germany. Marion Schöngarth doesn't love me, but she knows I'm making the right call."

Burgess said, "Good. Germany is important." He waited expectantly for more results from the meeting. "Mr. President?"

Ryan said, "My incredible powers of persuasion managed to win the day with Poland, too." Of course Poland would agree to the motion. It was in the same boat as neighboring Lithuania.

"That's not funny, Mr. President. Tell me you've got more."

"A lot of nations are playing this close to their vest. Canada will follow us, the UK as well. Most of the Central European countries voiced some support." Jack shrugged. "But that was a tough room."

Adler looked across the limo at his President. "I thought you'd do better than that."

Ryan raised an eyebrow. "This is a tough room, too, apparently."

"I'm sorry, Mr. President. I didn't mean to imply it's your fault. Almost everyone in that meeting already had their mind made up."

"I know, Scott. I feel like I was trying to herd cats in there. Let's start with who we know is going to come out against. Spain, Denmark, France . . . no way they will move NATO troops in advance of an Article Five violation."

Adler said, "At which point, just as was the case in Ukraine, the invasion is all but a fait accompli."

"Exactly. Italy looks doubtful, Iceland seemed skeptical it would do any good, but we might get a vote out of them anyway because they didn't express concern that it would do harm."

Ryan blew out a sigh. "We've got to get full consensus. Just because someone is against doesn't mean they won't raise their hand tomorrow. If they want to keep the integrity of the organization intact they might go along with it despite their reservations. But quite frankly . . . I don't think we're going to get our troops."

Bob Burgess was listening in via speakerphone. He said, "I've spoken with the Marine commander for Europe personally. He knows we're hoping to move NATO into Lithuania, but if that doesn't happen . . ."

Ryan said, "He's ready?"

"He's ready," Burgess confirmed. "The Black Sea Rotational Force will move to the eastern border."

Ryan cocked his head. "What about Lithuania's border with Kaliningrad? To the west?"

"We have a Special-Purpose Marine Air-Ground Task Force Crisis Response unit we will send from Morón Air Base in Spain. About seven hundred men in total. We will add to this force a FAST team, that's a Fleet Antiterrorism Security Team, in Rota, Spain. Another hundred twenty or so Marines, but all exceptionally well trained."

Ryan said, "Eight hundred Marines in total? That's even less than the battalion of the Black Sea Rotational Force protecting the east."

Burgess said, "True, but we are not expecting a big invasion by Russia out of Kaliningrad."

"Why is that?" Ryan asked.

"Simple, Mr. President. Poland. If the Russians hit Lithuania out of Kaliningrad, it will deplete their defenses in Kaliningrad. The Poles, who also have a border with Kaliningrad and a good military, could then attack Kaliningrad."

Ryan scoffed at this. "That's ridiculous. Poland doesn't want to invade Russian territory."

"We know that, but the Russians are paranoid."

Ryan thought it over and then nodded. "Something we can use against them, perhaps." He waved away the thought. "How long will the BSRF and the Marines on the Kaliningrad border be on their own before we can reinforce them?"

"The Marine Expeditionary Unit off the coast of Scotland has an LHD. Sorry, Scott, that means Landing Helicopter Dock ship. They have two other, smaller transport vessels as well. We'll have them join up with some warships for protection before they get into the Baltic. They can arrive in Lithuanian waters in five days. After that we have a brigade at Camp Lejeune ready to lift over. They could land in Vilnius in ten days."

Ryan thought this over. "Regarding the

MEU in Scotland. Any chance they can pack everyone up into their ships and head up the North Sea for a day? Make it look like it's part of their exercise? It would get them that much closer if we decide to pull the trigger, and it wouldn't necessarily look like we were considering using them."

Burgess said, "I'll talk to Nate Bradford, the Marine commandant. I think that sounds like a reasonable measure. If this gets any worse over there, hours will count."

Ryan said, "If somebody is killing CIA officers and trying to yank station chiefs over the border, then it *already* is worse over there. I think the only way to plan to succeed in Lithuania is to go ahead and plan on failing here in Copenhagen. Barring an Art Five violation before the consensus vote tomorrow, this one is in the bag, folks. We've lost."

As Ryan said this, just eight miles to his east, the Russian Severodvinsk-class submarine *Kazan* passed under the bridge that connected Malmo, Sweden, with Copenhagen, Denmark.

Directly above the silent vessel, European Union commuters passed in their cars between Denmark and Sweden, blissfully unaware that a massive predator skulked in the cold waters below them.

The *Kazan* was twenty-four hours away from initiating hostile actions off the coast of

Kaliningrad, and no one in the West knew it had even left port in the Arctic.

55

Twenty-four hours after the attempted kidnapping of CIA chief of station Peter Branyon, no one in Lithuania knew anything more about what had actually happened than they did during the event.

The two men of The Campus had spent the hours hard at work, beginning the moment Chavez and Caruso drove the wounded Branyon away from the border. Once they were out of range of whatever technology was jamming both cell and satellite signals near the border, Ding called Branyon's second-in-command at the U.S. embassy. When he got through he put Branyon himself on the phone with his deputy, and the CoS gave a sit rep and orders even as he fought vomiting from the pain and losing consciousness from the blood loss.

The Campus men delivered Branyon to the hospital and handed him off to a team of CIA security officers, another group of whom was already racing to Tabariškės, along with a contingent of Lithuanian troops, to collect Donlin's body and to check the location near the border where the gunfight had taken place.

Once Chavez and Caruso were clear of the hospital, they headed back to their safe house, conducting a long SDR in the process.

Chavez called Mary Pat Foley while still in the middle of the SDR. He didn't have to tell her about the incident because she'd already spoken directly with the deputy chief of station, but he filled her in on some key details.

When he was finished with his brief after-action review, Mary Pat said, "What do you think, Domingo? My first feeling is you both need to get out of there tonight."

Chavez replied, "Of course we'll do whatever you say, but I think there is still a role for us over here."

"I'm listening."

Ding said, "Right now you don't have a station chief in the city. I know Branyon and Donlin were burned, apparently by the network of agents run out of Tabariškės. I don't know how many more case officers at the embassy were known to that network and compromised, but we have no reason to believe we've been compromised to the Russians, or even to this other group obviously working on their behalf. Let us stay here in the field, continue working under the Data-Planet cover, and get the rest of our images knocked out during the day tomorrow. At night maybe we can support the local station in some way, even if it's just keeping an eye out here in the city."

Mary Pat said, "All right. That would be helpful, but I want you two to have a plan to get out of there."

"Trust me," Chavez said. "With the Russians peering over the walls on two sides, we are keeping our bags packed."

The next morning Chavez and Caruso were picked up by the DataPlanet van at six, same as every other day they'd been in country. When they climbed into the vehicle, however, they could immediately tell something was wrong. Herkus Zarkus sat behind the wheel looking ahead. He wasn't his normal laid-back self.

Caruso and Chavez both instantly assumed he knew about what happened the evening before somehow, and he was scared to be traveling with the two Americans who'd shot it out with some sort of foreign special mission unit.

"What's wrong?" asked Dom, but he thought he knew the answer to the question.

Herkus let the van idle while he turned to the other men. "Guys, I hate to do this to you, but I just came to bring you the van. I can't go out with you today."

Dom nodded sympathetically, certain now

Herkus didn't want to continue the relationship with the American intelligence agents. "I understand," he said.

But he did not understand at all.

Herkus said, "The president has asked everyone between the ages of eighteen and forty to join the national defense militia. I'm leaving today. I don't think they know what the hell they are going to do with us, but I figure since I have American military experience, they ought to make me a general or something."

He chuckled at his own joke, but the two Campus men could see his nerves showing.

Chavez realized he'd been wrong about Herkus. He wasn't scared of being around the Americans. On the contrary, he was going to volunteer to move even closer to the danger. "That's very noble, but you were an electronics-repair technician. What the hell good do you think you can do against a Russian invasion?"

Herkus said, "This is home now, guys. I can't ask you to understand, but I can't leave Lithuania to the Russians. Better that I die with a gun in my hand than driving my van around repairing the Internet."

Chavez put his hand on the man's shoulder. "Better you don't die, friend. Any idea where they are sending you?"

Herkus just shrugged. "I heard they are passing out thirty-year-old M16s they have in

636

their wartime reserves, and sending men to trenches being built at the border. Don't know if I'm going to the Kaliningrad side or the Belarus side." He shrugged again. "It's not like it matters."

Dom said, "An M16 isn't going to stop a tank, Herkus."

"I know." Dom could see the Lithuanian American was scared but resolute. Herkus said, "My decision is made, guys. I hope whatever it is they have you doing here, it helps us out."

Herkus drove the van to a streetcar stop near the Neris River, which bisected Vilnius, then climbed out of the vehicle, followed by the two Campus operatives. He already had a backpack ready in the back. He loaded up and shook Ding's and Dom's hands and climbed aboard a waiting streetcar without looking back.

Ding climbed behind the wheel, and the two men drove off for a day of high-resolution imagery.

Caruso said, "Is he brave or crazy?"

Chavez replied, "He's brave, for sure. I don't like his odds at all, but if this was my country, and my family could be twenty-four hours away from being ruled by a Russian puppet, I'd like to think I'd make the same decision."

Caruso shook his head. "I'd fight, but I

wouldn't fight with an old rifle in a muddy trench."

Chavez just shrugged. "Whatever we're doing here, I've got to think we're force multipliers. We're going to make the fight easier for Herkus and his side. The harder we work, the more chance he and a few thousand guys just like him make it out of their ditch alive."

John Clark had put in his second full day as a ship's captain, beginning at first light. Just after dawn the day before, he'd sailed into Scrub Island Marina and tied off at the back of a massive array of sailboats, easily seventy-five different vessels lined up in neat rows and bobbing in the peaceful water. He climbed into his dinghy and was halfway to the marina dock before he was able to rule out any chance that the *Spinnaker II* was in the mooring field. But still he tied off and went to shore, where he waited for the harbor services office to open.

As soon as attendants arrived, Clark filled up his dinghy's gas tank and, in a tone as nonchalant as he could make it, asked them if they'd seen a sixty-eight-foot gunboat. The men knew of the *Spinnaker II;* they said it was one of the fastest sailing ships in the Virgin Islands, and they told him its home port was Saint Thomas over in the U.S. Virgin Islands.

But the men said they hadn't seen it in the

BVIs in months.

Clark headed back to his boat and then uncoupled from his moorings. He had another dozen stops planned for the day.

Day one of his search for the cobalt-gray catamaran turned up nothing, as did the first six stops on day two. But on his seventh, this time at a dockside bar in Spanish Town in Virgin Gorda, he was told the cobalt-gray catamaran had arrived in the predawn hours, and had only just departed ninety minutes before he arrived. Clark asked if they'd seen which way the boat had gone. Of course, there was no way to pass his line of questioning off as idle conversation, but he was concerned he might not get another good sighting.

The captain sitting at the bar said he'd not paid attention, then he went back to his drink.

Clark left, and a man who had been sitting next to the conversation reached into his pocket and pulled out his mobile phone.

It was after six p.m. on a long afternoon of searching the cays, bays, and marinas around Virgin Gorda when Clark noticed a dive boat returning to the dock in Little Dix Bay. He assumed the boat might have run dives at one of the more remote locations near Virgin Gorda, so he carefully took his Irwin into the bay, following the dive boat toward the dock.

His persistence paid off. The captain of the

dive boat told him he'd seen the *Spinnaker II* sail into a remote cove of tiny West Seal Dog Island, an uninhabited rock a few miles northwest of the bay.

Clark knew he would have to make his approach carefully. The last thing he wanted to do was appear in front of the already suspicious men on the boat. He almost considered renting a new sailboat in Spanish Town to take into the area, but he worried this would just make the men on the *Spinnaker II* know he was up to no good if they recognized him on a different vessel.

After thinking it over for a long time, he decided he'd go to another nearby island and drop anchor for the night, far enough away from where the men were holding the Walkers that they couldn't possibly detect him. And then the following day he would move into position along with the other boats approaching the uninhabited West Seal Dog for a day of diving, fishing, and snorkeling.

There would be safety in numbers, he told himself. He'd try to stay out of sight and blend in with the rest of the crowd.

Clark had picked up provisions in Spanish Town, so he decided to spend the night in some secluded spot, just on the off chance that the *Spinnaker II* might leave West Seal Dog and head to a Virgin Gorda marina for the night. He found a suitable secluded spot on Mosquito Island just before sundown, and he dropped anchor.

Clark had decided he would take up watch on the catamaran the following day, probably from shore on West Seal Dog, and then make a scuba approach to the *Spinnaker II,* not at night but during the daylight hours. A night-time raid on the boat might have seemed to give him the most potential for success, but Clark assumed all five of the men he'd seen on his earlier surveillance of the catamaran would be on board during the overnight hours.

But if he arrived close enough to do surveillance tomorrow, he might well catch at least two of the men off the boat and ashore. Confronting three men who were wide awake but not expecting action was preferable to five men, even if some were asleep, especially if they had someone keeping watch.

Clark was all but exhausted from his full day of hunting for the *Spinnaker II,* but he'd achieved his objective. Now all he could do was get a good night's sleep, and prepare himself mentally for the confrontation to come.

56

Tatiana Molchanova had interviewed world leaders before, but she'd never met any foreign leader with nearly the power of her own president. Today all that would change, and this would be thrilling enough to her, but the added element to this evening's meeting with the American President had her positively electrified.

Molchanova spoke excellent English; she was the daughter of parents who'd immigrated to the UK in the early nineties, when anyone who had the means and the desire to get out did just that. She'd spent nine years in Sheffield, and she'd only returned to the land of her birth for college. She'd remained in Russia ever since, so she spoke her English with something of a British accent but she retained the lilt of Russian in her vowels.

It had added to her cachet in Russia that she had returned to the nation of her birth, eschewing the lures of the West because of the pride she felt in her heart in being a Russian woman.

This was a good selling point for Molchanova, but it had nothing to do with the reason she had really returned home. She wanted to be a broadcaster, and she knew her accent, while limited, would preclude her from making any name for herself in English because she was not a native speaker.

The interview was conducted in the living room of a suite at the Radisson Blu Royal Hotel in Copenhagen. It wasn't the President's actual suite, but rather one reserved for media broadcasts. A simple set had been assembled by moving furniture around, and behind the set was a window with a view overlooking the Tivoli Gardens.

President Ryan appeared right on time in the center of his large entourage of Secret Service agents and aides.

Molchanova was instantly struck by Ryan's physical size as compared to Volodin's — he was half a head taller — as well as his calm, relaxed mannerisms, again as compared to her own leader's. Ryan smiled easily and shook her hand gently and with deference.

She had an icebreaker prepared. "Mr. President, I know the people of Russia appreciate you taking time to give your view on matters important to both of our nations."

Ryan just nodded and said, "Happy to be with you, Miss Molchanova."

She said, "With your permission, we will

643

conduct our interview in English and interpreters will dub in the translations before this goes to air tomorrow evening."

Ryan then surprised the Channel Seven anchor by switching into slow but understandable Russian. "Unfortunately, I am forgetting more and more Russian every year. One needs to practice, and I have no time."

Molchanova had no idea Ryan knew a word in her language, and she was taken aback, but she retained the presence of mind to use the moment. In Russian she said, "Very impressive, Mr. President. I assume you learned when you were in the CIA?"

Ryan switched back to English and shook his head. "No, ma'am. In college." He smiled. "But since your English is flawless, let's stick with your plan to use the interpreters."

As Ryan was miked and Tatiana readied herself in the chair next to him, she realized she hadn't really known what to expect from the American President. She'd thought he would immediately try to get her to confirm that Channel Seven would play his comments unedited, or at least his aides would push her and her staff to commit. But the White House staff had been accommodating to the needs of the producers and technical people, much more accommodating than what she encountered when she interviewed mid-level Russian politicians in their offices.

And the President had said nothing on the

matter himself. She wondered if she had expected him to be some sort of thug, or if, perhaps, she was accustomed to interviewing thugs.

The cameras began to roll, and Tatiana Molchanova read her introduction. After this, with a large white grin and a sparkle in her eyes, she turned to President Ryan.

"Mr. President, thank you for your time this evening, on what is obviously a day that is very important to you."

"It's my pleasure to speak to Russians in their homes. Thank you for the opportunity."

"Of course." Her smile evaporated and she read her first question. "You are here, in Copenhagen, to ask NATO to move combat forces to the Russian border with Lithuania. How do you think this action will be received in Russia?"

Ryan said, "*Defensive* combat forces, Miss Molchanova. There is a difference."

"Will they be armed? Could not their weapons be used for both offensive and defensive actions?"

"Any weapon is just a tool. But NATO is a strictly defensive alliance. If it were an offensive alliance, I imagine NATO would have probably gone on the offensive at least once in Europe in the sixty-seven years since the charter was signed. It has not. I hope your audience understands that. For all the talk the West is at your door and about to knock

645

it down, the NATO nations that border Russia have the absolute least military presence in them."

"But you wish to change that by sending troops to Lithuania."

"I am requesting NATO move its Very High Readiness Joint Task Force into Lithuania, yes. Russia has twenty-five thousand troops on the eastern border there, and twenty-five thousand troops on the western border. The VHRJTF is five thousand, seven hundred men and women." He smiled. "Don't worry, Miss Molchanova. If your leader really wants to invade and conquer Lithuania, like he did in Georgia, like he did in the Crimea and Donetsk, like he tried to do in Estonia . . . I am sure he can pull it off. You will just have to come on television for him and explain to your viewers why they are suddenly at war with the West, why sanctions have been raised to the point where your only trading partners will be Cuba, Iran, and North Korea, and why no Russian will be allowed free travel outside their national borders."

Ryan could see it in her eyes: she thought she had a perfect riposte to his statement. "Such a long array of threats against the Russian people, Mr. President? Is that wise?"

"The threats will only turn into action when the Russian Sixth Army crosses into an independent state. If Russia remains in Russia, or even in its client state Belarus, no one in the West will act militarily against you. And that's a promise."

Ryan knew what she was thinking from the look on her face when the camera was on him. She hadn't penetrated Ryan's argument or his calm demeanor, and she was regrouping for another line of attack. He told himself to keep his cool.

"You say Russia is safe from the West if there is no war in Lithuania, but —"

"Well, you also have fifty thousand troops on the border of Poland, so we'd much prefer you didn't invade Poland, either."

She ignored him. "But all across Europe and even in your country you are calling for reprisals for the aircraft accident earlier in the week over the Baltic Sea. I don't see anyone threatening Sweden, the other country involved in the accident. Only Russia. Why is that, Mr. President?"

"Because the Russian military aircraft was flying without its transponder signal, meaning it was invisible to the other plane and air traffic control."

"International flying standards are very clear, Mr. President. Military aircraft do not need to fly with their transponder signals active. Often American planes fly in the dark just like the Russian aircraft. Surely you know this, so why the double standard?"

"Because no American plane has collided with a commercial aircraft. It is the pilot's responsibility to keep watch for planes in the sky who are playing by the rules. Russia has been conducting dangerous flights like this at an unprecedented rate. This was inevitable, and avoidable, and ultimately, President Volodin should be held responsible."

She rolled her eyes. "You think President Volodin asked his pilot to ram a Swedish commercial plane?"

"Of course not. But I believe, I *know,* he ordered his air force to increase incursions, his Baltic Fleet to harass commercial shipping in international waters near Kaliningrad. And he has turned the state of Kaliningrad into nothing less than a military base, with missile batteries ringing the entire nation."

"I've been to Kaliningrad, Mr. President. It is not a military base. It is a beautiful place full of wonderful people. Have you seen it for yourself?"

"No, Miss Molchanova, I confess you have had many experiences I have not had."

She raised her chin slightly in triumph.

"For example, I have never lived under a totalitarian regime. It's for this reason that myself and others like me, all over the world, see President Volodin's unilateral actions as dangerous to the world order."

To the Russian woman's credit, she did not get angry at the putdown. She simply said, "President Valeri Volodin is not running a totalitarian regime. His supporters would say he simply wants prosperity for every Russian. Some in the West seem to have great difficulty with that."

Ryan said, "One hundred eleven Russians are billionaires, while ninety percent of the nation lives below the Western standard of living. Apparently, in contrast to some of the reporting I've seen out of Russia, Valeri Volodin wanting something doesn't necessarily make it so. Another example would be Estonia. He wanted it, and he didn't get it. Now we know he wants Lithuania. This is why I'm in Copenhagen at the emergency meeting."

She said, "What the president said on my broadcast, and he was clear about this, was that since the Lithuanians have not been successful protecting Russian movement to our Kaliningrad Oblast, it was his duty to ensure his citizens were protected."

Ryan replied, "The event at the train station in Vilnius is under investigation, Miss Molchanova. I would avoid jumping to conclusions about who was behind that attack."

"I think the conclusions can be easily drawn. The culprits were Polish rebels working in collusion with the Lithuanian government to attack a Russian military transport."

Ryan said, "There have been a lot of attacks of late that are not what they seem."

"I don't know where you are getting your facts," Molchanova said, and she prepared to move on to the next topic.

But Ryan said, "I *do* know where you are getting yours. Straight from the Kremlin. Disinformation is a key part of Volodin's campaign of hybrid warfare."

Molchanova said, "You think what I am doing is warfare?"

With a smile he said, "That's exactly what it is. Information warfare."

She smiled herself and looked at the camera. "I have to say this is the first time I have been accused of looking like a soldier." She turned back to the President. "You recently declared today's Russia is more dangerous to the world than the Soviet Union in the 1980s. Would you like to explain that to the Russian people?"

Ryan said, "The Soviet Union had the potential to be more dangerous, but by the 1980s the Soviets were essentially satisfied with the world order. They had their part, we had ours. There would be struggles by proxy on the margins, but no major upsetting of the apple cart. Russia today is more brash, more dissatisfied with its standing, and therefore more unpredictable. Volodin is the manifestation of this unease, just as surely as Hitler was the manifestation of Germany's discontent after the First World War."

"So now we are more dangerous than the Nazis."

"No, I said —"

"Unfortunately, our time is up, Mr. President. Thank you so much for the interview."

Ryan nodded and smiled, unrattled to the end. The truth was, he knew she would end this with some sort of "gotcha" line, and she hadn't let him down.

The bright lights turned off, signaling the end of the interview. Tatiana Molchanova waited for her microphone to be removed, then stood and shook Ryan's hand.

Jack gave a perfunctory "Thank you" and started to turn away, but the Russian reporter surprised him.

"Mr. President, thank you very much for your time, but I would like to ask you for something else."

He was more than a little suspicious of this obviously brainwashed tool of the Russian state. "What's that?"

"I was wondering if we could go somewhere private to talk."

Ryan almost laughed. "No. That's not going to happen."

She leaned a little closer to him, and he knew Joe O'Hearn was about two steps away, just to the left of the set, ready to take the beautiful woman down to the floor like a safety dropping a wide receiver in an open field. But Joe contained himself and Molchanova whispered, "I bring a personal and private message to you from President Volodin."

Ryan just stared at her in disbelief for a moment, then said, "You know, there are avenues for that kind of thing. Statecraft isn't normally conducted through on-air personalities."

Molchanova smiled, her perfect white teeth shining bright. "I know, and I agree this is a unique situation. But the message is very real. I have been told you can contact the Russian ambassador to vouch for me. He only knows I have been tasked with conveying a message. He does not know what the message is."

Ryan sighed. He didn't particularly want a message from Volodin. It would have been welcome if there was any chance in hell it offered an off road to the impending catastrophe in the Baltic, but Ryan presumed whatever it was the woman had to tell him would only be another one of the Kremlin's patented stalling tactics, obfuscations, or misdirections.

He said, "Can you give me one moment?"

"Certainly, sir."

Ryan walked over to Arnie Van Damm. People were standing around, waiting to move with the President on to his next meeting, a coffee with the Canadian prime minister, but to Arnie's obvious surprise, Ryan spoke softly to Van Damm. "I need Canfield on the phone. Now."

The President was telling the chief of staff that he needed to talk to the CIA director on a cell phone in the middle of a hotel in

Denmark.

Arnie did as directed. It took a minute to make the secure connection, and since it was just five a.m. in Virginia, Canfield hadn't been expecting the call. Ryan didn't apologize for the early hour, he was too rushed.

"Jay, I need you to secure for me a hotel room in this building. I want it covered from top to bottom, left to right, with cameras and audio eavesdropping devices. I need it now."

Canfield did not hesitate in his response. "Room 1473. I'll let them know you're coming."

Ryan didn't understand. "What? How did you —"

"We've completely wired a couple of rooms there. Seriously, don't even think impure thoughts inside, because half the techs at NSA are going to know about it."

"What's it for? I mean, what is it for when the President isn't calling you asking for it?"

"You were CIA, Mr. President. Shit happens, remember?"

Jack smiled into the phone. "Room 1473. Thanks, Jay."

He hung up the phone and leaned over to Van Damm. "Hold my next engagement for a few minutes. The Russian reporter and I will be going to room 1473."

Van Damm's eyes went just as wide as Ryan thought they might. Van Damm leaned in himself and whispered back, "And I thought the *interview* was a bad idea."

"Don't worry. It will be fine."

"Nixon said that once, didn't he?"

Jack gave another little smile. "I guess he said it a lot."

57

John Clark had decided to bunk in the cockpit of his sailboat to keep more in tune with the sounds on and around the cove. There were certainly more comfortable digs down in the master stateroom, but down there he'd be completely unaware of anyone entering the area, or any threats that might arise. It was a little warm up in the cockpit, but Clark decided to give up a little comfort for a little security, so he slept on the cushioned sofa alongside the helm.

He knew his op down here would be a lot tighter with more personnel, but even before Sam's death it had been tough to work multiple operations at the same time. Since Sam had died, however, the concept of having The Campus's operational staff involved in three different areas of operation simultaneously was ludicrous. Still . . . Clark recognized, the enemy gets a vote, so here he was, while Jack was in Virginia on one task and Ding and Dom were in Lithuania on another.

Clark figured he had it the easiest, but that would be only until he boarded the gray catamaran and confirmed the presence of the Walkers on board. Then things down here would get interesting.

But not tonight. Tonight he just had to go back to sleep so he could be ready to hit the *Spinnaker II*.

He was somewhere between sleep and consciousness when he heard a noise and opened his eyes.

Clark lay there unmoving for several seconds, trying to determine what had stirred him. But he heard nothing other than the natural sounds of a healthy boat in a peaceful little cove.

He started to go back to sleep, but then he sat up, deciding that he needed to go to the head.

He stood on tired legs, took a pair of steps through the cockpit; his next footstep would have brought him to the top of the companionway down to the saloon. But he sensed something again, close. Not like before, this time he was certain enough to swing around, pulling his pistol out of his linen pants as he did so.

He didn't make it.

He never even knew it was a fourteen-inch steel-and-chrome marine wrench that dropped him. He heard the crack, felt the impact just behind his right ear, and sensed the loss of balance — the feeling of falling. He didn't realize he'd dropped the pistol. His hands were no longer under his control and he was unable to hold his body erect.

Weightless now, he didn't understand how he could possibly fall so far to the cockpit deck that had been right there, under his feet, just a second earlier.

The blow to the head, perfectly and savagely delivered, rendered him unconscious in just over one second, so he was out before he made his first impact with the companionway stairs, halfway down into the saloon. His body took blows in the arms, hip, and all across his middle back as he tumbled down, finally ending up in a still heap on the deeply lacquered floor of the saloon.

For several seconds Clark lay alone, still knocked out completely, but then he was joined by two men, who descended the companionway stairs into the saloon. They wore wetsuits but no other scuba gear; they were barefoot, their faces covered with neoprene head coverings that revealed only mouths, eyes, and noses. Only the glow from a few green lights on the radios and other electronics at the navigation console showed them their way around the saloon.

They stood over the body, looking down.

After a few seconds, the American drew his diving knife from the sheath on his ankle, knelt down over the shirtless man in the white linen pants, and lifted the head by a tuft of silver hair. He reached the knife around in front of the man's neck, placing the four-inch blade against the man's carotid artery.

"Wait," the South African said, looking around at the scene while he spoke.

The American responded, "But you told me to —"

"Forget what I told you. This is even better. When they find him they will think the old fuck bashed his head in rushing down the stairs in a panic. It will look like natural causes, so there will be fewer cops running around the islands asking questions."

"Why would he panic?"

"Because he realized he was sinking."

The American looked around himself now. He knew he was a subordinate on this op, the mercenary from Joburg called the shots, but the man from Cincinnati was bright enough to recognize this boat wasn't sinking.

Before he could bring up this rather obvious point, the South African said, "Disable the bilge alarm."

"Where's that?" The American didn't know boats, but the South African did.

"Never mind. I'll do it."

"You want me to snap his neck?"

"Is he out?"

"He's out, but he might still be alive."

"I don't want any more unnatural marks

on his body. Leave him just like that."

"I think we should kill him."

"I think you should do what I tell you to do, man. I cracked his skull like an egg, and a bloke this old will have broken every bone in his body falling down here. Even if he comes to, he won't be swimming to shore."

Together they lifted the access panel in the floor to the bilge pump and shut it off, then found the bilge pump alarm and disabled it. The South African found a second alarm, this under the table in the middle of the saloon, and he unplugged it, then tossed it on the floor.

While he did this the American found a large toolbox in the closet of the master stateroom, and he began to go through it.

Back topside the two mercs looked around the cockpit for a moment, checking the scene for any evidence they had been there. The American found the SIG Sauer .45-caliber pistol on the floor of the cockpit and he took it as a prize, and in another minute the South African had pulled two curtain rods off the curtains in the master stateroom. He joined his partner on the deck, then they both climbed back down the anchor chain and descended back into the water. Their scuba gear was lashed where they had left it, and they climbed back into their buoyancy-control devices and pulled on their fins.

The men descended under the boat and used the metal curtain rods to reach up through the intake hoses, then jam them in violently, breaking the seacocks and knocking the hose clamps off the seacock nipples.

They broke through the sea strainer as well, sending water gushing out near the bilge pump inside the boat, adding to the leaks.

All the damage was done below the floor of the saloon, the staterooms, and the hallway to the master stateroom; anyone diving on this wreck tomorrow would find no obvious evidence of any holes or breaches.

It took the two men much longer than they would have liked; they spent ten minutes jamming rods through the ports, but eventually they had created a dozen major leaks in the hull of the boat.

It was already listing to port by the time the men swam out of the area and back toward their dinghy, hidden in an inlet a quarter-mile away.

58

Tatiana Molchanova stood when President Ryan entered. There was real deference there, something she'd displayed little of during the interview. Ryan didn't know if she knew she'd been outplayed or if her behavior on TV was just an act to stay in the good graces of the Kremlin. He told himself he didn't have time to think about it. He wasn't going to change the thinking or the actions of those on state-run media, and it would be ridiculous to waste time trying.

Ryan crossed the room but stayed ten feet from the woman, as if she might be carrying a disease. He found himself more uncomfortable than he expected to be, and he knew he couldn't show it. He just said, "All right. I'm here and I'm listening, Miss Molchanova."

Molchanova seemed exceptionally proud and excited to be sent as an emissary between two leaders. With her chin high she said, "President Volodin is proposing a summit. A meeting, in secret. Between himself, yourself, and the leaders of Germany, France, and the United Kingdom. Only the five of you. President Volodin will be pleased to meet with you in Zurich as soon as you all can arrange travel there. If you prefer another location, he will entertain any ideas you have."

Ryan said, "I don't understand. Why is it secret?"

"He says the meeting will concern matters of state involving the future of the region. He assures you he will come prepared to make concessions for the mutual good of all Europe."

"Matters that involve all of Europe can't be discussed in front of all of Europe?"

Quickly Ryan saw in the woman's eyes that she had not been preloaded with answers to his questions. She just said, "I'm sorry, Mr. President. That was the message. Shall I give it to you again?"

Ryan shook his head. "I think I've got it. One more question, though. Is he making this offer in secret to the other leaders as well?"

"He asks for you to relay the message to the others."

Jack just gave a soft nod. He said nothing. Just looked at the wall for a moment.

Molchanova looked uncomfortable now. Finally she said, "Do you have a message you would like me to convey to President Volodin? If so, I promise you it will go from your mouth to his ear. I will not report on this, nor will I tell anyone about your message."

Ryan looked at her a long time before responding. "Yes."

She sucked in a small breath of air, her excitement obvious. Nodding, she said, "What is your message, Mr. President?"

"My message is this: Passing offers through a reporter for a secret summit is no way for national leaders to conduct business. I've seen more professional statecraft in my dealings with tribesmen in Togo. If he wants to be treated like the leader of a First World nation, he should try acting like one."

Her eyes widened and her jaw tensed, but she did not reply.

"You have my message, Miss Molchanova."

"Mr. President, I cannot tell him this."

Ryan shrugged. "Then don't." He gave the woman a little nod, turned on his heel, and left the hotel room.

Arnie Van Damm and Scott Adler were in Ryan's suite when he arrived five minutes later. "I hope you both heard all that."

Van Damm said, "Every word. Some response you gave her. She's probably shaking in her spiked leather boots, trying to figure out how to tell Volodin."

Ryan took off his suit coat and hung it from a chair, then sat down on a sofa across from the other men. "He wants to talk to certain

NATO members. U.S., France, Germany, UK. Clearly about Central Europe. But he doesn't want Central European nations present."

Van Damm asked, "Why?"

Jack Ryan knew the answer. "If you're not at the table, then you're on the menu."

Van Damm said, "Holy Christ! He wants to carve up Europe, just like in the Cold War!"

Ryan nodded. "It's Yalta all over again." The Yalta Conference at the end of World War II was a meeting between the victors to decide the geographical spoils of war.

Adler said, "You're not going to Switzerland, are you?"

Ryan said, "Of course not. If he wants to propose a summit he can do it through official channels. If we have one, it will involve delegates designated by NATO. This isn't 1945, and I'm not Roosevelt."

Adler said, "But he *does* think he's Stalin."

Ryan said, "He thinks *we think* he's Stalin. This whole damn thing was just a bluff to pump up his negotiating power when we sit down at the table."

Ryan looked out the window at the view over Copenhagen, and he shook his head in disbelief. "What an asshole."

An hour later Ryan sat in the suite of German president Marion Schöngarth. The two of them ignored the coffee service in front of them, while Ryan relayed his conversation with the journalist from Channel Seven.

When he finished, Schöngarth said, "He is after the redivision of Central Europe, a new redivision, to make up for what Russia lost after the Cold War. Thirty years ago they had no leverage to do anything but grant independence to virtually everyone who demanded it. But now, with Volodin in charge, he thinks he can reclaim some of what Russia lost."

Ryan agreed.

She added, "He wants the Baltic, and to get it, he is leveraging everything. He is threatening Poland, but Poland is his bargaining chip. It's as if he is saying, 'If you give me the Baltic, I will turn my tanks away from Poland.' "

"Exactly right."

She thought about the deeper ramifications. "But this means it's all a bluff, correct? Everything he has done till now is just him trying to up the stakes, to frighten the West into a place where we would be more amenable to a deal."

Ryan shook his head slowly. "Unfortunately, it doesn't matter if he is bluffing or not. Let's say he doesn't want to attack, he wants to win this with hybrid war simply by playing a game of geopolitical chicken with the West. If it fails, if we refuse to get out of his way, there is no way in hell he can ratchet down the saber rattling. He is expecting us to blink, but if we do not blink, he can't back down. He has arrayed all this potential energy at Lithuania's doorstep. How can he possibly set the stage for an attack, and then back away from it? He is a volatile individual who is using this volatility to leverage his power. He's mobilized his troops, he's brought his ships to combat readiness, and he's gone on television and announced the Baltic nations are illegal nonstate actors. If we don't back down, he will have to attack and hope that once the bodies start piling up, the West will lose its appetite for it."

Schöngarth said, "And it will only lead to one place." She paused. "We're about to go to war with Russia."

"It certainly appears that way."

She said, "The Russians have five hundred Iskander missiles in Kaliningrad. These missiles have nuclear warhead capability, although we don't know if they are armed with nuclear devices. The official range of the Iskander is four hundred kilometers, which places it below the five-hundred-kilometer threshold for the Intermediate Nuclear Forces treaty. But most experts agree the Iskander can reach targets at seven hundred kilometers, with an accuracy of five meters. One decision by Valeri Volodin, and the German parliament can go up in smoke."

"I know," Ryan said. "And right now there

is a Russian nuclear missile submarine some-where off the coast of the U.S. Its presence there renders our ballistic missile defense much less likely to be able to track and destroy an incoming Bulava rocket. It's there because Volodin wanted the United States in the same boat as Europe when he made his deal for a territorial summit."

The German president said, "Then you are in a similar situation as we are, Mr. President."

"Similar, but not the same. There is no threat of conventional attack against us like there is here, I recognize this. But I will put every single troop we have in Europe into Lithuania to stop this madman."

Just then, Arnie Van Damm apologized to the German president and leaned in to Ryan's ear. "The French president is on the phone. You need to take it."

Ryan excused himself and stepped over to a table with a phone already off the cradle. "Hello, Henri'."

The French president said, "Hello, Jack. I wanted to tell you personally. We will stand in the way of the deployment of NATO forces into Lithuania."

Ryan wasn't surprised, but he felt defeated. He'd spent most of a week on this goal, and it had failed.

The Frenchman said, "The Baltic States are untenable as NATO nations. When Russia was in NATO, well, yes, it made perfect sense. But with Russia as a threat, and small unprotected nations, all of which more naturally fall under the influence of Russia than they do under Western ideals . . . well . . . I am only concerned about Poland. We will make a counterproposal that NATO's readiness in Poland be upgraded. This will render an attack there less likely."

Ryan said, "And an attack in Lithuania more likely. We will be telling Volodin the Baltic is his as long as he doesn't try for Poland."

The French president said, "This is my decision. I have the backing of several other member states."

I'm sure you do, Ryan thought. He thanked the president for his call and said good-bye; there was nothing else he could do now.

He stepped back over to the German president, told her the news. In minutes he and his entourage were on their way back to his suite.

They did not speak during the walk, because the halls and elevators had not been declared clean by counterintelligence technicians. But the moment they got back in Ryan's suite, Adler asked, "What are you going to do now?"

Ryan said, "I'm going to go to Sweden. I want to appeal to non-NATO states to get some support for our actions. Show them we care about their concerns."

Scott Adler broke in here. "You thought that was a tough crowd. Sweden has all but shut down their military. They aren't going to want to do anything to upset the apple cart any more than Volodin is already doing. The fact Russia knocked their plane out of the sky has them pissed off, but other than a small but decent air force, they aren't much of a power anymore."

"How bad is it?" he asked.

"Sweden has a good air force, but that's it. Our view of Sweden's current defense condition is not optimistic."

"Meaning?"

"Meaning it is our belief that if Sweden decided to begin an aggressive program to build up its military, then in five years it would have the capability to defend itself in place . . . for one week."

Ryan said, "So Russia could steam west across the Baltic from Kaliningrad, or south from the North Sea, and they could claim Sweden as their own."

"At will, Mr. President."

President Jack Ryan rubbed his eyes under his glasses, pressing hard, as if to stanch the overwhelming frustration. "We'll go to them and ask for overflight rights. Air base access. Supply support for our Navy in the Baltic. We'll ask for their air force to support our mission in Lithuania. If we pull the trigger and deploy, then we'll need all the help we can get."

"That's not much, Mr. President."

"Well, it's all they have. I'd like to get Sweden into NATO down the road. If they help us now, I think both Sweden and the rest of NATO could see their way forward to allowing this to happen."

59

Clark dreamt of the pain before he woke to feel it. In his dream he had been at home in bed; Sandy might have been next to him but he could not turn to look. A truck had driven into his bedroom, slowly and without seeming to care, and it had driven onto his bed, pinning him down. His legs were crossed, one on top of the other, so they hurt the worst, but his back was twisted by the big tires, and the heat from the exhaust pipe burned the side of his head, just behind his right ear.

This was an awful dream, to be sure, but he preferred it to how he felt when he woke. His mind took in the feeling, his body alive with the pain, and his arms and legs were just as slow to operate as they had been when he'd been dreaming.

He was looking up through the companionway, so he saw a bit of the faint glow from a mostly moonless night, but other than that he was still shrouded in darkness.

He had no idea how long he'd been lying here, and he also had no idea how badly he'd been hurt, but the worst of it was the side of his head behind his right ear, so he forced his right hand up to touch it, praying the swelling would be on the outside of his skull, and not inside, where he ran the real risk of death, even hours after the injury occurred.

He touched his fingers to the center of the pain and he did, indeed, feel a massive knot there, which would have been good news, but Clark wasn't feeling any better about it, because as he'd moved his hand to his head he'd managed to splash himself in the face with seawater.

If he hadn't just suffered a concussion, if he hadn't just woken up from an unconscious state brought on by a violent blow to the head, then Clark would have recognized much more quickly that he was lying in pain in the bowels of a sinking boat. As it happened, it took him several seconds to work this out; only the taste of the water on his lips and the sense his ears were now filling with the wetness and blocking out the noises around him impressed on him how bad his situation had become.

Now the pain in his head and his back and his legs was all of minor importance. No matter how bad he hurt, no matter what condition he found himself in when he began to move, he had only one objective.

John Clark was a Navy man, true, but he found himself under no obligation whatsoever to go down with his ship.

His legs were probably just bruised; his right shin and his left knee had caught the stairs in the companionway. Clark didn't need a slow-mo replay of the event to know this. His back was killing him, it had seized in spasm, and he didn't know how the hell he was going to swim when one of the largest chains of muscles in his body refused to cooperate with the orders sent from his brain, but that was a problem he'd have to sort out in a minute or two. For now it was about getting out of the saloon, then out of the cockpit, and finally off the deck before this fifty-two-foot Irwin rolled over and took him down with it.

He pulled himself out of the water and up the companionway stairs in the darkness. To his right, circuits blew on his radio and weather center with pops and snaps and flashes of light as the seawater reached thigh-high.

John had watched boats sink before, and he knew the speed of the descent was unpredictable. A boat filling with a foot of water a minute could double or triple this rate instantly as the water found more non-waterproof openings, more ways to fill the air below the waterline. This very phenomenon was happening now, in fact. He'd been conscious no more than two minutes, and already the water had risen from a few inches over the deck of the saloon to three feet.

He made it up to the cockpit; here he put weight on both his legs and stood up for the first time. He felt weak and unsteady, his head was heavy like he'd been drugged, but he knew this was due to the blow to the head.

But not entirely. As he wobbled through the cockpit trying to find his gun and his mobile phone he realized the sailboat had begun a heavy list to port. He fought against it for a moment while he kept looking for the two items he did not want to leave the boat without, but quickly he came to his depleted senses and decided his luck of late had been far too bad for him to push it one second more.

Wearing only a pair of linen pants and boat shoes, he made his way out onto the main deck and leapt into the black water, fought against the agony in his back as he tried to swim away from the boat, at least far enough to avoid being slammed in the head by one of the masts as it came down.

He gave up on a breaststroke or a crawl, settled for a one-arm sidestroke because of his back pain, and was glad to see his faculties hadn't been damaged so much he could not still cover water rapidly and efficiently.

He took a break from his swim to shore, just long enough to watch a few more pops of electrical circuits blow on the deck, then the mast light flashed on and off in a shower of sparks.

Then the boat rolled over like a dying animal, revealing its keel in the low light of the moon.

Beyond the sad display a hundred yards away from him, he saw something that excited him for a moment. The lights of a boat in the distance. It was moving, but with no other reference points it was hard to tell if it was coming or going.

Quickly he told himself to curb his enthusiasm. The lights in the distance weren't going to be his salvation. He recognized the configuration of the masts from the masthead lights, and he realized he was watching the *Spinnaker II* round the northern tip of West Seal Dog Island. From the fact he could only make out the white light on the stern, he felt sure it was departing, motoring away to the northeast, perhaps for Anegada Island.

Not a sound made its way across the water to Clark's position as the catamaran left his view.

The lights disappearing in the dark took with them a mother and a child held against their will, their lives the key to unlocking a puzzle with global ramifications.

Clark started up his sidestroke again, telling himself to keep his mind on his personal situation. It occurred to him that he had no

675

way to prove anything untoward had happened here. His wounds would just make him look like some aging boat renter who slipped on his companionway as he rushed down to see about a leak. The fact that his bilge alarm had not gone off, screaming at 140 decibels, would mean nothing to most investigators, because for all they knew, the old renter of the Irwin probably hadn't tested it before setting out.

Well before first light, the battered and bruised body of a man — alive but too exhausted and broken to swim — floated the last two hundred yards through the gentle surf, washing ashore like trash in the water.

Clark crawled up the sand, through the morning coral and shell deposits, catching seaweed on his arms and knees as he did so.

He was exhausted and he was injured, and at the moment he was bereft of a plan. But as he sat there spitting sand out of his mouth, he told himself he'd get back in the fight. He didn't need a hospital. He just needed the three most important things he'd lost tonight — his phone, his target, and his motherfucking gun.

Jack Ryan, Jr., sat quietly, his body as still as a statue, his eyes locked on Salvatore as he sat at the lobby bar in the Stanhope Hotel. The Italian paparazzo had a drink on the bar in front of him and his mobile in his hand.

Jack stared intently at the man's face and did his best to gauge his mood, his intentions. Was he bored, intense, excited, scared? Was this just another day at the office for him, or was he being sent on some mission?

Jack leaned in, getting as close to the man's face as he could while still focusing.

Nothing. It was too hard to tell anything, looking at a man on a computer monitor.

Jack was sitting at his cubicle, and the security camera feed from the hotel was running on his center monitor in real time, pulled in by Gavin Biery's IT team.

This wasn't surveillance, what Jack was doing. In fact, he thought it was a joke. Unless and until Salvatore got up and did something obvious, Jack knew he'd have no idea what the hell was going on.

Jack had spent most of the workday looking into Salvatore in one form or another. He started with the man's history. In his career Salvatore had gone many places, taken and sold thousands of photographs all over Europe, almost all of them of famous people who were just trying to go about their day. It was typical celebrity smash-mouth paparazzo work. But in all these travels, Jack had not found one example of Salvatore working in Brussels.

Jack had also looked into the current status of dozens of other European-based paparazzi, using social media to determine their locations. Of the fifty or so he'd been able to pin down, not one of them had gone to Brussels, and this gave him the strong suspicion there was nothing going on there at the moment that would interest the paparazzi.

The Italian seemed to be on the world's most boring vacation, mostly just sitting around in the lobby bar at night and venturing out during the day, but not in some specific pattern like he was here for a nine-to-five job. No, he'd leave for an hour or two in the afternoon, then return to his hotel.

Jack had no idea what was going on, but he felt strongly that Salvatore wouldn't be here at all if he wasn't working in some capacity for the Russians, as he'd obviously been doing in Rome.

He had taken this information back to Gerry, framing it just as an FYI, an update on his progress about the Salvatore case. When Gerry didn't react to Jack's hints that perhaps it would be worthwhile for Jack to go over to Belgium after all, Jack went for broke, and point-blank requested approval again.

And as before, Gerry denied the request.

Jack went back to his desk and spent the rest of the day watching camera feeds at Salvatore's hotel, and that's where he finally found him, in the lobby, at ten p.m. Brussels time. The Italian was alone, he drank vodka on ice, and he played with his phone, either waiting for a message or just goofing off — Jack couldn't tell which through the security camera.

Jack couldn't tell much of *anything* through the security camera.

He realized then and there that he had to know what the man was up to, and there was just one way to find out. He couldn't wait for Ding and Dom to finish their work in Lithuania, or for Clark to finish his work in the BVIs. Whatever Salvatore was doing in Brussels was time-sensitive.

Jack decided he would defy Gerry Hendley's direct order to stand down, to wait for support from his fellow operators.

He would lose his job for his decision; he had no doubt in his mind. Gerry had allowed some indiscretions from Jack in the past. The younger Ryan had called audibles on missions that weren't exactly in the spirit of Gerry's orders, but he'd always done them in the heat of the moment, for the undeniable greater good of the mission.

But this was very different. He'd been expressly ordered out of the European theater and back to Campus HQ, he'd then requested to travel back to Europe to run a solo surveillance package on Salvatore, and Gerry Hendley, director of The Campus, had unequivocally denied this request.

There'd be no getting around it: When Jack climbed aboard a plane to Belgium, he would

be AWOL from The Campus and insubordi-
nate.

He'd be gone.

But Jack knew he was going to do it anyway.

60

John Clark sat in the saloon of a small sailboat, smiling at the middle-aged German couple who'd collected him from the shore of West Seal Dog Island an hour before. The husband was dressed only in a Speedo; he was as pink as a rose and as round as a beach ball, and although she was much more modestly dressed, his wife was no more svelte.

They smiled back at Clark, which told him they didn't get the hint that he wanted some privacy.

They'd rescued him from the rocky deserted island after he had sat there six hours in the sun, feeling the muscle spasms and the bruising and the swelling, and brooding over how nice it was going to feel to get the Walkers' kidnappers at gunpoint.

And then when the German couple brought him on board their thirty-five-foot Catalina, the *Frau* tended to his wounds with the boat's med kit and the *Herr* brought him a cold bottle of pilsner in an actual stein.

For a minute Clark thought his head injury was so bad his brain was playing bizarre and cruel tricks on him.

Almost immediately the couple asked to get a picture with the American, their catch of the day; they were so proud of their rescue Clark thought this would make the papers in whatever tiny hamlet they lived in back in Bavaria. He obliged reluctantly and then asked if he could use their phone to call his wife.

And here they were, Clark with the phone in his hand and Gerry Hendley's number already keyed into it, and the Germans smiling and grinning and beaming with pride, staring at him like they wanted to take him to a taxidermist and mount him and put him over their mantel.

Clark smiled even broader. "I'm sorry. I wonder if I could have a little privacy. I might get emotional talking to my wife, since I almost died last night. It would be embarrassing to me for you to see me cry."

"Ach so!" said the husband, and the wife quickly checked the icepack and the bandage on the side of his head, and then the husband shooed her up the tiny companionway and then followed her, even closing the companionway door.

Clark blew out a long sigh while he dialed the phone, then deleted his picture while it rang.

Gerry answered his mobile after a few rings. "Hendley."

"Hey, Gerry, John here."

"Jesus, John, I've been calling you all morning."

"Yeah, well my phone is probably getting humped by a lobster right now."

"I'm sorry . . . what do you mean by that?"

"It's at the bottom of the ocean." John told Gerry everything condensed into a minute of time, because he didn't know when the German couple was going to peek down on him and he really didn't feel like pretending to cry.

When he finished Gerry said, "Christ, John. We've got to get you out of there."

"I'm fine. I just need to be reequipped, and I need a new lead on the *Spinnaker II*."

"I'll pull the boys out of Lithuania to come help you."

"Please don't! What they are doing is important. This is important down here, but rescuing the Walkers isn't in the same ballpark as far as significance. I can handle this myself."

Clark realized he was beginning to sound like Jack Junior. He had something to prove that, one could argue, transcended logic and sense. Jack had to live up to the legend of his father. Clark had to live up to the legend of himself. Both he and Jack, Clark realized, were dealing with self-inflicted forces.

But that didn't make them any less real.

It simultaneously annoyed him and allowed him to lighten his criticisms of his younger operator.

Gerry said, "Look, when you didn't check in first thing this morning I got worried. I sent Adara down, she'll be landing around one-thirty."

"Gerry, I don't need —"

"Wait, just listen. It's done. Adara will support you. No arguments. You know what she's done in other ops. She is more than capable of providing operational support."

Gerry asked for no arguments, and Clark gave him none.

Clark's morning with the German couple ended when Adara Sherman picked him up in a rented helicopter in Spanish Town, Virgin Gorda. Clark had explained the attractive young woman in the red Robinson helicopter was an employee of the company he worked for, but he didn't explain how she happened to be down here.

As they flew back toward Tortola, Adara explained she had rented a small two-room house near the airport and she was taking Clark there now so she could check out his injuries.

Clark protested out of habit, but his entire body hurt like hell, and he was exhausted nearly to the point of nausea.

When they got into the house, a business-like Adara Sherman opened her rolling backpack med kit in the kitchen and ordered John Clark to take off his shirt.

Adara looked at his bruises and scrapes. "Good Lord! Did you fall down the stairs?"

"As a matter of fact, I did." He winced when she rubbed an alcohol compress on his back. "Is this where you and the other kids start talking about putting me in assisted living?"

It was a joke, and Adara had an easy laugh, even in tough situations, but she wasn't laughing now. She saw the knot behind his ear. "Oh . . . I get it. It looks like someone encouraged you to fall."

"That's my story, and I'm sticking to it."

"Was this a leather sap?"

"It felt like a hammer, but I'm not sure. I guess everything to the skull feels like a hammer."

Adara put ice behind his ear after tending to his other wounds. When she was finished Clark said, "We need to find that boat. I feel like they are still in the area, but it could take days to find it."

"John . . . we have an aircraft. We can fly across this entire chain in minutes."

"The Gulfstream can't make low passes over the BVIs looking for a boat. It will draw too much attention."

"Then I'll rent that Robinson we were just

685

on. On the way to pick you up, the pilot said he moves people all over the BVIs all day long."

"What's he going to say to flying a recon mission?"

Adara just smiled. "Trust me, Mr. Clark. I'll make up a good story. He told me he only had two short charters tomorrow, so I'll call him now, and first thing in the morning he and I will go out hunting for that catamaran."

Clark winced again as she cinched an ACE bandage holding an icepack around his head. "What about me?"

Adara said, "The only way this happens is if you take a couple days to recuperate. I see the pain you are in. You are lucky you aren't in traction in the hospital, or worse."

"But —"

"I can do the recon on my own. I know what I'm looking for. I can see better than you. No offense, but it's true. I'll find the boat if it's out there, and I'll report back to you. You lie around here for forty-eight hours, keep your ice on, and you will thank me when you get back in action."

"Ms. Sherman, I am really fine."

"Everybody says that the day after an injury. It's two days after, when the bruising circulates through the soft tissue, that the pain gets the worst."

John had learned this very fact from a lifetime of hard living. In retrospect, he wished he'd learned it from a book instead.

Adara added, "Let's let them think you are dead. If you go back out to the marinas and ports asking more questions, it won't take them any time to realize you are still alive and still hunting for them."

Clark realized Sherman was right. Still, he said, "What am I going to do for two days?"

"First, you're going to call your wife and daughter and tell them you love them."

Clark looked down at the floor, a little embarrassed. "Of course."

"Good. And you don't need me to tell you to do the other thing you have to do."

"What other thing?"

Adara Sherman gave John Clark a hard look. "You are going to plan your next meeting with the men who did this to you."

Clark nodded. No, he didn't need anyone to tell him this.

61

Valeri Volodin watched the helicopter carrying Tatiana Molchanova leave his front lawn, take off into a night sky filled with swirling snow, and disappear on its way back toward Moscow.

She'd delivered her message from Jack Ryan. She did it slowly, her voice cracking from nerves.

Fucking bitch, he said to himself. Ryan had bested her in the interview; she looked positively shell-shocked by the end despite a "gotcha" line or two. *And now she brings me this shit from the American President?* Ryan clearly felt bold enough to make such a tactless comment only because the woman he was talking to had turned to mush in front of his eyes.

Volodin would see that Molchanova was replaced on Channel Seven. She'd be live reporting street crimes in Grozny with her cell phone before the end of the month.

Volodin had given no outward reaction to

the insult when she delivered the demand from the American President that he should begin acting like a leader. Instead he thanked her and sent her on her way, masking his fury

Now Volodin would show Ryan how a leader acted.

The door to his office opened, and he felt the presence of his secretary. She stood there silently, waiting to be noticed, knowing full well her president looked out the window when he wanted to brood in peace.

Volodin said, "What is it?"

"I'm sorry, sir. Director Grankin is here for his meeting."

Volodin did not turn from the window. He just gave a curt nod and said, "Bring him."

Grankin was in the office and seated in the chair across from the desk by the time the Russian president finally did turn around to acknowledge him. Volodin sat back down, reached for his tea, and took a sip, all the while looking at the director of his Security Council.

Mikhail Grankin's nerves were showing, Volodin could see it plainly.

"What news?" Volodin asked.

"NATO will not deploy troops in Lithuania barring an Article Five declaration."

Volodin nodded. "They know Lithuania is defenseless, which means they know full well that the moment there is an Article Five violation it will be too late for them to respond. It is as I have said all along. Our pressure has convinced them they want no part in war with Russia. Lithuania is ours for the taking."

Mikhail Grankin's face remained inexpressive, but he nodded slowly. He then said, "Did the American President agree to the summit?"

Volodin shook his head. "Some incoherent babble about needing it to be processed through proper channels." Volodin waved his hand in the air like this key aspect of their plan was nothing but a trifle, as if it suddenly didn't matter. "Forget the summit. We will take Lithuania with only a few shots fired. It will be easier than Georgia."

Grankin said, "So we will begin the next phase?"

"The final phase of operation Baltic Winter Sixteen will begin immediately."

Grankin nodded, then said, "The aircraft collision was an unnecessary complication. We didn't need that."

Volodin nodded himself with a rare authentic expression of frustration on his face. "I only wish that fucking Ilyushin pilot was still alive so I could have him killed. In the larger picture this was a non-event. A complication, to be sure, but all the military air operations we have been conducting the last year have served their purpose. Russia is feared, and therefore Russia is respected. A single negative incident was a small price to pay for the power this has given us." He waved his hand. "Anyway, by this time next week, no one will be talking about an Airbus accident over the Baltic, I assure you of that."

Grankin cleared his throat, hesitating. Volodin saw he wanted to say something, but was not sure of the moment.

"What is it, Misha?"

"One of my best men. Vladimir Kozlov. He has been on special assignment to your office for the past month."

"Has he? Yes . . . I might have heard something about that."

Grankin cleared his throat again. "Well . . . with the operation in Brussels coming to a head, with Baltic Winter kicking off . . . I expect an increase in intelligence requirements very soon. I really need Kozlov back."

Volodin said, "You have other operatives in the Security Council."

"True, sir. But we have been careful to compartmentalize the larger aspects of our plan, keeping information away from FSB, away from GRU. Morozov is in Brussels. My man Kozlov is crucial now for other aspects of the operation."

Volodin shook his head. "Kozlov is your man when I give him back to you. For now he is my man. You will have to make do without him."

Grankin said nothing more on the matter.

He put his hands on the arms of his chair. "If you will excuse me then, I will make the calls to the necessary individuals to begin operations."

Volodin nodded, Grankin left, and then Volodin returned to his view out the window. The snow had picked up a little.

His mind left the operation in the Baltic, and he considered the operation in the Caribbean. He'd received a short text from Kozlov this morning, indicating all was going according to plan. He didn't go into any more detail, but Volodin didn't want or need it. All he needed to know was that in two to three weeks, his money would be out of the reach of all internal threats, and invisible to all external threats.

Volodin hoped he wouldn't have to touch it for a long time, but he knew what he was doing would make him either a hero of the Russian Federation or its most wanted criminal.

And he knew he had to prepare himself to play either role.

Peter Branyon's gunshot wound to his shoulder and his broken ribs had been stabilized in a hospital in downtown Vilnius, and then he'd been flown from Lithuania to Ramstein Air Base in Germany on an Agency Learjet thirty-six hours after the attempted kidnapping.

Ding assumed the CIA CoS had been out

of it for the entire time since the incident, but as he and Dom snapped the last of the 460 photos they'd been tasked to take by Mary Pat Foley, Ding found out Branyon had been busy, still working the phones, up until the moment he was given anesthesia to go into surgery to deal with his broken shoulder.

Ding's mobile rang at seven p.m., just as they were on the highway back to Vilnius. He looked at it and saw it was a Lithuanian number he did not recognize.

"Hello?"

A man with a Lithuanian accent spoke in English. "Mr. Chavez. My name is Linus Sabonis. I am director of the State Security Department."

Chavez realized he was getting a call from the Lithuanian equivalent of the director of the CIA. "How can I help you, sir?"

After a short pause, he said, "I think we should meet."

Chavez, Caruso, and Linus Sabonis met in a room at the Kempinski Hotel in Cathedral Square. Sabonis had a dozen armed men watching over him, so Chavez and Caruso were surprised when they were not searched, wanded, or run through any sort of security before finding themselves sitting in front of the nation's top intelligence officer. They just simply entered the room, shook hands with a few men, and sat down.

"My friend Peter Branyon told me what you did." Sabonis shrugged. "Not so much who you are, though, other than the fact you are not current employees of his organization."

The Americans did not respond.

Sabonis said, "I thank you for what you have done for my country already, but I would like to ask something more of you."

Chavez said, "We'd be happy to help in any way we can."

"We know of over one hundred Russian assets or agents here . . . I am speaking of Vilnius, not even the whole of the nation. FSB men and their informants, working in the city. They have a good operation to monitor SSD employees like myself, as well as CIA, MI6, and other agents friendly to our cause. It is truly their main role in the nation, neutralizing their opposition. Keeping our eyes down and our ears tuned in to the countersurveillance mission."

Dom said, "You are saying there is an intelligence stalemate here, which works to their advantage, because they can just wait for an invasion, at which point they can simply round the intelligence opposition up."

"That's right," Sabonis said. "Except there is an interesting wrinkle in the status quo. Another group of opposition here in the city. My men have tried to pin down who they are and what they are doing. Clearly they are on the side of the Russians, but they are not Russian, not from any of the other embassies here."

"How do you know about them?"

"We've heard rumblings, both out in the border towns and now here in Vilnius. These are not the Little Green Men who are actually Russian military. No, this is a foreign proxy force of some kind."

Dom said, "Like the guys who we came in contact with last night?"

"Exactly like those men you speak of," said Linus Sabonis. "I am thinking you two men might be the only people on our side of things who have actually encountered them."

"Any idea what they are doing here?" Dom asked.

"My feeling is they were brought in because the FSB is aware that they are known to us. This other force is being kept here in the city, ready to act in some way in support of the invasion. In what capacity, I do not know."

Ding said, "They were damn well trained. I was sure they were some sort of Spetsnaz force until Branyon insisted they weren't even Russian. I've got to assume they are here to disrupt any defense. Political assassinations, deniable actions. Obviously they are trained in kidnapping as well. You've got problems, Mr. Director."

"Which is why I wanted to talk to you. I'd like you to attempt to draw these men out in some way. Just enough to find out who they are. If we can identify another actor here in country, we can reveal this to the international media. Perhaps pressure whatever country these forces come from to withdraw them."

Chavez said, "I get it. You want to use us as bait."

Sabonis shrugged. "There is a benefit around here to not being known by the opposition. My first thought was to do this without asking your permission. Since I am known to the Russians, just walking up to you in a café and sitting down would put the eyes of the FSB upon you. At that point you would be marked by the opposition."

Dom didn't like the thought of this guy forcing them into playing bait like that. He said, "And the only reason you didn't was because you didn't know if that would just get the FSB you already know to tail us, as opposed to the other guys."

"Frankly, yes. These are desperate times for my nation, as you can imagine. My intentions are in the best interests of Lithuania." He leaned forward. "But now that I have told you how I want to use you, it might interest you to know I have a plan how you can attract the interest of the correct unit. Just to draw them out."

"How?" Chavez asked.

"Since the shootout at the border, a group of men has been outside the apartment of

Peter Branyon, conducting surveillance on the building. We received a report of this from a local, who was adamant these men were speaking some language other than Russian. I can only assume they found Branyon's home address when they kidnapped him. A key, a receipt, a laundry ticket, something on his person. They are not FSB, we are certain of that, because they are not in interaction with anyone we know here in the city, and we have the FSB in a stalemate.

"Our first thought was to get the local police to pick them up and check their documents, and to perhaps interview them, but it occurs to me they wouldn't be here without good cover stories and good-looking credentials. No, we need to catch them in the act of doing something . . . something where we will have some leverage over them."

Caruso said, "Again, you want to use us as a way to entrap them."

Sabonis nodded. "If the two of you went to Branyon's apartment and entered it, made it clear somehow that you had an objective of an intelligence collection or operations nature, then perhaps you would be recognized as the two men involved in the gunfight at the border. At that point, I can only assume you would be followed by the proxy force. They will want to know who you are. Their lack of knowledge about your existence the other day led to the deaths of five of them, after all."

Dom said, "And when these guys start following us, your men will swoop in and take them down."

Director Sabonis lit a cigarette. The Campus men had yet to encounter a soul in Lithuania who did not smoke. He said, "If it were that easy we would do just that. But my entire staff is being followed, as I said. If my men come to your aid, you will also draw the attention of the FSB."

Now Dom really didn't like where this was going. "So you want the two of us to reveal ourselves to some malevolent group we haven't identified, and then . . . what? We take them down ourselves?"

Sabonis shook his head. "No, of course not. You two are the carrot. You simply use other men from your organization to serve as the stick."

Dom had been sitting forward on the sofa, but now he rocked back, looked away in frustration.

Chavez just smiled. "For all intents and purposes, Director Sabonis, the two guys sitting in front of you represent the entire operational capacity of our organization."

The Lithuanian intelligence chief just sighed. He conferred with one of his men for a moment, speaking Lithuanian, of course, then returned his attention to the Americans. "If you can get the men to follow you, we can arrange for a police roadblock. The FSB isn't watching our individual policemen here in the city."

Caruso looked to Chavez. "Those guys we shot it out with at the border. They had skills. They were utterly ruthless . . . They would chew up a police roadblock in nothing flat."

Chavez nodded. "You're right. They had no compunction about killing, and they have been trained to do it well."

Sabonis waved his hand in the air. "I am not talking about the men who write the traffic tickets here. I can get a unit of ARAS, our Interior Ministry counterterrorism police. They are no good for surveillance duties, so we can't help with that, but they are serious gunmen. If you lead these mysterious interlopers to them, they will be able to arrest them . . . or do whatever they need to do to remove the threat."

Chavez nodded. "I don't know what choice we have, or what choice Lithuania has. Whatever this force's mission is here, taking some or all of them off the table is worth the risk."

Now Dom Caruso said, "If we do this for you, I think it's only fair you supply us with weapons."

Sabonis nodded. "No problem at all. You can choose from whatever ARAS has available." He stood. It was obvious he had other places to be. "Very well. I will leave you with my assistant to work out the details of the operation. I thank you for your service to Lithuania. I hope, when this crisis passes, you men can come back here and see what a nice and peaceful place this is."

The men shook hands, and the Campus operators expressed their wish to someday return, although both men wondered if this city was just days from finding itself behind the New Iron Curtain.

62

President Jack Ryan had done his best to get as much sleep as he could on the flight back from Europe so he would be ready to hit the ground running upon his return to D.C. He'd managed four and a half hours of rest, which was less than he'd hoped for but more than he'd expected, but his body clock was thrown off by the seven-hour time difference.

The international press had been hard on President Ryan's stop-off in Sweden after his failure with NATO. Many editorialized that it was cynical of him, and they characterized his actions as storming away from a failure. Insults flew from half the newspapers on the continent, accusing him of using the dead of the Swedish Airlines flight as pawns in his militaristic game.

But his meeting with the prime minister of Sweden had gone well. Ryan didn't mention the fact he was considering unilateral action in Lithuania, but he hinted that he was prepared to help the Baltic nation resist the

Russians in some way. The prime minister expressed his fury at the Russians for the deaths of his countrymen on SA44, and with a handshake he told Ryan he personally would do all he could to encourage his national legislature to support America should it get involved in the Baltic.

Ryan sat in the Oval Office now at four-thirty p.m., the fading light of the late-October day still glowing through the windows behind him, but with all the time changes he'd undergone, he felt like it was midnight after a full day's work.

And on top of his fatigue today was the worry about the two thousand Marines he was considering sending into harm's way. Two thousand versus fifty thousand was an oversimplification. The Lithuanians had a brigade-strength force of four thousand or so of their own troops, plus another five thousand volunteer militia who could be used for non-front-line duty: roadblocks, rear security, and the like.

And the two thousand Marines would be assisted by U.S. Air Force aircraft flying from all over Europe, perhaps even from B-52s and other platforms flown from the USA.

But still, the Marines heading into the Baltic were going to be seriously outnumbered, and a lot of them would die.

Ryan reached for his coffee and downed a third of it as his secretary came over the intercom. "Mr. President, Director Foley and Secretary Burgess are here."

Ryan tapped the intercom. "Send them in, please."

All three sat on the sofas in front of the President's desk. Ryan thought they would have some defense-related intelligence product to show him; he wasn't certain about their request for the quick meeting but had assumed it would only involve satellite photos over Belarus.

But they had nothing in front of them.

Mary Pat said, "Mr. President, technicians at the National Geospatial-Intelligence Agency have been working on a project for the past three and a half years that we would like to bring to your attention because we think it might be helpful now."

Ryan said, "I get briefings on ongoing NGA projects. Which one is it?"

Burgess said, "Actually, this is one you don't know about. It was something that seemed a little pie-in-the-sky a couple of years ago, from the viewpoint of the DoD, so it didn't get a lot of funding or attention. But now we at the Pentagon have seen what this system can do, and we want your blessing to use it."

Ryan raised his eyebrows. "Tell me more."

Mary Pat still had nothing to show him, which he thought was odd. She said, "The project is called EARLY SENTINEL. It melds the latest satellite and global-positioning data, signals and electronic intelligence information, along with high-quality battle-space imagery and ballistics and trajectory data."

"To do what, exactly?"

"To radically speed up the deployment process of troops into combat zones, and to increase the efficiency of the troops."

"It's . . . it's a computer program?"

"Yes, Mr. President."

"And it will speed up deployment by how much?"

"Compared to just four years ago, by a factor of five. What used to take a day can now be accomplished in under five hours."

Ryan was incredulous. "You're kidding."

Burgess said, "I've seen it in action. It's as good as the NGA advertised it from the beginning."

"How does it work?"

Mary Pat said, "I'm going to give you the simplest version of this I can give you, not to patronize you, Mr. President, but simply because I don't understand it all myself. NGA has put into their system all the data regarding Russian troops in position in both Kaliningrad and Belarus, including weapons systems and logistical needs, and dozens and dozens of additional criteria. And NGA also inputs all the ballistic and terminal data of the weapons of our troops. They've taken information from the Pentagon and DIA about our assumptions for the Russian plan of attack, and the specific terrain, geography, meteorology, architecture, soil composition, and hundreds of other pieces of data."

Burgess nodded. "Even humidity, the percentages of leaves left on the trees this time of year, even rainfall and wind data."

"Keep going," Ryan instructed.

Mary Pat said, "All this data generates specific positional deployment orders down to the level of the individual warfighter. We can tell a specific Marine rifleman, for instance, which window in a particular apartment building he needs to position himself in in order to have a line of sight on both a specific clock tower where a Russian sniper might hide himself and the highway, so he can report up to his command if heavy trucks pass. We've mapped out individual geometries of fire for every different weapon on the battlefield, including indirect-fire weapons, laser targeting devices, and other more technical weapons."

Burgess broke in again. "So when the time comes to deploy, we give information to the battalion commander, who tasks his company commander, who sends it down to his people, et cetera, et cetera. By the time the helicopters, Ospreys, and C-130s land in Lithuania, we will have a battalion of Marines with each one knowing *exactly* where he needs to be.

"The NGA has determined that the Russians' options for attack are extremely limited. Terrain is the culprit chiefly. Those tanks can't pick and choose where they want to cross the border. They have to do it somewhere high and dry enough for them to avoid getting bogged down.

"The logistics staff will have the most work, of course, but once everyone is in place, it will be down to the eighteen-year-old rifleman to know that, if he orients himself in just the right direction, he'll have the best situational awareness for his location."

Ryan was skeptical. "The map is not the territory."

Burgess said, "Very true, but this is not a map. We've had operatives in Lithuania in the past two weeks taking hundreds of high-level images that were input into the system to increase the precision even more."

Burgess had been ready for pushback from Ryan. "NGA had a lot of skeptics at the Pentagon, as you can imagine, myself included. And obviously we understand that several factors are involved that we cannot possibly control for. But our war planners who have been working on the Lithuania area of operations for the past several weeks, refining it the moment our satellites showed us just who showed up for the snap drill . . . they are convinced EARLY SENTINEL provides the most efficient and effective way

706

to deploy our assests to turn our Marines into a blocking force against an enemy vastly superior in numbers."

Mary Pat Foley said, "The most important feature of this program, Mr. President, is the deception element."

"Deception?"

"Yes, sir. With deployment sped up by a factor of five, we can hold our units in reserve until the moment we know the attack is imminent. The Russians will see no barriers ahead of them, they will formulate their movements accordingly."

Ryan said, "And then, when they get over the border, they are suddenly up against well-trained Marines who weren't there four hours earlier."

"Correct."

"I want to see how this works," Ryan said, his fatigue momentarily forgotten in the excitement of this new program.

Mary Pat did not look surprised. "I'd be very pleased to show you, Mr. President. I can have a PowerPoint worked up and I can deliver it myself."

Ryan shook his head. "You misunderstand me, Mary Pat. I want to go to the Pentagon, right now, or the NGA building in Springfield, if that's where I need to go. I want to sit at a desk, and I want to see this. I'm not going to micromanage our military in this. If the Pentagon wants to use EARLY SENTI-

NEL, then that's what we'll do. But I want to see it for myself."

Mary Pat nodded, still not surprised that Ryan, an ex–CIA analyst, required raw data in his face to make up his mind on how to proceed.

The *Granite* was an oil-products tanker hauling kerosene from Houston to Tallinn, Estonia, with a stop-off in Gdańsk, Poland. It had just left port in Gdańsk three hours earlier, and was now steaming northeast in international waters just west of Kaliningrad.

The captain of the *Granite* was South Korean, and his crew almost exclusively Malaysian. He had strayed east of the regular shipping lanes by design, hoping to avoid the high seas that would come from a storm passing to the east. He kept a keen eye on his marine navigation computers, kept himself clear of hazards and other traffic, as well as national boundaries.

He was vigilant, but he never saw the boat that killed him, nor did he see the instrument of his death. The boat was the *Vyborg,* a Russian Kilo-class submarine that had been in service for thirty-five years. And the weapon was the Type 53-65, a five-thousand-pound, twenty-five-foot-long torpedo.

The Kilo had been traveling astern of the *Granite,* not the best place from which to attack, but the massive oil-products vessel was cruising at only twelve knots. The Type 53-65, the captain of the *Vyborg* knew, would attack at forty-eight knots, and its acoustical homing equipment would have no trouble picking up the signature of the big and loud cargo vessel alone on this stretch of sea.

This was the eleventh boat the *Vyborg* had tracked in the past two days. The captain's orders had been to find a commercial vessel skirting the waters of Kaliningrad, ideally straying unequivocally inside, and to destroy the boat. If the boat was over one hundred meters in length, so much the better.

The *Granite* was 185 meters, it was within two hundred sixty meters of the territorial waters of Russia, and the captain of the submarine knew once it lost its ability to maneuver, its wreckage would drift well within the maritime exclusion zone.

So the *Granite* would die.

He fired a single torpedo. If the surface vessel had posed any kind of a threat whatsoever, the captain would have launched a salvo of at least two torpedoes, but the ship five thousand meters off his bow was so much more helpless than a sitting duck, because a sitting duck could, if it came down to it, flap its wings and fly away.

The torpedo was designed to defeat all manner of countermeasures, so this shot was akin to shooting fish in a barrel. It homed in on the unmistakable acoustic signature of its target, then as it got closer it began following the wake of the vessel, closed the distance between the submarine and the tanker, and neared the big vessel.

In the last phase of the weapon's attack, the torpedo dove from a depth of thirty feet to a depth of sixty feet and raced under the *Granite* to position itself directly under the hull, and then its electromagnetic fuse detonated.

The explosion of the *Granite* was impressive. The Kilo did not watch it in real time. No, it had followed protocol and dove after firing, it was eighty meters below the surface and far out of periscope depth, but the Kilo's sonar technicians listened to the detonation and the subsequent death of the vessel.

No one on board knew why they did what they had just done. The specific orders to track and kill had come from the Baltic Fleet commander in Kaliningrad, and in typical fashion no explanation was given for the order. But a rumor passed among the sailors on board was that Russian intelligence had determined that the ship they attacked was an American electronic-intelligence spy vessel, stealing information about Russian naval personnel off wireless communications bouncing through the air this close to the coast of Kaliningrad.

Others — not many, but a few — thought Valeri Volodin had gone insane and was begging the world for a fight.

The Kilo followed its orders and headed to the south, leaving the burning wreckage of the *Granite* to sink with all hands, and then drift closer to Kaliningrad.

63

The USS *James Greer* (DDG-102) wasn't looking for attention; in fact, the captain of the guided missile destroyer, Commander Scott Hagen, would have given a month's pay to be lurking silently anywhere else in the Baltic but dead solid center, surrounded by civilian vessels, the aircraft of half a dozen nations, and even the rented helicopters of a dozen of the world's biggest news outlets.

But they were here, finishing their fourth day at the scene of the crash of Swedish Airlines Flight 44, and the big powerful destroyer retrieving wreckage in the center of a very crowded sea had made one hell of an impressive shot for the video crews.

This would have been bad enough for Hagen, a realization of his worst fear of losing the element of surprise in an ocean full of very real threats, but now the officers' mess of his ship had been turned into an impromptu location to hold a press conference. Right now twenty reporters, photographers, and audio technicians were crammed tight, while three young sonar technicians, two male and one female, sat wide-eyed and uncomfortable at a table.

Three sailors — a petty officer 2nd class, a petty officer 1st class, and a senior STGC — had used a laptop computer and the ship's towed array sonar to create a "Black Box Detector" to search the deep water for the flight data recorder of SA44. They did this by taking the acoustic signature created by the black box's "ping" and sending it out to the towed array of the *James Greer,* telling it, in effect, to ignore every boat, fish, whale, and other sound in the sea, and to search for the telltale noise.

It had taken two days of running patterns in the area, but the box had been found. A research vessel that had been working at the site of a World War II plane wreck off the coast of Finland had joined the hunt, and they used their submersible to bring up the flight data recorder, allowing the other salvage equipment on station to concentrate on the recovery of larger pieces of wreckage.

And now the sailors involved in the successful search for the crucial equipment had their twenty-minute press conference to bask in their success to the world media, although all three of them looked like they'd rather be anywhere else in the world than here under the lights, carefully fielding questions without revealing one word of classified intelligence, all while their captain looked on from out in the passageway.

And if the three sonar technicians weren't exactly enjoying the moment, Commander Hagen was even more uncomfortable. He'd had to close off sections of his ship and position guards at doors in the bulkheads and hatches on the deck where they needed to be extra careful some intrepid reporter didn't try to leave the pack, and he had to watch his three young sailors to make sure they didn't drift into the no-man's-land of classified information; hard to do when they had zero experience giving briefings to the media.

But the Navy had ordered the event and the crew was doing their best to comply, while Commander Hagen just kept looking at his watch, wishing this day would end as soon as possible.

The worst part of all this wasn't the exposure, or the risk of losing a reporter down a ladderway, or the effort that had gone into finding the black box, taking his men and women away from their main mission here in the Baltic.

No, it was the bodies that bothered Hagen the most now, and it was the bodies that would stay with him the longest. The *Greer* had recovered thirty-one intact bodies or body parts in the past week, even though that had not been their main task here. Time and time again, reports from lookouts indicated floating debris in the water that appeared to be human remains, and while many times they would send out launches to discover clothing, suitcases, or colorful seats from the aircraft, thirty-one times his sailors had to retrieve the dead. Men, women, children . . . unidentifiable human remains.

Hagen knew this mission was important, he knew his boat was the right tool for the job, but the truth was . . . he hated this shit.

A tap on his shoulder pulled him back to the moment, and he turned to find his XO standing with a blue folder in his hands and a serious look on his face. He leaned over to his captain. "Message from the CNO, sir."

Hagen hadn't expected anything from the chief of naval operations, so he followed Lieutenant Commander Kincaid back to his own stateroom. Here he quickly opened the folder and began reading.

After a full minute he looked up at his XO. "A Russian Kilo has hit a Maltese-flagged freighter, possibly traveling in Russian waters off Kaliningrad."

"*Hit* it, sir?"

"Torpedoed. Sunk."

"Holy shit! On purpose?"

Hagen stared back at his second-in-command without comment. The XO held his hands up.

"Sorry, sir. You don't accidentally fire a

torpedo. I just . . . *Why?*"

"Not a clue. We are to make best possible speed for Lithuanian waters. It's a presence mission at the moment. Further orders to follow."

The XO said, "They have two Kilos in their Baltic Fleet, sir. I recommend we get the UH-60 Romeos far out ahead of us looking for them, erring on the side of caution."

"I agree. There is no reason for either of those Kilos to head as far north as Lithuania, but there was no reason for them to sink a Maltese oil-products tanker, either. Let's find them before they find us."

Hagen looked down the passageway at the media presence. "Phil, enough of the dog-and-pony show. I want those folks out of here, clear off the deck, within ten minutes. We've got work to do."

"Aye-aye, sir."

Thirty minutes later the *James Greer* had begun its transit of the Baltic Sea, but no message had been given over the 1-MC public address system as to their new mission.

Lieutenant Damon Hart, a thirty-year-old undersea-warfare weapons officer, noticed the change in the ship's engines, even down in his officers' quarters, several decks below the bridge. It was almost noon, but Hart had just climbed out of his bunk.

He had been working "five and dimes" all week. Five hours on shift, then ten hours off. He'd been on duty throughout the nighttime hours; he ate alone in the mess before climbing into his bunk to catch a few hours.

Now he was rested, but still coming out of his sleep. As he rubbed his eyes and sat down at the tiny desk he shared with another lieutenant, Hart heard running out in the passageway. He looked up at his door as it flew open.

One of his roommates, a communications officer named Tim Matsui, all but shouted, "Weps, you are not going to believe this!"

Because Hart was a weapons officer, everyone on the boat called him Weps, even the captain.

Hart yawned. "Dude, I know. It's Wednesday. Slider day. I can't wait." Wednesdays were especially big draws in the mess. The cook's cheddar cheese sliders were legendary.

The communications officer shook his head, a look on his face Hart had never seen from the man.

"It's not slider day?" Hart asked.

Matsui sat down on the bunk next to Hart. "A Kilo torpedoed an oil tanker off the coast of Kaliningrad at oh seven hundred. Left it just a smoking oil slick."

Hart blinked hard in astonishment. "No shit? Are they sure?"

"A Polish corvette was close by, it picked

up the torpedo signature before it even hit the ship. ID'd it as a Fifty-three, Sixty-five. *Had* to have been one of the Russian Kilos. It was in international waters, no question about it. We're heading to Lithuania to protect shipping at the border with Kaliningrad, and we might be sent into international waters to hunt the Kilo."

Hart had trained for this each and every day for the nine years he'd been in the Navy. But it occurred to him now that he never really expected it to happen.

Matsui said, "Did you hear what I just said? Looks like shit is about to get real."

Hart still found it hard to believe for a second they were going to actually start hunting a Russian sub. He thought they'd probably just flex their muscle in the area. Almost to himself, he said, "I can kill a Kilo."

It was an affirmation, but his roommate responded.

"You're damn right you can, Weps! You didn't get all those badges and shit for eating sliders."

The captain came over the 1-MC moments later, relaying his orders to move his ship toward Lithuania. He ended his briefing to the crew with a warning about operational security.

"We are on commo lockdown as of right now. No information out to anyone about our location, our destination, or our mission.

No one is to use social media at all for anything. Remember . . . Loose tweets sink fleets."

64

The Situation Room conference room was full. Cabinet-level national security officials ringed the table, and behind them their aides and other military officers lined the walls. Another six men and women stood in the corners.

Jack Ryan looked around at the crowd and thought he should be the President who finally had this room redesigned. It wasn't that the world's problems had grown past the ability of the physical dimensions of the room to deal with them since the Situation Room had been built in 1961; it was rather that the amount of information pouring into the room in times of crisis had become harder to manage. It took more people, more experts in more disciplines, more monitors, and more room for visual aids than did similar crises just twenty or thirty years ago.

Ryan had thirty people in front of him, and he felt like a quarterback of a too-large and too-unwieldy football team trying to play on a field that was way too small.

It was a stifling feeling.

SecDef Bob Burgess had the floor now, and he was on Ryan's direct left, speaking to the President, but careful to be loud enough to be heard all over the room. "The Russians are claiming the tanker sailed into Kaliningrad waters and refused to respond to radio hailing."

Ryan looked at the map on the monitor on the other side of the room. It was the only monitor he could see with the crowd against the walls. "What do the Russians say they thought the tanker's intentions were?"

"Terrorism. They are claiming they felt this was another attack on Russian forces in Kaliningrad, just like the attack in Vilnius."

"That's asinine."

Mary Pat said, "It's for domestic consumption. Volodin's about to go to war, he knows it, and he is hammering home the same nationalistic 'We're all under attack' line to his people he's been using for the past year. But now he's bolstering this assertion by claiming his people are literally under attack."

Burgess said, "Following your instructions, I've already directed the chief of naval operations to move the nearest surface assets toward Lithuania. First to arrive will be the *James Greer,* a guided missile destroyer."

Ryan said, "I saw the *Greer* on CNN this morning. It's helping with the SA44 crash."

"It was. It's already left the crash site, and now it's moving as fast as possible into position. It will be on station by seven this evening. The captain is awaiting orders. He knows he'll either protect Lithuanian waters or play a more active role in international waters."

Ryan nodded. He knew that decision was up to him, ultimately, but he wasn't going to be rushed into it.

Burgess said, "And there is news from DIA regarding the three generals we mentioned. Two from the Western Military District, and one in the Southern Military District."

Ryan said, "You told me DIA felt confident these men would be present in theater before an attack on Lithuania."

"Correct, and we've pinpointed all three. One of the generals is in Belarus, and one is in Kaliningrad."

"Where's the third?"

"He was in Belarus until the day before yesterday, then he left."

"Where is he now?"

"Believe it or not, he's in Odessa on vacation."

"Vacation?"

"He's at a new resort hotel set up for military officers. There was a story about it on TV this morning on Channel Seven. He and a few other top military guys were mentioned."

At first glance, this made no sense to Ryan. "What would his role be in the invasion?"

"Heavy artillery. That's what he's been involved with in all the other fights."

Jack smiled slowly now. It wasn't a look of happiness, just marveling at the situation.

"What is it?" Adler asked.

"This general . . . he's their Patton."

Burgess understood immediately. "A misdirection."

"Sorry," Scott Adler said. "Patton?"

Ryan filled him in. "Before the D-Day invasion, the Germans were keeping an eye on one man. America's most audacious general. They took it as a given that he would be involved with the invasion.

"Eisenhower understood this, so he sent George Patton up to the north of England, gave him a phantom army, used him as a complete misdirection. He wasn't involved in D-Day, because Ike determined he could serve best by turning the enemy's eyes away from the real attack."

Ryan said, "This Russian general is going to have capable senior staff under him who can do his job. The Russians send him off to 'club mil' in Odessa, make a big show about the fact he is nowhere near the theater, so we think nothing is about to happen."

Scott Adler understood the deeper ramifications of this news. He said, "In the past few weeks they've done everything in their power to telegraph the fact they were coming over the border. Now, suddenly, they apply some trickery." He didn't ask why, because he knew why. "The invasion is decided. The West caved like they thought we would, so they are going forward."

Jack Ryan agreed. "They *have* to go forward. They want us to let our guard down for a day or two while this old goat is sunning himself on the beach, which means that's when they'll come."

Burgess said, "I'll alert our ambassador to NATO. He can push again for a deployment."

"No," countered Ryan quickly. "NATO will only deploy when it's too late. That ship has sailed. They will only act, if at all, when the Article Five violation is well under way."

Adler asked, "What do you want to do?"

"We are going to deploy the Black Sea Rotational Force into Lithuania." He turned to Burgess. "They need to be moving ten minutes ago. Also get the Marine units from Spain on the way, and give the regiment at Camp Lejeune the green light. You said they could be in Lithuania in ten days. That clock is now ticking."

Burgess turned to an aide, a uniformed colonel with a nameplate that read BROWN. "Brownie, go." Burgess turned back to Ryan. "The MEU training in the North Sea?"

Ryan nodded. "Push them to the east —

toward the Baltic Sea. Obviously we've got some Russian subs to kill before I put two thousand American Marines in Russian waters. But it will take them days to get there." He turned to the secretary of the Navy. "You need to make sure our ships looking for those subs have everything they need. If you want me on the phone with Sweden or Poland, or . . . or anybody, to pull more assistance from foreign nations, you just say the word."

"Thank you, Mr. President."

"And Bob." He looked back to Burgess.

"Sir?"

"Keep an eye on this general in Odessa. If you remember, Patton wasn't involved in D-Day, but he sure as hell was involved a few months later, killing Germans at the Battle of the Bulge."

"I take your meaning, Mr. President."

The deployment of the Black Sea Rotational Force had been discussed for days, so when the orders came down through the Marine Corps Commandant to MARFOREUR, the Marine Forces Europe, at its HQ in Germany, the lieutenant colonel in charge of the BSRF, only had to give the "Go" order.

Lieutenant Colonel Rich Belanger was the battalion commander for the 3rd Battalion, 5th Marine Regiment of the 1st Marine Division. Known as the Darkhorse Battalion, 3/5 had spent the last fifteen years fighting counterinsurgency wars in the Middle East. At forty-seven, Belanger was a quarter-century older than the majority of his men. Defending his nation for so long would give him a different perspective from that of his younger men in most situations, but now his age had a special relevance. Back when Belanger was a young "butter bar" lieutenant, he spent virtually all his time getting drilled in the ins and outs of Soviet doctrine and Eastern Bloc military hardware. In the late eighties there was no secret who the principal enemy of the United States was, and where a potential war would likely be fought.

But for the young men in his battalion now, the world looked very different. Belanger's Marines with battle experience had learned the savageries of war in Afghanistan and Iraq, yet it was an altogether different kind of enemy, terrain, and warfare from what they would experience here in Central Europe if the Russians invaded a NATO country.

From the moment Belanger knew the storied Darkhorse Battalion would assume watch in the Black Sea Rotational Force, he'd gone to work on retraining and altering the mind-set of his Marines, impressing on them the different type of fighting they would do, because he alone appreciated what they were getting into.

Afghanistan sucked. The enemy was real

and the threats were pervasive. That said, *nobody* in Afghanistan *ever* talked about enemy tanks, or worse, enemy air.

Here in Europe, with Russia as an adversary, tanks and air was pretty much all anyone talked about.

A different kind of enemy altogether.

An insurgent's IED in Afghanistan could take out a squad, but a battery of Russian 2S19 artillery could take out a company.

As soon as he was given the heads-up that his force and his force alone might be heading into eastern Lithuania, Belanger did the unexpected. He spent almost all his time with his logistics and supply units, and left the finishing touches of precombat checks to his company commanders.

He gave his infantry leaders a detailed intent on what he wanted them to do, and trusted them to take care of business. Then he focused on freeing up the critical equipment he knew no one in EUCOM's area of operations would be willing to part with.

He knew this coming fight demanded a lot more of the big stuff.

He ordered his logistics and supply officers to get every antitank weapon they could lay their hands on. He chastised the logistics officer personally for his lack of audacity in the first twelve hours, put him on the shit list for taking his time, and told him he'd better get cracking and get creative immediately.

It worked.

One week later the Darkhorse had extra TOW missiles, extra Stingers, more machine-gun ammo, extra 120-millimeter and 81-millimeter high-explosive mortar rounds, and loads of smoke rounds. The logistics officer had somehow even teased out a stash of old Romanian land mines.

Lieutenant Colonel Rich Belanger's logistics officer had spent virtually every moment of the past week "augmenting" his battalion, both officially, by obtaining additional tanks positioned in Stuttgart but unattached to NATO, and unofficially, by procuring everything from extra encrypted radios to bandages from wherever he and his staff could scrounge them. They even "borrowed" extra American Javelin antitank missiles that had been stored in U.S. Army forward munitions bunkers.

Belanger looked down the final list of all the goodies his logistics officer had brought him, then looked up from his desk with a smile.

"You need me to sign for all this, Captain?"

The captain shook his head. "Probably better if you didn't."

With a wink Belanger said, "I like your style. You're off my shit list."

Belanger knew he'd be getting some phone calls later, but he also knew it was easier to beg forgiveness than to ask permission.

■ ■ ■ ■

When the time finally came to pull the trigger to move into Lithuania, the Darkhorse
Battalion moved faster and fatter than Belanger's wildest dreams. Days earlier they
relocated to Poland, to within three hundred
miles of their forward deployment positions,
and this gave BSRF the option of "organic
lift." Belanger task-organized his battalion so
they could arrive in the battle space ready to
deploy and fight immediately if need be.

The battalion consisted of a headquarters
and service company, a weapons company,
and three rifle companies: India, Kilo, and
Lima. Their tanks had been moved to the Polish border two days earlier, along with the
vehicles attached to the Headquarters and
Service Company, so it was only a three-hour
drive to Vilnius.

A dozen tilt-rotor V-22 Ospreys and six
C-130 Hercules cargo planes landed at
airports in Vilnius, Paluknys, and Molėtai,
beginning at midnight, with Harrier jets and
Cobra helicopters flying combat air support
during the lift to protect them if the Russians
moved air over the border. Belanger didn't
know how long he'd have the air cover, but
he appreciated it on the ingress, unsure what
he would find when he got into position.

The remainder of the H&S Company, along

with the beans, bullets, and Band-Aids, traveled in up-armored Humvees and seven-ton trucks from Poland. This ground force did not have a rifle company with them, but all Marine Corps units were trained to protect themselves, even the diesel mechanics and bulk-fuel operators who drove H&S's trucks. The Corps believed every Marine was a rifleman first, and the truckers always thought of themselves as riflemen and machine gunners who also knew how to turn wrenches, and not the other way around.

Rich Belanger did not travel with his H&S company. He entered Lithuania on the third Osprey to pass into Lithuanian airspace, and he wore the same basic loadout as the rest of his men: an M4 carbine, eight thirty-round magazines, a Beretta M9 pistol, and body armor.

The security of this operation had been as solid as the military could possibly make it, but there was no way to move twelve hundred Marines and their equipment into a nation the size of Lithuania, employing civilian airports, overflying cities, and rolling Humvees and tanks down the roads without the enemy getting wind of it. Belanger knew the Russians would be aware of this surprise deployment long before dawn rose over Moscow, and he wondered what this would mean for him and his men. Would the Sixth Army return to Russia from Belarus in the east, and go back to their barracks in Kaliningrad, or would the arrival of the Marines have the opposite effect, encouraging the Russians to attack when they would not have otherwise?

Belanger had been given the GPS coordinates to use for positioning created by the EARLY SENTINEL program at the NGA, although as far as he knew this was just information created by Pentagon planners, typical in any such deployment. Still, the specificity of the deployment order was a surprise to Belanger, his company commanders, and their lieutenants.

Belanger held his men back from these positions, however, and moved instead to positions just north of Vilnius. There were three camps in total, one for each of his three rifle companies; each camp also contained supporting tanks, Cobra gunships, and platoons of antitank weapons and mortars from the weapons company. From here they could quickly move into even more advanced staging areas, as intelligence about the location of the Russian forces on the other side of the border improved.

As soon as it was decided just where the Russian armor spearheads would breach the border, Belanger would task his three companies accordingly, filling in behind and around the meager Lithuanian forces already at the border and doing all they could to ready themselves for the Russians' assault.

Three hours after arriving in the country, Belanger paced around his command center. It was a high school gymnasium, and a hell of a lot nicer than most places where he'd worked on his half-dozen tours in Afghanistan and Iraq. Still, Rich Belanger knew he was in range of Russian missile batteries inside Belarus, as well as ballistic missile batteries in Kaliningrad.

As he paced, he thought over his tactical situation. He was the battle-space commander, but the reality was he knew if he stayed in fixed positions to fight, he and his twelve hundred men would be little more than a speed bump against the Russian onslaught.

Political forces would dictate Belanger's long-term prospects, but in the short term, he was in charge of his own destiny, and he knew there was only one way to success, one chance to outlive his opponents for the next seventy-two hours.

Shoot and scoot.

He knew he and his battalion would live longer if they kept moving, but for now, they just needed that critical piece of information that would tell them *where* to move to.

65

At eleven-thirty p.m. Chavez stood outside a locked metal gate under the archway of Pete Branyon's apartment on Ligoninės in Vilnius Old Town. Behind him was an open parking lot, and beyond that a small park, its trees bare in the cold. On the far side of the park was a row of old buildings, and in one of them, from what Ding had learned from Lithuanian intelligence, were an unknown number of foreigners who had been conducting surveillance on the building.

There was speculation as to whether these men were waiting to see if Branyon returned, or possibly even seeking information on the two men who'd managed to rescue Branyon the day before. Ding thought it could be the latter, since these men were obviously working with the Russians, and the Russians had probably assured the men they were watching all foreign intelligence operations in the area.

They would have been surprised by the fast

rescue of the CIA man, and probably very troubled by the fact they didn't have as good an understanding of the opposition as they had thought.

Branyon's home would be as good a place as any to be on the lookout for his mysterious protectors.

Ding took his time looking up and down the quiet street, lit only by the glow of streetlamps; then he unlocked the gate with a key provided to him by the deputy chief of station. He drew his pistol, then entered alone, disappearing under the arch. This led him to the small center court of the building, and here he took a stairwell to Branyon's apartment on the second floor.

In his earpiece Ding heard, "Okay, you've left my line of sight."

"Roger that," Ding said, and he kept climbing.

Dom Caruso was tucked under a graffiti-covered alcove on the same street as the men watching Branyon's house, just below and thirty yards to the right of their position. He sat cross-legged, a half-consumed bottle of beer in his hand and three more waiting alongside it. He was dressed like a bum, or what he thought a bum might look like in Lithuania, although he hadn't been here long enough to really know. He wore an old coat he'd bought at an outdoor flea market that afternoon, and an old felt cap, and he'd darkened the three-day growth of stubble on his face with charcoal, giving him more of a beard than he really had.

Most of the time Dom just sat there and nursed his beer, but he stole quick looks here and there with his binoculars and his FLIR monocular, both taken out of the inside of his coat each time he used them. On the first scan after Ding went into the building, Dom took a moment to center his glass on the Land Cruiser that Chavez had driven up in. It was parked in the lot near the entrance to Branyon's building, and through his binoculars Dom could make out the bullet holes even all the way over here. His hidden earpiece had a sophisticated microphone built in that allowed him to transmit even whispers to Ding's earpiece. He held his beer up to his mouth and said, "Driving over in a shot-up vehicle was a bit much, don't you think?"

As Chavez climbed the stairs he chuckled softly. "Nobody ever accused me of being subtle. We know there is a lot of oppo, and we know they are trained tactically . . . but we don't know if they are very smart."

"Fair enough," said Dom. "Carry on."

When Ding arrived at Branyon's apartment he began to turn on lights, telegraphing the fact he was there to the mysterious opposition, in case they hadn't noticed him.

Dom remained in the dark, scanning the area, searching for any signs of life.

Five minutes after Chavez entered the apartment, Dom saw two men walking through the park. One had a bottle in his hand, and they staggered a little while they walked, but Dom kept his eyes on them anyhow, in case it was a ruse.

The men kept going, and they walked out of the scene without ever looking in the direction of Chavez's location.

Another few minutes passed. Dom was switching between his regular binoculars, which worked fine here because of the street-lamps, and his FLIR monocular, which helped him scan all the windows, rooftops, and dark alcoves around the square for heat signatures, just in case someone was lurking there.

Ding opened the blinds on the second floor, then looked out over the little park.

Dom said, "Dude, you are silhouetting yourself. Giving them a target."

Ding replied, "I'm trying to get them to take the bait." He closed the blinds after a few seconds and turned out a light in the kitchen.

Caruso saw nothing that aroused any suspicions. He said, "If the watchers in the apartment on my left are interested, they should be looking at you right now."

Just then, Dom heard a car start in the parking lot on the far end of the alcove behind him. He knew this lot was used by people in the buildings all up and down this side of the street, meaning one of the unknown opposition team members might be behind the wheel. Dom quickly made sure all his gear was well tucked away, and he moved into the doorway of a hair salon next to the alcove.

Seconds later, a vehicle pulled into the tunnel from the parking lot behind. It had its lights off, and it stopped at the back of the tunnel, just idling there in position.

Dom said, "Okay, Ding. You called it. I've got some kind of a hatchback vehicle idling in the dark near my poz. Looks like two inside, but can't confirm that."

Ding said, "It's about damn time. I was thinking about making myself a sandwich." Then he added, "Keep an eye out for others."

"You've been spotted by the other side . . . Why wait around until a whole busload shows up?"

"I want to make it look good. I'm going to sit it out for a couple more minutes, then I'll roll out of here. You follow anybody following me."

"Got it," Dom said, and he sipped his beer.

Dom had a 2011 Honda CBR250R street bike parked against the curb a half-block up the street. It was an entry-level bike, nothing that was going to outrun any fighter planes, but for the twisting turning streets of Vilnius, it was agile, small, and, most important, it would not stand out.

After five minutes more Ding turned off the rest of the lights in Peter Branyon's apartment, then he appeared in the archway at the front of the building carrying two suitcases. These he put in the back of the Land Cruiser, before climbing behind the wheel.

Dom watched all this, and whispered behind his beer. "What's in the suitcases?"

"Just some books I threw in to make them look heavy. Do I still have eyes on me?"

"Affirm. The car is on my left, twenty-five feet away, but I'm tucked into a doorway and out of their line of sight. I won't be able to go back to my bike until they take off after you."

"Okay," Ding said. "But watch out for other vehicles. If they have the manpower and they are interested enough in who I am and what I'm doing, then they'll do a multicar surveillance package. Honestly, I'd just as soon get as many of these fuckers in one place at one time, lead them all into the police roadblock."

"Roger that," Dom said, and just as he transmitted he heard several car doors shut in the parking lot on the far side of the tunnel. "Careful what you wish for, Ding. You're about to be leading a parade."

Minutes later, Chavez drove off from the other side of the park, turning his bullet-pocked Land Cruiser in the direction of

Caruso and the opposition vehicles, then turning right.

As soon as he disappeared, three vehicles emerged from the passageway through the building on Dom's left. A gray Škoda hatchback, a black Ford four-door, and a black BMW SUV.

"Okay, Ding," Dom said. "I've got three vehicles following you." He described the vehicles as he rushed to his motorcycle.

"The BMW was in back, right?" Chavez asked over the net.

"How'd you know?"

"The Škoda and the Ford are full of labor, the Beamer is management. No team leader is going to sit in the back of a piece-of-shit hatchback while his muscle drives a BMW."

Dom whistled gently into his mike. "You have been doing this too long."

"Tell me about it," Ding said. "Catch up to us, but don't let them see you."

Chavez had to drive through late-night Vilnius pretending he did not see the three vehicles behind him. The men inside, assuming this was part of the same force he and Caruso had encountered at the border the night before, had proven themselves to be well trained with their weapons. But they were not terribly good at surveillance.

Chavez couldn't lose the three-car tail. The entire objective to this mission was to lead them to a police roadblock on the Drujos highway, just east of the Old Town. The location had been selected because it was close enough to the city that Chavez and Caruso felt confident there was little risk the tail would give up and just return to their apartment, and far enough away from homes, apartments, and public spaces that a shoot-out would not create a massive bloodbath of civilians.

Chavez spoke in a normal voice in the Land Cruiser, knowing Dom would hear him in his earpiece. "I'm two klicks out from the road-block. Still just the three vehicles tailing me?"

Dom had to speak louder, as he was riding on the bike, but his helmet muted much of the noise from the engine and the wind. "Affirmative. They are all lined up and following you like you're the Pied Piper."

"Good, keep an eye out for any joiners. We don't know how many of these guys there are, and we don't know their operational relationship with the Russians in the area, if any."

"Roger that."

The plan Chavez and Caruso had ironed out with the ARAS unit in charge of manning the roadblock to take down the foreign operators was for Chavez to drive his Land Cruiser under the pedestrian bridge over the four-lane road, then continue on past Vitebsko, a small street that ran off to the left. Once he passed, six ARAS police cruisers, each with two officers inside, would race out into the highway and block the road. Another half-dozen men would be up on the pedestrian bridge over the highway, armed with powerful spotlights, HK G36 rifles, and Benelli shotguns.

There were eighteen in the ARAS force in total, not ideal as far as Chavez was concerned, but it appeared the group following him in three cars would not be anticipating the ambush, so he thought the plan reasonable considering the threat.

Traffic was virtually nonexistent on this stretch of the highway now, and both Chavez and Caruso were thankful for this. The ARAS roadblock would catch anyone driving by once it was sprung, so if the men in the three cars tailing Chavez decided to fight it out, civilians might well be caught in the crossfire if there had been much traffic.

Ding called Dom over his earpiece. "Okay, I can see the pedestrian bridge ahead. You need to back off now so you don't end up downrange if the shooting starts."

Caruso did as Chavez instructed, slowing his motorcycle to a crawl on the road. He watched the taillights of the BMW SUV, the third of the three vehicles in the tail, get farther and farther away.

Dom decided to proactively block the road

so no one else got closer. He turned his bike around, and shined the headlight back toward any oncoming traffic. And he pulled out a flashlight from his jacket. He climbed off his bike and stepped into the next lane, then began waiting for cars.

Chavez passed under the pedestrian bridge that represented the opening jaw of the Lithuanian federal antiterrorist team's trap, and he kept rolling through, passing Vitebsko Street on his left, and continuing on. He looked in his rearview mirror and saw the lights of the first vehicle behind him, some 150 yards back. It was racing right into the trap.

The gray Škoda passed first under the pedestrian bridge, and just as it did so, a row of Lithuanian police cars raced out in front of it, covered all four lanes, and screeched to a halt. The Škoda skidded to a stop in the middle of the road, and behind it, the black Ford four-door did the same.

Men leapt from the police cars, swinging rifles out in front of them and leveling them toward the three vehicles, while just behind the Škoda and the Ford, the black BMW X3 pulled to a more controlled stop, just west of the pedestrian bridge that ran above the highway. Men on the bridge flashed lights on all three vehicles, some of them facing east to the two cars pinned in and others facing west to the BMW in the rear.

Eighteen men in black body armor and holding rifles or shotguns began yelling at the three drivers to turn off their engines.

The BMW was the first vehicle to move. Its tires screeched as it was put in reverse and the accelerator stomped to the floor. Men on the bridge yelled down to the driver, ordering him to halt, but the SUV launched backward, surrounded by the smoke from its tires. An officer on the bridge fired a shotgun blast at the hood of the vehicle in an attempt to knock it out of action, but the vehicle kept moving backward.

An order was initiated by the on-scene commander to open fire on the BMW, but before he'd finished giving the order, gunfire erupted simultaneously from both the Škoda and the Ford, two vehicles that were just twenty-five to fifty feet from the ARAS roadblock. Shooters inside the cars fired through the windshield and out the side windows, surprising the police force with both the audaciousness of the act and the volume of fire.

Black-clad ARAS men standing behind their vehicles returned fire, men on the bridge all shifted to the east to shoot down on the Škoda and the Ford, and the BMW, after receiving only one ineffectual shotgun blast, was all but forgotten. It raced backward out of the area, picking up speed as it backed westward in the eastbound lane.

Ding Chavez pulled the Land Cruiser over to the side of the road a quarter-mile from the roadblock. He heard the first boom of a shotgun, then the chatter of automatic rifles, and finally a cacophony of various weapons, easily twenty-five in number, all firing at the same time.

"Holy shit, Dom! It's gone loud!"

"I hear it," Caruso confirmed. He was a half-mile from the roadblock, and three-quarters of a mile from Chavez. "We can't approach without running the risk of being targeted by the bad guys and ARAS."

"Right. Stay right where you are. Watch out for any squirters."

"Too late, Chavez," Caruso said instantly. "The black Beamer is coming my way!"

Chavez slammed his hand into the wheel of the car. Ding had an MP5 nine-millimeter submachine gun on the seat next to him, and Dom, who was driving the motorcycle, was only armed with a borrowed Beretta nine-millimeter pistol, but there was no way Chavez could even get to Dom to help him without driving through the middle of the gun battle. He said, "Get off the road and out of their way. If you can, tail them, but do *not* engage."

"Understood."

Chavez slammed his hand again, feeling

impotent parked here along the highway, but then an idea hit him. He put the Land Cruiser in gear and then stomped on the gas, looking for a place to make a left off the highway. As he did this he flipped on the moving map on the Toyota's multifunction display. "Dom, I'm going to try and make my way through town back in your direction. You keep me posted on where they are going."

"Roger, they are passing me right now. I'm going to get behind them, and stick on them like glue."

The X3 had turned around by the time it passed Dom a minute earlier, but it continued driving the wrong way, west in the eastbound lane. A few other vehicles had been on the highway, all of which had run off into the median or at least slammed on their brakes as the BMW and the motorcycle chasing it passed.

Chavez had instructed Caruso to stay out of sight of the men he was following, but there was no chance of that. Dom's headlight was the one vehicle behind the BMW, as traffic had been stopped by the roadblock a mile back. Dom instead just kept far enough behind the BMW that he felt they'd have a hard time shooting him from the back window, and close enough to them that he could see where they were going. He hoped they'd pull off this road and into the bustle and narrower streets of the city, where he could be a little more discreet about his surveillance.

And Dom got his wish almost immediately. The X3 made a hard right turn at speed onto Aušros Vartų, a one-lane street that ran like a spine through the center of Vilnius's hilly and warrenlike Old Town. Dom followed into the turn, then tightened up on them so he didn't lose them. Dom and Ding's rented flat was only a few hundred yards from here, so he knew the area just well enough to know there were dozens if not hundreds of archways, breezeways, narrow alleys, and covered parking lots in which they could hide.

He spoke loud enough in his helmet for Ding to receive his transmission. "We're off the highway, heading north through the Old Town. Don't know if he has a destination or if he's just trying to shake me."

Chavez came over the net an instant later. "I'm hauling ass your way. If you can vector me in front of them I can try to pick up the tail."

Dom said, "Dude, you're the guy with the GPS, I'm the guy on the bike trying to read eight-syllable road signs at forty miles an hour."

Chavez said, "Point taken, Dom. Just give me north, south, east, or west, and let me know what you see. I'll try to figure it out from my map."

Dom followed the BMW north through the

Old Town. It had slowed to the speed limit but was clearly still trying to find a way out of the area, because it made a series of conflicting turns that led in various directions. Dom called them out to Ding one at a time, and Ding was even able to pan the map on his Land Cruiser's display over to the neighborhood and reroute Dom so he could give the occupants of the SUV the impression they had lost him.

Dom followed along with Ding's instructions, taking a parallel alley to the road the X3 was on, but when he came out on the other side, the black SUV wasn't there.

"Shit!" shouted Dom. "I've lost him."

Ding was using his map to help Dom while he drove closer to the area. "It's okay, there's only one way he could have left that road. Turn around, make a left on Subačiaus, and then another immediate left on Kazimiero."

Dom did as instructed, only to find himself in a perfectly dark, winding cobblestone passage. "He's not here."

Ding said, "Stay on that road, he's *got* to be in front of you."

Dom opened up the throttle, raced forward along the cobblestones at breakneck speed. He shot under a pair of passageways where the buildings that ran right up to the side of the pavement connected above the narrow road.

After thirty seconds of racing through the

dark, he looked to his right and saw the reflection of the BMW's taillights parked in the courtyard of a building. He started to slow to turn around, but he'd barely begun to do so when the BMW shot back out in the street, heading the other way. As it made the turn, just seventy-five feet behind Caruso, a single shot cracked in the narrow passageway. Feet above Dom's head, two-hundred-year-old masonry exploded from the wall of a building.

Dom took off after them, going back the way they had come. Another burst of gunfire kicked up sparks on the cobblestones in front of the motorcycle. Dom slowed and then turned hard through a covered archway that ran under a building, then shot out on the other side. Here there was a staircase that ran down in the direction the BMW had been traveling, so Dom began bouncing down it on his bike. "They are shooting at me. You see any other parallel routes where I can stay out of their line of fire?"

Ding vectored him off the stairs and back toward a road that headed to the south. Just as Dom raced onto the road, he saw the BMW in front of him, not fifty yards ahead on a one-lane cobblestone path with ancient walls tight on both sides. "Got them! South on Dvasios, they're hauling ass!"

"South on Dvasios?" Ding asked. "You sure?"

"Yeah, why?"

" 'Cause I'm heading *north* on Dvasios, and I'm hauling ass, too!"

"I don't know how long this road is, but you'd better plan on —"

Dom stopped speaking when he looked beyond the BMW in front of him and saw a big SUV race around the bend with its lights off. Both vehicles were doing fifty, and they were too close to avoid each other.

Ding Chavez had driven all over the Old Town in the past five minutes trying to put himself in front of Caruso and the vehicle he was tailing. And now he had finally done it, but he wasn't sure of his plan. When he was only twenty-five yards away from impact he let go of the wheel, dropped sideways across the center console of the Land Cruiser, and tucked his head down into the passenger seat. At the same time, he hit the brakes, but did not slam on them. He only wanted to slow down the impact to a survivable speed.

The crash with the big BMW SUV was violent. Chavez's body was wrenched sideways; glass shattered and metal tore like paper. The airbags in the Toyota had deployed, but they did so over Chavez, who was lying sideways with his head in the passenger seat. They deflated instantly by design, so Chavez sat up quickly with the MP5 in his hands. He leveled it over the dashboard, trained it on the vehicle in front of him.

The radiator of the big Land Cruiser was torn apart and hot steam erupted into the air, fogging the view between Chavez and any potential targets, but after a few seconds to take in the scene, he saw the driver of the BMW, just eight feet or so in front of him, fighting to get his deflated airbag out of his face, and his pistol up and out the shattered windshield.

Chavez flipped off the safety of his submachine gun and opened fire, raking the man in the head with nine-millimeter full-metal-jacketed rounds.

The front passenger got a shot off at Chavez but missed. Chavez used the muzzle flash to find his target through the heavy steam and smoke, and he fired several times, then he ducked down to avoid any return fire.

He unbuckled his seat belt, opened his driver's-side door, and bailed out, dropping all the way to the ground. Once he hit the hard cobblestones, with the smell of radiator fluid and engine oil prevalent in the cold night air, he swung his MP5 around and toward the BMW.

A man in blue jeans and a heavy coat had bailed from the back of the BMW, and was just now climbing off the ground, pulling a pistol from inside his jacket. Chavez leveled his weapon at the man. "Don't move!"

The man moved and Ding shot him in the

forehead, sending him falling back onto the cobblestones.

"Shit!" Ding said. He needed at least one of these men alive.

He clambered up to his feet now, thankful that his body was cooperating and he'd not been injured in the crash, then he carefully moved around the wreckage of the BMW, spinning around the back, low with his weapon up.

A man had been crawling from the crash on his hands and knees, and he was now in the middle of the one-lane road, thirty feet away.

Dom Caruso knelt over the injured man, his knee in the man's back, his Beretta pistol pressed against his skull. He looked up to Ding. "Hey, look what I found."

The last five minutes had been a logistical nightmare, but Chavez and Caruso had the wounded gunman alone, just the way they wanted him.

The only operable vehicle was the Honda motorcycle, so Dom climbed back on and drove over to the man lying in the street. The man had a broken ankle — somehow he'd injured it in the backseat of the BMW in the crash — and he was unable to walk or even stand, so once they searched him for weapons Ding secured his hands with tape, blindfolded him, and then put him on the back of Dom's motorcycle. Dom drove off to the south, with instructions from Ding to find a place for an in extremis interrogation.

Just on the other side of Daukšos, a main east-west artery a block away from the crash site, Dom motored up a private drive of a section of beat-up-looking old apartment buildings. Here, behind a parking lot and a row of garbage cans, he found a freestanding building the size of a one-car garage. It didn't look like it had been used in decades — it was surrounded by overgrown weeds and the window glass was broken out — but when he kicked in the loose wooden door and looked over the space with his flashlight, he saw the room would do for a short conversation.

Ding had been on foot, so he showed up five minutes later, out of breath from jogging. By then Dom had the man's coat and shirt stripped off him, and a flashlight balanced on the sill of a boarded-up window so it shined directly on him.

The man shivered and moaned in pain from his grotesquely swollen ankle, but Dom had done nothing to help him.

Ding entered the little room, looked around, then ripped off the blindfold. The man blinked several times, then looked around.

As far as Ding was concerned, the man looked like he could have been Russian. He was in his thirties, with a scruffy beard and mustache just a few shades more red than his auburn hair. He had a square jaw Chavez could make out even through the beard, and a flat nose like he was a boxer who lost a lot more fights than he won.

He had no tattoos or other distinguishing marks on his torso or arms.

"Do you speak English?" Chavez asked. The bare-chested man just looked up at the two Americans without reply, blinking from the 180-lumen flashlight in his face.

Dom knelt down over him now. Got in his face. In a voice designed to convey menace, he said, "Do. You. Speak. English?"

The man just shook his head a little, like he didn't understand, but he said nothing.

Dom sighed. "What do we do with him?"

From behind, Chavez replied, "He's worthless. Cut his dick off, shoot him in the head, and throw him in the river."

Dom nodded. "You got it."

"No! I speak English!" The man shouted it in a heavy accent, his eyes wide with horror.

"Would you look at that?" Dom said with a smile. "He's a quick study."

"I've been teaching that ten-second crash course in English for thirty years," Chavez replied, and he knelt down in front of the wounded man. "Okay, boss. Your buddies all made their choices, now it's your turn. Do you want to live or do you want to die?"

The man said, "I want to live." He seemed

certain in his choice.

"Good," said Chavez. "First, you're Russian?"

"Russian? No. From Serbia. We are all Serb." His eyes looked down a moment. "*Were* all Serb."

"Serb?" Dom said in surprise. "We're a thousand miles from Belgrade."

"But you are working for FSB?" Chavez said.

"No."

"Who trained you?"

"Serbian Army."

"Bullshit," Chavez said. "You've got Spetsnaz training."

The man said nothing for a moment, until Dom said, "The river's only two blocks away."

The wounded man changed his tune instantly. "Yes, there were thirty of us, trained in Russia. Tenth GRU Spetsnaz Brigade in Krasnodar."

"What are you doing here?"

The man shrugged. "We were fighting for Russia in Ukraine. Chetnik Battalion. The best men in our unit were taken to Russia for Spetsnaz training, and then told we would be going to the Baltic for destabilizing operations." He looked up at the men. "You said you wouldn't kill me."

"You tell us the truth, and we'll take you to the hospital."

"How can I trust you?"

"You know you can trust me to put a bullet in your eye like I did to your buddies."

The man looked down for a minute. "They told us Russia would attack. We were the vanguard."

Caruso said, "You tried to kidnap the American last night in Tabariškės."

He shook his head. "Other men in my unit. Not me."

Now Dom asked, "Did you blow up the *Independence*?"

"The what?"

Chavez and Caruso both thought the man looked genuinely confused by the question.

Chavez said, "What about the train?"

"Wha . . . what train?"

Caruso said, "*That* looked like bullshit," confirming what Chavez was himself thinking.

Chavez said, "What's your name?"

"Luka."

"Look, Luka. You can't be lying to us. I just killed three men. At this point, killing one more would actually make things easier. We don't have a car. I *really* don't feel like carrying you to the hospital."

Luka laid his head on the ground. "We were ordered to fire on the Russian troop transport. To wear the badge of the Polish People's Lancers."

Dom just mumbled softly. "Bingo."

A minute later, Ding left the little shack and stood in the dark. He called Linus Sabonis's mobile phone, ready to tell him to pick up the Serbian prisoner and give him the intel he just learned, but Sabonis didn't answer. He called back again, and again it went to voice mail.

Frustrated, Ding called Sabonis's second-in-command. He answered on the fifth ring. Ding started to tell him what was going on, but he didn't even get to the part where they tailed the BMW away from the roadblock before the man interrupted him.

"I'm sorry, I have to go."

Ding was surprised by the man's nonchalance. "You've got something more important going on?"

"Actually, yes." There was a slight pause. "Russian troops from Kaliningrad have entered Lithuania." The man hung up.

Ding reentered the shack and looked at Dom. He said, "It's showtime, brother. We are officially in a nation under attack."

Dom looked down to Luka. "You're on your own, asshole. Crawl down to the street and get a taxi to take you to the hospital, or else wait for the Russian tanks to save your ass. We're outta here."

"I'm hurt! I can't walk!"

"Sucks to be you," Caruso said, and he and Chavez left the injured man in the shack without another word.

66

Everyone thought the Russian attack on Lithuania would begin with rockets launched from over the border from Belarus and Kaliningrad, followed by tanks and troops moving through border crossings along the highway. Attack aircraft and helicopters, it was assumed, would support the ground forces, and artillery would pound the way ahead.

But the opening salvo was something quite different indeed.

A previously scheduled Russian military train passing through Lithuania came to an unscheduled stop at a railway yard in the Paneriai forest, just southwest of Vilnius, not far from the airport. Because of the Russian train's movement down the line, the massive rail yard's normal security had been augmented by a platoon of Lithuanian Land Force riflemen, but these thirty men plus the dozen or so lightly armed security guards were no match for ninety-six tier-one Special Forces commandos from Russia's Directorate "A" of the FSB Special Purpose Center on board the train. The dedicated counterterrorism unit was known in Russia as "Spetsgruppa A," or Special Team Alpha, but around the world they were known as "Alpha Group." These were the "Little Green Men" who had shown up in eastern Ukraine the year before, and the men Lithuanians had reported seeing near the borders for the past few weeks. Most of these sightings were erroneous; there were a few cross-border incursions, but the Little Green Men had waited till now to begin their direct action inside Lithuania's borders.

The ninety-six members of Alpha Group on this train had been given two crucial missions for this first night of the invasion. Forty-eight of the men would climb into vehicles waiting here in the yard and drive into the capital itself. They would break into eight six-man fire teams and begin quickly blocking roads, initiating checkpoints, and essentially showing themselves to the citizens of Vilnius as they headed to work in the morning. The Russians wanted to instill chaos in the nation, to give the impression the invasion itself had already made it into the capital before anyone knew they were at war. Eight separate teams working in eight predetermined choke points could make the news by dawn and grind the city, and perhaps the entire country, to a halt by mid-morning.

Like much of Russia's hybrid war, the operation was mostly for show, to create an *impression* of facts on the ground in order to change the *actual* facts on the ground.

The other forty-eight men of Alpha Group had a more direct operation planned. They, too, would climb into vehicles staged here at the station and then race to the east, taking back roads through the forest for the two and a half miles to Vilnius International Airport. Here they would break into four twelve-man units, with individual objectives. Two teams would hit opposite ends of the airfield to draw away the guard force and engage any military presence, while teams three and four would attack the terminal itself from opposite entrances, taking over the building and then setting up defensive positions in the shopping mall–sized space. The two fire teams would then attempt to link up and take over the control tower, thereby dominating the airport.

If all went according to plan, Russian follow-on troops from GRU (military intelligence) Spetsnaz units would land before dawn, resupplying and reinforcing the Alpha Group men already on site.

But first the Russians had to get off the train and to the airport. The Lithuanian troops defending the area were at first just confused by the fact that the big Russian train seemed to be slowing down as it approached the small station building in the center of the rail yard. The platoon commander's first order was for his second-in-command to call someone back at base to ask what was going on. It wasn't until the yard's security force, men who were used to the Russian train sailing through the station at 100 kilometers an hour, dove to the ground and hid themselves behind railcars and cinder-block walls that the Land Force soldiers had a clue that they were in danger.

The soldiers followed the security men to defensive positions, albeit slowly, and when the Russian men in black began to leap from the still-moving train, firing on anything that moved in the station, the twenty-three-year-old commander of the Lithuanian platoon realized he didn't have to wait for base to get back to him with orders.

He understood. The fucking war everyone in the nation had been talking about had just begun, right before his eyes.

Alpha Group snipers climbed onto the roof of several railcars and trained their long rifles, Sako TRG 22s outfitted with infrared scopes, on the scene before them. Within seconds they were picking off targets around the station and farther back in the rail yard, while below them the expert assaulters of Alpha Group began leapfrogging maneuvers to get distance from the train.

A Lithuanian machine gun began to bark

from the roof of the station, raking the train with 7.62-millimeter rounds. One Russian was hit squarely in the elbow, ripping his arm off at the joint and spinning him to the ground, where he would bleed to death in minutes.

But the big FN-MAG machine gun, the Lithuanians' most potent weapon at the scene against the now ninety-five invaders, was silenced after making the single kill. An assaulter on the ground lobbed a forty-millimeter high-explosive grenade from the underslung launcher below his Kalashnikov, and his shot landed perfectly in the sandbagged position, killing the Lithuanian gunner and wounding his reloader.

Within two minutes of the first shot at the rail yard, the lead squad of Alpha Group assaulters reached the station, having crossed several open tracks. They were down two men, and four other Russians lay dead or wounded on the tracks behind, but once the assaulters penetrated the station, the surviving Lithuanians, soldiers and security guards alike, were in full retreat, heading toward a pair of large warehouses to the northeast and then into the forest beyond.

The Russians did not pursue them; their orders were to conserve ammo; only the snipers remained on the train cars to scan with their infrared scopes to keep guard against a counterattack. While they did this, the assaulters rushed to a locked gate to the north-west of the station, shot it open with a shotgun blast, and then entered a large storage parking lot. Here, twenty brand-new Volvo XC-90 SUVs sat waiting for delivery to car dealerships all over the Baltic on two Peterbilt car carriers. Russia's FSB men working for a logistics company in Sweden had purposefully held up customs paperwork, keeping the vehicles stuck in port in Klaipėda until the day before yesterday, thereby timing their arrival by train here for delivery.

The commander of the Alpha Group men had multiple sets of keys, and he passed them out to the drivers. The operators jammed themselves and their heavy equipment into the Volvos, using all three rows of seats and every cubic inch of cargo space to do so, then the twenty vehicles left the station, minus the dead and wounded they lost in the infiltration operation.

Lieutenant Colonel Rich Belanger got word about the successful infiltration of Russian Special Forces the way he normally learned about fast-moving intelligence in the field. Piecemeal and with as much conjecture and false reporting as genuine actionable intel. His Marines were all positioned to the east of Vilnius, they didn't hear a word about the action at the train station until thirty minutes after the attack, and by that point the surviving Russian commandos were well clear of the station. No one knew where they had gone, but Lieutenant Colonel Rich Belanger realized that as troubling as enemy action behind him was, he needed to stay focused on his mission, the one thing he had some control over. The Belarusan border ten miles in front of him, and the 25,000 Russian troops positioned there.

The Lithuanians would just have to sort out the Russian deep-penetration mission on their own.

67

Chavez and Caruso neared the airport at two-thirty a.m., riding in tandem on the motor-cycle with only the Maxpedition shoulder bags they'd used during their operation this evening. They had other gear at their safe house in the Old Town of Vilnius, but they had decided to bypass it and expedite their escape from Lithuania. The men were well versed enough in OPSEC that there wouldn't be anything in the safe house that could lead back to them, and the laptops and other electronics were encrypted and set up by Gavin Biery so that he could wipe their drives remotely if called on to do so.

Leaving a safe house behind without scouring it wasn't optimal, but considering the fragmented news about an attack under way somewhere in the country, Chavez opted to pull the plug on his operation here and concentrate on exfiltrating the country while he still could.

The two men pulled over next to a grated

storm drain a few blocks from the airport and disassembled the weapons they'd been given by the SSD. As Ding let go of the receiver of the MP5 and listened to it splash below him, he said, "I wish we had time to go find Herkus Zarkus and give him these weapons. Couldn't hurt to have a backup or two."

Caruso tossed the pieces of his pistol in the water as well. "Realistically, the only thing we could do for him is knock him on the head and Shanghai him out of here."

They left their motorcycle in the lot next to the airport terminal and headed in to the security desk, and here the stress on the faces of the armed officers made it plain they knew their nation had come under attack. Just like Chavez and Caruso, however, these men had no real information. They just assumed the invasion had begun far to the west at the Kaliningrad border, or else twenty-five miles away at the Belarusan border. Bad news, to be sure, but none of them suspected they were in imminent danger.

The Americans explained they had a jet waiting for them at the airport FBO and a call was made from the terminal, and soon the men were directed through a metal detector and sent on their way.

Caruso noted the envious look from the men, who obviously wished they could simply climb aboard a private jet and leave the country.

Once the two Americans stepped back outside for the walk from the terminal building to the Gulfstream parked on the tarmac two hundred yards away, however, the Campus operators were surprised by the sudden wail of an alarm. At first Caruso thought they'd gone out the wrong door and triggered it themselves, but after a few moments a voice came over the loudspeaker in Lithuanian. Neither man understood what was being said, but whatever the announcer was saying, he sounded a hell of a lot more agitated than he would if he was just letting everyone know a couple idiots had passed through the wrong door at a sleepy airport.

Dom and Ding picked up the pace for the Gulfstream, which was bathed under lights in the distance in front of the fixed-base operator.

They were still one hundred yards away when the men heard a single snap from a rifle, far to the south, beyond the end of the runway. Both men looked out past the lights of the tarmac and saw several more flashes of light and then, an instant later, the sound of gunfire made its way to them.

"What the hell?" Dom said. "That can't be the Russians here already."

"Who says it can't?" Ding replied, and he broke into a run for the plane.

An explosion back at the terminal sounded to both men like the detonation of a forty-millimeter high-explosive grenade, and it was answered by staccato bursts and single snaps from automatic and semiautomatic weapons.

By the time the men were within fifty yards of their destination, they heard sustained gunfire from the northern end of the airfield as well.

Caruso said, "They've got the runway surrounded! Whichever way we taxi, we're going to be taking fire!"

Ding looked through the cockpit window and saw Campus pilot Helen Reid at the controls, and as he ran around the front of the plane he saw copilot Chester "Country" Hicks standing at the doorway with an HK UMP submachine gun down by his leg. He was looking to the south, the location of the nearest gunfire.

Even though Country wasn't trained in the security of the aircraft like the usual flight security officer for The Campus, Adara Sherman, he had been a Marine aviator, and he knew how to skillfully operate a number of different weapons.

The two Campus men raced up the stairs and past Country, who immediately began to close the hatch. Chavez ducked his head into the little cockpit of the Gulfstream luxury jet. "There is shooting at the terminal, and at both ends of the runway. What are you going to do?"

"Do they have SAMs?" Captain Reid asked.

"No idea."

"RPGs?"

"Unknown. I just heard automatic small arms and forty-millimeter grenades."

Chavez had to back out of the cockpit so Country could climb into the right seat, then he leaned back in. Reid was already applying power to the port engine to turn the aircraft to starboard. To her right, Country was belting in and scanning out all the windows, trying to decide on the best direction to go.

He said, "Most of the shooting is to the south right now. Looks like the Fourth of July over there. Once they get through the terminal, though, the middle of the runway will be under direct fire."

Helen Reid said, "Then let's not hang around. I'll take the high-speed taxiway to the middle of the runway, stop, hit full power while on the brake. I'll try a short takeoff to the north."

Chavez said, "Will that get you high enough to avoid the shooting at the north end of the runway?"

She was already taxiing at a speed that forced Ding to hold on with both hands.

Captain Reid answered, "No. We won't have any altitude by the time we hit the end of the runway."

Country said, "We can go hard right."

She nodded. "Hard right. As soon as the wheels leave the runway, we're going to climb to the east." She glanced at Chavez. "You and Dom better strap yourselves in."

Chavez rushed back into the cabin and sat in the captain's chair next to Caruso. Caruso was looking out the portal next to him. "What did they say?"

"They said the in-flight meal is going to be delayed."

Dom laughed despite the tension. "No problem. I have a feeling I'm about to lose my appetite."

The Gulfstream did not ask for takeoff clearance from Vilnius Tower, because Reid could plainly see the flashes of light from gunfire through the tower glass. There was a gunfight going on in there, and she'd never heard of well-armed air traffic controllers, so she assumed the tower would be in the hands of the Russians in mere moments. Instead, she applied the brake, pushed both engines up to full throttle, and waited for them to spool up to a scream.

She released the brakes, the sleek white aircraft lurched forward, and she drove it down the middle of the runway with her foot pedals. Chester "Country" Hicks read off her speed as she kept her eyes flitting between the centerline for reference and the flashes of light out of the dark at the end of the runway. The gunfire seemed to rush closer to her with each second as her aircraft raced toward a battle it could not avoid.

Reid normally kept a "sterile" cockpit on takeoff: no conversation, no talking at all other than what was necessary for the operation of the aircraft. But this was no ordinary takeoff. She said, "If we get hit, we need to know where we are going to put down to the south."

Country said, "Ninety knots . . . ugh, if it's bad enough we'll just have to find a highway. If we can limp over to Poland, let's do that. One hundred knots."

Reid needed 120 knots to rotate, but in front of her a shower of sparks began to explode across the runway. "They're shooting at us." She pushed down on her right pedal, taking her off the center line but racing her toward the right edge of the runway as the plane shot forward.

"One ten," Country said, and then he added, "You're running out of real estate."

The sparks picked up all around. Reid had no idea why the Russian Army was shooting at her, but she assumed the assaulters had been ordered to prevent all aircraft from leaving the country.

When she could no longer see any of the right edge of the runway in front of the nose of her aircraft, she waited an instant more, then began to put back pressure on her yoke.

On her right, Country said his next sentence as if it were just one word: "onetwentyrotate."

Reid pulled back harder, lifted the nose off the runway just feet before it rolled off the right edge and into the grass. The back tires left the hard surface even closer to the grass, but the plane was airborne now, just three hundred yards from the northern end of the runway.

As soon as they had any altitude at all, certainly they were no more than forty feet off the ground, Reid put her Gulfstream into a twenty-degree bank to the right.

Country said, "Gear up," and he retracted the landing gear himself.

The twenty-degree turn became thirty, the thirty turned to forty, and soon they were heading off to the southeast.

Lines of glowing tracers raced by Reid's left window.

One minute later Dom Caruso appeared between the two pilots. "I'm going to buy you both a beer, but not till we get where we're going."

Hicks just laughed, doing his best to play cool. Helen Reid, on the other hand, was not cursed with the same sense of bravado as the former Marine and the intelligence operator. She said, "Gentlemen, how about we stow the macho swagger until we get out of Lithu-anian airspace? For all we know, a couple of MiGs are hunting us down as we speak."

Caruso said, "You're right, but we'll be in Poland airspace in a couple of minutes."

She countered, "Correct me if I'm wrong, but a half-hour ago you had no idea Russia had attacked Lithuania. Do you know they haven't attacked Poland?"

Chastened, Caruso turned to leave the cockpit.

Reid called after him. "We'll be landing in Brussels in three hours. You guys should get some rest."

Caruso looked back at her. "Brussels? Why are we going to Brussels?"

Country snapped his fingers. "In all the excitement I forgot to tell you. Give Gerry a call, he needs you boys in Belgium."

68

Jack Ryan, Jr., stood at gate C3 at Dulles International Airport, waiting to take a five-fifty p.m. Lufthansa flight to Brussels. He was dressed in a suit and tie and he carried a roll-aboard, more to follow his cover-for-action appearance as a businessman on a business trip than for any operational reasons. He probably wouldn't wear the suit on the ground in Brussels; he fully expected that once he got to his hotel he would change into neutral-tone adventure clothing so he could follow his target through the city in a low-profile fashion that was also comfortable and warm. This was going to be a one-man show, after all, so he needed to be ready for anything.

The televisions at the gate were all displaying CNN, and all the reports were talking about nothing other than the Russian action in Lithuania. One journalist had just relayed unconfirmed reports that American Army forces were on the ground to the east and west of the capital, which, if true, surprised Jack, since the news had spent most of the past two days talking about how his father's attempt to get NATO troops into Lithuania had failed so miserably.

Jack wondered if his father was unilaterally helping to defend Lithuania. It sounded like something he might do. *Jesus, Dad. Good luck with that.*

The gate agent asked any families traveling with children to board the plane. Jack was in first class; he would be called soon, so he stood up and pulled out his phone to open the boarding-pass app, but when he looked down at it he saw that Gerry was calling.

He closed his eyes.

At first he considered not answering it, but he couldn't just ghost his way out of his job. He knew he'd be fired, but he also knew Gerry would not physically prevent him from going to Europe. It wasn't like he could scare up cops to pull him off the flight and take him to the White House to confront his father.

Could he?

Jack answered, tried to pass off a casualness in his voice that he did not feel, because he knew this was the moment when everything he had built for himself in his five years with The Campus was about to come crashing down.

"Hi, Gerry."

"It's your lucky day, Jack."

Jack didn't feel so lucky. "How's that?"

"Ding and Dom are leaving Vilnius as we speak. I just got off the phone with them, informed them of your situation. They will meet you in Brussels as soon as you get there. You have a green light to conduct a surveillance package on Salvatore."

Jack's knees weakened to the point that he reached out and put a hand on the wall. His brain felt the rush of new information, and he tried to process it as quickly and cogently as he could. He'd be relieved in a moment, but for now it was all about acting relaxed on the phone to Gerry. Finally, he coughed out a measured response. "Okay. Glad to hear the boys are away from that war zone. That's the most important thing."

"Right," Gerry said.

There was a silence over the line. Jack looked up and saw that the monitor at the gate read: "First class, welcome to board." He said, "Was there something else, Gerry?"

After a pause, the director of The Campus said, "I know where you are, Jack. I know what you are about to do."

Jack closed his eyes again. *Damn it.* "Yes, sir. I'm sorry, I really am. I don't want to be here, but I am *sure* I am doing the right thing."

"For the operation, perhaps. But not for the long-term good. You are running the risk of exposing yourself."

Jack said, "The only thing that matters is the op. The minute this organization's mandate involves watching out for me because of who I am, that's the minute I need to leave The Campus. There is too much at stake in this mission to turn The Campus into a babysitting service for the President's son."

Gerry's southern drawl remained soft and calm, but there was an edge to it. "Go to Brussels. Do what you have to do, keeping in mind that Ding Chavez is the operational commander on this op. When you get back . . . we'll sit down and talk."

"Yes, sir. Good-bye." Jack hung up and got in line, boarded the 777, and took his seat in first class. As soon as he was situated, he pulled out a notebook and began making notes about the op to come. Chavez could walk in and run the op, but he'd need Jack to get him up to speed.

Jack Ryan, Jr., realized this might well be his last operation with The Campus, so he wanted to make it count.

President Jack Ryan had never spoken with Belarusan president Semyonov; he'd seen little reason to. Belarus had chosen its role in world affairs — they were puppets of the Russians. Ryan didn't necessarily blame them, they were culturally and anthropologically related, they were a bordering nation with no ability to protect themselves from their bigger neighbor, and Belarus's western neighbors' long-seated problems with the governments of Minsk and Moscow had fomented enough mistrust that it made sense Semyonov would look to the east, not to the West, for protection.

There was a U.S. embassy in Minsk, the two governments did have diplomatic relations, but Ryan had not wanted to give the Belarusan vassal state the political clout of direct talks with the highest level of the American government.

But none of that made a damn bit of difference to Ryan for the purposes of this phone call. He was willing to talk to the Belarusan president, and he was about to play hardball.

This wasn't diplomacy; this was war.

As soon as the translator confirmed Semyonov was on the line, President Ryan gave a quick and polite-enough greeting, which was returned by the Belarusan president through his translator, along with a short statement about how concerned Belarus was about the reports of the arrival of American marine and air forces near his sovereign territory.

Ryan wasn't having any of it. "President Semyonov, I did not call you to listen to your criticism. I called you to talk. You have allowed twenty-five thousand Russian combat troops into your nation for the sole purpose of attacking a peaceful neighbor. Perhaps two peaceful neighbors. You have every right to let anyone in your country you choose, but I feel it is my responsibility to inform you of the potential consequences of your actions. I have already given my military forces an order about their rules of engagement in this crisis. I have told them that the moment any missile, rocket, aircraft, or bullet is fired or launched from inside the Belarusan border, American forces are cleared to fire on any military target within Belarus. That does not mean they will destroy a single missile launcher and then stop. No, Mr. President. It means the moment a single missile launcher fires on my forces from your nation, all my forces are cleared to engage any and all military targets within Belarus. We will make no distinction between Russian and Belarusan forces, Russian and Belarusan equipment, Russian and Belarusan command and control. We will target your bridges, highways, and airfields if we deem them military targets.

"You have chosen an allegiance in this, Mr. President, and you must accept responsibility for what will happen to your nation if your partner threatens the forces of the United States, or our allies the Lithuanians."

The Belarusan president clearly thought the American President had been calling to ask for his help to blunt Russia's passage through his nation, to offer him something to get him to deny the Russian military its freedom of movement.

But now he realized nothing of the sort would be forthcoming. This was just belligerence from Jack Ryan. Threats and aggression.

Semyonov said, "Mr. President, you know full well my small nation has no capacity to deny the Russian Western Military District *anything.*"

Ryan replied, "I see this as a political decision, President Semyonov. You have invited them in with open arms, and therefore you have facilitated President Volodin's crimes. I've seen nothing from you that distinguishes you from him."

Ryan's tone darkened, and he hoped the translator conveyed this. "Mr. President, it would be very dangerous, and very costly, for my forces to enter Kaliningrad because that is Russian territory. But we can, and we will, enter into Belarus if we see the need to do so."

"*What?* Invade my nation?"

"If we deem it necessary to reduce the threat to Lithuania."

There was silence on the line for a moment as the Belarusan president tried to think of something to say.

Ryan filled the dead air. "One last thing, Mr. President. My diplomatic leaders remind me that your private offices are in the Republic Palace. And my generals have notified me this is also the location of a portion of your military apparatus." Ryan let this hang in the air until well after the interpreter finished with his translation. Then he said, "For the duration of your war with your neighbor, I suggest you relocate for your own personal safety." Another pause, and then, "I'd hate to have to reenact this phone call with your successor in case of some sort of mishap."

The Belarusan president shouted into the phone. "Your comments are outrageous!"

Ryan now dangled the carrot. "If you publicly distance yourself from Valeri Volodin, not the Russian Federation, but only the current Russian president, and if you conduct tangible actions to limit Russian access to your western region, if only logistical, procedural, or political actions, I would see your nation's role in this conflict in an entirely different light, and the actions of United States forces would be adjusted accordingly."

After a pause he said, "But to date, you have shown yourself to be the leader of a vassal state, so I have little hope of your independent thinking. I only pray you prove me wrong, because the lives of millions of people in your region of the world hang in the balance."

The call ended there.

Ryan put the handset back in the cradle and turned to Scott Adler, who had been seated next to the President's desk in the Oval Office. Adler hadn't heard the translations, although he would be handed a transcript within moments. But he had heard Ryan's end of it, and from that Adler gave a thin smile. "And *that*, Mr. President, was a back-alley beating."

"There was a time for me to be chief executive. When that failed, I became the nation's chief diplomat. Diplomacy has gone by the wayside as well. Now it's time to concentrate on my role as commander in chief. I'm all for letting the State Department work night and day to try to stop this war, but my only concern is in winning this war. Semyonov is a two-bit thug, and he only respects bigger thugs. That's why he's Volodin's underling. I had to show him I wasn't the laid-back smiling guy on television, that I can crack a skull if I need to."

Adler nodded. "Not how I learned to do things at the Foreign Service Institute, but admittedly, not much of what I learned there has helped me with Belarus."

Ryan smiled, then stood. "All I've accomplished so far is pissing off yet another corrupt Slavic leader. We'll have to see what happens." He looked at his watch. "Sorry, Scott. I have a meeting with the Joint Chiefs now, then I'm heading over to the UN to announce the fact I've committed troops independently of NATO. I have a feeling that call with Semyonov will turn out to be the most upbeat and friendly conversation I have today."

Adler said, "Mr. President, in order for this conflict to remain isolated, short, and sweet, we have to get Polish forces over the border to help out Lithuania, we have to convince NATO to join us now that there has been an Article Five violation. It would also be damn helpful for Sweden to give us some air support. I see all three of these issues as things I need to be concentrating on."

"I agree. Let's talk tonight, see where we stand on all these issues."

69

Russia's next move on Lithuania took place not on land, but over water. With the sinking of the Maltese-flagged oil-products tanker *Granite* the previous day, Lithuania's tiny navy had come out of its harbors and littorals and up to the edge of its maritime borders, a show of force against any potential Russian incursion into its territory.

This meant the Lithuanians did exactly what the Russians wanted them to do. Vilnius did not understand that the sinking of the *Granite* was conducted simply to draw out as many Lithuanian naval vessels as possible into international waters so they could be destroyed without Russian submarines risking detection inside Lithuanian waters.

The first boat to fall prey to a Russian Varshavyanka — their name for the advanced version of the NATO designated Kilo-class sub — was the *Kuršis,* a Hunt-class mine-countermeasures boat the Lithuanians had purchased from the United Kingdom five years earlier. At 196 feet in length, it was an impressive-looking vessel, and it did have an older-generation but functioning sonar for detecting submarines, but other than mini-guns and machine guns on its deck, it had no real firepower, and nothing at all on board to combat an undersea threat.

But the *Kuršis* was sent out to show the Russians that Lithuania meant business, and in so doing it was promptly torpedoed just three hours after beginning its patrol southwest of Lithuania.

At nearly the same time the *Kuršis* was sunk, the Lithuanian ship *Žemaitis* was targeted by the other Russian Kilo. Unlike the *Kuršis*, the Flying Fish–class fast patrol boat the Lithuanians had purchased from Denmark did have significant antisubmarine capabilities, including modern sonar and advanced MU90 torpedoes. But the crew of the *Žemaitis*, distracted by the attack on the *Kuršis*, positioned itself to attack the sub that killed their countrymen, and this proved to be a fatal error.

The *Žemaitis* detected the Varshavyanka that destroyed the Lithuanian minesweeper, and it focused its attention on the identified contact, preparing to launch a torpedo over the side down the heading of the launch. But before the captain could give the order to fire, his sonar technician screamed a warning that two new torpedo contacts had been detected going active, and they were heading on a bearing that indicated they had been fired from out in international waters.

In the direction of the *Žemaitis* itself.

The *Žemaitis* had some torpedo countermeasures on board, and the captain had been trained to create large and confusing wake patterns to bewilder the Russian Type 53s' wake-homing sensors, but the torpedoes' electronic brains sorted out the attempt at misdirection. The first of the two torpedoes raced under the hull of the 175-foot-long fast patrol boat, and the ensuing explosion ripped the *Žemaitis* in two, and the second torpedo detonated under the fresh wreckage, ensuring that not a soul survived.

By five a.m., four Lithuanian naval vessels — two old minesweepers, the Flying Fish–class fast patrol boat, and a Storm-class fast patrol boat — were all resting on the sandy bottom of the Baltic Sea. The two advanced Varshavyankas had fired eight torpedoes between them, killed eighty-four men, and left another fifty-seven to be rescued, many with grave injuries.

And while all this took place in the Baltic just to the northwest of Kaliningrad, due west of the oblast, far out in international waters, Russia's secret weapon waited two hundred twenty feet below the surface. The Severodvinsk-class submarine *Kazan,* having just arrived on station from the Northern

Fleet, had been ordered to sit to the side of the action on the first day of combat so that it could save itself for the bigger fish.

The sonar technicians on board the *Kazan* tracked and classed dozens of active contacts, but they were concerned with only a few of them. To the south of their position, the Navy of Poland lingered not far from its territorial waters. Two larger Oliver Hazard Perry–class frigates and a Kaszub-class corvette were all significant threats to Russia's Baltic Fleet, but so far they had not made any aggressive movements toward Kaliningrad, so the *Kazan* waited silently and patiently.

Poland also had a submarine that could potentially pose a danger, but the GRU, Russian military intelligence, had recent pictures of it entering dry dock for a month of repairs.

The captain of the *Kazan* had come all this way for a fight, and he was looking forward to the challenges ahead, but he did not find himself disappointed at all that he had been held in reserve while the older Varshavyankas of the Baltic Fleet earned the glory today in the largest naval battle in decades.

No, not at all. Because he knew the real challenge would come in the form of the American surface Navy, as well as American antisubmarine aircraft in the sky above. He was saving himself for the Poles and the Americans, and if he did his job correctly, no one would know he was here until it was too

787

late for either nation to do anything to stop him.

The Varshavyankas of the Baltic Fleet would die in this war, he had no doubt in his mind. But he had every intention of surviving this and bringing his *Kazan* to port in Kaliningrad with a heroes' welcome as soon as the West sued for peace.

Jack Ryan, Jr., passed through Belgian immigration after getting his passport stamped, then walked by the luggage carousels without stopping. He'd only brought a roll-aboard and a backpack along for the trip, so he shaved twenty minutes off his arrival.

He was relieved to make it through customs without getting his bag searched, although it was loaded with only a few surveillance devices, like FLIR cameras, NVGs, and high-end binoculars. He figured any real check of his belongings would have pegged him as some sort of a nut, but nothing he had with him was in any way illegal, so he'd not been terribly worried. Still, he wanted to get started with his surveillance here, so he was glad to make it through without delay.

Outside the arrivals hall, Jack smiled the biggest smile he'd displayed in two weeks. Dom and Ding were waiting for him, both standing next to a new black Audi Q3 SUV. Jack hadn't seen either man in six weeks, so there was an energetic round of embraces and back slaps, then all the men loaded up into the Audi with Chavez behind the wheel, and they left the airport.

"When did you guys arrive?" Jack asked.

Caruso said, "Just long enough ago to pick up the wheels and unload at the safe house. We had some excitement getting out of Lithuania."

"How bad was it?" Jack asked.

Ding replied, "Let's put it this way. The G550 is grounded here till six bullet holes in the horizontal stabilizer get patched."

"You're kidding."

"Russian Spetsnaz attacked the airport in Vilnius just as we were getting out of there."

Again, Jack felt the pain of not being with his mates when they needed him. It was similar to how he was feeling about Ysabel now. She was less than 120 miles away from him in a hospital, but he had no plans to go see her until this entire affair was over.

She wasn't safe around him, after all.

Jack recovered and said, "Well, this op will probably be a little boring to you guys, considering what you just went through. We're going to follow a smack addict around in the hopes he meets with some assholes I ran into last week in Luxembourg."

Chavez said, "We don't mind a little quiet surveillance. Sherman rented us a place just a few blocks south of where Salvatore is staying at the Stanhope Hotel. We just have eyes on the front of the building from our poz, but of course Gavin still has us tied in to the hotel's security camera. We've been monitoring him on a laptop while waiting for you to land, and we're recording everything for playback, just in case something is missed."

"What's he up to today?"

"He hasn't left his room."

Jack said, "Yeah, he was out late last night. I watched him on the plane for a while. Drinks in the lobby bar, then he went out the front door around ten. Don't know what time he got back to the room."

"Three a.m.," Chavez said. "But he wasn't operational last night."

"How do you know that?"

"The bastard staggered in drunk. He was just boozing it up in a bar somewhere. Whatever he's doing over here, apparently it involves him waiting around a lot. If he's here to take pictures of some celeb, my guess is that celeb isn't here yet. And if there is some bigger reason for his visit, he's just in a holding pattern. Waiting on instructions, maybe."

Once they were all in the third-floor walk-up apartment they were using for a safe house, the three men sat around a table. Chavez said, "We want to know what you've been up to, and we have some stories to tell you about what happened in the Baltic, but my read of this op gives me the impression we don't really know what our timeline is here. For that reason we need to save the chitchat and get down to work."

Jack nodded. "Yeah. Salvatore has reserved his room at the hotel for three more days, but whatever he's up to could happen anytime. We need to act before he goes operational. I have no idea when that will be, but I want to be able to track him. I have a GPS tracker and a RAT to put on his phone so we can listen in to his calls and read his texts."

Chavez asked, "You know how you want to get that on him?"

"I thought about a direct approach. Confronting him about Rome, slipping the RAT and the GPS beacon on him while I did it. The only problem is —"

Chavez finished the sentence. "That your presence here might scare him enough to get him to blow off his mission. In which case we'd lose the chance to find out what he's up to."

"Exactly," Jack said. "I might be able to strong-arm him into giving me the intelligence I need, but there's a chance he won't talk, or he'll just lie."

Caruso said, "I have an idea, but we'll have to wait for his next drink binge."

Chavez replied, "We'll use today to get set up. Tell us your plan."

Salvatore drained the last of his Stella Artois

into his mouth and wiped foam from his lips; then he picked up his backpack off the floor and slung it onto his shoulder. He slid off the barstool and headed out the door of the little bistro.

He leaned against a signpost on the curb, looking at the large selections of brasseries, wine bars, beer pubs, Italian eateries, and even hamburger joints in view, trying to decide where to go next. It was just eleven p.m., so the Italian thought he'd hit one more bar, or perhaps two, here in the European Quarter of Brussels before returning to his room.

He realized he needed to relieve himself, so he turned into the next bar he saw, a rustic place on a pedestrian-only strip. He stepped inside, saw a few old men at the bar and a bunch of empty tables, and he passed them all, following a sign directing him downstairs to the men's room.

He took a narrow masonry staircase down to the basement, followed a turn around stacked kegs of beer, and pushed open the accordion door to the tiny men's room. He stepped up to the one dirty toilet, unzipped his fly, and closed his eyes.

He didn't hear any noise until the accordion door opened behind him. The restroom was large enough for only one person, so he started to tell the other man to fuck off, but before he could even see who was behind him the light flipped off and he was shoved past the toilet and up against the wall.

He felt the knife against his lower back.

The man whispered angrily into his ear, but it was something in a foreign tongue he did not understand. Salvatore said, "English? English?" and the man quickly barked at him again.

"Your money! Give me your money!" the man said.

Salvatore couldn't believe he was being mugged at knifepoint. He felt his wallet pulled from his pants, his pack ripped from his back, and he heard the sound of someone rifling through his belongings. He kept his eyes slammed shut, he didn't say a word, and he fought the urge to piss down the wall he was pinned against.

And then, as quickly as the man had appeared, he was gone. First Salvatore felt the pressure of the man holding him against the wall removed, and then his wallet was tossed in the basin of the sink on his right. Last, the knife was pulled away from his back. Before Salvatore could even think about turning around to look, he heard the noise of his backpack being dropped to the ground in the basement outside the bathroom.

A minute later he left the bar with his backpack over his shoulder. He'd not complained to the manager and he surely hadn't reported the robbery. He was here in town for reasons that precluded his filing police reports.

Twenty minutes later, when he was sitting back in his hotel room, he checked his wallet and saw all his money was indeed gone. But his credit cards were there, as well as his Italian driver's license. He opened his backpack and saw that he'd been relieved of a few euros he'd kept in an outer pocket, but his cameras were still there, as was his mobile. This would have comforted most people, but the Italian didn't care as much about either of these things as he did the other item in his bag. Frantically his hand fought his way to the bottom of his pack, and he pulled out his bag of smack. He breathed his first sigh of relief since the mugging when he saw his heroin had not been touched.

Dom Caruso ran a thirty-minute surveillance-detection route after his operation to plant the tracker on Salvatore's backpack and the surveillance software on his mobile phone. His route took him past both Chavez and Ryan, who each sat alone in outdoor late-night cafés drinking beer.

Once the team was convinced Dom was in the clear, they all returned to their safe house on Rue du Commerce.

Dom said, "It's not the most understated way to plant a bug on someone, but it will work. I had him convinced I was just a street criminal who had followed him into the john."

Chavez said, "You made a good call and did a good job."

"Thanks," Dom said, then held up a wad of euros. "And I scored sixty-five euros. Do we need to tell Gerry, or can I order us a couple of pizzas for dinner tomorrow?"

It was a joke, at which Chavez laughed, but Jack was already watching Salvatore's position on his laptop. "He's back in his room at the Stanhope." He then checked the app on his phone that informed him of any use of the man's mobile. "The RAT did its job. We've got visibility on both audio and text messaging, but he hasn't used either yet."

"What about photos, e-mails, that sort of stuff?" Chavez asked.

Jack looked at all the apps on Salvatore's phone, visible now on Jack's laptop. "There's not a single picture on his phone from Brussels. But he's got cameras with him, so that doesn't mean he's not up here doing some sort of recon. And he doesn't even have an e-mail app on this thing. Either he's one hell of a Luddite —"

Dom said, "Or he's practicing operational security."

"Exactly," Jack said. "He didn't impress me with his tradecraft at all in Rome, but this might be a different kind of op. We'll just have to keep watching him to see what he gets himself into."

70

Vlad Kozlov stood in the doorway of Terry Walker's bedroom, remaining stone-faced while Walker tearily said good night to his wife and son over the walkie-talkie.

The routine had been set since Kozlov's second night here in the islands. Each evening at seven-thirty he and his four security men would deliver Walker and Limonov back to the rented villa on the top of Saint Bernard's Hill, where Kozlov immediately checked in with the two men maintaining the safe house. Then all six Steel Securitas men would split into two-man teams. Two would sleep while two held inner security in the villa and two more patrolled the grounds.

Limonov would eat something and retire to his room, then Kozlov would enter Walker's room, hand him the walkie-talkie for three minutes for him to communicate with his family. Once three minutes was up, he'd take the device and leave the room, locking Walker inside for the night.

Tonight had been no different from all the others until he returned to the kitchen to pour himself a vodka from the freezer. As soon as he lifted it to his lips, his phone rang.

"Allo?"

He recognized the voice of President Valeri Volodin. "Give me a report."

Kozlov hadn't heard from the Russian president personally since before he and Limonov had left London.

He cleared his throat quickly. "Things are proceeding as planned, Mr. President."

"Walker is giving you no trouble?"

"None."

"And Limonov? He is proceeding as advertised?"

"Yes, sir."

"So . . . no problems at all?"

"No, sir. Well . . . yes. We did have a security issue, but it has been dealt with."

"I pay you so that we do *not* have security issues."

"My apologies, Mr. President, but you pay me to deal with them. A man, an American, took a special interest in the boat where we are holding the family of Walker. I sent mercenaries to warn him off, but he persisted. When it became clear he was going to be a problem, we eliminated the problem very quietly."

"Who was he?"

"Undetermined, but we made sure he was

798

alone. He is out of the picture now, there is nothing to worry about."

Volodin barked angrily. "Don't be a fool, Kozlov, he will have confederates who will come looking for him."

"If they do, they will not suspect us, and they will not find us."

"Listen to me! I order you to bring in more help. You know this is a matter of particular interest to me. If anything happens to this operation —"

"Nothing can or will happen, Mr. President."

"You interrupt me again and I will have Grankin send someone down to slice your tongue out of your mouth."

A short pause. *"Izvaneetya."* Sorry.

"If anything happens to this operation, I will hold you responsible. You can imagine what that means."

"I can, Mr. President. I will contact specialists who will add support, *another* layer of support, to assist in our operation here in the British Virgin Islands."

"You will do it now."

"Yes, Mr. President."

The Sikorsky MH-60 Romeo helicopter moved slowly, just barely more than a hover five hundred feet over the blue water of the eastern Baltic. The gray of the helo blended with the gray skies above, a nice feature for an aircraft that did not want to advertise its location to anyone on the surface, or anyone below the surface looking through a periscope.

This helicopter, call sign Casino One-One, did not own the sky here; it shared it with its sister helicopter, Casino One-Two, which patrolled twenty-three miles to the west.

The role of both helos was submarine detection, classification, tracking, and ultimately, destruction. To achieve this aim, every few minutes Casino One-One descended to within five hundred feet of the surface, lowered an AN/AQS-22 airborne low-frequency sonar from an umbilical, and dipped it below the ocean surface. The active sonar signal searched the waters for the two submarines identified the evening before.

So far neither helo had turned up any contacts beyond the surface ships in the area, of which there were many.

Each time Casino One-One turned back to the east on its pattern, the two-man, one-woman crew could plainly see the rescue mission continuing in the waters closer to the Lithuanian coast. Four ships had been sunk in a three-hour period the previous evening, and seeing evidence of the slaughter that had taken place on the ocean surface the night before instilled in the flight crew of Casino One-One a special dedication to the mission at hand.

They lived on a surface ship, after all, and their home was coming this way.

The *James Greer* (DDG-102) had no role in the rescue-and-recovery mission of the four Lithuanian naval vessels; that was left to others. The guided missile destroyer was the most dangerous threat to the Russian subs in the water, so it, and its two MH-60 Romeos, would focus on detecting, controlling, and engaging the enemy.

There were some assumptions made in this search by the American warship. For one, Russia's Baltic Fleet was known to have a Lada submarine, but it was currently undergoing repairs at the port of Kaliningrad. This meant the two advanced Kilo submarines, called Varshavyankas by the Russians, were the likely culprits of the five torpedo attacks of the previous two days.

Knowing the identities of the targets meant knowing their offensive and defensive capabilities. The Kilo fired Type 53-65 torpedoes, which had an effective range of 25,000 meters. This meant the two MH-60 Romeos had to dip the waters in a wide arc more than fifteen miles in front of its destroyer to ensure their ship was safe from lurking hunters.

At present the *Greer* was nearly twenty miles to the northwest of its two helicopters, so the MH-60 Romeos served as the vanguard with room to spare.

The *James Greer* itself had an impressive

array of equipment to hunt for undersea threats.

A hull sonar, a multifunction towed array, as well as variable-depth sonar that could dip below the various thermal layers submarines use to hide. All systems were currently configured to passive so the *James Greer* did not give away its location to the enemy, but since the Romeos were using active sonar, there was little doubt the Kilos knew there was a new component to the surface warfare hunt for them, and they would react accordingly.

That meant either they would run, they would hide, or they would attack.

Casino One-One made another dip into the ocean, and again the sensor operator on board reported negative contact. The Romeos were getting closer to Russia's waters off Kaliningrad, and the pilot of Casino One-One suspected the Kilos had bolted for the safety of their territory, but he didn't let his guard down for a moment. A Kilo lurking below him could possibly hear his rotors, and either descend deeper and run away or surface and attack the Romeo. It was known that Russian Kilos carried SA-14 man-portable air-defense systems, shoulder-fired antiaircraft missiles that could be launched by an operator standing in the conning tower.

The Kilos weren't just a threat to surface ships. Casino One-One's captain knew that his aircraft could fall prey to a Russian sub as well.

Commander Scott Hagen read his latest op orders from Sixth Fleet Command in Naples, and he blew out a long sigh. He'd have to classify the information as part good news, and part bad, but he told himself if nothing else it would light a fire under his butt, and the butts of his crew.

As if they needed more incentive for finding a pair of submarines that might just kill them.

The USS *Normandy,* a Ticonderoga-class cruiser, and the USS *Mustin,* an Arleigh Burke–class guided missile destroyer one generation older than the *James Greer,* were at this moment racing to join up with a Wasp-class amphibious assault ship in the North Sea. Already with the amphibious assault ship were a San Antonio–class amphibious transport dock ship, and a Harpers Ferry–class dock landing ship. The five vessels would form into an amphibious ready group, and then sail together around the Jutland Peninsula, through the Øresund Strait between Denmark and Sweden, and then finally into the Baltic.

It would take them two and a half days to arrive in the waters around Lithuania, and Commander Hagen knew that while the arrival of the big cruiser and the potent guided missile destroyer would be a tremendous help in the approaching fight against Russia's Baltic Fleet, the fact these two ships would be arriving just ahead of two thousand U.S. Marines on three other ships meant Hagen damn well needed to have these waters safe enough for an amphibious landing by the time the task force arrived.

And to that end he'd called for one of his junior officers. A knock at the door to his stateroom got his attention, and he looked up to see a fresh-faced lieutenant with blond hair and a nervous expression. Hagen had read the man's file again this afternoon, and he knew the man was thirty, but to Hagen he looked like he could have been sixteen.

Now even the LTs are starting to look like kids, he said to himself. *You're getting old, Scott.*

"Come on in, Weps. Take a seat."

Lieutenant Damon Hart did as directed, sitting on the chair in front of his captain's desk.

"I saw you in the CIC around midnight. You've been working all night?"

"Yes, sir."

"I'll keep this brief, and when I'm done with you I want you to get some chow and hit the rack. I need you ready when we get closer to Russian waters."

"We're going in after them, sir?"

"Not as of yet. But since they've been coming out after the Lithuanians, there's no reason to think they're going to stay in their territorial waters when we get close."

"No, sir. But I can't believe they'd really want to mess with us. Our torpedoes are better, we have air assets that can take them out at standoff range. I know their diesel boats are hard to find, but if they come out to play, even for just a second, we'll annihilate them. They know this, so there's no way they'd do that."

"I like your optimism, but you need to dispel any reliance on logic here. I'm sure the captains of those Kilos know we have a better weapons platform than they do. But you don't know what their orders are. For all we know, Moscow is on the horn with those Kilos right now demanding they make an undersea banzai charge right up our gut."

The lieutenant nodded, chastened. Damon Hart was a graduate of the Navy's new Naval Surface and Mine Warfighting Development Center, a Top Gun program for surface warfare officers chosen to be the best of the best, who were then given training to hone their skills to an even sharper point. Then they were sent back out into the fleet, with a mission to bring the level of naval combat up all over the Navy.

Hart's actual job here on the *James Greer* was as a warfare tactics instructor. It was his job to make certain every surface warfare officer on the ship knew everything he needed to know about every enemy weapon, tactic, and procedure, as well as U.S. Navy doctrine for finding and destroying undersea threats.

The fact Hart had the details down cold did not necessarily mean he understood the psychology of his enemy, and his captain wanted to make sure he was ready for war. War did not always follow conventional wisdom, or even rational behavior.

Hagen said, "Weps, you're the best-trained USW officer in the fleet and you're on my ship. I'm going to work you like a damn dog until this is over, and you are going to push everyone here, including me, if necessary, to fight these Russians the right way. Are we clear on that?"

"Yes, sir."

"Good. Now those Kilos hit all four of those ships during darkness last night. Doesn't mean they'll wait till nightfall to come back out, but they are going to be looking for every advantage they can find. If they hit again, it might not be till tonight. So I want you rested."

A few minutes later Hart ate chow in the officers' mess. He was tucked into a corner by himself, a half-eaten chicken salad sandwich on his plate and two large paperback books in his lap. On the bottom was his old dog-eared copy of the RP 33, the *Fleet Oceanographic and Acoustic Reference Manual,* a sort of bible of undersea science from a submarine and antisubmarine warfare practitioner's perspective. He basically knew the damn thing by heart, but he kept it close by all the time for quick reference.

On top of this was the latest edition of *Introduction to Physical Oceanography*. As he ate his sandwich he perused this, looking up some salinity equations he might need in this part of the Baltic.

Hart would read for a few hours, doing his best to push every bit of information needed for prosecuting an undersea target in these waters to the ready reserve in his brain. Antisubmarine warface moves fast, he knew, and seconds counted. If he ran into one of those Kilos tonight, Hart didn't want to have to pull out a pair of dog-eared books to remind himself what to do.

The troop transport train infiltration of Russian Spetsnaz forces into Vilnius County was eighteen hours old, and though the results were far short of the Russians' H-Hour+18 objective for the op, the plan did achieve the desired effect of wreaking havoc on the Lithuanian population. Rumors of battalions of Russians in the capital city were broadcast on radio and television, on social media, and throughout the foreign press.

As was often the case with late-breaking news, the truth was quite different from the reality. By seven a.m. at the airport terminal and tower, Russian troops were overpowered after a firefight with a combined force of ARAS federal counterterror operators and a company of elite military Special Purpose Unit troops. The Russians had better training, as well as solid defensive positions, but the Lithuanians had the advantage in sheer numbers and equipment, as well as massive amounts of tear gas.

Twenty-one of the Russians were killed in the three-hour-long battle, compared with forty-five Lithuanians, most in the initial attack and a disastrous counterattack conducted by well-motivated but outclassed airport security staff.

The airport remained closed for most of the day due to damage to the radars on the roof of the terminal as well as the persistent cloud of tear gas that hung in the stairwells of the control tower, but once the Russians lost control of the facility, the Russian troop transports circling to the east over Belarus were forced to return to the airport in Smolensk with their airborne troops.

The Spetsnaz operation to temporarily hold choke points throughout the capital city had fared better than the airport operation. Here, more than forty men reached their objective waypoints, causing pandemonium during the morning rush hour as small-scale gun battles between Russian Alpha Group and Lithuanian police seemed to flare up all over the city.

But here again, the Russian operation fell short of its goals. The unit's orders had been to spend two hours out in the streets creating chaos, and then melt away to a large wooded park in the north of the city, where a group of Serbian paramilitaries specially trained for the mission would be waiting with stolen vehicles, clothing, medical equipment, and other resupply. The Serbians had been infiltrated a week earlier with tourist visas, and as recently as twelve hours before the Russian military train arrived in the country, the Serbs had sent word that all was ready. But when the twenty-six surviving Russian special-operations troops arrived at their rally point in the parking lot next to the forest, they found only six Serbians in three vehicles, little in the way of supplies, and a story about how their mission had been undone by a police ambush the evening before where a dozen of their ranks had been killed or wounded.

As the remnants of the Russian and Serbian Spetsnaz men tried to exfiltrate the park, they were confronted by a company-sized element of Lithuanian Land Force volunteers, poorly trained and outfitted young men who had only numbers on their side.

In the ensuing bloodbath the combined Spetsnaz unit killed more than fifty men but suffered heavy losses itself. The few surviving

Spetsnaz, all Russian, retreated bloody and broken into the park when their ammunition ran out.

71

Lieutenant Colonel Rich Belanger had spent most of his first full day careening around in a light armored vehicle from his attached Light Armored Reconnaissance platoon, checking on all his Marines' preparations. He stopped at his companies' command posts to visit with each commander.

The CP of India Company, called "Diesel," was an old farmhouse with the men dug in out front in the woods. The CP of Kilo Company, "Sledgehammer," was in the rear in reserve with the tanks, ready to go into the counterattack when ordered. Lima Company, called "Havoc," was south of the others, in the woods in ambush positions looking out onto the E28, the main east-west highway that conventional wisdom said the Russians would use to drive straight through to Vilnius.

The weapons company, who used the call sign "Vandal," had their heavy M2 .50-caliber machine guns spread among the three companies and their 120-millimeter and 81-

millimeter mortars well to the rear of the battalion, prepared to fire a hail of steel rain over the lines and onto the Russian advance. The Vandal commander, during combat, would move into the Darkhorse combat command center, where he would control all his fires, including air and mortars. Also in the CP, Darkhorse's intelligence officer had just gotten the satellite comm systems up and running, and was trying to download the latest intelligence from EUCOM.

By early afternoon, Lieutenant Colonel Belanger, whose call sign was "Darkhorse 6," was confident his battalion was ready for a fight, but his concerns extended far beyond the twelve hundred men under his command. Small sporadic pockets of Lithuanian Land Force troops continued to surge forward, all over the eastern part of the country, without any real direction as far as he could discern from their attached exchange officers.

They moved around from south of Vilnius to halfway up to the Latvian border, and Belanger had been concerned he would be rushed into action only to be slowed down by having to push his way through roads clogged by their aging vehicles still trying to make it to the border regions or, even worse, by civilian refugees fleeing rearward in the face of the Russian advance.

And that was just one of his many burdens today. The USMC colonel in charge of him, the Black Sea Rotational Force commander, had tasked his intelligence officer with a lot of additional collection duties. Among the most pressing was keeping the BSRF regimental headquarters up-to-date with the latest information out of Vilnius.

All morning long and into the afternoon, Belanger's intel officer passed word to the regiment back in Stuttgart about a force of enemy sappers who had snuck in on one of the cargo trains and set about conducting sabotage operations in the city.

Finally, the intelligence officer called Belanger in his LAV C2 as he was touring the company engagement areas and suggested Lithuanian army reports had begun to coincide with the news reports they'd been watching on the Internet and CNN. Only a few Russian saboteurs remained; they had been flushed out and into the woods north of the city. Their infiltration game in Lithuania appeared to be over.

On television the Lithuanian government displayed a couple dozen Russian prisoners standing outside at the airport. Heads down in defeat, arms zip-tied behind their backs.

Belanger took one look at them and knew they were Alpha Group men, the best Russia had to offer. While most laypeople in Lithuania took their victory over the Russian commando unit as a sign that their nation could take anything the Russians had to dish out, the Marine lieutenant colonel had a more sober take on the news.

The fact the Russians had a hundred Alpha Group men they could sacrifice on what looked to be little more than a suicide mission into the center of Lithuania before the war even kicked off told Belanger that Russia had thousands of different GRU and Interior Ministry Spetsnaz troops to work with on the front lines. Troops he was certain to meet in the next hours or days, because he knew there were a lot more of those black-clad bastards just over the border in front of him.

Word came down through intel channels that some analysts at the Pentagon had identified a stretch of Belarusan border almost seventy-five kilometers long where the Russian army was mustering; this was likely where they would breach the border. Any farther north or south and they would find themselves away from trafficable roads, or too far from Vilnius, their main objective in the country.

Within this expanse there were four main arteries bisecting the border, and while Russian tanks didn't need to adhere to roads to attack, their truck-bound infantry, their supply, and the Russian heavy artillery would necessarily proceed on one or more of these roads, so it stood to reason the attack would emanate from one of these areas. Without the infantry, artillery, and a steady source of supply, the tanks would have a tough time in the thick forests and broken fields of Lithuania.

This narrowed down the location of the attack even further, Belanger and his intel officer surmised. To the extent Belanger had divided Darkhorse Battalion into three self-sufficient sections and placed them in three distinct locations near the four roads, they were prepared.

One rifle company could not stop a division-strength Russian invasion, of course, but Belanger had to have someone ready to engage the enemy while the intelligence officers checked the satellite data and confirmed this *was,* in fact, the spearhead of the Russian invasion, so the rest of his forces could maneuver onto the Russian advance.

The call he had been expecting for twelve hours finally came from EUCOM at dusk. Overhead platform surveillance of enemy troops in Belarus indicated a push to the border was under way, and it was happening in two places simultaneously: on the other side of the border from the Lithuanian town of Magunai in the north, and straight along highway E28, which led from Minsk to Vilnius.

Instantly Lieutenant Colonel Belanger knew his battalion would have to fight on two fronts, fifty kilometers apart. He dreaded it, but he would have to split his forces.

One half of all Lithuania's meager resistance force was already largely set up at the E28 at the crossing; it was Belarus's closest point to Vilnius, so the area was already defended by Land Force soldiers with World War II–era 105-millimeter howitzers, a few newer 155-millimeter howitzers from Germany, and dozens of mortars of different sizes. There were thousands of troops already in trenches, and sandbagged emplacements along the roads, but the space was wide-open enough for Russian tanks to use the fields and pastures to make their way toward the capital.

Belanger knew they could mow right over the Lithuanians unless the defenders received a lot of help from Darkhorse.

No, the local defense wasn't sufficient, but Belanger kept his India Company, along with a platoon from his weapons company and a few tanks and Cobra helicopter gunships, in the south at the predefined locations given to him from the EARLY SENTINEL deployment program. Each antitank missile, each mortar, each heavy machine gun, and each rifle squad was assigned a ten-digit grid and an azimuth of fire. Fighting holes were dug, equipment was moved under cover, and machine-gun and heavy-weapon range cards were drawn up to support integrated defenses.

Kilo and Lima infantry companies, and some heavy guns and antitank rockets and missiles from the weapons company, were ordered north to Magunai, where they were given defensive positions throughout the city and in the nearby farms and forests. Lima was in front, within sight of the Belarusan border, and Kilo stayed to the southwest, ready as Belanger's counterattack force, or to race all the way down to help India if absolutely necessary.

Belanger's intel officer identified that the expected northern breach zone for the Russians was virtually undefended by Lithuania, so the Marines would have to do the lion's share of the work to stop the Russian attack.

Belanger moved his forward command post into a supporting position behind his Lima Company, then ordered forward air controllers, plus a few JTACs — joint terminal attack controllers, scrounged from other units — to be split among all his company's strongpoint defensive locations.

By nine p.m. the Marines of India Company in the southern positions got word through their Lithuanian counterparts that they were seeing a mass of lights over the border from hundreds of vehicles. To the north, near Lima's zone and near Belanger's command post, they were able to see a wide glow over the rolling farmland as the Russian armor moved into position.

Belanger himself stood in the third-story

science lab of a shuttered elementary school in Magunai, as close to the front lines as any battlefield commander could possibly be. The lead elements of his battalion, his scout snipers, were in Prienai, one mile to the east, but his main force was spread out in the streets and houses and shops and out into the farmland of the tiny hamlet all around him. His heavy and medium mortars were a kilometer down a gravel road behind him, set behind a copse of trees.

Right in front of Darkhorse, intelligence estimates suggested there could be as many as eighty Russian T-90s, each complete with state-of-the-art targeting computers, night and thermal vision, explosive reactive armor, and sights that could see well out to ten kilometers. Belanger had studied anti-Soviet doctrine, and in the coming fight he was going to need all the information those old men in his Marine antiarmor schools had taught him. Most of those old-timers had fought in the Gulf War against second-generation T-72s. Hell, he'd seen a load of T-72s himself while fighting insurgents in Iraq, but they were all burnt out and picked clean by the Bedouins.

Belanger realized he had one thing in his favor, though. The same thing that had saved the bacon of his Army brothers in Bastogne. Amazing U.S. and coalition air support. Harriers, F-18s, and Cobra and Apache gunships were his for the tasking. And now, as the light grew in the east, he was fucking *certain* he would have a lot of work for them to do very soon.

A voice came over the radio set from his radioman's backpack.

"Havoc Six, Banshee Two, over?"

Belanger had been looking at a digital map with his operations officer, but he turned when he heard the call. Belanger knew Banshee Two was one of his best scout sniper teams, headed by Sergeant McFarland. They were positioned in a grove of trees next to an open field two kilometers from Lima Company's defensive positions in Prienai and a kilometer from his present spot in the forward command post.

Lima Company's commander was a captain named Ludlow, whose call sign was Havoc. Belanger listened to Ludlow's reply.

"Banshee Two, Havoc. Go for Six actual."

"Roger. Interrogative: Request Six actual confirm no friendly air-breathers southwest of phase line Red."

"Roger, Banshee, this is Six actual. I copy and confirm. Darkhorse-fires states all friendly aviation remains staged at their FARP's or on strip alert." The Lima Company commander was confirming all friendly helos were in their forward-area rearming points and the jets were ready for takeoff on the runways.

"Copy. In that case, be advised. Contact, enemy UAV. UAV travels east over phase line White. Will cross phase line Red in about three mikes. Altitude six hundred MSL. Rate of march approximately twenty-five kph."

Belanger listened while Ludlow asked a few more questions about the UAV. Its behavior, whether or not it was large enough to be armed or if it was enemy reconnaissance only.

After a few minutes of conversation, Belanger gave a long sigh of frustration, and took the headset from his radio operator. "Banshee Two, this is Darkhorse. Can you engage with SASR?" he said, referring to the snipers' M82 .50-caliber sniper rifle.

"Negative, sir. Its rate of march is too fast. Suggest either one of our crew-serveds or a Stinger. Otherwise it'll have free visual on all Lima Company's friendly positions in about two mikes."

Belanger said, "Banshee Two, Darkhorse copies all. Continue your mission, scan and report activity in your zone on this net. Break, break, Vandal Three, this is Darkhorse Six."

Vandal Three was the machine-gun section assigned to India Company.

"Go for Vandal Three," came the voice of the machine-gun section leader.

Belanger asked, "You have eyes on that UAV?"

"That's A-firm, Darkhorse."

Belanger did not hesitate. "Kill it."

Belanger actually thought he could hear a smile on the face of his machine gunner as he responded over the radio. "Vandal Three copies all. Engaging; time now."

The deep-throated thumping of the M2 echoed through the woods and into the village. It fired in short five-round bursts. Paused. Then fired again. Belanger couldn't see the shooting, but with his twenty years of experience he knew the gunner was using the linked four-in-one tracers in the five-round bursts to get a lead on the target. That kind of fire discipline is what he'd always preached to his company and platoon commanders. He thought for a minute, trying to remember who would be behind that weapon. He knew all his men pretty well, but there were so many, sometimes it took him a while to remember.

Yes. That was Sergeant Ascherbrock leading that machine-gun section. Ascherbrock knew his shit.

Within ten seconds the short bursts stopped.

"Darkhorse Forward or Darkhorse Six," came the voice of Sergeant Ascherbrock.

"This is Darkhorse Six, go ahead."

"Roger, sir. UAV is a KIA, in the field one klick west of our position. Do you need a grid?"

"Negative, we have the general location."

Belanger nodded and allowed himself a

slight smile. The men upstairs with him in the Darkhorse Forward CP pumped their fists in the air.

The lieutenant colonel rolled his eyes. "Congratulations, studs, now let's dial that shit back. We just killed the smallest speck of nothing in the Russian arsenal."

The intel officer looked up from his station and said, "Gotta start somewhere, sir, and I don't mind taking out some of the Russians' eyes."

"Yeah, Deuce, understood, but I'm certain their video feeds are playing back our front lines in Technicolor right now."

"Don't matter, sir, those fucks just got Darkhorsed!" said his radio operator.

Belanger suppressed a chuckle. If he survived this night, he knew he'd never forget it.

His chuckle didn't last, because he knew what was coming, and it came instantly.

The scream of incoming rockets filled his ears.

72

Martina Jaeger had complained to her brother incessantly for the past six days that she was bored to death because there wasn't a damn thing to do around Amsterdam. To this her brother Braam had pointed out helpfully that she had partied in the techno clubs around the city, she'd eaten the best meals, and taken the best drugs. She'd biked sixty miles through the countryside and she'd worn out her air rifle at the range.

Sure, she'd allowed, but still she'd grown accustomed to back-to-back operations for the Russians over the past several weeks, so the downtime felt especially slow and meaningless.

She needed some real action.

For Braam's part, he had enjoyed being back in Amsterdam. He'd worked out in his gym and wrestled in his local dojo, he'd biked with his sister and watched a lot of television. He figured he could stand another week of this easy living before he would feel the restlessness Martina had been showing since the second day back at home.

Still, for her sake he was happy to see a new instant message pop up on the TOR application on his computer this evening. He knew it would be the Russians, and he knew they never checked in to ask about the weather.

No, he and his sister were about to get a new contract.

Braam opened the instant message and read it. He found himself happy with the order, but he knew Martina would need some convincing.

He called across his living room, affecting a cheery voice. *"Goed nieuws, zus!"* Good news, sis. "They want us back in the BVIs."

Martina let out a groan of annoyance. "No! Tell them no way. We were just there, and it was just as dead as it is here."

Braam read the message aloud. "We request your immediate return to support an ongoing operation in the British Virgin Islands." He looked up. "It sounds like it's more action than the last time."

Martina sat up on the sofa. "Not to me it doesn't. When it's a wet operation they are always very clear on the target."

Braam said, "I'll ask for more details."

"Suit yourself, but I'm not going."

Braam typed for a moment while Martina looked on from the sofa. Finally, he said, "It says, 'Senior management is concerned about hostile actors in the area who are attempting to infiltrate our operation. Your expertise is required in eliminating the threat.' " Braam looked up at Martina. "That's a wet op."

"No, it's another babysitting mission."

" 'Eliminating a threat.' What else could that possibly mean?"

She looked at her brother for a long moment, sighed, then rolled off the couch as dramatically as she'd fallen onto it. Her brother could see she wasn't happy about taking the contract, but she would do it anyway.

She said, "It either means he has someone for us to terminate, or I am going to terminate him for wasting my time."

Braam shrugged. "I'm glad we're going back. You should try the Anegada lobster this time. It is really worth the trip."

Martina Jaeger shook her head in disbelief. "Flying halfway around the world for dinner is idiotic. Going that distance to kill a man for money — now, *that* is a trip worth taking."

Braam said, "I'll let you pull the trigger if you let me have my lobster. That way, we'll both enjoy ourselves."

She tousled her brother's hair as she passed him by at the desk, then headed to her bedroom to pack.

Jack Ryan, Jr., was sound asleep at noon,

wrapped in covers with a large pillow over his head to block out the light. He'd worked the night shift alone, eight entire hours of boring surveillance, while the pair just in from Lithuania got some real sleep, but now they were up and he was down, crashed in the back room on one of two twin beds in the third-floor flat.

His target had gotten drunk again last night after an afternoon in his hotel. Jack had even managed to get eyes on the man in the bar of the hotel down the street by using his spotting scope, although in truth the video feed from the hotel's house security camera gave him essentially the same information. Still, it was good to be over here, just one hundred yards away from Salvatore, after days of watching the man from 3,500 miles away in Virginia.

All through the night Jack kept one ear turned to BBC Radio on his computer so he could listen to the latest of what was going on in Lithuania. Of course, he would rather have been watching the news, but he never used the TV at night in the safe house because the moving light that shone through the windows could have drawn attention from those in other buildings or on the street involved in countersurveillance.

But BBC Radio was a good source of info, and by the time he went to bed at seven a.m. it had been confirmed United States Marines and Lithuanian Land Force troops were in heavy combat with Russian army forces inside the tiny Baltic nation. American Air Force and Navy aircraft were flying constant sorties, and even Poland was getting into the mix, flying F-16, MiG-29, and even old Su-22 aircraft on attack runs at Kaliningrad-based missile batteries.

Jack wondered if the American planes in the sky had trouble with MiGs flying on both sides of the war against the Russians.

Pundits on BBC Radio had expressed surprise that the Russian invasion had come exclusively from the east; the oblast of Kaliningrad had 25,000 combat troops poised to invade Lithuania from the west, but so far they had remained on their side of the border. Some suspected it was just a matter of time before they did push east, but others pontificated that Russia thought invading from Belarus would protect Kaliningrad from NATO retaliatory strikes if NATO eventually did get involved.

When Chavez and Caruso woke up, Jack passed them each a cup of coffee, then reported the news from Lithuania. Then he informed them they'd missed absolutely nothing in Brussels while they slept. Soon afterward he went to bed himself, hoping to be rested and ready when Salvatore finally did something, *anything,* that would make it worthwhile for the three Americans to have come over here.

He hoped that would be later today, and went to sleep with his fingers crossed.

He'd been asleep four hours when he felt someone grab his leg and shake it. He sat up quickly and balled his fists, coiling an arm back to throw a punch.

"Relax, cousin. It's just me."

His bleary eyes focused on Dominic, standing next to the bed in the dark bedroom, dressed in a black jacket and a brown watch cap. "It's on. Salvatore just got a call from someone who sounds like he could be his Russian contact."

Jack struggled to pull his jeans on as he rushed out of the bedroom, meeting Ding in the living room a moment later. Chavez was also wearing a dark-colored insulated jacket, along with a black knit cap. His car keys were next to him on the desk by the window.

Chavez said, "Listen to this." He played back an audio file on the laptop in front of him. An accented voice spoke in English. "You will go now to the Sofitel Brussels Europe, fifth floor. There someone will meet you and give you instructions. Just wait in the hall."

Then Jack recognized Salvatore's voice. "I understand. Where is it?"

"Take a cab. The driver will know where it is. Ten minutes from your hotel."

"I'm on my way."

Ding looked through the spotting scope in the front window. It was focused on the entrance to the Stanhope up the street. "He just climbed into a taxi. We need to move."

Jack put on his tennis shoes, then pulled on his brown leather jacket and pulled a gray skull cap over his hair.

All three men grabbed their Smith & Wesson M&P Shield nine-millimeter pistols and tucked them into Pistol Wear concealment holsters under their shirts. Each man also had his med pouch and two spare eight-round magazines slipped in the fabric band that held their weapons tight to their bodies.

In thirty seconds all three men grabbed their prepacked go bags by the door, and then they were rushing down the stairs of the building. Outside in the parking lot behind the building, they climbed into their black Audi SUV. Chavez got behind the wheel, Caruso in the front passenger seat, and Jack in the back. Both Dom and Jack had open laptops.

As they took off, Jack quickly texted Gavin, "Guest list at Sofitel Hotel. Run against KAs of Mikhail Grankin, KA of Andrei Limonov, plus any FSB, Kremlin, or Russian OC."

Jack knew Gavin had already created databases of the known associates of the different players in this operation, and Gavin also had a large and well-maintained file on Russian organized crime personalities. In twenty seconds he received a reply from Gavin acknowledging the request.

While Jack waited on Gavin, he pulled up the Sofitel's website, and looked at the list of conferences for the next few days. There was a meeting of a local symphony orchestra sponsors' group, a meeting of European estate attorneys, and a conference on gene therapy. Nothing that seemed like it would generate interest from either the paparazzi or Russian intelligence.

As Chavez drove he said, "Hey, Jack, don't know if it's relevant, but we're pretty much driving through the center of the European Union."

Jack looked up from his work, and out the windows of the SUV, and saw the massive Berlaymont Building, the headquarters of the European Commission. On the other side of the street they passed the Charlemagne Building, another office complex for the EU.

Dom said, "Maybe what we're looking for isn't at the hotel. That's just a rally point. Maybe there's going to be some sort of surveillance operation against the EU."

Jack said, "Could be, but there could be a thousand targets for Russian intel here. I'm sure they'd want to spy on every office in a ten-block radius if they could. We'll have to just see what Salvatore does."

Gavin called right back, and Jack answered

quickly, "Anything, Gavin?"

"Not a damn thing, Ryan. Sorry. If any known associate or Russian intel actor is staying at that hotel, they are checked in under a legend that has not been flagged by any of the Five Eyes intelligence agencies."

"Shit. Okay, Gav. Talk to you later." Ryan looked up again now. The Lex Building, another ultramodern EU high-rise, loomed over them. In front of it a group of protesters held signs. Jack couldn't read them, but it gave him an idea. "Wait! You still there?"

Gavin Biery had not yet hung up. "What's up?"

"Forget the Russians. Look and see if any known associate of Salvatore is staying at the hotel. Somebody in one of those protest groups he's been involved with. Greenpeace, antiglobalization, that sort of thing."

"Shit, Ryan, that will take some time. I don't have that automated like I do with the Russians."

"It's important, Gavin. You can send me half the names and I'll start looking them up."

Gavin said, "No, I can lump the hotel guests into a file and run it against Interpol, to see which guests have been arrested. Then I'll have to check the results one at a time to see what they were arrested for. There are two hundred twenty guests so give me about —"

Gavin stopped talking suddenly. Then he spoke with amazement. "Well, would you look at that."

"What is it?"

"One of the rooms at the Sofitel. Room 514. It's under the name Luigi Vignali."

Jack had heard this name before. He said, "Wait . . . that's Salvatore's real name."

Gavin's voice displayed his confusion. "Right. What do you think that means?"

Jack thought quickly, knowing time was in short supply. He'd listened to Salvatore get the message about coming to the Sofitel. He didn't seem to know where the place was. It made no sense that he was already renting a room there, in addition to the one in the Stanhope.

Jack looked up suddenly. The hotel was dead ahead.

He said, "It means Salvatore is being set up. Someone called him there so he'd be at that location. A location they've tied him to by taking a room in his name."

"But who?" asked Chavez from behind the wheel.

Caruso's head spun around and he looked at Jack. "The bomb at the LNG facility in Lithuania."

"What about it?"

"The body that washed up, the female diver. The Lithuanians thought she was just a patsy. Set up by the Russians, brought to the scene thinking she was part of some sort of protest and then killed. Just to throw off the scent that it was an FSB op all along."

Jack didn't know much about the bombing in Klaipėda. He hadn't been following it closely at all. As far as he knew, he was involved in an entirely different type of operation. "Are you suggesting someone is bringing Salvatore here to use him to take the fall for another attack?"

"We know that the Russians have used him before."

Jack looked down at his laptop and typed in "EU Brussels conferences" and the current date.

A quick glance showed him more than two dozen things going on in Brussels, most of them right here in the European Quarter in the various meeting spaces around the EU buildings. He scrolled down slowly, then his eyes locked on one event. He said, "The European Oil and Gas Conference kicked off this morning. It says it's an annual meeting with three hundred attendees, men and women at the pinnacle of the European oil and gas industry, as well as many government ministers from all over the continent."

Caruso asked, "Where is it?"

Jack typed the name of the conference center in Google Maps. While he looked it up Chavez pulled into a parking place on the Place Jourdan, right in front of the Sofitel.

Jack looked up from his computer. "The conference center is next door to the Sofitel. Right around the corner from us right now. He held his phone back to his ear. "Gavin, give me the real-time feed for the fifth floor of the hotel."

Nothing happened on Jack's laptop. "Gavin?"

Over the line he said, "It's not coming up. Someone else has hacked the feed, maybe? No, that's not it . . . The entire camera system in the hotel is turned off. It had to have been physically switched off from inside the hotel. Guys, I don't know what's going on, but be careful in there."

All three Americans then piled out of the Audi, unsure of what they would find on the fifth floor of the hotel in front of them, only certain now that Salvatore was not here to take pictures of celebrities.

73

Salvatore sat on the edge of the sofa in the middle of the suite, confusion on his face. He had no idea what was going on, only the suspicion that he had been tricked somehow, and now he was in a great deal of trouble.

Three minutes ago he'd been standing in the hallway when the door to the suite opened and an attractive brunette came out wearing a blue blazer and blue skirt. She smiled at him and took him by the hand.

He was confused, but pleasantly so, because he thought he knew her from somewhere, and she seemed so happy.

She led him back into the living room of a big suite with an explanation about working with the same Russian handler who contacted Salvatore, and the promise that what they were doing here in Brussels would be a great step forward for the environment.

The environment?

She said she knew about the work he had done in the past. The protests, the arrests.

Surely he wanted to do more.

Salvatore nodded distractedly, more interested in getting paid than in helping the environment. And then he looked over the large suite. The furniture had been moved around; a table and a chair had been placed close to the wall by the bedroom door on his right, in front of a white flag pinned on the wall. On the flag, planet Earth was represented by a globe-shaped maze of twisted pipelines, and an oil well protruded from the top. A red drop of blood dripped from the Earth at the bottom of the flag, just over the words *Le Mouvement pour la Terre.*

Salvatore blinked in surprise when the others entered the living room of the suite from the bedroom next to the flag. The men wore dark suits with ties, and the women wore conservative business attire. They were all young, not one of them appeared to be older than thirty-five, but other than that he saw nothing similar about them. One of the women was black, one Asian. Of the six armed men in the room, most wore short beards; a few were clean-shaven. A couple of the women, Salvatore couldn't help noticing, were very attractive.

He counted ten here in the room with him.

He didn't need to see the guns stacked against the wall by the bedrooms to know what was going on, but he did see them. There were ten rifles of some sort. Salvatore didn't know guns, but it didn't matter, because the flag told him something about what was going on. That flag on the wall filled in the missing pieces of this puzzle.

He was certain he'd seen this group before now. On television.

The explosion of the liquefied natural gas facility in Lithuania, the event that set off the events of the war that had just begun a two days' drive from where he now sat, had been conducted by this very group of men and women. The Spanish girl who'd collected him from the hall had been the masked woman reading the statement taking responsibility for the attack. He recognized her voice easily. Salvatore wasn't that dialed in to international news, but this story had been impossible to miss.

Now, while the others stood silently, the Spanish girl sat next to him and told him they had a mission, he had been chosen by the "Russian benefactor" to join them, and they would reveal it as soon as they recorded a video press release.

But the truth was, Salvatore didn't need them to report anything. He knew their mission, perhaps better than they did.

Salvatore's Russian contact had been using him all week to photograph the facility at the Albert Borschette Congress Center, to use his press credentials to get into other conferences and record the security, the placement of cameras, even the thickness of the walls and the makeup of the ceiling tiles.

He'd known all week the Russians were planning something with the Borschette Center, but he'd thought they were just going to bug it or install cameras of their own for the upcoming European Oil and Gas Conference.

Now he realized the men and women who blew up the LNG facility were a part of all this, and he knew they were in the hotel directly adjacent to the conference center. And he understood without a doubt what was happening. There was going to be a terrorist attack, right here, right now, and he would be complicit in it all.

He leapt off the couch, surprising some of the men and women around him, but not all. Others reached out for him, grabbed at his arms, and tried to pull him back to the couch. But Salvatore's sudden burst of adrenaline allowed him to pull away, knocking two of the women to the floor.

He bolted for the door, flung it open, and pulled away from more hands grasping from behind.

He stumbled halfway out of the room before he saw the large man standing in the hall in front of him, with a pistol pointed directly at his face.

The Italian raised his hands, and the men and women behind him tackled him and pulled him back into the hotel room.

His panic took hold of him completely now. His arms and legs flailed, he tried to scream, but a hand covered his mouth.

It was then he felt the hypodermic needle jabbed into the front of his forearm. He tried to pull away, but the Spanish girl threw her entire body over his hand and wrist, pinning his arm in place. He looked down to see a man press a plunger on the syringe, and a clear liquid disappear under his skin.

And in seconds Salvatore's terror melted away, replaced by a sense of calm. He knew he'd just been injected with heroin, and he knew this hit would be enough to kill him, but it felt nice already, so he just relaxed and closed his eyes.

While Ding took an employee elevator, Dom and Jack ascended the guest staircase to the fifth floor. None of the Americans drew their weapons, but all three opened their jackets and untucked their shirts, ready to go for their clandestine holsters if they needed to.

The two cousins made it out of the stairs, and peeked around the doorway to the hall. Jack leaned his head out first and found himself looking down a long hallway that ended in a right turn. There was no sign of life anywhere, so he hurried up the hall, with Dom right behind him. At the end of the hall he tucked his head out again. At the far end of the hall he could see Chavez signaling them. He was pointing toward the door to a room, and he had already drawn his weapon.

Jack and Dom arrived on his shoulder quietly. Ding kept his pistol trained on the door, but he leaned closer and whispered to them, "Saw one man. Forties, wearing a business suit. He was armed, aiming at someone in the room. Don't know who. He entered, and shut the door behind him. There are noises in there. Multiple pax."

The two other Campus men understood. They lined up in a tactical train to the right of the door, with Ding in front. He reached out and tried the door, and found it locked.

He nodded to Jack, who dropped to his knees and crawled low, below the peephole. Here he took off his pack, removed Gavin's unlocking device, and slipped the card in the card key slot. He activated it with a press of a button on the handset.

When the light on the lock flashed green, Dom pushed down on the latch. Jack scrambled to return to his position in the back of the train, then all three men burst into the large suite.

First they saw Salvatore; he lay unmoving on a sofa in front of them in the center of the room. To the right of the sofa, a huge group of masked and armed individuals stood in front of a bright light. On the opposite side of the room was a camera, and behind the camera a man in a business suit who wore no mask.

The three Americans had walked into the middle of a film shoot.

The three Campus men did not know what they would find when they hit this hotel room registered to Luigi Vignali, but none of them expected to see ten people standing around with assault rifles.

Chavez, Caruso, and Ryan raised their weapons as they filed into the room, but the group on the right — Ding was in near disbelief at the sheer number of gunmen — were all wielding AK-74s with collapsible stocks. When they saw the door fly open they spun around in surprise.

Chavez started to shout an order for everyone in the room to drop their weapons, but in a heartbeat he realized this would be wasted breath. This was some sort of a terrorist outfit, and the way they moved showed Ding this wasn't going to be a negotiation.

Nope, this was a gunfight — the only thing missing was gunfire.

An AK cracked from the back of the room, removing any faint chance anyone could be talked out of a fight.

The first Campus man to fire was Chavez, principally because he was the first in the room. He hit a tall man square in the chest, knocking him back against the wall. Others in the room charged their rifles as they dropped to the floor. Caruso shot the older man in the suit. He'd been ducking down behind his camera's tripod, and the round hit him in the back of his shoulder. He spun to the floor, then disappeared into the bathroom to the left of the suite.

By the time Jack entered the room he found himself under fire. A 5.45-millimeter rifle round tore a piece of the door frame off in Jack's face. Still, he was able to fire over the sofa, hitting one of the gunmen ducking there in the chest.

And then the AKs opened up in full force, turning the doorway into a fatal funnel of fire. All three Americans dove for the ground and scrambled back out of the room.

In the hallway they stayed low, as bullet holes above their heads rained wood and plaster down on top of them.

And then the explosion came. A massive eruption that blew smoke and debris out the door to the suite, blew over the three Americans lying on the ground, forced them to cover their heads as more plaster fell on them from the ceiling of the hallway.

It sounded to Chavez like it might have been some sort of improvised explosive device. The volume of the detonation was way more than any grenade or RPG he'd ever heard, even taking into consideration the closed space of the hotel suite.

It took at least ten seconds for the dust to

clear, but when it did, Jack chanced a quick glance around the door frame back into the suite. As soon as he was able to see across the room in the smoke, he noticed a light behind the sofa that he had not noticed before.

He waited a few more seconds for the smoke and dust to dissipate, then looked again, and only then did he realize what he was looking at.

A hole blown in the wall of the suite behind the couch large enough to drive a small car through.

And the shooters were gone.

Security was especially tight this year here at the European Oil and Gas Conference in the Albert Borschette Congress Center. Among the three hundred attendees would be government ministers from all over Europe, as well as the leaders of million- and billion-dollar energy corporations.

The politics of the event also added to the heightened security presence. Aside from the typical environmental protesters ubiquitous at all European meetings of energy policy officials, recent conflicts in Ukraine and Lithuania had many in the industry concerned about the security of those present.

To accommodate the large crowd of vulnerable guests, the Belgian government sent uniformed police and special-tactics teams, and the EU brought in extra site security in the form of contractors.

Getting into and out of the Congress Center required X-rays, baggage checks, identity badges, and bomb-sniffing dogs.

It was Europe in 2016; security could be achieved, but only at the price of convenience.

All over the facility attendees were enjoying the last minutes of break before the one p.m. lunch session began. Men and women checked their e-mails in the atrium or chatted in the coffee shop. Many were still out in the courtyard smoking, careful to keep their badges displayed at all times so they could make their way back through the heavy security.

Dozens more filled the restrooms on the three lower floors.

The massive conference room where lunch would be held was less than ten percent occupied with attendees when a ten-by-six portion of the southern wall at the back of the room exploded inward, launching cinder-block debris two dozen yards across the tables just set for lunch.

Men and women in the large room reacted to the explosion, of course, but more out of surprise and disbelief than any real fear. After all, what terrorist would plant a bomb in a wall and then detonate it in a barely occupied conference hall?

It wasn't until the masked figures in the

suits and ties appeared in the hole, then began climbing through, that people started to react with terror. A waitress who'd been pouring water at the table nearest the blast had been knocked down and bloodied. The men climbed over her as they entered the room, ignored her still form as she lay there, but they immediately lifted their weapons to their shoulders and began training their sights on the big room in front of them.

Gunfire boomed in seconds, and screams of panic erupted throughout the room.

Masked women in business attire climbed out of the hole now and passed through the dust cloud in front of it. A female conference attendee who'd arrived early to her table huddled behind a felled chair, but an armed female in a blue blazer and skirt combo opened fire and shot her dead where she crouched.

The eight gunners had hit their objective too early, this they knew as soon as they saw all the empty tables, so within moments of the attack several of them were running for the exit to the atrium of the conference center.

Two more masked gunmen climbed through the hole, then used the cinder-block wall as cover so they could engage the three men armed with pistols who'd surprised them in the hotel suite and forced their early attack.

74

Ding Chavez had used the cover of the dust and smoke cloud to enter the suite. He rushed left, all the way to the bathroom, where the older man with the wound to his shoulder had entered a minute earlier.

When he entered the bathroom he found the man lying by the toilet. A detonator lay on the marble floor next to him, and blood smears were all over the toilet, the white marble floor, and the wall. He'd been in the process of tying off his injury with a towel when Chavez surprised him.

The man reached for the blood-covered handgun next to him.

Ding shouted, "No!"

But the man lifted it anyway, and Ding shot him in the face.

Outside in the suite, two gunmen with AKs crouched low over the lower edge of the hole in the wall. They held their weapons over the side and fired in at the doorway where Dom and Jack were. Ding saw what they were doing, realized they hadn't seen him enter, so he moved out of the bathroom and made his way to the back wall.

He stood here for a moment, out of sight of the men firing through the jagged cinder-block hole from the Congress Center side. They were twenty feet away, but before he got any closer to engage them, he wanted to make sure his two teammates knew what he was doing.

Ding wasn't about to rush the hole in the wall and attack the men there as long as there was a chance Caruso or Jack Junior was going to stick a compact pistol around the corner and open fire.

Just then Jack leaned out through the doorway to take aim at the threats. He looked up to see Ding in the far left corner of the room. Jack nodded to him, then raised his pistol at the hole just as both gunmen stood up with their AKs at the ready.

Jack fired three rounds, hitting one of the men in the hand, then ducked away as the other returned fire.

This was Chavez's opportunity. He holstered his pistol, went low against the wall, and crawled on his hands and knees across the floor. Just under the hole in the wall he rolled onto his back, drew his pistol again, and waited.

In seconds he saw the barrel of an AK jut

through the big hole, just three feet from his face.

He pulled his watch cap off his head, used it as an oven mitt on his left hand, then reached up and yanked the hot barrel of the gun forward, pulling the user off balance. He sat up as he controlled the weapon, used his right hand to aim his little pistol at point-blank range under the chin of the astonished man.

Ding blew the top of the terrorist's head off with a single hollow-point round.

He ripped the gun away.

Back at the door to the hall, Dom yelled, "You're clear!"

All three Americans began rushing toward the hole in the wall. Dom and Jack vaulted the cinder blocks, and here Jack saw the man he'd injured in the hand as he sat cross-legged, trying in vain to switch his slung rifle to his off hand.

Jack shot him twice more with his pistol, emptying his magazine with the final shot.

Dom raced by next to him. "Take his AK, but give me your spare mags."

Jack scooped up the Kalashnikov and ran alongside his cousin. He had only one spare to his pistol remaining, but he pulled it out from under his shirt and tossed it to Dom as he ran through the big conference hall, heading toward the sounds of gunfire just beyond the exit to the atrium. Dom reloaded and ran along, leaving Chavez behind.

Twenty-five-year-old Spaniard Nuria Méndez was the leader of the Earth Movement. Today's attack was to be the culmination of her life's work against the oil and gas industry, larger than the attack in Lithuania just two and a half weeks earlier.

As in Lithuania, her heart pounded with pride, so honored was she to be taking part in this event, even though this was not her plan. As in Klaipėda, her Russian benefactor had arranged everything down to the last detail; he'd even found other members to join her. Some of the men in this group — actually all of them, she realized — were not environmentalists at all. They were just some sort of gunmen from somewhere in Eastern Europe, taking orders from the Russians.

Nuria didn't care in the least, she was happy to have them. The end result would mean those who controlled European oil pipelines that were destroying the earth's natural habitat would suffer and die today, and she would make deals with the devil for this opportunity.

She ran along the atrium and shot at a man as he ran up a hallway, missing just over his head. She was no seasoned terrorist herself, but she was smart enough to know the promises the Russian benefactor had made to her about today had been lies. There were not three hundred men and women sitting "like sheep for the slaughter." Instead she now ran down an escalator, far beyond the nearly empty conference room where all the killing was to take place, doing her best to control the recoil of the big and unfamiliar weapon. At most she'd actually hit only four people — a far cry from the shooting gallery she'd been promised.

She hoped the men from Eastern Europe were somewhere else in this big complex exacting a huge toll on the evil men and women all around.

Just then she looked to her left and saw the glass doors leading to the courtyard. Out there, from what she could see from the escalator to the first floor, were dozens and dozens of men and women trapped in a small area.

She turned and ran back up the escalator, hoping to fire down on them all.

Jack Ryan, Jr., ran down a hallway on the third floor of the conference center, waving along the men and women who came rushing toward him, their eyes wide with shock. Jack carried the same weapon as all the terrorists killing people here in the building, but he wasn't wearing a mask, so few seemed to notice the rifle in his hands.

He was halfway up the hall when a door to the side opened and a portly man with silver hair and a gray suit rushed out and then lurched forward, slamming face-first into the wall opposite the door. The booming gunfire told Jack the man had just been dropped with an AK.

He knelt down, aimed at the doorway, and watched a masked woman in a red skirt and white blouse step out, turn the other way, and then take aim on a middle-aged woman who had peeked out the door of an administrative office. Jack shot the female terrorist in the left side of her rib cage before she could fire; she pitched to the side and fell to the ground, her weapon cartwheeling away from her.

Jack stood back up and raced on, pushing through more civilians, some wailing, some screaming, and many near catatonic as they moved through the hallway.

Dom Caruso scored himself an AK after he shot a masked man in the back of the head, stepping out of a coffee shop. When Dom scooped up the weapon next to the body, he looked into the little shop and realized he'd been too late. There were five people inside, and they all appeared to be dead.

Suddenly he heard more gunfire right outside the shop, and he looked out. A female terrorist toppled to the ground, and in seconds she was passed over by Belgian police, who raced through the first floor now with guns high.

Dom put his AK back where he found it, uninterested in getting shot by the good guys today.

Domingo Chavez made it down to the ground floor faster than his two teammates had, by chasing a terrorist into a stairwell off the atrium. As soon as he entered he heard gunfire, so he took cover for a moment, but when he started down again he saw a man and a woman, both wounded in the arms and legs. He passed them with a promise to send help, then descended another floor after hearing another shot. Here Ding saw a dead man lying on the stairs; next to him was the terrorist's Kalashnikov. Chavez picked it up, expecting to find it empty, but the magazine was half full.

He was confused for a moment, but then he realized the dead man lying next to the gun wasn't wearing his neck badge.

Instantly, Chavez understood. The terrorists were dumping their guns and their masks, then taking ID badges to melt into the crowd of escaping conference-goers.

Chavez dropped the rifle back on the stairwell and holstered his pistol, then ran down the stairs as fast as he could.

Chavez stood at the bottom of the escalator a minute later, looking up at dozens of men and women rushing down. Gunfire continued upstairs. His eyes settled on a woman in a blue blazer and a blue skirt as she descended with the others, packed tightly in the middle of the conference attendees making their escape past the now huge police response.

Ding could see the neck tag around her neck, but it was facing in, not out.

She reached the bottom of the escalator and started toward the exit.

Ding began to follow her out onto the street. Something about her demeanor got his attention; she was just a little too casual compared with the others around her. He couldn't say he remembered her outfit from the hotel room at the Sofitel, but he also could not rule it out.

As he walked he noticed the woman continued past where many of the conference-goers were milling around. She took the sidewalk all the way past the entrance to the Sofitel and onto the Place Jourdan, then she turned and looked back.

Ding stared right at her, just seventy-five feet away.

She turned away quickly, and he knew she recognized him.

She was one of the terrorists, he had no doubt.

He closed on her as she reached the end of the square and made a left turn.

Once she left his sight, Ding began to run

toward the corner, afraid she would climb into a vehicle and make her escape. As he came around the corner, however, she was standing right there, a short knife in her hand. She swung it up as Ding passed, slashing at his throat, but he caught her little wrist easily, wrenched her hand behind her back, and yanked up. She let go of the weapon before he dislocated her shoulder, but when she cried out, screaming in French for someone to help her, Ding threw a shoulder into her back and knocked her, forehead-first, into the brick wall of a bistro.

She dropped to the sidewalk, dazed, and he scooped her up and threw her over his shoulder.

75

The *Spinnaker II* had spent the last two days anchored off Salt Island in a remote cove. The six-man security team watching over Kate and Noah Walker had seen no threats to their operation whatsoever, and they'd reported the lack of action to their employer, the Russian who called himself Popov.

Still, Popov told them to keep their guard up, so to this end one of the Steel Securitas men was positioned on the flying bridge at all times with a pair of binoculars in his hand. A second lookout remained on shore, high on a hill overlooking the cove.

As far as they were concerned, the measures they had taken were already an absurd over-kill. Yes, they'd killed the old man following them around the islands, but since then their jobs had given them plenty of time to work on their tans.

Be that as it may, Popov had informed the men the night before that the following day the Dutch couple who'd been involved in the original kidnapping would return to add another layer to the security.

The South African in charge of the operation pointed out to the Russian that there was no place for two more people to sleep on the boat, but he was informed they would stay on their own boat, nearby but out of sight, and they would be used in case of any new threats.

Now it was six a.m., and only a faint glow above the hills over Salt Island revealed the morning. The South African was in his bunk, as were the German, the Chilean, and the Romanian.

The American was on watch on the flying bridge, and the Cuban was up on the hill overlooking the bay. Both sentries were awake, but neither was quite alert.

After all, there was nothing to worry about.

John Clark ascended the last few feet under the dark water; then he placed his hand on the bottom rung of the ladder next to the sea stairs on the bow of the *Spinnaker II.* He took a moment to listen to the noises of the boat here, checking for the sound of any voices.

When Adara found the cobalt-gray catamaran the afternoon before, she'd also noticed the man sitting on the hill above it. She'd taken pictures of the entire scene, and from these Clark had confirmed this man was one of the mercenaries taking part in Kozlov's operation, so he knew he'd have to board on the far side of the boat from the island.

This, he saw, wasn't going to be a problem. The catamaran had swung around with the morning tides to the point that Clark could ascend the sea stairs without fear of being seen by the man onshore.

He wasn't so sure about the man on the flying bridge, however.

Once he climbed onto the ladder he let his scuba gear sink to the bottom. It was only thirty feet deep here in the bay, so he could retrieve it if he had to, but for now he wanted to leave no hint that he was on board until he was ready to reveal it for himself.

He wore a shorty wetsuit and this he peeled off to reveal black cargo shorts and brown T-shirt. He'd kept his dive knife strapped to his ankle, and Adara had given him her compact Glock-26, which he'd just tucked into a side pocket of his shorts. He rose from the water and crouched low behind a dinghy suspended at the back of the boat, and he looked to the flying bridge ahead and above.

He could just barely make out the top of a man's head there, but from what he could see, the moment Clark stood up, the sentry would see him easily.

Shit, Clark thought. He considered slipping back into the water to try to climb up at another part of the hull, but the gunwales were higher on the side, and there were no ropes or ladders.

If he were twenty-five years old he could board this damn boat fifty different ways, but those days were behind him.

He sat tight, watching the sky get lighter as he willed the man above him to turn around.

At six a.m. he got his wish. The sentry on the flying bridge stood up, stretched, and gave a quick wave to the man a hundred yards away on the hill. Clark couldn't see if the wave was returned, but soon the lookout climbed down from the bridge and disappeared into the cockpit.

Clark couldn't believe his luck. He drew his pistol, remained low, but rose to a crouch and then headed toward the cockpit behind the sentry, his back aching from the wounds he'd received three days earlier.

It was darker in the cockpit than it was on deck, but Clark realized the man he'd seen above had climbed down into the saloon. Clark trained his weapon on the space, then made his way over to the helm. Quickly he looked over at the controls, determining in just seconds that he'd have no trouble piloting the boat.

He heard noise on the stairs and he stood there in the half-light calmly.

Clark recognized the American who'd called himself Joe. Along with the South African he had come aboard Clark's Irwin the other day to threaten him. Now Joe had a cup of coffee in his hand, and he was moving carefully so he would not spill it.

He was all the way up the stairs in front of Clark before he looked up and saw him.

Clark spoke softly. "Put the coffee on the table. Raise your hands."

The man did as he was told, but he raised his hands only to chest level. "What do you want?"

Clark smiled a little. "How about we start with my pistol?"

The American looked down to the waist-band of his board shorts and saw what Clark was referring to. The grip of the big SIG Sauer handgun he'd taken from the sinking boat the night he left the man in front of him there to die jutted out of his pants.

There was no way the man who called himself Joe could deny he'd been on board when the man was attacked, and that meant, to the American mercenary, anyway, that he was going to have to make a play for the pistol.

"Look, sir," the American said, playing for time, hoping to find an opening.

Clark said, "You going to tell me you were out for a swim when two pounds of steel floated by?"

"No, sir." Clark could tell the man was thinking about a move.

Clark said, "If you give me the gun, and you tell me where the Walkers are, without raising your voice, I will let you live."

The man said nothing.

"Or don't. You can guess what happens then."

The American seemed to relax a little. Clark saw him glance back down at the full cup of coffee on his right. "You won't shoot. It will make too much noise."

"I'll shoot. Then I'll hang out up here with my gun on the companionway, drop the next asshole that comes through."

The American shook his head. Still weighing the situation. "They'll kill the hostages."

"No," Clark replied calmly. "Only an idiot would do that, give up their one bargaining chip, knowing a killer is waiting up here with a tactical advantage. They might be that stupid, but I'm going to guess that you are the idiot on this crew."

"What makes you say that?" Before he finished speaking the man's right hand went for the coffee mug, he got his hand on it, and started to fling it up toward the man by the helm.

Clark shot the man in the forehead. His head snapped back and he dropped to the floor of the cockpit.

"The first guy to die usually is."

The sixty-seven-year-old man moved quickly now, rushing to the dead man on his back, pulling the SIG from his waistband and the radio from his front pocket. He then returned to the helm and began to flip switches, powering the navigation aids, starting the engine.

A second man appeared at the companionway stairs. Clark shot him dead before he could even focus on the situation.

He heard shouting from the hill now, and then over the radio a man with a Hispanic accent called for a status report.

Clark crouched behind the helm, pointed his gun at the entrance down to the saloon, and keyed the radio.

"I want to see guns tossed up out of the saloon. A *lot* of guns. Then I want you up here one at a time, hands high. I have a feeling you boys are working for a paycheck. Trust me, now that I'm on your boat, you aren't getting paid enough for this shit, so I'm going to let you quit."

He doubted he'd get the response he wanted, but he waited for a moment. Then he heard a woman scream.

Braam and Martina Jaeger stood at the Beef Island/Tortola heliport, watching the pilot of the Robinson helicopter conduct his preflight walk-around of his aircraft. The Dutch brother and sister yawned and stretched their arms; it had been a long flight in the rented Falcon from Amsterdam.

Braam's mobile began ringing. "Hello?"

"It's Popov! Listen carefully! The boat is

under attack!"

"Where?"

"I'll send coordinates to your phone. The crew is under fire. They have control of the hostages but haven't been able to remove the threat. Get there and fix it."

Braam hung up the phone and took Martina a few feet away from the pilot. Seconds later, both came back to him.

Martina asked, "Where can we get parachutes?"

The pilot seemed surprised by the question, but he said, "There's a skydiving club here. Their shack is over by the terminal, but it won't be open today till eight."

Martina turned and headed for the terminal.

Five minutes later she returned with two packed chutes. The pilot said, "What the hell? Did you steal them?"

Braam produced a Steyr handgun from inside his luggage. He leveled it at the pilot. "Take us here." He held up his phone with his other hand, showing a spot on a digital map next to Salt Island.

John Clark watched the head of Kate Walker appear up the companionway stairs. Just as he expected, there was a pistol jammed against her throat. Behind her, Clark recognized the South African, struggling to keep as much of himself hidden as possible.

When they were at the top of the stairs, the mercenary said, "Drop your fucking gun or I'll shoot this bitch."

Clark rose up behind the helm and took careful aim.

"No you won't," he replied.

"The *hell* I won't, man. I'll shoot her!"

Tears rolled down Kate's face. Clark saw this and said, "Ms. Walker, don't worry. He's not going to shoot you. He's going to get himself in what he thinks is a better position, then he's going to turn the pistol on me and use you as a shield. When he moves the barrel of the gun off of you . . . I'll take him, and this will all be over."

The South African said, "You're fucking crazy, man! I've got three more men who aren't going to let you out of here."

Clark said, "They can't wait for you to die so they can get away from this fucked-up mission. C'mon, asshole. Go ahead. Turn your gun on me."

Clark wasn't focusing on the man's eyes, he was just looking at the front sight of his weapon, making sure it was centered on the little piece of forehead he could target to the right of Kate Walker. But he knew what he'd have seen in the man's eyes. Panic, indecision, and then . . . slowly . . . determination.

The barrel of the man's pistol shot out toward Clark. Clark fired a single round, and the man lurched back, tumbling backward down the companionway.

Kate Walker collapsed.

Seconds later, pistols began flying up out of the saloon and dropping on the deck at Clark's feet.

Five minutes later the two surviving mercenaries on the boat had tossed the bodies of their three mates overboard, raised the anchor, and then themselves leapt off over the gunwale into the bay. Clark turned the boat around expertly and pushed the throttle forward, moving the powerful engines up to full power, and leaving the three mercenaries behind on the deserted island.

Kate went downstairs to untie Noah, and Clark called Adara Sherman to let her know he'd be at the marina in Tortola in just over an hour. He then called Gerry and gave him the news. Gerry told Clark the other operatives were on their way back from Belgium on a U.S. government Learjet, after capturing a terrorist tied to Russian intelligence.

Clark said, "And I thought I was the one having all the fun."

Gerry laughed and hung up.

Soon Kate was back on deck with Clark. "Noah will be up in a minute, but first I have questions."

"I can imagine."

"What do I call you?"

"Call me John."

"Who are you?"

"I'm a friend of your husband."

"My husband doesn't have friends like you." She said it flatly. A challenge to Clark.

He did not disagree with her. Instead, he said, "It's not too late to change that. He's been dealing with some dangerous people, but the people who took you did so because he wanted nothing to do with them. He can help us out now that you are safe, and he has promised to do so. I just have to get you out of here, then we just have to get Terry away from his captors."

She looked him over for a long time. Clark had a feeling he knew what she was thinking, and when she spoke, she confirmed his suspicion.

"By yourself?"

Clark looked out to the open water in front of him as he manned the helm. "God, I *hope* not."

Twenty minutes later, Kate brought John a cup of coffee and then she and Noah went back down below. Clark sipped slowly while focusing on getting as much out of the engines as he possibly could. His speedometer on the multifunction display of the boat read thirty knots, two and a half times faster than the top speed of the Irwin he'd sailed around the BVIs earlier in the week. It was an impressive machine, Clark thought, except for some blood on the floor and the pervasive scent of a half-dozen mercenaries.

He'd just taken a sip of coffee when he heard an unmistakable thud on the aft deck of the boat. More curious than concerned, he flipped on the autopilot, scanned the water ahead for a moment, then went to investigate.

He had just passed through the rear cockpit door when he felt something grab him from above. A line from one of the sails had been lowered around his neck, and now it choked him as whoever held on to it pulled him so hard his feet left the deck.

Straight ahead of him, at the stern of the boat and just in front of the dinghy, he saw a woman with auburn hair unfasten a parachute harness. She already had a pistol in her hand, and she raised it at Clark.

Clark struggled with the line around his throat, and while he lurched his head back, trying in vain to break the hold, he saw a man lying on the flying bridge just above him, reaching over with the line and heaving it with all his might.

The woman said, "Who else is on board?"

Clark couldn't have replied if he wanted to, he just held on to the line digging into his throat, trying to keep his airway open. For one brief moment he reached down to his cargo pocket trying to pull his Glock, but the auburn-haired woman recognized what he was doing, so she stepped forward and removed the pistol before he could get to it.

She racked the slide, ensuring there was a round in the chamber, then pointed it at Clark's face. "How many more of you on board?"

Clark's hands went back to the line, clawing into his own skin to get some relief from the pressure against his windpipe. He was seconds from losing consciousness. He'd left the SIG in the cockpit, and he couldn't reach the knife on his ankle.

From nowhere, Noah Walker appeared in the cockpit just behind Clark, his eyes wide with terror when he saw the woman who had kidnapped him days earlier.

Martina Jaeger saw the kid and rolled her eyes. She took a step to the side and raised Clark's Glock pistol toward the boy; she didn't give a shit if the Russians wanted him alive anymore, because clearly the Russians couldn't manage one *fucking* aspect of this operation.

Her gun arm reached by Clark, a foot from his left shoulder, and when he saw this he kicked with both feet, swinging as hard to his left as he could. He dropped both hands from the noose strangling him to death, and these hands fired out toward the Glock, surprising the woman aiming at the boy.

Clark grabbed the woman's wrists, yanked back and torqued them around, and shoved the hands and the pistol they held under the lip of the flying bridge above him, slamming the barrel into the ceiling of the cockpit directly under the big man lying there above him holding the line around his neck.

The force of the impact between the pistol barrel and the cockpit ceiling caused the woman's finger on the trigger to jerk, and the weapon fired, point-blank, into the ceiling. The bullet went through the wood, into the flying bridge, and directly into the chest of the man lying there holding the sail line around Clark's neck.

The big man released his hold and Clark dropped to the ground, still holding the woman's wrists, controlling the gun only enough to keep it away from him and the boy.

Noah disappeared down the companionway.

Clark and Martina wrestled on the aft deck, but only until the big man above them called out in a hoarse shout, *"Ik ben neergeschoten!"* I've been shot!

Martina Jaeger let go of the gun and stood, raced up the ladder to the flying bridge, and knelt over her brother.

It took Clark nearly half a minute to stand back up, since he could still barely breathe. When he stood he raised the Glock and saw the blood dripping into the cockpit through the bullet hole in the ceiling.

Above, the woman knelt over the wounded man, sobbing hysterically and then screaming in rage.

What the hell? Are these two assassins a couple?

Clark couldn't see her, he could only hear her. He had no idea if there was a gun up there, so he retreated into the cockpit, directly below her.

Kate appeared in the companionway now, and tried to come up on deck, but Clark sent her back down, told her to take Noah back into the stateroom and lock the door.

This wasn't over.

Clark knew he could fire through the ceiling again, and perhaps hit the woman, but if he missed he would go a long way toward revealing his exact location. Instead he moved out of the port side of the cockpit and tried to sneak a look above. Just as he did so, he saw the woman standing with a silver automatic pistol in her hands. Clark ducked back into the cockpit as a shot rang out. He had his Glock in his hand and pointed up at the ceiling, but he still didn't dare fire up into the flying bridge above him, because she could easily return fire and kill him. He was a sitting duck below her.

As he considered retreating down to the saloon, the woman fired down, sending bullets into the sofa of the cockpit.

Clark aimed at the origin of the shots and opened fire now, dumping round after round straight up through the lacquered wood.

After nine shots he heard the woman's

pistol fall and bounce on the flying bridge above him. He ceased fire, listened as carefully as his assaulted eardrums would let him. Seconds later the woman fell off the bridge and onto the foredeck, slamming hard on her side. Clark kept his pistol on her as he approached, but soon he lowered it. She was unarmed, lying on her back with a gunshot to her stomach, and two more in her legs. Tears ran freely from her eyes, and blood filled her mouth.

Clark knelt down, laid the Glock on the deck behind him, well out of her reach, and lifted her by the head.

She looked up at Clark, blinked away tears. "Help me, sir. Please. I beg you."

Clark didn't know if there was much he could do, but he lowered her head back down and pulled out his emergency medical kit. There would be more first-aid supplies somewhere on the boat, but he didn't want to take a chance looking for them. He opened a thick wad of bandages to put pressure on her stomach, then looked to the woman, saw her looking back at him through the tears. Clearly she realized she was being helped by the man she had just tried to kill, and she seemed surprised by this, but happy.

"Thank you, kind sir. Thank you so —"

Her eyes flitted away from Clark, focused to a point over his shoulder.

The eyes widened now. "No!"

Clark spun around on his knees. Above and behind him he saw Kate Walker, standing with the Glock pistol in her hand, leveled coolly at the wounded woman on the deck of the *Spinnaker II.*

"No one threatens my child and lives. No one."

She fired once; the gun jerked and sprayed smoke and fire. Clark ducked down low, falling away from the wounded woman onto the deck. When he looked back, he saw that Kate had shot the woman high in the chest. Her eyes remained open, locked on the Australian mother standing above her, while a low, guttural gurgle came from deep in her throat.

Her eyes rolled back in her head and her breathing stilled.

"Give me the gun, Kate," Clark said, holding his hand out for the pistol.

She did as he asked, then turned away, went back to the cockpit, and sat down on the sofa.

76

Rich Belanger stood on the second-floor balcony of the small farmhouse he'd chosen as his command post, feeling the cold, wet night blowing across his exposed skin. On his right was his sergeant major, and both men held binoculars to their eyes. They peered off into the dark, in the direction EARLY SENTINEL had predicted for the Russian armor advance.

There wasn't much to see. Although there was a moon above broken clouds, most of the scene at ground level was obscured in the predawn by a heavy fog bank coming off the river basin and from the soggy fields all around them.

"What do you think, sir?" Sergeant Major Garcia broke the silence in a hushed voice.

Belanger replied, "This isn't the location I would have picked. We've got good ground to protect, but our view of the village on the other side of the river is going to suck, even when the fog clears."

"It's a little late to move," the sergeant major said. They'd spent the last four hours getting into position and digging in.

Belanger kept peering through the glass. "Couldn't if I wanted to. This EARLY SENTINEL voodoo told us to come here and do this, and my orders are to follow EARLY SENTINEL, even if that means driving off a cliff."

"Don't worry, sir. If EARLY SENTINEL turns out to be a complete clusterfuck and we all get caught up in a Slavic meat grinder, I bet that computer can write a nice letter home for all our loved ones."

"You always make me feel better, Garcia."

Sergeant Major Garcia had been in the Marine Corps longer than Belanger, and was the oldest man in the battalion. He'd seen many commanders in his time, and his duty was always to remind them of the price of making a poor tactical decision. The sergeant major had been around Belanger enough to joke easily with him about everything from the ubiquitous Marine Corps equipment shortages to their Marines' personal quirks. But when the sergeant major took his eyes away from the binos, he saw that his chief was really struggling with the issues at hand.

"What's bugging you, sir?"

"Yesterday when we met the Russians at the border, their rockets pushed us back before we could engage. Since then our Harriers and F-18s have come through for us, and we think they've knocked out a lot of the enemy's capability to hit us at real distance. The Russians are stalled in the south because of U.S. and Polish air mostly. But we don't have air up here for the next hour. If the Russians figure that out, they'll come and they'll come hard."

"That bridge is a bottleneck," Garcia said. "They'd only try to cross if they thought they were clear of opposition."

Belanger nodded. "That's what I was thinking."

EARLY SENTINEL had told them to focus their fire on a patch of woods to the north and on the two-lane bridge to the northeast. This put them in the town of Punžonys, Lithuania. Its sister village of Punžionys, with an *i,* lay across the Neris River to the east. The heavy bogs in the area made the ground soft, and the thick pine forests gave the infantry a distinct advantage. Belanger had walked through as much of the forest as he could during the day, and he and his operations officer had spent four hours personally inspecting every fighting position of the two companies dug in behind the wood line around him.

Belanger didn't really trust that the computer program had put them in the right spot, but if it had, he felt they were ready.

The Darkhorse forward operations center

had brewed some coffee using the farmer's stove and an old coffeepot they had scrounged. All the locals had fled, leaving everything in place, including weak, flavorless coffee. A lance corporal brought a mug each for Belanger and Garcia on the balcony. Belanger took a sip and called out to the lance corporal as he headed back toward the kitchen. "I should have you court-martialed for this shit."

The nineteen-year-old saw the half-smile on his lieutenant colonel's face, and he left the balcony knowing his life wasn't over just yet.

Belanger stepped back inside and looked at the Blue Force Tracker computer map of the area. The terrain seemed right. The bridge between Punžonys and Punžionys appeared capable of holding heavy armor, but the small villages lay at no major intersection. Regardless, if the intel was correct, there might be a hell of a lot of tanks and fighting vehicles headed into their lines somewhere, and soon.

Belanger knew his job seemed complicated, with a thousand moving parts. But at its essence, his responsibility was very simple. He was here to kill tanks.

And *that,* he was certain, he could do.

A Javelin system, operated by one Marine, weighed upward of fifty pounds. It was "fire and forget," unlike the TOW system, which was wire-guided and required the operator to guide it all the way into the target. That made the TOW gunners vulnerable the entire time they engaged the enemy tank.

Belanger had positioned Lima Company, code-named "Havoc," in two engagement areas at the bridge east of Punžonys. One on the east side of the bridge, and another on the west. He put India Company, code-named "Diesel," on opposite sides of a rail bridge farther to the south of the villages on the Neris.

The weapons company, call sign "Vandal," had spread their combined anti-armor teams, CAAT-1 and CAAT-2, out between the various positions, and Vandal mortars were far enough back to drop shells in both villages as well as east of the river.

Belanger had his engineers laying mines and both his rifle companies rushing like hell to form ambush positions at the moment, but there was little for him to do now except wait.

He forced himself to drink the full mug of coffee while he stood over his map. Just as he put the empty mug on a table, his radio man called out to him. "Sir, you have Diesel Six on the net."

"Okay, thanks." Belanger walked over to the radio room and picked up the handset. "Six" was the commander of the unit, in this case the captain in charge of Lima Company, the force Belanger had positioned well to the south of the villages, near the rail bridge.

"Diesel Six, this is Darkhorse Six, send your traffic."

"Copy, sir. We're seeing movement along our phase line Jenna."

Belanger stretched the handset back to the intelligence officer's map. The intel officer was pointing out the area Diesel 6 was talking about.

"Copy, Diesel, looking at it now. I have no friendlies at that location. Havoc, concur?"

A new voice came over the radio. "Roger, sir, this is Havoc Six, we're still getting all elements into place on the east side of the bridge."

This was followed by new radio traffic.

"Darkhorse Six, Diesel Six. My lead platoon is telling me they are hearing the sound of armor coming from near Punžonys . . . or Punžionys . . . whatever, sir, the village with an *i,* up near Havoc's sector."

"Shit," said Belanger. He directed his response to Havoc 6. "Havoc, I don't care how well your positions are set on the east side. Get to the far side of the bridge and prepare your ambush. The enemy is on his way." He pointed to the operations officer and weapons commander to get ready to start battle tracking.

The enemy attack was on.

Minutes later a report came from the team

setting their ambush on the eastern side of the river. "Havoc Six, this is Havoc Two. I have a SPOTREP to follow. I identify a reconnaissance element of four BTR-90s and approximately forty, that is four-zero, troops moving through the eastern village, inbound my vicinity from phase line Jenna to phase line Hanna."

BTR-90s were armored troop carriers. The fact there were forty troops on foot around the vehicles told Belanger they had dismounted to patrol through the little village and across the bridge, looking for enemy positions or booby traps. He looked out the window at the predawn while he spoke into his radio. "Havoc Six. I want you to let that force pass through you."

"Sir?"

"Your cover in the woods adjacent to the bridge will prevent him from seeing your positions. He's going to recon the bridge, then mount up and push west. I want to draw in the tanks. I want their report to go back to their commander clean. Let them say they just seized the Punžonys bridge."

"Copy. What are my instructions after that?"

"Well . . . if I'm right, then you get to be the first Marine on this continent to kill a bunch of Russian tanks."

"Copy, sir," said Havoc 6, sounding less enthusiastic for the second task than he did for the first.

Another call came over the radio now. Belanger knew it was going to be a morning full of interrogatives and orders. "Darkhorse Six, this is Reckless Six." It was the Headquarters and Service Company commander, but the captain was an infantryman, and he was being tasked with all sorts of odd jobs today.

"Go ahead, Reckless."

"Copy, sir. Me and the engineering-O just finished laying all the mines. I think in broad daylight they'll be visible, but for now, they are set up where you wanted them."

"Okay, good work. Get back through friendly lines. I want you manning fifty-cals and ready to deal with dismounts."

"Copy. Reckless Six out."

Minutes later the lead rifle company commander came back over the net. "Darkhorse, this is Havoc Six, be advised, the enemy recon has passed our positions and is over the bridge. They mounted back up in the BTR-90s and are headed your way. Also, we hear those tanks now. They are near the cemetery on the east side of the river. Northeast of the bridge."

There was no way Belanger would have known to look toward the little cemetery on the far side of the Neris. There were so many other places in the area that seemed to offer a better approach for Russian armor. It occurred to him that if this sighting was, in fact, enemy tank contact, then EARLY SENTI-NEL had already proven its worth in the field.

Just then the same voice came over the battalion tactical net. "Break, break. All stations off the net. Flash report, this is Havoc Six. Confirmed. Positive ID on enemy armor . . . and they are *not* T-90s. They are fucking T-14s! Say again . . . Russian T-14s!"

No one had faced T-14s in combat; the T-14 was a brand-new tank and its capabilities weren't fully known by NATO forces. One of the weapons had famously broken down the first time the tank had been revealed to the world in a May Day parade through Red Square, but Rich Belanger knew better than to hope Russia's new fifth-generation tank would just stall out and die at its first contact with the enemy.

"Copy, Havoc. How many?"

"Three . . . Negative. Four. I think there are also T-90s behind them. They are still in the village of Punžionys and I can't say numbers yet."

Belanger called his India Company commander: "Diesel, are there tanks in your zone as well?"

"Negative, sir. Not sure this rail bridge can hold the T-14s, but we're tracking and our ambush positions are set."

Belanger thought over the picture of the entire battle space quickly. "Okay, Havoc, listen up. I want you to kill those T-14s using volley fire. Make sure your CAAT team uses their TOWs in conjunction with your Javelins. If these assholes disappear off their radios it will make the Russian commander halt and think over his situation. When that happens you will move all your forces to our side of the river, and occupy your final engagement positions. Acknowledge."

"Roger, Darkhorse, I copy all."

Belanger tuned his second radio to Havoc company's net. He had given the order, and now, as if tuning in to the big game, he would listen in as the India Company commander and his men did the job.

Havoc's lead gunner was armed with M27 machine guns. The M27 was an awesome weapon against troops in the open, but it wouldn't scratch the paint off a Russian main battle tank.

"Havoc One, what's your range to the lead T-14?" the company commander asked Lieutenant Munyon, his first platoon commander.

"Havoc Six, they sound like eight-zero-zero distance. But sir, I'm dealing with a *lot* of fog here."

"You've got tracers in your M27?" the captain asked.

"Yes, sir."

"Nail that fucking tank, Devil Dog. Light the way for the antitank guys. ATs, are you all copying my traffic?"

The antitank platoon commander took to

the radio now. "Sir, this is Shitty-Kitty. Roger on all. I can't see much in this fog with my thermals, but if they can reach out and touch the target with tracer fire we'll take the shots."

Belanger ran to the balcony. His sergeant major was already out there, pointing off to the east. From their elevated location in the farmhouse the two might have seen out to the northern bridge in perfect conditions, but the darkness and fog ensured they couldn't make out anything at that distance now.

Within seconds, however, Belanger saw a bright red streak of light shoot across and toward the village on the other side of the woods in the distance. It looked like it was impacting near the cemetery on the far side of the Neris. Another red streak followed shortly behind it. The report of the machine gun rolled across the countryside and back to them in a loud burp.

The tracers began arcing skyward after impacting with metal near the cemetery. Belanger knew they were raking the tanks with lead.

"Havoc Six for Shitty-Kitty. You got eyes on that location?"

"Copy, we see vehicle movement in the fog at the end of those tracers."

"At my command I need you to fire off a volley of TOWs at the two lead tanks. Havoc Two, are your Javelins set?"

"Ready to rock, sir."

"Fire on my order." There was a moment's delay, then the command came: "Fire!"

From the farmhouse two kilometers from the river, the sky to the east flashed too many times for Belanger to count. He saw the streaks of light of multiple Javelins, but because the TOW missiles raced along a wire-guided path close to the ground, he was unable to follow them across the undulating landscape between his position and the bridge.

One long, single bright red flash illuminated the fog near the cemetery. The lieutenant colonel knew multiple targets were being hit multiple times, but it looked like one long detonation from where he stood.

Then dozens of low booms from the explosions finally reached him at Darkhorse command.

His radio came alive. "Darkhorse Six, this is Havoc on battalion tac. It looks like the T-14s' reactive armor went off. Only the Javelins' two tanks were destroyed. None of the TOWs hit their targets — they were all destroyed in flight by the Russians' antimissile system. Break . . . There are a pair of T-14s still alive. They are moving to engage."

Now Belanger saw tracer rounds coming out of the village on the other side of the Neris, streaking over the woods and into Havoc's position.

"This is Havoc Two! We're taking fire!"

Belanger pressed down on the radio call button and ordered Havoc 6 to move his men. "Displace to your secondary defensive positions on our side of the river."

Just then, Belanger heard a clatter of heavy gunfire two hundred meters from the farmhouse he was using as his CP. The enemy's reconnaissance element had found his secondary machine guns, manned by his Headquarters and Service Company.

He heard the H&S commander calling for 81-millimeter mortar fire on the Russian recon-element men who were dismounting from their troop carriers, and Vandal company acknowledging that high-explosive rounds would soon be on the way.

More Javelins were fired at the Russian tanks at the cemetery, but again the tanks survived the onslaught by using automatic anti-air missiles and reactive armor that detonated in front of the inbound missiles, destroying them before impact.

The radio reported T-90 tanks appearing at the cemetery as well, farther away than the T-14s. The sounds of battle, both near and far, made Belanger's adrenaline pump, but he had to keep cool, continue directing his forces.

"Sir, this is Havoc, be advised: Those tanks are pushing across the bridge, we're not set up yet. Permission to drop a shitload of smoke."

"Copy. I'll get Vandal on the net to take your call for fire." Belanger couldn't lose that bridge. EARLY SENTINEL had said the point of penetration was at the bridge, and it had been right. Now it was up to him to do his work and hold it.

He heard three quick *whumps* in succession, followed by five distinctive *cracks*.

Enemy tanks main gun, thought Belanger. *Shit.*

The battle raged all around for a dozen minutes more, until Belanger got a call he'd been expecting for more than five of those minutes.

"Darkhorse Six, this is Havoc Six. We're out of Javelins. The enemy is sending more tanks. I am taking casualties. Their 120-millimeter guns are working over my positions. Sir, I have only AT-4s and SMAWs left and I don't think they are going to do shit against the T-90s."

"Roger. Stand by." Belanger knew that AT-4 rockets and shoulder-launched multipurpose assault weapons would be highly potent against a multitude of armored threats out there, but the Russian tanks were just too big and high-tech to be threatened by either of the weapons. He turned to his fires officer, who confirmed that they were firing continuous 120-millimeter smoke and high explosive onto the far shore of the Neris, but it wouldn't do a thing to the remaining T-90s except slow down their advance.

Belanger realized he needed to get his reserves moving into position to help Lima.

He pulled his radio back to his mouth. "Sledgehammer Six, Sledgehammer Six, this is Darkhorse."

"Sir, Sledge Six, I read your mind. I'm Oscar Mike already," said the company commander, clearly itching to get into the fight. "With your go, we can make the bridge in five mikes with the tanks and put the main guns into action."

"Go now!"

"Roger, on the way. Hooorah!" said the commanding officer of Kilo. Belanger knew only a U.S. Marine in a Humvee could get excited charging into the teeth of the lion. At least he knew he'd guide those M1A1 tanks into a good position.

Havoc then called on the battalion net. "Darkhorse Four, I am retrograding out of the woods now. I need medevac for a lot of my men. I can self-lift them to the medical exchange point, but no further. I need you to take them. These enemy tanks just keep coming."

Five minutes later the Kilo Company commander came back over the net. "Havoc Six, this is Sledge Six. I have the fight. You boys get out of there. The T-90s will be on your heels smelling blood and I'll fuck them up!"

Belanger stood over the map now, and worked out with his weapons company commander a final firing solution for the 81- and 120-millimeter mortars. He knew they needed a hellacious amount of smoke both to get Havoc out and to obscure Sledgehammer's tanks as they moved into position to the west of the bridge.

If they could just clobber a platoon of enemy tanks, Belanger knew, he could get the Russians to grind their advance to a halt. No one, not even the Russians, could stomach losing one full platoon at a pop. It would make the enemy back out of the area and regroup, hopefully buying enough time for Belanger to reposition and rearm.

"Sir, this is Sledge. We see T-90s on Havoc's heels. They have spread out and are leaving the cemetery, coming this way, but my attached tankers are ready."

"Okay, you are clear to fire."

"Copy, rounds on the way."

Belanger listened. There was a terrible pause, and he imagined they had again lost the targets in the fog, or maybe the smoke had drifted.

Then a *crack,* then *crack-crack-crack.*

The tank battle went back and forth for a full minute in the distance, and while this was happening, the H&S Company commander reported that all four Russian BTR-90 reconnaissance vehicles had been knocked out, along with the forty troops. He was transporting multiple wounded of his own back to the battalion aid station.

Finally, Sledgehammer 6 called in. "Darkhorse Six, this is Sledge Six. I have three burning Russian tanks, and a fourth that stopped but has no movement. Say again, four T-90s are down. Break . . . The rest are backing out of the cemetery! Their explosive reactive armor is no good against our tanks' main gun rounds. Sir, permission to advance and counterattack."

"Roger, clear to advance. But no further than our side of the bridge. Hit them till you can't see them in retreat any longer."

"Copy that, sir."

Belanger looked around the CP one more time. In the red light of their battle lanterns, with the grip of fatigue setting in, the men looked like zombies, but they had done it. And more important, they were ready for more.

Belanger left the second story of the farmhouse with Sergeant Major Garcia minutes later, mounted up in their Humvee, and headed to the battalion aid station. He knew the "docs," as they affectionately called their Navy corpsmen, would be working frantically on all the wounded from Kilo and Lima companies, but he hoped his other Navy personnel, namely the chaplains, wouldn't be performing any last rites.

His hope was in vain, as he knew it would be. You don't battle tanks without taking losses.

77

Terry Walker had been told nothing about his family's escape, but he could see the panic on the faces of Limonov and Kozlov, and he knew something had happened. He sat at his computer, making his trades, sending billions of dollars into invisible accounts, quite possibly for the Russian president. But while he did this he kept one eye on the Russians, trying to figure out what was going on.

Soon the four security officers were taken aside by Kozlov, and then they moved out into the hallway. He didn't know what they were doing at first, but when he asked to go to the bathroom Kozlov himself drew his pistol, then led Walker down the hall, past the four men, all of whom had their guns out and trained on the elevator and stairs.

He'd asked Limonov what was up, but the Russian bean counter would not speak to him at all. He just chewed his fingers and made his trades, argued with Kozlov in Russian, and looked like he might have an aneurysm at any moment.

When it was time to leave for the day, all seven men moved down the stairs and out to the vehicles. Walker walked in the middle of the group; he was the only man without a gun.

As soon as one of the security men put his key in the door of one of the Land Rovers, laser beams shined lines of red light from several directions. The security men raised their pistols high; then the men began spinning and dropping to the ground, one after another.

All four were dead in under two seconds; flashes of light across the parking lot were the only indicator of the source of fire, but Walker hadn't heard a single gunshot. He dove to the ground. Above him Kozlov fired a single shot before he too tumbled facedown onto the parking lot.

Walker lay next to the man, their eyes locked together, Kozlov's empty with death.

Limonov tried to run, but pieces of the parking lot kicked up in front of him and he stopped, raised his hands. Limonov's chest was covered by the red dots of lasers.

Walker shut his eyes and prayed this was the end of the horror.

Soon after he opened them, he sat with his wife and son on a sofa in a luxury Gulfstream jet. The three could not hold one another tight enough, and Walker promised the very serious men on the aircraft with him that he would answer any question, provide any assistance, or reveal any detail to the world that they wanted from him. He'd leave the BVIs and never return; he just didn't want to have anything to do with the man tied to a chair at the front of the cabin.

Jack Ryan, Jr., sat in front of Andrei Limonov. Limonov might have been able to recognize the President's son, it happened from time to time, after all, but the Russian wore a blindfold.

He looked white from terror, so Jack decided to play on his fears.

Jack said, "Limonov, you've got no choice. You are done."

Limonov licked his dry lips. "Actually, I do have a choice. To me this is quite simple. I am infinitely more afraid of Valeri Volodin than I am of Jack Ryan."

Jack was momentarily stunned. Then he realized the man was talking about his father.

He recovered and said, "You misunderstand the situation. We aren't taking you to the USA. You aren't going to Guantánamo. You are going home. Back to Moscow."

Limonov's chin rose slightly, and Jack thought he detected a tremble in his lip. "I don't understand."

"No? I bet you'll figure it out. We're going to plop your ass in the middle of Red Square the same morning the news gets out that a top Russian financier with Kremlin ties has been in the BVIs moving eight billion, and you have turned over the account numbers to American Feds."

"What? Wait, that's not what happened. I didn't give you anything!"

Jack leaned forward. "Your boss might own the press in Russia, but he doesn't own it all over the world. It won't take any time for Volodin to learn what happened here, or maybe I should say our *version* of what happened. No matter the circumstances, what do you think he'll do with you?"

Clark had been listening from across the cabin, but he stepped over for a moment and leaned down, just behind the Russian's left ear. "No, Limonov, don't even bother to think, because you can't imagine it. Volodin has spent decades learning the best ways to exact payback on those who fail him, and I'm pretty certain when he finds out the U.S. has access to his money, he's going to be a lot more pissed off than he's ever been."

Clark said, "Your end will be a fucking horror movie, pal. And your death will be the best thing that ever happened to you in your whole life."

"No!"

"If you will work with us, give us the accounts and the details of your network, you will be protected. If you don't . . . well, like I said, it's back to Moscow for you. This time next week someone will be digging your eye out with a pair of tongs."

Limonov just nodded slowly. "Take me to America. I'll tell you about Volodin's money."

Ryan looked to the back of the plane and gave the others a thumbs-up. Nobody was going to Moscow, but the threat had served its purpose.

The USS *James Greer* (DDG-102) sailed south at twenty-two knots. The ship was rigged for quiet but the relatively high speed negated much of the hard work the engineering department put in to keep the vessel stealthy. The twin screws of the Arleigh Burke–class destroyer were designed to reduce noise, even when under significant power, but at twenty knots, those with ears in the ocean ahead would be able to tell something was coming.

Commander Scott Hagen knew he was taking a calculated risk with his tactics, but he thought it worth the gamble. After days patrolling Lithuanian waters, essentially taking the place of the significant portion of Lithuania's Navy that had been sunk in a two-and-a-half-hour period earlier in the week, he had finally received approval to patrol out into the open sea. As soon as these orders came through from the Sixth Fleet commander, he sent both of his MH-60

Romeo Sea Hawk helicopters out in front of him to clear the way, and he ordered his engine room to give him the highest speed they could manage without rendering the towed array completely ineffective. Doctrine would have him picking his way a lot more slowly and carefully — as it was, the SQS-53 hull-mounted sonar's effective range was cut by two-thirds — but Hagen saw tonight's objective less as a typical sub search and more as a race against time, so he pushed on.

He also had a strong suspicion he knew where danger prowled in the Baltic, and it was dead ahead, out of range of his vessel, at least for a short while longer.

Thirty miles south of the *James Greer*, the Polish Navy was in a fight right this minute, and although the Poles seemed to think they had the upper hand, as far as Hagen was concerned, they just had a tiger by the tail.

For the first few days of the conflict the Poles had stayed in their own waters, but the northern coast of Poland lived and died on the basis of its Baltic seaports, and ever since the submarine warfare kicked off with the sinking of the Maltese cargo ship *Granite*, few ships of any type had dared enter the south-eastern sector of the Baltic Sea. Seeing the economic imperative of opening their coast back to commerce, the Polish government ordered its navy out to ensure the safety of ship traffic.

They sent a search-and-attack unit — a collection of integrated surface vessels and aircraft with antisubmarine warfare capability — out to comb the waters west of Kaliningrad in search of the Russian submarines. An Orkan-class fast attack boat had been positioned to the east of the rest of the group. Above it, one of Poland's Mi-14 helos with antisubmarine dipping capability had detected an undersea contact but had not been able to designate it as a threat with any confidence, so the Orkan began moving closer to join the helo in the hunt.

Without warning, a pair of torpedoes were launched from the location of the possible contact, and though the captain of the Orkan managed to avoid one of them with evasive maneuvers, the second inbound Type 53-65 blew his small boat all the way out of the water, killing every last one of the thirty-two on board.

The Poles also had another helo in the area, an SH-2G Super Seasprite. It locked on to the undersea contact, declared it hostile, and dropped a pair of Mark 46 torpedoes into the black water.

A Polish corvette received the data pulled from the integrated targeting system of the Seasprite helicopter, and it launched a pair of its own torpedoes at the target. With four weapons converging simultaneously at one target from two directions, the Kilo had little chance.

The sonar technicians on the *James Greer* heard the death of the Russian sub in their headsets, and even though they were still some twenty-six miles from the action, it felt like they were right there in the submarine with the doomed men.

While it was natural to empathize with the dying, every one of the sonar technicians on the *Greer* knew the horrific sounds in their headsets were the sounds of justice. The Russians had started this shit, after all, and they'd killed a lot of innocent people.

Commander Hagen played no part in the celebration. He stood in the CIC quietly while the overhead speakers and the digital dead-reckoning tracer table in front of him gave him the news about the kill of the Russian sub, and he thought about the other undersea threat out there, the second Kilo. In their previous attacks the two enemy vessels had worked in tandem, so he expected it was just a matter of moments before one of the two Oliver Hazard Perry–class frigates in the Polish SAU found out that the other Russian submarine was also here in the sea north of Gdańsk.

He also knew the only reason the Polish helo had detected the Kilo in the first place was that it had been moving into position, preparing to fire on the Orkan, so Hagen wanted to be close enough to detect the other Kilo's attack when it came.

Hagen was pleased to see that his USWE, or undersea warfare evaluator, on duty, Lieutenant Damon Hart, played no part in the brief celebration in the CIC. Instead, Hart loomed over the dead-reckoning tracer table, his eyes rapidly scanning the contacts and tracks, taking in headings, speeds, directions, and even coastline features.

The commander saw Weps was as focused on finding, fixing, and finishing that other Russian sub as he was.

Hagen shouldered up next to the young man and scanned the display himself now. As NATO members and close allies of the U.S., the Poles were on the same tactical data-exchange network as the U.S. Navy, and this made coordination between the two nations' fleets and aircraft as seamless as Hagen could possibly hope for. The Northrop Grumman Link-16 network allowed every designated track of every surface or subsurface contact — friend, foe, civilian, or unknown — to be immediately shared with every allied system in the hunt. The Polish helos and ships, the American helos and ships, all had the same near-real-time visual understanding of the battle space, and they were all rendered on the digital map on the big table.

Lieutenant Hart glanced up quickly at his captain. "That other Kilo is out there, sir."

"I know it is, Weps. The question is, will he attack this entire SAU while he's alone?"

Hart said, "I sure as hell wouldn't." He followed that with a "Sir."

"I wouldn't, either, unless I got a little blue communications folder from Naples ordering me to. Remember, this isn't just about the psychology of the Russian captain, or the conventional doctrine of submarine warfare. This is about his orders. Politics is driving this fight. Not the military minds under the sea."

Hart nodded. "The right move for him, if he is alone, would be to play it safe. If he doesn't play it safe, if he does attack, it must mean there is another element to this fight I haven't figured out yet."

Just then, the ASW tactical air controller came over the speakers. "All stations. Casino One-Two is reporting passive broadband contact, bearing zero, zero, eight. Initial classification of contact is POSS-SUB, confidence level high."

Hart said, "Designate Contact-Enemy Sub One-One." A red V-shaped indicator showed up on his digital dead-reckoning tracer table a moment later, east of the Polish SAU and eight degrees off the starboard bow of the *Greer.* This went instantly to everyone on the Link-16 system, meaning all the Polish ships saw the contact from the MH-60 Romeo, as well. The allied vessels only had a single bearing, not enough to identify the track of the submarine.

Seconds later, Hart heard a voice in his headset. "USWE, Sonar. Polish contact designated Friendly Surface Zero Five has gone active sonar."

"USWE, aye." Hart looked up to his commander. "That's one of the two Polish frigates, the *Generał Kościuszko.* He's exposing himself to that Kilo."

Seconds later the same voice said, "USWE, Sonar. Friendly Surface Zero Five has launched two torpedoes. Heading one, eight, eight."

"USWE, aye. Are they acquiring?"

"Sonar, negative. Not yet."

Hart and Hagen stood there, hoping like hell the Polish frigate took out the Kilo before it had a chance to fire back. Now that the frigate was actively pulsing the water hunting for echoes, the Kilo would have no difficulty launching Type 53-65s right at it.

Hart said, "The frigate is firing the fish to keep the Kilo on the defensive. We'll be able to launch an ASROC at the same contact in three minutes, but we're still out of effective range for now."

Hagen just nodded.

A radio operator just feet away in the CIC spoke loudly into his mike: "All stations, I have one . . . correction, I have *two* undersea missile launches. Popping up on the surface.

I say again, two Vampires in the air!"

It was quiet in the CIC for two seconds while this information was processed. The Russian Kilo was not known to have undersea missile launch capability. It only had torpedoes and mines.

The commander spoke calmly over Hart's shoulder. "What bearing?"

Hart asked the question into his mike. "What's the bearing on the launch?"

"Bearing zero, three, one."

Hagen and Hart looked down at the display. The missile launch had come from a completely different bearing from the designated contact.

This could mean only one thing. It was a different sub.

Hart said, "Jesus Christ! What the fuck is over there?"

"Calm down, Weps," Hagen said, then he spoke over the 1-MC net. "All stations. General Quarters. Condition Zebra. Missiles inbound off the starboard bow. Set Aegis to ready-automatic. CWIS to auto-engage. All hands prepare for impact."

A confirmation of the orders came over the net a moment later.

Hagen looked up at one of the two big Aegis display screens on the wall. A pair of missiles were in the air, forty miles from the *James Greer,* but only thirteen miles from the Polish frigate that now pinged active sonar. He called over his headset. "EW, this is the captain. Can you ID those Vampires?"

The electronics warfare technician came over the net an instant later. "Captain, EW. Missiles in the air appear to be P-800s. They are not heading for us. Looks like they are going after Friendly Surface Zero Five."

Hart and Hagen exchanged a glance. Hart said, "That has to be a mistake. The P-800 is the Oniks. The only sub that carries those is the Severodvinsk class, but the Baltic Fleet doesn't have a —"

Hagen said, "Trust the data in our hands now, Weps. Not the intelligence reports."

"USWE, Sonar. Passive sonar from friendly Air Zero Nine designates contact at bearing zero, three, one. Initial classification, POSS-SUB high. No cross-fix information. Evaluating acoustics now."

"USWE, aye," Hart said, the distraction in his voice noticeable. "We have to get close enough to get a cross fix on that target."

"USWE, Sonar. Both torpedoes launched by Friendly Surface Zero Five failed to acquire, break. We have solid track on the Kilo."

"Range to target Enemy Sub Zero One?"

"Range, twenty-four thousand yards."

Hart spoke softly, not exactly to his captain, not exactly to himself. "That's just barely in the launch window." He took a couple of calming breaths and said, "Fire Control,

USWE. Launch two ASROCs on Contact-Enemy Sub Zero One."

A female voice replied instantly. "USWE, Fire Control. Launch two ASROCs on Contact-Enemy Sub Zero One, aye!"

On the deck of the *James Greer,* a hatch sprang open, and a cloud of white smoke billowed out. From within the smoke, a fourteen-foot-long RUM-139 VL-ASROC antisubmarine rocket launched into the cold night air above a pillar of flame.

Two seconds later another missile cell on the deck launched a second weapon, and it chased its teammate up toward the stars.

Inside the housing of each missile was an MK-54 torpedo, but it did not splash into the water to begin its search immediately. Instead, it lifted high into the sky, pitched over on the heading of the Kilo submarine directly off the ship's bow, and climbed to a height of 10,000 feet. At the apex of its flight path the missile broke apart and the Mark-54 dropped in free fall toward the water above the submarine contact. Shortly before the Mark-54s hit the water, parachutes deployed from each torpedo, but the devices still hit the water hard enough to descend far below the surface from gravity alone.

Once in the sea, both torpedoes came alive, started up and ran diagnostics of their systems, reported back to the *James Greer,* and began searching for the exact contact they had been sent into the water to seek out.

Hart was up against two enemy submarines at the same time. As soon as he saw good start-up on his weapons targeting the Kilo, he looked back at the Aegis displays on the wall, just as the Polish frigate *Generał Tadeusz Kościuszko* was hit midships with an Oniks. The 550-pound warhead detonated into the side of the 444-foot-long vessel, creating a fireball that lit up the sky twenty miles away from the *James Greer*.

The camera on the top of the *Greer*'s mast broadcast the explosion to the men and women in the CIC, causing them all to stop what they were doing for a moment.

But not for long. Just as the missile hit its target, the radio operator came back over the net. "All stations, I have three missile pop-ups, bearing zero, four, two! More Vampires in the air! I think they are coming for us."

"God almighty," Hart said softly.

78

Marine Lieutenant Colonel Rich Belanger wiped sweat from his eyes, though it couldn't have been thirty-five degrees here in the back of the LAV-C2 tracked command-and-control vehicle. He'd opened the hatch to let some cool air in, though the cramped conditions and the incredible stress were causing his perspiration.

He'd lost a lot of men in the past two and a half days, but his battalion had done its job. They hadn't held any sort of a line — no, the Russian armor had been too strong and the mobile multilaunch missile batteries too accurate for Belanger's battalion to stick to any fixed point for more than a couple of hours. But by giving ground, moving from one configuration of EARLY SENTINEL positioning points to the next all over the eastern part of Lithuania, his weapons company and his three rifle companies had inflicted a disproportionate level of damage on the Russian invasion.

They weren't doing it alone, of course. The battalion commander realized two factors had worked in his favor in this endeavor. For one, the EARLY SENTINEL program had made it appear to the Russians that the initial breach of the border was going to be all but uncontested, to the point they'd fired only a very limited amount of rockets and artillery in advance of their movements, hoping to limit the damage to the roads, bridges, and other conveyances to keep their attack moving through the nation. This had proved to be a disaster on the first day of the attack, as the Marines had been in position, ready and waiting, when the armor entered their sectors. In the first four hours of the attack, two dozen Russian tanks were destroyed, both by TOW rockets and air strikes, and this bottlenecked the advance both in the south and in the north. By the time the Russians began heavily assaulting Lithuanian territory with MLRVs, 155-millimeter artillery, and air of their own, the Marines and even most of the Lithuanian Land Force personnel had withdrawn a few miles, and made themselves impossible for the Russian spotters to fix.

The twisted armor blocking the highways just inside the border had created serious logjams for the Russians, logjams that were exploited by American Harriers and F-18s as well as attack helos firing from standoff distance.

After the first two days there was more damage done to the Russians inside Belarus than there had been in Lithuania.

The other component to the battle that had worked in the favor of Belanger and his men was the ferocity of the Lithuanian and Polish forces. He had not seen a single Polish aircraft himself, but his net was alive with reports of Polish F-16s striking well into Kaliningrad behind the other front, disrupting the Russian attack there and taking up more Russian air assets, reducing the threats to Belanger's front.

And though the Lithuanians had no air to speak of, their ground units had fought heroically with their limited weapons. They'd suffered unspeakable losses, especially in the south near the E28, but they'd killed a lot of Russian armor, and by attacking into the advance, they'd provided the Marines both time and a better tactical picture of the Russian battle plan.

But the good luck the Marines had been enjoying ran out at the end of the second day, when a storm front brought little rain but black low-hanging clouds into the area, severely limiting U.S. and Polish air assets' ability to prosecute their counterattack.

The Black Sea Rotational Force had spent the last twelve hours getting pummeled by T-90 tanks that had advanced faster and faster. 3rd Battalion, 5th Marines had repositioned; they'd counter-attacked in hit-and-run operations that even included the Headquarters and Service Company calling in mortars and engaging dismounts with their M4s, but it had been nothing but small steps forward in a half-day full of large steps back.

Belanger sat in the back of his command vehicle now, looking at the disposition of his units on the Blue Force Tracker screen and enjoying the smell of pine out the open rear hatch. Outside he could just see a bit of the thick forest around him from the red glow of the lights here in the interior of his vehicle.

He was in a thick wood near a village called Balsiškės, although he knew he wouldn't be here for long. The Russian tanks were approaching up rural route 5227, just a few miles away, and they'd be on him by dawn if he didn't pull back yet again.

He didn't want to give away more ground. Looking at his digital map he recognized he had only two more fallback positions before he'd be in the outskirts of Vilnius itself, and at that point the Russian advance could take any one of dozens of routes to get around him, to cut him off from escape, and then to lock his force into an area small enough to destroy it with ease.

He'd moved his field hospitals back into the suburbs of Vilnius already, but he did not want to move his fighting forces into the city. No, he wanted to stay out here, mobile and ready to keep chipping away at the enemy.

Just then a noise roared; flashes in the sky and in the forest around him caused Belanger to launch toward the hatch of his command vehicle. Explosions throughout the woods blasted his eardrums, and he recognized the sound of Russian 300-millimeter rockets raining down around him, ripping into the forest and the village next to it.

Eight explosions within less than ten seconds told him a 9A52-4 Tornado multiple rocket launcher vehicle either had a specific fix on his position, or just general orders to flatten the village in advance of the T-90s' arrival.

Either way, it didn't matter. He needed to get his men out of here.

He grabbed the latch of the hatch and started to pull it closed, but quickly he looked back into the red glow behind him. He saw three of the four Marines who'd been riding with him. His radio man was out taking a leak.

"Flagger!" he shouted, and the young Marine appeared in the dark, rolled into the command vehicle, and the tracks began turning in the mud. Belanger shut the hatch, ordered his driver to take them south, and ordered all elements on the net to fall back yet again.

This wasn't any sort of combat he could recognize. Belanger was essentially being chased down by rockets and tanks now. He'd have to get on the roads to stay ahead of the hot pursuit, and the Russians knew how to read road maps. They merely had to pulverize the escape routes back to Vilnius, and then they would kill the retreating Marines.

Belanger knew his force had punched above its weight for two and a half days, but he suspected they wouldn't make it till dawn unless something stopped the T-90s.

A new sound tore the sky directly above his vehicle, so loud all the men with him ducked down. He turned and looked at his roof-mounted camera, flipped it to infrared, and panned the lens back and forth looking for the source of the noise.

A pair of unusual-looking fighter planes raced by just above treetop level, heading west to east.

"What the fuck, sir?" one of his captains shouted over the noise.

Just then explosions erupted to the northeast, right at the spearhead of advancing Russian armor.

Belanger looked at the image of the aircraft in the distance, then another pair roared right overhead, this time on a slightly different heading. He looked the planes over as they raced by. These two dropped bombs over the Russian spearhead before banking off to the north.

Belanger said, "Those are Saab Gripens."

His captain asked, "Who flies those weird-looking birds?"

"Sweden. Just Sweden."

More explosions erupted over the Russians.

"Sweden is in this war?" the radio operator asked.

"Guess so," the lieutenant colonel said.

"Whose side are they on, sir?"

"Well, they're blowing shit up to the east, genius. What does that tell you?"

The radio operator looked at his lieutenant colonel. "All hail Sweden?"

Belanger fought a smile, then began ordering an immediate halt to his battalion. He could take advantage of this attack to mount a new defensive line, utilizing the EARLY SENTINEL positions in the area. With a little luck and a lot more Gripens in the air, he realized, he might actually have a shot at holding the Russians out of Vilnius until the weather cleared.

79

Lieutenant Damon Hart always wondered how he would feel if he actually destroyed a submarine. He'd been training for it since he'd joined the Navy, he'd served on cruisers and LCSs and guided missile destroyers with that one objective in his mind, but he never knew how he'd react if the moment ever came.

And now that moment came and went in an instant. The sonar supervisor had just spoken over the net to announce the second ASROC Hart had ordered launched at the Russian Kilo had struck it dead center. The sounds of explosions, cavitation, and metal wrenching under pressure reported by the sonar technicians erased any doubt at all that Hart had just done his duty for his country.

But at this auspicious moment Lieutenant Hart had no time to think about his kill.

Instead all his attention, every synapse of his brain function, immediately turned to something else. He looked up at the Aegis screen, focusing on the tracks of the missiles in the air. While he did this he keyed his mike. "EW, USWE. Talk to me about the Vampires."

There were five missiles flying, every one fired by the submarine at bearing 031, now 26,000 yards off the starboard bow of the *James Greer.* He could see one of the missiles was on terminal flight, rocketing down toward the second Polish frigate. On one of the two Aegis displays on the wall it showed the flight path of this Oniks missile as it converged with the ship.

There was nothing that could save that frigate from taking a direct hit.

The second Oniks launched at that vessel had veered off course somehow. From its erratic track on the Aegis display, it appeared to all that it had suffered a mechanical malfunction of some sort.

But there were three more launches where tracks had not shown up on the display yet. But Hart had a sinking suspicion he knew where they were going.

"USWE, EW. Three Vampires are inbound on our heading. They are tracking, convergence in forty-two seconds."

On Hart's left, Commander Hagen broadcast on the 1-MC network, sending his booming voice through almost every compartment on the ship. "All hands, inbound Vampires. This is *not* a drill. Prepare for evasive action and impact."

Hagen then called Weapons Control. "WC, Captain. Stand by on chaff. Send broadband jamming strobe."

"Captain, WC. Standing by on chaff. Sending broadband strobe, aye!"

The captain then ordered his XO on the bridge to turn into the missiles, reducing the radar cross section of his ship, and this order was confirmed as well.

Just then, the tactical air controller monitoring the two MH-60 Romeos broadcast over the net. The helo had been dropping sonobuoys to the north of the second contact, designated Contact-Enemy Sub Zero Three.

"USWE, TAC. Casino One-Two reports good cross fix and firing solution on Contact-Enemy Sub Zero Three. Request permission to engage. Reports his loadout is two Mark-54 torpedoes."

Hart couldn't jam his transmit button fast enough. "TAC, USWE. Casino One-Two is cleared batteries released. Engage with two Mark-54s."

The TAC confirmed the order.

Hart grabbed on to the side of the display table as the *James Greer* began heeling hard to port. Up in the bridge the executive officer was positioning the warship in the best defensive position against the incoming missiles.

The TAC's voice came over the net. "Casino One-Two reports two weapons away."

915

A report over the net from starboard lookouts announced the sighting of two pinpricks of light above the water. Everyone in the CIC realized these were two of the three inbound Oniks, and all eyes looked to the left Aegis screen, which showed the video display of the mast-mounted sight on the *James Greer.* But instead of the incoming missiles, they could see only a massive fireball in the distant night as the second Polish frigate was hit by a missile.

Seconds later the *James Greer* vibrated, and Hart grabbed the table even tighter. He knew the Aegis system, set up on auto-engage, was launching RIM-174 extended-range active missiles from its aft missile deck. They were the *James Greer*'s main defense for antiship cruise missiles. It would be hitting a bullet with a bullet, and Hart knew that no RIM-174 had ever engaged a Russian P-800 Oniks, so this would be a first.

Hopefully.

The Aegis system launched a total of six missiles off its aft missile deck in rapid succession, and within seconds of the last launch, the report came across the net that all launches were successful, and there were no apparent casualties on board the ship, a standard report for any launch.

Hart knew three state-of-the-art missiles were inbound on him at Mach 2.5, but he had to keep his focus on his job, which was

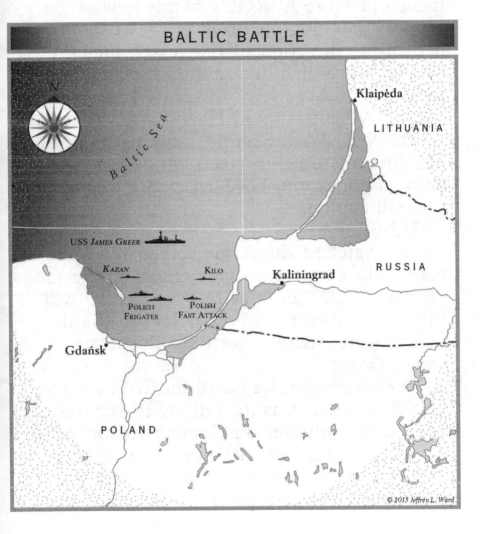

BALTIC BATTLE

N

Baltic Sea

Klaipėda

LITHUANIA

USS JAMES GREER

KAZAN   KILO

RUSSIA

Kaliningrad

POLISH
FRIGATES

POLISH
FAST ATTACK

Gdańsk

POLAND

© 2015 Jeffrey L. Ward

the attack on the Severodvinsk-class sub to his southeast. He ordered Casino One-One into the area to launch its two torpedoes as well, and he prepared the *Greer* for the launch of more ASROCs at this new target. He was planning on firing every weapon he had in the direction of the vessel, including his ship's five-inch deck gun, if it came down to it.

The TAO interrupted Hart's concentration — "USWE, TAO. Second inbound Vampire has lost altitude, thirteen thousand yards away. It appears to have suffered a mechanical malfunction."

"USWE, aye."

Hart watched the Aegis screen for a moment. He saw the missile track of the six outbound RIM-174s as they converged with the two remaining inbound Oniks missiles, which were steadily getting closer to the *James Greer.*

Over his headset he heard the TAC's voice. "USWE, TAC. Casino One-One reports a good firing solution on Contact-Enemy Sub Zero Three, and is requesting batteries free."

This was the other helo. Hart said, "You have batteries released. Launch two Mark-54s."

The tactical action officer spoke now. "One inbound Vampire destroyed. Remaining Vampire has made it through the ERAMs and is inbound. Impact in twelve seconds!"

Captain Hagen was on his net with the WC and the bridge. "Launch chaff, increase to flank speed!" Then he broadcast again on the 1-MC: "All hands, one inbound Vampire on terminal attack. Brace for impact."

Hart bent his knees, slacked his jaw, and held tightly to the table, but he kept his eyes on the digital dead-reckoning tracer table in front of him. He could see four torpedoes active, and the Severodvinsk sub was taking evasive actions, trying to avoid its own destruction.

At the same time, the USS *James Greer* was doing exactly the same thing.

It occurred to Hart then and there that each combatant in this fight was about to kill the other, and everyone would die.

He heard a low, whining sound above him now, loud enough that he squatted down for an instant as if to take cover. Soon he realized what he was hearing. The Phalanx close-in weapon system — abbreviated CIWS and simply called "C-whiz" — was a missile-defense system, an automatic cannon that used the Aegis radar and a Vulcan 20-millimeter Gatling gun to attack inbound antiship missiles with 4,500 rounds a minute. It was the last defense on the destroyer, and when it fired, it meant an antiship missile, in this case one moving at two and a half times the speed of sound, was only seconds from impact.

The C-whiz sounded to Hart like the world's largest lawn mower, and it roared above him in four two-second bursts. After the last burst, Hart heard the sound of impacts all over the ship. He felt a jolt, and lost his footing and dropped to the deck of the CIS.

Commander Hagen knelt next to Hart, and he spoke to the bridge, calling for a status report. When none came, he dropped his headset and ran out of the Combat Information Center.

Hart stood back up slowly. He wasn't sure what the hell had happened, but he was pretty certain the *James Greer* did *not* just get hit by an antiship missile.

That was noisy and disruptive, yet they hadn't been blown to pieces as if they'd been slammed into by an Oniks.

He had just looked down at the table when he heard, "USWE, Sonar. I have cavitation at heading zero, zero, two. Contact-Enemy Sub Zero Three. Torpedo impact!"

Across the CIC men and women began cheering. The Severodvinsk had managed to avoid three of the four Mark-54s fired at it, but the last one detonated below its hull, and tore the submarine in half at a depth of two hundred meters.

On his display Hart watched a Polish corvette turn toward the location of the explosion and begin steaming closer to inspect the wreckage. It was only three and a half miles away, and it would be there in minutes.

The celebration was quick; it was subdued in the CIC when moments later the two Aegis display screens went dark. Calls over the 1-MC requesting firefighting personnel and medical teams began soon after.

Hart made his way up to the main deck minutes later, and by then he had heard the news. The last of the three Oniks missiles fired at the *James Greer* had been destroyed by the C-whiz just 525 yards from impact, but the kinetic energy of the inbound missile had sent hundreds of pounds of shrapnel against the ship, ripping through radar systems, destroying communications equipment. Debris had ripped into the bridge, killing three outright and injuring eleven more.

Hart saw small fires and torn metal, blood on the deck, and wounded carried by in the passageways.

He figured this was only a hundredth of the effect of the Oniks had it slammed into the hull, but this was still bad. His vessel was wounded enough to severely curtail its operations until it could limp back to port and go through repairs, and men and women were dead and wounded.

Hart walked back down to the CIC, knowing he needed to evaluate the status of the warship's fighting capabilities. He had no idea if other dangers hid in the waters below him, and he knew the Poles had just lost their two largest naval vessels.

Exhausted, disheartened by the death around him, he realized his work would not end until he was home, or politicians in Moscow and Washington somehow figured out how to end this war.

President of the United States Jack Ryan hung up the phone with the president of Poland, then he looked at Scott Adler, sitting in his customary position across his desk. "It's settled. They've agreed."

Adler blew out a long sigh of relief. "Good."

He then turned to Secretary of Defense Bob Burgess and DNI Mary Pat Foley, both sitting farther away on one of the sofas in the seating area of the Oval Office. "This had better work."

Mary Pat said, "It's our best play. The most direct way to affect things over there."

Burgess nodded. Said, "While you were on your call, I spoke with Secretary Hazelton. The naval battle is over. We had damage to our destroyer, and the Poles lost two frigates and a fast attack boat."

Ryan sighed. "And what did that get us?"

Burgess cracked a hint of a smile. "Three subs. As far as we know, everything they still had in the water over there that poses a threat to our Marine landing ships."

"Thank God."

The SecDef added, "The destroyer that sank the *Kazan,* their most advanced attack sub?"

"Yeah?"

"DDG-102. The *James Greer.*"

Admiral Jim Greer had been Ryan's mentor at CIA.

The President cocked a slow, sly smile. "Funny damn world, isn't it, Bob?"

"Sure as hell is, Mr. President. I think Admiral Greer would get a kick out of it."

Ryan said, "Let's give it to the Poles."

"I'm sorry?"

"The *Kazan.* We'll give the credit for the kill to the Polish Navy."

Burgess said, "A lot of good men and women on the *James Greer* gave their all to win that sub. Handing it over to the Poles diminishes the work of the U.S. Navy in all this."

"They didn't get into that work to be famous."

"Still, Mr. President. It's the biggest naval success in a generation, and the Poles deserve a lot of recognition, but robbing the *James Greer* of their part in it seems wrong."

"I'm not robbing anyone of anything, Bob. I'm just aware of how important a diplomatic coup it would be if the world, and the Russians, thought the Poles did this on their own."

Burgess was not happy about this, and Ryan saw it. "Bob, you're pissed, and I appreciate that. But this is the right move. When the smoke clears and the *James Greer* gets back home, I'll go out and visit them and make a big deal about their efforts in the Baltic, without being specific. I'll talk about their sinking of the Kilo. I'm going to be unpopular around the Navy on this one, I understand, but I'm only thinking about discouraging Russia from attacking its neighbors."

Burgess blew out a long sigh. "You're still popular with the Navy, Mr. President." He chuckled. "Maybe you'll let me stand behind you when the *Greer* gets back to port so I can give the sailors a little wink, let them know we know what they did."

Ryan agreed to this, then stood and looked at his watch. "It's almost time to go on TV. If I'm going to do this I want it to be ready for the news in Moscow. I'll spend an hour with the speechwriters and then I'll go on-air."

80

President Jack Ryan wore a blue suit with a red tie, and he sat at his desk in the Oval Office and looked into the camera. His comments would be broadcast live all over the world, certainly even in Russia, although some there wouldn't see him.

After a serious greeting and a little background on the short land war in Lithuania, he said, "From here on, I will refer to the actions of the Russian military currently under way in the Baltic as Volodin's invasion. While he enjoys the support of the majority of the Russian population, I am aware that the information on which the Russian population is basing its support for Volodin is carefully manipulated." Ryan placed the palms of his hands on his desk and looked down at them. For a moment it looked like the teleprompter had stopped and he was lost.

Then he said, "No. Not tonight. Tonight I am going to change the manner in which I address you all. I apologize in advance for my frank tone, and my lack of diplomatic nuance, but millions of lives are depending on an understanding of what is going on.

"To the Russian people: You are being lied to, manipulated, tricked, used. Valeri Volodin was a product of the Soviet Security Services; he was born and trained to use deception. He is very good . . . no, he is better than that. He is the best I have ever seen.

"But it is not possible to tell a lie well enough to make it true.

"Volodin's invasion has failed. His tanks have stalled east of Vilnius. His three most dangerous subs in the area are all at the bottom of the Baltic Sea. A large and growing coalition of nations is standing up to this illegal attack. Armies are moving into Poland and now Lithuania to assist the defensive actions of local forces and the United States Marine Corps.

"Valeri Volodin went into this thinking NATO would hand him the three nations of the Baltic in exchange for a promise that he would leave Poland and the rest of Ukraine alone. That plan is up in smoke now, but instead of him just losing this conflict, a conflict he started, now he is about to lose a lot more.

"What I am about to say might make many of you angry. I ask you to keep an open mind. As we speak, the armed forces of Poland are preparing to launch an attack into Kaliningrad. Russian territory. The Russian defense there is weak at the moment, because they have been focusing on Lithuania. Further, NATO has agreed today in special session to immediately send its Very High Readiness Joint Task Force to defend Poland in the case of attack there. And in the sea off Kaliningrad, where Volodin's Baltic Fleet is still smoldering, multiple amphibious assault ships carrying thousands of United States Marines have been moving into position to land." He looked in the camera. "I thought I would be sending them to defend Lithuania. But now? Now I am considering sending them into Kaliningrad Oblast."

Ryan looked hard into the camera. "These are indeed difficult times.

"Please understand, all these tens of thousands of armed men, all these aircraft and ships and special operators and missiles and tanks, all NATO and NATO-allied forces, will begin to turn around and go back to their bases the *second* Valeri Volodin gives the order to his army to quit Lithuania and quit Belarus, removing the threat of an invasion of Poland. Despite everything you have heard in the Russian media, and despite everything you will no doubt hear from the television pundits waiting for me to finish my speech so they can hastily discount everything I say here, we do not want one inch of Russian territory. Not now, not ever. It belongs to you, the Russian people. But we can't let a madman like Valeri Volodin go on threatening his neighbors.

"We will invade Kaliningrad to stop war in the Baltic, but we will return Kaliningrad to Russia, when we achieve our aims.

"My message to Valeri Volodin is a simple one. You have, once again, overplayed your hand. Get out of Lithuania now or lose long-held Russian territory.

"And if you dare employ any weapon of mass destruction, nuclear, chemical, or biological, we will be forced to respond in kind. Launch a nuclear weapon at us, at any of us *anywhere,* and Moscow will open itself up to devastating retaliatory strikes. I want to speak plainly. I will not fire first, Mr. Volodin. But I *will* fire last."

Ryan took a sip of water. "One more message for the good people of Russia: As I said before, the moment I stop talking, you will be lectured to by a number of well-trained disinformation specialists from the Kremlin, attractive men and women with a gift for selling whatever Valeri Volodin has to offer. But moments from now, when they begin talking, you will notice something different about them. A bit of confusion, a measure of caution with their words.

"Why is this?

"Because while I have been speaking with you, all Russian media outlets have received a statement from a Kremlin banker from Moscow. This man was Valeri Volodin's personal cashier, and the statement is backed by evidence to prove his assertions that for the past several months he has been moving the personal assets of Valeri Volodin out of Russian control, and into a series of offshore accounts. He was captured in the British Virgin Islands along with a Kremlin security official, and he is revealing all the information about Volodin's crimes against his own nation.

"Your president has been stealing money from Russia, and then hiding this money in overseas banks to the tune of billions of dollars, ladies and gentlemen. He even hid it from insiders within his own government, creating an escape in case this war did not turn out his way. Long before the first shot was fired in the Baltic, Valeri Volodin had been preparing to leave Russia behind if he needed to.

"Your media will still mock me and disagree with me, to be sure. You can't retrain a parrot in a number of minutes, but prepare yourself to look confusion in the face when the Kremlin's spin doctors posing as unbiased journalists show themselves in about thirty seconds."

Ryan signed off moments later.

All across Russia, the image of President Ryan sitting at his desk at the White House switched to that of a panel of Russian journalists. As predicted, they seemed confused by the accusations, but they did their best to carry the water of their leader.

At least for now.

Five minutes later the cameras were out of the Oval and they were replaced by Ryan's national security staff.

Mary Pat Foley said, "Mr. President. This puts significant pressure on Volodin. You add that to the announcement you are about to make and . . . I think you should consider what Volodin might do."

"You are talking about the Borei somewhere off the coast. You are saying Volodin might order a nuclear launch."

"The captain of the *Knyaz Oleg* is a pro-Volodin zealot. Very political. He'll do whatever his president orders."

Bob Burgess added, "He is literally the worst person we'd want to have commanding a nuclear submarine off the coast of Washington."

Ryan said, "And still no hint of where it is?"

Burgess replied, "Finding a submarine off the Atlantic coast is like finding a specific pebble in the bottom of a lake. As long as it sits there quietly and doesn't draw attention to itself, we will not find it, Mr. President."

Mary Pat said, "I think you need to think

about leaving Washington until this crisis passes."

Ryan shook his head immediately. "No, I'll stay here. I'm not jetting off to a bunker in Colorado."

Arnie Van Damm had sat quietly behind the conversation. He said, "I've been thinking about a vacation to South Dakota. Or maybe Micronesia. Wonder what Tierra del Fuego looks like this time of year. I'd like to take a lengthy sabbatical."

Jack chuckled. "Request denied. Hell, I'm protecting you. You are in no shape to hike the southern tip of Argentina. Better take your chances with the inbound nukes."

"Funny, Jack."

The café on Krivokolenny Lane had hosted dozens of these meetings, but never once in the fall. Usually these were springtime occasions, every year at the same time.

Volodin would have preferred the tradition remained. It was another half year to the next scheduled meeting, and in a half year Volodin was certain he'd be in a better place than he was now.

But he *had* to come tonight. Diburov was powerful, he had called the meeting, and Valeri Volodin knew all the *siloviki,* not just Diburov, were restless and they were angry. The events of the last several weeks would just play into this anger.

The *Kazan* was sunk, this was true, and the action in Lithuania was stalled. But the Northern Fleet had more subs, and reinforcements were on their way to Belarus. He saw the failures as mere speed bumps.

More damning, perhaps, was the fact that Western media was parading around a female Spanish terrorist who claimed Russia had organized the attack against the European Oil and Gas Conference and the bombing of the LNG facility in Klaipėda. Volodin knew this to be true, and it was in line with his assertions during the last *siloviki* meeting that he would engage in a campaign to boost energy prices in order to raise Russia's standing in the world, but Grankin had assured Volodin the Russian contact with the Earth Movement group could in no way be tied back to the Kremlin.

Volodin could deny this to his *siloviki,* and he planned on doing just that when he got inside. They might not believe him, but he had to try.

No, Volodin did not want to come tonight. He knew things were dangerous for him politically, and here he would have to face the rage of the most powerful men in the nation.

But he had to come tonight. He had to come because *fucking* Limonov had run off with all his money.

In the spring when these affairs took place

at Café F, the security was locked down tight. But tonight things appeared altogether different. He assumed the late word of the meeting was the reason that there was no roadblock at the end of the street and that he saw a few passersby walk down the lane as if it were just any other night.

Volodin wasn't worried about security. His detail was here with him. They would protect their president. The other men could go to hell, for all he cared.

But his security officers were livid about the lack of controlled access to the street. They made phone calls and demanded answers about when the road would be blocked off.

Once the motorcade pulled up to the alcove in front of the café, Volodin looked in the window of the door. He saw Grankin at the bar, and next to him was Diburov.

Volodin's security men told him to wait. He did as they said, sitting silently, thinking about what he would say inside, while his security men argued over mobile phones.

Finally Grankin walked to the window, looked out at his president, and motioned him in. Volodin just nodded in response, then he turned to his security men in the limousine with him.

"What the fuck is the problem?"

His lead security officer leaned back to him. "Mr. President, I don't want you to leave the motorcade until they block off the street. I don't know what is going on, but this isn't the protocol."

Volodin sighed. This was turning into a train wreck.

Diburov came to the window and looked at Volodin sitting there in his car, and Volodin looked back at him. He knew how this made him look. Weak, scared, afraid to face the music.

Volodin shouted at his men around him. "Damn it to hell! I'll just go in. No one will say Valeri Volodin was afraid to meet with his own supporters."

"It's not safe, sir."

"They aren't going to shoot me, Pasha. They might want to, but they would never get away with it. They know that. Plus, they are weak men. They would never dare."

Pasha said, "I'll go with you."

"All right, but only you. Security men are only allowed in the front room by the bar. I will *not* look scared in front of these bastards."

"Yes, sir."

Pasha opened Volodin's door, and together the two men crossed the sidewalk and stepped into the alcove in front of Café F. Normally, one of the security men inside the building would hold the door for the president here, but the door did not open, so Pasha had to rush forward and do it himself.

The door seemed to be locked.

Pasha yanked again, embarrassed. Volodin looked through the glass at Grankin and Diburov. They just sat at the bar and stared back at him blankly. Volodin then turned to look to the right, at the main room of the café. He couldn't see this space from his motorcade.

It was empty. No security, no *siloviki,* no waiters.

"What the fuck is going on?"

Pasha turned toward the president, took him by the shoulder, and spun him around. "Let's go."

A gunshot cracked close in the alcove, and Volodin recoiled all the way back to the locked door. His big security man on his right lurched back, blood splattered the glass behind his head, and he slid down the door to the pavement.

A figure with a gun stood in the darkness to one side of the alcove, just feet from Pasha's crumpled body. Volodin froze in fear, but for only an instant. Then he started for his limousine, fifty feet away. He could see doors open up and down his motorcade and his detail rush forward. They would be with him in seconds.

He'd been so focused on the man with the gun in front of him, and his security men in the street, that he'd not seen the other figure in the dark, hidden on the other side of the alcove. This man stepped forward to Volodin as if he would give him a hug, and the Russian president flinched when he felt the presence.

The second man in the alcove drove a knife into Valeri Volodin's gut.

The Russian president's eyes shot open and then softened, his knees gave out and he dropped onto them, and then he pitched forward, the blade still protruding from his body.

The two men left standing in the alcove looked at each other for an instant; then the gunman shrieked, *"Allah'u akbar!"* and he shot his compatriot, the assassin of Valeri Volodin, in the forehead. Then the gunman turned his weapon on himself and began the pledge again, but before he could finish it he was cut down by a hail of bullets from Volodin's protection detail.

Arkady Diburov and Mikhail Grankin left Café F via a back door moments later. They climbed into separate Mercedes sedans and rolled off into the night in opposite directions.

One hour later, Channel Seven news anchor Tatiana Molchanova appeared in the homes of most Russians watching television at eleven-thirty p.m. Her eyes were rimmed with red as if she had been crying.

"Ladies and gentlemen. Late-breaking news

from Moscow. President Valeri Volodin has been assassinated at the hands of Chechen terrorists this evening, just blocks from the Lubyanka, the building where he worked as a young man to build a greater Russia. Apparently the president became separated briefly from his security detail, and he was attacked in the street. He received a knife wound to his stomach, and even though his bodyguards immediately killed the savage terrorists and took their president to the hospital, he could not be saved."

Tatiana Molchanova wept openly on camera.

81

The President of the United States sat at his desk with the complete dossier on Arkady Diburov lying open in front of him. The new Russian president had been in office only four hours, and already he was going to conduct his first red-phone call with the President.

Ryan thought it a little awkward that this man was under economic sanction by the U.S. Justice Department, but the dossier spoke for itself. As the director of Gazprom, he had been the beneficiary of hundreds of millions of dollars that had been rerouted from oil receipts into shell companies around the world.

The guy was a crook, just like the man he replaced, Ryan knew. But Ryan did not yet know if the guy was a crook who would be willing to make a deal.

He's *siloviki,* a billionaire, shadowy, but perhaps less so than Valeri Volodin.

I can work with that, Ryan said to himself.

And Ryan also didn't know if he would be

able to fool the man into thinking the Russian ballistic missile sub off the American coastline was currently being targeted by the Navy. The truth was he had no idea where it was, so Ryan felt his best option was to feign a position of authority with the new president, to negotiate America's way from the brink of nuclear war.

He heard a sound through the phone in his ear and then a man speaking Russian. The translator conveyed a few words of introduction, and then Diburov said he hoped the two nations of Russia and the U.S. could have better relations.

Ryan said he felt the same way, but things would only improve when Russia obeyed international agreements and norms.

After a pause, Diburov said, "President Ryan, I am disappointed you think you can bully me in our first conversation."

Ryan replied, "My intention is to state facts, because if we both understand the facts, our nations will be better off. Fact one . . . we know where the *Knyaz Oleg* is. We can destroy it right now if we want."

Diburov said, "You said it is time for facts, but that is *not* a fact. That is a threat, Mr. President."

Ryan replied, "If you aren't interested in threats, President Diburov, what is that submarine doing off our coast? Why hasn't it turned around and returned to Russia?"

There was no response from the Russian president.

Ryan said, "It would be an extremely helpful first step in reconciliation."

"My feeling is we have nothing to reconcile. My administration is not the administration of Valeri Volodin."

"No, it's not. But *your* administration is the one with the ballistic missile submarine parked off the U.S., so you have to accept responsibility for any actions we might take. Things went bad for Volodin when the *Kazan* was destroyed. You won't be able to wrap yourself in the excuse that it's your predecessor's fault when your *other* most advanced warship sinks."

After a long pause Diburov said, "I will need significant concessions from you if that is to happen. Very significant, indeed."

Ryan thought to himself that this clown wasn't ready for prime time, but he was now in charge of the nuke codes in Russia, so by that factor alone he deserved some respect. "President Diburov, stop your attacks on all fronts, and then we'll talk about a deal."

"I'm sorry, Mr. President, but I refuse to be ordered around by America."

The phone went dead.

Twenty-four hours after the acrimonious phone conversation, the Russian ambassador requested a meeting with the President of the

United States.

That it took an entire day for this to happen worried President Ryan and his secretary of state. Diburov was shrewder than they'd given him credit for. He hadn't folded like a cheap suitcase during the phone call with the President, nor had he waffled under the pressure of an impending American invasion for twenty-four hours. Ryan and Adler were beginning to think they had totally misjudged the man's mettle, so they were hard at work on the next phase of prosecuting the diplomatic situation, planning ways they could crank up the statecraft nearly to the level of war.

The last thing Ryan wanted to do was to lose the Baltic. But the second-to-last thing he wanted to do was to invade the sovereign territory of the Russian Federation. He'd send troops over the border if he felt it was his only option, but he was acutely aware of the consequences.

Very quickly into their conversation, the Russian ambassador said, "I firmly believe there are agreements we can come to, Mr. President."

Ryan knew where this was going, but he played dumb. "I'm very happy to hear you say that, Mr. Ambassador. I wonder if you have something in mind, something that would be to Russia's benefit, but not jeopardize the security of other nations."

The ambassador spoke as if this were just coming to him spontaneously, although Ryan knew the man's script was well memorized. "I won't go into detail about Russia's economic fortunes of late."

Here it comes, Ryan said to himself.

"The economic sanctions against prominent Russian businessmen are stifling the growth of our nation. We see it as illegal and against the norms of diplomacy. The president feels the West's removing the holds on the finances of the nation's top businessmen would go a long way to showing fraternity between East and West." A slight smile from the portly man. "We don't need to be fighting one another."

Yep, Ryan thought. Diburov takes the reins of power in the Kremlin, and his first action is to send his ambassador to tell America he will stop a war if America gives him all his money back.

Humans, despite all the artifice around them, could be such simple creatures at their core.

Ryan played his part in the little game now. As the ambassador had pretended to just think of this, Ryan pretended to just mull over the consequences of the request. He took thirty seconds before he responded.

"Mr. Ambassador, do I understand you to say a loosening of international sanctions would result in Russia moving its forces in Lithuania back to their barracks in Kaliningrad and their forces in Belarus back to sovereign Russian Federation territory?"

The ambassador nodded. "Simply put, Mr. President, we need to get our economy flowing again. This is more important now than the crimes perpetrated by the West against Russia."

No, Ryan thought. *Diburov* needs to get his personal assets flowing again. Diburov and the other men under sanction kept all their money in offshore accounts. Releasing every cent of this would help the economies of Luxembourg, Cyprus, Monaco, and Singapore more than it would Russia.

But Jack Ryan's objective at the moment wasn't about Russia's domestic prospects, it was about Russia's international expansion. And it looked like there might be a way out of this.

No, Ryan thought, he and Adler had not misjudged Diburov's character. He was exactly what they took him for. The twenty-four-hour delay had nothing to do with the man's resolve to continue the fight with the West. It was probably just the time it took for the new leader to figure out how to ask for what he really wanted, access to his piggy bank, without looking like what he really was.

Another kleptocrat.

EPILOGUE

Jack Ryan, Jr., sat in Gerry Hendley's office, his hands folded in his lap. Gerry was behind his desk, elbows propped on the edge. They'd been talking for twenty minutes, mostly about Brussels, but now that the conversation had slowed and an intensity had grown on Gerry's face, Jack got the idea there was something he wanted to say.

Something Jack wasn't going to like.

He'd rather not be here now, at all. Ysabel had arrived in the United States the evening before, but Jack had not been by to see her at the hospital yet. He'd been working most of the night, and this morning's one-on-one meeting with Gerry was something he knew he couldn't beg out of.

So here he was, suddenly aware that this was the moment of truth.

Gerry said, "We've spent the last twenty minutes talking about what happened in Brussels. You did great work, again, and I appreciate that very much."

"But?"

"But I'm not sure you understand the danger you put The Campus in over the past few weeks. From the contact with the Italian paparazzo that went unreported, to the exceeding of your analytical work in Luxembourg, to your unilateral decision to betray your stand-down order and return to Europe on your own."

"I did what I thought was right, Gerry."

"Exactly, Jack. But you are not a one-man band. You are an operator and analyst, but you are not an executive. You don't make the rules, you have to be able to follow orders, and I have to be able to depend on you. Your personal security in the field affects everyone at The Campus, and the well-being of our organization affects the security of the United States of America."

Jack just nodded. He understood, in theory, but he felt like he'd made the only reasonable calls, considering. "I know, Gerry. And I shouldn't have gone against directives, but I don't want to be treated like the President's son around here."

"Well, you are. And neither of us can change that." Gerry drummed his fingers on his desk, then said, "I'm suspending you, Jack. Six months. Take some time, figure out what you want to do, whether or not you want to be a part of this team."

"Six months?" Jack had been hoping for

two weeks.

"Yes. I hope you come back at the end of that time with a new attitude. An appreciation that the risks you take have to be for the good of the unit as a whole. I hope the man who sits before me in half a year's time will understand his role on the team."

Jack said, "Does Clark know?"

Gerry said, "I am in charge of The Campus, not John Clark. But to answer your question . . . yes, he knows. Clark and Chavez are ex-military, they understand that orders and chain of command serve the whole. And they understand your violations should be taken seriously."

Jack nodded. He was angry, he felt Gerry was going too hard on him, but he understood Gerry had to put his foot down somewhere.

Jack stood, reached across the desk to shake Gerry's hand. "I'm sorry I put you in this situation. I'm not sure I'll be back here in six months, but I appreciate the opportunity you gave me here."

Gerry stood and shook Jack's hand. "The world in six months is going to need a man like you working in a place like this. Keep that in mind."

"I will." Jack headed back to his cubicle to start packing.

Ysabel Kashani sat in the chair next to her

hospital bed, looked down at the soup in the styrofoam bowl, and frowned.

Christine von Langer saw the expression from her chair across the room. "I thought you ordered the alphabet soup."

The Iranian said, "I did. We don't have this where I am from. I assumed from the name it would have something from every letter of the alphabet in it. You know, asparagus, beans, cilantro . . . like that." She just stared at the soup. "But . . . it just has watery tomato sauce and little letters made out of dough."

Christine laughed. "Yeah, that's it."

Ysabel took a bite. "It's hot, anyway. The food in Luxembourg was better."

"You're in Baltimore now, Ysabel. I can get you some crab cakes, but not from the cafeteria here."

Ysabel didn't want to put Christine out. The woman was helping her in so many ways, tending to her dressings better than the nurses, walking with her to the bathroom to keep her steady, keeping her company through the long days and nights cooped up in a hospital room.

But she'd never even heard of a crab cake, and looking down at her alphabet soup, something else she'd never heard of, she thought it sounded amazing right about now.

Jack Ryan, Jr., opened her door, his face hidden by a bouquet of two dozen roses. He saw Christine first and gave her a wink, then lowered the roses and looked at Ysabel.

"Well, look who it is," she said. Her tone made clear he'd taken his time in coming to see her.

He crossed the room and kissed her passionately but carefully. She still had a bandage on her neck, and the doctors were monitoring her concussion even now.

"Sorry, had to go by the office. I knew you were in capable hands."

Ysabel said, "Christine has watched me every step of the way. I think I have a friend for life now."

Christine stood and headed for the door. "And this friend for life knows when it's time to step out for a few minutes. I'm going to go hunting for crab cakes."

Jack knelt down next to the Iranian, stroked a hand through her hair while she smiled at him. He asked her how she was feeling and tears formed in her eyes.

She did not reply.

Jack held her close. "This was my fault. I am so sorry I pulled you down into something I didn't understand."

She shook her head. "I went down willingly, Jack. You can't blame yourself. You and I both felt indestructible after what happened to us in Dagestan." She shrugged. "Luxembourg was a wake-up call, I guess." With a sad smile she said, "We're not indestructible. Not at all."

948

Jack nodded, then kissed her again.

She said, "Thank you for getting me over here. I was surprised when you suggested it."

"Johns Hopkins has the best doctors in the world. I should know, my mom is one of them."

"Yes, she dropped in on me this morning."

Jack's eyes went wide. "What? How did she —"

"How did she know about me? Something about you asking your dad about helping with my visa so I could come over and get care. He said something to her, she came looking for me. It was cute. They are very conspiratorial about meeting your very exotic but slightly defective girlfriend."

Jack had gone to his dad for help getting Ysabel into the country for care, but he hadn't mentioned they were in a relationship. He guessed his mom just happened to pop in on her to check her out, and now that his mom and Ysabel had had some alone time, there was no doubt both his mom and dad knew everything.

Ryan groaned inwardly, but he hid it.

"You aren't defective. You are just in the shop for a few repairs."

He kissed her and she laughed.

Jack wasn't sure what would happen with him and Ysabel, but he knew he would do everything in his power to make sure she recovered quickly and completely. After that . . . well, he could always ask Clark and Gerry if they were interested in a multilingual asset who knew tradecraft and had proven herself in the field.

As if on cue, John Clark opened the door, giving a half-knock as he did so. Jack just looked at him for a moment. "Is there *anyone* who doesn't know about this?"

Clark laughed. "I was in for a checkup on my back. Ran into Cathy, she mentioned Ysabel. Hi, Ysabel. I'm John."

The two shook hands. Jack just smiled a little and looked at the door, expecting at any moment to see a bunch of men in dark suits and sunglasses come in as the advance team for a visit from his dad.

Ysabel said, "Oh, Jack, by the way. Your mom invited us over for dinner. Just as soon as I get out of here. Christine is coming, too. Hope that's okay."

Jack just laughed. "Sure. That sounds great."

ABOUT THE AUTHOR

Mark Greaney's debut international thriller, *The Gray Man*, became a national bestseller and was nominated for a Barry Award in the Best Thriller category. There are now four books in the series. A feature film adaptation of *The Gray Man* is in development by Columbia Pictures. He is the #1 *New York Times* bestselling author of *Tom Clancy Full Force and Effect* and also *Tom Clancy Support and Defend*. He is the co-author of #1 *New York Times* bestsellers *Threat Vector* and *Locked On* by Tom Clancy with Mark Greaney, as well as the co-author of *Command Authority* by Tom Clancy with Mark Greaney.

Mark Greaney has a degree in International Relations and Political Science. In his re search for *The Gray Man* and *Tom Clancy* novels he has traveled to dozens of countries, visited the Pentagon and many Washington, D.C. intelligence agencies, and trained alongside military and law enforcement in the use of firearms, battlefield medicine, and close-range combative tactics. He lives in Memphis, Tennessee.